Coffee

with

Cowboys

"In the rodeo world, the competitor is the stock or the clock, not the other rider. We help each other and cheer each other on…and pray no one gets hurt."
-- Delaney Rawlins

One thing about raising bucking horses, there was no instant gratification. You had to wait YEARS, and patience was NOT something I was known for.
-- River Westmoreland

I realized how comfortable it all was; as if I had been doing it all my life. I turned back and looked at the small group and wondered why I was walking away. So, I went back and had coffee with cowboys.
-- Lacie Jae Madison

This book is fiction.
The characters, properties, and dialogues are from the author's imagination and are not to be construed as fact.
Real people with dialog have been used by approval.

ACKNOWLEDGEMENTS

You cannot write a book like this without a great research rolodex. I am truly thankful for the encouragement and willingness to help by the people below.

Tracy Hammond
Crystal Longfellow
Devan Reilly
Kirk & Katie St. Clair
Brody Cress
Ike Sankey
Cody Yates
Lewiston Roundup Association
Trenten & Maria Montero
Jessica Gates
Dillon Holyfield

Lindsey and Chad Hutsell
Brady Portenier
Tate Owens
Johnny Espeland
Martee Pruitt
Lori Smith
Darryl Kirby
Rylee Potter Hansen
Kim Grubb
Amberleigh Moore

ISBN- 9781733952811

Coffee

with

Cowboys

Gini Roberge

THE
INTRODUCTIONS

CHAPTER ONE

Delaney

My fingers gripped the rail of the metal fence panel so tight my knuckles hurt. I concentrated on my breathing; deep intake, slow release. I stared across the arena floor with such intensity my eyes began to burn.

Deep intake, slow release...I stared at the steer in the chute.

"Our next rider is Evan Rawlins..." The announcer called out and the crowd cheered as my father walked his horse into the box. With reins firmly in his grasp to hold back the anxious horse, he watched his competition...the steer in the chute. Dad looked calm...as if our whole world didn't depend on this run.

My mother's year-long illness before her death had created over two hundred thousand dollars in doctor and hospital bills. We had spent the last six months selling what we could from the ranch and using the money Dad had won qualifying for the National Finals Rodeo to keep the creditors at bay...until now. We were on the verge of bankruptcy and losing our livestock, land, and our home; my home the entire seventeen years of my life.

There were ten nights of rides, ten steers to turn...with our life hanging on each one. He had placed in the rodeo seven of the last nine nights, but the big win we needed was the average. The rider with the lowest combined time over the ten nights could earn almost $50,000 on top of the winnings from the other nights. With all the money combined, he would save our home.

This was the tenth night, the final ride. He was second in the average going into the night with the man in first having already run. He had to throw the steer in under 6.3 seconds.

The murmur from the crowd and the chatter from the announcer faded away as I stared at dad. He could do this...I believed with all my heart that he could do this.

He nodded to release the steer and my lungs froze. The horse bolted with dad already sliding off the side and to the steer's shoulder; his arms stretching out to the horns. He was down; legs stretched out in front of him as his heels dug in to brace for the stop and turn. With a roar from the crowd, his body fell back with the steer's nose in his arms...they landed on the ground, and the steer's legs turned to the sky. The judge's flag went down and I searched for a penalty flag; there wasn't one. He slowly stood and tipped his hat to the crowd that was celebrating his 4.3-second run.

With hat in hands and over his heart, he walked back out of the gate.

I ran to find him with tears sliding down my face and found him in the alley under the bleachers. When he saw me, his arms opened, and I jumped into them.

"You did it, Dad," I whispered. "I knew you would."

CHAPTER TWO

RIVER

I wrapped my arm around the wooden fence post, gripped the gate pole, then braced myself and pulled hard. The barb-wire gate stretched out over the dirt road. With my other hand, I tried to stretch the barb wire loop that was attached to the pole over the top of the post. The wooden post painfully dug into my shoulder. A few swear words and a grimace gave me just enough extra energy to slide the loop over the pole and close the gate.

Taking a step back, I cussed the damn gate again. Why did Dad and Caleb have to stretch the wire so tight?

With an exasperated huff, I turned back to the horse that was waiting for me. We had just purchased the mare at the Billings Livestock sale in Montana, and I couldn't have been more pleased. The dark brown mare was 16 hands tall, broad at the shoulder, and wide at the hip. Her rump was huge for a quarter horse. There were several racehorses in her lineage, which would suggest she would have the speed along with the strength. I'd spent the last three days working her in contained areas; corrals, arena, and stockyard. Now was the chance to get her out on the range and see how independent she was and if she had a solid mindset. So far, I'd been pleased with her performance.

At 5' 5", I didn't have long legs to easily step into a stirrup on a horse her size, but she stood still as my leg stretched high. Not even a flinch as I rose into the saddle and settled in.

"We need a good name for you, Sweetheart," I ran a hand down her neck then nudged her to the rise in the pasture on our left. The stock tank I was checking was just over the hill.

She moved without hesitation and with a curiosity to see what was on the other side. My grin of pride widened. I was only seventeen, but my father trusted my horse-sense and allowed me to purchase her for a working ranch horse to help with the cattle and bucking horses we raised. She was proving me right.

When we crested the hill, I looked out over the vast range-land as far as I could see. A bright blue cloudless sky hovered over the green pastures, jagged ravines, and the winding river that flowed along sandy beaches and tall canyon walls. The cold breeze tinted my face a deep pink. I zipped my jacket and adjusted the wild-rag scarf around my neck. My shoulder-length dark brown hair was all the same length, even the bangs. I used a hat most of the time to keep it from falling forward. It was now captured in a warm beanie cap with a leather patch tooled with the Westmoreland Livestock brand; WML. I pulled it down lower over my ears.

When I turned, I was surprised to see Dad's truck and horse trailer by the stock tank. He had said the tank needed to be checked but didn't tell me he was doing it.

I nudged the brown mare into a trot down the hill.

As we neared the truck, the mare let out a short neigh. I wondered which horse he had brought and was excited to go riding together.

I smiled as he appeared around the back of the trailer. His eyes widened.

"River? What the hell are you doing here?" He shouted in surprise.

The horse stopped, and I felt her body stretch and back end lower. It was a familiar feeling…that of a mare releasing a

4

mixture of urine and mucus showing a stallion she was in heat and ready to be bred.

"I just released Chinook!" He turned to disappear around the trailer, but it was too late.

His prized stallion trotted out in front of the truck with head held high, tail lifting to the sky, and legs prancing. The magnificent beast of a horse was seventeen–hands-high and a deep reddish-brown with black legs, mane, and tail. There was no halter; he was free, and he knew it as his head lowered, and he started toward us. I adored Chinook, had all my life, and knew he wouldn't intentionally hurt me, but we weren't taking any chances in his eagerness and the mare's willingness to breed.

My heart leapt to my throat as I turned the mare away and kicked her into a run. Thank heavens she didn't hesitate or refuse. I looked back over my shoulder to see the stallion thirty yards behind us. Dad was between the truck and horse trailer.

I turned back and looked ahead of us…the gate was useless. I could not get it open and closed before the stallion would be on us. I had no choice but to push her out to the open range. Another glance and the horse was barreling towards us, Dad's truck was pulling away from the trailer.

I kicked the mare faster, "Go, girl…go…" I whispered to her and leaned forward as if a jockey in a race. She flew across the barren ground with her strong legs pounding against the dirt. The sound was thunderous and made my heart beat stronger.

I looked across the land. Where to go? Where would it be safe away from him?

I knew Chinook was afraid of water, so I turned her to the right where I knew a creek meandered across the pastures. It was early April, and the snow from the mountains was just beginning to melt, so the water wasn't wide or deep this time of year, but maybe it would be enough to stop him.

I could see the dip in the ground, which signified the creek. The mare galloped down the slope and jumped to fly across the water. My heart was pounding in my ears! I turned back to see the stallion jump the creek without hesitation.

"Damn!" I gasped. There was only one more option. "I hope you're not afraid of water," I called out to the mare and turned her toward the far trees where a large pond nestled.

Another glance back, and I could see Dad's truck blazing across the ground right behind the stallion who was closing in on us. The horse didn't carry an extra 130 pounds, and a saddle on his back like the mare did.

"Hurry…" I kicked the mare and tried to judge the distance to the stallion's speed.

It was going to be close unless the mare wouldn't go into cold water. I was just going to have to dive off and hope the stallion didn't ruin my saddle in his eagerness.

The blue of the water came within sight, and I glanced back. Chinook was twenty yards back…Dad was twenty yards behind him.

My hands gripped the reins and entwined into the horse's mane. With lungs tight, heart racing, and body tense, we approached the pond. I prepared for the horse to slide to a stop or duck away, but she ran right into it with water splashing over us. I gasped as the frigid water splashed my bare face and my body was instantly drenched. I had to lift my feet up high out of the stirrups and up high to keep them out of the snow-cold water.

I pulled the reins to stop the mare from running through the pond and twirled back to see what the stallion was going to do. He was skidding to a stop but sliding into the water with his hooves dancing unhappily. Dad's truck skid sideways to a stop twenty feet from the horse with the door flying open. He jumped out with shotgun in hand.

"Don't shoot him!" I yelled.

"If it's between him or you, what would you like me to do?" He growled back.

I laughed, which made him shake his head and lower the gun.

"I'd have just shot in the air to get his attention. You cold?" He asked with a smart-ass grin.

"Getting there," I turned the mare to face the prancing stallion and humored father. "Did you see her? How fast was she going?"

"Not as fast as Chinook," He shook his head. "I brought him out so he could get a good stretch of the legs and play a bit. This wasn't what I had in mind."

The stallion reared into the air and slid down the slope toward the water again. He squealed in excitement.

"We need to breed them," I said confidently.

"River, we're not rewarding that damn stallion by breeding them out here after he charged after you."

"He didn't charge after me; he went after a mare in heat, and THAT wasn't a no," I shivered.

"No…it wasn't," He nodded with that grin again. "They both proved they had some speed along with their size."

"Powerful, Dad," I told him with the excitement growing. "Let's get them home. They are going to have a great foal…big and strong."

He stood with hands-on-hips and looked at the prancing stallion then back to the wet mare standing in belly-deep cold water.

"That mare has no buckers in her background," He mused.

"But Chinook is dominant so…I have faith, Dad."

"And what happens if we put 5 years into a horse and he doesn't buck?"

"Then I'll have one really tall saddle horse," I grinned.

He watched the stallion pacing back and forth at water's edge, then turned and looked at my mare.

"Have faith, Dad," I insisted. "Just believe…"

He stared at me a moment then shook his head with an exasperated sigh, "I'll go back and get the trailer. That leaves you in the pond for another fifteen, twenty minutes."

"I'll survive," I grinned through clenched teeth. "Maybe a little whiskey to warm me up?"

He chuckled. "You're seventeen; you have four more years before you're legal drinking age."

"But not for 'soaked to the bone in freezing pond water' legal ranching drinking age." My grin widened as I shivered.

He just laughed and turned to his truck.

While I waited, I ran a hand down the mare's wet neck as we watched the stallion prance, buck, snort, and rear up in the air. His mane flew wildly just as it had when he was bucking in the rodeos.

"He's a beauty," I whispered to the mare. "And so are you. You're going to have the best foal…a star. Your baby is going to be the future of our rough stock herd." My hand slid back over her large brown rump as the stallion grew closer to the water. "I have dreamed of raising a horse that will rise to fame…rising to the top of the line…going to the National Finals Rodeo…bucking horse of the year…" I whispered with a sense of awe and belief.

Chinook stepped into the pond but recoiled back, which made him slip and fall onto his side. Mud splattered across his hide, and he looked like a gangly teenager trying to get himself up. I smiled as the mare, and I watched him slip back down and nearly break his neck, trying to stay away from the water.

"He really is an elegant stallion…superior NFR bucking horse in his own right."

I knew it was true, but his goofiness could not have been convincing his new girlfriend.

Three hundred and sixty-three days later, a long-legged broad-chested dark brown bay colt was born. Just like his sire, a wide white blaze ran from his forehead down to his nose.

"Chinook and Destiny…we'll have to rebreed them this year," Dad said from behind me as I rest a hand on the brown mare's hip.

"Nice stud colt," Caleb grinned. "You're right, Sis. He's going to be superior."

"You have a name yet?" Mom asked me.

"Yeah…" I whispered and reached out to touch the colt's nose that was curiously stretching out to me. "Destiny's Ignatius…Iggy for short."

"Ignatius?" Caleb huffed. "Where the hell did you come up with that?"

I just grinned, "It means fiery one and because he's gonna light a fire under those cowboys."

My parents and twin brother stepped out of the stall when I heard Caleb speak, "That's going to be one of the most pampered, spoiled horses ever to roam the earth."

They chuckled, and I grinned because we all knew it was true.

CHAPTER THREE

Lacie Jae

"Are you freaking kidding me?"

"Lacie Jae, the shuttle was leaving, so we hurried and jumped on at the last second."

"Camille! I don't even know where I am! How am I supposed to get there now?"

I looked around the expanse of the Las Vegas MGM Grand Casino. People...it seemed like thousands! I wasn't very tall, just 5' 1" and I was being bumped and was too short to look over the people in front of me. I had been following behind my sister and her two friends when they suddenly disappeared, leaving me lost in the maze of aisles around the casino.

The noise from the band playing at the corner bar and the slot machines rattled my already shot nerves.

"Just follow the signs. There should be another shuttle in just a few minutes," my sister said. I could just see her rolling her eyes at her two friends, Eve and Kendra.

I was forever the brunt of her jokes as she tried to impress them.

"I don't see any signs, or I would have been with you," I growled in exasperation and a bit of desperation. "Why would you leave me?"

"You're twenty-one..."

"What the hell does that have to do with anything?" I cried out with a bit of panic rising. "I've never been to Las Vegas! I've never been in a casino and try to find my way through these confusing aisles that seem just to go nowhere, then take you in circles."

"Ask someone for directions or forget about the rodeo and just go back to the room."

The call ended.

I wanted to scream and cry as I glared at the screen of my phone. How could she just leave me behind? Sure, she didn't want me there to start with, but to abandon me in the middle of "Sin City" by myself?

Another bump from behind, and I was jolted out of the daze. I gripped my tiny purse tighter. It was just a wallet that hung around my neck and across my chest. There wasn't any way that someone could swipe it, but holding it close made me feel a little more secure.

My lungs began to hurt from the shaking breaths that escaped.

I looked around at the mass of people, gambling tables, slot machines, stores on the edge of the building, and the signs hanging above the aisles. There was no sign directing me to the shuttle that would take me to the Thomas and Mack Center to watch the National Finals Rodeo. Another glance around, and nothing looked familiar. We had arrived at the casino in time to change clothes and try to make the first shuttle of the night. We wanted to spend as much time at the center as possible in the "Fan Zone" and exploring the building.

I took a deep breath and looked for someone official. There was a cocktail waitress in the tightest, skimpiest skirt, tights, and corset, but she disappeared into the midst of the slot machines.

"Can I help you?"

I felt a sigh of relief until I turned around to one of the biggest men I have ever seen. The top of my head barely reached his armpit. My grip on my purse tightened for that imaginary security.

My gaze rose to curious and concerned brown eyes. A black cowboy hat allowed just a hint of black hair to peek out the bottom. He wore one of the grey jackets with all the patches on it like dozens of other women and men with cowboy hats were wearing. He was broad...so broad he was at least twice as wide as me.

"Are you lost?" He asked. "I know it's confusing in here. Can I help direct you somewhere?"

I took a deep breath as I leaned away from him.

"I was headed to the rodeo," I stammered. "But..."

Was I telling this behemoth of a man that I was just abandoned by my sister and alone?

"Were you looking for the shuttle? Are you with someone?" His eyes moved around us, then came back to me.

I just stared at him. What was I supposed to say or do? I wanted to go to the rodeo, but now the fear coursing through me was quickly convincing me to run back and hide in the room. My breath shook as I tried to contain the tears that were rising.

"Logan, you're scaring the hell out of her," a woman appeared at his side. Her dark blonde hair was thick and fell below her shoulders. It framed a slender face under a black cowboy hat, and she was wearing one of the grey jackets, too. There was an air of comfortable confidence about her. Something in the way she smiled at me made me relax...a little. "Sorry," she said to me. "His size is a bit intimidating to some people and as tiny as you are, it must be that much worse."

I tried to smile as my eyes went from her to him then back.

"Well, I'm sorry if I scared you," he smiled. It was a great smile that reached up into his eyes.

I relaxed a little more.

"We're going there now," she said. "We can show you where to catch the shuttle, or you can ride over with us. We're headed out to catch an Uber car."

"Do you have someone with you?" Logan asked.

"They are on the shuttle already...on their way," I exhaled as my nerves began to relax.

"They left you behind?" The woman asked in disbelief.

"Yes…" I huffed. "She figured I could catch the next shuttle, but I don't have any idea where it is, and I can't find a sign."

"Who is she?" Logan asked.

"My sister," I grumbled with an exasperated sigh. "…and her two friends."

"I'm guessing an older sister, and you're the odd one out," The woman smiled.

"You have no idea," the tension left my muscles as I rolled my eyes. "All three of them are at least four years older than me, and they are at least six inches taller, and they are wearing boots with heels!"

The woman laughed, "I know that feeling." She looked at Logan. She was taller than me but not near his height. "We need to get to the center. What would you like to do?"

I looked between the two of them with the realization that I wanted to go with them and not on the shuttle. Driving away with strangers was one way of getting kidnapped, tortured, raped, and murdered.

The woman smiled in understanding, "There are cameras all over the place in here, and we're going in an Uber."

"Alright," I said with a bit of apprehension. "I'd rather ride in an Uber than a shuttle."

"Let's go then," she said and turned.

They both had long legs, and I found myself jogging after them, just like I did with my sister.

Within minutes, we were walking out the front of the hotel with a blue SUV waiting for us.

Logan motioned for me to sit in the front seat.

"Thanks," I smiled. "But your legs will need the extra room. I'll ride behind you since I don't need much space."

He grinned, and my body sighed.

The woman and I slid into the backseat and smiled at each other.

"I'm Lacie Jae Madison," I said to her as the vehicle moved forward.

"Do you go by Lacie or Lacie Jae?" Logan asked.

"Lacie Jae," I answered. "My mother's name was Lacie, too, so it helped."

"Delaney and Logan Rawlins," she said. "Nice to meet you. Where are you from?"

"Redding, California," I answered. "And you?"

"Bend, Oregon," She looked up at her husband then back to me. "Have you been to the finals before?"

I looked at her curiously, "Finals for what?"

Her lips rolled together. I was sure she was trying not to smile. "The rodeo we're headed to...the NFR ...National Finals Rodeo.... The Finals..."

I felt my cheeks warm, "Oh, my gosh, that is embarrassing. I've never been to a rodeo before."

She huffed with a grin, "You've never been to a rodeo, and you start with this one?"

"So...I'm guessing this is like the Super Bowl for football?" I asked.

"Yes," She chuckled. "So you've never been to the Thomas and Mack Center? Where the rodeo is held?"

I shook my head.

"Let me see your ticket, and I'll walk you through how to get to your seat," she said.

"Thank goodness Camille gave me the ticket before we left our room tonight," I said and handed it to her. Then the realization clicked. Our father had paid for the tickets with Camille carrying the envelope they came in. She gave me my ticket before we left the room, but I didn't see her give Eve and Kendra their tickets.

She had planned on leaving me behind. That tall bitch! I huffed to myself. My father paid for the tickets for the three friends with the condition that I was to go with them. She was pissed and probably had the plan of abandoning me the whole damn time.

"Lacie Jae," Delaney whispered. "You alright?"

"Yes," I huffed and looked at her. Well, I would just show my sister and show up at her side and piss her off that I made it. First was finding out all the information I could from the pair.

14

She told me how to get through the "Fan Zone" then up into the building, how to find the right door to go into the large arena, and then how to get to the seats.

"If I remember right, the shuttle back to the MGM is number 2," Logan said from the front seat. "You'll see the signs when you come back through the "Fan Zone" and just follow the crowd onto the bus."

"Then follow the crowd back into the casino," Delaney said. "Let me see your phone, and I will put my number in it. If you get confused again, then you call me."

I handed my phone to her with a confident smile. How did I luck out to find this husband and wife team? This was going to piss off Camille when I knew what I was doing and didn't need her.

The driver stopped as she handed me my phone.

"Thank you so much," I said with an appreciative grin. "Thank you both for coming to my rescue."

"I'm glad he didn't scare you off," Delaney smiled.

I opened my door then turned to the building as it closed. After a moment of looking at the crowd, I turned back. Neither of them had gotten out of the car which was nowhere in sight.

"Well...OK then," I mumbled to myself and took off with a confident stride.

I followed Delaney's every instruction and made it to my seat. My three travel companions were nowhere in sight, so I settled onto my red seat and looked around. We were up in the balcony seats, but at the lower rows so there was no problem seeing the action. There was a laser light-show making animals and words on the ground.

A vendor walked by selling water and beer. Having just turned twenty-one, I thought I'd be 'grown-up' and have a beer at the rodeo. I chuckled to myself. Of course, he had to check my ID. He looked at the image on the license then looked back up at me.

"I like your hair short," He smiled as he handed me the beer.

"Thanks," I had just cut off my shoulder-length white-blonde hair to just above my ears. It was longer on top so I could create a stylish swish over the top. The shorter hair allowed my silver loop earrings to be seen. I liked it more every day.

Camille was just the opposite since she looked like our father, and I looked like my mother. Camille's hair was down to her waist, dark brown, and thick. With her height and looks, she could have been a model.

"Well, look who made it," Kendra's voice was full of amusement. She had long black hair and always wore dark red lipstick. Eve had short blonde hair and was looking at me with a teasing smirk. I ignored them and didn't even look at my sister.

They chatted between themselves as I watched people until the rodeo started.

Watching all the competitors on horseback come running into the arena made my heart race. There were so many of them, and it looked like they were going to collide. The crowd was cheering, and the announcer was yelling out the names and states the competitors lived. I was trying to see everything at once and my heart raced in exhilaration.

All the horses ran back out of the arena then the big screen in front of us showed a horse in the bucking chutes. I watched the screen as the first rider and horse bust out into the arena before I realized the action was happening just below the screen. I had to laugh at myself.

Watching the cowboys holding onto the bucking horses while gripping just a small leather handle was exciting until one fell onto the ground. I gasped right along with the crowd. The cowboy stood and jogged out of the arena as two cowboys on horseback tried to catch the bucking horse.

The action moved to the other end of the arena as cowboys began riding in next to a small cow in a metal cage. I heard the announcer say he was in a chute not a cage. Again, I chuckled at myself.

A cowboy's picture appeared on the screen; Tyler Waguespack. I looked down at him in the area to the right of the cow that was in the chute. Another man on horseback was on the other side, but they weren't holding ropes.

"What are they...?" I started.

Tyler nodded, the cow with horns was let out of the chute, and the two cowboys took off at a run with the cow between them.

"What the...?" I gasped as Tyler slid off his red horse and landed on the cow with his arms wrapped around the horns.

Within seconds...3.7 to be exact, the cowboy turned the cow, and they both fell onto the ground.

Kendra, who was a barrel racer and the reason the rodeo was the vacation of choice, yelled with a fist-pumping in the air.

I looked at her in amazement then back to the screen as they replayed the cowboy tackling the cow.

The next pair of cowboys rode into the areas by the chute. The name Will Lummus and his picture shown on the screen. Why did they put up only his name when there were two cowboys chasing the cow? How did they choose which one tackled the cow?

I was curious enough to ask Kendra, but when I turned, Will nodded and the whole process happened again in 4.3 seconds.

After four more cowboys were announced and cows tackled, I realized that only the cowboy that showed on the screen jumped off their horse.

I wondered if they actually did that on ranches. Did they jump off their horses out in the open range and stop the cow? I chuckled to myself as I lifted the beer can to my lips. The next name and picture was shown on the screen, and I barely got my hand up to cover my mouth as I choked on the beer. All three of my companions looked at me in disgust.

"Your first beer?" Eve laughed.

"She can't even handle one beer," Kendra shook her head with a self-humored yet condescending chuckle.

"That's the guy that gave me a ride over here," I whispered and looked at the picture of Logan Rawlins. "He and his wife."

All three of them laughed. I ignored them and watched Logan back his horse in next to the chute. My heart was pounding in a sudden burst of energy and surprise. He nodded and his brown horse took off running...Logan was already sliding off the horse and onto the cow. He was down and had the cow on the ground in 4.8 seconds. The crowd cheered, making my heart race even more.

Kendra turned to me with a smirk, "You're going to sit there and tell us that a world champion gave you a ride over here?"

Camille shook her head. She glanced at Kendra then to me, "Why don't you be a more embarrassing little sister?"

"It was him," I muttered through gritted teeth.

They just laughed then ignored me the rest of the night, which was fine because I was ignoring them and enjoying the rodeo. I may not know everything that was happening, but it was exciting and fun to watch...until the cowboys on the bulls rode out. That was scary and exhilarating.

When the rodeo was over, we stood and made our way down the steps.

"Let's go to the rodeo party at the MGM," Kendra said. "We can do the buckle ceremony tomorrow night."

"OK," Eve said. "What's a buckle ceremony?"

At least I wasn't the only one that didn't know everything.

"Every night, the winner of each event is given a go-round buckle for their win. After the rodeo, they have a big party at another casino to award it to them." Kendra answered. Of course, Kendra explained it to her without an attitude. If I'd have asked, she would have sneered with a roll of the eyes.

"Ooh, that could be fun," Eve said. "Maybe Lacie Jae's new boyfriend will win tomorrow night, and we can watch him get one."

They all three laughed. I turned red and knew they thought I was embarrassed. I wasn't, I was pissed. Why did they assume I was making it up? And why and the hell would I?

Kendra leaned over to whisper into Eve's ear. They both laughed and nodded. Then Kendra whispered in Camille's ear, and they all laughed and ignored me.

When we stepped out of the building, I trotted down the stairs and left them behind this time. I followed Delaney's instructions to the charter bus and was there five minutes before the trio of snotty women. I rode on the first bus back to the hotel and they had to wait until the next. Following the crowd, I was able to find the concierge desk and they told me how to get back to our room. It was 10:00 when I stepped into the room.

There were two double beds and a sofa-bed. I pulled out the sofa-bed and cuddled under the covers with the phone in hand to Google Logan Rawlins.

I was a bit embarrassed and shocked at what I found. He was a four-time qualifier to the finals and was the returning champion. They must have thought I was nuts for not recognizing him. But, then again, I did tell them that I had never been to a rodeo.

He was so polite for someone that was a champion, so was his wife.

Just for fun, I signed onto Facebook and looked up the NFR pages that would replay the rodeo. He had placed second for the night and first last night. After muting the volume on the phone, I re-watched Logan's run a couple of times. Each time my heart raced and I would cringe as he fell off the horse. Who would purposely do that?

I heard the lock on the door click and dove under the covers to pretend I was asleep.

They giggled and whispered as they tried to decide who got to sleep alone and who had to share a bed. Camille won the single bed since our father had paid for the tickets. I glanced at my phone; it was 1:00 in the morning.

The room went silent...for about 5 minutes, then one of the could-be-a-model women started a low rumbling snore. Yikes!

I was up, showered, hair done, and dressed before the trio began to rise from their beds.

"You're going shopping with us at Cowboy Christmas?" Kendra asked me.

"That's all the vendors at the convention center?" I asked.

When they all nodded, I shrugged, "Sure."

I'd just pay attention to how we traveled there, and if they were rude, I would just go on by myself. I had the comfort of Delaney's telephone number if something went wrong.

"I'll get you some coffee while you're all getting ready," I said and left the room.

As the door closed, I could hear them all giggle. It was a conspiratory giggle that made my stomach ache. I could leave them, I told myself, and gripped my phone tighter.

We rode the tram to the convention center, and I couldn't get enough of looking out on the city. Buildings everywhere, cement everywhere, and lights everywhere. It was mesmerizing, and I was so glad I was above all of it.

When we arrived at the convention center, the three of them walked into the building in front of me. They had been walking just enough to stay ahead of me, but not slow enough I could catch up.

"Preifert?" Eve whispered as they walked up to a map of the room.

I had no idea what that word meant.

The building was huge, with shopping vendors spread way to the back and up onto another level. There were hundreds! I had been looking forward to shopping, so I jogged down the steps in anticipation and headed for the first booth. It had the grey jackets with all the patches that Logan and Delaney had worn the night before. It would be my souvenir that would remind me of them when we went home.

"We're going upstairs first," Kendra called out. "Come up with us."

I turned back and looked at her in surprise. Eve and Camille were nodding in agreement.

"Alright..." I said and turned to walk to the escalators with them.

When we walked through the doors on the second level, all three walked right past dozens of booths. I wasn't sure what they were doing, but I wasn't uncomfortable, yet so I just followed.

They stopped next to a line of blue metal fencing panels that said Preifert on them. A row of people was standing in-line. They looked like they were waiting for something. My three companions walked to the line and stood in front of me.

"What are we doing here?" I asked.

They just smiled and didn't say anything to me; they chatted amongst themselves about the party at the bar the night before.

The line moved forward, and I was beginning to get bored when the three women giggled again and stepped away from each other. They had been blocking a table with Logan Rawlins sitting on the other side signing an autograph for a teenage boy who was grinning and nodding. It was obvious Logan was his hero.

The boy walked away and Logan turned to look at my companions.

My heart was racing, palms moist, and stomach-turning. What if he didn't recognize me?

His eyes connected with mine.

CHAPTER FOUR

"Lacie Jae?" Logan grinned with clear delight that I was standing in front of him.

My companions were silent.

"Hi," I smiled. My mind raced on what to say, so I didn't sound like an idiot, like I didn't know he was going to be there. "I just wanted to come by and thank you again for the ride last night. You and your wife."

He stood and towered above me. "Delaney is my sister," He said as he walked around the table. Ignoring the three silent women, he stretched out a hand to me.

I slid my hand in his and hoped it wasn't trembling.

"I feel a bit silly that I didn't know you were tackling cows in the rodeo," I said.

His grin widened, "It's called steer wrestling or bulldogging."

I shook my head in more embarrassment. "I'm sorry..."

"Don't be," He said and squeezed my hand tighter. "You said you'd never been to a rodeo, so it's understandable."

"I think I better start Googling all about rodeo before we go out tonight," I laughed softly.

He was just so nice and big...muscular big.

"We'll have to get together so I can do a quick tutorial with you." Logan grinned.

"I would love that," I gushed. "Is Delaney in the rodeo, too?"

"Not this year. She's roping out at the World Series," Logan answered. "She'll be here in a few minutes if you would like to come into the booth. I need to get back to signing."

"Sure," I gasped in surprise and excitement.

I turned to my companions, but they weren't there. I wanted to laugh.

The line to visit Logan didn't seem to end. After a few minutes, he had turned to me and asked if I would take a picture of him and one of his fans. Of course, I said yes! He handed me the fan's phone and smiled at the bright, proud eyes of the teenager standing with him.

I spent the next hour taking pictures and listening to him talk and laugh with the people. He was as charming as he was tall.

Delaney appeared and was very surprised to see me.

"Lacie Jae, so good to see you," She said as she stood next to me. Her dark blonde hair was in a braid down her back, and she wore jeans, a straw cowboy hat, and the grey jacket with the patches over a white shirt. She looked so western and beautiful. "Did you enjoy the rodeo last night?" She asked me.

"Oh, yes," I nodded. "But Logan informed me it is steer wrestling and not cow tackling."

We all three laughed.

"Oh, that's so funny," Delaney sighed. "We need a rodeo lesson."

"Logan said the same thing," I giggled. "I would love it!"

"Are you going tonight?" She asked.

"Yes…" I hesitated. Camille had my ticket. After their little trick failed, would she still give it to me?

"Sis," Logan said and turned to Delaney. "These ladies would like you in the picture, too."

She smiled and stepped forward to stand in the middle of four women that looked in their twenties. Logan was right next to her. I had to take a picture with all the women's phones.

Why didn't I look up Delaney last night too? The first chance I had, I'd do just that so I didn't look or sound like an idiot again. Logan said she was roping at the World Series, but I thought the World Series was baseball.

Logan continued to sign autographs for the next half hour with Delaney occasionally requested to join them. She always did with an appreciative smile.

The line for Logan had diminished until just minutes before another cowboy showed up, and the line of people increased again.

"Who is that?" I whispered.

"Kaycee Feild," Delaney whispered. "He's a bareback rider."

Logan and Delaney shook his hand and relinquished the autograph table to him.

"How did you do?" Logan asked his sister.

"Paid the way here plus a bit extra," She said with an amused smirk to him.

"I did that the last two nights," Logan huffed.

I looked at the two of them in open confusion.

"She won money roping this morning," Logan explained with a smile.

"And he won money by placing the last two nights at the rodeo," Delaney said.

"So you were roping this morning at somewhere called the World Series? That isn't baseball." I grinned that I at least knew that much.

They both laughed. It was a comfortable laugh, and I had the reassurance they weren't laughing at me, just with me. It was refreshing, and I was enjoying the fact I was entertaining them with my ignorance.

"What are your plans for the rest of the day?" Delaney asked. "Where's your sister?"

"Shopping somewhere in this big building," I answered.

"Are you meeting up with her?" Logan asked.

"Just long enough to get my ticket for the rodeo tonight," I answered.

"Logan has some interviews he's late for, so why don't you come with me out to the roping?" Delaney said with a smile.

"I would LOVE to!" I bounced in my shoes. "But you'll have to teach me what I'm watching."

24

"No problem," She said and looked at her brother. "We'll meet up with you at the rodeo tonight."

He stared at her a moment then nodded his head before looking back down to me, "You enjoy your day."

"Thank you," I grinned. "I will and good luck tonight." I looked between the two of them. "Is that the right thing to say or is it like theater and I'm supposed to say 'go break a leg' or something?"

"No!" They looked at each other then back to me.

"No 'break a leg' around steer wrestlers," Delaney shook her head.

I wrinkled my nose at them and grimaced, "Sorry…good luck then." I giggled to him.

"Thanks," He said with a grin, then turned and walked away.

I watched him a moment, just long enough to see him turn back and look at us over his shoulder and smile again.

When he disappeared around a corner, I turned back to Delaney.

"Do we have enough time so I can go to our room and see if I can find my rodeo ticket?"

"You know where you're sitting?"

"Up in the balcony, around the same place as last night."

"I have better tickets. You can sit with me, and I'll explain rodeo to you as we watch."

I gasped in surprise, "Really? Oh, I would love that."

"Looks like we're spending the day together then," She smiled. "Did you want to shop first?"

"No…not really…except maybe…" I looked around at the vendors.

"What are you looking for?"

"I saw the booth this morning that sold the grey NFR jacket like yours. I'd like to buy one."

"Well, let's go get you one."

The small was still too big for me, but I bought it anyway.

In the Uber car, on the way to the World Series, she told me about the SouthPoint Hotel and Casino and that it had many arenas for the roping competition. Thousands of horses and riders were expected to take part in the roping, and over twelve million dollars would be awarded over the week-long event.

We drove to the back of the hotel where her horse was stalled.

"This is Ketchum," Delaney said as she stepped into the stall. "He is my roping horse."

I stepped to the door and glanced inside to see a big white horse. He had his head down and was eating hay until he turned to the sound of her voice. Then he walked to the short door and stuck his head out.

I took a nervous step back as Delaney smiled and ran a hand down the horse's nose. "He's very nice; you can pet him."

"I've never been around a horse before," I whispered. "Especially not this close."

I watched the horse's eyes as I stepped closer to him. They were large, brown, curious, and warm. With a hesitant trembling hand, I touched the end of his nose. It was soft. I caressed his nose as Delaney had done. Ten minutes with the horse and I was running a hand down his neck and over his shoulder…what I could reach with the stall door closed.

"How many horses do you have?" I turned my attention back to my guide.

"Between the ranch, roping, and barrel horses? Forty-one at various ages and training."

"Oh, my gosh!" I gasped. "Are they all as nice as Ketchum?"

"I would like to say yes to that," She chuckled. "But we don't spend as much time with some of them."

We made our way into the SouthPoint Hotel and Casino. I was shocked to see two arenas *inside* the building. Delaney was stopped a dozen times to congratulate her on her morning success.

"What…how…did you win?" I asked her.

She glanced at her watch then nodded to the rows of red seats that surrounded the big arena.

"Let's sit in the stands and watch the roping, and I'll walk you through it."

"Are you sure I'm not keeping you away from something?"

"No…not really…nothing I should be doing anyway," She shrugged and settled down onto a bleacher seat.

Within minutes, a small group of people sat next to us, and Delaney was pulled into a conversation. I watched team after team ride in and rope a steer, but I listened to the people talking so I could learn more about my companion. What I learned surprised me. The year before, she had come in fourth in barrel racing but won the average; I had no idea what that meant. The morning roping she had won was worth fourteen thousand dollars! She had won with her partner Kim.

She was riding and competing again the next day. I gasped in delight.

"Lacie Jae?" Delaney turned to me. "You OK?"

"We're not leaving until Saturday morning, so can I watch you rope?"

"Of course," She smiled and glanced at her watch again.

My phone alert rang out, and I nodded apologetically and pulled my phone from the jacket pocket.

Text from Camille: Where are you? We're ready to go back to the hotel.

Text to Camille: I am at the SouthPoint Hotel with Delaney Rawlins.

Text from Camille: Really? You couldn't have told me you were going?

Text to Camille: You couldn't tell me about Logan this morning instead of trying to trick me?

Text from Camille: I'll leave your ticket in the room.

Text to Camille: Thank you. I will be sitting with Delaney so she can teach me about the rodeo.

There was no response.

Delaney was standing and saying goodbye to the people around her when I slid the phone in my pocket.

"Shall we head to the other arena?" Delaney asked as we made our way up the steps.

"Take me where you will," I giggled.

We walked through more vendor booths that were selling clothes, horse tack, jewelry, horse feed, and much more as we made our way to the other indoor arena. I had to stop and buy a blue shirt with sparkles and a matching necklace. They were souvenirs to remember my day with Delaney.

"That blue will be pretty with your blue eyes and blonde hair," Delaney said.

"Have you already shopped here?" I asked since she seemed almost immune to all the vendors.

She chuckled, "Yes...plus, you wouldn't believe the closet I have at home full of clothes and jewelry I've purchased from here and other rodeos. We built a walk-in closet in my room to handle the overflow."

I smiled, "I don't have a lot of clothes and jewelry. My life is a bit boring, and I don't really need much."

"What do you do at home?"

"I'm a barista manager. I manage three coffee shops and twelve employees."

"That doesn't sound boring. It sounds like a lot of work."

"I've worked there since I was sixteen so it's routine to me now, but my life is just home and the coffee shops." Until this day, it had all been fine with me.

We walked through a door that looked like we were going outside, but two arenas were in front of us. They weren't surrounded by seats like the other arena; the viewing area was between the two. Two riders were roping a steer to our right, and there were dozens of riders in the arena to our left. They were just riding in a big circle.

"What are they doing?" I nodded to the arena.

"Warming up the horses," she answered as we made our way down the steps. "Everyone goes in the same direction, so there are no collisions...hopefully."

Instead of walking to the raised platform with seating between the two arenas, she walked along the side and stood next to the fence. Another two riders were chasing a steer with ropes whizzing above their heads.

A dozen teams rode in while she explained team roping to me. It went from a bit boring to watch to more intriguing as I understood the dynamics and what would go right and what would go wrong with a run. It was more challenging than I first thought.

A beautiful yellow horse trotted into the arena followed by a pure black horse. Two men were riding them and swinging their ropes to the side.

"Oh, my," I gasped. "Those horses are beautiful...and the cowboys adorable."

Delaney chuckled, "The palomino is named Silas and the black is Warlock."

"You know them?"

"They roped at a lot of the same jackpots and circuit rodeos when I was barrel racing." She smiled at me. "I recognize a lot more horses than I do riders."

"Well, those two are just beautiful."

The riders burst out of the box and chased after the steer. Silas' rider swung the rope and it twirled perfectly around the horns...the rope tightened and Warlock's rider caught the back hooves. The horses turned to face each other and the cowboys turned to the judge holding the flag.

"That looked good," I said as the time of 7.05 was announced. "That yellow one really turned fast."

"That is called 'facing' when he has to turn and face the heel horse to stop the clock. It was good, which is to be expected. They are leading our circuit standings."

"What does that mean?"

We walked over to the fence by the arena where the horses were going in a circle.

"The country is separated in different circuits...like territories. Oregon, Washington, and the upper half of Idaho are in the Columbia River Circuit. We ride in those rodeos and the more money you win the higher you are in the standings. We've all qualified for the circuit finals rodeo, which is in January. If you win there, then you go to the National Circuit

Finals in Florida and compete against all the winners in the nation."

"Who is we?"

"My brothers and I and those two," She said and nodded to the two horses, Silas and Warlock.

"Your finals rodeo doesn't happen to be close to Redding, California, does it?" I asked with a wishful grin.

"No, it's in Yakima, Washington, mid-January."

"Ah…" I moaned.

"There is another large conference room down the hallway filled with vendors," she smiled. "Want to shop a little more before we go to the rodeo?"

"Yes…" I giggled.

We had to stop at the MGM casino so I could drop off my shopping bags while Delaney waited for me in the car. My roommates weren't there, but I hid the bags behind a chair to try and make sure they didn't go through them. I trusted Camille. I didn't trust the other two.

My ticket was sitting on the desk under the television. I picked it up and put it in my wallet.

As we rode in the Uber car to the Thomas and Mack Center, I turned to Delaney.

"How long have you been roping?"

"Since I was born, it seems," She leaned back against the seat and relaxed. "My parents owned a ranch, but I didn't start competing until I was twelve. My brothers started when they were young, but once I started, I was hooked. We rode the school rodeo and a couple of clubs with roping and me with barrels, of course. Our younger brother, Brodie and his best friend Craig, started mutton busting, riding sheep, when he was five, then progressed to steer and are now saddle bronc and bareback riders. Logan grew too big to be a roughie, so he concentrated on roping and steer wrestling."

"What the heck is a roughie?"

"Someone who rides anything that's trying to buck you off," She chuckled. "Sheep, steers, bulls, horses…those are called rough stock."

"Can I ask? How old are you?"

30

"Twenty-four to Logan's twenty-six. Brodie is twenty-one."

"I just turned twenty-one, but you two seem so much more mature than me."

"Maybe more traveled," she shrugged. "But to be a manager at your age is pretty damned mature."

"I guess…" I sighed and looked out at the buildings. "Maybe that's what I need…to travel more."

"Have you done much besides coming here?"

"No…none really, besides going to Disneyland and Sea World, which are both in southern California when I was ten."

"Some people don't ever travel and stay in their home towns their whole lives."

"I don't want to do that," I said with wide eyes.

"Then, start making a list of places you want to go and plan for it."

Our conversation ended when we arrived at the center, but I knew she was right. I needed to explore the world a bit more.

CHAPTER FIVE

Our seats were six rows up from the arena! I was so shocked and overjoyed I couldn't stop grinning. The chute that would hold the steer Logan would be chasing was right in front of us.

"Oh, this is going to be so exciting!" I giggled to Delaney.

"Better than the balcony," She chuckled. "The team ropers will often end in this corner so we get a great view."

We had purchased hamburgers, fries, and beer before settling into our seats.

"These are the best fries ever," I said and shoved more into my mouth.

"I agree," She nodded. "I look forward to them every year."

I pulled my original ticket out of my wallet and looked at the seat and section number, then looked around to find where I would have been sitting and tried to see Camille, Eve and Kendra. I was not going to miss sitting with them.

I turned to Delaney as the announcer's voice boomed around the arena.

"Are your parents here, too?"

She shook her head, "My mother passed away when I was sixteen. My father is in one of those suites up there." She pointed across from us to rooms that separated the lower and upper levels of the seats. "He's up there with his old buddies."

"You weren't invited?"

She smiled and her gaze seemed to search for him. "No...just a bunch of old cowboys not wanting a young cowgirl to overhear their raunchy stories."

She paused as her eyes stopped moving...as if she found her father.

The lights went off and the laser lights danced around the arena as the rodeo started.

Her gaze moved to the horses running into the arena.

We sat quietly until the parade of competitors began and my heart rate increased.

"So you rode in that last year?" I asked.

She nodded and pointed as Logan rode into the arena carrying the flag for the state of Oregon.

"The last two years...it's exhilarating," she grinned.

I watched Logan run by with just a glance over to us. He grinned then disappeared into the mass of riders. It made me feel a bit special that out of all the people in the arena, he looked at us. All the riders formed a U-shape as the announcer talked about the night.

I glanced at Delaney but she was looking up at the area where I imagined her father was sitting with his buddies. So, I took the moment to look at Logan. He was big; muscular big to go with his height; other men around him matched his size. They had to be steer wrestlers, too. I took a quick picture with my phone.

I looked around at all the cowboys in the area. They were all different ages but they all seemed so mature.

"What are you thinking about so hard?" Delaney asked.

I shrugged a shoulder and smiled at her, "That they all look so...mature...or experienced is what I mean."

She nodded slowly and looked at the group around her brother and the whole group of men and women. "They have all gone through a very long year to get here. Lots of travel, competing, victories and failures, away from family, injuries...just a lot," she smiled. "It has a tendency to age you."

The group of riders began their run out of the arena and the rodeo began!

Delaney explained bareback riding to me as the horses busted out of the chutes. Her brother Brodie's best friend, Craig, was a bareback rider, but they didn't qualify for the NFR.

As the last rider was desperately holding onto his riggin', it was announced that steer wrestling was next and the gate that blocked the chutes was opened. Two cowboys rode out from under the tunnel and took their places in the area next to the chute; the box.

After two competitors ran, Logan appeared and backed his horse into the corner of the box. His eyes were on the steer in the chute.

"Tyler is the hazer on the other side," Delaney said. "His job is to keep the steer in line so it doesn't move out of Logan's reach."

"They go so fast," I whispered as Logan nodded.

The chute opened and the horses bolted...my heart jumped!

He slid off the horse and his right arm wrapped around the horn as his left hand gripped the top of the other horn. His boots dug into the dirt while his body leaned back...arm moving around the steer's nose and they fell back onto the ground...all in 3.6 seconds!

"Like I said!" I yelled over the applause as I clapped for him. "It goes so fast!"

"His fastest time in this arena is 3.4 seconds," Delaney clapped.

Logan stood and looked to the opposite side of the arena where their father would be. He tipped his hat then turned to walk back to the gate at the chutes. At the last second, he turned and looked up at us. I waved then clapped, which brought a wide grin to his face.

After another rider competed, I was quite surprised when Logan rode back into the arena on a sorrel horse.

"What's he doing?" I asked.

"He's going to come out and haze for Tyler now."

"But...aren't they competitors? He's going to help him?"

"In the rodeo world, the competitor is the animal stock or the clock...not the other rider. We help each other and cheer each other on...and pray no one gets hurt."

"Oh," I exhaled in surprise. "That is so awesome."

Logan hazed for three other riders, including the last rider of the night who could have beaten his winning time. He didn't though, and the arena crowd erupted in applause as

Logan rode the haze horse and led the other horse out of the arena. Before he disappeared through the gate, he took his hat off and waved it to the crowd…the applause increased.

"Dad has got to be thrilled," Delaney sighed. "So glad he made it here to go to the buckle ceremony."

"Can I go with you?" I asked hopefully.

"Are you kidding?" She grinned. "We've spent all day together…you think I'm letting you go before the day is over?"

"I'm so excited!" I bounced in my seat. "This is the best day."

I excitedly looked back to Camille and the other two. I couldn't really see them, just that the seats weren't empty.

Text to Camille: Are you going to buckle ceremony?

Text from Camille: Yes, are you going with your new friends since he won?

Text to Camille: Yes, Delaney invited me to join them. I'll see you there.

Text from Camille: Have fun

I didn't see her all night.

*****

"You don't worry about me," I said to Delaney as she stepped up on the big beautiful light grey horse. "I'm just going to sit on the bleachers and watch."

"Alright," She smiled down. Her hair was in a ponytail down her back and was held down by her black cowboy hat that matched her black shirt that was covered in patches. Her eyes were hidden behind dark sunglasses. "I'll rope in this arena twice, and then we move over to the other arena for the third. When we make the short-go, which means the top twenty fastest teams, then we'll be back to this arena."

"I can watch down there, too?" I looked across the arena and could just make out a second one.

"No bleachers there, but you can stand and watch," she said, then turned to look down the road that led back to the hotels. "I'm not sure if any of my family will be here…they have a busy schedule today, but if they show up, I'll introduce you so you're not alone."

"I'm OK being alone," I told her but didn't explain that I spent a lot of my time alone at home.

"Alright, I'll check in when I can."

She rode toward the back of the second arena.

I love to people-watch and this was such an unknown world for me that the time just flew by! There were hundreds of riders, horses, and spectators to watch. I squealed in excitement the first time I heard Delaney's name called. She was all in black on top of the light grey horse, so I could see her well. I had watched a lot of people using their phones to video the riders, so I pulled mine out to do the same for Delaney. There was a spot next to the fence. So I could get a closer video, I trotted down the bleacher just before she entered the arena.

She and her partner burst from the chute and followed the steer with ropes blazing. I was shocked when they caught it right in front of me! I squealed in excitement and turned off the video.

I repeated the process for all four of her runs then sent them all to her phone.

My phone alert rang out just as the last video sent.

Text from Camille: We need to leave the hotel for the concert by 5:00. Where are you?

I huffed in frustration. I wanted to stay with Delaney, but I also wanted to go to the concert. Since Dad had purchased the ticket, I didn't have a choice. He'd be upset if I didn't go.

Text to Camille: Watching Delaney rope at South Point Casino. I will make my way back to get ready.

I stood at the top of the bleachers and searched for Delaney. She was right behind the cook shack with her team roping partner. Both horses were watching the crowd as the two women hovered over Delaney's phone.

They were watching the videos I had sent when I arrived; that just made me feel useful.

36

"Damn it," Delaney grumbled. "Damn thing just jumped right out of the damn loop."

"Not much to do on those," Her partner shook her head and looked up at me. "Hi."

"Hi," I giggled and then grinned at Delaney when she looked up.

"Kim, this is our videographer, Lacie Jae," Delaney smiled. "We really appreciate these."

"Thank you," Kim reached out a hand to shake.

"I'm glad I could be helpful," I answered and looked back to Delaney. "I forgot I had a concert I have to go to tonight with Camille."

"OK," She turned and waved at a girl driving a golf cart. "Can you take her to the stalls behind the hotel and I'll meet you there?"

Twenty minutes later, Delaney was driving her truck away from the stalls.

"Who are you going to watch?"

"Shania Twain," I answered.

We chatted about the different concerts and events she had been to over the years until we approached the hotel.

I let out a disappointed sigh. "We'll be home late tonight and fly out first thing in the morning, so I won't see you again."

"Never say never," Delaney smiled at me. "We have a rodeo in Redding every summer and you are more than welcome to come up to the ranch for a visit."

"Seriously?" I squealed.

"Of course, any time you want and we're home," Her smile was warm and inviting. "It has been wonderful meeting you and spending the last two days together."

I slid out of her truck and looked back, "Thank you so much for making this vacation so memorable. Please tell Logan goodbye for me…and good luck."

"I will, and you have my number. Call me anytime."

"Thanks."

With that, I shut the door and she drove away. I was going to miss her.

There might have been four of us going to the concert, but I felt like a fifth-wheel the whole time.

The trip home was just the same.

Camille dropped me off at the house that I shared with our father. I quietly walked in. It was completely silent so I tiptoed to my room and turned on the television in time to watch the last performance of the rodeo. I shouted at the TV when Logan turned his steer and won the Championship.

I covered my mouth quickly and listened to any sound outside of my room, but there was silence. I sighed in relief.

After working all day Sunday, I watched highlights from the rodeo in my room for the rest of the day. I still hadn't seen my father since I returned. The whole trip to Vegas seemed like a dream. The videos and pictures I had taken of Delaney riding and Logan at the rodeo kept it real for me. I put on the jacket I had purchased with Delaney and watched them over and over again.

At 10:00 Monday morning, I arrived home from the early shift at the coffee shop. I walked through the front door of the house and stopped to look for my father. I didn't hear or see him, so I closed the door without making a sound. I walked around the house looking for him but didn't call out in case he was sleeping.

My phone ringing made my whole body jump. With trembling hands, I pulled it out of my pocket…it was Delaney! My heart jumped in excitement as I pushed the accept button.

"Hi, Delaney!" I said excitedly.

"Good morning," she answered and I could hear the smile in her voice. "You made it home alright?"

"We did, and we got home just in time, so I could watch the rodeo on TV. Tell Logan congratulations for me."

"I'll do that."

"I was so nervous," I admitted with a laugh. "I screamed at my television."

Her laugh was low and amused.

"I am so glad Camille abandoned me so I could…"

"SHE WHAT?" My father's angry voice roared behind me.

CHAPTER SIX

I jumped away and twirled to see him glaring at me. My heart was racing as I gasped and stepped away from him.

The front door opened with Camille taking a step in. She stopped when she glanced at my shocked face then to our father as he turned to her.

"You abandoned her?" He growled and stumbled toward her.

Her eyes widened as she looked at me and without a word, she turned and slammed the door behind her. Screaming her name, he stumbled to the door, but by the time he fumbled it open, she was already in her car. The engine roared as she backed out of the driveway.

I turned and ran out the back door and ended the call as I made my way down the steps of the back porch.

Our father was an alcoholic...had been all our lives. Camille was born of his first marriage and I was born from his second. My mother died when I was sixteen and his drinking increased. The worst part was when he was angry...he was mean.

I was nineteen the last time he had hurt me by grabbing my hair and throwing me into a wall. It took a week of hiding the large bruise and bump on my forehead before it healed enough I could go out in public.

Camille was the only one that knew what happened because she had pushed him away from me so we could both escape. We had never talked about it and now, when he got angry, we just ran.

The need to take care of him when he wasn't drinking kept me living in the house. Camille only came over to make sure I was alright, but she hated it. She refused to talk to him and after making sure I was alright, she would leave. She resented me for keeping her connected with him.

Now, I was running through our backyard to the hidden trail through the shrubs and into the neighbor's yard.

My phone started ringing and I glanced to see Delaney's number calling again. I declined the call as I reached the next road and turned to look down at the corner where Camille had stopped her car. It was our designated rendezvous spot.

"Why in the hell did you tell him that?" Camille screamed at me.

"I didn't!" I panted as I slid into her car. "I didn't know he was there...I looked. I was on the phone talking to..."

"Damn, Lacie Jae," She was red from anger, frustration, and rising tears. "You have to get out of there because I am never going back."

"I..I..." I stuttered. "Who would take care of him if...?"

My phone rang again and I declined the call.

"It's not your responsibility," Camille yelled. "He is a grown man that needs help and neither of us can do that. He doesn't care about us enough to get help and his anger towards us just gets worse every month."

"But..." I sighed and fell back against the seat. "I know you're right, but I just...I don't know what I'd do."

"I know a lady that rents out one of her rooms. You have a job and she doesn't charge much." She glanced over at me. "I'm taking you there now."

I sighed and nodded in defeat. She was right...we had tried for years and there was nothing we could do to help him. "Maybe Father Litton can help him."

My phone rang again.

"Who is that?" Camille asked.

"Delaney...I was on the phone with her..."

"No doubt, you scared her."

I nodded and pushed the accept button. What was I supposed to say?

"Lacie Jae!" Delaney gasped. "What the hell happened? Are you alright?"

"Yeah," I sighed. "Can I call you back?"

"You're alright? Are you alone?" Worry dripped from her every word. Sadly, it made me feel better.

"I'm alright…I'm with Camille and we're going over to her friend's place," I answered.

"Can I help? Are you hurt?" She asked with a shaking sigh.

"No, we're both fine," I answered and the need to have her at my side was overwhelming. "I promise I'll call you back."

"OK, I'm giving you one hour to call me back, or I'm headed down there. I can be there in four hours." She said.

Tears rose at her mothering and protective tone.

"OK," I whispered. "I'll call back."

I ended the call and stared out the window as Camille drove the ten minutes to my new home. We were both silent.

When she pulled her car in front of a large blue house, she turned off the engine, but neither of us made a move.

"I don't have anything," I sighed. "How am I supposed to go to work tomorrow in the same clothes?"

She exhaled and her hand shot out to my wrist and squeezed.

"That is the first time you actually said you were moving," she turned in her seat. Her dark brown eyes were pleading with me. "You are going to follow through with this before he hurts you again or kills himself or one of us."

"Alright," I nodded. "I promise I will, but I need my clothes and car."

"He's probably already asleep…passed out," she corrected. "Let's go meet your new landlady, then we'll go back and get your clothes."

"Alright…" I sighed with my stomach feeling hollow.

I don't know what I expected my 'new landlady' was going to look like, maybe a little old grandma, but I didn't expect the woman in black slacks and emerald green blouse that was almost hidden by an expensive black wool coat. Her dark hair was in a tight, stylish chignon and diamond earrings finished the image. She looked more like a bank executive than a grandma…or landlady. It was a three-story home with a view of the lake and a pool in the back yard. It looked cold now, but it would be wonderful in the summer. Would I still be here?

She walked us to a small house in the backyard that she had converted to a guest house. It was cute with blue, white, and yellow Mediterranean decorations. It looked like the ocean should be right outside the door. After a wave around the house telling us to make ourselves comfortable, she left.

I stood in the middle of the adorable house and felt so out of place.

"You said a room," I tried to smile at Camille.

"That's what she called it," She chuckled. "If I weren't headed to Fresno with Eve and Kendra, I'd move in here."

"You're moving?" I gasped and looked at her with wide eyes.

She nodded with a bit of a guilty grimace, "I just needed you away from him before I could move."

Tears of disbelief rose, "So you're just leaving me by myself?"

"Lacie Jae," She huffed. "You have three coffee shops full of employees who are also your friends. Since you don't have to take care of Dad anymore, you can start accepting their offers to parties and movies."

"But..."

"No buts, it's time for you to have a life and enjoy your twenties," she turned and walked to the door. "Let's go get your clothes and car."

After pulling into the driveway, in front of the house I was raised in since I was born, we closed the doors as quietly as possible.

"I'll go..." I started, but she threw a hand in the air and shook her head.

"We'll both go in," She said and stepped in next to me as we walked up the brick pathway.

"Even if he is awake, he probably won't remember we were even here," I said as my hand hit the doorknob.

I turned it and slowly pushed the door open. From the front door, we could see into the living room, dining room, and part of the kitchen. He wasn't in sight, so we cautiously walked in and started down the hallway toward my bedroom. The sound of his snoring rumbled from his bedroom, which was ten feet farther down the hall than my own.

"That's his 'totally passed out' snore," I whispered.

"We'll take no chances," Camille pushed me down the hall. "We'll hurry and get out of here."

Fifteen minutes later, all my clothes were stuffed in two plastic garbage sacks and my personal items were stored in my suitcase. The last items I put in the case were the framed pictures of my mother. I would never leave those behind.

Camille carried the bags out of the front door.

I set the suitcase on the top steps of the walkway, then turned and walked back into the house. I made my way down the hallway toward my father's room. The snoring increased in volume and vibration...it was deep down from his lungs.

With a slight hesitation, I pushed his door open and peered inside. He was lying on his back across the foot of his bed in just his jeans that were two sizes too big...he was so skinny. An empty bottle of Jack Daniels was lying on the floor next to the bed. A half-empty bottle set on the bedside table.

The room smelled of old socks and alcohol-sweat, so I tiptoed to the window. My eyes were on him the whole time...waiting for him to rise. We could never know whether he would wake angry or in a decent mood...he was never happy.

Even though it was cold outside, the house furnace would keep him warm while the fresh air would help with the smell.

On my way back to the door, I stopped and looked at him. His grey-streaked black hair was too long and a mess...sweat moistened it to his skin. At least a week's worth of whiskers gave him a rugged, homeless look. He wasn't a big man, but when my mother was alive, he didn't drink as much and looked healthy. Every year that went by he looked worse...for five years and there wasn't anything Camille or I could do about it.

A deep sigh released from me. Camille would be waiting at the car, so I walked to the door and hesitantly looked back.

43

This wasn't right...leaving him like this. He was safe in a warm house with food filling the cupboards and refrigerator, but just going without talking to him first; it just didn't seem right. But what would he say? And what would he do?

The thought made my hand go to my forehead as if the last bruise and bump were still there. He could have easily broken my neck when he slammed me into the wall. My stomach trembled as I took a step out of the door. He rolled on the bed and snorted. Fear raced through me as I fell forward out the door, bounced off the wall, and tumbled onto the floor. I scrambled to my feet and nearly ran to the front door.

If he raised that much fear in me by just snorting, then I was doing the right thing. I would call the minister at the church and let him know Dad was on his own. Father Litton would check on him and make sure he was alright.

I locked the front door before shutting it and picked up my suitcase to carry it to my older Ford Escort. Camille was standing next to it, waiting for me.

"I just got off the phone with Kendra. She is arranging interviews for me in the morning. I'm going to my apartment now to pack then drive down tonight."

"That fast..." I sighed.

"You'll be fine in that cute house and taking care of your coffee shops," She leaned forward and gave me a quick obligatory hug before turning to walk down the driveway. When she opened her door, she turned back to me with a very somber expression. Her eyes went to the house then back to me. "Stay away...he'll only hurt you. Christmas is a week away, but you don't come here. You stay away from him."

"What are you doing for Christmas?" I asked softly with a bit of hope she would be here.

"Mom bought me a ticket to fly to Georgia and spend it with her," Camille shrugged. "She's put the money out, so I'm not backing out now."

I just nodded as the tears started to rise. I was losing my father and my sister within minutes of each other. But...in reality...I had lost both of them a long time ago. We were just in a stalemate with life.

"Lacie Jae?"

"What?" I whispered.

"I am very proud of you and your coffee shops. You're smart...you'll be fine."

Our eyes met and I felt our whole childhood played in the look. She never really liked me, always picked on me, and the fact she was proud of me shocked the hell out of me. She slid into her car and backed down the driveway without a glance back to me or the house she grew up in since she was three.

With a sigh of something that felt like defeat, I set my suitcase on the back seat then slid into the car. I drove away while staring at my home until it disappeared.

When I stopped in the driveway in front of my 'new' home, I stared at the adorable little house. It should have been exciting to live there, but I just felt so lost and out of place.

My phone chimed and I slid it out of my pocket. I prayed that it was Camille changing her mind, but it was Delaney.

"It's been an hour. What's going on? Are you alright?"

"I'm OK," I sighed.

"What can we do to help?"

My gaze moved from the house to the road in front of me, "You said that I could come visit. Is that invitation still open?"

"Of course!" Her voice was full of excitement and relief. "I've already checked the road conditions and it's clear all the way."

"Can you send me the address and I'll put it in the GPS into my phone?"

"We'll have dinner waiting."

*****

As I drove out of town, I called Father Litton and he assured me he would check on my father. Then I called the owner of the coffee houses and let her know I'd be gone. It

45

was the middle of winter and still busy but not as hectic as summer when all the tourists were in town. I had a lot of vacation time accumulated so she just told me not to worry about returning until after the first of the year.

On the drive, I thought of Vegas and the National Finals Rodeo. It entertained me until the GPS chimed and said I had arrived.

The sun was just going down over pine trees in the distance. I stopped under a log opening that had a black metal sign hanging from it that was an outline of a steer head with a bar running across the inside with an R resting on it. In the distance, at the end of a long driveway, were buildings. Wood fencing on each side of the driveway led me to the house, barn, and lots of metal panels. They created two arenas and numerous corrals.

I slowed down as I approached the buildings because I wasn't sure where they would be. A relieved sigh released when both Delaney and Logan stepped out of the large barn. I drove towards them as if they were life preservers.

"Just in time," Delaney grinned and gave me a big welcoming hug.

Logan was right behind her and although he wore the black cowboy hat, he looked so different in a ranch jacket than his competitor's jacket. He was more earthy and if at all possible, more masculine.

"Just in time for what?" I asked in surprise.

"We have babies to feed and you don't want to miss that," Logan grinned and swept an arm toward the barn.

I was still in the clothes that I had worn to work and my comfortable slide on shoes.

"Should I change first?" I asked.

They both looked at my feet and grinned again.

"I don't think any of us have feet as tiny as yours to borrow boots," Logan chuckled. "Do you have any with you?"

"I don't ever wear boots," I admitted.

"Well, we'll try a pair of mine," Delaney turned to walk in the house. I followed.

There was a long wall of windows looking out over the pastures and corrals, but we went to the side and through a small door. There were shoes and boots spread out along the base of the wall; mud, cowboy, snow, tennis shoes, slide-on, and in different sizes. Coats hung on hooks on one wall and dozens of cowboy hats, baseball caps, and beanies hung from the opposite wall.

"This is the mudroom," Delaney said. "Let's take you for a tour before putting on boots."

"Ok," I said excitedly.

Her hand hit a door in front of us, "Bathroom." She continued down a hall and hit the door on her right, "Laundry Room...then this door is Dad's suite."

We walked out of the hall and into an elongated room that started with the kitchen in front of us with a long kitchen island with six chairs on the opposite side. Just past the island was a long dining room table that could comfortably seat twenty people. Then a large sitting area with three dark leather sofas and two cream-colored recliners creating a U shape in front of a large television. Wood tables with black wrought iron details were between the furniture and against the walls. Turquoise and red gave the room color in pillows, blankets, lamps and a large rug in front of a stone fireplace. Western art hung from the walls.

"This is spectacular," I whispered in awe. "It looks like a western showroom."

Delaney grinned, "Every year we go to the NFR, we bring back a nice piece of furniture."

"Or two," Logan added from behind us. "We have also won a few items we've added."

"So, it is kind of a showroom for the NFR vendors," Delaney chuckled and walked through the kitchen to the other side of the house and turned right. "To our right is the only bathroom, besides Dad's, that has a tub. We each have a bathroom in our rooms but no tubs. Then on the right is the office and on the left is Martin's room."

"That's your brother Brodie's best friend, Craig's dad?" I giggled.

"Yes," Logan nodded. "He is pretty much a second dad to all of us."

"The original house was what we just walked through," Delaney explained. "When Martin and Craig moved here, the rest of the house was built."

"Martin is an architect," Logan added. "And we can all swing a hammer so we added rooms for each of us."

"Including Craig," Delaney added. "They have their own house about ten minutes away but some nights it's just easier for them to stay here."

"And there is a guest room that has three bunk beds in it," Logan added. "We cater to the homeless cowboy every once in a while and want to make sure we have somewhere for them to sleep."

"Oh, that's nice," I smiled then gasped in surprise when we walked into the 'new' part of the house.

There was a wide-open space that contained two rows of saddles on stands and shelves with trophy buckles. The walls were covered in framed pictures of the family in rodeo action shots and their official NFR portraits.

At the end, just before glass double doors that led back outside, sat a lot of exercise equipment, including three treadmills. "Three?" I looked at them with wide eyes.

They both chuckled.

"Dad got tired of us fighting over them, so we bought a couple more," Logan smirked.

"So," Delaney said as we stood in the middle of the hall. She pointed to the corner to our left. "Brodie's room, then Craig, Logan's, mine, and to the left is the spare room you can stay in while you're here. We call it the 'Bunk Room' because of the beds."

"Oh, my gosh, thank you," I stammered. My heart was racing at the thought of staying in this house.

"How long do we have you?" Delaney asked with a smile.

I giggled at her phrasing, "I really don't know. I just..."

"As long as you want," Logan said. "Let's get you into a pair of boots and go feed."

"What are we feeding?" I followed them back down the hall as I looked at all the pictures on the walls. It was all so overwhelming…the lives they had led compared to mine.

"Baby calves," Delaney answered.

"Calves?" I gasped in excitement. "I've never fed animals before."

"And we're experts and can show you," Logan laughed.

I slid on a pair of Delaney's boots and a hooded sweatshirt to cover my work clothes.

I tripped on the 'too big' boots as we made our way out to the barn. Logan politely held out his arm for me to hold as we walked. It kept me from falling on my face at least three times.

Just inside the barn and to the right was odd equipment I had never seen before, "What is that?"

"Brodie and Craig's practice equipment," Logan answered. "The piece that looks like slabs of plywood is a spurring board. The red padded barrel looking thing is called a *Mighty Broncy*. You can use the springs underneath to get it moving, or someone grabs the handle that sticks out the back to move you up, down, and around.

"You use them?" I asked Logan.

"Nah, I have other equipment that's in a shed behind the barn. I'll show you tomorrow." He answered.

"Ok," I turned, and my heart melted. Four black calves were looking at us from over a low fence. "They are so cute." I gasped.

Their long tongues began to stick out and lick their lips and up into their noses. They pushed against each other, trying to get closest to us since they knew we were there to feed them.

"Can I touch them?" I asked, hopefully.

They both chuckled, and Logan stayed next to me as I nervously reached out a hand.

"They are so soft," I giggled and looked up at Logan. "This is going to sound so silly, but I can't believe I touched a cow!"

He smiled warmly with amusement dancing in his eyes, "Well, let's get you feeding them, too."

"How?"

Delaney was holding big white bottles that had long red nipples protruding from the top. Logan showed me how to position the bottles for the babies. I laughed until all four were well fed and plopping down in the straw.

"Looks like your job while you're here," Delaney grinned. "They need to be fed every four hours."

"Oh, yes!" I giggled in delight. "Even at night?"

She nodded, "I do the midnight feeding, and Logan has the 4:00 in the morning feeding."

They gave me a tour of the barn and introduced me to the horses that were stalled inside before we went back into the house.

"Where's your dad and brother?" I asked as we took off our coats and slid out of the boots. "Your dad isn't going to be upset that I'm here, is he?"

"Of course, not," they both answered.

"They went down to Texas to visit with some friends before coming home," Logan explained.

While Delaney started a fire in the rock fireplace, Logan dished three bowls of stew from a crockpot, and I wandered around the room to look at all the paintings.

Dinner was comfortable at the long kitchen island then we moved to the sitting area with each of us taking a sofa to ourselves. Delaney was stretched out on the middle couch, so Logan and I were across from each other. I tucked into the pillows and watched the fire dance. I had woken at 4:00 in the morning to go to work, and I was now sitting 4 hours away from home just outside of Bend, Oregon, in a house I had never been to, yet I felt more comfortable here than I did at home. How was that even possible?

I glanced at the television show they were watching then over to Logan. His eyes flickered from the television to the fireplace, then to me. When our eyes met, we both smiled. I relaxed back into the pillows even more. My gaze went to the dancing flames.

My eyes opened into the dark. The television was off, the fire was just burning embers, and the house quiet. A heavy blanket lay over the top of me. I didn't move but just looked around at what I could see from light filtering into the house. Because I rose early to get to the coffee shops, my internal clock had me wide awake.

Down the hall, I heard a door open then footsteps moving toward the kitchen. It was much too heavy for Delaney, so I knew it was Logan. He passed through the kitchen and to their mudroom.

What was he doing up so early? Then I remembered they had to feed the calves every four hours. Well, I didn't want to miss that!

I slung off the blanket and quickly made my way down the hall. He was just opening the outside door when I appeared.

"Are you going to feed without me?" I teased as I slid on the boots. "I thought that was my job while I was here."

His grin was welcoming, and it made my whole body relax. He was so…comfortable.

"I didn't want to disturb you on the first morning of your vacation."

"I can sleep any day; I can't feed those cute little babies every day."

He helped me slide on the coat, then pulled a bright blue knitted beanie from the wall and pushed it on my head for me. He smiled as he adjusted it.

I held his arm as we slowly made our way out to the barn.

"I think I need to go buy some boots today," I giggled the third time I nearly fell.

"You'll still have my arm to hold any time you need," his words were honest and sincere.

My arms squeezed his in response since I couldn't get a word to form in my head.

In the barn, he taught me how to mix the calf supplement. Bottle holders were attached to the short stall wall that I set three of the four bottles in so the little black calves could drink while I held the bottle for the fourth. It was fun, and I couldn't help but laugh as the calf's eyes would roll back into his head, and milk speckled his nose and whiskers.

As I giggled and enjoyed the feeding, Logan cleaned the dirty straw from their pen and replenished it with fresh straw. When the babies finished eating and lay back in the pile of new bedding, I watched them for a few minutes then looked at Logan.

"Can I go in the pen with them? Is it safe?"

"Yes, they won't hurt you."

He held out a hand and led me through the door, so I could sit in the straw between two of the babies and stroke their backs as they began to fall asleep.

Logan leaned against the short wall and smiled at me. "You look natural there," He whispered.

I laughed, "Honestly, it feels like I have done this my entire life, and yet I've only fed them twice."

"Then you are a natural."

I stroked the back of all four then looked up at Logan, "What will these four grow up to be?"

"Those are my future training partners in steer wrestling."

"So, you're not going to eat them?"

"Eventually...somewhere down the road," he said honestly. "Until then, they will have a quiet life wandering the ranch and eating all they want with an occasional run in the arena."

"So I shouldn't give them names," I stated thoughtfully.

"That is a slippery slope."

Logan lowered down onto the straw with his back against the wall. When he stretched his very long legs out in front of him, his boots were just inches from mine. I held back the urge to playfully tip my boots against his.

"Many people do and don't have a problem with it," he continued. "Some people name them, raise them, then sell them when it's time."

"So, if I'm only here a few days, then I can name them since I won't be here 'when it's time'?" I gave him a teasing smile.

He chuckled, "So, what are you going to name them?"

I looked at the four black calves again then shrugged, "I've never named anything before."

"Not a dog or a cat?"

"No, we only had one cat growing up, and Mom had named him, Bert."

"I've named dogs, horses, cows, cats, and one rangy coyote when I was a kid."

My eyes widened, "a coyote?"

"Yeah," Logan grinned. "He must have been injured when he was little and couldn't get around very well, so he wasn't any danger to our animals. He never got close to us, but he just wandered around the barns and edge of the trees."

"Did you call him Wiley?" I giggled.

Logan laughed, "Nah, his name was Buster."

"What happened to him?"

"He was around for about six months then just wandered into the hills one night and never came back."

For an hour, he told me stories of the animals he had as a kid. I felt like I had stepped out of my coffee-making, care-taking world and fell into a bubble, as if the outside world didn't exist anymore.

"Have you two been out here all night?" Delaney appeared at the stall door.

"Just a couple hours," I smiled.

"Well, you want to be introduced to the ranch or sit around here on your asses?" She grinned.

Logan laughed as he stood and offered a hand to help me up.

"Let's get you in the side-by-side," He said.

"Is that like a pushme-pullme in Dr. Doolittle?" I asked with an innocent grin.

They both laughed, and it set the mood for the whole wonderful day. After the next calf feeding, we went to town so I could buy boots and a warm coat.

We made it home for the next calf feeding, and I had my new boots on as we stepped out the back door. Logan still offered his arm, and I happily took it.

It wasn't until that night, as I lay in bed and stared at the ceiling, that I thought of life outside of this bubble I was living in. Even if she wasn't the nicest to me, I missed Camille. Just the thought of not having her pop-in to check on me brought a hollow feeling to my stomach. My last vision was of Dad lying at the foot of the bed passed out and snoring. It brought tears to my eyes, so I rolled over and buried my face in the pillow to make them stop.

Did he wake and think I abandoned him? What would he think when he saw all my clothes gone? What would he do?

I could only pray that Father Litton managed to talk with him.

*****

For two days, I lived in the ranch bubble while I was with Delaney and Logan then ventured back home at night in bed to think of the loss of my family; Mom's death, Dad's drinking and dwindling health, and the fateful day that Camille decided to switch colleges. I will always curse the day she met Kendra and Eve, and the two women took away what relationship my sister and I had.

The tears would guide me into sleep until my alarm went off at 4:00 in the morning to help Logan feed the calves while he told me stories of his childhood. The stories would pull me back into the blissful bubble.

Friday morning, the full-of-milk calves were sleeping in their fresh straw and Logan had disappeared. I wandered around the large barn until I came to the stack of hay in the corner. As if I was a little kid, I climbed up the bales of hay then jumped off the side into the aisle of the barn. On my fourth climb, I heard the distinctive sound of a horse's hooves hitting the brick flooring.

I climbed to the middle of the stack and slid my legs over the side to sit on the edge and look down the aisle at his grin.

"Playing in the hay?" He teased.

My face flushed, "Yes, it's just another thing I have never done before."

He came to a stop next to me, and due to the height of the haystack, we were eye to eye.

"We'll have to find more of those fun things for you to do that makes your eyes light up," He said softly.

He was so handsome, so big, so kind. What would it hurt if I was brazen just this one time?

"There is one more thing I can think of," I whispered.

"And what's that?" His voice was smooth, caressing.

I took a deep breath and looked at him shyly. I just hoped he felt the same way.

"I've never kissed a cowboy before."

His dark brown eyes warmed as the smile spread across his face.

"That, Little Lady, I would be more than happy to remedy."

My pulse quickened, face warmed, and breath barely escaped as our eyes locked and he leaned forward. Just as I felt his breath on my lips, I closed my eyes and let his touch surround me. His masculinity made my body tremble as our lips came together in a soft kiss that hinted at the beginning of the exploration of these new emotions. My head swirled to the point I leaned into him with my hands rising to gently caress his jaw with my fingertips. The feel of his whiskers made my body sigh with the need for more.

I had been kissed before but by boys, not a man like Logan.

He leaned back way too soon, so I wrapped my hands behind his neck and pulled him in for one more.

When we finally leaned away from each other, our eyes locked for a shared, bliss-filled moment.

The tractor started just outside the closed barn door.

"Hmmm, damn sister," Logan grinned, and his hands wrapped my waist to lift me from the bales of hay.

We walked to the hitching post where I stuffed my hands deep in the pockets of my coat and leaned against the wall to quietly watch his every move as he saddled the horse.

Delaney had a large round bale of hay speared on the front of the tractor and was moving to the gate by the pasture. I stopped watching Logan and jogged to open the gate for her. She mouthed a thank you as she drove through. Logan was on his horse and walked by me with a hand stretched out. I reached up, and our fingers barely touched, and gaze met as he rode by. It was enough to make my whole body sigh in anticipation.

Wanting to remember the moment, I reached for my phone to take a picture of him riding into the pasture, but it wasn't in my pocket. I had left it in my room.

It was ringing when I opened the house door. It was the first phone call I received since I had arrived at the Rawlins ranch, so I ran to it in anticipation of talking to Camille.

But it wasn't her.

CHAPTER SEVEN

"Hello, Father Litton," My fingers gripped the phone tightly. I had been so worried about my father. He would have answers.

"Good morning, Lacie Jae," His voice was low and held the professional tone he used in church.

"What's wrong?" I lowered down onto the bed, and my gaze went out the window. I could see Logan and Delaney out in the herd of cattle.

"I went to your house this morning to talk Wayne into working at the church with me today," he answered. "He offered the other day to do some volunteer work…painting and such."

"He really needs that," I sighed. "He needs something to do."

"That was my thought after talking with him." There was a very long pause. "He still thought you two girls were at the rodeo."

"Oh…" I sighed and closed my eyes. "He's losing so much time. Maybe…I…maybe I should come back…"

"Lacie Jae, he didn't answer this morning…I had to go to the back door to get in."

My heart clenched, and tears tingled behind my eyes.

"Is he OK?" I whispered even though I knew he wasn't.

"He passed away overnight…in his recliner…peacefully."

A sob escaped. If I had been there, maybe he wouldn't have died. The guilt made my stomach hurt. Tears slid down my cheeks.

"If I had been there…?"

"I don't believe it would have made a difference," he said softly. "He looked normal yesterday morning when I was there. It wasn't that he was sick...or physically sick anyway."

Silence hung in the air.

"Where is he now? Is he still...at home?"

"No, he's at the coroner's office, then I'll have him transferred to the mortuary."

"Thank you," I took a deep breath. "I'll leave here soon, but it will take me four hours to get back."

"Would you like me to call Camille?"

"No...thank you..." Another deep breath. "I'll call her now."

"Call me when you arrive."

"I will," I whispered and ended the call.

Before I could think too much, I pushed the speed dial button to call her.

"It's early," she answered with a huff.

"Dad died last night," I said bluntly, so I didn't burst into tears. "Father Litton found him this morning. He said he died peacefully in his sleep."

"Where are you?"

"In Bend, Oregon with Delaney and Logan Rawlins...at their ranch."

I could hear her exhale, "So you stayed away. I was worried about that."

"But, if I'd been there..."

"This is not your fault in any way," Her voice rose in volume and urgency. "He was slowly killing himself...it just took five years for him to do it."

"Camille..." I sighed.

"He wanted to die after your mother's death...we both know that. He just gave up and with you leaving..."

"He didn't realize I had left. He thought we were still at the rodeo."

"Oh...well, I don't know..."

I sighed. I didn't know either.

"I'll be headed home, but it will take me four hours to get there."

"I'm on the south side of Fresno, so depending on traffic, it may be six hours before I can get there. I could take a flight…"

"I don't think that there is any reason to hurry."

"True…and I'd rather have my car. I'll meet you at the house."

"Alright," I sighed. "Father Litton is taking care of his…of him."

"The obvious question is what do we…where do we…?" Her voice faded.

"When we buried Mom, Dad bought the space next to her…he said to cremate him and just bury him with no funeral."

"Oh…well…I guess that's the toughest decision…and he made that."

I looked back out the window to see the Rawlins pair making their way back to the corrals.

"I need to go say goodbye to Delaney and Logan; then I'll head home."

"Alright…"

The call ended.

I walked back to the bathroom and wiped the tear streaks away. I didn't want a long goodbye with them, so I stuffed my clothes back in the sacks. My suitcase had remained in the car.

With a heavy heart, I carried the bags out of the house and down the stairs toward my car. Delaney had parked the tractor by the barn and Logan was tying his horse to the hitching post.

"Lacie Jae?" Delaney's voice called out as the pair quickly walked toward me.

They both looked shocked and worried.

I felt the tears rise again and fought hard to keep myself in control as I placed the bags on the back seat and turned to wait for them.

"You're leaving?" Logan exhaled in disbelief. There was hurt in his eyes.

"My father died last night," I blurted.

The hurt changed to dismay.

59

"Oh, Lacie Jae," Delaney wrapped her arms around me and pulled me close.

I leaned into her and absorbed as much of her warmth as possible.

"I'm so sorry," Logan said as he stood next to us.

I looked up into his warm brown eyes...the memory of our kiss made my heart hurt.

"You want me to go with you?" Delaney asked as she stepped back.

"No, I talked to Camille...she's headed home too. There's a lot to do...or figure out...and it will be up to the two of us."

"I can drive down with you and come back..." She offered with sincerity in her voice and eyes.

"Thank you," I hugged her again. "I'll miss you."

"You are a joy to be around...you're welcome here any time you need to get away," She said and stepped back. "We'll always need a calf feeder."

"Oh," I had to swallow hard to keep the tears down as I imagined the sweet little calf faces looking at me. "I'll miss them."

I turned to Logan...his arms opened to invite me in and I nearly jumped into them. I sighed into him and soaked in the comfort his arms gave me as they wrapped around me and squeezed. I wanted to stay there safe and warm in his arms forever. It took everything in me to lean away from him and step away. I couldn't look up at him. I just needed to leave.

"Thank you both so much for the best vacation..." The word drifted away. It hadn't felt like a vacation.

Logan opened the door for me and I slid in and started the car, so I could roll down the window and look back up at them.

"You let us know if you need anything," Delaney said softly. "We're here for you."

"Thank you," I said as the tears rose again.

Logan knelt by the window, so we were eye to eye.

As if it had a mind of its own, my hand rose, and fingers caressed his jaw.

"Come back," he whispered. There was worry and understanding in his eyes but also a bit of loss.

I smiled longingly then lowered my hand.

"Good-bye," I whispered and forced myself to drive away.

*****

I called Father Litton as soon as I parked in the driveway, then sat and stared at the house. The whole drive home, I wondered what this moment was going to be like. Dad wasn't there anymore...never would be again. The early years in the house with my mother were wonderful...most of the time. As hard as she tried, she couldn't get him to quit drinking and hellacious fights would occur. Camille and I would cower in our rooms or hide in the basement until it was over.

But now, I needed to try and hold onto the good times as I opened the door to the car and stepped out. My stride grew wider and faster up the brick walkway as I thought of Mom sitting in the dining room with a cup of coffee in one hand and a book in the other. When I opened the door to the house, I was almost expecting her to be there but, of course, she wasn't. Only dirty plates and three empty bottles of Jack Daniels were at the table instead of my beautiful mother.

Although it was chilly outside, I left the front door open to help with the stale odor of the house. Nothing in the house had changed since I had left, except the bottles that were on the table. I slid my coat off and tossed it on the back of the sofa as I walked down the hall to his room. I don't know why I was going there first...maybe just to confirm the fact he was gone.

Peering around the door to his room, it was confirmed...he was not there. The hollowness that had filled me was beginning to harden. I was going to need that to make it through the next few days.

The window I had opened before I left was still open. All of the whiskey bottles were gone from the room and I was

61

sure Father Litton had picked them up and set them on the kitchen table.

My bedroom door was closed and since he never went in there, he wouldn't have known I had left. Each day would have blurred into the next.

Not knowing what else to do, I pulled a garbage bag from the box under the kitchen sink and began picking up the whiskey bottles, half-eaten food, pizza boxes, and other garbage in the house. By the time Father Litton arrived, I was washing the last of the dishes.

"Lacie Jae?" He called out from the open front door.

"In the kitchen," I answered.

The older man with deep-set eyes, wide clean-shaven jaws, and a mass of black hair under a winter cap walked around the corner. He gave me a condolences nod before leaning against the counter as I finished the last dish.

"So…" I said with a sigh. "Where is he? What are we supposed to do next?"

"He's still at the coroner's office, then he will be transported to the mortuary when the autopsy is completed."

"He wanted to be cremated and buried next to my mother with no funeral."

"Is that what you want?"

I turned and looked at him with a bit of irritation, "No, I WANT my beautiful mother and my sober father to be here so I can sit and talk to them or give them a hug or…"

I forced myself to stop.

He took a deep breath with a nod, "I understand."

"But that won't happen and doing what he said he wanted, keeps us from having to decide what to do."

"Where is Camille?"

"She's driving up from Fresno."

"Would you like me to stay here with you?" He asked.

"No…that's not necessary," I answered and looked past him and into the portion of the living room I could see. "But…if you would…"

"What can I do?"

"You said he died in the recliner...can you please get it out of the house?"

His phone rang before he had a chance to answer me, "Do you mind?" He asked. "It's the coroner's office."

I just nodded.

He answered the call and was quiet at first, then he sighed and nodded, "I'm with Wayne's youngest daughter now." He handed the phone to me.

I did not want to do this! I did not want to talk about my father's dead body, but I took the phone with a trembling hand.

"Yes, this is Lacie Jae Madison."

"I'm sorry for your loss," The man's voice said. "I have finished the autopsy and have concluded that an aneurysm is the cause of death."

"Due to the alcohol," I sighed.

"Yes, the liver was failing and there were signs of high blood pressure...between the two, an aneurysm occurred."

I did not want to hear this...I did not want to imagine his last moments...I did not want any of this.

"Now what?" I asked. "What am I supposed to do? He wanted to be cremated, but I don't know what to do."

"We'll handle that for you," he said. "You'll need to meet with the funeral home director so you can make arrangements for the burial and sign papers."

"Alright, thank you," I said and handed the phone back to Father Litton.

After he slid the phone back in his pocket, he turned to the living room.

I could hear him moving the recliner, but I kept myself hidden in the kitchen.

"It's in the back of my truck," Father Litton called out from the door.

I hesitantly walked around the corner and into the living room. The carpet that the recliner had covered was a crisp light grey, unlike the rest of the room, which was very dingy and stained.

"When do we go to the mortuary?"

"I called and talked to them before you got here. They are ready to take care of everything. They just need signatures."

"Let's get it done before Camille gets here," I walked out the door.

The paperwork was signed, arrangements made, and I was back home before my sister arrived. The kitchen was clean, refrigerator emptied of the few items it had in it, and I was carrying empty garbage sacks to his room when she walked in the door.

I just glanced at her then continued down the hallway.

As we emptied the dresser drawers and closet of clothes that hadn't been worn in years, I told her of the arrangements. Then, in silence, we cleaned out the whole room; mattress, bed frame, dresser, tables, everything until it was all sitting on the lawn in front of the house.

Camille was surprised when I walked back in his room and began to rip up the carpet, but she just took a grip and pulled too. I don't know how many times I had cleaned vomit, spilled alcohol, and food off the floor. It was just gross. We rolled the carpet, and with extreme difficulty, we pulled it out of the house. We repeated with the grey living room carpet.

I called Father Litton, and he generously found volunteers to remove everything from the front yard.

Then, we showered, ordered pizza, sat on the patio furniture on the back deck with heavy blankets around us, and stared out at the lake view as the sun began to set. I would never be able to count the times we had looked out at the lake. It was a beautiful view, no matter what season.

"We need to go in Monday morning and meet with the financial advisor," I sighed. I wanted this over with and to move on.

"You do, I don't need to." Camille shrugged.

I turned and looked at her, "I can't do it by myself."

"You're very capable of…"

"No, Camille," I turned in the chair to face her. "I literally can't do it without you and your signature."

Her brow rose in confusion, "It was your mother's house, then your father's, so now it's yours."

64

My jaw dropped in amazement, "Dad never told you?"

"Told me what?" Her voice was impatient as if she wanted to leave.

"About the house and the investments…"

"The only investment I know about is our college fund, which I have used mine already. He said what I didn't use would just be yours."

"It doesn't work like that," I shook my head in amazement.

"He said that the money would go to you," she repeated.

"I don't understand why he would tell you that."

"Because he was an alcoholic, abusive father, who didn't like me because I wouldn't take care of him and because I was born from the wrong wife," Camille abruptly stood and walked in the house, slamming the door behind her.

I thought of what she said and was very sad to admit the truth…she was indeed right on everything. With a sigh, I rose to follow her.

She was standing at the front window, staring out into the night sky.

"I admit, you're right," I walked to stand next to her; she didn't move. "But, to me, he was an alcoholic, abusive father, who only tolerated me because I took care of him, but hated me because I reminded him that the right wife was dead."

Her shoulders lowered, but she still stared at the stars in the sky.

"But, my mother loved you, and you know that," I sighed, and when she nodded, I continued. "The amount in your college fund is yours. Mine is totally separate. Mother set up a bank account for Dad, with my name too, that would deposit $3,000 monthly and would pay for anything he needed. The house was paid for, so it was only utilities, food, and his bottles that came out of the account." She still didn't move, so I continued. "Since he barely used that amount monthly, let alone the large amount it started at, the account has just been building. There is over $200,000 in the account now."

She turned to me with wide eyes.

"Mother gave Dad living rights to this house until the day he died, and then the house belongs to both of us."

She gasped, "She did that?"

"Yes, because she loved us," I said softly. "The worst thing she did was give Dad no reason to work and earn money, yet enough money he could drink himself into oblivion. The best thing she did was to make sure we could go to college and make a living for ourselves. With the house, we would be financially OK after he died."

She looked around the dingy walls, carpet-less floor, old lights, and furniture, "I don't want his house."

I didn't need to look around; I already knew. "I don't either. I think we should use half of the money in the bank to have it modernized, then sell it, and split the equity."

"I agree," she whispered.

My mother had died as the executive of a chain of banks, so the house set in a high-end neighborhood. With the $100,000 put into the house, I estimated it would sell for at least a million dollars. Camille and I both knew that, we didn't need to speak of it.

"I have a friend that is a designer and real estate agent," Camille turned to look back out into the sky. "I can contact her tomorrow and she'll be able to handle all the remodeling and the sale of the house, so we don't have to."

"I agree with that," I sighed. "I may hate the house, but I don't want to be here during the remodel."

"We'll meet with the advisor and her in the morning," Camille turned from the window.

"Alright," I nodded. "Have you talked to your mother?"

Her shoulder rose in a half-hearted shrug, "No, why bother? I'll just tell her when I get down there."

"You're still going?" It was barely a whisper.

"Yes," she answered and walked down the hall to her old bedroom.

With my father gone, I had no other family but her; she knew that and yet she was still leaving. I walked to my own room and shut the door. Laying down on the bed, I stared up at the ceiling. Had it really just been hours since I was in that blissful bubble kissing Logan?

I hated this reality and hated the fact that I was now an orphan. I curled into myself and let the tears flow.

Sunday morning before church, we met Father Litton and three other men at the cemetery next to my mother's grave. In the grave next to hers, a small hole had been dug to hold the urn that held our father's ashes.

I knelt next to my mother's headstone with tears threatening to fall. It was a pink marble two-foot-tall stone that held the words: Lacie Janine Madison, Beloved Wife and Mother, 1977-2014. I carried a dozen yellow roses for her and placed them at the base of the headstone.

I missed her. Every fiber in my body wanted to scream at the need for her. I wanted to hear her voice, see her smile, feel her loving arms around me! I wanted to run away from this reality, but I just turned to the hole in the ground. Without looking at anyone, I waited until the urn was set on a pedestal next to the hole.

Father Litton said a prayer then spoke briefly of a man that had been lost in the world and had lost his world when my mother died. He spoke of my father's love for his daughters. Neither Camille nor I said anything.

When Father Litton nodded that he was finished, we both turned away and walked toward Camille's car. Half-way there, I hesitated then turned back to the graves. I stopped between the two and slowly knelt. With a trembling hand, I took two of the yellow roses from my mother's headstone and placed them next to the pedestal holding my father's urn. I needed to believe he loved his daughters and someday I was going to need to forgive him.

I stood and looked between the two graves. My heart hurt, my body hurt, my mind was going numb. I didn't want this. I hated this. I wanted to scream and cry, but instead, I turned and walked away.

On Monday, we met with the designer first thing in the morning then financial advisor late in the afternoon.

That night at the house, Camille and I stood in the living room in silence. Memories of the house flooded through me. It was where we had lived as a family with my mother when we were young. It stopped being a home when she died.

I wrote Camille a check for a quarter of the amount that was sitting in my father's bank account; $52,348.

The check sat like a beacon on the table. Other than the final check for the house, it was the only thing that bound the two of us together.

"I want you to know something," I whispered to Camille.

She didn't reach for the check. Instead, she stood at the back door and looked out at the lake view. "What?"

"We are family," I exhaled as I stared at the check. "I do love you, but you are choosing your mother, Kendra, and Eve over me." I stood and took a deep breath. "You are throwing away the wrong person."

There was silence as I walked down to my room and shut the door.

In the morning, the check had been replaced by a note:
I'll contact you when I get back. Merry Christmas Sister

All the life and energy drained out of me as I walked to the front window to see her car gone, only my old Ford sat in the driveway.

I turned to look back at the house then to the Ford. I needed to find somewhere to stay while the work was completed on the house, so I dressed and stuffed all my clothes back into the garbage bags. The suitcase with my mother's pictures was still in the trunk. I drove away from the house knowing I would never return but with no real destination in mind.

Then, I passed a car dealership, and without much thought, I drove in.

I sat in the 'new to me' RAV4 at the parking lot pull-out to the road and had nowhere to go. I wasn't expected at the coffee shops for work for another two weeks. I had no home to go to and no family to go to, so I sat and watched the cars pass.

I could go to Texas for the winter months. I'd always wanted to see the Alamo. Or I could fly to New York and be in Times Square for the New Year celebration. Maybe drive to San Francisco and catch a cruise to Hawaii. Or fly to Miami and go to the Bahamas. With my large college fund and the $52,348 in the shared bank account, I could do whatever I wanted.

PART ONE

DELANEY

6 Months Before

CHAPTER EIGHT

"Delaney!"

"Dad!"

"I put new tie-down straps in the truck toolbox."

"Happy for ya!" I chuckled to myself as I stepped up into the back of the truck. Even though I couldn't see him, I knew he would take the teasing with a laugh.

He appeared around the end of the flat-bed trailer that was piled high with thousand-pound round bales of hay. Two rows of five, set at the bottom, and he had just used the tractor to place four more bales on top.

His grin greeted me as he walked toward me. "You're a bit of a smart ass."

"You know, everyone says I take after you."

"That's not necessarily a good thing."

"Funny, that's what I tell them," I smirked as I pulled the new straps from the toolbox and tossed them to him.

We chuckled at each other as we both threw a strap over the top of the highest bales. Well-practiced at strapping the load down, we worked without talking until the last crank of the ratchet handle was closed across the back row.

"You want tractor or truck?" Dad asked.

I shrugged, "Truck, I guess, my phone is already in it."

"Humph," he huffed. "And my phone is in the tractor."

"See ya at the barn," I smiled at him and watched him turn and walk down the length of the extended trailer.

When he disappeared around the end, I slid onto the seat of the truck and started the engine as my hand went to my phone. I quickly checked for any message from Brodie, Craig, or Logan, who were at the Sunday afternoon performance of the Coulee City rodeo in northern Washington. The message stated Brodie placed third in saddle bronc and in bareback; Craig won bareback and placed second in saddle bronc; and Logan won steer wrestling. I was so proud of them and knew the three of them were going to have a good drive back home.

I shifted into drive and pulled forward. The back of the trailer rocked and my eyes shot to the side-mirror in time to see the top back bale of hay roll off onto the ground and bounce as the second bale rolled off behind it.

"Son-of-a-bitch," I threw it back in park and turned off the engine.

Walking toward the back, I stopped next to the hole in the trailer where the ratchet had been fastened. The brass was now in pieces on the ground, and the strap stretched out behind the trailer and under the escaped bales.

"The ratchet broke," I yelled out and started walking around the back of the trailer. The sound of the tractor's engine sounded odd...muffled.

"Dad?" I called out as I rounded the trailer.

Two of the bales had rolled against the tractor.

There was no sign of my father. I instantly broke into a run as my heart pounded in rising fear.

"Dad!"

The tractor was precariously tipped on the two wheels on the far side—one bale against it and the other pinning him between it and the trailer. I couldn't see him under the bales.

"Dad!"

I ran to the roof of the tractor and peered underneath. My heart sunk. His chest lay on the seat of the tractor with his body and legs pinned between the machine and the thousand-pound bale of hay. It looked like he had dove into the tractor.

A deep moan of pain escaped from him.

"Dad?" I had no doubt the tractor could continue the fall at any second, but that didn't stop me from crawling under the roof and stretched a trembling hand to him. He was unconscious but moaned deeply. His breaths were exhaled in obvious pain.

There was no way I could move him by myself. Kneeling on the ground with one hand gripping his shoulder, I called 911.

It took three tractors to release him as the medics stayed at his side. One tractor braced the roof of the trailer so it couldn't move, while two other tractors were hoisting the bales at the same time. Within minutes, he was on a backboard and carefully being loaded into the ambulance.

I crawled in next to him with my phone gripped tightly in my hands. On the ride, I called my brothers.

In the hospital waiting room, I was surrounded by the men that had helped in the rescue. Their families arrived as well as Craig's father, Martin. With his arm firmly around my shoulders, we waited for Craig, Logan, and Brodie to arrive.

"Have you heard anything?" Logan asked after running down the hall.

"No," I whispered and held onto him for support. I took Brodie's hand in mine. "They've been back there with…"

My words faltered when the door opened and a tall older man in blue scrubs walked out. He looked around at the nearly thirty people that were waiting in the small room.

"Rawlins?" He asked.

"That's us," All three of us stepped toward him.

He nodded and took a deep breath, "Both femurs were broken and his pelvis."

"Oh, God…" I exhaled as the tears rose.

"Is he going to be OK?" Brodie asked.

The doctor nodded with a deep frown and stern look between the three of us, "Those will heal."

I gasped and tried to brace myself.

"There is also damage to the lower spine," He continued. "He was unconscious when he arrived and still hasn't woken, but we don't have any reflex from his legs."

"He's paralyzed?" Brodie exhaled.

"We'll know more when he wakes," The doctor nodded. "But, there is a strong possibility he will be paralyzed."

"But he'll live?" Logan's hand tightened around mine.

"He has a long road of recovery ahead of him," The doctor answered with a grim expression. "There is no head injury, nor did we find internal injuries. The bones will heal and we'll have to wait for the spine."

"Can we see him?" I asked, hopefully.

"As soon as we move him to his own room," he answered.

It was an hour of waiting and praying before the three of us were escorted back to his room. It was another hour before his eyes opened. There was confusion followed by fear then relief when he saw me.

"What happened?" he whispered.

"The ratchet came apart," I answered. "The bales rolled off and pinned you against the tractor."

"Thank God you were in the truck," He whispered as tears filled his eyes. "Thank the Lord…thank…" He closed his eyes as the emotion overwhelmed him.

The next 48 hours were a blur of doctors, phone calls, turning well-wishers away from his room and trying to rest when we could. We didn't leave the hospital as we waited for the reality of his paralysis to set in with him.

"Just give me a fucking percentage," Dad growled at the doctor. His eyes were glazed and voice slurred from the pain killers. His body was covered in a cast from his chest to his ankles.

"It's too early to tell," The doctor said. "You have to give it time to heal…you have to…"

"YOU," Dad yelled. "Have to give me the percentage to start with."

I stepped in between them and the glare he had directed to the doctor turned to me…then slowly faded as I smiled at him and squeezed his hand.

"It's only been two days," I whispered. "Let's give it another week before you start pissing off doctors and making them quit."

"Two days?" He asked as his eyes started to close. "Feels like months…"

His body sighed back into the bed, and within moments, his snores took over.

"I'm not leaving," I huffed at Dad.

Only four days after the accident, he glared at us from the hospital bed.

"Delaney…" He grumbled.

"No, I am not leaving. I have no event I need to be at this weekend. I'm not worried about the Circuit Finals, nor am I trying to qualify for the NFR this year…so, again, I am not leaving," I said.

He glared at me then turned to Logan, Brodie, and Craig. "You will not be standing here by my bed doing nothing. I know your schedule for the next couple of months; Central Point this weekend, Sisters next weekend, then Cowboy Christmas."

All three stood uncomfortably silent.

"I'll be here as well," Martin added. "Delaney and I will take care of Evan as you three take care of business."

All three men looked dejected.

"Dad..." Logan exhaled.

"If you don't go, tell me what you're going to do while I'm lying here in bed sleeping or watching movies," Dad growled.

They just looked at him in rising frustration.

I stepped to the side of the bed and turned to them.

"Martin and I will take care of him," I said in understanding.

"There is nothing to do but lie here and heal for the next 6 to 8 weeks," Dad said. "And you three...and Delaney after this weekend will just bother the hell out of me."

Their shoulders lowered in defeat. He gave me this weekend; I wasn't going to argue about the coming weeks until I had to.

A week later, I had to, and I stood in just as much defeat as Logan, Brodie, and Craig had.

"I may be broken on the lower half, but the upper half still works pretty damn well," Dad grumbled at me from his bed. "Sisters rodeo is this weekend and there's no damn reason you're going to miss it."

Four weeks after the accident, two days before Logan, Brodie, Craig and I were leaving for the rodeo in Prineville, then Meridian, and Mountain Home, I walked toward Dad's bedroom. Martin greeted me in the hall as I knocked on the door.

"Get your asses in here!" Dad called out.

I looked at Martin in concern then nervously turned the handle to enter the room, which was more of a suite with a sitting area, large walk-in closet and expansive bathroom.

When we entered, there was nothing out of the ordinary. Dad was laying back in the bed with food on one end table and water on the other. He had the remote in hand, held in mid-air as he pointed it at the television, which instantly became quiet.

"What's wrong?" I asked and stepped into the room.

"Nothing," he smirked. "My feet are hot and I need the blanket off of them."

I shook my head in disbelief as Martin grumbled.

"Why the hell didn't you call?" He asked our patient as he flipped the covers off his feet. "I'm twenty fucking steps away."

"Where are the boys?" Dad asked without even acknowledging that Martin had spoken.

"In the kitchen, getting ready to go move the heifers," I answered.

"I need to talk to them, too," Dad growled with an impatient huff.

"Fine…" I mumbled under my breath and called down the hall for the three men.

They walked in with shoulders high, lips rolled into grim lines, and eyes darting between me and Dad, who looked between the five of us and took a deep breath.

"The next eight weeks, between the rodeos this weekend then into the Cowboy Christmas run all the way to Pendleton Roundup, you four are going to be busy," He said.

"Yeah, but we don't…" Brodie started.

"Don't interrupt me, Son," Dad said to him. "I just want you to know that while you're out on the road, Martin has agreed to be here…and I'll be hiring a part-time nurse…"

"Dad…" I sighed.

"And you don't be interrupting me either, Daughter," Dad smirked. "You four will be busy, and I'm going to be sitting here twiddling my fingers…" He paused and grinned. "…and my toes."

With that, he wiggled all ten toes for the first time since the accident.

I don't know how that room could hold the amount of emotion that flooded out of us.

"How's your dad?"

I coiled the rope then leaned down to attach it to the saddle. The team roping jackpot was over.

"Getting anxious," I answered as I turned my grey horse toward my roping partner, Kim. "He's been pretty patient the last six weeks, but the cast is removed on Tuesday, and he says he's going to keep it and make a scarecrow out of it."

She laughed, "I can see Evan doing that!"

"Me too," I chuckled. "He has a lot of physical therapy ahead of him, but he's keeping his sense of humor."

"Are you going to Calgary?"

"Logan is after the rodeo in St. Paul with Brodie and Craig. Then the pair are hitting the road pretty hard."

"And you?"

"I want to be with Dad the first weeks of therapy, so I'll hit the Circuit rodeos as I can…depending."

She gave me a smile of understanding, "Give him my best."

"They are bringing him up from x-ray now," the nurse said as she walked into the room.

Martin and I both turned to her.

"Did they say anything?" I asked nervously. "It's been so long…hours."

She shook her head, "They removed the cast and gave him a bit of a sponge bath…"

As if on cue, the door opened and Dad was pushed into the room in a wheelchair by his doctor. That surprised and worried me. Dad's expression was pensive.

"Dad?" I whispered.

He looked up at me and gave me a slightly forced smile but didn't say anything.

I looked to the doctor…who was unreadable.

"We've conducted a few initial tests," The doctor said. "Evan asked me to explain it to you."

He continued as the words just ran together and I stared at Dad's expression. It was up to Martin to remember the technical words, but what it came to was his femurs healed well. He could move his legs and would begin therapy for the broken hip immediately. During the initial testing, his attempt to stand was painful…unbearable. There was the possibility that even with movement and therapy, he may still be confined to the wheelchair.

The longer the doctor spoke, the harder my father's expression became. For the last week, we had planned and dreamed of his journey to get back on his feet and on a horse, maybe never steer wrestling again, but at least on his own two feet.

From the narrowing of his eyes and the increasing rising of his chest, he was realizing the chair was his future. He was working hard on not saying a word.

My heart ached for him as I looked at the doctor, to the nurse, then to Martin.

"Can we go home now?" I asked and stepped between the doctor and my father. Without waiting for an answer, I pushed Dad out of the room and down the hall.

Martin and the doctor walked next to us.

"He has an 8:00 am therapy appointment." The doctor said.

"Alright…" I nodded without looking at him. I stopped at the elevator and pushed the button with a trembling hand.

CHAPTER NINE

"Well, that interview took forever," Logan grumbled as he walked out the door of the meeting room. We strode quickly down the hallway of the MGM Grand Casino.

"He sure stuttered a lot. Like he didn't really know what he was talking about," I said.

"Yeah...when he asked if it hurt when I jumped off my horse, I kind of figured he was a bit lost," Logan chuckled. "We're late getting over to the arena, but Brodie is warming up Fred for you."

We stepped out into the main casino with the noise and cigarette smell assaulting our senses.

My phone rang, "Hold on." I stopped and pulled the phone out of my jacket. "Hey, Dad."

"You're supposed to be the sane one getting those boys to the places they are supposed to be on-time," He shouted over the cows mooing in the background.

I grinned, "One of those lost interviewers that we couldn't get to shut up, so I finally just stood and walked to the door. The car is waiting for us and we're headed over now."

"Just talked to Brodie, he said there are a few anxious people waiting for last night's buckle winner to interview," Dad yelled.

"We're on our way," I assured him with a loving smile. He was always looking out for us.

"Call me back when the steer wrestlers are up."

"Will do...love ya, Dad."

"You too, Darlin'."

I slid my phone in my pocket as I looked for Logan.

He was walking toward a girl that was standing in the aisle looking around her like she was a terrified kitten surrounded by dogs. Her hands gripped her purse as if she was ready for someone to rip it out of her hands at any moment. She was tiny, had short white-blonde hair, large blue eyes, and she looked totally disoriented and out of place.

"Are you lost?" Logan asked the girl. "I know it's confusing in here. Can I help direct you somewhere?"

I had to smile as the girl leaned away from my brother who, at 6' 5", towered over her.

"I was headed to the rodeo," She stammered. "But…"

"Were you looking for the shuttle? Are you with someone?" He asked and I was sure the girl was going to burst into tears.

"Logan, you're scaring the hell out of her," I turned to the girl who I thought was only a teenager but was actually older…maybe twenty or so. "Sorry," I said. "His size is a bit intimidating to some people and as tiny as you are it must be that much worse."

Her eyes flickered between us as her lips twitched into somewhat of a smile.

"Well, I'm sorry if I scared you," Logan said in his soothing voice as if to a frightened colt.

Her shoulders lowered and her grip on her purse relaxed.

"We're headed there now," I said. "We can show you where to catch the shuttle or you can ride over with us. We're headed out to catch an Uber car."

"Do you have someone with you?" Logan asked.

"They are on the shuttle already…on their way," she answered.

"They left you behind?" I gasped. Who in the hell would do that?

"Yes, she figured I could catch the next shuttle but I don't have any idea where it's at, and I can't find a sign." She nodded.

"Who is she?" Logan asked.

"My sister," The blonde grumbled with an exasperated sigh. "…and her two friends."

"I'm guessing an older sister and you're the odd one out," I said.

"You have no idea," Her whole body relaxed as she rolled her pretty blue eyes. "All three of them are at least four years older than me and they are at least six inches taller and they are wearing boots with heels!"

"I know that feeling." I chuckled at Logan, who was eight inches taller than me. "We need to get to the center. What would you like to do?"

I could tell she wanted to go with us, but I'm sure her common sense was kicking in about going somewhere in Vegas with people you didn't know.

"There are cameras all over the place in here and we're going in a public Uber," I assured her.

"Alright," she huffed nervously. "I'd rather ride in an Uber than a shuttle."

"Let's go then," I said and pulled out my phone to glance at the time. Damn, we were really running late.

I slid onto the backseat behind the driver and the blonde buckled up next to me. We smiled at each other and the little inkling of a happy soul shown through.

"I'm Lacie Jae Madison," She said.

What a freaking cute name and her looks matched it perfectly.

"Do you go by Lacie or Lacie Jae?" Logan asked.

"Lacie Jae," She answered. "My mother's name was Lacie, too, so it helped."

"Delaney and Logan Rawlins," I said. "Nice to meet you. Where are you from?"

"Redding, California," she answered. "And you?"

"Bend, Oregon," I glanced up at Logan and could just see a smile. "Have you been to the finals before?"

"Finals for what?" She asked with a slight confused frown.

My lips rolled together to keep from grinning. "The rodeo we're headed to...the NFR ...National Finals Rodeo.... The Finals..."

Her cheeks flamed red, "Oh, my gosh, that is embarrassing. I've never been to a rodeo before."

"You've never been to a rodeo, and you start with this one?" I asked with a chuckle.

"So, I'm guessing this is like the Super Bowl for football?" She asked with a humored grin.

"Yes," I answered. "So you've never been to the Thomas and Mack Center? Where the rodeo is held?"

She shook her head.

"Let me see your ticket and I'll walk you through how to get to your seat," I would love to take her, but there just wasn't time.

"Thank goodness Camille gave me the ticket before we left our room tonight," she handed me the ticket.

She suddenly looked pissed with her face turning red and nostrils flaring.

"Lacie Jae," I whispered. "You alright?"

"Yes," She huffed and a determined glint shown from her eyes.

I gave her specific instructions on how to get to her seat and even typed my phone number into her phone in case she was lost again.

"Thank you so much," she said with an appreciative grin. "Thank you both for coming to my rescue."

"I'm glad he didn't scare you off," I chuckled and looked up at Logan.

She stepped out of the car and closed the door.

"Hurry," I told the driver. "To the back, and we're running really late."

"Who was on the phone?" Logan asked.

"Dad, telling us to get our asses in gear and get over here."

"Brodie tattle-taling again," Logan huffed.

"Little brothers…"

As soon as the Uber stopped, we both shot out and weaved between the horses, riders, family members and staff.

Our little brother's eyes were full of relief when he saw us.

"Son-of-a-bitch!" Brodie cried out. "What the hell took so long? I've had everyone and their families over here trying to find Logan."

"You going to ride in the grand entry for him?" I laughed.

I knew how much he wanted to be part of that grand entry, but in his own time and under his own name. I had no doubt it was going to happen; we all believed he would make it.

"They would have to have football pads for me to pass off as him," Brodie grinned and stepped out of the saddle.

"Where's Craig?" I stroked the nose of the buckskin gelding, Cinco. This wasn't the first time this horse had been to this rodeo and ridden in the grand entry. He had been my father's steer wrestling horse and Logan had ridden him in the entry his first two qualifying years, then I rode him the last two years.

"He's meeting us at the seats," Brodie answered.

"Well, let's get out there," I said to him and turned to Logan. "Kickass."

"Don't fall on your face," Brodie gave him a smart ass grin, which made those people around us laugh.

I sat between Brodie and Craig as the parade of riders ran onto the dirt. The arena was full of horses, flags, riders, and excitement. I'd ridden in that entry the last two years and I knew how heart-pounding it was…truly an unforgettable experience.

"We'll see you two there next year," I said to the pair of best friends.

"I believe!" They shouted in unison as if on a church's pulpit. We all laughed.

The pair met when they were little cowboys at a junior rodeo and both riding sheep. Even without knowing each other, they had encouraged the other to hold on and ride hard. Every junior rodeo and clinic they attended the two would pair-up for the weekend.

Craig's parents divorced when the boys were eleven, with Craig choosing to live with his dad. Martin moved them closer to Bend and the two boys became inseparable.

As soon as they turned eighteen, they bought their permits for the PRCA and hit the road. They both wanted to win, so they flipped a coin to choose who would ride Saddle Broncs and who would compete in Bareback. There were no better nights than the few times they had managed to both win their event on the same night. Occasionally, they would compete in both events to try and earn more money to keep on the road.

Having been on the road himself, and helping Logan and I fulfill our dreams to ride at the NFR, Dad always made sure they had just enough money in the bank to make it to the next rodeo.

The only 'problem' with their friendship was Craig's undying crush on me. I saw him as a little brother; he always teased about wanting more.

He was a good looking cowboy, same 5' 10" as Brodie, slim but muscular. They kept themselves in good shape even when they were on the road. Both were joggers and found swimming holes anywhere they could find them. They also used yoga to help stretch and strengthen their bodies. Craig's mother was of Indian heritage, which meant his complexion was darker than Brodie's but, from the back, you could barely tell them apart.

At the moment, Craig was slowly maneuvering his right arm over the back of my chair and across my shoulders.

"You really want me to make a scene with all these cameras around here?" I asked without looking at him.

They both chuckled.

"Someday..." Craig sighed in false hope as his arm was lowered back to his side.

"Someday, you'll find a girl that doesn't think of you as a kid brother," I told him.

"I've said it before," Craig grinned. "Just give me one chance to show you I'm not your kid brother."

"Eeeww," I crinkled my nose at him.

He just laughed; his dark brown eyes danced in humor.

The grand entry and national anthem were completed, and all eyes went to the bucking chutes.

Our seats were next to the roping chutes, so the full length of the arena was between us and the riders as they burst out of the chute. Both my companions would grunt, swear under their breaths, moan or cheer as the bareback riders competed. There were a number of whispered disagreements with the scores given.

Although most people wouldn't notice it, there was clear longing in their voices to be out in the arena riding the bucking horses.

"Next year," I whispered to the pair.

Neither responded more than a slight nod of the head.

As the last bareback rider burst from the chute, I turned back to the roping boxes to see the mass of steer wrestlers behind the panels. I took out my phone and started the video chat with Dad and Martin so they could watch the event live instead of the delayed national broadcast.

Logan was the seventh competitor and we watched and quietly critiqued the first six. Other than being his friends, they were the best in the world and Logan had to be top of his game to retain his world champion title. His win the night before propelled him into second place overall and first place in the average.

He knew exactly where we were sitting, but not once did he look in our direction. His full concentration was visualizing the run. It was something Dad had taught all of us, even Craig. Visualize the positive-winning ride that you want to make.

I tried to stay relatively calm as his horse, Fred, carried him into the arena, but my racing heart proved it was impossible. No matter how many times we had watched each other compete, it was always heart pounding at this level. Logan, Brodie, and Craig had all told me they held their breaths each time I had competed in barrels the previous two years. I found myself holding mine as Logan backed the brown horse into the box.

Memories of Dad doing the same thing in this same arena made me smile a bit. I took Brodie's hand and squeezed. He was only fourteen the first year Dad had competed here and, in doing so, had won enough money to pay off the debtors trying to take our land.

Brodie squeezed back without a glance or word.

Logan nodded and everything froze for that 4.8 seconds until he was on the ground letting go of the steer.

"Yes!" Brodie screamed.

"Way to go, Logan!" Craig yelled.

"Way to go, Fred!" I yelled and was still grinning when Logan finally turned to glance up at us.

He tipped his hat toward us, but the three of us knew it wasn't for us. It was to Dad, who was cheering on the phone.

I flipped it around and looked at Dad and Martin, who were beaming in pride.

"He'll keep second," Dad said with a confident nod.

"We're only halfway there," I chuckled.

"He's got it...flip me back around so we can see the rest," he ordered.

I did as he said, and we watched as his prediction came true. Logan took second for the night and remained second overall and kept his first in the average.

When I flipped the phone around and saw my father's smug mug, I had to laugh.

"I love you, Dad." I chuckled.

Craig and Brodie leaned between me and the phone with big grins.

"We love you too, Dad," they sang out.

Dad and Martin laughed.

"Good luck in the morning," Dad said to me.

"Thanks...you're still coming tomorrow morning?" I asked, hopefully.

"I'll be there and in time to see you rope and Logan ride the last two nights," He nodded.

"Lots of people are looking forward to seeing you," I smiled, but his shoulders rose. "They want to see you; they don't care about the wheelchair."

He just nodded, "Have fun."

The call ended as the first team of ropers backed into the box.

"He just needs to get in front of them," Brodie exhaled.

"We'd have just as much apprehension if it was us," I sighed.

"Don't be too much of a cushion for him," Brodie turned to me. "Don't babysit him."

"I have no intention of doing that," I sighed again. "He'll be OK; they will all welcome him with open arms, and by the end of the weekend, he'll accept it that little more."

"And be here ALL next year as the two of us ride here," Craig added.

Without hesitation, all three of us threw our arms in the air and yelled, "I believe!"

"Why don't you just stay in the condo with us?" Craig asked as we walked through the doors of The Grandview Hotel we called home for the two weeks in Vegas.

I looked at him as if he was insane for even asking, "One woman, three men...five after tomorrow...no thank you!"

All four of us laughed, but mine ended with a big yawn.

"Last night's late buckle party and up early this morning, I need a night of solid sleep," I sighed and followed them to their door.

"It's only 10:30," Brodie complained.

"You go out if you want, but I'm going to bed," Logan said and opened their door.

"Want me to walk you to your door?" Craig asked with the light of humor in his eyes.

"Yeah…no…" I huffed and shook my head. "I'm not letting any of you know where my room is."

He grinned again, "Ah…"

"Text me when you get to your room," Logan ordered and shut the door behind them.

I quickly turned to sprint down the hall to the stairway. My room was one flight up…nearly over the top of theirs.

I sent a text as I jogged up the stairs: 60 seconds.

I received an immediate text back: I'll be there in 2 minutes.

My pace increased and hand dipped in my pocket for the key. In a flash, the door was open, and I was shedding my coat, shirt, boots, jeans, and running into the bathroom to run a wet towel over my face and brush my hair.

I quickly sent a text to Logan so he wouldn't worry.

Barely five strokes of the toothbrush made it across my teeth before I was rinsing out my mouth. My hand hit the towel to dry my lips when the door lock clicked.

I hustled to the sofa and threw myself on the cushions. With hand sliding my hair back out of my face, I turned as the door opened.

He was in quickly, and pushing the door closed behind him as his head turned to me. A wide excited grin spread across his face as his eyes roamed from my bare legs to my tousled hair…then there was the lacy blue panties and bra.

"I have been envisioning you in those since you sent me the picture of them lying on the bed this morning," He kicked off his boots.

"I wore them all day thinking of you," I purred.

"You wore lace while roping?" He shed his shirt then went for the buckle on his jeans.

"Yeah," I giggled. "I may have lace rash."

"Well, I'll just have to thoroughly check that out for you."

His cowboy hat hit the end table seconds before he fell into my arms.

CHAPTER TEN

My team roping partner, Kim, and I sat on the horses behind the fence of the arena and watched the steer break out of the chute. The pair of ropers were right behind it.

"They've been great steers all week," Kim mused.

"Straight but fast," I nodded. "We'll need to hustle."

"I'll push the barrier…just stay up with us," Kim glanced at me with a smart-ass grin. Her eyes were covered in dark sunglasses under the white straw cowboy hat.

It was sunny, only 60 degrees but at least it wasn't raining. We were four teams out, so I removed my coat and handed it down to Craig. My hair was braided down my back and laid over a crisp white-collared long-sleeved shirt that was covered in patches and embroidery from my sponsors.

I stretched out my arms, relaxed my shoulders, and took a deep breath then pushed my cowboy hat tighter on my head.

"Have you seen them yet?" I asked Craig.

"Nah, got a text from Brodie that they were leaving the airport," he answered.

"Well, will you record it for him just in case?" I asked as I adjusted my sunglasses then shifted my hat again.

"Of course," he turned and took off at a jog to the bleachers for a good view of the arena.

"Kim Havens and Delaney Rawlins are next in, then we have…" The announcer's voice boomed over the speakers.

I calmly nudged my grey horse, Ketchum, forward and looked at the steer in the chute. Just another run, I said to myself. I visualized the run…the feel of the rope, my arm positioned perfectly and the throw as the rope slid out of my hand and across my fingers. Tip of the rope aimed perfectly, so the loop would dance around the back hooves of the steer...arm jerked back to take up the slack and trap the hooves before dallying around the horn.

I visualized the perfect throw again and remembered the way it felt as I backed into the box. Ketchum stood completely still, but alert as his ears twitched in anticipation of the run. The horse loved to chase cows.

I turned and looked at Kim; she was concentrating on the steer, rope balanced perfectly in her hand. She glanced at me, and I nodded to let her know I was ready. The steer was calm, looking straight ahead and Kim nodded. Instantly the rush of the run tingled through me as my legs squeezed the horse's sides and lifted me up in the stirrups so I could lean just enough to see the hooves of the steer. Kim's rope was around the horns and she turned the steer giving me an angle for my throw...it was already flying to trap the hooves. I leaned back while wrapping the dally and stopping the horse to tighten the slack. The hooves lifted from the ground as Kim and her horse spun around to face us. All in 8.2 seconds.

A quick tremble of elation and relief swept through me as I turned to Kim with a grin.

"Nice! One down," I said as we trotted out of the arena.

Our second run was even better at 7.9 seconds and we won the short-go, winning just over $14,000 each.

The nerves that had been resting in my gut began to bubble. With years of guidance from Dad, I always managed to keep them at bay until after I was done running, whether with roping or barrels. Focus first, stress after.

I turned to look for dad or anyone in our group.

"How is your dad?" Kim asked as if reading my mind.

Wanting to keep full concentration on the roping, we didn't discuss him all morning.

"Health-wise, he is fine. He's been in physical therapy four times a week and is growing in strength." I answered. "But he is still mentally getting used to being in a wheelchair."

She nodded as we stepped off the horses and led them through the trucks and trailers.

"As active as he was all his life...the roping, steer wrestling, ranch life..." she sighed. "I couldn't even imagine it."

"Well, he says at least he had 46 years of activity and adventure before he landed in it," I said as I searched for them by the food truck and bleachers. "And, of course, he was glad it happened after mom had passed away."

"Tough years and he's a tough man. He'll make it through; you're a strong family."

"Thanks, I agree, but this is his first trip to any jackpot or rodeo. He didn't want to miss being here for Logan, even if it meant facing all his old friends."

"They'll want to see him and not care about the chair."

"That's what we've been telling him. He just needs this first time...then it will be better."

"There she is," I heard the familiar voice approaching from the side.

Martin was walking toward us, but he was alone.

I smiled hesitantly, "Good to see you, but where is Dad?"

He gave me a quick hug, "Once he rolled up next to the bleachers to watch, half-a-dozen cowboys came over to visit with him. He hasn't stopped talking for the last half hour."

Relief ran through me, "did he see our run?"

"Saw the last two," Martin nodded and turned to my roping partner. "Haven't seen you in a while, Kim. Nice runs...congratulations."

"Thanks, Martin," she shook his hand. "It felt good...we were on a roll."

"One more on Friday," I added. "But, we got this."

Craig appeared with a hand stretched out to me. "Let me have the horse and you go see your dad." He smiled as if holding in a secret.

I handed him the reins but turned to Kim, "I'll contact you later for practice."

We nodded to each other in shared respect, then I turned to follow Martin down the dirt road and toward the food truck and bleachers.

"How was the trip down?" I asked.

"He managed it pretty well," he said softly. "He was pretty anxious but determined to see your runs and be here for Logan."

"I am so glad he is here. Now he'll see that people want to see him."

"Oh, he's getting the picture," Martin chuckled and tipped his chin up to point toward the bleachers.

Dad was sitting in his chair, leaned into a conversation with his hands motioning wildly. Five other men were staring at him and hanging onto every word he said. I stopped and gripped Martin's arm. Tears welled as laughter erupted from the group of men.

"Oh, Martin…" my voice quivered.

"It's all good, Hon," he whispered and patted my back reassuringly.

Brodie appeared at my side with a broad smile, "They are having a luncheon and I'm taking Dad to it."

"He's OK with that?" I gasped.

Brodie nodded, "He was pretty apprehensive when I helped him from the rental car to the chair…"

"I see he brought the 4x4," I said of the all-terrain wheelchair with large wide tires he used to get around the rough ground of the ranch. There was a wide platform for his legs to sit on instead of standard footrests. It was a combination of a 4-wheeler and a wheelchair.

"He was more worried about getting around out here than anything else," Brodie nodded.

"You should have seen the looks in the airport," Martin smiled. "We checked this one into baggage claim and they moved him to one of theirs for getting on and off the plane."

"But it went OK?" I asked in concern.

"He was treated like a king," Martin nodded. "I don't think he'll have a problem flying again."

"And this," Brodie nodded to the group of men in deep conversation. "He'll hit the road with us this year and not hideout on the ranch," he turned to me. "Don't let him lean on you too much…make him…"

"Depend on his own independence," I interrupted. "I know."

"I'll stay with him today," Brodie continued. "You go check on Logan and his autograph sessions."

"OK, I'll keep my distance…today," I conceded.

Dad glanced right at me. The joy and pride on his face and illuminating out of his eyes made my breath catch. He'd looked at me like that many times before and it always made my heart swell, but this was the first time since his accident that he looked truly happy.

I nearly ran to him and fell into his outstretched arms.

"There's my girl!" He called out. "Damn fine roping."

Leaning back, the look in his eyes again made my whole body tingle with love and pride. I could not have a better father.

"Thanks, Dad," I managed to whisper as I finally looked away from him and at the beaming group of men around him.

Dad's longtime friend, Darryl Smothers, smiled at me, "We were just telling Evan that we're all going to get one of his chairs and go four-wheeling and fishing together."

The laughter around me just filled my heart as I looked down at Dad.

"I know I promised to hang with you today," Dad said. "But I'm going to head over to the hotel and join a luncheon. I know you wouldn't want to spend your afternoon with a bunch of old cowboys."

I beamed in pride at him, and I could see the flicker of understanding in his eyes. "You know I would love to hear all your stories, but I'm going over to the convention center and see how Logan is holding up."

Dad nodded, "Good idea."

I kissed him on the cheek and gave him a firm hug. When I rose, I stepped behind him and looked at every cowboy around him and silently thanked them all with a look.

"Here's your coat," Craig said and handed it to me.

"Kicking me out of the all-boys club here?" I teased him.

He laughed and nodded, "Yes…yes, I am."

"Alright," I looked around the group again, ending on my father. "I'll see you tonight?"

His face scrunched in humor, "About that..."

"We have a suite," Darryl said. "And he's agreed to join us tonight to watch the rodeo from there."

"Wonderful!" I grinned at him. "Then, I'll see you after?"

"Yes, absolutely...I'll keep in touch," Dad said and patted his pocket where he kept his phone.

One last smile at the group of people and I walked away with a side glance to Brodie.

All was good; my whole family was here now even though we would be spread out all over the Thomas and Mack Center.

After getting my horse back to his stall, I rode in an Uber to the convention center where Logan was signing autographs. I glanced at my watch as I arrived at the center. I had an hour to get back to the South Point Hotel for the indoor roping I promised to watch just before a final kiss at three in the morning.

I was smiling at the memories of the overnight visit when I approached the Preifert booth, where Logan was set up. I was very shocked to see the woman we had given a ride to the day before was taking pictures for him.

"Lacie Jae? Good to see you," I smiled and looked at the very pleased grin on my brother's face. He was very smitten with this young woman. "Did you enjoy the rodeo last night?

"Oh, yes," she nodded with wide excited eyes. "But Logan informed me it is steer wrestling and not cow tackling."

Now, that, was funny. I liked her, and it was obvious Logan did too, so after the autograph session, I invited her to spend the day with me. It would help me keep my mind off Dad and help her have a great time since her sister abandoned her.

Brodie would be in a suite with Dad and Martin, and Craig was helping Logan with the horses, I was left with 2 extra tickets...so I invited her to join me at the rodeo.

It was a very relaxing, fun day and evening with Logan winning the night.

Friday morning, she joined me to watch the team roping. She smiled the whole morning and into the afternoon. It wasn't until she was walking up to me late in the day that a frown creased her brow. She had to leave, but it was clear she didn't want to.

I missed her cheerfulness and smile the moment I dropped her off at her hotel.

Saturday night, Dad, Martin, Brodie, Craig, and I proudly watched Logan take the stage again to receive his second gold buckle as the World Champion Steer Wrestler. When he stood behind the trophy saddle, he turned and looked up at us and pointed to Dad. With the assistance of Craig and Brodie, Dad slowly rose from the chair and gave Logan a brief standing ovation. Logan's hand went over his heart as tears filled his eyes.

Sunday morning, around the breakfast table, the energy and excitement of the long two weeks and the previous night's late celebration had taken its toll and we were all quiet as we ate.

Dad looked around all of us, and with a loud exhale, he spoke, "I'm not going home."

CHAPTER ELEVEN

We all looked at him in concern until a slight smile escaped him, "Darryl asked me to come down to Stephenville and spend some time there before Christmas."

I exhaled in relief, "Bit over-dramatic there, Dad."

Everyone chuckled.

"Wanted to make sure I had your attention," Dad smirked. "As much as I would like to just travel down there myself, I have to be realistic and admit I need someone with me, but Martin has work to do this week."

"I'll go with you," I offered.

"Makes more sense for me to go," Brodie said with an apologetic look to me.

"You're not going without me," Craig huffed. "You might find a rodeo to enter while you're gone."

I knew immediately Dad would take up their offers. There were times he didn't want his daughter helping him.

"I'll go with you," Logan added.

Dad smiled, "I love ya all, but since Logan and Delaney have their horses here, they should have responsibility for getting them home."

Logan and I nodded our agreement.

"So," Craig grinned at us, "you two go home to the 30-degree weather and we'll head down to the 70."

Martin huffed, "but you'll all be home before Christmas Eve."

It was a long, boring drive home. Taking our time and giving breaks to the horses, we didn't arrive until one o'clock in the morning. Mark, a family friend, had taken care of the ranch while we were gone and helped us with the horses then left with a congratulation to both of us.

After sixteen days on the road, crawling under the covers of my own bed was like heaven. I barely remembered lying down before I drifted off to sleep.

Monday morning, Logan and I sat in Dad's office with Brodie on the video chat. He was standing in Darryl's barn, so Dad couldn't hear us checking in on him.

"He did fine," Brodie assured us. "A bit apprehensive at first, but he settled in."

Logan was leaning back in his chair and, like usual, was doodling on a piece of paper as we spoke. He always had to be moving or doing something.

"When are you flying home?" I asked Brodie.

"We booked a flight on Sunday morning," he answered. "I'll send you the itinerary, but I've got to get back in there."

The video chat ended, so I turned off the computer and looked over at Logan.

"Did I remember to tell you?"

"What?" His eyes narrowed.

"Congratulations, on your year," I smiled sweetly but a little smart-assy like a little sister should.

He laughed as he stood and playfully slapped me on the back of the head as a big brother should, "Thanks, Sis."

I leaned back in the office chair and swiveled around to look at the pictures that covered the office walls. Rodeo pictures were in the hall; these were family pictures from ranch life and vacations. There were lots of pictures of Mom, including my parent's wedding portrait.

Dad had begun traveling to rodeos with his father when he was young, and there was a picture of the pair of them at the first rodeo where they had competed against each other in steer wrestling. Grandpa won with Dad in second place, only a half-second apart.

And now, Dad was our rodeo manager. The only thing on the wall that wasn't family pictures was a poster-size calendar showing each month. The calendar was full of our travel plans, with each of us having a different color of pen used except Brodie and Craig because they always traveled together.

I glanced down at the paper Logan had been doodling on. It wasn't his normal horse or steer head picture, he was writing a name. I leaned closer to see "Lacie Jae" written in different spellings at least a dozen times. One had big block lettering and a big underline underneath.

He was quite taken by the young woman. I had to admit I had really enjoyed the two days I had spent with her. She was fresh, innocent, and just a joy to be around.

Leaning back in the chair, I pulled out my phone to call her and make sure she arrived home, alright. I couldn't really say I trusted her sister and friends.

"Hi, Delaney!" She answered with a voice full of excitement.

"Good morning," I smiled. "You made it home, alright?"

"We did and we got home just in time, so I could watch the rodeo on TV. Tell Logan congratulations for me."

"I'll do that."

"I was so nervous," she laughed. "I screamed at my television."

I chuckled.

"I am so glad Camille abandoned me so I could..."

"SHE WHAT?" The voice was male, loud, and full of anger.

I shot up out of the chair and gripped the phone tighter.

"Lacie Jae?" I gasped.

"You abandoned her?" The man's voice bellowed through the phone.

My heart was racing, "Lacie Jae?"

The line went dead.

What the hell? I called her again, but it only rang twice before going to voicemail.

I began pacing the floor. What was I supposed to do? I had no idea where she lived except Redding, California. I could call the police and maybe they could track her phone.

Pushing her number again, it rang twice then went to voice mail.

I jumped back to the chair and turned the computer on to search the Redding police phone number. I wasn't sure about calling 911...I wasn't really sure what was happening.

I tried calling her one more time; this time she answered with a low, troubled voice.

"Lacie Jae!" I gasped. "What the hell happened? Are you okay?"

"Yeah," She sighed. "Can I call you back?"

"You're alright? Are you alone?" My voice trembled in worry.

"I'm okay...I'm with Camille and we're going over to her friend's place."

"Can I help? Are you hurt?" I wasn't fond of Camille and could only hope she was there actually helping.

"No, we're both fine. I promise I'll call you back."

"OK, I'm giving you one hour to call me back or I'm headed down there. I can be there in four hours."

"OK," She whispered. "I'll call back."

I stared at the phone when the call ended. She said, 'we're both fine'. Did that mean they had both been in danger? He yelled about Camille having abandoned Lacie Jae, so it did make sense. Who was 'he'?

My stomach was sick with worry, pulse racing, and my mind couldn't stop wondering what was happening.

I paced the floor a few moments, then walked out of the room, out of the house, and directly to the barn.

Damn, Logan was already riding out in the pasture toward the cows.

I stood at the door of the barn and watched him ride and kept glancing at my phone. We had a skiff of snow on the ground, not much, but would the roads be clear enough I could

get to Redding if she needed me? I searched the internet for
the road conditions; all was clear.

I began pacing again; in and out of the barn and looking
out to Logan.

Precisely 59 minutes later, I called again.

"It's been an hour. What's going on? Are you alright?"

"I'm OK." She sounded stronger but a bit wistful.

"What can we do to help?"

There was a pause before she spoke, "You said that I
could come to visit. Is that invitation still open?"

"Of course!" I knew my voice was full of relief and I
would do anything to get her out of whatever situation she was
in. "I've already checked the road conditions and it's clear all
the way."

"Can you send me the address and I'll put it into the
GPS in my phone?"

"We'll have dinner waiting."

I immediately sent her the address and looked out to
Logan. He had disappeared into the trees, so I quickly saddled
my barrel horse, Gaston, and rode out to meet him.

Four hours later, we were pacing in the barn and staring
down the road. The only break we had taken was Logan
throwing together a dinner for her in the crockpot.

"Call her," Logan demanded for the tenth time.

"Give her time," I tried to sound patient. "We don't
want her answering the phone while she's driving."

"She said she's coming?"

"Yes, I told you that. It's the last thing she told me."

A small car turned down the driveway causing loud
exhales of relief from both of us.

"DAMN!" Logan yelled.

I jumped a foot and looked at him with wide eyes.

"I had to get the stress out before greeting her," he
huffed with a loud exhale of tension.

We calmly walked out the door together.

She greeted us with a smile…as if nothing was wrong.

For the few days she was with us, she did not once
mention what had happened, so neither did we.

Friday morning, I parked the tractor next to the barn and caught a glimpse of her carrying her bags of clothes out of the house. My heart sunk; something must have happened.

Her eyes were red-rimmed from crying when we walked up to her.

"Lacie Jae?" I asked.

"You're leaving?" Logan exhaled in disbelief.

"My father died last night," She blurted.

"Oh, Lacie Jae," I wrapped my arms around her.

She was holding on so tight; I didn't want to let her go.

"I'm so sorry," Logan sighed.

"You want me to go with you?" I finally stepped back.

"No, I talked to Camille...she's headed home too. There's a lot to do...or figure out...and it will be up to the two of us," She answered.

"I can drive down with you and come back..." I hoped she would say yes.

"Thank you," She hugged me again. "I'll miss you."

"You are a joy to be around...you're welcome here any time you need to get away," My heart was breaking for her. "We'll always need a calf feeder."

"Oh," Tears glistened in her eyes. "I'll miss them."

She turned to Logan and fell into his arms. His face tightened as it did anytime he was trying to hold back his emotions.

"Thank you both so much for the best vacation..." Lacie Jae whispered as she stepped away from him.

Logan opened the door and she slid in only to roll down the window to look back up at us.

"You let us know if you need anything," I said with sincerity. "We're here for you."

"Thank you," her eyes glistened.

Logan knelt by the window and her hand rose and fingers caressed his jaw.

"Come back," he whispered.

I was not surprised at the tender farewell they shared.

"Good-bye," she whispered.

Logan and I watched her drive down the long driveway and turn onto the road. Neither of us spoke when he turned to the barn and I went into the house.

It was already too quiet without her beaming smile and cheerful laugh.

CHRISTMAS EVE

I stood on the porch and watched two cars slowly make their way down the long driveway.

"We're going to have to direct traffic this year," Dad said from beside me.

I looked down and smiled, "Your Christmas gatherings are getting bigger every year."

"And I wouldn't have it any other way," he grinned. "No one should have to spend Christmas sleeping in their car or truck or in a rundown hotel."

Since the Christmas after mom died, he had invited any traveling cowboy to stop by the ranch to stay for the holiday. The first year, we had five guests. With the group coming down the driveway we were at nine.

Brodie and a small group of cowboys wandered out of the barn in time to eagerly welcome the newcomers with a big grin and welcoming wave.

Logan was in the house cooking. He was the only one of us that liked to cook so he dutifully prepared lots of food. Currently, there were five cowboys in the kitchen, helping him taste-test.

A round of laughter echoed out of the house.

"And that's why," Dad smiled at me.

"I'm right with ya on that," I sighed.

Sharing the holiday and listening to laughter from men and women that would have been alone for the holiday made it easier not to have mom with us.

Another truck turned down the driveway. I could see the outline of two cowboys in it.

"I'll go see if Logan needs me to run to the store for anything," I turned into the house.

When I stepped into the kitchen, I was met by a broad grin from my brother. We all liked these full houses.

"Two arrived a few minutes ago and two more coming down the drive," I informed him. "You need anything?"

"Nah, Martin is stopping by and picking up the four turkeys Mrs. Anderson cooked and she added a couple of hams, too. So we should be good with the steaks I have marinating and the roast that's in the oven," he answered.

"He's got about thirty pounds of potatoes on the barbeque, too," one of the cowboys said and they all laughed. "We helped wrap them in foil."

"Putting you to work this year," I teased and glanced out the window in time to see an SUV pull down the driveway.

The vehicle stopped, started again, then stopped again. Then it slowly made its way to the house. I walked back out to the porch to see who was so hesitant to join us and hopefully make them feel welcome.

Dad was talking to the driver but blocking the view of who it was, so I walked out to him.

I gasped in delight when I saw the smile from the blonde in the driver's seat.

"Lacie Jae!" I nearly shouted. "It is so good to see you." Relief flooded through me at the knowledge she really was alright.

Her eyes were filled with tears as I made my way down the stairs to greet her. Her father had just died days before. Where was her sister?

"Hi Delaney," she smiled. "I just wanted to come by and say thank you, but it looks like you're having a family dinner."

"It's an open-door get-together," Dad said. "Go park your car and come inside."

"I really don't want to interrupt," she said hesitantly.

"You're not," I said earnestly. "Please, stay. I'm beginning to get outnumbered here, and another female would really help me out."

"So far, she's the only female here with about a dozen men," Dad smirked. "Go park your car."

"Ok," she said and looked up at me. "But I have a gift in the back for you, and we don't want to carry it too far."

"Lacie Jae! You didn't have to get us anything," I gasped.

"It's a thank you gift for my vacation last week," she stepped out of the car and looked hesitantly between us.

"Lacie Jae, this is our father, Evan Rawlins," I said and walked down the stairs to help her.

She opened the back of the SUV and I gasped again.

"What is it?" Dad called out and drove his wheelchair to the back of the vehicle.

"I've been a coffee barista for a few years and I know Delaney and Logan like their coffee, so I bought you a new machine," she answered with a smile. "It's like the one I bought for home, The Barista Express from Breville."

"That's a hell of a machine," I huffed.

"Damn," Dad looked up at her. "I want one."

We laughed, and I could see her shoulders lower as she relaxed.

"Dad loves coffee more than Logan and I," I said and lifted the box from the back to reveal a second box. "What's that?"

"I brought different coffee beans and flavors for you to try out," she explained. "I wasn't sure what you all liked."

Brodie and two other cowboys appeared at the back of the vehicle. After introductions, they carried the boxes in the house.

I walked in with Lacie Jae hidden behind me.

"What's all this?" Logan asked as he pulled a tray of fresh rolls from the oven and set them on the counter.

"We have a visitor," I grinned and stepped aside.

The look on my brother's face was pure shock that quickly changed to genuine happiness.

"Merry Christmas," Lacie Jae giggled softly.

Her eyes sparkled when she looked at him and her cheeks turned pink when he leaned down to give her a quick welcoming hug.

"Damn, girl," he grinned. "I was expecting another rough cowboy face...yours is much better."

She giggled again, "I brought you and Delaney...your whole family a thank you gift for my mini-vacation last week."

"A coffee machine?" Logan shook his head. "You didn't have to do that."

"I know, but I wanted to," she blushed.

"And I'm still waiting for my cup," Dad rolled in next to her with an expectant raise of the brow.

She spent the day in the kitchen with Logan preparing different coffee drinks for everyone in the house while he cooked.

Brodie and I were setting the table with 21 plates in all. We were able to fit most around the formal dining table but some were happy enough to sit at the kitchen island.

With Christmas music playing in the background and food being devoured around the table, Dad looked content.

When dinner was over and the dishes cleaned, everyone gathered in the living room and watched *Prancer* with Sam Elliot then *Die Hard* with Bruce Willis; our traditional Christmas movies.

In the morning, they all woke to a Christmas stocking filled with assorted nuts, candy canes, and oranges, just like Mom used to fill our stockings when we were little. There was also an envelope inside containing a $30 gas card to help get to their next rodeo.

Lacie Jae making coffee, laughter, movies, and games filled the morning until each of the cowboys departed, leaving just family and Lacie Jae at the end of the day.

Just the two of us were feeding the calves in the barn when we finally had a chance to talk alone.

"How are you doing?" I asked.

She just smiled and shrugged, "Fine."

"And your sister?"

"She is visiting her mother in Florida for the holidays and she lives in Fresno."

She didn't look upset, but she looked a bit lost.

"Lacie Jae, you told me your mother passed away and your father just died...do you have any other family."

"Just work friends," she whispered.

The calves wandered off to lie in the straw and we quietly walked to the house. I really liked this young woman and hated to see her alone in the world. I couldn't imagine what it would be like not to have Dad and my brothers.

I didn't see the men as we entered the house and started cleaning the bottles in the mudroom sink.

"When do you have to go back to work?" I asked.

"I don't know if I'm going back to the coffee shops," she said. "I have enough money in the bank. I don't really have to work for a while. Maybe I'll do some traveling first."

"By yourself?"

She shrugged, "Sure, after we talked in Vegas, I decided I wanted to travel more, so I was thinking maybe go to Texas and see the Alamo or maybe go on a cruise."

I smiled, "Those are pretty diverse choices. Are you sure that's what you want to do?"

She just shrugged again, which told me she truly was lost in the world.

"Why don't you stay here with us until you make up your mind about what you want to do?"

"I don't want to intrude on your life," she sighed.

"Lacie Jae, you wouldn't be intruding, we truly love having you here."

"Those baby calves would really miss you," Dad said.

We both turned in surprise.

He, Logan, and Brodie were standing behind us.

"You have to train us on that coffee machine," Logan smiled.

"Between the ranch and rodeos we don't have a lot of time for training," Brodie added with a grin. "It may take a while."

Tears glistened in her eyes again.

"I really like having another woman on the ranch with me," I said honestly.

"The guest room is yours as long as you want it," Dad said.

"Stay here," Logan said bluntly.

Her gaze wandered to each of us then stopped at Logan. After a moment, she took a deep breath and nodded, "OK, I really want to stay."

CHAPTER TWELVE

I lowered the stirrup down the side of the horse and turned to lift my lariat out of the bag that lay on a bale of hay.

My phone sang out. The picture of Val Kilmer as Doc Holiday appeared on the screen.

I stopped and quickly glanced around before answering.

"I'll be your huckleberry," I purred into the phone.

"Oh, damn," he chuckled. "I'm calling every five minutes so you can answer the phone like that."

In my smoothest voice, I sighed, "Oh, Sexy, I look forward to every call."

"My Delaney, I could listen to you read the PRCA rule book."

We both laughed.

"What's up?" I giggled.

"Just missed your voice, texting is good, but I love hearing that seductive voice of yours."

"Hmmm," I sighed. "Personally, I prefer it face-to-face in bed."

"Oh, baby," he laughed. "Next week, I'll talk all you want."

"Talk? Talking is the last thing I want from you next week."

"Well, how are you going to be able to escape when you're sharing a room with Lacie Jae?"

"I don't think I'm going to have to worry about that. In the last two weeks, I don't think she and Logan have been apart from each other more than a couple of hours."

"Does that surprise you?"

"Not really, he's been giving her riding lessons on Brutus. He's half Clydesdale and huge. She looks so tiny on him. It took a lot of persuading by Logan to get her to even sit on the saddle. The horse is the most gentle I have ever been around, and after the second lesson, she fell in love with him. Logan has even had her on his dummy-horse, wrestling down the dummy-steer behind the ATV. He walks behind her with his hands on her waist and helps her slide from the horse to the steer head until she gets her legs in front of her. Then, she just lets herself get dragged. She laughs the whole time."

"That's funny as hell. Did you get any pictures?

"Pictures and video," I chuckled. "I'll send them to you."

"Ah, damn, I gotta go, Sweetheart," He sighed.

"I'll call tonight."

"Go practice."

"I am. Bye, Darling."

Next week couldn't come fast enough.

I slid the bridle on Ketchum, and we walked down the barn aisle to the echo of his hoofbeats. I loved that sound.

Lacie Jae was sitting on the tractor near the barn door. It had been a lot of fun the last two weeks watching her become a ranch girl.

"See that!" She was holding her phone out in front of her and talking loudly.

"What is that?" A voice asked from the phone. She turned the phone to look at the screen.

"That's a tractor! I'm sitting on a tractor!" she laughed.

"Oh, what a fun adventure you're having," A woman's voice said from the phone.

"Logan let me ride with him in the arena this morning when he tilled the ground. I think he called it grooming though."

"They groom the ground?" The male voice asked.

Lacie Jae giggled, "It means chopping up the hard ground and dirt clods, so it's better for the horses to run in."

"Isn't it cold up there?" The female voice asked. "And they are going to ride horses in the cold?"

"Yes! It warmed up to 30 degrees today," she answered.

"I'd just die in that weather," the woman groaned.

"They wear long-johns, and jeans, then chaps, then a long coat over that when they ride." Lacie Jae informed them. "And warm hats and gloves."

"Sounds like you would be too bundled to move," the man chuckled.

"And they find it enjoyable?" the woman asked.

Lacie Jae laughed, "It's what they do, and as Logan said, 'it's the cowboy way of life'. Hot or cold they have work to do, but yes, I do believe they enjoy it, too."

"They are just crazy!" the woman said.

Lacie Jae grinned, "Well, I'm starting to go crazy too because I'm loving it, especially when I get to ride on the tractor!"

"We have to go, but you don't freeze to death up there," the woman said.

"Have fun on the tractor!" the man called out.

Lacie Jae giggled, "I will! Miss you both."

She lowered the phone and smiled out toward the arena as her hands gripped the steering wheel and turned it like it was moving. She looked like a little kid enjoying playing grown-up.

Listening to her description of something I took for granted just made me smile. I always enjoyed being around her and seeing my life through her eyes; it was amazing the little things that she noticed. Her life had been so sheltered, and her awakening to the ranching and rodeo world was fun, but the way she described it to her friends was so hilarious I could listen to her all day.

She heard the hoofbeats and turned.

"Roping again?" She gasped.

"It's my job," I answered. "I take advantage of this weather all I can. We have the finals coming up and I need to be ready."

"Circuit Finals in Yakima; you told me about them in Vegas and I'm so excited to get to go," she nodded with a wide grin.

"You can come with us anytime we go anywhere."

"Logan says I can go with him to Denver after the circuit finals. That will be so much fun."

"I would love to see you discovering the Denver Stock Show," I grinned.

"Are you going, too?"

"No, I'm staying here. Dad is going with Logan. Brodie and Craig are headed for the Texas and Oklahoma rodeos, too."

"Gonna be the boss lady?" she teased with a wide grin.

"Something like that," I laughed. "But I truly will miss seeing you discover life on the road and Denver."

"I am so excited," her grin beamed happiness and excitement.

"You'll have to add me to your video chats," I smiled, then an idea struck me. "Do you remember the podcast we listened to at New Years?"

"Yes, that Devan guy. Logan listens to all his interviews."

"Blazing Trails and Telling Tales," I nodded. "He's a bareback rider…a friend of Brodie and Craig. He knows all about rodeo and the industry, so he has a great show."

"I love listening to him."

"And I love listening to you talk about this place and what you're experiencing when you talk to your friends."

"So, why did you bring that up?"

"What would you think of doing a podcast about your discovery of rodeo and the industry?"

"What? Really?" She gasped. "I can't interview anyone!"

"I don't want you to interview anyone. Just talk like you do with your coffeehouse friends on the phone. You will just tell people what you're seeing and learning."

She just stared at me with wide eyes.

"I don't want to miss your discoveries in Denver, and this way, we can all hear them. I am already looking forward to your stories."

"You really think I could do something like that?" She whispered; a bit in disbelief.

"I absolutely believe you can do it," I nodded. "We'll contact Devan and see if he can help you get started. Your podcast will be distinctively different than his. If you just tell your stories like you're talking to your friends at the coffeehouse, you'll be a huge hit."

"Delaney," she looked at me warily. "I've never done anything like that."

"You just did," I pointed out. "And we'll use the Circuit Finals as your debut."

"But, I never, ever thought of doing something that would be so...with people actually listening to me?"

"Yes," I nodded firmly. "You're branching out in the world. More opportunities and adventures are in front of you. Don't stay in your past when such a bright, fun future is right in front of you."

"Oh...Delaney," Tears sprung to her eyes. "I've been so lost the last month...looking for something that truly mattered...that made a difference...this is it. My heart is racing with excitement...I just..." She sprung off the tractor and threw her arms around me.

As little as she was, she had a strong grip.

The morning we were due to leave for Yakima, I pushed the button to increase the speed of the treadmill and my strides instantly widened. Sweat slid down my neck and back. The thumping of foot to treadmill increased and doubled in sound when I looked over at Brodie, who was on the machine next to me and pushing the button, so his was going faster than mine.

"Everything is a competition to you," I puffed.

"Can't let big sister run faster than me," he laughed.

For twenty minutes, we ran next to each other and looked out the expanse of windows showing us the front pasture with horses grazing from a large round bale of hay. The blue sky was a beautiful contrast to the fresh layer of new white snow.

Behind us, Dad was riding an incline stationary bike. With so much of his life sitting in the wheelchair, he didn't want his leg muscles to lose their strength. With weights in each hand, he did upper body exercises while he wore a headset and watched reruns of the television show *Longmire*.

I decreased the speed of the treadmill, and ten seconds later, so did Brodie. We just looked at each other and grinned...such competitiveness in our sibling life.

When we finally stopped, so did Dad. We waited for him to transfer to his wheelchair then made our way into the kitchen. All three of us turned to look across the living room. Logan was sitting on the couch, his back tucked into a corner, and his legs stretched out in front of him and crossed at the ankles. Nestled onto his lap and tucked into his shoulder was Lacie Jae. Logan's arms were wrapped tightly around her, his chin resting on the top of her head, and they were sound asleep.

"Well," Brodie whispered. "Feeding the calves this morning must have been exhausting."

Dad and I chuckled.

"It's about time one of you twenty-something-year-old children of mine finally got hooked up with someone," Dad huffed.

"He's been hooked up with one hell of a lot of someones," Brodie smirked.

"Longer than a night," Dad clarified with a shake of the head.

"If the past is any indication," I sighed. "She's got a lot of exes to overcome."

"Hopefully, he has been honest with her about that, so she knows what to expect," Dad whispered. "And when the time comes, and it will, we'll need to be there to help her because there are times that women can be true bitches when it comes to him."

Brodie and I just nodded. We had witnessed women in physical altercations when it came to getting Logan's attention.

"I like that girl," Dad stated. "As opposite as they are in size, they emotionally fit each other perfectly."

"I agree," Brodie and I added.

"This trip to Yakima will be her first challenge," I sighed.

"We'll work on keeping those two hooked up," Dad said then looked up at us. "And figure out how to get you two hooked up with someone."

Brodie huffed, "We may get hooked up, but good luck getting us out of the house."

Welcome to my first podcast for Coffee With Cowboys!

I'm Lacie Jae, a relocated city girl who will be adventuring into the ranching and rodeo world...the cowboy way of life. Until a few weeks ago, I had never been around a horse or a cow, and now, that's changed.

I'll be sharing with you my adventures and discoveries as I travel with the Rawlins family. They are a three-generation rodeo and ranch family and also National Finals Rodeo qualifiers and champions. They have lived the cowboy way of life all their lives and are now generously letting me tag along and share their adventures.

To start, I want to explain the title of the podcast. I have been a coffee barista for the last five years and the last three as a manager over three coffee houses. So, obviously, I love coffee.

And so do cowboys!

The other morning at the Rawlins Bar-R ranch, it was bright, beautiful blue skies and white frosted ground as they moved a small herd of cows into their corrals. I delivered coffee to them as they sat on their horses, stood in the dirt, or leaned against a gate. To clarify, when I talk about the Rawlins, it includes Craig, who is best friends and rodeo traveling partner to Brodie Rawlins and Craig's dad, Martin. They are family, too.

So, I delivered coffee to dad Evan, the beautiful Delaney, Brodie, Martin, and Craig...and, of course, Logan, who is also my boyfriend.

As I walked away from the six of them drinking their coffee and talking about the cows they had wrangled and the horses they used to round them up, I realized how comfortable it all was, as if I had been doing it all my life. I turned back and looked at the small group and wondered why I was walking away. So, I went back and had coffee with cowboys.

This morning, I'm standing in the ranch house kitchen because it is ten degrees outside. The Rawlins have already been outside and finished the chores and are now sitting at their kitchen table drinking coffee and talking about the ranch...cows and horses...and about the next couple months of rodeos...who is going where and when.

I'm standing here just watching them and am so thankful that I get to be part of this cowboy way of life. My podcasts will share with you these moments and fun adventures on the ranch and rodeo trail. First on the list of rodeos is the Columbia River Circuit finals in Yakima, Washington.

It's a cold winter's day outside but a warm family atmosphere inside...so...I'm going to sign off now and go have coffee with cowboys.

"That is perfect! I absolutely love the name," I said to an anxious Lacie Jae. She had been staring at me the whole time I listened to the recording. "I am so excited for you."

She giggled with a wide grin, "I wanted you to hear it first to see if I needed to make any edits before sharing with anyone."

I shook my head, "As I said, it is perfect. Let's share it with the family."

It was my turn to stare at her as she nervously watched the family who was gathered around the long kitchen table listening to the podcast. Her fingers were held into a tight grasp as they twisted anxiously, and her face was flushed. There was no doubt she really loved what she did and was excited about the whole opportunity. She wanted this so bad her whole body was trembling.

After the last words of the podcast rang out into the room, Dad turned to her with a big grin. He started clapping, making her giggle and tears to rise. The rest of us joined in.

"I can't wait for the next episode," Logan said proudly and wrapped her in his arms.

Lacie Jae adopted my dad and Martin. Whenever Logan was busy, the girl was always taking care of the two men, and it was easy to tell they adored her. They sat on the bleachers of the arena together, ready to watch my breakaway runs of the morning.

Pulling my attention from the trio, I watched the first five riders break from the box and chase their calves. Three caught in under three seconds, and the others missed. When I rode forward to the box, my twitches were evident; twirling the rope a few times over my head, shoving my hat down tighter, tipping my head to each shoulder to loosen my neck, then spinning the rope one more time. It was a habit, and I couldn't get myself to do it any other way.

I backed my blue roan horse, Archer, into the box and concentrated on the calf as the horse settled.

"GO DELANEY!"

It took all my concentration not to smile at Lacie Jae's cheering.

Another deep breath and the nod; Archer and I propelled forward with rope twirling and hooves pounding...for 2.3 seconds. Relief tingled in my stomach. It was only the first of three runs for the competition, but I was thankful the first was a good run. The second and third were just as fast and my trio of fans in the bleachers hollered as I followed the third calf to the stripping-chute to retrieve my rope.

As I returned to the waiting area of the arena, I could see Lacie Jae standing between the two men, arms up to the sky and she was wiggling back and forth to her cheering, "Yeah, Delaney!"

She earned a smile from everyone around her.

When the last rider broke from the box, I rode to the edge of the arena and watched as Martin walked just in front of Dad as they slowly stepped down from the bleachers. Lacie Jae was at the bottom waiting with the wheelchair ready. Once Dad was settled into his chair, the trio looked back to me.

"Yeah!" Lacie Jae danced over to the arena fence.

"Good job, Daughter," Dad grinned proudly.

"You looked pretty calm out there," Martin added with a smirk.

"Well," I huffed. "I was not."

They laughed.

"We're headed to lunch," Dad said. "You want us to wait until after your meetings?"

"No, who knows how long those will take," I answered. "I'll meet you at the hotel when we're done."

Two hours later, I was walking down the steps from the meeting rooms with two large bags of gifts; one from barrel racing and the other breakaway. The circuit finals jackets from the two events were slung over my arm.

Just as I placed all the items in my truck, a phone alert chimed.

Text from Huckleberry: Nice Ass

I chuckled and closed the door of the truck and inconspicuously looked around the parking lot. I spotted him near the opening to the contestant's entrance to the building. Walking as if I didn't have a care in the world, I made my way to the building. He turned as I approached and walked through the door and down the long hallway. I followed fifteen feet behind him until he suddenly opened a door and disappeared to my right. I glanced over my shoulder then down the hall to make sure it was clear as I approached the door then quickly slid into the room and right into his arms.

The announcer's voice echoed in the building, "Thanks for coming to the rodeo tonight, folks. Finals will be tomorrow, where we'll award our Circuit Champions and announce those competitors who will be traveling to Florida for the National Circuit Finals in Kissimmee. Before you go, stop by the autograph tables at the end of the arena. Tonight, you get a chance to meet the finals leading team ropers, Jess Corday and Ryle Jaspers, and the finals leading bareback rider, Craig Houston. The Rawlins siblings are also there, which includes World Champion Steer Wrestler Logan, NFR Qualifier as well as this year's Circuit Breakaway champion, and she's third in the finals this weekend in barrel racing, Delaney Rawlins. Their brother Brodie will be there also, and he is currently holding the high average for the weekend in Saddle Bronc. Stop by and say hello, and we'll see you tomorrow for the championship round."

I saw the tall brunette coming from half an arena away. Her eyes were focused on Logan, who was sitting on my left at the end of the autograph table. To my right was Brodie, who I nudged with an elbow. When he glanced at me, I turned my eyes to the tall brunette that was barreling in on the table.

He nudged his chin to our left. I turned to see Logan's last girlfriend, Anna, standing at the edge of the crowd and watching him with a smile that left no doubt she had all intentions of connecting with him after the signing.

I leaned over to Logan to whisper. "You see them, don't you?"

He just nodded and concentrated on writing his name on the picture.

We kept signing and talking with the fans but kept an eye on the two women.

Lacie Jae was innocently standing to the side with Dad and Martin. They were out of view of the two women.

As the crowd thinned, the two women slowly inched their way forward. No one was standing in front of Brodie, so he quickly stood with Craig, who was sitting on the other side of him, having to catch his chair from falling. Logan turned to his left and looked at Lacie Jae. As Brodie made his way around the table, Lacie Jae grinned at Logan, who tipped his head to invite her over to the table. Brodie approached Anna, Lacie Jae approached Logan, and a fan walked up to the table just in front of the tall brunette.

Brodie leaned to whisper into Anna's ear. Logan turned just enough to move his leg out from the table then wrapped his arm around Lacie Jae's waist to pull her in to sit on his leg as he talked to the fan and signed the picture.

Anna's cheeks turned red, and her head jerked to look at Brodie with furious eyes before turning to disappear into the crowd. The fan thanked Logan and stepped away. The brunette was left standing in a bit of shock in front of a smiling Lacie Jae perched on her target's leg. There was a long pause as the brunette's eyes widened in a pit of panic.

Even though she was standing in front of Logan, I spoke to her, "Are you interested in breakaway or barrels?"

Her eyes darted to me, and she shuffled toward me, her cheeks turned pink, "I just wanted to congratulate you on your win this morning."

"Thank you," I smiled brightly.

She hesitated then walked away as Brodie returned to his chair.

Craig leaned to Brodie, "What did you say to Anna?"

He turned with a sneer, "If I had said it to Delaney, she would have knocked me on my ass."

"Oh…" I gasped and Craig chuckled.

When the crowd finally disappeared, Lacie Jae leaned around Logan with a smile, "That was very kind of you."

I wondered if she had been aware of the impending collision.

"Well, maybe it's time to make this official," I said and pulled out my phone as I stood.

She was still sitting on his lap but leaned into his chest while Logan wrapped one arm around her waist and the other relaxed across her thigh...very intimately. They both grinned for the camera and looked extremely happy.

"You other three get in there for a picture," Martin said and took my phone from me.

We all posed with wide grins.

"Now, I want one of all of you," Lacie Jae giggled.

Logan sat in the chair but leaned against Dad's wheelchair, Brodie, and I stood to one side with Martin and Craig on the other.

"Now you get in there," the event's official photographer with a large camera said.

Lacie Jae hurried to stand between Logan and Martin. The photographer took the picture with her camera then one with my phone.

After the pictures were finally finished, Dad rolled away, "I'm hungry."

"Party at the hotel?" Craig asked as we all followed.

"That's up to you," Dad answered. "I'm headed for pizza and beer."

It was another family dinner around the table at the pizza parlor. After ordering, we all posted the picture of Lacie Jae and Logan together on our social media sites.

"That should ward off any possible attacks tomorrow," Martin chuckled.

Logan looked at Lacie Jae in concern. She whispered in his ear, causing a wide grin to appear.

CHAPTER THIRTEEN

Welcome to Coffee with Cowboys with me, Lacie Jae.

Greetings everyone! Lacie Jae with Coffee With Cowboys here. I'm a relocated city girl who will be adventuring into the ranching and rodeo world … the cowboy way of life.

We just finished the Circuit Finals Rodeo in Yakima, Washington. The first time I met Delaney, she had told me about the rodeo, but I would never have dreamed I would actually be here. It's been only five weeks since I met this wonderful family, and I'm learning so much every day.

The first thing I learned was that there is a lot of preparation to travel miles away from home with horses and competitors. The family is so used to staying in hotels that it didn't really faze them, but I was so excited I could barely keep from smiling the whole time. That, people, is how sheltered my life had been.

The second thing I learned is when the arena is quiet, and the competitor is backed into the box and ready to nod, you don't yell really loud at them. Martin and Evan thought it was distracting, but Delaney didn't even acknowledge it and caught the calf really fast anyway. So, I warn you now, Delaney, I will be yelling again. (giggles)

So, we drive away from the Yakima Sun Dome with the year-end Circuit winners in breakaway and steer wrestling, and the finals average winner in barrels, and bareback. What that means is a trip to Florida for the National Circuit Finals! I've never been there, but I've heard so much I can hardly wait! I mean, who hasn't watched CSI Miami and seen all the beautiful people and places?

Logan, Delaney, and Craig qualified to go, but Brodie didn't, he was just 2 points away. I was so disappointed for him, but it didn't seem to bother him. He said that is the way rodeo is. Sometimes you draw a horse that will help you get to the top and sometimes you don't. It wasn't his time, he said. Honestly, I'm still disappointed for him.

Evan says it builds character to learn how to lose and win with dignity.

It's going to take me a while to get used to handling losses like how these rodeo people do.

I hope you enjoyed this little bit of a peek behind the curtain of traveling with the Rawlins and Houston family. The next stop will be the Denver Livestock and Rodeo next week. I'm so excited to share everything I learn and see with you. When I get back from Denver, I'll work on a social media site or website where I can share pictures and videos I take along the way.

But for now, the horses are loaded into the trailer and everyone is ready to go home for a couple of days. With three full thermoses, I'm loading up and having Coffee With Cowboys!

Text from my Huckleberry: Listened to the podcast, it's fun hearing about you

Text: You know everything about me, more than anyone else

Text: But I get to hear it from someone else; a third point of view. Sounds like she is having fun

Text: She is, more than me right now. I'm getting ready for my second so-called date with Mark

Text: You had fun last night

Text: We were roping then had dinner. Was about the same as usual just without all our friends with us. Then I got to go home and video chat with you. That was fun.

Text: All your friends will quit pushing you together now

Text: Peer pressure. At twenty-four you would think I would be past that

Text: Maybe by the time you're 50

Text: LOL, probably. We're meeting for breakfast at the café then I'll give him the 'let's just remain friends' request.

Text: Two dates and out

Text: Yes, my family will be thrilled I broke up with another guy

Text: Well, I am ☺

Text: You're the one that told me to finally go out with him

Text: Never thought I would see the day I told my girlfriend to go out with another guy

Text: LOL, well I need to go so I can get this over with

Text: Have fun, I can't wait to see you again, I miss holding you in my arms

Text: I am so ready! I'll call tonight after I go look at that horse Dad told me about

Text: More horses ☺

Text: Other than being with you, looking at new horses is my favorite thing to do

Text: I would have to say the same thing, be careful in all that fresh snow.

Text: I checked, roads are clear

Text: Bye, My Delaney

Text: Bye, Huckleberry

"Excuse me."

I turned to the voice to see large, perfectly highlighted brown eyes looking at me with a very concerned expression. She was a good three inches taller than me with long brown hair flowing down her back over a crisp navy blue shirt. Denim jeans, black knee-high fashionable snow-boots, and a wool jacket slung over her arm gave an elegant aura.

"Yes?"

"Are you Delaney Rawlins?"

"Yes…"

She turned and tipped her chin toward the table next to the door, "Did you come in with the man in the cowboy hat and red shirt?"

I glanced over at Mark then turned back with narrowed eyes, "Yes."

"Is he a relative?"

"No…"

"You're on a date?"

"Yeah…"

"Well…I…" She sighed with her bottom lip caught between her teeth. "I just went through the same thing…"

"Same thing as what?"

"My best friend…well, I thought she was anyway, seduced my boyfriend."

"What the hell does that have to do with Mark?" I huffed.

She glanced to him sitting at the table reading his phone then back to me, "While you were in the restroom, he asked me out for dinner and drinks tonight. He wanted to show me the town."

"He what?" I gasped.

"I'm sorry…but I wish my other friend had told me when she had found out about it, but she just kept her damn mouth shut and let the situation build up and explode."

I wanted to ask her what happened, but I was still processing Mark hitting on her. Our dating was just a 'show' for my family and would never be serious. Mark didn't know that, yet he asked her out. That was a bit irritating. He could have broken it off with me first or at least not ask her out when we were on a 'date'.

I turned and looked at him. There was no doubt he hadn't seen us together. Looking back to the beautiful brunette, I knew what I wanted to do, "Did you say yes?"

"He's a pretty damn good looking guy, and normally I would have said yes, but no, I saw him come in with you."

"I'm going to go over and sit with him. Would you come over and tell him you changed your mind?" I gave her an innocent smile.

The brunette grinned, "Yes…love to."

I casually walked back to the table, then slid onto the chair next to him.

"So, what would you like to do tonight?" I asked with as sweet of a smile as I could muster.

He shrugged, "You want to go rope?"

I had no doubt that if we really were a couple, that is all we would ever do…which was fine with me but…

The tall brunette walked up behind him and slid onto the chair across from me.

Mark turned to her, and his expression froze. He glanced at me as I was looking at the brunette and his whole body shrunk down into the chair.

"I just wanted to let you know my evening has cleared so I can take you up on that offer of showing me the town tonight," She grinned at him and acted like she didn't see me at the table.

I tipped my head and looked at him with a raised brow.

His eyes flicked between me and the brunette a few times before they stopped on me.

I said nothing. I just waited to see what he was going to do which was stand up without a word and walk out of the restaurant. The woman and I just watched him go.

"Well, a gentleman would have at least thrown some money on the table to help pay the tab," I muttered and leaned back against the chair, feeling a bit relieved. At least, now, I wouldn't have to make up a reason to break up with him.

"Gentleman…no, not what I would call him," the brunette gave me an apologetic smile. "Was it serious?"

"He takes care of our ranch when we're not home, and we have lots of mutual friends. It was more pressure from them to try dating," I answered with a sigh. "He was a nice guy…but…"

"Yeah," She huffed with a roll of her eyes. "I keep trying to tell myself that too, but my irritation is more for my so-called best friends than Matt."

"What happened?" I asked and picked up the cup of coffee, relaxed back into the chair, and crossed my legs. Now that Mark was gone, I had time to kill before going to look at the horse, and I was curious about her story.

"My best friend and boyfriend started sleeping together while I was at work and pretending like nothing was going on while I was around. For two damn weeks before she finally told me."

"Oh, damn," I grimaced. "Two damn weeks she was having sex with him knowing he was sleeping with you too? Yuck…"

"That's what I thought," She grimaced. "How can you do that to someone you call a friend?"

"What did you do?"

"I told her exactly what I thought of her, packed up and left. I went back home, and…well…I didn't want to be there, so here I am," She shrugged and looked around the café.

I watched her for a moment, then remembered she knew my name. Maybe she recognized me from rodeo or roping, maybe barrels, but I knew I had never seen her before.

"How did you know my name?"

She turned and looked at me with a heavy sigh escaping her, "I guess we never did meet in Vegas."

"No…"

"I'm Lacie Jae's sister."

"Camille?" I gasped.

CHAPTER FOURTEEN

"Yes," she nodded and looked up at the approaching waitress. "I haven't eaten so..."

"Me either," I mumbled as I tried to wrap my head around this woman being Lacie Jae's sister. The one that abandoned her in the middle of one of the largest casinos in Las Vegas and after their father died.

I was shocked when she ordered waffles, bacon, hash browns, and a tall glass of orange juice to go along with the coffee.

She looked at me with a shrug and a smirk, "Pity-party binge."

"Well, I'm in too," I chuckled and looked at Susan, the waitress. "I'll have the same, but would you add your wonderful buttermilk biscuits and gravy, too?"

"Oh, good call, add it to my order too, please," Camille smiled and set her coat and purse onto Mark's empty chair. "Whole damn pot of coffee, too."

Susan walked away with a shake of the head.

"Lacie Jae is here...isn't she?" Camille asked hesitantly, but hopefully.

"Yes, she arrived on Christmas Eve."

"How is she?"

There was a warm but nervous look in her eyes.

"She's doing quite well," I answered. "She has adopted all of our orphaned calves and has learned to ride a horse."

Tears shimmered in her eyes, "I am so glad she is happy. Baby calves, she must be in heaven."

"She's enjoying it...and other things."

"Is it presumptuous of me to ask if it's your brother company she's enjoying?"

"Enjoying each other, that's for sure," I huffed with a smirk.

Susan dropped off the pot of coffee and the tall glasses of orange juice.

"The first time I saw him was when he was signing autographs," she smiled. "We tricked Lacie Jae…she had no idea he was going to be there. Kendra was convinced she had lied about him giving her a ride to the rodeo and thought she would…" Camille sighed again. "Stupid thing to do, Lacie Jae would have no reason to lie. I seriously cannot believe I agreed with their stupid plan."

"Gang mentality?" I asked.

"I guess…," she sighed. "But when he saw her standing in line? The look on his face? Yeah, I knew he was head over heels for her."

"I saw it too…from him," I admitted. "It took a while for Lacie Jae."

"My fault…Dad's fault…our screwed-up life," Camille placed a hand over her face to rub her forehead then swept it through her hair.

There seemed to be a heavy weight on her mind.

"She was a bit lost, seems like you are too," I said softly.

She nodded with sadness and regret in her eyes, "The last thing Lacie Jae told me was I was throwing away the wrong person. She was so damn right. I was lost and held onto Kendra and Eve, who I thought were my bridge to life, but they were just…"

Susan placed the waffles, hash browns, and bacon on the table. We both reached for the bacon first. After it was gone and after a few bites of waffles, I placed an elbow on the table and my chin in hand and looked at her.

"Lacie Jae doesn't talk about her past, any of it. She just closes down."

Camille's eyes shimmered again as she nodded. She finished the waffles, and her fork began to play with the hash browns. She looked and probably felt like she lost her whole world. Between her friends, father, and sister, in a way, she had.

This woman needed someone to be there for her.

"Talk," I whispered.

She took a deep breath, glanced at me then away.

"My mother and father divorced when I was three, and Mother left me with him when she moved," she said before Susan interrupted long enough to drop off the biscuits and gravy, then Camille continued. "They got married because she was pregnant with me. The day after the divorce was final, he married his high school sweetheart, who he should have married to begin with."

"Lacie Jae's mother?"

"Yes," she glanced at me, then her fork dipped into the biscuits and gravy. After a few bites, her fork waved in the air. "But…even then, Lacie…the mother…my step-mother, couldn't keep him from drinking. After Lacie Jae was born, I was on the back burner, and she was everything. When Mother Lacie died, Dad's drinking escalated, and Lacie Jae was everything, and I was nothing to him."

Wow…not what I was expecting. I tried to keep my surprise hidden. We finished the biscuits and gravy in silence. I wondered if her two friends had ever let her talk to them like this. I really doubted it.

"But…" She finally paused with fork in air and eyes on the gravy stained plate. "He took his anger, his loss…his alcoholism out on us…"

"He…" My stomach clenched, and my own fork stopped mid-air. "Did he…?"

She shook her head and the fork went to the last of the hash browns, "He never touched us…inappropriately. He would swing an angry hand and hit if we didn't duck fast enough or run fast enough." Her fork stopped again and her shimmering brown eyes bore into mine. "He nearly killed her because of me."

"Why?" My heart ached at the look in her eyes.

"I threw away a bottle that still had whiskey in it and since she was the one that took care of him, he thought she did it. He had her by the hair…shaking her…I was running to them…down the hallway when he slammed her head into the wall. I ran into him to get him away...he fell to the floor and stumbled. When he tried to get up, I kicked him down again. Lacie was lying on the floor...I thought he had broken her neck." The tears slowly slid down her cheeks. Her breath shook when she paused; her gaze dropped to the plate of hash browns and her fork started playing in them again. "I picked her up and we ran. From then on, when he got mad, we would just run."

"Why didn't you call the police?"

She plucked a few napkins from the dispenser and wiped away the tears.

I was stunned by this story. Lacie Jae was so...innocent...sweet...who would have guessed she had this past? Had gone through so much?

Camille sighed and looked out the window. "I asked myself that a dozen times and so did Lacie Jae...but...you know...he was our father. Neither one of us even suggested it. I took her to the urgent care clinic and we told them she fell down the stairs. She had a concussion."

"They believed you?"

"Why wouldn't they?" She sighed again.

"It could have been so much worse."

Her eyes flicked back to me, "Yes...and well...I had already moved out, but after that, I came by every day to check on her when I knew she wasn't working. She refused to move away until after the rodeo when he overheard her talking to you, and he went after me."

"I heard him yell," I admitted. "Scared the hell out of me, I can't imagine what it was like there with him."

"I was there for about two seconds before we both ran. Neither of us saw him awake again...before...he died."

"How did he die?"

Her brows rose in surprise, "Lacie Jae didn't say anything?"

"Not a word to me other than he died and you were in Fresno. She could have told Logan, but he hasn't mentioned it either."

The waitress arrived to clear away the empty plates. We both had half the plate of hash browns left and Susan walking away with the dishes caused both our forks to dig back into the food.

"He died of an aneurism in the middle of the night caused by his saturated, over-abused liver and high blood pressure."

"I'm sorry for your loss," I said, but somehow it just felt empty.

She shrugged slightly and set her fork down on the empty plate. After a sip of orange juice, she looked out the window. "Like I told Lacie Jae; he had been slowly killing himself for five years. He wanted Mother Lacie. He wanted to leave then but had us girls to take care of, even though Lacie Jae took care of him." She paused, then looked over at me. Her eyes were sad but resolved. "We are all better off with him crossing over."

I wasn't really sure what to say so I just nodded. After a long silence I finally spoke, "Then Lacie Jae came here and you went back to Fresno?"

She shook her head, "My mother had bought me a ticket to fly down to Georgia to spend Christmas with her. After Dad died, I considered staying with Lacie Jae and probably should have, but I had always been angry with Mom, that she left me with him, so with him gone and a ticket in hand, I flew down and confronted her."

"Must have made for an interesting Christmas," I whispered.

She huffed with a slight smile, "Yeah, she was pissed I did that," Then she shrugged. "Couldn't compare to all the abandonment feelings I've had through the years, so I really didn't care and still don't care."

"You thought she abandoned you?"

She nodded and leaned back in the chair.

My phone alert rang out, and I considered not looking, but Camille was staring out the window in silence, so I glanced at the message.

Text from Mark: I called and paid your bill. You seriously ate that much? I'm sorry, but I wasn't under the impression you were into a relationship.

Text to Mark: A bit of indulgence this morning, thank you. I can pay you back. I'm sorry too. I should have been more open.

Text from Mark: Peer pressure dating

Text to Mark: Yeah…that's what I called it too. Are we good then? You forgive me?

Text from Mark: Funny, you're asking for my forgiveness. I was in the wrong this morning.

Text to Mark: Let's just be friends again and forget this happened.

Text from Mark: I'm good with that. See you at the arena Friday.

Text to Mark: I'll be there.

I set the phone down and looked back at Camille.

"You OK?" I asked.

She nodded with a deep sigh.

"That was Mark…he paid for our breakfast."

"That must have surprised him," She said with a slight smile.

"It did," I pulled a ten-dollar bill out of my pocket and placed it on the table for a tip. "So, now what?"

"I don't know," she sighed and dug into her purse to put another ten dollars on the table. "I need to see Lacie Jae and apologize to her. Then? Well? I just don't know."

"She's not here."

Her eyes widened, "You said she was here."

"She is here, as in all her stuff is in our house, but she is in Denver."

"Denver?" Camille gasped.

"She's there with my brothers and father," I couldn't help but smile at the shocked but delighted expression. "They are at the stock show and rodeo."

"Why didn't you go? But, Lacie Jae got to go?"

"I wasn't competing this year, besides someone has to stay and take care of the place." I chuckled. "And she was so thrilled to be going. She is hanging with my dad while Logan, Craig, and Brodie compete."

"I am so happy for her," Camille smiled with sheer delight in her eyes. "Denver; it must be so exciting for her, but when will she be back so I can talk to her? Should I call?" She hesitated then shook her head. "No, I need to talk to her in person." Her body deflated back against the chair. "Now, what am I going to do?"

I smiled at her as I stood and pulled my coat from the back of the chair.

"I'm headed to Madras to look at a horse. You can come with me," I turned and waved at Susan, "Thanks, Lady!"

Camille was right behind me as I walked to my truck.

It had only been six weeks since I had invited Lacie Jae to join me for a day in Vegas. I can't say I had liked Camille, at all, before today and would not have believed it if someone had told me I would be inviting her to stay also.

There was one thing about the two sisters; they were the epitome of not judging someone without knowing their story.

"What about my car?" Camille asked as she slid onto the seat of my truck.

"It will be fine here until we get back."

"How long is she going to be in Denver?" Camille asked.

I turned the truck onto the highway and started the hour drive to Madras.

"Hopefully, to the end of next week, if at least one makes the finals."

"So, what am I supposed to do until she gets back?" She mumbled. "I guess I could go back home." She said the last part as if she was going to the dentist.

"I can always use a hand at the ranch."

She laughed, "I've never been around a horse or a cow."

"There is a lot to do on a ranch that doesn't have anything to do with working cows and horses."

"Alright, but, I'm not sure about Lacie Jae knowing I'm here waiting for her."

"I understand," I nodded. "I don't want to interrupt or affect her work."

Camille's head jerked to me, "What work? She's working? I thought she was just traveling with your family."

I chuckled as I pulled the truck off to the side of the road. I plugged my phone to the truck speakers and started Lacie Jae's first podcast:

Welcome to my first Podcast! I'm Lacie Jae, a relocated city girl who will be adventuring into the ranching and rodeo world...the cowboy way of life. Until a few weeks ago, I had never been around a horse or a cow, and now, that's changed.

Camille chuckled, laughed, and cried through the podcast.

"How did this happen?" She wiped away the tears.

I told her about the phone calls to the coffee shop workers and how much enjoyment we got from seeing our life through her eyes.

We listened to more podcasts until we were five minutes away from the Parkston ranch in Madras.

Camille sighed as she stared out the window. "She started at those coffee shops when she was 16. After graduating, she basically took them over. I kept telling her how smart she was, but she never believed me."

"Maybe it was something that she just fell into. With the podcasts, she truly believes she is bringing enjoyment to people even while they laugh at her...or rather, with her. She is having fun."

"After her mother died, she had been taking care of our dad and just worked. I couldn't get her to go out with her friends from the coffee shop or from school. She'd occasionally go to a movie with me, but that's it. For her to be finally out having fun…" Camille's voice quivered, but it was also full of excitement. "I don't know what to say…I'm so happy for her."

I turned down the long driveway to the ranch. White fencing created two large snow-covered pastures that set in front of the house and massive stables. Both buildings were made of stained golden pine with a dark stone accent at the bottom and had snow on the roofs and smoke puffing from a chimney.

"I feel like we're driving into a painting," Camille whispered.

A large metal building set behind the stables and seemed to blend into the white pastures. I knew from their website that it was their indoor arena. As we neared the buildings, I could see even more pastures stretching out behind the buildings. White fencing created five long narrow pastures. Each had a round-bale feeder filled with hay in the middle and dozens of horses around them.

"Wow, that's a lot of horses," Camille whispered as her head turned from one pasture to another. "Have you been here before?"

"No…first time, although I've seen it on their website. I'm sure the stalls in the stable are full of horses, too. They would keep the ones in training in there." I turned to park next to the house.

Jeremy Parkston walked out of the house and down the wide wood steps. He was a tall, slender cowboy who I knew to be one of the finest cutting horse trainers in the country.

"He looks so western and handsome," Camille whispered as if he could hear her.

"Yes, but very married with a son living in Texas showing their horses and a daughter with a passion for barrel racing. She's quite good, they both are."

"Isn't the phrase 'born in the saddle'?"

"Yes."

We both stepped out of the truck to a blast of chilly air. It was moments like these that I appreciated my long thick hair and its ability to help keep my neck warm. From the center console of the truck, I pulled out a stylish beanie cap and chose a dark blue one for Camille and tossed it to her.

"Thank you!" She grinned and slid it on over her brunette hair. She was in stylish snow-boots, not working winter snow-boots, but they would still suffice the short time we would be outside.

I slid on my mint green beanie and zipped up my coat. I'd worn my knee-high snow-boots in anticipation of the walk to the barn, which was covered in five inches of fresh snow. If I needed my riding boots, they were laying on the back seat next to my saddle.

"No horse trailer?" Jeremy asked with a wide grin and an outstretched hand.

"Don't you deliver?" I teased and shook his hand. "Jeremy, this is Madi, she's helping out at the ranch while everyone is off playing."

Camille didn't flinch at the name; she just stretched out a hand and smiled brightly.

"Nice to meet you, Madi," he shook her hand then looked back at me. "How is Evan?"

It seemed that it was always the first thing people asked.

"He's doing very well. We finally have him traveling."

"That's fantastic," he said and turned toward the stables. Camille and I followed alongside him. "I called a couple of times after the accident but haven't been able to make it down to see him."

"With these horses and the ones in Oklahoma and Texas, I think getting a phone call in is pretty thoughtful of you," I said honestly.

He stopped just outside the stable door and pulled a halter off the hook and handed it to me with a smile.

"You didn't even catch him for me?" I teased with wide eyes.

"And if I did, you would have thought there was something wrong with him...as in why I called your dad about him when I heard you were looking," Jeremy chuckled. "By going out and catching him in the pasture, well, you'll see..."

"I would have trusted you," I smiled.

"Now you'll know," He opened the gate to the first corral. No horses were there, so we walked through the next gate and to the pastures. "This is the weanling pasture or I guess now they are yearlings. Then the two-year-olds in the next, then the three and four-year-olds together."

"And the six-year old I'm looking at is in the farthest pasture?" I asked with a lifted brow and the five inches of snow crunching under my feet.

"Well, you know me, I wanted to show off my horses," He gave me a grin, but there was something in his eyes that said he wasn't really teasing.

At the sight of our walking through the gate, a dozen young horses trotted down the long pasture toward us.

I heard a squeak escape Camille before she stepped to the side, putting Jeremy and I between her and the excited horses.

I asked her with my eyes if she was alright and she just nodded slightly, so I turned back and looked at the colts and fillies that were crowding each other to see us. My hands went to each one to play with an ear, glide down a neck or over their backs.

All of them were fuzzy in their long-haired winter coats, and they were of all colors; black, buckskin, sorrels, and a handful of palominos. A little colt stood to the side in full profile so I could see his large rump, deep girth, short neck, and intelligent eyes. He was a light creamy yellow with dirty white forelock, spiked growing mane, and a stubby growing tail.

"Look at that butt," I whispered as I took in his whole conformation.

"You're looking at his butt?" Camille asked.

I couldn't take my eyes off him as I responded to her, "Quarter horses are known for their speed in a quarter-mile sprint. It stems from the large butt and powerful chests. If you're in an event that needs sudden speed like barrel racing or breakaway, you need that fast burst."

"Oh, that makes sense," she whispered.

"He's going to have a strong bust out or fierce turn," Jeremy said with a pleased tone.

139

"Very bulldog," I nodded and continued to play with the younger horses.

Camille's hand finally left her pockets to reach out to a little red filly with a wide white blaze down her face. She giggled softly as the filly's nose touched her fingertips. Within seconds the horse stepped in for more, and Camille was copying my stroking of the horses. Her hand slid down the neck and across the back.

"Seriously, Jeremy," I said. "You have the nicest foals...or yearlings."

"Don't horses carry for a whole year?" Camille asked. "You breed them in January? In this cold?"

"No," Jeremy answered. "Most were born in April and into May. But, no matter what month they are born in, once the next January 1 passes they are considered yearlings."

"Even if they were born in December?" Camille asked.

"Yes," Jeremy nodded and turned to walk to the gate for the next pasture. "Thoroughbred breeders like to foal in January so their 2 and 3-year-old racehorses are the biggest they can be to start."

"Wow," she said and stepped through the gate with another dozen horses slowly walking through the snow toward her.

Camille froze in place until I stepped between her and the larger approaching horses.

With one hand gripping the back of my coat, she followed me as I walked around the horses. Her other hand would reach out and pet a nose or hip that walked by.

Into the third pasture and the larger three and four-year-olds, Camille was gripping the back of my coat with both hands.

I chuckled, "You want to watch from the other side of the fence?"

"Ummm...I so want to say yes, but I'm trying to brave it out," she giggled and finally let go of my coat with one hand to pet the nose of a black horse.

A tall filly pushed her way through the other horses to nudge her nose under my hand. She was stunning. Her body was dark gold with white patches under her belly, and her back

140

legs were white up to her hocks. Her mane and tail were a mixture of white and black while her long forelock was just black. It hung over a wide white blaze that flowed down her nose and covered her whole face. Large soft brown eyes looked to me for attention. She was a striking buckskin paint with a bald white face.

"She's a full sister to the gelding I called you about," Jeremy said.

"She's tall…14.3 hands already?" I asked.

"How old are they when they stop growing?" Camille asked as her hand moved from one horse's nose to the other. She still had a firm grip of my coat with the other.

"Height-wise, they can grow up to five or six, then they begin to fill out in the body," Jeremy answered.

"Here I am holding a halter and rope and they are all trying to get to me," I said. "That's impressive."

"My daughter, Sammie, takes it upon herself to halter break and gentle the horses. She does a fine job for preparation for training which my son and I do," Jeremy said and stood patiently as I gave the horses attention. "Except for barrels, she does the training."

"They are beautiful," I said as my gaze wandered to each one.

"Yes, so big, beautiful, and gentle," Camille nodded with a hand sliding down the neck of a large black gelding.

Jeremy grinned proudly and moved to the next gate and another set of horses had lined along the fence waiting for their turn at the attention. "We best keep moving. My wife is making lunch and will meet us in the indoor arena so you can ride."

Camille and I shared a quick glance. How were we going to get another bite into our very full stomachs?

I knew I wanted the gelding the moment I saw him. The videos and pictures didn't do him justice. His body was muscular, broad, and the same white and buckskin color as his sister I had just met. Her body was mostly buckskin with a splash of white, but he was a bold pattern of white and dark gold. Her blaze covered her face while his was just a strip down the center. He had a strong, wide jaw, shorter strong neck, broad shoulders and a wide back that led to a large, but well-proportioned hindquarters. His mane, tail, and forelock were a mixture of white and black. But it was his eyes and the way he held his head that I loved.

"Which one?" Camille whispered as she hid behind me.

"It's OK if you want to go on the other side of the fence," I smiled but pointed to the striking gelding.

"Thanks," she turned and Jeremy opened a gate for her. "And that horse is cool looking!"

"Yes," I said breathlessly.

To test the horses, I lifted the lead rope and halter in the air and they nosed it, attempted to chew it, and one large black gelding dipped his head under it and shook it around.

"Jeremy..." I sighed. "Just impressive."

He grinned proudly.

Without a flinch, the paint gelding let me slide the halter on him and fasten it. My hand found its way down his long nose, which dipped into me.

"This is what you wanted me to see?" I gave Jeremy a knowing grin.

He just laughed and walked to the gate. Camille was standing on the lowest rail of the fence and leaning over the top to pet the horses.

The gelding strode calmly next to me as we walked out of the pasture and to the wide driveway which led to the barn. As we walked, I looked out at all the horses we walked through and wondered why. If we could have just come down the driveway and to this gate, why did he walk us through the horses, especially when he could clearly see Camille was uncomfortable?

Fifteen minutes later, I was putting a boot in the stirrup and lifting up onto the gelding's back. It wasn't exactly warm in the indoor arena, but it was protected from the wind, so it was comfortable. I'd seen videos and trusted Jeremy enough that I didn't worry about groundwork prior to getting on a horse I didn't know. After one lap around the arena at a soft trot, Jeremy's wife, Alana, had joined the group. She was pulling sandwiches out of a cooler.

After a few moments, everyone faded away as I concentrated on the horse. Every move, turn, speed of gait, and little cue I asked for he accomplished flawlessly. At six, he had already had extensive training toward a cutting career. The fact that he was so large and broad-bodied was the reason he was up for sale. He was too big for a high-end competitive cutting horse, but he would make one hell of a roping horse. Shorter horses, with shorter strides, made my backache. Too long of a stride and he wouldn't have the stop I was looking for. But this horse had a comfortable stride and I felt in-sync with him from the start.

I loped to the far end of the arena and stopped him. Turning his butt into the wall, as if in a roping box, I kicked him into a fast run for twenty yards, then leaned back quickly to bring him to a stop. He was nearly perfect. There was no doubt in my mind that with practice, he would have a great stop. Then there was the fact that he was trained as a cutting horse, which meant he was already used to being around cows.

I came out of my haze and trotted down to the horse's owners who were chatting with Camille as if they had known her for years. Alana greeted me with a pleased smile and a hoagie sandwich. Camille's hand instantly went to the horse's jaw to caress it gently. She had definitely had an introduction to horses...lots of them and she had a natural instinct to touch them.

"You two looked great out there," Alana said with eyes brimming in pride at the horse.

"A high-quality horse like I expected from you," I took the sandwich but didn't think I could eat it.

"Have you swung a rope around him?" I asked.

They both shook their heads.

"Just cutting and trail rides," Jeremy answered.

"Well, I'm sure it won't take much," I stepped down from the saddle and the horse's nose turned to me. He bit half the sandwich before I could move with the other half falling to the ground.

We all laughed, and I silently thanked him.

"What's his name?" Camille asked.

"Memphis," Alana answered. "That's his barn name. We bought him as a two-year-old and his sister as a weanling."

Jeremy walked to a side table and picked up a black binder. He opened the cover and handed it to me while he took the reins of the horse. It was filled with dozens of plastic protective sheet covers that held a picture on one side and registration papers of the horse on the other.

"Here's his paperwork...the one on top," He said and looked pointedly at his wife.

There was silent communication between them, which ended when Alana stood and looked at Camille. "Madi, can you help me with the hot chocolate while they talk business?"

"Of course," Camille said, and after a quick glance to me, she followed the woman out of the barn.

I walked Memphis over to the hitching post and began removing my saddle.

"Delaney?" Jeremy's voice was almost a whisper.

"Yes?" I slid the saddle off and set it on the hitching post then turned to him.

"Are you still barrel racing?" There was a hesitant hitch in his voice.

"Yes...occasionally...not as much as I used to," I admitted with my stomach beginning to ache.

"You're just roping now?"

"Mainly, yes, but looking at keeping my foot in the door with barrels."

He nodded thoughtfully then took a deep breath, "When I told Sammie you were coming here to look at Memphis, she just about flipped that she wasn't going to be here to meet you."

I smiled, "That's nice of her."

"She went on a 30-minute diatribe of you and your horses, Gaston and Pepper."

There was something in the way he said it that made a knot form in my stomach. "They are great horses."

"You three made it to two trips to the finals...almost three...that first year only missing by a couple of thousand

144

dollars." He smiled slightly, but there was tension in his eyes. "Part of Sammie's lecture."

We missed it by $1,639. It was a heart breaker. "Yeah, it was tough but we made up for it."

There was 30 seconds of silence between us as I stood quietly and waited for him to speak.

"I don't know what your intentions are..." he finally said. "If you had plans on running barrels again this year or not...or just roping. But Alana and I talked about it, and no, Sammie doesn't know...but we talked and..."

My stomach clenched.

"Well," He squared his shoulders and stood taller. "We want to know if you're interested in selling them to us for Sammie."

I just stared at him in stunned silence. Sell Gaston and Pepper?

CHAPTER FIFTEEN

"We believe, without a doubt, our girl will make it to the NFR and we honestly believe that your horses can take her there."

"I..." Sell my boys? The thought had never crossed my mind.

"No hurry...or rush," He said quickly. "But Alana and I did some research and think we came up with a fair deal."

My face flushed as my stomach soured.

He continued when I didn't say anything.

"They are quality, proven themselves a number of times and are still healthy...sound."

I nodded slightly, which he must have taken as my considering selling my horses and his voice rose in tone and volume.

"We'd like to do a trade with you," He nodded to the horse that was standing calmly next to us. "Memphis is quality and has the pedigree...he's won a bit in the arena, but we know he isn't the value...yet...of Gaston so we'll throw in a yearling and a couple three or four-year-olds. The horses of your choice from that book. Pepper...well, we know he isn't the value of Gaston so, to be fair, we were thinking Memphis and a couple two or three-year-olds with training...of your choosing also."

That was why he walked us through all four horse pastures instead of going directly to the one that held Memphis. He paraded me through his horses so I would have a preview for their offer.

"Delaney?"

I looked up at him, still, a bit stunned and with an aching stomach.

"Is that something you would consider? We weren't sure if you were keeping them since you didn't really race last year."

"Well," I managed to say. "The thought of selling either of them never crossed my mind."

"Oh," His shoulder's lowered and he looked a bit deflated. "We had really worked ourselves up with hope. Sammie was so enamored with them, but, as I said, we didn't tell her about the idea. We were hoping Gaston for her; she was saying he was pretty special."

"Yes, he is," I said and snapped out of the shock to turn and remove my bridle and replace it with the halter.

"Well, if the time comes and you consider selling either of them, would you give us first chance?"

I nodded as I slid the brush down the horse's back. Sell Gaston?

"So, what do you think of Memphis?" He smiled, even though the disappointment floated in the air between us.

"He's what I've been looking for," I said honestly. By the time I had finished the ride, I was looking forward to having him home and working with him. I realized it was the same feeling they had for Gaston and Pepper for their daughter, who, even though I'd never met her, was one hell of a rider and racer.

"Let's let him cool off in the stall over here before taking him outside," Jeremy said and walked to the corner of the barn.

I led the horse in and with a final stroke down his neck, I stepped out of the stall and looked back at Jeremy.

"Sorry for my response, but the thought of selling my boys caught me by surprise."

"I understand, we just didn't know, but wanted to make sure we made an offer or were first in line if the opportunity comes up," He turned and picked up the notebook he had handed me earlier. "Alana put this together last night. It, of course, doesn't include the horses showing down south."

"Of course," I nodded.

His shoulders rose a bit as he held out the black binder, "Take it with you."

"I..." My hand slowly rose to take the binder. What the hell was I doing? Giving them false hope? I wasn't going to sell my horses.

When we walked out of the stables, I looked back at Memphis, who had his head down in the hay feeder. I wanted him; why didn't I bring a trailer with me? Now I was going to have to come back and face them again.

As hard as I tried not to, when we walked out of the barn, my head turned to look over the horses out in the pasture. They were all quality horses with big futures ahead of them. I couldn't go wrong with any of them but...sell my boys?

"I'll come back for Memphis tomorrow," I said as we walked to my truck to place the saddle, boots, and the binder onto the back seat.

When we walked into the house, Alana and Camille were hunched over a large laptop. Camille was pointing to the screen, and Alana was nodding.

"What are you two up to?" Jeremy picked up a hot chocolate filled mug and handed it to me, then lifted one for himself.

The first sip seemed to ease the hollow ache in my stomach.

"Madi is a web designer and I asked her to look at our websites," Alana said and turned to me. "We have a couple of different ones then all the social media sites."

"They aren't all connected together," Camille/Madi said. "It's key to showing the size of your operation, and your horses need to be laid out better."

I listened to them for a while as I sipped the hot chocolate. I had no idea what she did for a living and was pleasantly surprised at her confidence as she spoke. Even without knowing horses, she obviously knew business and product placement.

I knew the Parkston family was highly respected in the horse industry, whether cutting, reining, or barrels, and their horse business was obviously profitable. The home was full of exquisite furniture that made it elegant but comfortable.

I caught a look between Jeremy and Alana; hers was hopeful, and his was disheartened. He whispered to her and her shoulders lowered as she looked at me with a slight smile.

"We thought we should try," She finally said.

Camille's eyes finally left the laptop and darted between us.

"I understand," I smiled in understanding. "I just had never thought of selling them, so it caught me by surprise."

"But she promised to let us have the first option if she does," Jeremy added. "And she'll be back for Memphis in the morning."

"He'll be a great breakaway horse," I glanced at Camille with a silent 'time to go' look.

She stood without a word and followed us out the door.

As I turned the truck and drove back down the driveway, Camille turned to me.

"Why did you call me Madi?"

"Short for your last name Madison so I could remember what I said," I turned onto the main road. "They are friends with my father, who made the arrangement for me to come here today. Just in case they talked, I didn't want them mentioning a Camille being with me and Dad mentioning it to the group back there."

"Oh, makes sense, thanks for that."

As if on cue, my phone sang with Dad's face appearing on the screen. It was a habit to set the phone on the holder and connected it to the speaker system as soon as I slid into the truck. It was aimed toward me so there was no way they would know Camille was there unless she spoke.

I pushed the accept button and his concerned face appeared.

"What's up?" I asked and relaxed back in the seat for the hour-long drive home.

"Just wondering what's taking you so long to call and tell me about the horse," he said.

"I just left...literally just turned out of the driveway," I glanced at the phone and wondered if I should mention the trade offer.

"What's that look? Wasn't he what you wanted?"

"I'll be coming back for him in the morning," I smiled pensively.

"Then what?"

I took a deep breath and slowly released it. *Thinking* it was bad enough, *saying* it out loud made it real. "They offered a trade."

"For what?" he glared.

I hesitated.

"Spit it out," he ordered.

"They want Gaston and Pepper for their daughter," His only response was his eyebrows rising in surprise, so I continued. "They want to trade the gelding, and three others of my choice for Gaston. For Peppers is the gelding and two trained horses of my choice."

"Six for two…" he whispered.

"But that's an awfully big TWO," I sighed.

"What did you say?"

I shrugged and felt the tension rise in my stomach again. "I told them I hadn't considered selling them but ended up taking the binder full of horse pictures and registrations with me."

"So, you're considering it?"

I just stared down the road for a moment then slowly shrugged.

"You didn't barrel race as hard last year and then there was ranch work, but Gaston is a competitor. Pepper almost as much."

"I know…" I whispered.

"Do you have any plans right now of taking them to a race or rodeo?"

"We qualified for Houston and San Antonio next month and The American, then I was thinking Moses Lake and Walla Walla this April…Pendleton for the big July race…"

"The tournament rodeos then just a few for the summer; is that fair to them?"

I swallowed the lump that was rising in my throat and my eyes hurt from staring so hard at the road.

"You and Gaston did well together because you're both warriors when it comes to competition."

I glanced at the phone to see his thoughtful look.

"You accomplished the dream that included him and Pepper," he continued. "Now you're on to the next; roping, which doesn't include them."

"I could re-train them," I said and even to me, my voice sounded weak.

He shook his head with a huff, "Gaston doesn't like ropes, he is a barrel horse…that's his passion and if you were going to re-train Pepper, you would have already and not just bought yourself another roping horse."

"So, you think I should do it?" I sighed and a little part of me wanted him to order me one way or another, so I didn't have to make the decision.

"No, Darlin', that decision is all yours."

I sighed, "They have both been such a big part of my life and accomplishments."

"Been…they have 'been' not 'are' a part of your current dreams."

My heart ached and it must have shown on my face.

"Delaney, you don't have to make the decision now, but if you were ever to decide to, the Parkston's would be the family to get either of them back in the Thomas and Mack."

"I told them if I decided to sell, I would give them first opportunity."

We were quiet a moment, then his image on the phone wiggled as he repositioned it.

"I'll let you concentrate on the road and think," he said. "You drive safe and let me know when you get to the ranch."

"I will, love you, Dad," I said.

"Love you, Darlin', be safe."

The phone went dark and I just stared out the window.

Camille glanced in the back of the truck then leaned over to grab the binder from the back-seat.

"Do you mind?" She asked.

I just shook my head as I reminisced about all the miles Gaston and I had traveled to get to the famous yellow arena.

All the excitement of being at the National Finals Rodeo as a contestant and not just there for Dad, but it was mostly the miles and companionship the horse and I had shared over the long trips and nights. Then the hours we spent conditioning and practicing.

He never let me down. Was I letting him down now by not racing him?

"Kendra said you had been a barrel racer at the NFR, so I looked you up when Lacie Jae came here the first time," Camille said as she flipped through the pages of horses. "Watching you and those horses run was pretty spectacular; so were all the other ladies. I'd have been scared to death."

"I missed going the first year I bought my card. At the beginning of the second year, I added Pepper to the team to give Gaston time off."

"What does "bought my card' mean?"

"You can buy a permit to compete in WPRA rodeos so you can get experience. Then, after two years on a permit, or until you finish college, you have to buy a card which enables you to enter in and get a draw in the bigger rodeos. Then you become eligible for the NFR."

"Why did you stop?"

"I reached my goal," I whispered as my mind replayed Gaston turning each barrel at our last race in the famous yellow arena. "Pepper ran and placed two of the ten nights to give Gaston a break, but Gaston won two go-round buckles and the average our final day."

"Not the championship?" She glanced over to me.

"Wasn't my goal; although it wouldn't have upset me either," I huffed with a smile. "My grandfather raised Dad with the focus on consistency in the arena then Dad taught us; being consistent over ten days of rodeo at the NFR. You win the overall average, which brings home more money."

"But doesn't winning the championship mean you earned more?"

"Yes, you earned more throughout the whole year. With the average, it's for just those ten days. That's what was ingrained in us. With Grandpa, Dad, Logan, and me winning it, it's now a family tradition that Brodie will be looking for in the next couple years."

"So, you won the average last year and your focus changed?"

"Yes, to roping. I enjoyed barrel racing, but it was the only way I could get to the NFR. Roping is my passion...which they don't have women's roping at the NFR, but they do at the World Series of Roping which is held at the same time."

"And your new goal?"

"World Champion Roper with the WPRA," I answered with conviction and the warmth of the dream spreading into my heart.

The conversation died as she looked at the horses in the binder and I drove us back toward the diner.

"So, can you recommend a hotel?" She asked and set the binder back on the seat as I drove in next to her car.

"Sure...Hotel Rawlins," I smirked. "It's a bit snow-covered, but it has pretty cows and horses to look at."

"Delaney, I..."

"Camille...I've been in the house by myself for four days and I have at least another ten to go. Consider it a favor to me and I'll just work your butt off during the day in payment of room and board."

She chuckled, "Alright, since it sounds so inviting."

"How does a hot tub sound?"

"Like heaven; I'll stop and buy some wine."

"I already have a couple of bottles," I admitted. "But we still have work to do."

"I'm not sure I have anything to wear to 'ranch' in."

"Other than the length of your legs, I'm guessing we're about the same size, and I have plenty of clothes to 'ranch' in."

"What are those?" Camille stopped just inside the barn in her borrowed jeans, boots, and dark blue sweatshirt under a brown Carhart jacket. Gloves covered her hands, bright red wild rag scarf around her neck, and the knit beanie cap covering her dark brown hair. All of it was mine and used, but somehow she made it all look like she was ready to shoot the cover of a magazine. When I wore it, it did not.

"Training equipment for bareback and bronc riding," I answered.

"Oh...," She said and looked it over again before following me to the trailer that was attached to the ATV.

"We'll load hay onto the trailer and drop to the horses inside the barn then take some out to the ones in the pasture."

She stepped right up to the bales and started to lift one. There was no hesitation, and that impressed me.

"Is Gaston here?" She asked as we slid onto the seat of the machine.

"Yes," I answered with a sigh. I'd managed to keep my mind on Memphis coming to the ranch and not the idea of Gaston leaving it. "The horses we want to keep in competition condition are kept here at the barn and a few of the older ones, so they get extra pampering."

We slowly moved down the aisle of the barn and fed the anxious horses.

"This is Gaston," I said and stepped into his stall.

The tall red roan nudged me in the arm then stomach as he asked for attention. As always, my heart sighed when I touched him and I couldn't help but smile. Thousands and thousands of hours we had spent together in the last eight years. Many of those were just the two of us as we traveled from one race or rodeo to another.

"He's beautiful," Camille said as she stuffed his feeder with hay then dumped a can of feed in the bucket hanging on the wall.

"Inside and out," I ran a hand down his neck as his head dipped into the bucket. "Heart of gold...of a champion...a once in a lifetime horse."

I stepped out of the stall with one look back at him. Sell him? How and the hell could I do that? What would it be like not to have him in the stall?

"So, which other ones are your competition horses?" Camille looked down the aisle at the horses leaning over stall doors waiting for their food.

"Next is Archer. He's a blue roan and my current breakaway horse."

She ran a hand down his nose then tossed hay in the feeder as I poured the grain.

"Memphis is replacing him?"

"Never replacing," I smiled at the horse. "Once Memphis is ready, it will allow Archer to retire and just become a ranch horse."

She moved to the next stall, "And this white horse?"

"That is Ketchum and he is actually considered gray. You'll be able to see that a bit better when he sheds out this spring. The three of them are my main horses, and then Pepper is Gaston's backup...he's the bay in the next stall."

"Pepper and Gaston are your barrel horses, Archer and Memphis your breakaway...but just Ketchum for team roping?"

We continued down the stable to feed the remaining horses.

"We all have roping and ranch horses we use for competition."

"So, your brothers rope too?"

"Yes, we grew up team roping together with Dad."

After finishing feeding in the barn, we used the tractor to haul large round bales of hay to the feeders in the pasture. I was amazed at how hard Camille worked. We closed out the daylight of the day with an ATV ride to check stock tanks in the back pasture. She insisted on learning how to drive.

"I can't believe I'm going to say this," she said as we walked back into the barn. "But, I'm actually hungry."

"Cupboards and pantry are full and I hate cooking," I smiled. "Feel free to make whatever you want. I'll finish out here, then come in and get the hot tub going."

"Sounds like a plan."

I watched her walk to the house, then turned and walked to Gaston's stall. He was standing at the door to the outside run and looking out at the pasture and horses in the distance.

I crossed my arms over the top of the stall door and just looked at him. He turned to me then turned back to stare out at the darkening night. It was as if he knew we should be in Denver racing. Guilt settled into my stomach. For the last three years, we had competed at that rodeo and I was sure he felt as left out as I did.

According to my phone, it was six o'clock our time, which would make it seven o'clock in Denver.

So, I sent a text: Hey, Handsome. INU

The phone rang with a picture of Val Kilmer as Doc Holiday appearing on the screen.

"I'll be your Huckleberry," I purred.

His chuckle was deep and made my whole body warm.

"Damn, I wish you were here," he said in a deep, caressing voice. "INU makes me nervous. You OK?"

"Where are you?"

"In the truck. We were checking on the horses before heading to the hotel."

"How did today go?"

"Just practice, and you didn't give me the 'I need you' code to talk about my day so, my Delaney, what's going on?"

"I think…maybe…I'm going to go back to barrel racing."

There was a pause before he spoke, "Didn't you go look at the gelding today?"

"Yeah, I was going to go get him in the morning, but I don't have to…I'm not sure I should."

"Sweetheart, what's behind the change? Are you going to be happy backing out of roping? Don't you have a full calendar of events this year?"

"Yeah…" I sighed and visualized the large wall calendar that hung in the office. Nearly every weekend was full. It hurt my heart just thinking of throwing it away and recreating one with barrel races…even if it was with the beautiful gelding in front of me.

"Tell me what happened," he whispered. "…this have to do with your date with Mark?"

I chuckled softly, "No, we broke up at breakfast when he hit on another woman."

"Are you fucking kidding me?"

I chuckled again and told him about the whole day from Camille to the offer for the horses to the horse standing and ignoring me at the door in front of me.

"Well, that's a bit of an overwhelming day," he huffed.

"I know, and I'm so tired of thinking."

"Hmmm…well, the thing with Mark is understandable if he didn't get the feeling you were into a relationship."

I could almost hear his smile and the tone was a subdued smart-ass and it made me smile.

"So, Lacie Jae's sister…I thought you didn't like her."

"We obviously didn't know her; just Lacie Jae's side of the story. Camille was so lost at first, but around the horses, she tried and pretty much succeeded in showing her inner-strength then outer-strength as she helped with chores. She didn't hesitate in anything and she's catching on real quick."

"Sounds like you like her."

"I have to say, I do, so far. Right from the start, she wasn't anything I expected."

"What do you think her sister is going to say when she shows up?"

"Hmmm….well…I don't know, but I don't think she will be happy she's here and probably feel betrayed that I do like her. Maybe she'll feel angry that Camille showed up in her new life after kicking her out of her own."

"Well, that's another ten days down the road. So, what about Gaston and Pepper?"

I leaned against the top of the stall and watched Gaston stare out the door.

"What was your first reaction?" He asked.

"Shock at the thought."

"Not a yes or no right away?"

157

"Well, no…" I admitted and kicked the ground while silently hoping he would give me the answer.

"Delaney, why in the hell would you ever consider selling Gaston?"

"I wasn't…I don't think. You don't think I should?"

"Of course not!" He huffed. "How many times did we talk about breakaway being added to the big rodeos now? Isn't that one of the reasons you went to look at Memphis?"

"Well tons…that's why I haven't been racing."

He laughed in disbelief, "Delaney, you are not thinking straight. Gaston with barrels and Archer and Ketchum in roping? You can kick some ass and take a handful of all-around cowboy awards home."

"Oh," I shook my head in disbelief. How could I forget that?

"But is Memphis the rope horse you've been looking for?"

"My gut says yes."

"And did he get your heart rate up and you couldn't wait to get him home to start training?"

He knew me so well.

"Yes, I wanted to just ride him home and grab a rope."

"Gaston on barrels, Archer breakaway roping with Memphis as a backup, you can kill it out there on the rodeo trail this year. Then throw in Ketchum with team roping…damn, I can't wait for this year."

"Oh, Darlin', I'm so glad I called," I giggled with relief flowing through me.

"Me too," He laughed. "If I was there, I'd kick your cute butt for even thinking of selling him."

I flushed at the thought as I grinned at Gaston, "Kinky…"

He laughed again, then his voice quickly changed serious, "What about Pepper?"

"He'll be on the back burner unless something happens to Gaston," I stepped into the stall and Gaston turned to me. "If I was only running races, then I could run both. But I want to rope and I can do that at jackpots and rodeos. I have to be realistic about what I can and cannot do."

"You think Memphis will be ready?"

I shrugged into the darkness and ran a hand down Gaston's neck. "He's never had a rope around him so we'll see. I'll start working with him, but I'd still take him with us to get him used to traveling and the excitement of rodeos."

"I know of the Parkston family and they are pretty damn respected. What is the daughter like?"

"I don't know her; just that she's a great racer and has done an excellent job working with the younger horses."

"Why would you even consider trading Pepper to someone that you don't know?"

"I...don't...know...?

"I agree with your dad that it isn't fair to Pepper if you're not going to use him and he's just going to sit in the pasture or do ranch work. He's an NFR horse and still young...he needs to be running."

I sighed and closed my eyes.

"But, don't even consider trading him without meeting her."

"I won't," I sighed.

"They are a perfect family for him, just make sure she's the right human for him."

I smiled and felt a sense of relief, "I'll call and see if we can meet in the morning at the arena in Marsland."

"*Then* you decide," he said confidently.

"There's no hurry to sell him," I agreed.

"You feel better?"

I grinned as Gaston rubbed his head across my chest as if he knew the tension and frustration were gone. I slid a hand down his nose and neck, and my whole body relaxed.

"Yes, I knew you would help."

"I wish you could come over here," his voice lowered, and there was a touch of loneliness.

"I thought about it last night, but now with Camille here..."

"Yeah, you can't leave her there or bring her here," he sighed.

"Well, I'll call you every night and do what I can to help you fall asleep."

He laughed and the sound just filled my heart.

"Good night and thank you, my Huckleberry," I whispered into the phone.

"Good night, my Delaney."

I sighed and ended the call, then called Jeremy. I couldn't tell if he was upset when I informed him Gaston wasn't for sale, but he immediately agreed to meet when I told him Pepper was an option.

"That's quite a little coffee nook you have," Camille said as I walked in the door.

"Lacie Jae brought the coffee maker to us right before Christmas as a thank you gift. My dad and brothers built the nook just for that machine and all the supplies she said they would need."

"So, then she stayed."

"I think, at first, it was more of a hostage situation as they weren't letting her leave without a destination and plan."

Camille nodded and stirred the pasta while I pulled the plates from the cupboard.

Once we both were sitting at the long kitchen island, she turned to me, "Do you think she'll be mad I'm here?"

"I don't know."

Dinner was finished in silence.

"I'll get the Jacuzzi going," I stood. "I have swimsuits in my dressing room, a couple brand new that you can use. I have one in the laundry room I'll change in to."

She stood without a word and disappeared down the hall.

I was the first to the hot tub and slid in with my phone and a glass of wine; the bottle was close by.

After a long swig, I leaned back and closed my eyes as the pulsating water relaxed my muscles. The conversation in the barn made my heart sigh. After the thousands of hours we had talked on the phone over the months, he knew me and my dreams more than anyone else in the world.

I stretched out my legs on the side of the tub and tried posing them sexily and held the camera to make them look longer. The swimsuit had high sides, so it looked like I was naked, which made me giggle as I sent the picture to him.

It only took a minute before I received a text: Next week can't come fast enough.

A mischievous giggle escaped as I set the phone down and lifted the wine glass as Camille walked into the room. Her long dark hair was piled in a messy ponytail on top of her head and she wore a black one-piece swimsuit that showed her long sleek figure.

"I left our house in Redding at 3:00 this morning and never would have dreamed how this day would turn out." She slid into the bubbling water and sighed as she leaned back.

She held out her glass, so I could pour the wine for her. "You exercise?"

"Oh, yes," she smiled. "I'm a California girl that likes her beaches and boats. Redding has a river and lakes and the ocean is only 3 hours away. I still do Pilates and have or had a treadmill in the house for a good morning run."

"Well, my morning runs are usually chasing after loose cows or horses."

We both chuckled.

"Feel free any time to use the equipment in the hall. We try very hard to stay in as good of shape as we expect our horses to be. Dad still works with a therapist who comes out here most of the time."

"It was your father when Jeremy mentioned the accident?"

"Yes," I took a long drink of wine. "He was pinned by one of those large round bales we moved today. Pinned between the bale and a tractor, it broke his legs and back."

"I didn't see a ramp anywhere for a wheelchair. Is he paralyzed?"

"He has movement and can stand for short periods of time, but it becomes excruciatingly painful, so he is bound to the chair. There is a ramp off to the side he uses if he is in a hurry but he would rather make his body work in climbing the couple stairs. The shed up on the deck stores his wheelchair for inside the house. After the accident, the owner of the business which built the ratchet that broke and caused the accident, showed up at the hospital. He paid for everything medical and after Dad was home, he brought a dozen different wheelchairs for Dad to choose from."

"Wow, that's pretty upstanding of him."

"Very and he is a very nice man. Everyone in the company was horrified at what happened and they have all been helpful. Dad has a smaller chair for in the house and a couple of different ones for outside depending on what he is doing. Then, of course, he has a modified four-wheeler and his van."

"How is he dealing with being in the chair after such an active life?"

"He has had his moments," I whispered.

We both took a long drink of wine.

"What's on the agenda for tomorrow?" She asked and relaxed back into the pulsating jets.

"Feed, then meet Jeremy and his daughter."

"Really?" She gasped. "You decided to sell them?"

"Not Gaston, we'll rodeo together this year but maybe Pepper. I just don't want to make a decision without meeting Sammi. If she's some kind of pretentious little snot then there is no way I would let Pepper go to her."

"I didn't get the impression from her parents that she would be that way."

"Yeah, I haven't heard anything about her, but we don't run around the same crowd, so I don't really know."

"And if she isn't?"

"I don't know. I just need to see them together before I decide."

CHAPTER SIXTEEN

The next morning, we drove into the Marsland arena with Pepper in the trailer behind us. Loading him was such a natural thing to do and I kept myself from thinking that it would be the last time. My heart hurt every time the thought crept in. I just had to keep telling myself this was the best for him.

Jeremy walked to us with a long stride and anxious look on his face as we parked.

"We didn't tell Sammi anything," he said as soon as I opened the door. "She thinks we just came here to give you Memphis...he's inside."

"How do you want me to play this then?" I asked as Camille walked up next to us.

"Maybe that you wanted to exercise him here while you had the indoor arena?" He said anxiously.

"Alright," I nodded and walked to the back of the trailer to unload the horse. "I already have him saddled because I planned on doing just that."

Jeremy held open the door into the building as Camille walked through with Pepper and me following.

The building was large, with metal panels around the large arena. To my right was a long set of bleachers and to my left was a large open area for those waiting to go into the arena.

I could see Memphis tied to a hitching post in the corner with Alana and Sammi standing next to him. The horse made my heart beat faster. He was 'cool-looking' as Camille kept saying, but he also had a gentleness to him and an intelligent eye.

Alana smiled at us, making Sammi turn. Her eyes couldn't have widened more and her jaw dropped, letting out a muffled squeal. She was nineteen, only a few years younger than me. She had a unique combination of blue eyes and red hair that was straight to her shoulders but covered with a black knit hat.

"Sammi, this is Delaney Rawlins and Madi. Ladies, this is my daughter." Jeremy smiled.

I held out a hand to her as I approached. Pepper's head was at my shoulder and her eyes bounced from me to him as her hand rose to take mine.

"I am so honored to meet you," she grinned.

I was always a bit embarrassed when people said things like that, so I just smiled, "Your parents said you did the initial training with the horses. I'm very impressed."

Her cheeks blazed red, but her smile could not have been any wider.

"I just love horses and working with the young ones," she said.

I didn't want to just sit around chit-chatting; I wanted to get to my answer.

"Well, to start," I said to her. "I'd like to ride Memphis one more time before I sign papers, so would you mind riding Pepper for me?"

"What?" She gasped with jaw dropped. "I can ride him? Yes…yes, of course, I will!"

I chuckled. "If you'll get your saddle, I'll move mine over to Memphis."

The words were barely out of my mouth before she was running for the door.

"Thank you, Delaney," her mother said. "Whatever you decide, at least she gets to ride him."

I didn't say anything, my stomach was swirling and nerves were shaking. The only thing that made me feel alright with this was they hadn't told her their expectations. I couldn't have imagined telling her no if she knew.

The door opened and she walked in with the saddle cradled in her arms.

Her face was full of excitement and so was her voice, "I brought in the bridle I've used with Memphis so you can see."

Her hand was trembling when she handed me the bridle.

Instead of taking it, my hand slid over hers and squeezed.

She looked at me in surprise.

"Just relax," I smiled. "Take a breath and relax."

Her eyes widened again, "You don't understand," she whispered. "I have dreamt about this moment since I was little...since I first watched the barrel racing on TV when I was a kid. I've dreamt of riding a horse that was ridden at the NFR. Dreamt and believed that someday it was going to happen for me."

There was pure honesty in her eyes and awe in her voice. This girl was not a pretentious little snot like I had hoped, so my decision was easier to make. This girl was a dreamer and a believer and had the desire, work ethic and, most importantly, family support to reach her dream.

The nervous ache in my stomach eased.

"Let's just ride for a bit so you can get used to him," I smiled in understanding.

I watched her as she prepared the horse for the ride. She talked to him constantly. When she was ready to step in the stirrup, she turned and smiled at her grinning parents then turned to me with a fire and light in her eyes.

She stepped up and relaxed into the saddle with a wide grin. A hand reached out to slide up his neck.

"Ready?" I asked.

"Oh, yes," She said breathlessly. "What should I know about him?"

That impressed me.

"Stay off his face, loose reins. Use your legs lightly...he's touchy and will respond with the lightest touch."

We were silent the first lap of the arena, but with the second, the questions started and came in rapid succession.

"What was your favorite rodeo?"

"What was your fastest time on a standard pattern?"

"How was riding Gaston different than Pepper?"

"What was your biggest disappointment?"

"How much did you practice?"

"What was it like on the road all the time?"

"What was the biggest advice I could give her?

I answered all, and once she relaxed, I moved us to trot. The questions continued and she never once interrupted my answer and she hung on every word.

By the end of the ride, it was quite easy to tell that Sammi would be good for Pepper. The decision was made, and I felt very confident it was the right one.

The next morning I stepped out of the shower, tossed a very supportive athletic bra on the bed, then my usual riding panties that were more like tight boxer shorts. I chose a flannel shirt and lined jeans and threw them on the bed next to the underwear. I thought of the image of the blue lacey panties and bra set that I had sent to him in Vegas and giggled. For fun, I sent him the picture of the very unsexy underwear.

By the time I had all the clothes on, I had received a response.

Text: Knowing the body they are covering and how much I would like to take them off it...they are so fucking sexy.

I was giggling as I made my way down the hall. Camille was already at the stove in the kitchen.

"You're up early," I made myself a cup of coffee.

"Matt called last night, and I finally answered," she said and slid an omelet onto a plate and handed it to me. "He said he didn't sleep with Kendra, wouldn't have because he liked me and she was a bit of a...bitch...his word."

"And...?"

She flipped the omelet remaining in the frying pan before answering. "I told him I believed him, but I must not have liked him well enough to confront him before I left. I wished him well, hung up, and called Eve."

"And...?"

"She said that Kendra had told her she slept with him and had no idea why she lied."

"She's still friends with Kendra after what she did to you?" I asked in surprise.

"No, Eve moved out of the house we shared in Fresno, so Kendra is on her own now."

"Why would anyone lie about that?"

"I have no idea."

I took a bite of the omelet and leaned back in the chair, "Why did you finally answer his call?"

She slid the omelet out of the frying pan and to the plate then set it on the table. After settling onto the chair she looked at me from across the table, "Because I realized it didn't matter anymore. Kendra is out of my life, and what he had to say didn't matter because I am not going back. It was just right to hear his side, then tell him goodbye."

"So, what are your future plans then?"

"The Parkston's also called last night and asked if they could hire me to redo all their social media and websites."

"That's fantastic!"

"I really like them," she nodded. "I can do the work from here when you're busy practicing."

"Sound like a great plan."

"There is just one thing, but I know that I've asked a lot from you already."

"Really, Camille?" I laughed. "What exactly have YOU asked of ME? Seems like I pretty much just made you come with me while I checked out a horse, made you work for your board and keep, and kept you here to keep me company…and cook for me."

We shared a humored giggle.

"So, what can I do for YOU?" I said.

"I would like to learn how to ride a horse," she answered with a determined nod.

"Well, that's easy enough," I laughed and stood to put the dishes in the sink. "We'll feed then catch Brutus. He's a great teacher. Craig drew for tomorrow night, but both Logan and Brodie ride tonight, so we want to be in to watch them this afternoon."

"Let's get busy then," Camille said and stood.

After feeding, I did a quick pass with the tractor in the arena to clear a space for us to ride. The snow was only inches thick and only an inch or two of the ground was frozen, but it turned well and was good ground to ride. The temperature just hit 40 degrees, so it was still comfortable. Camille caught Brutus while I haltered Memphis then I showed her how to saddle the horses.

The woman was a natural. Not once did I see any fear in her as there had been with Lacey Jae. Even the horse's size didn't intimidate her. She followed every direction I gave her from the one-rein stop to posting at a trot. She began with a glare of concentration, but it quickly turned to smiles and by the end of the lesson, she was laughing.

For me, by the end of the lesson, I felt like I had ridden Memphis all my life.

Our arena lesson was followed by a ride out in the pasture to check the stock tanks and ride through the herd of roping cattle.

The rest of the day was full with checking fences on the side-by-side ATV with Camille driving. There seemed to be a weight lifted off her shoulders and she relaxed more with every hour that went by.

Dinner was in front of the computer as we watched Brodie take second for the round while Logan nearly missed the horns and had to fight to get the steer down. He was fourth in the round but still made it to the semi-finals.

"How does he handle that?" Camille asked.

"We've all learned that we won't have perfect runs every time. There have been times that he's totally missed the steer and hit the ground or started to drop and the steer got too far away and he had to try to climb back on the horse. Lots of different things have happened. Every event in rodeo has the potential for disaster."

We moved into the Jacuzzi to finish our day with me telling her stories of our greatest near-misses, misses, and total failures when it came to ranching and rodeo. As I turned off the jets from the tub and we made our way to our rooms, I had to laugh.

"Did I just scare you away?"

Camille shook her head, "Not in the least. It just shows how protected and boring our lives were growing up. Other than boating, we never really lived…which is what you guys did."

I had to nod in agreement. We did live. We had full childhoods, happy childhoods, even when things didn't go our way.

"Another lesson in the morning?" Camille asked. "Can we gallop too?"

"Sounds like fun if the weather holds out and we'll move you to Embers. She's a good solid horse."

I closed my bedroom door behind me just as I received a text.

He didn't write anything; it was just a video of his bare legs and feet standing in a shower full of muddy water swirling toward the drain.

I laughed and fell onto the bed. The phone rang with Val Kilmer's image appearing again.

We talked for an hour before I finally closed my eyes for the night with a contented smile.

The next morning I found Camille in the hall in front of the wall of photos of my family, which dated back to my grandfather riding in the NFR. She silently sipped a cup of coffee as she walked around the room.

She stopped in front of the photograph of Gaston and me in full stride as we won the Sandcup barrel race in Pasco, Washington.

I walked up beside her and looked at the image. It was one of my favorite wins, yet the worst day.

"I'll tell you a secret about that photo, which no one else knows," I said.

She turned to me with a raised brow, "Why would you trust me with a secret?"

"Why wouldn't I?" I asked in a bit of a surprise.

She stared at me a moment then turned back to the photo, "Alright...did you win?"

"The race, yes, it was my first big win at that level and really gave me a huge confidence boost," I said and nodded to the image. "Everyone focuses on me in the picture..."

"Naturally..."

"But if you look behind me, to the guy in the red jacket."

"I can't see his face, who is it?"

"His name is Tim Croft, my boyfriend. We'd been together for about six months."

She leaned in closer to inspect the image then glanced at me, "He isn't watching and he..."

"...has his arm around another girl flirting with her." I sighed. "That was one of the best wins. I was so excited about it until I saw that picture. Tim and I had talked getting married, but I kept putting it off."

"Looks like a logical decision, but why, out of all the pictures I'm sure you have, would you have this one on the wall showing him doing that? Doesn't your family know?"

I shook my head, "They didn't know that jacket, so they didn't know it was him. As I said, everyone just looks at Gaston and me."

"Then why keep it?"

"It reminds me of how, even when you're at the top of your game...winning...there is still someone or something trying to pull you down, make you lose focus. I was devastated, but it wasn't enough to make me give up. I never let a win get to my head because I know the next second it could be gone."

The next two days were filled with chores, riding lessons, and me working with Memphis around the lariats and training equipment.

Friday night, Camille walked Embers toward the back of the horse trailer. She was determined to do everything herself when it came to the horses. I admired her for that. She looked like she had ridden all her life in her black western jacket with a red wild rag stuffed perfectly into the collar. Her hair was loose and hanging straight down her back. Framing her pretty face and big brown eyes was the navy blue stylish beanie hat that I had given her the first day.

I probably should have told her that Mark was going to be at the jackpot, but I just couldn't get myself to do it. There was a little bit of fear she wouldn't go with me and I was enjoying having someone, another female, to do things with.

"Are you taking Memphis?"

"Not this time," I walked Ketchum into the trailer as she stepped out. "Next time, so he can get used to the crowds and all the ropes whizzing over his head."

"You sure Embers and I will be OK?"

I stepped out of the trailer and she closed the gate.

"I wouldn't let you ride her if I thought there was going to be any problem."

She nodded confidently, "I should have thought of that. I trust you."

A little twinge of guilt hit me. Maybe I should tell her about Mark.

A half-hour later, I still hadn't and we were riding the horses into the arena. I quickly searched the people for Mark; I didn't want to miss his reaction when he saw Camille.

"Just trust Embers," I reminded her as we rode through the crowd and into the arena to warm up the horses.

"I'm just sticking by your side until it's time to just sit and watch," she smiled.

On the third lap around the arena, Mark walked in on his large bay gelding. We were only twenty feet away…if he turned just a little, then they would see each other. I glanced at Camille, who was running a hand down Embers' neck.

171

I glanced at Mark, who was just turning…he looked back and smiled at me. You would think it would be awkward…considering we were on a date when he asked Camille out but it wasn't. I smiled in return just as his gaze moved to Camille.

"Isn't that the guy from the café?" Camille asked and looked at me.

"Yes, it's Mark," I answered.

The only reaction Mark had was the slight drop of a jaw and his eyes darting back to me…questioning me.

I turned to Camille to find her glaring at me. Her cheeks were red and there was no doubt she was upset.

CHAPTER SEVENTEEN

"What is this?" She growled. "Payback for Vegas?"

"Vegas?" I had no idea what she was talking about.

"...our blindsiding Lacie Jae with your brother? You're doing some kind of payback?"

I gasped in surprise, "I never even thought of that."

She must have been holding in a lot of guilt for that to be her first thought.

Camille glowered at me.

"I was afraid you wouldn't come with me if you knew he was going to be here," I said quickly. "I really wanted you to come with me."

"Really?" She huffed. "You asked me to join you. I would have come whether he was here or not."

Guilt washed over me, "I'm sorry."

"Well, I'll accept that as long as we always talk to each other from here forward," she said through clenched teeth. "No more games. I'm so damned tired of games."

Mark suddenly appeared between us.

"You two knew each other?" He accused.

"No," I said quickly and explained the meeting at the café.

I glanced at Camille, who was staring at him as he listened to me. Her face was still flushed but I had a feeling it wasn't from anger anymore. Mark was good looking with dark hair under his black cowboy hat. He wore a black vest over a brown shirt, making him tall, dark, and handsome.

She was quite smitten with him.

When I turned back to Mark, his eyes darted between Camille and me then settled on her.

"Let me officially introduce you two," I said. "Mark Callahan, this is..."

"Madi Madison," Camille smiled, and her eyes lit with laughter. "Delaney gave me a nickname based on my last name."

Mark grinned, and his handsome meter rose.

"Well, Madi Madison, do you rope?" He asked.

"No," she chuckled. "Delaney has been teaching me to ride. I've never been around a horse or cow before this week."

"Really? You look so natural there." He said in surprise.

"She is a natural," I said. "I'm going to go sign in. Keep her company for me."

I don't think he even heard me as they walked the horses away.

Just after I paid my entry fee for the night, my phone beeped, indicating a video call. I walked Ketchum to a back corner where it was relatively quiet then positioned the horse, so he was looking over my shoulder and held up the phone. Dad's face appeared and instantly started laughing when he saw the long nose of the horse sniff at the phone.

I laughed. I loved my dad, and seeing the laughter in his eyes always made me happy.

"Delaney, why such a long face?" He grinned.

I nearly choked at the old corny joke.

"Where are you?" He asked.

"At the Friday night jackpot, where are you?"

"Denver," he grinned. "About to watch your brother fall off a horse."

I chuckled, "How did Craig do?"

"He made it to the finals," Dad said proudly.

"Fantastic," I said excitedly and looked out to the arena to find Camille. She was still on the horse but standing along the fence watching Mark lope in circles. She turned and searched for me, then smiled and waved.

"Want to watch Logan?" Dad asked.

"Yes, of course, but when? They are about to start here."

"Tyler is up now, then Logan."

My phone beeped again and I lowered it to look at the message. It was a weather alert.

"Did you just get that too?" Dad asked. The whole family had the weather alert app on our phones.

"Yes, big snowstorm predicted for tomorrow night," I answered and looked over at the arena. "I'll ask Mark to come over tomorrow and we can get the cows moved closer to the barn."

"You want us to fly home?" He asked in concern.

I smiled at him, "No, we can handle it. You just stay there…"

"Oh, hell, almost missed Logan."

The phone flipped around just in time I saw my brother bolt out of the box and slide from the horse.

"4.4…" Dad announced. "With the 5.8 the other night, it will put him in third going into the short-go tomorrow night."

"I'll be online watching," I sighed and felt the unease again for not being there with them.

"Wish you were here, too, Darlin'."

I smiled at him. He knew all three of us so well.

"We'll all be together in Texas next month," I sighed with a slight smile.

"Martin will be there too, so we'll need to see if Mark will take care of the ranch."

"I'll talk to him," I nodded and looked back out at the arena. Mark and Camille were on their horses just outside the arena. They were talking and smiling at each other. "They are starting. Text me when Brodie is about to ride, and I'll see if I can watch."

"Will do, have fun," he said and ended the call.

I had just enough time to lap the arena three times before the first team backed into the box, so I rode outside for a while to warm up Ketchum to my satisfaction. When I rode back into the building, Mark and his partner were chasing a steer across the arena. Camille was still along the fence watching closely and didn't even see me ride up next to her.

After Mark's rope wrapped the back hooves of the steer for a successful run, she relaxed back into the saddle and turned.

She grinned sheepishly when she saw my amused smirk.

"OK, so he's handsome and nice," She said. "No games. Is this awkward for you?"

"Not at all," I assured her. "He and I have been friends since high school. If something were to happen between us, it already would have. Just friends…"

"OK," She nodded and smiled at him as he rode in next to us. "Yes," She said to him.

His grin widened as he looked up at me.

"Yes, what?" I asked cautiously.

"I asked her out tomorrow night…you know…to show her the town," he grinned and we all three chuckled.

I was so relieved we could just laugh about the café.

"There is a snow storm coming, and I was going to ask if you'd like to come over and ride with us to move the cows," I said.

"Delaney!" The announcer called out.

I turned quickly and flushed in embarrassment when my drawn partner was sitting in the header box waiting for me.

"I am so excited about watching you!" Camille giggled excitedly.

"Oh, the pressure," I laughed and trotted to the box.

With relief, I trapped the back hooves for a good run.

"We need a volunteer to help strip the ropes," the announcer's voice rang out.

Camille turned to me with excitement, "Is that something I can do?"

Mark and I chuckled.

"Sure," I nodded. "The steer run into a small chute so you can take the rope off the horns or back hooves."

"OK, I'll do that," she nodded eagerly.

"Come with me," Mark stepped out of the saddle with a wide grin.

Camille looked at me in excitement as she slid out of the saddle and quickly followed him.

I watched her as I waited for my next run. She eagerly took the long hook that was used to slide through the panel to the steer's legs to hook the rope and pull it free. The riders took to her right away. They always thanked her and a few rode down to give her a beer. Every once in a while, her laughter would echo in the building and I couldn't help but be happy and proud of her. I took her picture as she was removing one of the ropes.

My third run I caught the hooves and my rope ran off with the steer. I trotted down the arena and watched her remove the rope with the hook, then she turned to me. Her brown eyes were sparkling with happiness.

She held out the rope to me but held on for a moment.

"Thank you so much," she beamed. "This is so much fun and I feel...so..." She looked like she was ready to burst.

"At home? Helpful?"

"Yes," she laughed and let loose of my rope. "Everyone is so nice...everyone is thanking me for jumping in to help."

The rest of the night was full of laughter, roping, cowboys, and horses, a perfect night in the arena.

It was late when I backed the horse trailer next to the barn.

"Delaney, I have had so much fun tonight," Camille nearly danced to the back of the trailer. "More than I have had in years. All those people were so nice and welcoming and the horses are so much fun."

"I thought Kendra was a barrel racer."

"She is, but I never met her horses. I was never invited to anything to do with them." She opened the back door of the trailer.

Ketchum backed out by himself and I reached out and grabbed the lead rope I had thrown over his back when I loaded him.

I huffed, "Well, that was a foreshadowing."

"What do you mean?" She said as she stepped into the trailer to open the divider in the trailer to release Ember.

"If she is a serious barrel racer, then her horse is her world."

Camille shrugged, "Well...you're right. I should have known."

"How long did you know her?" I asked as we walked into the barn.

"We met my third year of college. She didn't have her horse there."

"Hmmm…" I shut the door to Ketchum's stall and looked into Ember's stall.

She had one hand on the horse's shoulder as she stared blankly at the ground. Camille's good mood was gone.

"I'll be right back," I said and walked over to my living-quarters horse trailer.

When I returned, I handed her a white bottle.

"Rumchata?" Camille's smile returned. "Oh…yummy."

After taking a long swig, she handed it to me and I matched her swig.

She closed the door on Ember's stall and we shared another long swig.

We were relaxed and giggling about Mark as we walked back to the main doors.

She stopped at Craig and Brodie's training equipment.

"How does this work?" She asked.

She pointed to the spurring boards that looked like two pieces of plywood angled together. A leather bareback rigging was strapped to it.

"Here, hold the bottle," I said, then lifted a leg and swung myself up to straddle the boards.

Camille laughed and took another swig from the bottle.

"You grip the handle like this," I demonstrated. "Then lean back, free arm up high, legs stretched out high up the boards; toes pointed out, then you slide your heels along the board all the way back to your ass." I slid my legs up then slammed them back down. "Slow up to run the spurs up the hide, then fast back to do it again. When you're on the horse, you want to time it, so your feet are stretched over the horse's shoulders when the front hooves hit the ground." I did it a half dozen times until my legs and the rum told me to quit.

We both laughed, but I could see she was impressed.

"Your turn," I lifted a leg over the side and jumped down.

"Oh, I'm absolutely trying that," she laughed.

She barely got a leg over and couldn't get herself lifted up, so I pushed her butt to help and nearly pushed her over the side.

We were both laughing and had to take another swig each before she finally wiggled up to the rigging and gripped the handle with legs dangling straight down.

"Lean back, toes out, legs straight in front of you as if you were on the horse," I instructed and adjusted her body to the proper position.

"Damn, kind of like extreme planking." she giggled, took another swig, then handed me the bottle.

"Free arm up by your ear, like this," I demonstrated.

Then, I gripped her feet and slid her boots up toward her butt then stepped back so she could slam her feet down the boards, but she didn't quite make it and nearly fell off. The laughter, giggles, and swigs continued until she finally gave up.

"Let's try the one with the saddle instead of just the bareback riggin'," I said and pointed to the equipment in the corner. "Here, jump on the dummy,"

Camille turned to me with wide innocent eyes. "But Mark's not here."

I laughed so hard my sides hurt.

"Well, this one looks easier," she said and again attempted to jump on the long barrel-shaped dummy. I had to push her on that one, too. "Now what?" She said as I took a long swig.

"Put your feet in the stirrups...heels down, toes out to keep the stirrups from flying off," I helped her slide the boots into the stirrups. "Damn, your legs are as long as Brodie and Craig's."

"All my height is legs," she grinned. "Wonderful for dresses, shorts, and swimsuits, but it's a bitch finding pants long enough."

"What a terrible curse...long legs and a nice ass," I teased with a roll of the eyes and another swig in the nearly empty bottle.

"You ain't slacking with that tiny waist and nice rack." she huffed. "And that ass…"

"It makes buying jeans interesting," I grinned.

"See! We're both cursed."

We both giggled.

"Hold the rope in your left hand, as you bounce and spur, pull it up toward your right ear."

She looked at me with confused eyes, "How the hell am I supposed to bounce on this?"

I chuckled and walked to the controls. "It's electronic." I twisted the knob to the first level. "Lift the rope to help you stay in the saddle."

Camille shrieked in laughter and barely kept herself from falling off.

"The challenge is to stay on when Logan works the barrel," I laughed. "He's so freakishly strong and can get the barrel going up and down and left and right, that he's almost worse than a real bucking horse."

Her body was moving with the rhythm of the dummy, but she wasn't moving her legs.

"There is a spur out rule where you have to have your spurs above the shoulders of the horse when the front hooves hit the ground out of the gate." I pulled her legs and set them up high. "Then, you curl your legs back to your butt while you lift the rope."

She did and very slowly slid off the side of the dummy with a high pitched screech.

I jumped forward to grab her so she didn't hit the ground, but we both ended up on our butts.

We looked at each other and laughed again.

"I don't think that is meant to learn while you're filled with rum," she giggled.

"Probably not," I conceded and stood to turn off the machine. "Let's try one more."

I pulled a concrete block over to her. It was only six inches wide and ten inches long, but it was heavy.

"Put this between your feet," I pushed the block to her and grabbed her boots to assist her in placing her heals in the grooved sides.

"OK," She finished the bottle and set it aside. "Now what?"

"Toes out, lean back and lift it."

She finished three lifts.

"Now, the same thing, but bend your legs to lift it toward your butt."

"Seriously?" she drawled with narrowed eyes.

"Yes," I laughed. "That's how they strengthen their legs and stomach.

She managed to lift it to her butt then back.

"It's like extreme Kegels and planking at the same time," she laughed and let the block fall.

"Works your butt real well, too," I laughed. "I have another bottle in the trailer."

She rolled up and stood just to fall back against the dummy, "Yes," she giggled. "I need more alcohol and to pee."

"Trailer has that, too."

Turning off the light, we stumbled toward the trailer. Just inside the door was a small sofa that turned into a bed. Stepping left was a door into the bathroom that led to a feed room that also led to the outside or to the horses. Going right was the kitchen and the dining booth that also turned into a bed. Across from it was the couch, which was another bed. The big bed was up a few stairs and hovered over the back of the truck. It was literally my home away from home.

I turned on the furnace while she was in the bathroom. After my turn in the bathroom, I found her looking at the pictures I had pinned to a corkboard.

"You have lived such a full life already," she slurred.

"Yet, so much life more ahead of us," I said pointedly. "And it starts with chocolate."

"You have chocolate?" She twirled around to me and had to grab the counter to keep from falling.

I giggled and crawled up onto the bed, "M&M's on the counter, but the good stuff is hidden up here or my brothers and Dad would it eat."

I stretched out on my stomach to pull a box of chocolate-covered caramels from the cupboard. Camille joined me and I handed her a couple to start.

We giggled and rolled onto our backs to look at the ceiling of the trailer which was just a few feet away.

After a few moments of silence, while we enjoyed the chocolates, she turned and looked at me. Her eyes were lost again.

"What do you think Lacie Jae is going to say when she finds me here?" Her eyes glistened. "Do you think she'll be mad?"

"I don't know, but why would she be mad?"

"Because I abandoned her when she needed me, then followed her," Camille whispered and looked at the ceiling again.

"You came looking for her. That will mean a lot. If you had just called, it wouldn't have meant so much. Actions mean more than words."

She stared at the ceiling, a tear slowly sliding down her temple. She looked utterly sad.

"Camille?"

"Yes?"

"I'm very straight."

More tears fell as she slowly turned to look at me. "Me too, but why would you say that? Because we're laying on a bed together?"

"That and the fact you really need a hug and I want to give it to you without you thinking I was hitting on you." Her eyes pleaded with me as more tears fell. "From what you've told me...you're not the bad person here. You are as much a victim of your father as she is. You've lost your step-mother that raised you and you feel that your mother abandoned you." I looked at her in understanding and sympathy. "You're not the bad person here."

"But I abandoned Lacie Jae," Her lips rolled into a thin line as her chin quivered.

"It's not the same as you and your mother and you've come looking for her."

I rolled onto my side and opened my arms. She cuddled into me and cried.

The warmth of the furnace, the rum coursing through me, and the comfort of holding her shut down my senses and I fell into a deep sleep.

I woke to the special alert I put on my phone when Lacie Jae posts a podcast.

CHAPTER EIGHTEEN

I squinted at the phone then to Camille, who was curled into a pillow on the opposite side of the bed. Her makeup was smeared under her eyes and onto the pillow, but she looked peaceful.

I carefully slid down the bed of the camper and walked to the table where my phone sat. I had missed a call, but he had sent a message.

Text: Took first, jackpot must have run late. Text me when you wake.

With a look back to Camille sleeping soundly, I silently stepped out the door and into the cold. My whole body shivered.

There was no time to listen to the podcast now because the phone said 28 degrees and I could see storm clouds on the horizon. The scent of snow touched the air. Mark would be arriving to help move the cows in the next 30 minutes, so I jogged to the house and down the hall. The shower was just long enough to rinse off the arena dirt and the alcohol sweat from the night before.

As I jogged back down the hall, Camille was just coming in the back door.

"Why didn't you wake me?" she said as we passed in the kitchen.

"You looked peaceful," I smiled. "I'll get Ember ready for you. Use what you need in my dressing room. Just make it warm because it looks like we'll be pushing in the snowstorm."

She had disappeared down the hall, so I jogged out to the barn.

I sent a quick text.

Text: Hey Handsome, sorry I missed your call. Headed out to push cows closer to the barns and off the mountain before storm hits. I'll call when we return. Proud of you on the win!

Ember and Gaston were saddled when Mark's truck and horse trailer turned down the long drive. Camille was walking out of the house wearing a waist-length jacket.

"Well, you're going to need to be warmer than that," I said and walked into the tack room. I returned with chaps and a lined ankle-length outback coat.

"You want me to wear those?" She gasped in surprise as I wrapped the leather chaps around her waist. They belonged to Brodie, so I knew the length would be fine, but I did have to tighten the waist as much as I could.

"You'll appreciate the extra warmth and protection," I said as I lowered behind her to buckle the straps.

"Kind of sexy," she giggled.

"Wait until you see Mark in them," I grinned.

"Morning, Ladies," Mark waved as he buckled his chaps then walked to the back of his trailer to unload his horse.

"Good morning!" We called out.

Camille's grin was wide and cheeks red and I'm sure it wasn't all from the cold air.

"You were right," she whispered.

I stepped into the saddle, "Stay with either Mark or myself. Ember is good in the snow. You'll stay behind the cows to keep them moving while Mark and I ride out the sides to gather."

She listened to me intently and nodded her head.

"You have a headache?" I grinned as she rose in the saddle.

"Little bit," she admitted with a smile.

"Nothing better for a hangover than fresh air," I said and turned to Mark as he rode up next to us. "Thanks for coming. We'll move the young heifers that haven't calved yet to the barn. The herd with the small calves need to be in the pasture to the back so they can get into the barn or trees."

We had the herd of young heifers in the corrals before the snow began to fall. Halfway to the main herd, the snow was heavy and hard to see through. I turned to Camille, who was covered from head to toe and had pulled her coat collar up and over her nose. Only her eyes were visible.

"You OK?" I yelled.

She turned and waved with a thumbs-up. Only four days in the saddle and she was riding through a snowstorm pushing cows. She impressed me. I took out my phone and tried to take a picture then shoved it back in my pocket.

The cows moved through the gate from the back hillside to the main pasture where we wanted them. I stepped out of the saddle to shut the gate and heard a muffled yell.

I turned to see Camille pointing behind me. Three cow and calf pairs were walking toward the gate, so I stepped out of the way while Camille and Mark trotted back to retrieve them. Mark continued to ride out into the field and disappeared into the wall of snow.

Camille pushed the cows through the gate then looked back where Mark had disappeared, but there was no sign of him.

"He'll be OK," I told her. "He's just checking to make sure we didn't leave any others behind."

Gaston's red hair was nearly covered in the white snow. I brushed the snowflakes away from his eyelids.

As we stared into the snow, a black form finally rode toward us. Mark and his horse appeared and I glanced at Camille to see her eyes smiling. I had to admit, he was quite the cowboy vision.

They rode through the gate and waited for me to step into the saddle before starting to ride toward the barn. We tucked Camille between us to keep her protected.

The snowstorm was in full force as we approached the barely visible barn so we rode straight into it with heads down, blocking the snow from hitting our faces. An odd ache rumbled through my stomach as we walked into the barn and out of the storm.

I stepped out of the saddle and handed Camille my reins.

"Stay here, I want to check the heifers," I said and turned before she could respond.

Mark was right behind me as I stepped into the wall of falling snow in the corrals. Just as I had feared, two heifers had calved while we were gone. Mark swooped one of the calves up into his arms and ran to the barn with the worried mom right behind him. I carefully walked up to the second newborn calf that was huddled next to its black mom. Waving my hands in the air, the cow spun nervously in circles until she finally followed the other cow toward the barn with the baby wobbling next to her.

Both calves were soaking wet from birth and snow. Camille had found towels to start drying off the first calf as Mark gated the momma cow away.

The second cow and calf were barely in the barn when he swooped the calf up and through the gate before the cow knew what happened.

"Well, that's a hero move if I've ever seen one," Camille teased with sparkling eyes.

He grinned at her as he set the calf on the ground.

I chuckled at the pair as they rubbed the two shivering calves. The mothers were standing on the opposite side of the gate, staring and mooing at their babies. Flipping the switch to the radiant heater, we moved the newborns next to it to help keep them warm.

"We'll keep the pairs in the barn for the next couple days," I said. "I'll get a couple of bales of straw." As I walked away, I looked over my shoulder to find Mark and Camille smiling at each other.

I took out my phone and took a picture. It was cute. I swiped to the one taken of Camille in the storm and was pleased how it turned out, then one more swipe to the image of her the night before at the arena.

No matter what happened between her and Lacie Jae, I was determined Camille would have pictures to remember all the new adventures she had accomplished. Removing ropes from the steer at the jackpot, riding in a snowstorm, and taking care of freezing calves with a good looking cowboy…they were good images for her to cherish.

While placing the bales of straw on the cart, I thought of Camille's sad eyes the night before and the tears. It was such a raw moment; my heart ached for her.

My phone alert rang out.

Text from Dad: How is it going?

Text to Dad: All cows moved, heifers in corral, two born and in barn. We got this.

Text from Dad: I know you do. Proud of you.

He made me smile.

Text to Dad: Will call when we get into the house to check how everyone is doing there.

Text from Dad: I'll take notes

I laughed and slid the phone back in my pocket.

The storm began to ease with our third trip out to check on the calves. No new babies had been born but six little ones had been taken to the barn for their safety.

Camille was all smiles and laughter with ooohs and aahs to the babies. I don't think I could have talked her into leaving them…just like Lacie Jae.

"I'm starving," I walked to the door. "I'll bring some food out."

"Thanks," they both chimed.

They didn't miss me the hour I took to make sandwiches, heat soup to put in thermoses, and talk to my man on the phone.

I reluctantly ended the call and took the food out to the starving ranch hands.

Mark was talking as I stepped into the side door of the barn.

"Camille, can you see if there are any other towels in the tack room?" He called out.

I was halfway to them when I realized he had called her Camille instead of Madi. I looked at her with a raised brow.

"No secrets, no games," she explained as we passed in the aisle.

As much as I agreed with her, I was going to miss the name Madi.

The rest of the day was spent checking the herds and taking care of the babies. Just before dark, the skies cleared and the temperature dropped into the teens.

"You want me to stay or go?" Mark asked.

"Well," I glanced between the two of them and there was no doubt both wanted him to stay. "Aren't you two supposed to be going on a date tonight?"

Camille's eyes widened, "I am not leaving you in freezing temperatures with all the snow and all those animals."

I grinned at her protectiveness, "You two go in the house, fix dinner, and have your date. I'll stay out here in the trailer and go through the horse book from the Parkston's."

"You sure?" Mark asked.

"It's been a couple of days now, and I really need to give him an answer," I nodded. "It will help me concentrate if I do it by myself and you two can...entertain each other."

"Alright," Camille conceded. "But I'll bring you dinner."

"Fair enough," I switched off the barn lights and we separated.

After retrieving the black horse book from the truck, I started the furnace in the trailer, turned on the lights, and quickly thumbed through the book of at least 40 horses aged one to six. I would love to have all of them. Second time through and I texted ten images to my Huckleberry.

Text: You have time?

Text from Huckleberry: Give me fifteen minutes to get to hotel.

My phone alert went off, indicating the incoming video chat just after Mark brought me a covered plate of steak and potatoes.

A warm trailer I considered home, steak, pictures of horses, and my man on video, I was in heaven. For three hours we talked and chose the horses I was going to bring home.

We talked until I heard Camille giggle and Mark laugh as they approached the trailer.

Both their eyes seemed to glow with happiness as they stepped through the door. They slid onto the bench seat across the table from me.

"Did you pick any?" Camille asked.

"All three," I nodded and stood to pull a bottle down from the upper cupboard.

"More Rumchata!" Camille squealed.

"You have any…?" Mark started.

I pulled out a bottle of Roca Patrón Silver and handed it to him.

"Which horses?" Camille pulled the book around to flip through the pictures.

I smiled, "Memphis' little sister."

"Oh, I just love her…she's cool looking, too." Camille flipped to the filly's picture to show Mark.

I smiled as he nodded his approval, "And, I'm going to call her Madi."

We all three laughed as the first shot of the night was toasted on the horse's name then devoured.

Four shots later, we were out at the training equipment with Camille on the bucking barrel, Mark pushing the lever up and down to make her lift in the air while I tried to hold her on.

We played on the equipment until midnight, then we did one last check of the cows for the night before Mark retired to the trailer and Camille and I went to the house.

Side by side, we made our way down the hall. As I reached for the doorknob to my room, I turned to her with a smile.

"And did you kiss him at dinner?"

She smiled as she opened her door and looked at me, "Thoroughly."

We shared a giggle before disappearing into our rooms.

CHAPTER NINETEEN

Welcome to Coffee with Cowboys with me, Lacie Jae.

Greetings everyone! Lacie Jae with Coffee With Cowboys here. I'm a relocated city girl who will be adventuring into the ranching and rodeo world ... the cowboy way of life.

It's going to be a little different today. When I started the podcast, I was determined to just stick with observations. A documentary style of the podcast about my discoveries with rodeo and ranching, but, I'm going to change that just for today.

I have, of course, spent time with Logan and Delaney Rawlins, and while I was exploring Denver's Stock Show, I spent time with the two dads, Evan and Martin. However, I haven't spent much time with Brodie or Craig, so today they are here in the trailer with me, just us three, and I'm going to interview them.

I cheated a bit and gave them a look at some of the questions I was going to ask but the last ones they haven't seen. Because I haven't, ever, interviewed anyone, I have all my questions written down so I don't sound foolish ... or as inexperienced at this as I am. So here it goes.

Lacie Jae: Say hello Brodie Rawlins and Craig Houston.
Brodie: Hello!
Craig: Good morning!
Lacie Jae: So my first question is for Brodie. How old were you
      when you started riding rough stock?
Brodie: Five, both my granddad and dad were steer wrestlers and
      sometimes they team roped together in the rodeo, too.
      Logan and I started going with them when I was five and he
      was nine.

Lacie Jae: Just the four of you?

Brodie: Oh, yeah. Those memories of traveling as the 'four men' of the family, those are special. Not everyone has a three-generation story like that. We have a lot of photos on the walls at home that are of the four of us traveling together. Granddad always insisted we take pictures in front of the rodeo arena signs so we could see where we had been. We traveled until Granddad passed away.

Lacie Jae: Did you completely stop traveling?

Brodie: We didn't travel as far or over as many weekends. Dad cut back and let Logan and I take over with clubs and high school rodeo, with Craig, too.

Lacie Jae: How did you meet Craig?

Both men laugh.

Brodie: The very first, close to home, rodeo I went to. They had mutton busting, which is riding sheep. Granddad asked me if I wanted to do it and I said yes. Anything he asked me, I would do.

Lacie Jae: Did Logan ride sheep?

Brodie: No, he was too big. He rode a steer that day.

Lacie Jae: So, how did Craig come into the story?

Brodie: In our hall at home, is a picture on the wall of me in the chute for the very first time. I was pretty nervous sitting there on the sheep. It stunk a bit and I was gripping the wool so tight my knuckles were white. I was scared but sure as heck wasn't going to tell Granddad. Anyway, in the picture behind the chute helping me balance on the sheep was Dad, right next to him was Logan grinning like the Cheshire cat because he knew I was scared.

Lacie Jae: Big brother ... (giggles)

Brodie: Oh, yeah. Granddad was taking the pictures because he wanted to be able to show Mom that it was safe and I had fun; his justifying not telling her beforehand. Off to the left of the picture, you see a man's legs. Those are Martin's legs, Craig's dad. But kneeling at the chute, right at the sheep's head, was Craig. He had just ridden and did real well and was talking to me ... encouraging me.

Craig: It was my third time riding, so I'm more experienced then him. I was sharing my five-year-old wisdom.

Both men laugh.

Lacie Jae: What did he say?

Brodie: He told me that all I had to do was squeeze hard with my legs and balance like I was riding on a bike and, of course, hold on to the wool and don't let go. And he told me the one thing we have used as our motto, mantra, and guiding light. He said, "My Pops says you have to believe ... you just got to believe you can do it before you can do it.'

Lacie Jae: That is awesome. So did you ride it?

Brodie: Oh, yeah. All the way down the arena and halfway back. They had to run to catch me and pull me off the sheep.

Craig: He had this big grin on his face and marched over to me and we high-fived and yelled, 'you just gotta believe'.

Lacie Jae: You still say that all the time.

Both Men: We believe!

Craig: We both have it written down on cards, and it's in our pocket when we ride. It's also stitched onto our travel bags and the cuff of our competition shirts. We focus on believing. You have to believe you're the best and can ride anything to be successful.

Lacie Jae: So, you two have a picture of the moment you met?

Both men: Yeah.

Craig: The Rawlins and Houston's traveling and rodeo circus; just us men until Granddad passed away and then Delaney was allowed to travel with us.

Lacie Jae: She couldn't rodeo with you?

Brodie: No, Mom wanted us men to have those memories and Delaney was more than happy at home taking care of the ranch with Mom. She started competing when she was eleven or twelve and never looked back. But, even today, I would say Delaney is more of a rancher than a rodeo competitor.

Lacie Jae: So, back to you, Craig. How did you start riding rough stock, starting with the sheep?

Craig: Dad and I were in the car one day and saw a bunch of people and horses at the fairgrounds. I asked him if we could go see what was going on and so he stopped. I got on that day for the first time and was hooked.

Lacie Jae: Neither one of your mothers knew you were getting on a sheep before you did it?

Brodie: No, not until we got home and they showed her the pictures. She took one look at how excited all four of us were and she was fine with it.

Craig: I rode in four kid's rodeos before we told my mother. Since I was an only child, she was a bit overprotective of me and barely let me out of the house.

Lacie Jae: What made you finally tell her?

Craig: I didn't ever want to stop. I wanted to move onto the steers, but Dad put it on the condition I talked to Mom. He said if I wanted it that bad, then I had to face her. I did, she hated it, they fought, but I continued. When I was eleven and still riding steers and mini-horses and ready to go to mini-bulls, they had a huge fight and got a divorce. The judge asked me what I wanted and I told him that I loved my mother, hated TV and being inside a house, loved my father and wanted to continue to ride rough stock until I was a hundred. So, he gave them split custody but residential custody to my dad so I could continue.

Lacie Jae: Wow, I have to ask since I feel it wouldn't be complete for everyone without knowing the answer. Where is your mother now? Do you see her?

Craig: I talk on the phone with her a couple of times a week. Always have. Weekends I didn't rodeo, go to a clinic, or practice were spent with her until she remarried when I was seventeen. Now we just see each other once or twice a month and talk on the phone but NEVER discuss my riding.

Lacie Jae: Well, that's a heck of a history and so different between the two families.

Craig: Lilly, the Rawlins mom, was from rodeo family and she was married to a steer wrestler so she knew all the positive and negatives that came with rodeo life. My mom is a city-girl and had never been around rodeo and was just too scared to accept it.

Brodie: Nature or nurture ... doesn't matter when it comes to rodeo. Whether you were born to it or it didn't come along until you were a teenager, it still gets in your blood. Johnny Espeland is a bronc riding friend of ours. He didn't start riding until he saw a flyer for a Rodeo Bible camp when he was a teenager. He thought it looked fun and went to it and has been hooked since.

Craig: One of the best riders in our Circuit.

Lacie Jae: You have a lot of friends in rodeo. What is your best story from on the road with them?

Both men laugh

Craig: Something to do with rodeo, drinking too much, being locked out of a hotel ... completely naked.

All three laughed

Brodie: My best memories are traveling with my brother, Granddad, and Dad. Nothing can beat those memories.

Craig: There was the time in Winnemucca that Brodie and I decided to turn-in early and get some rest before Saturday's performance.

Brodie: I'd like to say we did that often in our early days ... but honestly ... I can't.

All three laugh.

Lacie Jae: How did going to bed early have a good memory of that night in Winnemucca?

Craig: The rodeo had a competitor's tent and served free breakfast and since we were younger, we all tried to make sure to get the free stuff so we could save our money for more important things.

Brodie: Entry Fees and fuel

Craig: Exactly. So we walk into the tent and all our buddies that had gone out partying were there; with black eyes, split lips…

Brodie: Bruises, scratches, sore necks…

Lacie Jae: What happened?

Craig: They got in a massive fight at the bar.

Lacie Jae: With who?

Craig: With each other!

All three laugh.

Brodie: And the best part is none of them knew why they were fighting or how it even started.

Craig: And the worst part is we didn't get to join the fun. We were sleeping!

All three laugh.

Lacie Jae: You have a lot of friends that are competitors. I also know that you two get along really well. Do you see each other as competitors?

Both men: Oh, yeah

Brodie: Absolutely. The first long trip I went to was in Sheridan. Granddad and Dad were steer wrestling. Dad clocks a damn respectable time and takes the lead but within a couple of minutes, Granddad beats him out and wins the rodeo. Talk about being happy and disappointed at the same time. (laughs). Granddad got it that year and Dad had to wait for his until he got back into rodeo after Mom passed away. Other than the NFR, Sheridan, Cheyenne, and Pendleton are my big goals. Those three are historic and both my dad and granddad won them.

Lacie Jae: Are you two the same way when one beats the other?

Craig: In our last year of high school rodeo, we decided we both wanted to win and we couldn't do it by both riding in the same event. So, we flipped a coin to see who rode bareback and who rode saddle bronc. That way we could both win.

Brodie: We both won a couple of rodeos at the same time but the best was last year when we both won the Sisters Rodeo. It was one of those weekends you have fire in your gut and not only believing but knowing you're going to ride anything they put in front of you.

Craig: We still compete in both events at some of the rodeos. I like both and didn't want to totally give up saddle bronc.

Brodie: Yep, and as to your question on if we're competitors to each other, when we're riding the same event, my drive to beat him fires up the ride; I'll do anything to beat him.

Craig: (laughs) Same here, trying to out-ride each other makes us more focused and better riders overall.

Lacie Jae: Brodie, you mentioned your Dad getting back into it after your mother passed away. He had backed off after your grandfather passed away. Can you talk about him getting back into it?

Brodie: Yeah, I guess. We don't really talk about the why, but time has passed enough; hopefully, Dad won't be upset.

Lacie Jae: We don't have to. I have other questions.

Brodie: No, it's OK. My mother was sick for over a year. When she passed away, we had hundreds of thousands of dollars in bills to pay. We were on the brink of having to sell the whole ranch. Dad decided to rodeo again because that was what he was good at and could bring in the money we needed in a relatively short time. He called a couple of friends and talked to them.

Craig: No one in the industry knew this.

Brodie: Both his friends took him on the road with them for months without telling a soul that they were paying the way; gas, food, and entry fees. They did it so Dad could send any money he won home to pay the creditors. I was fourteen and traveled with the three and took care of their horses and cleaned stalls. Logan and Delaney took care of the ranch with Craig helping and Martin working the books and paying bills.

Craig: All three men were on the road for months, hitting every rodeo humanly possible.

Brodie: Dad wouldn't let them just loan him the money; he had to earn it. After the season was done, and the bills paid off, Dad paid them back for all the entry fees, fuel and gas then found horses for each of them and trained 'em then gifted them to both men as a thank you.

Craig: Both horses helped take the men back to the NFR for years after that.

Brodie: Mom and Dad were high school sweethearts and married right out of school. It was a tough time for all of us but for Dad … after going through Mom's initial diagnosis … (long pause) and the year of her illness knowing there was nothing he could do … she was the love of his life. Well, then he had to deal with her death, and having to go on the road leaving Delaney and Logan at 16 and 18 in charge of the ranch and trying to raise three teenagers while trying to save their home...well … he … Dad is the toughest person I know. (long pause) Lacie Jae, you can't be crying in an interview and mess up my train of thought and get me crying.

Lacie Jae: (whispered) I'm sorry, we can cut this out.

Brodie: No, that's alright. If a man doesn't tear up when talking about his mom's passing, then he isn't much of a man.

Craig: After everything Evan went through, then having the accident last spring that landed him in the wheelchair, well, he is the type of man that everyone should aspire to be.

Brodie: Dad AND the two men that helped him out that summer. As far as we know, they have never said anything to anyone about Dad's desperation to save the ranch.

Lacie Jae: I'm not going to ask who they were, that's up to those three men to say. But let's move on to another topic.

Both Men: OK

Lacie Jae: So, these are the questions you didn't know I was going to ask. Which of you is older?

Craig: Me, by two months, but we didn't get our permits until after October 1st, so we had a full year on the first year on permits. Then this is our first year on cards.

Brodie: This is our rookie year.

Lacie Jae: Who is the better saddle bronc rider?

Both Men: Me

Lacie Jae: Who is the better bareback rider?

Both Men: Me

Lacie Jae: (Giggles) Who is better looking?

Both Men: Me

Craig: I have been called more exotic because of my Indian heritage.

Brodie: You were 19, and she had to be at least 40 and was trying to get you to bed.

All three laugh

Lacie Jae: (Giggles) Well, I'm not going to ask if she did.

Silence

Lacie Jae: OH! That innocent question took a wrong turn! (giggles) On to another subject! Brodie, you said Pendleton, Sheridan, and Cheyenne were your favorite rodeos because of the history. Craig, what is yours?

Craig: I like Sisters because it's like a hometown rodeo for me.
        Then I'd say San Antonio because I like the city itself and
        the rodeo is pretty cool and Pendleton.

Lacie Jae: Brodie's biggest goal was those three rodeos. Craig,
        other than the NFR, what is your biggest goal?

Brodie: Women younger than 40.

All three laugh

Craig: Dad having to add another room to the house because I
        won too many saddles.

Brodie: He loves saddles more than buckles.

Craig: I'd like the Big 4 saddle for winning the most points in
        Pendleton, Kennewick, Lewiston, and Walla Walla.
        Because we grew up in the Pacific Northwest, I feel that it
        would be like winning a hometown award. It would be a
        unique saddle to have.

Lacie Jae: I know Logan wears his first NFR go-round buckle as
        his main everyday buckle, and Delaney wears her Nampa
        Snake River Stampede buckle, Craig, which do you wear?

Craig: Sisters … it was a huge night.

Lacie Jae: Brodie?

Brodie: I don't have a set one, just kind of changes with my mood,
        but when I ride, I use my grandad's spurs.

Lacie Jae: Very special. Who has had more injuries?

Craig: Ankle, knee, rib, and fingers

Brodie: Concussion, leg stress fracture that made me sit-out half of
        my sixteenth year, ankle, and rib.

Craig: He dislocated his shoulder, too.

Brodie: Oh, yeah, then there was your groin pull.

Lacie Jae: So about the same, you're both just broken

Both Men: Life of a roughie

Lacie Jae: Dream bucking horse to ride?

Craig: Craig at Midnight, of course, and probably Killer Bee …

Brodie: Virgil is an ultimate.

Craig: Medicine Woman, Womanizer

Brodie: Khadafy, 303 Spring Fling, and Grated Coconut, if I could
      go back in time.

Craig: Lunatic from Hell

Lacie Jae: Well, that one just sounds scary.

Brodie: He can be. There are so many good ones out there now
      you can make a 90 point ride.

Craig: The stock contractors have been doing a phenomenal job
      in their breeding programs. Dozens of new horses come
      out every year that help get you a check.

Lacie Jae: Who would Delaney say she would rather team rope
      with?

Craig: Oh, damn … that's a good question.

Brodie: Probably me just because we've done it more.

Craig: Yeah, I agree.

Lacie Jae: Who would Logan rather travel to rodeos with?

Both men laugh

Brodie: I'd say Craig because Logan likes to sing when he's tired
      and Craig harmonizes better than me

Craig: Brodie has a terrible singing voice

All three chuckle

Lacie Jae: Favorite western to watch when killing time

Both Men: Lonesome Dove

Lacie Jae: Logan and Delaney both said to ask you what your
      personal theme songs are.

Brodie: It ain't my fault

Lacie Jae: What isn't your fault?

Craig: It was too.

Lacie Jae: What?

Brodie: The song by Brothers Osborn, 'It Ain't My Fault'

Craig: It was your fault

Lacie Jae: (Giggling) Explain, who did what to who?

Brodie: The two of us and Logan were traveling together last year
      and we stop at some truck stop in Oklahoma. One of those
      places with a laundry mat. Logan goes in and gets food

while we get our laundry started, then we go in and get food while he starts his. I get back first and Logan is digging in Craig's bag.

Craig: This is where it is his fault.

Brodie: It wasn't my fault (chuckling). Logan pulls out Craig's riding pants and ...

Lacie Jae: What? What are those?

Craig: I have a football girdle that is skin tight and holds my ... well; it holds everything tight to the body when I ride. They're under the jeans, so no one knows they are there.

Brodie: (chuckling) except us and Logan pulls them out and throws them in a washing machine before Craig gets back from the store. I had no idea what he was doing until he put something in with them.

Craig: Again, your fault

All three chuckle

Brodie: Logan even manages to get them dried without Craig knowing. He puts them in his own bag until Craig isn't looking then stuffs them back in Craig's under his clothes.

Craig: I get to the rodeo that night and we're behind the chutes where no one can see us, so I was changing clothes. I wear tight bike shorts so I'm not completely naked, but I go to put on my riding pants and they are fucking bright yellow!

Lacie Jae: (Laughing) Yellow and not pink?

Craig: Yellow, fucking yellow.

Brodie: (Laughing) Logan found food coloring in the grocery store and also dumped a huge bag of lemon heads in the machine. They were so bright and Craig was so pissed as the cowboys around us were just ... speechless.

Craig: Speechless because they were laughing so fucking hard, especially when Logan peeked his head around the corner and started laughing.

Brodie: He was so pissed he rode like a maniac and won the damn rodeo.

Craig: The worst part is I started sweating, and the food coloring soaked into my skin. I was told I looked jaundice down there.

Lacie Jae: Who would know that?

Low chuckles

Lacie Jae: Oh! You two! Making my innocent questions go bad.

Laughter

Lacie Jae: Brodie, what is your theme song?

Both Men: The Gambler

Lacie Jae: Why?

Brodie: I'm playing poker with a bunch of people, including Delaney. We get to a hand between her and I and Brody... Cress, suggests making a bet that doesn't include money.

Craig: It ends up with Delaney having to clean his bronc saddle or Brodie riding Gaston around the barrels at competition speed.

Lacie Jae: I'd never do that! Those turns look scary fast.

Both men laugh

Brodie: Oh, they are... I know, because I lost.

Craig laughs

Brodie: I made it around the first barrel OK, then decided to take the second one wider but Gaston knows what he's doing and didn't go as wide as I wanted and I nearly toppled out of the saddle.

Craig: We have video of the third barrel.

Brodie: That horse turned so damn fast both my feet came out of the stirrups and no matter how tight I held that damn saddle horn, the g-forces had me flying.

Craig laughing: In grand style.

Lacie Jae: Did you get hurt?

Brodie: No, but I did walk away with more respect for Delaney's riding ability... which I already had respect for.

Craig: And he doesn't let anyone talk him into gambling for anything but money anymore.

Laughter

Lacie Jae: Last question and I want both of you to answer. If you were sitting in front of a dozen teenage cowboys that were headed on the road, what is the best advice you could give them?

Both Men: Believe

Craig: Believe in yourself, never stop learning or trying. Get to the point that your believing in yourself is just a way of life, not a goal to reach.

Brodie: That and don't give up. Life is not always on top. It is a freaking roller coaster. You can have the best ride of your life in the afternoon, then that night get bucked off a 70 point horse.

Lacie Jae: We couldn't end this interview on a better note than that. Thank you both for taking the time out of the day for this interview. I'll talk to Evan on whether he wants me to edit out the part about why he got back into rodeo.

Craig: Thanks, Lacie Jae, you did an excellent job for your first interview.

Brodie: Thanks for talking with Dad about that, and I agree, you did a great job … but you're still going to make us coffee, right?

Thank you, everyone for listening. I hope you enjoyed learning about these two best friends as much as I did. I am so incredibly lucky to have the Rawlins and Houston's in my life and you can now understand why. I'm going to sign off now and have Coffee with these two Cowboys. Have a good day and a great cup of coffee.

CHAPTER TWENTY

"Well?" Mark asked with a grin as we sat on the bales in the barn after listening to the podcast. "Who would you choose?"

I laughed, "It is split; Craig as a header and Brodie as a heeler."

"You didn't even have to think about it?" Camille asked.

"No, I have at a dozen jackpots we've gone to," I stood and reached for my gloves. "I'm going out to check the herd."

By the end of the morning, two more newborn calves and mothers were tucked into the barn. The temperature was down to 15 degrees, with the three of us taking turns napping in my horse trailer or watching over the cows in the barn. The older horses were in their stalls with their doors to the outside closed to stop all drafts throughout the barn.

While Mark slept in the trailer, Camille was busy on her laptop, so I worked in the tack room oiling saddles and cleaning bits.

The day passed peacefully but cold. Before dark, we saddled the horses and rode out through the herd then out to the pastures and hills to make sure no cows were lost, injured, or birthing. We pushed through the fresh eight inches of fresh snow that fell the day before. I was able to capture more photos of Camille riding through the snow or sky-lined on the hill against the bright blue sky. She was a natural rider and trusting of the horse.

We watched the rodeo while they fixed dinner and I texted with my Huckleberry. At dinner, I broke out a bottle of Captain Morgan's Spiced Rum. It was still with us as we went to the barn to check on the cows and play on the practice equipment.

Monday morning, the temperature rose to thirty degrees and a light snowfall began again. Water troughs were checked, cows were watched over, and the horses pampered in their stalls.

Mark left to go to his engineering job, but he and Camille texted throughout the day.

"Is it OK if I go riding out to the pastures?" Camille asked after we fed the last calf his lunch.

"Of course," I answered while washing out the supplement bottle. "Go anytime you want...you don't have to ask."

Twenty minutes later, I was walking through the corrals checking on the young heifers and could see her ride out toward the trees in the distance. She began to trot in a large circle, then tightened it with every lap and created a spiral of sorts in the snow. Another large circle in fresh snow and she did it again the opposite direction. It made me smile that she was practicing.

I took another picture. You really couldn't see her; she was just a dark spec in the snow in the image but it would bring up the memories for her. After walking through the rest of the herd, I turned to walk back into the barn and glanced out at Camille. She was off the horse and standing at her side. Worried something was wrong, I retrieved binoculars from the tack room.

She was leaning against the horse's shoulder with her face resting in her hands. There was no doubt she was crying again. Damn, it just broke my heart. The woman was riding one heck of an emotional rollercoaster. I lowered the binoculars when she started wiping the tears away. By the time I had put the binoculars away and stepped outside, she was back in the saddle and walking the horse to the barn so I walked out to greet her.

There was no sign of the tears as she approached. Her lips were rolled into a straight line and her eyes looked determined.

"Delaney, I need to ask you a favor," she said and stepped down from the horse. Embers instantly turned her head and rubbed against Camille's arm. After quickly removing her gloves, she stroked the long nose and neck of the horse.

"What is that?" I asked and shut the barn door behind her.

"No matter what happens with Lacie Jae, I want to continue to ride and be involved with horses," she smiled with a deep soul releasing a sigh. "I love them...I love Embers. Whether here or somewhere else, if she doesn't want me around, I will be involved with horses."

"She will..."

Her hand rose to stop me.

"Neither of us knows what she is going to say or do, but I've decided you were right. Actions speak louder than words, so I have put that into motion, but I need a favor from you."

"OK..."

"Will you teach me how to rope? Like in breakaway?"

"Yes!" I squealed in delight. "We can start right now!"

Her grin widened and excitement sparkled in her eyes, "And I'd like to buy Embers."

My smile faded, "No...never...she's not for sale."

Camille's shoulders lowered as her hand rest on the brown horse's shoulder.

"But...why? I really love her."

"We all do," I hoped this didn't change her mind about riding. "But there is no way she will be for sale...ever."

"Why?"

"Because she was my mother's horse," I said softly and felt the tug on my heart as I thought of the last moment my mother had touched the horse. It was the day before she died. Logan had carried her outside on the deck while Brodie walked the horse to her so they could spend time together. Embers had been calm while nuzzling her softly then stood quietly at her side...as if she knew something was wrong.

Camille's eyes widened in surprise, "You let me ride her?" She gasped.

"Of course," I smiled and tried to calm my heart. "Embers needs to be ridden and she's perfect for a beginner to learn."

"Oh…" She turned to the horse and ran her hand down her shoulder. "Well…"

"Let's get started on the basic roping," I said and started walking down the aisle to get her moving forward again…literally and hopefully figuratively. "Embers will be your training partner and when the time comes, we'll look for your next partner."

"Are you sure?" She asked and I could hear hoofbeats on the ground as she followed me.

"Yes," I chuckled. "You put Embers away and I'll go pick out a rope to get you started."

She laughed, "How do you pick one rope from the hundred you have on the wall?"

"And that will be your first lesson!"

We spent the first half-hour talking about the ropes; softness, core, color, brand, stiffness, length and how the weather and ground affects them.

I'm not sure which one of us was more excited the first time I dropped a lariat into her hand. She blushed and giggled with her feet tapping on the ground.

"Hold the coils in your left hand, take the first coil and flip it around to create your loop," I demonstrated. "And the knot that the rope threads through is the honda…"

We spent hours with her learning to twirl the rope over her head and when she threw the loop at her first dummy steer, we both squealed in excitement.

Mark arriving surprised both of us…the time had sped by. The look on his face when she told him what we were doing and demonstrated how she could throw well, the man had already been falling for her and now she was quickly becoming his perfect woman.

By the end of the night, she was sitting on the dummy 'horse' and throwing at a dummy 'steer'. We were all so excited we had forgotten to break out the bottles in the cupboard.

One last check on the herd and I walked to the house by myself to give the pair of them some time alone.

I was already in the hot tub when I saw her room light turn on.

I received a text from my Huckleberry and my whole body sighed.

Text from Huckleberry: How is my Sweetheart tonight?

Text to Huckleberry: I spent the day teaching Camille how to rope. She did so well!

Text: Well, you two must be getting along.

Text: Oh, yes. One moment she is happy and excited and then she will suddenly drop to a low point and cry. Breaks my heart.

Text: Teaching her to rope will keep her focused and attitude high.

Text: That's what I thought.

The light in her room went off.

Text: She's coming...I have to go.

Text: Call me when you crawl into bed

I giggled and quickly removed the wide naughty grin that flashed.

Text: I will

I set the phone down as she walked into the room with a smile and carrying two glasses and a wine bottle.

"Perfect," I drawled.

She set both glasses on the side of the tub and twisted the corkscrew into the top of the bottle. Her body was swaying to imaginary music.

"Delaney," She grinned at me and the cork released with a pop that echoed above the sound of the water bubbling. "I haven't been this excited and motivated for years."

The wine was quickly poured and we rose the glasses into a toast.

"Here's to you and your equine infection taking over," I laughed.

Wednesday morning, Mark arrived with a box for Camille. She quickly took it into the house before they rode out into the herd to check on the cows. I began moving bales of hay from the hay barn to the shed at the horse stable.

I was driving the ATV past the house and toward the barn when a movement to the right caught my attention. Slowly coming to a stop, I watched Dad's van pull down the driveway.

"What the hell...?" I whispered and waited. They weren't supposed to be home for days.

The van came to a stop with Dad driving and Martin in the passenger seat. They both grinned sheepishly at me.

If it was just the two of them...but the door behind Martin opened and a cute blonde head appeared with a big grin.

My stomach clenched as I looked at Lacie Jae then slowly turned to look across the corrals and into the pasture. Mark and Camille were trotting toward the barn. From the dip in the ground and the angle they were riding, I had no doubt they didn't see Dad's van arrive.

"Well, daughter?" Dad said with a smile as he opened his door. "Surprised to see us?"

No matter my feelings on the impending collision of sisters, I was always happy to see him and returned the smile.

"I said I could handle the ranch," After one more look to the two riders approaching the back of the barn, I slid off the ATV.

He didn't need help, but I still liked to be close as he maneuvered the wheelchair from the van to the walkway. He rose and used the railing to brace himself for the three steps up to the porch. Martin carried the chair to the top so Dad could sit again.

"Surprise!" Lacie Jae giggled as she tip-toed through the snow then up the steps. She was bundled in a blue coat with a white fur-trimmed collar, which emphasized her big blue excited eyes.

"Yes, it is," I nodded with another glance to the barn.

All three of them turned to see what I was looking at.

"That's Mark, isn't it?" Martin asked.

"Yeah," I nodded.

"Who's with him?" Dad asked.

"His girlfriend," I said truthfully.

They all three turned to me in surprise.

"I thought you and Mark were dating?" Lacie Jae gasped.

"It didn't work out," I shrugged. "We're just friends."

"Then who is that and why is she riding Embers?" Dad asked again.

I turned to see the pair, still on horseback and now holding hands, ride out of the barn. They were looking at each other and laughing. It was easy to see for everyone that the pair were quite happy.

"Delaney? Who is that?" Dad repeated.

"Well," I hesitated.

"That looks like...and that laugh...sounds like..." Lacie Jae tipped her head to the side and narrowed her eyes. "No...she doesn't know how to ride."

"Who?" Martin and Dad asked at the same time.

"She wouldn't be here..." Lacie Jae said firmly but leaned toward the approaching riders.

They both turned and looked to the house and their smiles melted away with Mark looking at Lacie Jae then to Camille.

The two sisters stared at each other with Camille looking worried and Lacie Jae looking confused.

She turned and glared at me, "Is that HER?"

"Who?" Dad and Martin asked again.

I nodded and looked back to Camille, who had stopped the horse in front of the van and was now stepping down from the saddle.

Mark had also dismounted and held out a hand to take Embers' reins from Camille. She didn't look at him as she dropped them in his hand and kept walking toward the porch. She slowly walked up the steps until she stopped one step down from her sister, so they were eye to eye.

"What are you doing here?" Lacie Jae huffed with cheeks a deep pink.

211

Camille smiled slightly, but I could see the worry in her eyes, "I came looking for you."

"Why?" Lacie Jae's voice was low, gruff, and her eyes were narrowed.

"I wanted to make sure you were alright and to tell you something," Camille answered.

"What?" Lacie Jae snapped.

"That you were right," Camille tipped her chin up slightly. "I didn't intend to abandon you or throw you away, but you took it that way and I am so sorry. I was so angry at Dad and at my mother. I didn't choose her over you; I went down to confront her. As for Kendra and Eve? Kendra is a bitch and Eve...well...she was as blind to her as I was."

"What does that mean?" Lacie Jae glared.

"It means that after I left Fresno, so did Eve and neither of us has anything to do with Kendra anymore."

"Why?" Lacie Jae put her hands on her hips.

Camille shrugged slightly, "We can discuss that later but once I left Fresno and went back to Redding, well, I didn't want to be there, so I came here looking for you. To tell you, I'd made a mistake and to make sure you knew how damn sorry I am."

Lacie Jae's lips rolled together as she looked at her sister with doubt and distrust.

Camille glanced at me then swung a hand back to Mark, "I ran into Mark and Delaney at the café in town and Delaney invited me to spend the day with her."

Mark and I shared a quick glance and a slight smile at her description of our 'run in'.

"How long have you been here?" Lacie Jae asked with an accusing glance to me.

"Since the morning I went to look at Memphis," I answered. "She went with me; then I invited her to stay until you got back."

"That's over a week," Dad grumbled.

I looked down at him to see accusing eyes looking back at me. Damn, I wasn't expecting that.

I shrugged, "Yes..."

"We decided not to say anything about my being here so we didn't spoil your trip," Camille added quickly.

"You knew I'd be mad or upset you were here?" Lacie Jae said in disbelief. It was a bit forceful and very much sounded like she was mad.

"I had no idea how you were going to feel," Camille answered. Her gaze didn't leave Lacie Jae. "When we drove to look at Memphis, Delaney told me about your podcasts and we listened to them. I've listened to all of them a couple of times." She smiled and the light in her brown eyes sparkled. "I am so proud of you."

Lacie Jae huffed disbelievingly.

Camille's jaw dropped and the smile faded. Her cheeks reddened. "I've told you that before about the coffee shops. You were a great manager...everyone loved you. I came to..."

"You never wanted anything to do with me, Camille," Lacie Jae growled.

Camille took in a deep breath and slowly released it, "Well, that's not exactly true...I just did a real bad job of showing it to you." She paused, then continued. "Can we go in the house and I'll show you?"

"How are you going to do that?" Lacie Jae glared.

"I could probably stand here all day and talk to try and convince you, but I don't know what I could say that would make you believe me. But, maybe if I show you...let me show you," Camille begged with hope in her eyes.

Lacie Jae shrugged and turned to the house. Without waiting for anyone, she walked down the porch and through the side door to the kitchen.

While the sisters were talking, Mark had replaced the horse's bridles with halters and tossed the lead ropes over the hitching post.

Camille turned to him and held out a hand. He smiled slightly as he took it and walked with her into the house.

"What the hell were you thinking having her stay here?" Dad growled.

I looked at him in surprise, "I was thinking you don't judge someone by what other people think of them...you be the judge yourself. You never know the true story unless you see if for yourself."

"Using your words against you," Martin chuckled and held the door open.

Dad glared at both of us as he rolled through.

We found Camille walking down the hall with Mark and Lacie Jae standing quietly by the table.

Lacie Jae turned to Dad, "You still want coffee?"

"There are more important things…" he started.

She shrugged and turned on the coffee machine, then filled the water tank as we waited. She had just poured the coffee beans into the container when Camille returned carrying the box that Mark had delivered.

He rushed forward to take it out of her arms and set it on the table for her. Camille smiled her thanks then opened the top flap of the box. She smiled nervously at her sister, who was staring blankly at her.

Camille's hand dipped into the box and pulled out a tall white paper coffee cup that had a black sipping lid on top. Lacie Jae's eyebrows rose and her chin dropped slightly.

On the side of the cup was written the name of Lacie Jae's podcast: "Coffee with Cowboys" and just underneath was the Rawlins' steer head and bar-R brand.

"I have a friend that creates these and he did a few for me the other morning and over-nighted these samples. I bought these paper ones," Camille set it on the table then dipped into the box again. "But I also bought a half dozen mugs, too." She pulled out a tall mug that was reminiscent of the campfire cups. She held it out to her sister, whose hand trembled slightly as she took it. Camille turned and looked at me then to my dad. "I hope you don't mind; I put your brand on it. It was on her t-shirt she had on in the pictures from Denver, so I thought it would be OK."

"It is," Dad said and nodded to Lacie Jae. "That one is mine. I'll take that cup of coffee you're making in it, so I can test it for you."

We all smiled…even Lacie Jae as she walked to the sink and washed the cup.

"Camille Madison," she stuck out a hand and shook Dad's hand.

"Evan," Dad said. His demeanor had changed slightly with shoulders lowering.

"I want one," Martin tipped his head to look into the box.

Camille smiled and handed him one.

"Martin Houston," he smiled as she shook his hand.

"Me, too," Mark whispered and was pleased to have one handed to him.

Camille looked at me and I grinned and gave her the proudest look in return.

Her eyes glistened as she handed the cup to me.

"Logan, Brodie, and Craig will want one too," Dad said. "We should get more ordered."

Camille looked pleased, as well as she should be. Her sister walked back to the small group and finished making Dad's coffee.

"I also…well…" Camille stuttered.

"What?" Lacie Jae asked. The animosity in her voice was gone. It was clear that Camille recognized that and her shoulders rose in confidence.

"You kept saying in your podcast that you would work on a Facebook page or website when you had time…after Denver." Camille said.

"Yeah…" Lacie Jae nodded.

"Well, since that is what I do for a living, I went ahead and created one or a whole social network so you wouldn't have to." Camille smiled. "I can always adjust whatever you don't like."

"Can I see them?" Lacie Jae smiled.

Dad was already rolling to the monitor on the wall that was attached to the laptop we used for watching videos at the table.

Camille sat in front of the computer with a 'thank you' glance to him. "Of course, I haven't published any of them."

Lacie Jae handed Dad his cup of coffee, then took the chair next to her sister and leaned toward the monitor. Mark,

Dad, Martin, and I stood quietly and amazed at the website and social network pages she had created in just a few days.

Once they began to make adjustments, I stepped away and took Mark's arm. We walked out of the house as Dad and Martin moved down the hallway to leave the sisters alone.

I couldn't have been happier for the two sisters. I really liked them both. They still had a long road of healing in front of them, but at least they were both in the same place to try and make it happen.

Welcome to Coffee with Cowboys with me, Lacie Jae.

Greetings everyone! Lacie Jae with Coffee With Cowboys here. I'm a relocated city girl who will be adventuring into the ranching and rodeo world... the cowboy way of life.

Hello from Fort Worth!

Food! People, there is food everywhere! If you look hard enough, you might find something healthy but oh the fried food!

Between Denver and Fort Worth, I have gained 10 pounds! On a five foot small frame that's a lot! I have this weird little belly pooch that's tightened my jeans to the point I want to leave the top button open or even wear tights instead. Ugghhh! The food is so good! Have you heard of chicken-fried bacon? I hadn't, so Evan Rawlins introduced me to it. I now call the man 'the fried devil' because I can hardly stay away from it.

Elephant ears too! Not the real animal (giggles), but the fried ones with sugar on it. At least five of my extra pounds are from elephant ears! They are like flat doughnuts that are as round as my whole head! (More giggles).

Fried ICE CREAM! (squeal of laughter) Evan talked me into trying that, too! So good... and to be honest, it really doesn't take much to get me to try food. Martin absolutely insisted that I try alligator on a stick and it was good. Delaney and my sister, Camille ... oh! My sister has come up from California, too, and she is joining us for the rest of this Texas trip, which is weeks we get to spend together! Anyway, Delaney and Camille stick with Haystacks that are like taco salads. Once a day, they have something real fattening, then ride horses or jog to work it off. I don't have discipline like that. Delaney said she has had to really work on it and Camille has ALWAYS been like that. She's more addicted to shopping than food.

Talk about shopping! Anything you can imagine is crammed into every building available here in Fort Worth. Clothes, jewelry, furniture, towels, boots, hats, beautiful rugs, horse tack, and purses! I have found I want to use a different purse every day ... kind of like a different shirt every day (giggle) so I splurged a bit and bought three more yesterday. I have no doubt that by the time we go through San Angelo, San Antonio, and Houston, more will be coming home with me.

Camille has boxes of clothing and jewelry going home with us, but I swear the only thing Delaney has purchased was this cool sign that says "I'LL BE YOUR HUCKLEBERRY". I guess that's from a movie. Logan has informed me we'll be watching it one of these nights he's not riding. Delaney had to remind me that she's been at the rodeo life since she was young, so she has just about everything ... but not that sign. I'm now curious to what this huckleberry thing is.

Back to the thousands of people here for the stock show and the rodeo ... the carnival and so much more ... this is such an adventure. Something I never dreamed of doing. My heartbeat has strengthened in just the few days we have been here so far. If I was back in my old life, I'd be standing in a coffee shop brewing coffee and talking to customers or I'd be home. There isn't anything wrong with that as long as you add an adventure in every once in a while. We all need balance, but I didn't have that. Now I do.

Find your balance by adding fun into your life, whether it's an adventure like the Fort Worth Stock Show and Rodeo or a movie or going to the beach or... just anything that gets you out and enjoying life again. We only have one life to live, so make the best of it.

Of course, if I have much more of this fried food, mine might be a bit shorter! (Giggles)

I'm signing off because Camille and I are going to the carnival while everyone is working horses, practicing, or getting interviewed before the rodeo tonight. It's going to be a busy day, so I'm headed back to the trailer to have coffee with the cowboys and get it started the right way!

One thing I hated most in life was driving thousands of miles only to hit a damn barrel with my foot and knock it over. Unless all the other fifty plus racers knocked over a barrel too, it took me out of any chance to win the Fort Worth Rodeo. It added money into the overall year-round standings, which really didn't matter if I wasn't riding to make the National Finals. Of course, winning for a round put money in the bank so I could travel and rope more. I tried very hard to keep my perspective and dignity when I was in public with cameras around us, but when I arrived at the trailer, with no one to hear or see, I let my frustrations out. If I didn't, I'd go insane.

"A poker brunch?" Camille asked the next morning as she helped me set up the table and chairs outside of our trailer. "I've never heard of such a thing."

"Kills time," I chuckled. "Non-physical competition that keeps our energy up and focus strong; we are competitive against each other no matter what it is. Logan went to buy snacks. Brodie and Craig will be here soon."

"I am looking forward to meeting those two," She set the poker chips on the table.

"Well, be prepared. Even though I told them you were dating Mark, they'll still hit on you...mostly for fun."

"I love fun, innocent flirtation," she giggled.

With perfect timing, the long white SUV drove in behind the trailer. Both men grinned broadly when they looked at Camille in her new figure-hugging Wranglers and high-collared red shirt under a black vest that emphasized her slender waist. Her long dark wavy hair flowed down her back. Large feather earrings, she had purchased from a vendor at the rodeo, swayed as she waved at them.

"You're teasing them," I chuckled.

"But, of course," she giggled.

The doors opened and both men stepped out with full attention on Camille.

"If you two stink, you stay away from her until you have showers," I yelled out to them.

All three laughed with eyes bright with anticipation.

"We took showers before we drove up," Brodie stretched out a hand.

Craig shot his hand forward, so he reached Camille's hand before Brodie's.

"You must meet the beauty before the beast," Craig drawled and stepped between the pair.

Camille's flirtatious laugh made their teasing grins wider.

"My goodness, Miss Delaney," Camille said in a deep southern drawl and offered her free hand to Brodie. "You didn't tell me these cowboys were so ruggedly handsome."

"Oh, brother," I rolled my eyes in feigned exasperation.

"Aren't they cute?" Lacie Jae stepped in next to her sister with a wide happy grin.

"Stop..." I groaned as the men beamed. "They are going to be full of themselves all day."

"They already are," Logan set full grocery bags on the table. "Have been for years."

219

Logan and I endured the three flirting through hours of poker while Lacie Jae giggled in pure enjoyment.

"They are staying in your trailer," I told Logan as we put everything away to get ready for the rodeo.

"Not a chance in hell," he huffed. "Dad and Martin will be here tomorrow and they'll be staying with us."

"You're going to make me live with the three of them?" I moaned.

"You've lived through worse," he chuckled. "Remember that chick with the palomino in California?"

I grimaced, "Yuck." She not only talked in her sleep, but she was a slob that left dirty clothes on the floor and hanging from the cupboards. Then there were the men she would 'host' in the back end of the horse trailer making the whole truck and trailer shake. I made her find another travel partner after only four days.

"Those three don't seem so bad now," He laughed and took Lacie Jae's hand to walk to their trailer.

My three roommates just grinned, making me shake my head in exasperation as I walked to the stalls.

I placed third in the rodeo to bring in a check while Logan was second for the night.

The next night, after a day full of the six of us shopping, napping, and watching movies all day, I won the night but didn't qualify to move onto the semi-finals. I spent the days training Memphis, practicing with Archer, and just riding Gaston to keep him conditioned. The nights were sitting on the bleachers with Camille, Lacie Jae, Martin, and Dad cheering on Logan, Brodie, and Craig.

Fortunately, I placed in the San Angelo rodeo to build my confidence before going to San Antonio.

CHAPTER TWENTY-ONE

Welcome to Coffee with Cowboys with me, Lacie Jae.

Greetings everyone! Lacie Jae with Coffee With Cowboys here. I'm a relocated city girl who will be adventuring into the ranching and rodeo world ... the cowboy way of life.

I'm going to call this podcast 'raw and edgy' because that's how my voice sounds. It's a bit raw from over abuse last night so bear with me. (clearing of throat) I'm also not going to edit this; I'm just going to post when done so if anything goes wrong, well, you get to hear that too.

So, we're here in San Antonio at our trailer at the rodeo grounds. There are three different brackets with this rodeo and the competitors ride for three nights in a row before moving on. The four best in the average of those three nights move to the semi-finals. Logan and Brodie are in the first bracket and last night was their third night. I'm proud to say Logan won the average in his bracket and moves on to the semi-finals and Brodie came in second and gets to move on, too.

Craig and Delaney don't ride until Tuesday in Bracket Three. So, basically, we had the night off since none of us had to be anywhere today. We celebrated Logan's win with a night out at a local bar. What a night it was! (throat clearing). Sorry, tender throat.

So, we're at the bar after the rodeo drinking, a little dancing, and lots of teasing fun. You know how family can be ...

The band, drummer, keyboards, and a guitar player take the stage but no singer ... they start playing and still no singer but everyone, and I mean everyone in that bar knew the song the band was playing. Within a minute, the crowd is singing the song because the singer isn't there. Now, I've been on the road long enough with this group that I had heard this song dozens of times … enough I felt comfortable singing with them.

I have to admit the crowd was doing a great job … until the original singer walked on stage. The place freaking erupted. The type of eruption that makes walls shake, windows tremble, and I don't know how that roof stayed put. You have not lived until Toby Keith crashes a party.

He walked on stage with a swagger, straw hat, guitar over his shoulder, and that red solo cup in his hand to join the crowd in singing 'Whiskey for my horses". Crazy!

(Throat clearing and a cough with a big exhale and continues in a hoarse voice)

Now, I'm a short person, and it didn't take long for the crowd in front of us to block my view, so Logan, Mr. Six Foot Five, let me crawl onto his back so I could watch the show. Legs wrapped around his waist, one arm around a wide shoulder and one holding my glass in the air as I screamed in his ear. It was so freaking fun. Every song was a favorite and the whole crowd sang along.

To have a man like Toby Keith walk into cowboy atmosphere … people, you just haven't lived until you've been through a moment like that. (Slight pause, light clearing of voice)

Toward the end of the night, Toby played only one slow-ish song. It, of course, was "Kiss Me Like That". At that point, Logan wiggles me around, so we are now face-to-face with my legs still firmly attached around his waist, and now his hands are on my … bum holding me up. Hundreds of people are around us singing with Toby, but for me, it was just Logan and I singing it to each other.

Not only did he 'look at me like that', but he also 'kissed me like that', the whole world disappeared around us.

(Throat clearing and a long pause)

Sorry, I had to take a drink of water.

Even though it was in public, it was such a private moment, and I could have just gone on and not mentioned it here, but I wanted to share ... wanted people who had given up or were about to ... or people that were lost in this world ... yes ... lost is what I want to say.

I was literally lost when Logan found me. I was figuratively lost when the Rawlins family took me in.

(A pause)

When Logan found me lost in Vegas, I couldn't have imagined how THAT moment was going to change my life. (Another pause with a shaking exhale) I'm now in the world that I feel like I was supposed to be in. He not only found me, but he gave me that ... my life.

When the family took me in at Christmas and wouldn't let me go into the unknown, well, that absorbed me into this cowboy world. I may not be the best at sitting a horse or swinging a rope, but I can be the best at living this toughness, the honesty, the camaraderie that surrounds these people; cowboys, rodeo, ranching.

So ... my point is ... don't give up in finding the life that you were meant to be in. There were millions of people in Vegas that night, yet that one moment that he saw me lost ... it was just a MOMENT our paths crossed, and my life changed. Somewhere down the road is your moment. Don't give up, keep fighting through, because your moment will come.

Logan and his family are my life now. I'm never letting them go. When Logan and I were singing that song to each other last night ... the words just melted me inside. The honesty and emotion in his eyes just made my heart sigh.

I'm going to sign off now; hopefully, I made some sense and didn't ramble. And now, on this quiet morning with everyone sleeping off the whiskey and the singing, I'm going to go have coffee with my cowboy.

When my phone alert rang, my hand slowly stretched out from under the covers to look at it. Lacie Jae had posted a new podcast.

"Are you fucking kidding me?" My voice was barely over a low grumble.

"What?" Camille's voice was just as low and hoarse.

"Lacie Jae is up and posted a podcast already."

"What time is it? She did it already?"

"It's 6:42…I don't think we've been in bed for maybe four hours."

"Well," Camille sighed. "Now, I'm curious."

"Yeah…" I pushed the play button and turned the volume up so she could hear it, too.

Lacie Jae's gruff low voice echoed into the trailer.

There was complete silence throughout the entire podcast.

When she signed off to go have coffee with her cowboy, I closed down the podcast app.

"Kendra had grabbed my arm and pulled me into the mass of slot machines and card tables," Camille whispered. "I had no idea what she was doing. I had never been to Vegas, but she had a couple of times, so I thought she was taking a short cut. I didn't realize Lacie Jae wasn't behind us until we were stepping into the bus. When I tried to turn back, Kendra just pulled me along saying Lacie Jae was smart and now twenty-one so I should quit babying her…quit treating her like a child. I just kind of repeated what she said to Lacie Jae, then Kendra grabbed the phone and hung up on her. I was sick to my stomach all the way there and was so damned relieved to see her in the chair when we arrived."

I was trying to fight my mind from wanting to go to sleep so I could talk.

"The next night," she continued. "After Logan won the round, I talked them into going back to the MGM after-party instead of going to the buckle ceremony, so they didn't do something to ruin it for her."

I was grasping at consciousness, "So…we can thank Kendra for *that moment* they met and changed both your lives."

224

She chuckled and rolled over onto her stomach and curled into the pillow.

My mind shut down as I thought of Logan and Lacie Jae singing to each other. *What a special moment for them* was my last thought until my alarm chimed an hour later.

The banging on the door started the second my feet hit the floor. Half my hair was down, with the other half still bobbing loosely from my ponytail. Camille was sitting on the edge of the bed with her hair a tangled mess on top of her head.

We squinted at each other through mascara smudged blood-shot eyes.

More banging.

"Stop that!" I tried to call out, but my voice was low and barely a whisper.

"Who the hell?" Camille growled.

"Probably, Dad," I whispered and opened the door to his grinning face.

"Good morning, my…uh…beautiful daughter?" he laughed.

"Coffee," I squinted at him.

"You probably don't know it, but Lacie Jae posted…" he started.

"We heard it," I interrupted.

"Then you understand why I'm not knocking on their door. So, it's the Keurig machine this morning." He slowly rose from the chair and gripped the handles to the trailer then shuffle stepped up the flat platform. He slowly walked to the kitchen bench as Camille scrambled to remove her bedding from the couch.

"Good morning, Sunshine," he grinned at her.

I chuckled and started the first cup of coffee.

"Good morning," she smiled and stuffed her blankets up onto my bed.

I helped her change the bed back to a couch.

"Sounds like I missed a hell of a night," Dad said as his eyes shot between the two of us. "Looks like it, too." He chuckled.

"Funny man," I rolled my tired eyes and handed him the first cup of coffee.

He patted the seat next to him with a look of invitation to Camille.

She looked a little shocked then smiled sweetly as she sat next to him.

"I have to admit, last night was pretty epic," she said. "I haven't had a night like that since my first two years in college."

"What happened after that?" Dad asked.

"I transferred to another college," she answered.

"Why did you transfer?" I asked and set the second cup of coffee in front of her.

She grinned, "Something to do with those epic nights."

We all chuckled, which made me cringe at the tingle of pain in my throat.

I pulled out the top drawer and grabbed a handful of cough drops to toss on the table.

Camille quickly popped the first one in her mouth. "Gives a bit of a minty kick to the coffee."

"So, Toby Keith crashed the party," Dad said.

"Oh, yeah," she nodded. "We were already dancing with the whiskey and rum flowing, but he came on and the singing was non-stop... unreal energy."

"After the first couple of songs, everyone started dancing again," I started my cup of coffee and leaned against the counter. "I'm not sure sweet little innocent Camille there sat down even once."

"I don't think I did either," She looked at Dad. "Your Brodie can sure cut a rug. Damn good dancer."

Dad grinned proudly.

"And you're talking to the man that taught him," I slid onto the bench across the table from them. "He and Mom won a number of contests and made sure all three of us carried on the tradition."

"You must have taught Craig too," Camille added. "I don't think he sat down either."

"The brunette with the red shirt?" I asked.

"For the first part," Camille said. "But I think he finally gave up on her after the third or fourth dance."

"What's that mean?" Dad asked.

"Brodie promised Mark he'd watch over me," Camille answered. "So, he danced with me all night and the brunette was boring a hole in my back. She was all eyes for Brodie. Craig finally realized it and moved onto the lineup of girls that were waiting for him."

"And, at the end of the night, disappeared with a girl in a pink shirt," I added.

"And you?" Dad raised a brow to me.

"I danced and sang every song with a shot of Pendleton whisky between each one," I informed him with a raised cup of the coffee.

"Good girl," he smiled. "Have fun in life."

"I got to thinking last night," I glanced at him then smiled at her. "Camille, if you want, I'd love to have you use my companion pass."

"Oh, that's a great idea," Dad nodded with a pleased grin. "You'll have fun."

"What is that?" She sat straight up.

"You get to go to the competitor's area with me and in the lane as my help," I answered.

"Yes!" She growled with a laugh.

"But there is one caveat," I warned.

"What? I want to do that, I'll do anything," Her hands pounded on the top of the table. "Oh! Seriously, what do I have to do?"

"You have to be in complete western dress code, including the cowboy hat," I answered. She had refused to wear a cowboy hat and become a cliché because of her looks, fashion style, and because she didn't believe she had earned it.

"Just at the rodeos, no problem," she giggled excitedly. "I'll just borrow one of yours. What do I get to do?"

"She'll walk you through it later, but for now, she has work to do," Dad answered.

"For what?" I stood to brew him another cup.

227

"Other than stall cleaning, you brought him, so you need to get Memphis out and worked around all this commotion," he answered.

"Yeah…I do," I pushed the button for the next, much needed, cup of coffee.

"So, while she gets her butt going," Dad said to Camille. "Tell me your epic college stories."

Camille giggled a bit devilishly.

The first night of competition for me in San Antonio and my heart was racing as Gaston and I made our way to the entry lane. I loved these big rodeos and all the extravaganza that went with them.

My nerves were tingling, so I stopped at the end and took a deep breath. In my head, I was telling myself not to hit a barrel with my toe again.

"Have you two even raced this year?" The next rider, Tanya Morgan, asked.

I turned and looked at her. She was mounted on a big sorrel with a white blaze and nearly perfect socks on all four legs. He was tall, muscular, and stunning to look at.

Tanya had long dark hair flowing down her back over a crisp white shirt. It looked sharp, but her so-called 'innocent' eyes tried unsuccessfully to hide the bitchiness behind the question.

"Yes," I answered without elaborating.

I hated bitchy dramatic people.

Her name was announced, and I smiled politely at her, "Good luck, run hard."

"Thanks," she said over her shoulder as she rode down the lane as Kathy Grimes trotted out of the exit gate with a run time of 15.2 seconds.

The bitchy rider, Tanya, left the barrels up, but each turn was wide, and she came in over 18 seconds. When she rode out the exit gate, her face was contorted in anger, and she yanked on the horse's reins making his head jerk to the right. A shiver of irritation ran down my spine. I looked for the race official, but his back was to her.

The announcer called out, "Jamie Hamilton will be our next rider followed by Delaney Rawlins."

I leaned forward and ran a hand down Gaston's red roan neck. Taking deep breaths, I ran the pattern in my mind. Not just any pattern, but the perfect pattern...the last run at the NFR. I could feel every move as my body swayed back and forth.

"You got this, Jamie," Lauren, her mother, called out as she trotted down the lane. "Just remember to lift his shoulder on the second."

I glanced over at Lauren standing proudly with dark eyes beaming in high expectations. She made my gut ache.

Jamie trotted through the exit gate while patting her horse's large rump. She had a respectable 14.9 and her mother was grinning proudly at her.

I could feel the excitement in me begin to drain as I watched the pair.

"What am I supposed to say to you?"

I turned to see Camille looking up at me in concern. "What?"

"I'm supposed to say something encouraging like she just did," She smiled. "What's your favorite pep talk? What am I supposed to say?"

"Kickass, you got this, trust Gaston..." I answered. "I've heard just about everything."

"Ok, well," She put her hands on her hips and looked at me in all seriousness. "I am so damned excited to be here and watch you run...so don't let me down."

I laughed as my name was called and I nudged Gaston down the lane.

The noise of the arena faded as my heart rate increased. My energy rising made Gaston begin to prance. The perfect pattern was completed in my memory again.

The entry gate was open and we ran. It felt good even if it was only for 14.11 seconds. Camille was bouncing with an arm pumping in the air as we came to a dramatic halt at the gate.

"Did I let you down?" I asked as we pranced through the gate.

"No! That was so exciting!" She jogged next to us. "You're second!"

"Two more nights," I puffed.

"Oh, you're making the semi-finals," She declared.

"Top four in the average after three runs," I reminded her.

"You two are NOT letting me down," Camille looked up at me as we walked toward the back pens. "I want to watch you in the finals."

"I'll do my best," I said and truly meant it.

The second night, I was the first rider out of the lane and into the arena. All day, I had analyzed the run the night before by watching videos from different angles and replaying the feeling of the run in my mind. I had no doubt I could shave time off the run as long as the barrels stayed up. With Camille yelling behind me, and the rest of the family just behind the third barrel, Gaston killed the pattern by crossing the line at 14.01.

Camille was jumping and yelling when we rode through the gate. You really couldn't ask for more honest support than that; I mused as we trotted past the other racers waiting their turn. Only one rider was faster, leaving me second again.

The third night, pressure tapped me on the shoulder as I stepped up into the saddle. One more ride 'all you have to do is clock a decent time and you're in the top four' it said to me. My stomach churned. Damn, I hated that. I took a deep breath and slowly released it as I rode toward the arena. I nodded to Jamie as I passed her and didn't even acknowledge her mother standing there.

Camille was walking alongside of me.

"What's wrong?" she asked.

I just shrugged.

"Well, I just want you to know how much fun this is," she smiled slightly as she looked up at me. "But, no matter what happens with your ride tonight, you're just not going to top the Toby Keith night."

The tension laughed right out of me as I trotted into the lane then arena.

I topped my time the night before with a 13.97, which gave me the lead in the average, the win for the night, and the step up to the semi-finals.

My hand slid down Gaston's neck as we pranced through the gate. I loved this horse and was beginning to love the lady that was pumping both fists in the air as we approached. Until that moment, I didn't realize how much I had missed having someone like her on my sidelines. I had my brothers who would cheer from the crowd when they were at the same rodeo. Most importantly, my father would be standing where Camille was now, grinning at me, as she was now. The wheelchair stopped that and I missed him but I was pleased with this new friend.

Camille jogged back to the arena to watch the bull riding and get settled for the concert afterward.

I took my time taking care of Gaston for the night and making sure he had everything he needed then feeding the other horses. With a final loving pat down his neck, I closed the door of the stalls while I searched for my Huckleberry. There was no doubt he was going to be there, I just had to find him.

It was the green can of Jose Cuervo margarita that led me to the end stall. I picked it up and looked around. There was a red margarita can at the back of the closest trailer. I followed the trail of margaritas and had five cans cradled in my arms when I finally saw him at the feed door at the back of my own trailer. The door was open and he was stepping inside by the time I reached him. I attacked the second the door was closed.

"So damn glad you're coming back next week, too," he grinned as he pulled his pants back on.

"Back at ya," I slid my foot in a boot. "Brodie didn't make it to the finals, but Craig and Logan did."

"I want a whole night with you. We have to figure that out."

My phone alert chimed.

Text from Dad: You joining us in the stands? Want food?

Text to Dad: YES! No burgers

I tucked in my shirt and picked up my cowboy hat to settle it back on my head.

"I have to go…"

The words were smashed into a kiss one last time before I scurried out the door and jogged toward the arena.

Gaston stood as a statue as I listened to the crowd react to Amberleigh Moore's run. We were down the tunnel and couldn't see the arena. I took a deep breath and slowly released it. In my mind, I replayed the three runs I had already completed to make it to the semi-finals. The top five riders of tonight's bracket would move on to the final round. We didn't need just a good run, we had to have a championship run to make it. The nerves tingled down my back again.

The announcer called my name, and I nudged Gaston forward. His whole body rose in anticipation with ears pointed forward as he looked for the barrels. These big rodeos with loud crowds really fed his energy and he began prancing. He was ready and he knew his job. After another deep breath and the knowledge I had done this run thousands of times before and succeeded, I was ready and I knew my job, too. Working as a team, we sprinted into the arena with the first barrel in our sights. Three fast turns later, we were flying down the arena to the timer.

The crowd roared and my head twirled to read the clock as the announcer called out the 14.07 time. My hand immediately stroked up and down Gaston's arched neck as he pranced to celebrate our second-place run. We qualified for the finals and my heart pounded in pride for my horse. Damn, I missed this feeling this last year.

When I returned to the stall, Camille had already cleaned it and spread fresh bedding. With a hand full of treats for Gaston, she greeted us with a proud grin and a squeal of excitement.

Championship night, I stood next to Gaston just before the gate into the warm-up arena staring at the video on my phone. Everyone in our group but me was in the bleachers watching Craig lower onto his horse in the chute. He was the last of the bareback riders in the finals to go. Frontier Rodeo's Full Baggage was a winning horse and could give him the ride he needed to take over the lead from Orin Larsen, who had already scored a 90.5 and was sitting in first. Craig needed a higher score to earn more money to get his winnings above Orin's total. The man with the highest earnings from the whole tournament-style rodeo would be the champion.

My fingers squeezed the phone as I stared at the video. My whole body tingled in the desire for him to win the whole damn thing.

Craig leaned back with gloved hand wedged into the riggin and the other resting on the top of the gate. His body wiggled slightly to position himself on the horse. With chin tucked to chest, teeth clenched and arm rising in the air, he nodded and the gate swung open.

The first jump out, Craig was tight on the horse's back, spurs high on the horse's neck and body ready for the first lunge from the chute. The second the horse's front hooves hit the ground, Craig was pulling his boots back to the riggin. Down and back his boots and spurs moved along the shoulder as the horse's powerful kicks took them in a straight line until the last few seconds when he turned to the left but Craig looked strong and in control.

"Ahhh…" I growled at the phone and my feet started dancing as the buzzer went off. "Yes, Craig! Yes!" I shouted and with breath held, I waited for the score.

The 90 point ride was just short of Orin's giving Craig a second-place finish for the finals and for the whole tournament. One damn point and he would have had it!

Dad turned the phone back around and his big grin greeted me, "Damn good ride, proud of that boy."

"Me, too," I exhaled in a mixture of triumph and defeat. "Call me when Logan's up."

I slid the phone back into my pocket and stepped up into the saddle. Just a few laps around the arena and the phone ringing had me trotting to the exit.

Logan was already in the box when I answered.

"He's third in the standings right now," Dad said. "Needs a solid run here."

Fred, Logan's brown horse, jumped from his stance and they swirled in the box three times before he settled down.

"Oh my, I am going to have a heart attack," Lacie Jae was sitting right next to Dad.

Logan nodded, Lacie Jae squealed and Fred shot out of the box with Logan's whole body pushing the horse to move faster. He slid from the side, arms reaching for horns, the steer's front-end bounced high in the air and the hard forehead between the horns hit Logan in the face. Through the momentum, Logan finished the wrap of arms around horns, legs stretching out and putting on the brakes, then leaning back to turn the steer on his back.

I'm not even sure Logan saw the flag go down through the blood that was flowing down into his eyes. He let go of the steer and fell back onto the ground with his arms falling to his sides.

CHAPTER TWENTY-TWO

"Logan!" Lacie Jae cried as the steer trotted away.

"He's alright," Dad said in a soothing voice and the video moved from the medical team running out into the arena to the bleacher and their feet.

"DAD!" My fingers tightened on the phone.

The video wiggled until it showed his face, "Sorry, the medics are out looking at him. Go warm-up and I'll text you what's going on."

"Ok," I whispered in a bit of a pout.

The screen went black and I gripped the phone, but I couldn't get myself to move. I took a deep breath as the image of the blood on his face and his fall back onto the ground flashed in my mind. Damn, that was a lot of blood and flowed so fast.

My phone alert echoed and I quickly looked.

Text from Huckleberry: Your family is making their way to the back, so I thought I'd let you know he is sitting up and looks like he's talking.

I took a deep breath and nodded to the phone as if he could see me.

Looking at the arena, all I wanted to do was run inside.

Text from Huckleberry: He's up now and walking toward the gate on his own.

Text to Huckleberry: Thank you

I turned and stepped up into the saddle. I needed the motion of Gaston's movement to get myself to relax. Instead of going to the warm-up arena, I rode toward the main arena. I wasn't even halfway there when I saw Martin, Camille, and Craig walking toward me.

All three looked like they were expecting me.

"Evan said you would be coming," Camille greeted me.

"He's fine," Martin added. "It split his head just below the hairline and he's going to need stitches."

"And he'll have one hell of a headache and won't be drinking to celebrate coming in third," Craig added.

I looked down at them and took another breath.

Martin looked up and patted my leg, "He'll be fine, just won't be wearing a cowboy hat for a few weeks."

"OK," I nodded and turned to Craig. "I'm so proud of you."

Eyes bright, grin wide, and face flushed he laughed, "One damn point."

"It's a tournament," I said. "And getting second is one hell of an accomplishment."

"Well," he huffed. "Go warm-up and we'll be waiting to watch you kick-ass."

"Alright, I'll see if I can beat you," I turned Gaston to the sound of their laughter.

As I rode back to the warm-up arena, I looked back over my shoulder to see the three of them walking to the arena. We didn't share blood in our veins, but they were family.

My body relaxed and mind cleared.

Gaston and I waited patiently and listened to the crowd yelling as Kathy Grimes raced in the arena. We were a corner away from being able to see her 14.07 run.

I kept myself focused on the ride by replaying our last run. As we made our way into the arena, my eyes laser-focused on that first barrel.

"Let's ride," I exhaled and leaned forward.

Gaston's hooves dug in the dirt, propelling us to that first barrel. Every movement we made together was rehearsed, fine-tuned, and in-sync as we slid around each barrel then the final charge out of the arena and into the aisle.

Through the pounding energy echoing in my ears, I could just make out the announcer yell a 14.02 time. A rush of emotion flooded through me, stomach swirling in pride, heart racing, and grin widening, I leaned down to pat my spectacular horse that just took us to the top of the leaderboard. One more racer entered the arena and as I turned my horse in circles, I listened.

"Stay here," a woman to the side yelled at me. "We'll need you in the arena immediately."

I wanted to answer that we didn't know if I won or not, but by the time the words formed the announcer proved her right.

Within minutes, I was standing at the edge of the arena, boxed trophy buckle in my trembling hands, people standing to the side of me with prizes as pictures were taken. I could hear my family yelling behind me, so I turned. My heart swelled at the pride on their faces. Damn, how I had missed this feeling.

"Good thing you don't have to go to the qualifiers," I grimaced at the 15 stitches across Logan's forehead. I slid on the bench seat of the trailer next to Dad.

Logan huffed through squinted eyes, "Yeah, I got two weeks to heal before The American and Houston."

"That's gonna hurt to wear a hat," Lacie Jae winced. She was sitting on the couch next to him, honest concern in her eyes. She hadn't left his side since he had walked out of the arena the day before.

"Darryl is taking all the horses you don't need this week to his ranch," Dad told me. "You're just taking Gaston and Archer up to Fort Worth?"

I nodded, "That will help me concentrate a bit better."

"We were thinking about flying back to the ranch for a couple of days," Lacie Jae said then turned to me. "When are you going to be at the ranch again?"

"We have branding after we get back from The American then the next weekend I have breakaway in Redmond then the National Circuit Finals in Florida then the next weekend back in Redmond," I answered.

"Busy girl!" Lacie Jae grinned. "Good thing you didn't let a little ol' steer bonk you in the head."

Laughter boomed throughout the trailer.

Welcome to Coffee with Cowboys with me, Lacie Jae.

Greetings everyone! Lacie Jae with Coffee With Cowboys here. I'm a relocated city girl who will be adventuring into the ranching and rodeo world ... the cowboy way of life.

I once thought I had moved from city life in California to ranch life in Oregon, but now I believe I have actually been transported to a Texas girl on the rodeo trail. It's like we've been here forever! Fort Worth, San Angelo, San Antonio, Houston, and now back to Fort Worth then to Arlington for the American rodeo. We did escape to the rodeo in Arizona, where Logan took first place before getting bonked in the head by a steer on the final night in San Antonio. After going to the doctor, it was decided to give his minor concussion time to heal before getting in an airplane, so our planned trip back to Oregon was postponed ... for two more weeks. It's a good thing I like Texas, but I think I'm getting a bit of a twang in my accent, y'all. (giggles)

It's Monday afternoon, and I have been sitting in the bleachers of this arena all freaking day. All the barrel racers and breakaway ropers that qualified to be at the American are here this week trying to earn their way to the Semi-Finals rodeo this coming Thursday through Sunday. The top riders from there will compete the next week at the finals on Saturday and Sunday. There are thousands of horses and riders here.

At this arena, I watched Delaney and Gaston run barrels this morning and take second place and will be going to the semi-finals this weekend. Then they started with the breakaway ropers.

Over FOUR HUNDRED ropers are here and they will run today then tomorrow and the two times will be added together. The forty riders with the lowest combined total get to compete at the semi-finals. Delaney qualified twice and she is number 234 and 301; which means after she ran barrels we had lunch, took a nap, and now she's warming up her blue roan horse, Archer, to get ready to compete.

So, that's where I'm at ... and my sister Camille has been going between helping Delaney to now sitting here next to me, watching all these ropers compete in something she is just learning to do. Her goal is to be here competing next year.

I didn't say that. (Camille)

But it is anyway because it should be. We all need goals in our life and that just seems like it should be yours. (Pause) She just rolled her eyes at me. (giggles)

As for the rest of the family, since he doesn't compete this week, Logan is out at another arena helping with the steer wrestling qualifiers. His dad and Martin are with him. Brodie and Craig were at another rodeo over the weekend and are driving to Texas today. They both compete on Wednesday as part of the qualifiers.

So, basically, we're kind of all over the place right now. I guess that is rodeo life; traveling and never being home. I'm the youngest of the crowd, so we don't have little kids to worry about. That would be so hard if you were a competitor, man or woman, and had to leave them behind at home to rodeo ... which as Delaney keeps reminding me is a job. They practice, train, and work at it to earn money for their families and home. It is a job. There is no difference in going to a football game or basketball game and watching the professionals do their jobs. Rodeo athletes, professionals, are doing the same dang thing ... just at a professional level they aren't getting paid near the amount, don't have much of a down-season, and for most, have an equine partner they have to pay all the bills for and have others in training. So, why do they do it? Because, they love it.

Delaney is two out. (Camille)

I'm going to sign off and watch, then come back and let you know how she did.

And, I'm back. She has a time of 3.55 with run A and a time of 2.22 with run B.

We are now done for the day. We'll be back at it first thing in the morning, because we love it. Now, I'm going to go have coffee with my favorite cowgirls.

Have a great day and I'll check in later in the week.

Lacie Jae was sitting in a lounge chair outside of the trailer watching Camille throw the lariat at the dummy steer as I walked toward them. The horses were tucked safely in their stall for the day.

"Well, we sure as heck know I'm not moving back to California," Lacie Jae was saying. She was moving her wallet from a large bag to a new one she had just purchased that was covered in little steer heads. She turned and looked up at me as I approached. "Great runs today!"

"Thanks," I sat in the lawn chair, stretched my legs out, and sighed back into the chair.

After the second day of competition, Gaston and I qualified for the semi-finals in barrels and Archer qualified us for breakaway. It was a good couple of days but now I could relax for a day or two. I let out another sigh as Camille coiled her lariat.

"You really do get stressed," Camille grinned. "You always look so cool, calm and collected."

"Focus first, stress later," I smirked. "And what's that about moving back to California?"

"I'm not," Lacie Jae shook her head with wide eyes. "I'm perfectly content with Logan and your whole family."

I looked at Camille with rising disappointment.

She just shrugged as she sat across from me, "I haven't really stopped to think about the future. I just know that I'm enjoying myself and I surely do not want to leave Lacie Jae right now."

The sisters smiled at each other, then turned and smiled at me.

"We received a phone call this morning from the lady that is selling our house for us in Redding," Camille continued. "They had the open house last weekend and received five offers."

"Well, that's great," I said honestly. "Did you accept?"

"Yes," they both answered.

"One came in a bit higher than the others with no contingencies, so we accepted that one," Lacie Jae said.

"They already sold their place, so they had cash," Camille continued. "It should go fairly fast."

"Not like we're in a hurry for it," Lacie Jae shrugged. "What are we doing now?"

"Done for the day," I answered. "And nothing until tomorrow night when we're going to watch the roughstock slack."

"Dinner with everyone at the steakhouse tonight," Camille added.

"So…," Lacie Jae looked between us. "Shopping?"

"Yes!" Camille turned to me. "Are you up for it?"

"Maybe after a drink," I grinned.

"I found cans of Jose Cuervo margarita in the feed room and put them in the refrigerator," Camille stood. "Want one?"

"Two, and give me a half-hour to chill, then we'll attack San Antonio," I said.

Saturday morning, I sat in the bleachers to watch the team roping at the second performance of the semi-finals. Lacie Jae had heard of a twelve-year-old boy riding with his uncle and a seventy-nine-year-old man riding with a younger woman and she wanted to watch. I relented because it wasn't fair to her to suffer because I didn't want to watch that younger woman rope.

"His name is Pete," Lacie Jae was saying excitedly then turned to look at me. "Do you know the other lady?"

"Yes, she's a champion roper. Her name is Lauren Conners."

"Is that her grandfather?" Camille asked.

"No, the news report said it was her fiancé's grandfather," Lacie Jae answered.

"What about the twelve-year-old?" I asked.

She chatted for ten minutes about the boy she didn't even know.

"Oh, dang," Lacie Jae sighed. "Pete only got one leg."

"At this point, you have to catch both to move on," I said.

"Well, they seem pretty happy," Camille added. "Still, getting to the semi-finals is a great accomplishment."

"So I've heard," I huffed.

She and Lacie Jae chuckled.

"You and Craig will make it back next year," Lacie Jae sighed. "Besides, it was only three-one-hundredths of a second."

"It could have been an hour and have the same result." I grinned at her reasoning.

She giggled, "I'll mention that in my next podcast."

"And how are you going to describe the breakaway?" Camille asked with a smirk.

"All about that luck-of-the-draw," Lacie Jae giggled again. "One stops and the other should be put in the Kentucky Derby for cows."

Camille and I laughed.

"And Craig's 3.5-second dismount as artistic moves that would make any gymnast jealous," she continued.

We laughed so hard people turned and looked at us.

We waited another half-hour before the twelve-year-old backed into the box. I watched him with a silent prayer that he was able to catch, but his uncle was the header and missed the steer. They received a loud round of applause.

"I really love how this industry supports each other," Lacie Jae sighed as she stood. "Are you going back home or staying for Logan and Brodie next week?"

I followed the sisters down the bleachers and up to the aisle, "There are a number of jackpots I've entered for barrels and breakaway next week, so we'll be here until the end."

By the time The American rodeo finals began, Memphis had earned three checks. They weren't a lot, just enough to pay for his board and food while we traveled, but they were a beginning.

By the end of the rodeo, Logan and Brodie earned checks, too. Theirs were substantially higher since Logan placed third overall and Brodie was sixth. They easily paid for their own room and board, too.

Welcome to Coffee with Cowboys with me, Lacie Jae.

Greetings everyone! Lacie Jae with Coffee With Cowboys here. I'm a relocated city girl who will be adventuring into the ranching and rodeo world … the cowboy way of life.

Today I have something important to say. Last week I talked about how I took care of the men who were riding in the rodeo or just watching when Martin and Evan are here. Delaney too, but we'll come back to that. I stated how I made sure the men were fed decent, laundered their clothes, and I also clean the trailer while they are getting ready for the rodeo so it's nice when we get back at the end of the night.

You will NOT believe how much crap I took because of that podcast. Well, let me tell you something, I LOVE TAKING CARE OF THEM. It's what I do and what I want to do. None of you women's libbers or feminist activist, male or female, are going to shame or guilt me into doing anything else. If you have a problem with how I DECIDE to conduct my life and take care of the people around me, then just FREAKING MOVE ON!

I love taking care of them. It's not something they expect of me, pay me to do, or force me to do. It's what I WANT to do.

On the flip side of that is my friend and my boyfriend's sister, the beautiful Delaney Rawlins. She is one of the toughest humans I know. She is a part of the "Cowboys" when I say "Coffee with Cowboys". Cowboy doesn't just point a finger to a male that rides a horse. Cowboy is a way of life. It's the way you conduct yourself, your code of honor, the people you surround yourself with, and, most of all, it's who you are inside. It's being tough on yourself and honest with others. It's working hard and playing hard in a world that has no forgiveness. That means even on the coldest winter's night or the hottest summer's day, or having to miss family events, you take care of the animals and the land that makes you who you are.

Delaney is alongside the toughest of the tough. She is as strong on the inside as she is beautiful on the outside. She doesn't like to do laundry or spend much time in a kitchen unless it's to eat something over the sink because she doesn't want to wash a dish. She doesn't expect anyone to take care of her and she'll expect you to take care of yourself. Living with two brothers, a dad, and a surrogate brother and dad, she's been outnumbered 5 to 1 for the last seven years. She holds her own whether working on the ranch, throwing a rope, doctoring a cow, or riding in the rodeo.

Hold no judgment over her because she doesn't want to be in the kitchen, barefoot and pregnant, as the saying goes. Hold no judgment over me because I so look forward to the day that I am in the kitchen, barefoot and pregnant.

Hold no judgment over anyone, but yourself and that judgment should be whether you are doing what YOU want to do in life and not what other people tell you to be or judge you to be, or guilt you into being. Be who you want to be.

So, I'll wrap up this chat by saying I'm not only going to sign off and go have coffee with cowboys, but I'm going to proudly serve it to them too!

Have a great day and a good cup of coffee.

"Girl's got moxie."

"She always has," Camille beamed. "She's got you pegged, too."

I laughed, "She caught me eating mac and cheese out of the pan...over the sink."

"So, guilty as charged?"

"Oh, yeah," I yelled over the mooing of the cows in front of us.

All of us were home for four whole days together. It would be the last time for another couple months. We took the time to work two hundred and twenty-one cows to be separated from their calves so we could brand, dehorn, vaccinate, and castrate.

I was in the ATV side-by-side with Camille driving. Lacie Jae was riding Brutus right next to Logan on his horse. They slowly pushed the cows closer to the corrals.

"I don't think she will ever ride another horse besides him," I pointed to the pair. "She looks so tiny on top of him."

Camille nodded, "I've really been looking forward to today. You guys have talked about branding day so much."

"Lots of work, tiring work, but we've had lots of stories to tell, too."

The flat-bed truck rolled up alongside of us with my grinning father behind the steering wheel and looking down at Camille, "You think you can get that thing moving a little faster?"

Camille laughed, "It's bumpy out here!"

"You're going to bump whether you're going fast or slow," he countered.

"It's just how high we fly off this seat when we hit those bumps," Camille grinned.

"Well, go a bit faster, bump a little higher, and get those gates opened at the north corral," he pointed where she needed to go.

"Yes, Boss!" She yelled and hit the accelerator. The bump we hit nearly made our heads hit the roof but our laughter was lost to the mooing cows and the roar of the engine.

Two hours later, the corrals were full of calves and the pasture full of mooing cows looking for them.

Brodie and I were on horseback to rope the calves and bring them in for branding and shots. Martin, Logan, and Craig were on the ground to castrate, dehorn, and brand them. Dad was at the back of the flatbed on his 4x4 wheelchair filling the heavy-duty repeater syringes for the double shots that Mark was showing Camille how to give the calves.

Lacie Jae had an ear tag applicator in each hand that Dad was keeping filled. She had finally given in and let Logan buy her a pair of dark blue chaps and a straw cowboy hat for the day. With a black jacket and mud boots, she looked like a boy. Luckily, Lacie Jae was the one that pointed it out so we could tease her. Her name became LJ for the day.

Camille was wearing my old dark brown chaps that had a black cross over the thigh on each side and a black shirt under a dark brown work vest, but she wouldn't wear a cowboy hat. Her long hair was in a braid down her back and covered by a Bar-R baseball cap. As the day progressed and mud and manure covered her, she still looked like she could be on the cover of Western Horseman magazine. Dad was taking pictures with a regular digital camera and I had my phone. We took numerous pictures all day long of her and Lacie Jae. Their first branding was going to be thoroughly commemorated in pictures.

The best picture of the day came when the last few calves were roped. The sisters were standing side by side, Lacie Jae, with an applicator in each hand and Camille with the large syringes in each hand. Standing in the middle of the corral, they were splattered with mud and manure but were looking at each other with the biggest grins. They were happy, and they looked like they had been in a branding corral all their lives.

Logan and I grinned at each other as I showed him the picture on my phone.

Dinner around the large table was filled with laughter and stories from both women.

"You going to help us in the morning?" Craig asked them.

"Yes!" They both answered with wide eyes of excitement.

"You even know what we're doing?" Martin smirked.

"No!" They both laughed.

"Working the horses tomorrow," Dad informed them. "They all need spring shots, wormed, manes and tails brushed out, teeth and hooves checked."

"Yes!" The sisters called out again.

We all laughed, especially when, a half-hour later, they had both fallen asleep on the sofa.

The next morning, Dad, Logan, Martin, and Lacie Jae drove to town for supplies while Craig, Brodie, Camille and I rode out to wrangle the horses.

"What's this horse's name?" Camille asked Craig as they brushed the mane and tail of a sorrel horse.

She had asked for all their names and made sure to greet all of them.

"This is Popover," he answered with a smirk. "If you're not careful, you'll pop over his shoulder and land on your ass on the ground."

"He is the horse we trained on when we were younger," Brodie added while giving a bay mare a squirt of wormer.

Camille looked at both of them with brows drawn in confusion, "Trained for what?"

"Bucking horses," Craig answered.

"You train on the horses, too?" she asked in surprise. "Not just your equipment in the barn?"

Brodie shook his head, "That allows us to strengthen, practice technique and style, but we trained on horses because each one will give us something different."

"To have a horse moving under you...not knowing what they are going to do...is better practice than just boards or dummies," Craig said.

"How come I didn't know that? How come I haven't seen you guys practice here?" she asked.

"Because we've been down south running the winter circuit while it was winter up here," Craig chuckled.

Camille looked at the sorrel horse that looked half asleep while they brushed him.

"This is a bucking horse?" she asked warily. "I thought they were all wild."

Craig laughed and pulled out his phone. I grinned because I knew what video he was going to show her.

She leaned over his arm to look at the video and gasped. With wide eyes, she looked at me, "Is that you?"

"Yeah," I laughed.

"You rode a bucking horse?" she gasped.

"Well, I couldn't let them do something without me trying it, too," I smirked.

She watched the video again then looked at Craig with a question in her eyes.

Craig laughed, "You want to try it?"

She took in a deep breath and stared at him pensively.

"You're killer on the practice boards and machine plus the bucking dummy even with Logan trying to buck you off," Brodie nodded. "You can do it."

"Just think of the story you can tell everyone," I encouraged.

"You think I can do it?" Camille whispered to me.

"Of course, you can," I nodded. "You can do any damn thing you want. It's not like Popover is NFR quality, but he'll give you a good taste of what a bucking horse is."

"You just have to believe you can do it," Craig said. "Believe it, then do it."

"Ok," She grinned with nervous yet excited eyes.

"Hell, yeah!" Brodie laughed. "She believes!"

"We believe!" Craig and I called out.

Camille laughed, "What do I need to do?"

"You watch the video again and pay attention to how the horse is bucking and what Delaney is doing...how she is moving," Brodie said. "As Popover bucks, you move your body as if you're on his back."

"We'll get the horse in the chute," Craig added then looked at Popover. "After we wake him up."

I tossed the mane brush into the grooming box and excitedly pulled out my phone.

The second the chute gate opened, Popover's head rose with ears perked. With little encouragement, the horse loaded into the chute. He loved to buck.

Craig and Brodie readied the horse with saddle, halter, and rope while Camille watched the video again. Her body was swaying with the motion the horse was bucking on the video.

"Climb up on the back platform," Craig told her. "Brodie is going to get his horse and be your pick-up man."

"He's your out," I said as she climbed the panel and stood behind the chute. "He'll help you any way he can."

"Have a seat first," Craig told her. When she sat on the rails next to him, she looked at him with wide eyes. "How do you feel?" he asked.

"Nervous," she said quickly.

He grinned and his eyes lit up, making her smile and her shoulders lower.

He nodded slightly and their eyes locked, "Look me in the eye and tell me you believe you can ride a bucking horse."

"I can," she nodded with a deep breath.

"Camille, you can't just say it, you have to believe it," he said earnestly. "You don't get on a bucking horse 'thinking' you can do it. That's how you get hurt."

"You think I can do it," she said. "Delaney and Brodie do, too."

He smiled slightly, "That is because we truly believe you can but YOU have to believe you can."

She looked down at the patient horse.

He continued, "When Delaney races into the arena, she knows she and Gaston can win the race. When she busts out of the box, she truly believes she can catch the calf or steer."

She glanced at me then back to him, "We all believe she can."

"Yeah, we do," he smiled at me then looked back at her. "If you don't believe in yourself, believe you can do whatever it is you're trying to do, then don't even bother. You're going to get hurt or hurt someone else."

She stared at him, clearly thinking over his words.

"You watched the video," he said. "You've been able to hold on and even spur a bit when Logan tries to get you off the dummy."

"Yeah," she nodded with her jaw clenching.

251

"After watching that video, was Popover moving anywhere near what Logan was doing?" He asked.

"No," She smirked and her body relaxed. "He was like an extreme rocking chair in an earthquake."

Craig grinned, "Very extreme, but do you think you can ride that extreme rocking chair?"

"Yes," She returned his grin with determination.

"What was that?" he asked with raised expectant brows and a tilt of the head.

"I BELIEVE!" she yelled.

"WE BELIEVE!" Craig and I yelled.

"Let's get you on that horse," Craig stood.

Camille's face was set in a determined grimace as Craig helped lower her onto the horse's back. There was no doubt; she was not going to back out now.

Brodie rode in on his horse as I anxiously waited on the ground just outside the chute and took lots of pictures.

Craig showed her how to measure the length of the rein and how to hold it with fingers laced through it. The stirrups didn't need to be adjusted since her legs were as long as Brodie's and Craig's.

"He's pretty patient in the chute," Brodie called out. "You can move your body around, practice moving your feet a bit."

"Remember to move just like you do on the dummy," I encouraged. "You're great on it, you can do this."

"We believe!" Craig, Brodie, and I called out.

"Yeah…I can," Camille chuckled with a death grip on the buck rein.

"You believe?" I asked her with a grin.

Her shoulders lowered and her body relaxed, "I believe I can."

"What?" Craig and Brodie hollered.

"I believe!" she hollered and we all laughed.

"She believes!" Craig, Brodie, and I called out.

"Let's do this!" Camille shook her shoulders and leaned back in the saddle.

"Shove your feet hard in the stirrups, toes out to keep your feet in them and brace," Craig said and gripped the flank strap. "Don't worry about spurring; just keep your feet in the stirrups. Remember to lift on the rope to hold yourself down and to balance."

"I'll be out here with you," Brodie said. "When you're done and if you're still in the saddle, just grab the buck rein with both hands and I'll ride in next to you."

I turned on the video on my camera and set it on top of the fence post.

"Nod when you're ready," Brodie told her. "Not a second sooner…take the time you need."

I pulled the gate rope tightly and prepared to unlatch the handle.

A deep breath and her hand holding the rein rose just a bit higher; the freehand was high in the air over her head…she nodded.

I swung open the gate and Popover made his first jump out of the chute and she held on.

With her braid flying in the air, she pulled the rein up to full tension and lowered it as the horse moved his head down. Her feet were down each time the horse's front hooves hit the dirt so she could brace herself for the impact. Popover didn't have a strong "tossing cowboys" type of buck but he still got a little height.

"Go, Camille, go!" I screamed and ran out into the arena.

"You got it!" Craig yelled and jumped into the arena to run out next to me.

Brodie rode to the side as she completed a dozen bucks before her free hand came down to grab the rein. He swooped in next to her and they reached for each other. As if she had done it a thousand times, she slid off the horse and landed on her feet on the ground as Brodie let her go, then she tipped back and landed on her butt in the dirt.

"Yes!" I screamed.

"I did it!" She scrambled off the ground with a laugh and a grin and jumped in the air. "I did it!"

"Damn right!" Brodie yelled from the horse as he trotted toward Popover.

"You believed!" Craig laughed and pumped his fist in the air.

Camille and I ran to each other and high-fived twice!

It was then that we heard the screams and applause from the side of the arena. Dad, Martin, Logan, and Lacie Jae were cheering for her.

"Aahhh!" Camille screamed, and we high fived again.

She ran to the fence and crawled over to hug her very proud sister.

"I was so shocked!" Lacie Jae laughed.

Brodie had caught Popover and was leading the calm horse over to the fence while Craig jogged over.

Camille was up and over the fence again to wrap her arms around Craig then nearly pulled Brodie from the horse to hug him, too.

"I so understand now!" She gushed to them. "I will never call you crazy for getting on a bucking horse again. It was so exciting! Heart pounding fun!"

Laughter rang out.

"Camille!" Dad yelled and we all turned. "Get over here."

Without hesitation, she was crawling back over the fence and grinning at him.

"You have pushed cattle during a snowstorm, bottle-fed and kept alive orphaned calves, learned to rope, given shots during a branding, and now you've ridden a damned bucking horse."

She laughed with utter happiness vibrating out of her.

"So," he continued. "You think you've earned that cowboy hat you've been refusing to wear?"

"YES!" We all yelled, and she leaned down to give him a firm embrace.

"Get your ass in the truck," Dad huffed. "We're going into town."

On the morning of the last day of our four days home as a family, I stood at the fence of the horse corral and watched my horses grazing peacefully. It was a beautiful crisp morning with barely a cloud in the sky. In the distance, a cow was mooing and birds were calling out. It was peaceful.

These days-off in a pasture were good for the horses. It helped reset their brains just like it did for me.

I watched Gaston effortlessly lower himself onto the ground for a good roll. As much as I was loving the prospect of roping all spring and summer, I really missed running him every week. I missed traveling with him. The trip to Texas and success in San Antonio just dusted off the memories of us together.

I heard the 4x4 wheelchair approaching and turned to him.

"What are you thinking about so hard?" Dad handed me a cup of coffee.

"How much I miss traveling with Gaston," I sat on the rail of the tractor so we were eye level.

"Florida is coming up with him soon."

"Yeah, the Circuit rodeo," I took a sip of the coffee and sighed.

"You want to go on the road again?" he asked as if reading my mind.

"I don't know what I want. Two months ago, it was all about roping with some barrels thrown in. Now, I just don't know. Last year...well..."

"Yeah, my accident pretty much stopped that," It was his turn to sigh and look at me thoughtfully.

"I had already decided to just ride for the Circuit and not go for the NFR."

"Is that what you want this year?"

"I don't know. I thought I had it all figured out and even sold Pepper, but that Texas trip just got my blood pumping for the rodeo road again."

"Well, winning does do that to you," he smirked.

I chuckled, "Yeah, it does, but it isn't just that. Being with the family and friends at the rodeo and on the road...well...I miss that."

"Roping will get you around to a few of them with the boys."

My stomach swirled in doubt as my mind jumped from memories of roping and rodeos, I just couldn't decide which I wanted more. "I feel so scattered and uncertain," I finally admitted.

"You're twenty-four, that's how life is at that age."

I just shrugged.

We sat quietly watching the horses until he turned and looked at me.

"It's who was there with you in Texas," he said.

"Yeah...family..."

He shook his head, "No, we were only a part of it. It was your traveling companion that was by your side whether at the trailer, shopping, and most importantly in the lane with you."

As if on cue, the woman walked out of the door of the house and toward us.

"Good morning!" She smiled and took the seat next to me. "Am I interrupting?"

"Not at all," Dad answered. "We were just talking about Delaney's travels this spring and summer."

"Well," Camille huffed with brows coming together. "That's what I came out here to discuss."

"What's that?" Dad said.

I sat quietly and prayed she wasn't moving back to California.

Her eyes darted between us.

"You know Lacie Jae and I sold our house a couple weeks ago," She said and we both nodded. My heart sunk. "Well, the money was deposited into the bank yesterday and it's enough to last a while unless I go on one hell of a spending spree."

They both chuckled, and my stomach soured even more.

She turned to me, "I wanted to know, since I can take my work with me anywhere I go, and I have money to take care of myself, if I…" She hesitated.

My heart rose in anticipation.

"When you go to the jackpots, races, and rodeos…can I go with you?" She asked. "I'll do anything you need. I'll be the groom and trailer cleaner. I know you don't like to cook, so I'll do that, too."

Her eyes were anxious but hopeful.

I glanced at Dad, who had a bit of a smirk as he looked back.

The memory of her jumping up and down in the lane when I rode out of an arena made my heart beat just a little faster.

"Does that help you decide?" Dad asked.

I nodded.

"Decide what?" Camille asked.

"I was trying to decide since we've done so well so far this year, and we're already in the top five, that maybe I should change my mind and get Gaston back to the NFR."

She gasped, "So, not as many jackpots?"

"There will still be roping, because it's what I love to do," I answered. "But I also love running Gaston and between San Antonio and Fort Worth, they just kind of shook up that competitive drive I put on the backburner last year."

"So barrels and roping?" She asked pensively.

"That means weeks on the road," I said calmly even though my heart was pounding in anticipation. "Basically, the whole spring and summer."

"All the way through September, traveling through Florida, California, Wyoming, Texas, Montana, Canada, Idaho…" Dad added with a suppressed smiled.

Her eyes darted between us.

"It's not like these tournament rodeos where we're at one rodeo for a week or more," I warned. "It's more like six rodeos in a week…lots of traveling."

"I'm OK with that…I want to travel more," she nodded.

"It would be helpful to have a cook with me to keep me away from junk food," I smiled.

Her back straightened and eyes widened, "I can go with you?"

"It is long weeks, long nights, stressful if I travel for miles or hours and knock down a barrel or break the barrier," I warned. "I get a bit bitchy."

"Delaney, I want to go on this adventure with you." She was glaring at me, but her lip was twitching.

"Alright, but don't say I didn't warn you," I grinned.

She squealed in delight.

"Alright, you two," Dad grinned. "Let's get in the office and plan out your year."

We stood to follow, but she turned back to look at the horses in the pasture. She was looking at Ember.

"It's a five-horse trailer," I said. "I have four spots filled, which means Ember is coming with us."

She squealed again and laughed.

"You still have training to do, and part of that is getting you into a few competitions," I said. "It starts this weekend and goes to mid-September, Saturday afternoon at Pendleton. You sure you're ready for this?

"Yes! Delaney! This summer is going to be EPIC!" She shrieked.

CHAPTER TWENTY-THREE

Welcome to Coffee with Cowboys with me, Lacie Jae.

Greetings everyone! Lacie Jae with Coffee With Cowboys here. I'm a relocated city girl who will be adventuring into the ranching and rodeo world ... the cowboy way of life.

So, I'm a couple of months into this rodeo life and so far, as you know, I am loving it. There are challenges like rushing to make one rodeo then another then another. Then there is the challenge of eating healthy ... remember that 10 pounds I told you about? Eating healthy and exercising ... yes! It's a challenge ... especially with those cinnamon and sugar doughnut things they call elephant ears. To die for!

Anyway, that's some of the challenges ... then come the rewards.

Last night at the rodeo, they held military night. Now, we went to the Denver Rodeo and Stock Show back in January and I was at their military night, too. Last night's celebration reminded me of that night and I realized I hadn't discussed it here yet.

Well, the pride in the arena last night? In those stands? The looks on people's faces? It was goosebumps all night long!

There was a big dinner for all the rodeo contestants and a large crowd of active military personnel. The room was buzzing with excitement and shared stories. The cowboys hung on every story the military people told, and the military people laughed and enjoyed the stories from the cowboys and their families. Then there was a section reserved for any military person and their family to watch the rodeo for free. It was packed, not a seat empty.

People were coming over to that section and thanking everyone. The whole rodeo gave them a standing ovation before the rodeo started! Military people helped roll out a massive flag in the middle of the arena as two military captains sang the national anthem. It was so beautiful! I don't believe any other industry gives and celebrates the military like the rodeo industry.

I take pride in being part of that community now.

Pride … five little letters that combined means so much. Whether for the military, your kids, your sports team, projects at work, or just anything. Take pride in them and, most importantly yourself. If you're proud of someone, let them know! Every day if you have too!

I was so proud of my sister, Camille, going to college and graduating with honors, and she was proud of me for becoming a manager over the coffee shops when I was only eighteen. But, we didn't convince each other of that and it drove a wedge between us until this last winter. We're closer now and celebrate each other's accomplishments, whether it's this podcast or her learning to ride and rope.

A couple of weeks ago, I came home to Camille sitting on a bucking horse in a chute. I thought she was just seeing what it was like, but to my surprise Craig was there coaching her on how to ride the darn horse. And she did! Just like at a rodeo, the gate swung open, the horse bucked, and my beautiful, adventurous sister rode that horse for more than 8 seconds. It was so shocking, exhilarating, and just plain fun. I'm not sure who was more proud, but I know I was bursting with it and I made sure she knew.

Be proud, whether on the grand scale of the military or the more personal scale of your family and yourself.

I'm proud of Logan every day for the way he loves his family, the way he treats his horses, and the way he'll help everyone that really wants to learn. Right now, he is out in a practice arena with five teenagers wanting to learn how to steer wrestle. They hang on his every word and he is honest, sincere, and lets them all know when he is proud of what they are doing and the energy they have to do it.

Share your pride people. You never know what that will mean to someone.

Now, I'm going to make myself a cup of coffee and go watch the training in the arena. It's today's version of Coffee with Cowboys.

"You got this," I patted Embers' shoulder and looked up at Camille.

The lariat was held to the side at shoulder height and dangled comfortably from her fingers...perfect, practiced position. Her eyes were focused on the rider in the box.

We were in the line of waiting competitors inside the arena.

The metal clang of the chute echoed and the calf darted out with the rider right behind it with rope swinging.

"That's 3.1 seconds," the announcer yelled. "Now, we have Camille Madison on Embers."

"Remember," I walked alongside her as she walked the horse toward the chute. "We are here for practice. You aren't competing against anyone in this arena, but you."

She looked down at me and nodded...shoulders lowering inches.

"Just be better than I was yesterday," she whispered and walked into the box.

I had searched for the perfect spot to video her and gave a young rider ten dollars to use my phone while Camille was warming up Embers. Her mother promised to video it too to make sure we captured Camille's first competitive breakaway run.

I stood on the opposite side of the chute and watched her back the brown horse into the corner. Ember's butt leaned against the metal railing. Camille's eyes focused on the calf in the chute while lifting the rope and swinging it once, her chest rising in a deep breath.

"You got this...just relax," I said soothingly. "We're just practicing in another arena...just another swing."

Another deep breath and she nodded.

My whole body tensed as the chute clanged open. The calf bolted with Camille and Embers following. My breath caught as she chased him halfway down the arena before she threw the rope. It hung over the calf's head then slowly fell to wrap around its neck. Embers came to a halt with Camille's arm flying backward to pull the slack, then her hand let go of the rope. After 6.8 seconds, the rope broke from the saddle horn and flew in the air.

"Yes!" I screamed and bounced with fists pumping in the air.

Camille turned to look back at me as she trotted down the arena to retrieve her rope. Her grin was wide.

"YES!" I screamed again and held a big double thumbs-up to her with tears of happiness threatening to fall.

"Way to go, Delaney!" One of the riders called out.

I turned and looked at her, "It's all her! She just learned how to rope. It's her first jackpot…any competition."

"Then I want to take roping lessons from you," One of the other riders laughed.

I grinned and quickly made my way back along the fence and behind the waiting riders. I very impatiently waited for Camille to return.

I was so proud of her my feet couldn't stay still. After the next roper missed her calf, Camille slow-loped the horse down the side toward me.

I don't think either of our grins could have been wider.

"Way to go!" I called out.

"My heart!" She squealed as our hands slapped in a high five. "So damn exciting and nerve-wracking."

I laughed, "I know the feeling."

"I think I'm a little addicted," She giggled.

"Replay that last run and analyze everything."

"It felt good even if it wasn't fast."

"You're just starting! That was fast!" I gasped. "You have to get the feeling before you get the blazing speed. Replay that in your head…over and over."

She nodded and watched the next rider rope the calf in 4.2 seconds.

"She was a little more left…" Camille started.

"It depends on the calf and horse," I said, and we analyzed the riders one at a time and compared to how she ran.

The second time she walked into the box, my heart was pounding just as hard as the first. She looked cool, calm, serious, analytic…ready. She was so focused; I had no doubt she had forgotten all of the other riders were watching her.

The nod and my body tensed again…for 7.3 seconds, when the rope broke from the saddle horn again, then it jumped in the air as the scream escaped.

We spent the next half hour analyzing her first two runs before she walked into the box for the third and last time of the night.

We were both more relaxed because we couldn't have been prouder of her day already.

"Just relax and feel the rope…watch the calf," I said from the opposite side of the chute.

Her lips rolled, rope bounced in the air, deep breath…she looked confident as she nodded.

It was a fast calf, but Embers was right on his heels with Camille standing in the stirrup twirling the rope…then the throw. My heart caught until the horse slid to a stop and Camille leaned back as the rope broke free from the saddle at 5.7 seconds.

"YES!!!" I screamed and leapt in the air with arms flying.

Laughter rang out around me, but I didn't care as I crawled over the fence and ran for my phone; the lady who videoed it was grinning.

"That was pretty exciting," She handed me the phone. "What's your number and I'll forward the ones I took with my phone."

"Thanks," I gushed as my feet danced.

I made it back to the arena as Camille trotted down the side fence.

She slid off the horse and ran to me for an elated embrace.

The night was filled with laughter, margaritas, and half a dozen new friends outside the trailer.

I woke the second the sun hit my eyes. They opened slowly to see I was still in the lounge chair outside the trailer with Camille curled up in the chair next to me. Four girls were in sleeping-bags on the ground next to what was remaining of our campfire. Three blenders were sitting on the little side table with what was remaining of the margarita ingredients scattered across the top. I could smell their sweet, tangy aroma, and it made my nose crinkle.

Twisting in the chair, I sat up to listen to the sounds of the rodeo grounds coming to life. My phone fell off my lap so I slowly lowered to pick it up. Squinting through the ache behind my eyes, I looked at my last text.

His text: Good night sexy, see you tomorrow night.

I read through the conversation, which wasn't much more than jumbled words and him finally LOL'ing in the text and telling me to go to sleep.

My heart warmed at the thought of seeing him again. I just had to figure out what to do with Camille so I could spend the night with him.

But first, I needed to concentrate on getting ready for the rodeo. I'd sent the text at 2:12, and it was now 7:30. The rodeo started at 1:00, and I was running breakaway and barrels during the performance.

I stood from the lounge chair and no one else moved. I chuckled to myself and stepped into the trailer to change into loose yoga pants and a big t-shirt. The muck-boots were next as I made my way to the horses. They were fed, watered, and stalls clean when I walked back to the trailer. One girl from the sleeping-bags was gone, but everyone else was still sleeping.

I stepped into the trailer to take a shower.

By the time I stepped out, refreshed and ready for the day, Camille was making an omelet.

"How are you feeling?" I grinned at her.

"Spectacularly hung-over and happy," She chuckled. "I'll finish this then go feed."

"Already fed and cleaned this morning," I sat on the sofa and braided my hair.

"Well, aren't you the damned rock star this morning."

"Wow, margarita hang-overs give you a potty-mouth," I teased with a big grin.

She laughed then squinted her eyes, "Don't make me laugh."

I chuckled, "The rodeo should be over by 4:00. We can be on the road by 4:30."

She nodded, "Mark texted this morning and he has the late shift tomorrow so he is flying in to celebrate my roping last night."

I secretly cheered.

"He has a room booked so you are on your own tonight," she glanced at me. "You're OK with that?"

"Why wouldn't I be? I love it when you and Mark can get together and the fact he wants to celebrate your big accomplishment."

"It's not like I won anything."

"Are you kidding?" I huffed. "You just started roping a couple of months ago...in the middle of winter. You catching all 3 at your first competition is a huge accomplishment."

She turned with a grin, "I am as thrilled with that as I was riding that bucking horse."

"We all are," I slid onto the dining bench as she set the omelet in front of me. "Damn proud of all the work you put in with the horses and roping."

"Thank you, Delaney," she sat across from me. "So, what are you going to do without me?"

"Nothing," I grinned. "I am going to lie on the bed, watch a movie, and do absolutely nothing. It's going to be weeks before we have a chance to do that again."

"After the roping tomorrow, we head toward Wyoming for the week," she nodded. "That will be a busy week."

"The whole family is going to be there at some point."

It was only a three-hour drive to our next destination and it was an upbeat laughter-filled ride after Gaston carried me to first in barrels and Archer and I taking second in breakaway. There was a new All-Around saddle sitting in my tack room.

Mark appeared in a rental car five minutes after we had the horses tucked into their stalls for the night. They disappeared ten minutes later and the back door of my trailer opened within five minutes and my Huckleberry's arms wrapped around me. An hour later, we were lying in bed watching a movie and doing absolutely nothing but cherishing the feel of each other.

I could feel his warmth down my side. I was lying on my stomach, so I rolled over and up on top of him so our backs and butt cheeks were against each other. He had released my hair from the braid the night before so now it was flowing around his head.

"Your hair is in my face," he whispered.

I grinned with a sigh, "You said you liked it when my hair was in your face."

"That's because it means we are together, in-person, not electronically."

I giggled and rolled off of him and onto my back. He rolled on top of me so his back was to my chest. I giggled again and slid my fingernails down his side and up around his waist to his very flat abs. His body shivered then rolled and I rolled with him so his stomach was flat on the bed and my chest was still on his back.

"I don't think that's the right way," he chuckled.

I smiled and sat up with my knees on each side of his hips. I slid my fingers up his back then started giving him a back massage.

"Ah, damn Sweetheart, that feels good," he whispered, and his body relaxed into the mattress.

The sounds of the equestrian park waking reached us; generators were starting and horses being walked down the road.

"Ok, I'll see you in a couple of days."

I turned quickly and looked out the window, "Damn, that's Camille already. She isn't supposed to be here for another hour."

"Shit," he muttered and rolled to the side of the bed and tucked his head and feet under the covers.

Normally, we stuffed his clothes and boots in the cubby hole at the foot of the bed just in case I had unexpected visitors. It was still dark in the trailer, and I couldn't see where his clothes were.

"Damn," I whispered and lay back on the bed, pulled the covers over me, and stared at the ceiling.

I could hear the key in the door then the snap of metal as the door opened. There was a step in, then another which was followed by a faint thud and gasp.

"What...? Whose boots...?"

There was silence a moment as we both lay still wondering what she was going to do.

"I think I should go get a cup of coffee first," she whispered.

There was the sound of her foot hitting the step of the trailer then the door closing firmly.

I rolled to the side and moved the curtains just enough I could see her walking toward the food truck that was serving coffee.

"Clear," I whispered and threw the blankets to the side.

We both scrambled off the bed in the midst of chuckling and he dressed quickly while I watched for her. She was in the light of the vendor truck, so I could see her turn a couple of times and look at the trailer.

"I'll see you at the jackpot this afternoon. I'm looking forward to seeing Memphis run." He whispered and stepped through the bathroom to the feed storage and back door. I gave him a very firm good morning kiss before he opened the door and slid out.

Camille was reaching for her coffee from the vendor when I glanced out the window, so I quickly checked for any other evidence of him being there then stepped into the bathroom.

I was in the shower when I felt the trailer tilt slightly when she stepped in.

I dressed in a t-shirt and running shorts before stepping out of the bathroom. She was at the stove and glanced over her shoulder with a slight smile then returned to stirring the eggs in the pan.

"The jackpot doesn't start until noon," I said nonchalantly. "Want to join me for a jog?"

She hesitated a moment then nodded, "Sure, why not?"

"I'll go feed the horses while you get ready," I said and stepped out of the trailer with a smile.

"Memphis' first competition!" she called out. "I'm pretty excited."

"Me, too!"

At six-years-old and having competed at cutting shows, Memphis had a mature attitude. Although his head was up and watching the activity in the arena, he responded to each of my requests without hesitation.

It had only been a couple of months since the weather had changed so we could get practice runs completed in the arena. He was also put on the back seat of training while I competed with the other horses. The jackpots were good to start since we roped at least three instead of just once like the rodeos.

We backed into the box, and he remained still and broke out the second I needed him to. It was a great run even if I waited too long to throw, and we placed 4th. The next go, he nearly ran over a slower calf, but I managed to get the catch. The third and final go was smooth for a 2.2 second time. It was a 2nd place for the round and took us to 4th overall. I knew, in my heart, this horse was a treasure. I was so lucky to find him and my belief in him grew.

As we trotted down the arena, I looked for Camille. She had the camera up and pointed our way so I gave her a grin and wave.

When I retrieved my phone from her, there were four missed messages from my Huckleberry.

Text: You look sexy on that horse.

Text: You look sexy on any horse.

Text: You don't need a horse to look sexy.

Text. You just SEXY

I started giggling and very casually looked at the crowd around the arena. Just as quickly as I caught his eye and grinned, I looked away.

CHAPTER TWENTY-FOUR

"Logan's truck is here, so they are back from the airport," I pointed to show Camille.

We had the horses exercised, stalled, and fed before walking back to the trailer.

"That's a long flight from Portland. I hope Evan handled it well," she said.

When we stepped into the trailer, there was a bright yellow gift bag with blue tissue paper sticking out the top sitting on the table.

"What's that?" Camille asked as I lifted the card on the side.

"Don't know, but it has your name on the card."

She reached for the package as the door opened behind us. I was pleased to see Martin's grinning face.

"Did she open it yet?" His eyes were full of excitement as he stepped into the trailer.

"No," Camille answered. "What is it?"

Martin chuckled, "Open it and find out. I had it made yesterday."

She smiled at him and lifted the tissue paper out of the package then dipped her hand in to pull out a shirt. It was a yellow t-shirt with large blue numbers across the front.

"Three hundred and forty-three?" Camille looked at him in clear confusion.

I knew exactly what it meant and couldn't have been prouder of him at that moment.

Martin laughed, "No, it's 3, 4, 3."

Camille's head slowly moved side to side, "I don't get it."

He grinned. "You had your first jackpot yesterday, and you caught all three."

"You were *three* catches *for three* tries," I explained.

Camille gasped as she looked down at the numbers on the shirt. After a moment, tears welled in her eyes as she took in shaking breaths. She slowly turned to him.

"You...you had this made? For...for me?" she stuttered as the first tear fell.

The excitement in his eyes quickly turned to concern, "Yes...don't you like it?"

She slowly lowered to sit on the sofa.

"Since Lacie...mother Lacie passed away, no one has ever done anything like this for me...thought of me enough to...to have something made specifically for me. It means so much..."

My heartstrings were pulled again and my own tears rose. They fell when Martin sat next to her and opened his arms. Camille melted into him as her tears increased to little sobs.

I turned to walk out of the trailer. To try and get my emotions in control, I walked down the dirt road toward the stalls then walked back.

After fifteen minutes, the door opened and Martin stepped down the stairs.

"She's trying on the shirt," he smiled.

Our eyes connected in emotional understanding.

The door burst open with Camille grinning broadly. The yellow shirt looked phenomenal on her, and the blue 343 was blazoned across her chest. She looked like she was ready to explode with happiness.

Welcome to Coffee with Cowboys with me, Lacie Jae.

Greetings everyone! Lacie Jae with Coffee With Cowboys here. I'm a relocated city girl who will be adventuring into the ranching and rodeo world...the cowboy way of life.

We're home on the ranch today. Logan and Evan have left to help some friends for the day, and I'm sitting out on the fence, leaning my back on the large corner post of the cattle chute and

I'm drinking a cup of coffee in peace. The sky is a bright blue with just a few small clouds in the distance. The air is brisk, but it's promising to turn out to be a beautiful day in the 80's.

The pasture in front of me is a bright green with thick grass and some pretty happy dark brown cows grazing on it or sleeping in the sun.

The horses are to my right in a pasture behind the barn and a few are lying flat out and sleeping as the morning sun shines on their shiny hides.

Birds calling out in the distance is the only sound besides an occasional moo from a mother looking for her calf. (a deep sigh)

So, darn peaceful.

Hmmm, I'm not alone. Delaney just walked out of the house. Dark blonde hair piled on top of her head, a bright blue tank top with San Antonio written across the front, loose black yoga pants that look like they are ready to fall off her hips are tucked into the top of styling mud-boots. All that and she is still beautiful. (giggle)

Delaney and Camille drove in this morning around 2:30, then it took them a while to get the horses unloaded and taken care of for the night. It's barely 7:00. I'm shocked she is awake and outside. This road stuff can be exhausting and I'm just talking about the driving part.

This is their first time home since the somewhat successful trip to the National Circuit Finals in Florida in March. Delaney was second in barrels, Logan second in steer wrestling, while Craig was fourth in bareback. Brodie didn't qualify, so he was in Texas and Oklahoma with friends hitting other rodeos. They can't take a weekend off when there is money out there to be won. (giggle)

So what does a champion cowgirl do on her first day home in 6 weeks? Well, she stepped into the camper part of her living-quarters horse trailer a minute ago and she's already walking out dragging two large duffle bags. Which I know are dirty laundry bags. No doubt, they are full of rodeo shirts that have to be washed, dried, ironed, and hung up. Plus, the woman has dozens of jeans.

Well, I'm going to sign off and go make her some coffee ... oh, wait, here she comes out of the house. Now what the heck? Why isn't the woman sleeping?!

She's opening the tack room door of the horse trailer ... you know, I should just tell her I'm here and go help but (giggle) I'm curious what she does. As a reminder, I am sitting on the fence, leaning against the old wood cattle ramp so she probably has no idea I'm out here. She would have waved if she did.

Back to what she is doing ... oh, she has unloaded three saddles. Those are the saddles she won in the six weeks she was gone. The one that she won team roping in Arizona was shipped up here already with a friend of Evan's that was coming this way. In this rodeo and jackpot world, it's like you meet a person one time and they are family. They can be as close as a brother or sister or there are the ones that you just 'acknowledge' you know ... you know ... like family. (giggle)

She has carried two of the saddles into the house and is returning for the third ... but first something from the tack room. Oh! Statues and champion spurs mounted on a plaque. I tell you, the woman was focused the last two months and it shows. Being focused is one thing, but truly believing you can win is another. Right now, she and the whole family are believers.

Truly believe in yourself, and you too, can be dragging a new championship saddle or three into your house. (giggle)

And she's back outside and walks to the garden shed. Hmmm ... a long wand brush thing and, seriously folks, she is now dragging a hose and the long brush to the horse trailer.

Oh, here comes Camille in shorts and a t-shirt. I kind of figured she was still sleeping (giggle), but no, she made coffee and is walking a cup out to Delaney. I'm proud to see they are my podcast cups.

273

Her long dark hair is pulled into a braid in the back and she's rocking the mud boots, too. Without a word, she handed a cup to Delaney and took the brush from her. While Delaney sips her coffee in one hand, she is spraying the trailer with the hose. Camille is brushing right behind her.

I'm tired just watching them. So, while they are washing down the horse trailer, I'm going to sign off. I may be back...

...and here I am an hour later. They have finished the outside of the trailer and cleaned the inside. Camille has disappeared back in the house, and Delaney has disappeared into the barn. I'm not sure what... oh, wait, here she comes. She went in for Gaston, her barrel horse. The pair just rocked nearly every rodeo they competed in. Lots of firsts and seconds, which included those spurs mounted on the board she took in the house.

She tied the red roan gelding up at the hitching post and disappeared into the barn again... and... she just came out again with Archer, her breakaway horse. Last weekend the pair came in second at the jackpot and qualified for the American rodeo! We're heading to Texas again next February. I can't wait, it was so much fun. (Giggle) I loved Fort Worth and the Stockyards then going over to the excitement of the AT&T stadium. Being the world champion, Logan will be going on an exemption so he can't try for the million dollars... just the hundred thousand. But Brodie and Craig will be trying to qualify this year too.

Just a sec... (long pause)

There are times I have heard people say things how the cowboys just use their horses for nothing more than winning... that they don't really care about the animal. Well, I just had to take a picture of Delaney. She has no idea I am out here watching her... more like stalking her (laughs softly). All the time I have been talking, since she brought Archer out, Delaney has been petting, massaging, kissing, leaning her forehead on theirs and smiling like she is in heaven.

Now, like I said, she has no idea I'm out here. There is no one else here but Camille and she's in the house.

This is the moment when people say you can tell the true character of someone by what they do when no one is looking. Well, she is still loving on those two horses and they are fighting for her attention. This woman loves these two horses and it's returned.

With a final hand down their noses, she walked back into the barn.

The pair she just loved on helped her win those three saddles she took in the house a little while ago. They are all-around horses and all-around teams.

And here she is with the big white... I mean a grey horse called Ketchum. That horse is so sweet. She stopped just inside the barn where the other two horses can't see her and she is loving on Ketchum now. Kisses on the nose, playing with his ears, rubbing his neck and back then laying her forehead on his. The horse is just standing there taking it all in and the pair at the hitching post are staring at the door, no doubt they can hear her.

She finally moved the horse to the hitching post next to the others then walked into the trailer. They really are a beautiful trio of horses; blue and red roan and a white... oh! She has a red, white, and blue horse! Even if the white is technically grey... how funny is that? She's come out of the camper with a camera in her hand and she's taking a picture of the three horses as they look at her.

I just love her. (Sigh)

She has such a good heart and wants to help those around her... like helping Camille learn how to breakaway rope. If you haven't seen the videos of her cheering for my sister, please go onto the podcast website and check them out. You would think that Delaney had just won the world championship!

She went back in the barn...

And here is Memphis! He's been traveling and learning at a few smaller jackpots. He's done pretty well so far. She tied him up on the hitching post on the other side of the door and went back in ... so who this time? (pause) Oh, it's Madi, Memphis' sister. They are both buckskin paint horses. Real cool looking. Well ... there she goes in again.

I wonder what she is doing? The two younger horses are looking over at the three older horses. I wonder what they are thinking? That they have big shoes to fill? I know Memphis is Archer's backup in breakaway, but Delaney isn't sure yet with Madi. She wants to work with her a while then decide if she will be a barrel or rope horse.

Seeing these five horses makes me think of Logan and his horses. Fred is his main steer wrestling horse while Bubba is his hazing horse. If you ride horses in the rodeo, you don't just have the horse people see in the arena; there are always more in the background as backups or in training as a replacement. So, that's more feeding, training, vet care, and farrier work. It's costly and time-consuming.

Whoop! There she is ... and we have Embers. That's the sweet brown horse that my sister Camille is riding and learning to do breakaway. She really improved while they were gone.

So, Delaney has her main three horses to the right of the door, Embers and two young horses on the left of the door and I have no idea why. Oh, she's bending over and ... dang, this woman. She's working on their hooves. Six horses!

She stood and turned ... oh ... (giggles), speaking of farrier cost ... here comes the farrier truck on his way down the driveway. So ... now we know. I'm going to sign off for a bit while they work the horses.

OK, we're three hours later and I'm sitting on the lounge chair in front of the house and they still have no idea I'm here. I'm sure they think I'm with Logan and Evan. While the farrier worked, Delaney and Camille cleaned and oiled five riding saddles and all the tack that goes with them. They just put all the tack back in the trailer and the noise you hear is the tractor Delaney is driving. She's at the stack of hay that is designated for travel. Logan said it was certified weed-free hay so they don't take weed seeds to other states. It's required in lots of places.

Anyway, Camille has loaded the front of the tractor with bales of hay and now Delaney is moving over to the horse trailer. Camille is climbing up to the roof to unload the hay into the carrier.

Wow... there really is a lot of work that goes behind that run in the arena. I can't imagine how tired these two are but here they are getting ready for the next run. I'm not even sure they slept for longer than three hours.

Hay is stacked and Camille is tying it down while Delaney moved the tractor into the barn. And she returns with the front of the tractor piled with a couple bags of grain then stops to put a couple more bales of hay next to the grain. I know that will all be going into the feed room of the horse trailer.

It's a good thing these two get along so well. Just like me and Logan ... and Brodie and Craig. It would be awful and so stressful to travel with someone that you didn't mesh with.

Your traveling partner is almost closer than your spouse or girl or boyfriend.

Back to a day with Delaney. The trailer has been scrubbed and looks new. The animal feed has been loaded and she is parking the tractor. All six horses are still tied to the hitching posts and the pair walked back into the barn pushing wheelbarrows and hay rakes. They are cleaning stalls now. Goodness... I'm tired. (Giggles)

I signed off and we're an hour later with the pair done in the barn and they disappeared into the trailer. Not sure if they are napping yet, but the horses are still tied to the hitching posts.

No naps! They just walked out of the trailer after changing from the yoga pants and mud boots to jeans and cowboy boots.

The three older horses are being led to the back pasture. Looks like they get to go run and graze in the green grass. Now they are saddling Embers and Memphis. Goodness, I'm just tired watching these two. I'm beginning to think the only time they really have off is when they are on the road between rodeos and have nothing to do but wait.

... and they are off into the arena with Camille riding Embers and Delaney riding Memphis and leading Madi. I'm going to sign off while they practice but I'll take a couple of pictures and load them onto the website.

And we're back again. I was getting ready to start up again since they put the younger horses out to the pasture with the older ones but then they left in the truck. Practice was about two hours and they left two hours ago and they just pulled down the driveway and backed up to the trailer. I can say the truck exterior was washed while they were gone and now they are unloading bags of groceries into the trailer.

During their practice earlier, Camille was roping with the dummies, and Delaney was working Memphis in the box. He doesn't like the barrier rope he has to run through. Well, he didn't. By the time they were done it didn't bother him at all and he has a tremendous breakout. Delaney was pretty happy with it.

She rode Madi too but it was more just riding in circles and walking in and out of the box. Then she trotted her around barrels and poles.

Remember those competition dress shirts I was talking about? Well, the pair are inside the house ironing them and already have a dozen on hangers. Music is playing, and they are singing and laughing.

It's now 4:30 in the afternoon. They went to bed around three this morning, outside at seven, and currently still going. If I had time, I'd make a pool for everyone to bet on when they will crash.

I hear a truck (long pause). I had to sneak around the corner to see who was here and it is Camille's boyfriend, Mark. He started to get out of the truck but stopped when Camille ran out the door toward him. She has her purse and a large overnight bag so I'm guessing she won't be back tonight. (giggle)

After a couple of long kisses ... seriously, now I really feel like a creeper after watching that. (giggles). The pair are driving down the driveway and Delaney is walking out the door of the house.

So, she thinks she is totally alone on this ranch ... what is she going to do? As she walks to the barn, she is texting on her phone ... must be something good because she's giggling with a big smile.

She's disappeared into the barn, so I think it's time to go talk to her. If you've heard this podcast today, then you know she approved me sharing her day, if not ... YOU'LL NEVER KNOW! (laughter)

CHAPTER TWENTY-FIVE

His lips barely touched my skin as he moved down my jawline to the curve of my neck.

"If I remember right," he whispered and his breath caressed my skin, causing goosebumps all over my body. "You and I were texting right after Camille left your ranch."

The guilty giggle bubbled out of me as I tilted my head back into the pillow.

"Yes, you were texting me what you had planned for tonight...what we just did and are about to do again."

He twisted his head and lightly bit my jaw, "You giggled then and you giggle now."

I giggled again as my fingers tickled down his bare back until they came to a halt at the sheet that barely covered his firm butt.

I turned to whisper in his ear, "Giggling is how complete happiness escapes me."

He rose just enough we could look into each other's eyes. We grinned at each other and both giggled before our lips brushed together.

"Now," I exhaled. "It's time to show me the rest."

His fingers tangled into my hair to tip my head back, then his lips took mine in a deep passionate kiss.

"Where has the time gone?" I turned onto the Highway 80 exit away from the Laramie rodeo grounds.

"May and June were just a flash, a really fun flash. Traveling to five towns in six days for rodeos this last week just makes them fly even faster," Camille sighed back into the seat of the truck. "But, I'm going to miss Wyoming and Colorado,"

"Spectacular here," I agreed but my mind was reliving the full week of nights sleeping next to my Huckleberry. That's what I was going to miss. "I'm sure it helped with Mark there all week."

"Hmmm…" An elbow rest against the door, her temple resting on hand and she just stared out the window. "Yes, it was eye-opening."

"What does that mean?"

"We haven't had this much time together in months and it wasn't exactly…well, we had a lot of time to talk and I don't think our individual goals match a joint future."

I huffed, "That sounds like business mumbo jumbo."

She shrugged with a bit of a distant look, "It's been seven months now and I think he is looking into the future, and I'm looking at now. I want to spend a few years playing and traveling, enjoying life with this new outlook I have. I want rodeos and jackpots and seeing how far I can go with roping."

"He's not seeing that?" I sighed in dread.

"No, he's seeing kids in the next year or two, buying a house and settling down."

"He already has a house."

"Yeah," she exhaled. "So, one of the three is done and next on the line are kids. I'm way down the line on that and not sure I just want to become a housewife or mother in one place. I'm not really seeing that for a long time."

"You told him that?"

"Yes, this morning before he left. The first couple of days we were together here was just having fun watching you and your brothers competing. I loved you winning Casper and yesterday in Laramie but Brodie winning in Sheridan? Well, his reaction was just heart-pumping fun and I just don't want to miss that." She sat up in the seat and turned toward me. "Sitting in the bar yesterday with dozens of friends and watching Logan compete in Calgary; it was just so much fun."

"And even though Craig didn't win, he actually pulled a check-in each rodeo so that will really help in the standings." I nodded. "I am so looking forward to Lacie Jae's next podcast about her adventure up there."

"It was her first time out of the U.S." Camille smiled. "I thought she was going to have a heart attack when he told her they were going."

After a few minutes of silence, she glanced at the clock on the dash.

"We're stopping tonight in Elko on our way to Salinas?"

"Nine hours today, then we'll leave early in the morning from there for another nine hours to Salinas on Tuesday."

"Giving us Wednesday off..."

"Sort of, I have a couple of hours in the afternoon for practice, then we have the day off. Thursday is slack and we run twice. We're 73rd so middle of the pack on both runs. We have performance Friday night and off Saturday but doing the horse trailer sponsor photo shoot."

"Then you have the short-go finals round on Sunday."

"Then Monday, we have a nine-hour drive home where we meet up with the family and go on the Oregon, Washington, and Montana five day run."

After another few minutes of silence, she sighed, "I'm just not at a point, and don't see it for a couple of years, that I want to miss all this travel and adventure. I was so anchored before and I feel like I was released...well...like I'm flying in a hot air balloon...released out into the world."

I loved the image and thought it fit for her and Lacie Jae.

"And Mark knows that?"

She exhaled and her body slumped into the seat, "He does as of this morning. We're just not in the same place in our lives right now."

"So, how did you leave it?"

"We parted ways saying just that. Now we're taking a week to decide if one of us is willing to give in."

Damn, I would never tell her, it was her own decision to make, but I truly believed she would always regret not continuing on her new journey if she stopped now to raise a family.

Five minutes went by in silence before she turned to me. "I need ice cream." It was said in all seriousness.

I chuckled, "It's only 8:23 in the morning."

"Time is irrelevant in matters of ice cream."

I had to agree, "Google a place to stop."

Camille's head was turning from one direction to another. "So, the rest of the rodeo is over there in the arena while the barrel racing is going on here on the race track?"

"Yeah," I tightened the cinch around Gaston then looked over my shoulder. "During the performances."

"Well, I'm glad the family is in Nampa this week. It would be frustrating trying to watch you all at the same time."

"Running slack this morning allows us to watch them on the live-feeds tonight."

I stepped up into the saddle, "We run in the performance on Friday, then hopefully we can watch one of them Saturday night on the live-feed if they make finals in Nampa."

She looked up at me, "Why did you decide to come to Salinas instead of staying closer to home in Nampa with the family?"

I looked down at her and lied, "I've won the Stampede. I haven't won Salinas. They both have a good payout, but I want the Salinas buckle."

I trotted away.

Gaston was full of energy as I rode him in the warm-up area. He loved to run on race tracks, which fueled his impatience. Knowing that I didn't have to pull him to a stop against panels filled my impatience because I loved to run him on the race track.

Only six riders in a set were allowed at the starting line at a time. We were in the second set, so I walked Gaston along the rail behind the stands.

The sound of the tractors firing to life to groom the barrel pattern brought me out of my haze and I looked around at the other five riders in my set then over to Camille in the bleachers. She had her camera focused on me so I gave her a quick smile.

She lowered the camera and waved then turned away. After months of being together, she knew I liked these few moments alone with Gaston.

The other riders in my set and I walked along the side of the track to the starting line.

"Delaney Rawlins!"

I turned to the voice and saw the mounted outrider waving me over.

"You ready?" He asked.

"Yep," I nodded.

"As soon as they park, I'll let you know when you can go."

The tractors neared, and Gaston began to prance. Left then right…he rose on his back hooves and lowered. This horse was ready to fly and it made my heart beat a bit faster.

The tractors were parked and became quiet. The voice of the announcer faded away.

"When you're ready," the outrider said.

That was all Gaston needed; he rose on his back hooves again and I relaxed the reins…he shot down the arena with laser focus on that first barrel. It was a perfect turn followed by a whipping turn on the second and a deep dig to the third, which he slid around without hesitation.

Head lowered, eyes focused on the back fence, we flew down the track and didn't slow down until we were twenty feet past the laser timer.

I instinctively listened for the time and heard it and Camille yelling. I smiled at both.

I trotted down the track to lower our heart rates and when we returned, she was walking through the gate, hands clapping in the air, and grin happy and full. It might be awfully selfish, but I did not want her to go back home with Mark.

"Your dad was watching on the live-feed and called just before you took off, so we got to yell together," She laughed. "16.07! He is so excited! They all are."

Before I even had a chance to climb down from the horse, she had lowered and began removing his boots. She handed them to me as she took them off and chatted the whole time.

"We have a couple of hours to wait for the second run," I stepped down from the horse when we reached the stall. "Let's get something to eat."

"Where are we shopping after your run?"

I grinned; the woman was a fiend when it came to shopping, "I thought we were headed to the beach?"

"Shopping today and the beach tomorrow!"

An hour later, I was walking Gaston back onto the track.

"Congratulations!" A rider waved as she trotted by.

I sat up in surprise and looked over at Camille. She was tapping on the front of her phone. She paused, then squealed, "You were first in the first round!"

"Good start," I said calmly and stroked Gaston's shoulder. My pulse rate had doubled with a bit of excitement and anxiousness for the next run.

Camille giggled and walked back to the bleachers.

I stood next to the outrider and watched the racer before me trying to calm her horse before the ride.

"Beautiful horse," he looked down at Gaston. "I love a red roan."

"Me, too," I grinned. "Wish he was a mare so I could have an offspring from him."

The racer took off to the first barrel.

"That's the worst thing about geldings," he grinned. "They become a one and only."

"That he is," I slid a hand down Gaston's neck as the rider knocked over the third barrel and raced for home. A woman ran across the dirt to upright the barrel.

Gaston began prancing with a rise of his front hooves again.

"He's raring to go," the outrider chuckled.

I laughed and nudged the horse to the middle of the track.

Once the woman was back along the fence-line the official spoke, "Go when you're ready."

I loosened the reins and we raced to the first barrel with a turn just as smooth as the first time. Nearly a perfect second barrel was turned before heading to the third.

Around the last barrel, I leaned forward to push on his neck to encourage him to give it his all…and he did; 16.12.

I was sure I looked calm on the outside as I patted Gaston's rump then forward to his shoulder but I started grinning when I heard Camille holler. Yeah, I would definitely miss her.

After the last rider had run, we walked to the barn as the leader for the day.

Four horses and riders were ahead of us as we walked through the gate off the track and to the stalls. I looked down at Camille, who was walking alongside us with Gaston's boots swinging in her hands. She was still smiling and nearly dancing as she kept pace.

"Watch out!"

I looked up in time to see the front horse shoot back toward us, with the other two skittering to the side. I barely had time to turn Gaston when the out-of-control horse's shoulder slammed into the front of us.

Having relaxed enough in the saddle, the force of the hit sent me off Gaston's shoulder, and I had to grab at the saddle horn and grip it tightly as I swung off the side.

"Delaney!" Camille screamed.

Gaston screeched.

CHAPTER TWENTY-SIX

The reins and saddle horn ripped from my hands as I fell with a thud to the ground while frantically looking for the out-of-control horse. The sorrel horse with four white socks was running down the track with his rider running after him.

"Delaney!" Camille yelled again.

She had ahold of Gaston's reins, but the horse was rushing backward. Scrambling to my feet, I ran after her.

"Whoa, boy…whoa, boy, whoa…" I called out in a rising panic.

He stopped with head high, nostrils flaring, and his right front hoof held in the air.

"Son-of-a-bitch," I gasped and reached for his reins.

"He's hurt," Camille's hands trembled as she dropped the reins in my hand.

"I'll get the vet!" Someone yelled from behind us.

I ran my hand down the horse's neck and shoulder while trying to access the injury. A long strip of hair was missing down his lower leg, where the horse had stepped on him. A deep scratch ran down his hoof wall.

"It's not bleeding," I whispered and lowered to run a hand down the slim bone.

Gaston pulled it away and took a limping step back.

With reins held in a death grip in my hand, the other hand resting against his shoulder, I lowered my head and closed my eyes. Panic was beginning to take over, and I needed to get into control.

"Delaney," Camille whispered. "Are you alright?"

My stomach was sick, as if I had the flu and needed to vomit. Three deep breaths to regain that control, my heart rate decreased and skin stopped tingling. The queasiness remained but not as overwhelming.

"Yeah," I exhaled and opened my eyes.

We both caressed the horse and tried to get him to calm down, but the people scampering around us added to the energy.

"It's OK, boy," I whispered until his body began to relax.

I handed Camille the reins and lowered to look at the leg again.

An inch wide strip of hairless skin ran down the front of his cannon bone. I gently ran a hand down, but he still pulled it away from me.

"Here's the vet," Camille huffed.

I stood back and watched the veterinarian examine the leg. We walked the horse down the dirt road then back. The limp was evident, making my stomach swirl again.

"He's going to be sore but it's not broken," The veterinarian concluded. She turned and looked at me. "Do you have another horse to run?"

It felt like a punch to the gut, and the air exhaled out of me.

"No," I whispered.

"It's your call," the veterinarian said. "But, my suggestion is to give him a couple of days off. Do you have a poultice? That could help."

I nodded, "I do. I'll get it on him when we get to his stall. Thank you."

I slowly walked to his stall with Camille at our side. Without a word, we finished stripping the gear from him and filling his food and water buckets.

I covered his leg with the poultice and wrapped it carefully then sat on the ground at the back of the stall to lean against the wall. Camille was at my side.

"The first year I ran for the NFR, it was just Gaston and me so I had to give him a few rodeos off to rest. We missed making it to the finals by $1639," I sighed. "I found Pepper that winter and I was able to balance the rodeos, so Gaston didn't have to work so hard. The three of us made two Finals together before last year when I decided not to run again." I pulled my knees up and rested my arms across them as we watched the horse eat.

"You concentrated on roping," Camille nodded. "That's why you bought Memphis as Archer's back up…so one wouldn't have to do all the work."

"No win or dollar amount is worth over-working your horse and, in this case, taking the chance of hurting him more."

"So, you're pulling out of the rodeo?" her voice shook with emotion.

"I'm not riding Gaston for a couple of days."

"And if you had Pepper, you wouldn't have to."

"Yep," I sighed again. "By not riding Friday night, it takes us completely out of the chances of making it to the finals on Sunday."

"Is there a way of renting a horse? I mean, like Pepper."

I shrugged, "It would be leasing, but Pepper and Sammi are in Nampa this week competing there."

We sat quietly again until Camille turned to me.

"A fucking roller coaster," she sighed. "Just like Brodie said in that interview. Your best ride in the afternoon, then you get bucked off at night."

"Life on the rodeo road."

I pulled out my phone and hit his speed dial.

"Congratulations, Daughter," Dad answered with a happy lilt in his voice.

"Thanks, Dad," He brought tears to my eyes.

"What's wrong?" He asked.

I told him about the accident as I fought back the tears.

"Well, son-of-a-bitch," He whispered then in a muffled voice repeated the story to whoever he was with him. "What?"

"What?" I huffed.

"No, Delaney, hold on…" He said and his voice was muffled again. "Darlin', you have Embers with you."

"Yeah…"

"She was your mother's barrel horse, Delaney," The energy in his voice made my back straighten. "She may not get you a check, but if she gets a good enough time Friday night, it could get you to the top 12, then Gaston can run on Sunday."

I glanced at Camille, "She's been ridden for months and is in really great shape."

Camille's brows rose.

"Go take her for a run, Darlin'," Dad ordered. "Then call me back and let me know what you think."

"Love you, Dad," I said as I stood and ended the call before I heard a response.

"Who are you...?" Camille followed me out of the stall.

"Embers," I opened the horse's stall door with a spark of hope rising in my heart. "She was Mom's barrel horse as well as breakaway. As you know, she's fast. What she loses around a barrel turn, she can make up in speed on the way home."

A half-hour later, I was loping laps around the practice arena on the bay horse with Camille standing anxiously by the fence.

By the time I was done, I felt confident we would make it around the three barrels the next day without embarrassing ourselves. Just that little bit of light made me feel better.

Two women were standing next to Camille as I walked to the gate.

"Well?" Camille asked.

"We'll give it our best shot; just need to go wide around the barrels," I answered with a quizzical look at the two women.

"She looked like she was dropping a shoulder around the second," The woman on the left said. "I'm Jessie Nordstrom, this is Vera Fulton, we are here investigating how your horse was hurt."

I stepped out of the saddle and Camille instantly reached for the reins.

"A horse ran into us and I didn't have time to react," I answered. "It looks like the horse's hoof ran down the length of the cannon bone. It's bruised and sore but he'll be alright."

"You didn't see what caused the horse to come at you?" Vera asked.

"I was three horses back when he started," I answered.

"Alright, thanks for your help," Jessie began to turn. "Good luck tomorrow."

"Thanks," I smiled. "Who was the rider that lost control?"

"Her name is Tanya Morgan," Vera said and the two women walked away.

"Damn...damn...damn...damn," I muttered and started walking to the stalls.

"Isn't she the one from San Antonio you were irritated at?" Camille asked.

"Yeah, and a couple more times, if I'd have pushed it then this wouldn't have happened."

"But you didn't have any evidence and no one else saw it."

"Well, let's keep an eye on her with our phones handy the next couple days and see what happens."

Camille nodded, "I'm sure we won't be the only ones watching."

The next morning, it was hard walking away from Gaston with Embers right behind me. He whinnied a couple of times, making my heart ache.

"He'll be OK," Camille muttered.

The ache and depression stayed with me through the warm-up and I worked Embers for an hour before I felt confident enough to leave for the day. We spent a couple of hours shopping then made our way to the beach with the ocean in front of us. The waves rolling in helped calm my nerves.

Before the rodeo, Camille took her position on the bleachers as I sat quietly, visualizing the run and trying to focus. There were two sets of 6 riders in each performance of the rodeo. Tanya Morgan was in the first set of riders who made their way to the starting line. Vera and Jessie were along the fence watching her.

I shook my head and tried to think of Embers and visualization...how I had to ride her differently than Gaston.

I heard the tractors come to life and watched them make their way out to the barrels. Camille was on the bleachers looking out to the steer wrestling event.

I was the last of twelve riders to go, which meant the dirt would be deeper around the pattern. I knew Gaston wouldn't have an issue but I was concerned with Embers.

The tractors silenced and we made our way to the starting line.

Embers' ears were up, eyes searching, and body ready to go. That was a good sign. Mom had trained her and they were working well together until she became too sick to ride.

The reality of riding my mother's horse hit me hard. The emotions began to make my lungs tight and tears well. It was a beautiful clear evening with just a slight breeze but sweat formed across my brow and I could feel it trickling down my back. This was the reason we weren't riding in Nampa.

"Delaney Rawlins," the outrider called out.

I rode next to him and he looked down at the bay horse but didn't say anything. He just nodded.

The arena was ready, barrels set, horse prancing, and my heart aching with the loss of my mother. Tears slowly slid from my eyes as I nudged Embers into a run.

The first turn was wide, the second closer, and the last a bit wide but her speed had us flying to the finish line. I had no doubt that most of what she had lost in time going around the barrels was picked up on the final run. We clocked a respectable 17.17; outside the money and we dropped to fifth in the average but qualified for Sunday's short-go.

We ran down the track and away from everyone. Trotting in circles to cool the horse down, I let the tears and sobs escape me. In my mind and in my heart, I could hear my mother talking to me; soothing my troubles like she had thousands of times before. I could almost feel her touch.

Once the tears stopped, the sound of the rodeo invaded my senses and I looked around. Camille was nowhere to be seen; I found her back at the stalls.

I led Embers into her stall with Camille right behind us.

When the horse was stripped of her gear, brushed, loved, and food in front of her, I walked to Gaston. He was standing peacefully eating his hay so I knelt to run a hand down his leg. He didn't flinch, but it was warm to the touch.

"Well, you just hang out in here and have a good day off," I whispered to him.

He turned and nudged his nose to my hip, then went back to eating.

"Are you alright, Delaney?" Camille whispered.

A deep breath, "Yes, I'd say let's go have a drink, but I have the photoshoot in the morning and alcohol makes my face puffy."

"Water," Camille declared. "Water to flush your system and cucumbers to flush the water. You think there is a spa open this late?"

"It's eight o'clock on a Friday night."

"Well, we need to go to the grocery store," Her stride to the truck widened. "We'll have a spa night in the trailer. I know everything we need to get you ready for a photoshoot."

"You refuse to model anything," I grinned. "How would you know?"

"I took a modeling class."

We stepped into the truck.

"Why don't you like to model then?"

"Because I took a modeling class," she chuckled.

"Your skin is so soft," The makeup artist said.

"We had a spa night."

We were sitting under a large canvas tent as she applied the last touch of gloss to my lips. It was still dark since the creative director decided he wanted the sunrise behind us but I didn't mind. I was used to getting up early and loved the idea.

The horse trailer and truck I was modeling next to was parked in front of a remote deserted gas station that must have been built in the 1950's. The photographer and an assistant were setting up the large lights in front of it.

"We're running out of time," I heard the director say on the phone behind me. "How far out is she?" There was a long pause. "Are you kidding? Not only will we miss the sunrise but we will miss the entire morning light. It's the only damned day we can get Delaney for the next couple of months due to her rodeo schedule." Another long pause. "We're not waiting for her, we're shooting Delaney right now by herself and we'll discuss the sponsorship of your daughter when I get back to the office." Another pause. "Delaney raced last night at the Salinas rodeo, yet she has been here for an hour and is already done in wardrobe, makeup, and hair a good 20 minutes before the sunrise."

The makeup artist took off the makeup 'bib' she had placed around my neck to protect the high-collared white shirt I was wearing with my sponsor's logos. I wore white denim jeans with blue stitching decorating the sides that matched the stylish brown boots with blue stitching. A dark blue cowboy hat was ready to be perched perfectly on top of my long hair that was left down but 'fluffed' so it was in its full thick glory down my shoulders and back.

I glanced at the director who was looking out at the truck and trailer. Camille was leaning against the front of it with her denim encased legs crossed at the ankle. Short ankle boots, flat-brimmed cowboy hat, and a red short-sleeved shirt finished her very elegant and casual look. Her long dark hair was braided down the front of her left shoulder. The damn woman always looked like a model no matter what she wore.

I looked at Camille then to the director then back to Camille. My brow rose as my idea formulated.

The director ended the call and walked to me.

"Well, we can't get anyone out here in time to go with the original plan so we're going to focus just on you unless..." he smiled hopefully then glanced out at Camille again. "We've asked her a couple of times and she's said no...you don't think she would now...maybe if you asked her?"

I shrugged and gave him an encouraging smile then walked out to my traveling partner.

"You look hot," Camille grinned. "Love those pants. Do you get to keep them?"

"I can find out where they got them and buy a pair," I smiled with a bit of a devilish intent behind it.

"What?" Her eyes narrowed.

"Here's the thing," I started with a flip of the hand. "The other racer isn't going to get here in time so they wanted to know if you would fill in for her."

"I don't want to model," She huffed.

"Well…that I know…but…if you look at it a different way…"

"Modeling is modeling."

"Yes, we'd be modeling for them and the horse trailer but we would also be modeling for us, too."

"What's that mean?"

"Well, we are having that epic summer you wanted and having professional pictures taken to commemorate it would be fun. But, you have to admit, if we did it ourselves, it would just look damned weird. But, if we were so-called modeling together in a picture for my sponsor, then we'd get our pictures taken for free and no one would be the wiser." I grinned with a full conspiratory gleam in my eyes.

Her eyes narrowed, "You're right."

My grin widened.

"But you have to tell everyone you blackmailed me or something so no one comes asking me to do it again."

I squealed quietly.

"Tell them I get the choice of wardrobe," Camille stood away from the truck.

I laughed, "I don't think they are going to have a problem with that."

We celebrated the successful photoshoot with an ice cream and Kahlua party in the trailer while we watched the finals of the Snake River Stampede. We screamed and cheered when Craig took second in bareback, then when Logan won steer wrestling, and Brodie took home a check with third place. It was a fun and fattening night.

CHAPTER TWENTY-SEVEN

From the moment I stepped onto the saddle, I gauged every step Gaston took. There was no heat in the leg indicating soreness, nor did he move with a limp.

"He looks good," the veterinarian nodded. "Glad the bay mare was able to keep you in the rodeo."

"Me, too," I smiled in relief.

"Good luck," she waved and walked away.

"I love Embers that much more," Camille grinned as we walked toward the warm-up arena.

"Me, too," I whispered. The tears of my mother's loss had been shed, it was now time to celebrate the mare's accomplishment. "She kept us in the average, but Gaston would have to shatter the arena record to win."

"Well, get some money in your standings, then we'll come back next year to try and win it again."

I just nodded but also caught her words of 'come back next year'. Did that mean she had made a decision about Mark? Now wasn't the time to discuss it, we had a nine-hour drive home after the rodeo to talk.

When the warm-up was done and we approached the waiting area, Gaston began to prance again. After his two days of confinement, he was ready.

I caught the grin from the outrider as he watched us approach. We were the 6th to run.

"Good to see him, he looks raring to go, again," he chuckled.

"Oh, he is," I nodded.

Any doubts on Gaston's recovery were quelled when he turned the first barrel. It was faster and tighter than the two before. His third time through on this race track proved to be his fastest at 15.93. We didn't win the rodeo but his performance gave us third place and I couldn't have been prouder of the two horses.

An hour later, I turned onto the highway with horses tucked safely in the trailer, Camille hooking her phone into the speaker system for our music, and relaxed back into the seat for the nine-hour ride home. We had changed into comfy shorts, tank-tops and sandals. Baby carrots, licorice, grapes, bottled water, and our filled "Coffee with Cowboys" cups nestled on the console between us.

"I have two questions before you put the music on," I said to her.

"Mark and what else?"

"Modeling…"

"What do you want the answer to first?"

"Modeling, because we had a lot of fun yesterday."

"I agree, that was fun, but just because you're good at something doesn't mean you like to do it."

"Did you have a bad experience modeling?"

She shook her head and leaned back into the seat. "When I was a sophomore in high school, I had a bunch of boys tease me that I was going to be nothing but a whore in college."

"WHAT?" I gasped.

"Their reasoning was, I was tall, slender, my hair was as long then as it is now, and I always styled it. I also wore just enough makeup to highlight but not to 'yell' I was wearing it."

"I don't understand. You're beautiful so they thought you'd be a whore?"

"They said that when I got to college, I would be beautiful enough that hundreds of guys were going to want me and I could sleep with a different guy every night. That was paraphrasing what they actually said."

I cringed in disgust, "What an awful thing to say."

She chuckled, "They actually thought they were complimenting me."

I gasped again.

"Anyway," she continued. "I went home, washed off all the makeup, found the ugliest, oldest clothes I had and put them on and stuffed all my good clothes in garbage bags. When Lacie...Mother Lacie got home I was standing in front of the bathroom mirror, cutting my hair off."

"Oh! All of it?"

"Just above my shoulders," she nodded. "We were both in tears as I'm hacking away and telling her what the boys said."

"Oh, that's so sad," I moaned.

"Well, she took the scissors away from me then we went on the back porch and she sat me down and held me until I stopped crying. She explained to me that they were just jealous because I wouldn't go out with them so they said mean things to me instead. Girls did the same thing and even adults would say awful things to me just because of the way I looked."

"Because you were better looking than them."

She shrugged, "Beauty truly is in the eye of the beholder. I'm not good looking to everyone. Those that thought I was just said I was, those that didn't think I was had to point out why I wasn't; eyes too close together or too far apart, mouth too wide, chin too narrow, and one said my ear lobes were too short."

I just shook my head in amazement.

She continued, "Being a teenager, or even in my early twenties, every time someone said something like that to me, it just tore me down. I fixated on each thing they said was wrong with me."

"Camille, that's awful," I groaned.

"The sad thing is most of them didn't know what they were doing."

"Sadder is those that did," I sighed.

"That day on the back deck, Mother Lacie told me I would have to be a different person for all the different people who liked or hated me all because of my looks, whether they were old, young, male, or female, jealous or indifferent. When I asked her how I was supposed to do that, she told me that the only person that mattered was me. She explained that I was only with other people for a fleeting time in my life, but I was with myself forever, so I was the person that I needed to please and make happy."

"That is so true."

"She asked if I liked the short hair or the old clothes I had on. I told her it was horrible and I hated it. I started crying again because I was mortified I had cut my hair and I was going to have to live with it for years waiting for it to grow back. Luckily enough, it all happened on a Friday so she took me into a very high-end salon the next day and they weaved in extensions into my hair and no one knew what I had done. Then, she did the opposite of what I did by trying to hide my looks, she took me to a wardrobe stylist who taught me what and how to wear different outfits and how to do my makeup for different occasions."

"What a wonderful woman."

Camille sighed with a slight melancholy smile, "Lacie Jae gets her heart from her mother. She is all heart even after everything she went through…her mom's death, dad's alcoholism, and my basically abandoning her. Now, we're closer than we have ever been. I don't know what I would do without her and if anyone dared hurt her, I'd rip them apart."

"Logan and the rest of us would be there with you but, what does that have to do with why you don't like to model?"

"I do what I want and look how I want for me. It was a hard road, but I learned not to care what other people think of my looks. I did the modeling school right out of high school and didn't really care for all the attention. The clothes they made me wear…well, some of those were just awful and I didn't want to wear them. I had been a bit of a loner in high school. Then I partied too hardy the first two years in college to make up for it. When Mother Lacie passed away, I took a hard look at my life then moved to the other college to do a restart."

"Which led you to Kendra and Eve."

"Yeah, poor naïve, beautiful, mentally screwed up Camille got picked out of the crowd by one manipulative bitch. I was obviously immature and looking for someone to be a friend and like me for who I was and Kendra saw that."

"Well, to be honest, I really didn't like you after Vegas, but after we met at the diner and spent the day together, I like you whether you're beautiful or not."

She chuckled, "You let me be me…all my screw-ups and mental breakdowns and all."

"We all have those moments," I whispered.

"Yes, but other than Mother Lacie, I didn't have anyone that ever listened to me. You did the one thing that most people would never do for someone they didn't like. You told me to talk and when I broke down, you listened, and when I was really falling apart, you literally opened your arms and held me while I came apart and you've been there every minute while I try to put my life together."

We were quiet a moment until I finally smiled, "You are so different now than when we first met."

"That leads to the conversation of how we met in that café…Mark."

"And?"

She sighed, "I truly, honestly, care for Mark, but I'm not willing to give up this life on the road or even settle down right now. So, if I'm not willing to do that for him, then I'm obviously not truly in love with him."

After a few more miles down the road, I whispered, "Now what?"

"I need to talk to him."

"You know," I glanced at her with a smile. "This is how team ropers get themselves in trouble."

"What's that mean?"

"Conversations like this one," I explained. "When you're a team roper and you travel so much with your partner, you're bound to get into deep topics."

"So?"

"Then they end up in trivia competitions where people ask, 'who knows you better, your wife or your partner?'."

"Well," Camille grinned. "I certainly hope they all lie and say it's their wives."

We both chuckled.

"So we have you stinky *'boys'* with us for four days?" Camille playfully wrinkled her nose at Craig and Brodie.

They both chuckled.

"We'll try to keep the farting, bad body odor and breath to ourselves," Brodie grinned.

"Speak for yourself," Craig huffed. "The only thing I will commit to is *TRYING* to watch my language."

"Well, you fucking better," I grinned, making them all laugh.

I slid behind the wheel of my truck with Brodie quickly jumping into the passenger seat up front.

"You suck," Camille slapped the window next to his head then slid on the seat behind him.

Craig sat behind my seat and quickly shoved his knee into the cushion and into my back.

"Jackass," I chuckled and turned the key.

"Stupid boys," Camille teased.

Logan, Lacie Jae, Dad, and Martin were in the trailer just in front of us as I drove away from the ranch to start our rodeo trip to Joseph, Oregon, Cle Elum, Washington, and Libby, Montana.

With the entire family traveling together, it was full of laughter and success. Logan, Craig, Brodie, and I took a check away from each rodeo. I was thrilled that Gaston led us to another victory in Joseph, one of my favorite rodeos. Brodie had won the rodeo, too.

With the run of success over the winter, through the Wyoming trips and over the week, Brodie and Craig, for the first time, were both officially in the top 15 of the world. I was still sitting 5th and Logan was 9th. It was celebrated that evening in one of the downtown bars in Joseph.

We were gathered around a large round table that was full of empty bottles, glasses, dirty plates, and our two winning belt buckles.

A blonde with hair down to her figure-hugging jeans and a tiny white tank-top hugging very full breasts continually turned and looked at Brodie and Craig. Considering Lacie Jae was sitting on one of Logan's knees, the girl's gaze never wandered to him.

"So, do you just flip a coin in these situations?" Camille grinned.

"Whatever do you mean?" Craig feigned innocence, which brought a round of laughter from the table.

"Well, she'd take either one of you at this point," Lacie Jae quipped.

I shrugged with a laugh behind my glass filled with Pendleton whisky, "Craig's got his 'exotic Indian' looks but Brodie has the gold buckle so…"

Dad laughed, "Exotic…that's just too damn funny."

We all laughed again.

"Well, what about you two?" Camille pointed a long finger at Dad and Martin.

"What about us?" Martin huffed.

"When was the last time you two got laid?" Camille asked.

I choked on my Pendleton, Brodie, and Logan spewed beer, and Craig fell back in the chair, hitting the ground with a thud. All that happened as Lacie Jae and Camille burst out in laughter and Martin and Dad leaned back in their chairs, grins wide and heads turning left and right.

"I'm serious?" Camille chuckled. "You're both great looking men, still relatively young, and…"

"Relatively?" Martin huffed.

"Yeah," Camille giggled. "If I were a bit older, I'd be looking at you two like that blonde is looking at Craig and Brodie."

Logan stood without a word, took a giggling Lacie Jae's hand and pulled her out of the bar. Craig, Brodie, and I rose to walk to the bar and order another round of whisky. It was easy to hear the laughter of the three remaining at the table as we downed the shots of Pendleton.

We finished the night in a circle of chairs in front of the trailer. Around two in the morning, I stumbled into the trailer and slowly climbed up on the bed. The last thing I remembered was hearing Camille and Craig's giggles from the lawn chairs before everything went dark.

Somewhere in the night, I heard more giggles, this time inside the trailer then I drifted to sleep again.

My head was pounding from the whisky making my eyes squint as I tried to open them. I slowly lifted my hand that was still clutching the phone. It was 6:50 in the morning and the last text I sent my Huckleberry was at 1:49. Damn, these short nights were killing me. Brodie was going to have to drive the next stretch so I could sleep.

Slowly, I rose from the bed and had to brush my hair out of my face and a few strands out of my very dry mouth. Blah…

I turned to look if Camille was awake and caught my breath.

CHAPTER TWENTY-EIGHT

She was asleep…cuddled into Craig's arms. Granted, they were both still clothed with her under the covers and him lying on top of them. What the hell was she thinking? What the hell was HE thinking?

Brodie, who was on the bed in the far back, rose on an elbow and looked at the pair then to me. He lowered his head to type on his phone.

Text from Brodie: What the hell?

Text to Brodie: No, Shit

I looked at him with wide 'no shit' eyes.

Text from Brodie: Did you know about this?

Text to Brodie: No, did you?

Text from Brodie: I knew he liked her, since branding and riding Popover, he talks about her all the time.

Text to Brodie: Damn alcohol

He looked up at me and nodded, then nudged his head to the door.

I slid off the bed and walked out of the trailer with him.

We were both still dressed in the clothes from the night before, so we slid on our boots and walked to feed the horses.

"She ever say anything to you about him?" Brodie asked.

"Nothing more than usual," I sighed. "Well, I guess, they have talked more since Popover."

"Doesn't mean they haven't been texting."

"True…" I had become pretty covert in hiding my relationship.

We cleaned the stalls and fed the horses in silence.

"I like Mark," Brodie sighed as we slowly made our way back to the trailer.

"They've been trying to decide whether to break it off or not. They have different goals in life right now."

305

"Then make the break before moving on," he grumbled.

"This is a hell of a situation to be in."

"I don't want to lie to Mark if he asks. Damn, why did they have to get us involved?"

I huffed and glanced over to him, "Maybe because we are their best friends."

"Shit…" He sighed.

The door of the trailer opened with a smiling Camille and Craig appearing.

We stopped and waited.

Camille shook her head and looked apologetic, "I could blame it on the alcohol but I truly just needed to be held last night and Craig was willing to oblige with no strings attached."

Craig smirked and looked at me, "If you had a choice between cuddling with Brodie or Camille, which would you choose?"

"Damn man," Brodie groaned. "Don't use cuddling in the same sentence as my name again."

The tension burst and we all chuckled.

Sunday night, as we pulled out of the rodeo grounds in Libby, Montana to go home for three days, I received a text from Logan.

Text from Logan: Did you know tomorrow is Camille's birthday?

What? Brodie was driving with Camille and Craig in the back seat. I turned and looked at her with wide eyes but the two of them were looking at the travel calendar for the next two months.

Text to Logan: I had no idea.

Text from Logan: LJ just told me they hadn't done anything special since her mother died.

Text to Logan: When is LJ's? And we'll be doing something special to make up for it then, I just don't know what, yet.

Text from Logan: LJ's is November. It's late Sunday…nothing is going to be open for shopping.

Text to Logan: Give me a bit to think of something…besides a cake…horse-shaped…with little girl horse toys on it.

Text from Logan: LJ laughed and agreed.

I slid the phone into my pocket and stared out the window as we drove. I thought of all the time we had spent together from meeting at the café, riding and roping lessons through her rejoicing at my win in Joseph.

It wasn't until we were just outside of Hermiston that the idea struck me like a kick from a mule. Damn! She was going to love it.

I pulled out my phone and began sending texts. The more excited I got, the faster I typed and the giggles escaped.

"What are you doing? Who are you texting?" Brodie asked.

I shook my head with a grin, then glanced over my shoulder. Camille was leaning against the door, sleeping and Craig was sleeping against the other door. Turning up the music in the truck, I leaned over and whispered in Brodie's ear. He started nodding and grinning.

Text from Dad: You have a good heart Darlin', we're all in

As tired as I was, the excitement running through me would never let me sleep. It was midnight when we arrived home singing the famous song from the movie Jaws, "Show Me the Way to Go Home" as Brodie drove down the driveway. When we stopped and the doors opened, we still continued singing and the four from the other truck sang with us as the barn lights were turned on and the horses released from the trailers.

As we walked to the house, Martin and Craig walked to their truck.

"Aren't you staying here?" Lacie Jae asked in mock surprise.

"I have a meeting in the morning," Martin said and gave her and Camille a quick hug goodbye.

"And I have a morning to sleep through," Craig added.

As they drove down the road, everyone but Camille knew that they weren't going home. They had a secret destination.

At four o'clock in the morning, as everyone in the house slept, Logan and I were waiting at the end of the driveway next to the road. Martin and Craig returned then drove away ten minutes later.

At nine o'clock in the morning, as the family was gathered around the breakfast table, the father and son returned again. They nonchalantly meandered into the kitchen as if nothing special was about to happen.

"I was too tired and just postponed the meeting until later," Martin greeted the happy sisters.

As the eight of us had breakfast and chatted, we waited for Dad to signal the beginning of the party. He rolled back away from the table and everyone but Camille shifted chairs back. She looked around curiously.

Dad leaned down and we all leaned down, as he rose with a small wrapped package in hand, we all rose with a small wrapped package each and set them on the table in front of us.

"Happy Birthday!" We all yelled.

Camille squealed in surprise with her face turning red. She looked accusingly at her sister who just laughed and handed her a present.

With laughter and near tears, Camille opened the first box. She lifted out a piece of paper.

"What is this?" She giggled.

"It's a treasure hunt!" Craig explained with a laugh. "What's it say?"

Camille read the paper: The War Room

"Go!" Lacie Jae laughed.

Camille was quickly up and ran to Dad's office. She returned with a beautiful turquoise necklace and hugged her sister.

The next box was from Brodie and it sent her to the treadmills. She returned with a new saddle pad for her horse.

From Logan, she was sent to the front porch and brought back new feed buckets. Brodie sent her to the guest bathroom, where she brought back a new halter and lead rope. Craig's box sent her running out to his truck where a grooming box filled with brushes was waiting for her. Martin's box sent her to the washing machine where a long white box was waiting. She carefully set it on the table and opened it to reveal a birthday cake covered in small plastic horses and candles. She cried when she saw it and had to wipe away tears as she hugged him.

"And now," Dad said happily and handed her his box with a wide grin.

She hugged him before taking it and then quickly opened the box and read the note: "Delaney"

She looked curiously to Dad then back to me...so I handed her the last box.

She read the note out loud: "Gaston"

"Really, Delaney," she laughed. "You're giving me Gaston?"

We all laughed as I shook my head.

"Not hardly, but he does have the gift from Dad and I."

We all excitedly walked out to the barn with her leading the way.

As we neared the stall, her breath caught with a hand going to her chest. Tears filled her eyes as she turned to look at us.

"Really? Mine?" she whispered. We all nodded.

Camille reached out and touched the red muzzle.

"You recognize her?" I asked.

Camille nodded as the tears fell, "She was at the Parkston's ranch."

"She was the first yearling you touched when we walked out into the pasture," I smiled so hard my cheeks hurt.

"The first horse I ever touched," Camille cried and ran a hand down the horse's neck.

"That's how you get the equine addiction," Dad said proudly.

I stood in the doorway of the barn and watched Camille lead her new horse around the arena. Craig was walking beside her as they talked and laughed. There was something new between the pair, and I had a gut feeling the Joseph night they spent in each other's arms had been just the beginning for them.

Camille was 25 to Craig's 21 but from his experiences in travel and the way he was raised, he seemed older than her. Age really didn't matter, it was chemistry. As much as Camille had it with Mark at the beginning of their relationship, she had changed. Mark was still the same man but Camille's awakening to the world had changed her. Her chemistry now was quite evident with Craig.

"There is only one other person I've seen him look at, like he looks at her," Brodie said as he stepped next to me.

"That blonde in Denver?"

Brodie chuckled, "Not hardly; just you, sister dear, just you."

"He's my brother."

"I know, and he does, too. He kind of got over the crush with that blonde in Denver, he just likes joking with you."

"And I him," I smiled. "I guess those little 'couples' remarks are over now."

"Oh, yeah. Have you heard even one since she rode Popover?"

I turned and looked at him in surprise, "No and I hadn't realized that."

"Well, Joseph rodeo solidified it for him."

"She said nothing had happened."

"So did he, at that time, but it looks to me that 'something' is going to be happening soon."

"She won't without talking to Mark," I sighed. "And she told me last night she was having lunch with Mark today."

"And there you go," He walked out of the barn and toward the house.

As I followed him to the house, I realized it could be fun having Camille and Craig together as a couple.

The four of us with Logan and Lacie Jae were leaving on a 10-hour drive to Preston and Idaho Falls, Idaho, and after those rodeos, it would be another 10-hour drive to Sandpoint, Idaho then the drive home; which was another 8 hours. No doubt by the end of those we would know.

"Do you miss us already?" I grinned at Dad and Martin on the video chat as I stood at Gaston's side at the Preston rodeo.

They both laughed.

"Let's say it's pretty damn quiet around here without you noise-makers," Martin answered.

"Well, since I've been in a damn truck with the other five noise-makers, I know exactly what you're talking about," I chuckled. "Talk about a bunch of chatterboxes."

"Beats traveling by yourself, now, doesn't it?" Dad huffed.

I nodded in agreement, "Yes, I enjoy the moments with my brothers and new sisters."

"We called because Dillon from Lewiston is on the opposite path as you six," Martin said. "He's going to meet up with you in Idaho Falls Friday night then pass by here on his way to a jackpot."

"Ok...?" I muttered.

"There is an antique frame I'm buying from a friend over there that will be going in the business office I just finished," Martin explained. "I need Craig to go give the money to the seller and give the frame to Dillon to deliver it Friday night on his way by here."

"Simple enough," I nodded.

"Good, you have his number to connect with him, so go get your ass busy and win the damn rodeo," Dad ordered with a grin.

"Yes, sir!" I saluted just before the phone went black.

I didn't quite make it as we all placed second in the rodeo. It made for a slew of second-best jokes as we drove from Preston to Idaho Falls.

We arrived in the middle of the night and happily crawled into the trailer for a good night's sleep. Because of his size, Logan was sleeping on the large bed with Lacie Jae, Brodie and I slept on the converted sofa, while a giggling Camille and Craig cuddled on the converted table.

"Stop giggling," Logan ordered.

"You're not my boss," Camille giggled.

"But I'm big enough to throw you out of this trailer," he threatened.

"I'd just go to the window next to your head and start tapping on it all night long," Camille giggled again.

"Like being haunted," Brodie added.

We all chuckled and it grew quiet in the trailer until the muted whispering began from the back bed.

"Stop it!" Brodie yelled.

Camille and Craig giggled.

"I'm big enough to throw both of you out of the trailer," Logan warned.

"Hmmm," Craig hummed, drawing giggles from Camille and Lacie Jae.

The trailer was quiet again until Logan began to snore.

"You think, between all of us, we can throw him out of the trailer?" Camille whispered.

We all giggled.

Friday night, Idaho Falls War Bonnet rodeo started with Craig pulling a second-place check, Logan drew a first-place check, followed by Brodie's second place. Archer and I had to chase the breakaway calf half-way down the arena before I could get a decent throw. The rope was just inches from going over the calf's nose but slid up and it ended as an illegal catch around the ears. Frustration bubbled from me. I ran a hand down the horse's neck then rump as we exited the arena. Camille was there with Gaston already saddled and ready to take care of Archer for me.

A half-hour later, I sat on Gaston just outside the entry gate determined that I was not going to be the only one going home without a check.

As I waited for the barrels to be set up in the arena, I looked around. I loved the history of the rodeo, the atmosphere of the old buildings and the energy of the crowd.

"Delaney, isn't that the gal that caused the accident in Salinas?" Camille asked from beside us.

I turned to look and saw Tanya Morgan trotting toward the warm-up area on the large sorrel gelding with tall white socks.

"Yeah, that's her," I whispered with a glare. "She's on that same horse, too."

Camille pulled the day-sheet from her pocket and read the list of contestants.

"You're first and she's last," She said and looked back at the rider.

"Keep an eye on her," I said as the truck that had carried the barrels into the arena drove past us.

"First up is Delaney Rawlins…" The announcer's voice boomed.

I turned back to the lane and swore at myself for getting distracted. Holding Gaston tightly, I took my time walking up the lane toward the gate. I visualized the run, the feel of the turn, and heard my brother's teasing jabs if I screwed up. That couldn't happen. My focus was intense as I loosened the reins and aimed for that first barrel. Only 16.95 seconds went by before we were running past the timer.

"What a way to set the pace!" The announcer called out. "That was last year's winning time so let's see if the next rider can beat that. We have Amberleigh Moore..."

His voice faded as I trotted away from the arena. I was searching for Camille but didn't see her as I cooled Gaston in the warm-up arena. She appeared just as I was walking back to the stalls.

"Where are the guys?" I asked.

"Meeting with Dillon to get that frame for Martin."

As we walked by the arena, Tanya rode in for her run.

"Go cowgirl, go!" The announcer called out.

A loud 'ahhh' rang out from the crowd. Camille and I both turned to the arena in time to see Tanya run out on the large sorrel gelding and her face twisted in an angry growl.

The announcer continued; "It was a good run until that 3rd barrel fell, which leaves our first runner of the night taking home the win. Congratulations, Delaney Rawlins."

"Yeah," Camille muttered as we both watched Tanya trotting off between the horse trailers.

"Thanks," I answered but was concentrating on the horse and rider.

At the last moment, Tanya yanked back on the reins and jerked the horse's head to the left.

"Go get an official," I told her and gave her Gaston's reins and pulled out my phone.

I ran down the length of the trailers and nearly ran into Craig.

"Follow me," I ordered. "Get your phone out...video."

We jogged down to the end of the row of trailers and peered around the last one.

"What's going...?" Craig started but stopped.

Tanya was still on the horse's back and pulling his nose to her knee and kicking his sides then a boot to his muzzle. We stepped out from behind the trailer as she yanked the reins the other direction. The horse shook his head and stumbled backward.

"Tanya! Knock it off!" I yelled and jogged toward her with phone video recording.

Her head jerked around and she instantly released the reins. She knew she was guilty and caught red-handed.

"Mind your own fucking business," she growled and jumped off the horse.

"This is mine and everyone else's business."

"I'll train this horse the way I want," she jerked the reins again and my stomach clenched.

"That's not training, that's abusing. You waited until you hid back here, so you know it's wrong," I growled and tried to get between her and the horse.

When I leaned in to take the reins from her, an elbow swung out and hit me on the jaw, causing a flash of anger to swarm over me.

"The rodeo officials are on their way and my camera is recording this," I hissed and rubbed my jaw.

Tanya turned to look back at the arena so I unbuckled the throat latch on the headstall. Knowing the reins were still around the horse's neck so he couldn't run away, I pulled the headstall over his ears and the bit fell out of his gaping mouth.

I turned back to see Camille still pulling Gaston behind her as they jogged toward us. Two men were right next to her.

CHAPTER TWENTY-NINE

It was two o'clock in the morning and we were three hours from Idaho Falls on our way to Sandpoint when the video chat alert echoed into the truck.

"Told you he would call you," Brodie said from the back seat.

Camille was tucked in between him and Craig with Logan driving and Lacie Jae between the two of us on the front seat.

I lifted the phone and accepted the call with a deep breath.

He was sitting in front of the home computer glaring at me.

"Hey, Dad, you're up late," I said in a low flat tone and smiled at him on the screen.

"Delaney," he huffed. "What the hell?"

"What do you mean?" I answered in as innocent a voice as I could. "Didn't Dillon get there?"

His head tipped down and eyes narrowed, "You know damned well he did and just why I'm calling you."

I just smiled.

"Damn it, Daughter," he growled. "Imagine my surprise when Dillon handed Martin the frame then walked to the back of his trailer just to unload another damned horse."

"Why would you think it was my fault?" My hand went to my chest in false shock. "There are six of us in this truck."

His shoulders rose and lowered as he took in a deep breath, "What the hell am I supposed to do with him?"

"Craig is sending you a video on your phone," I relented.

There was silence until his phone alert went off then we heard my voice yelling at Tanya.

316

Once the video concluded, he looked back at the screen with a glare that I knew was not meant for me.

"Put him out in the pasture and let him be a horse until next spring," I said. "Anything, but putting another bit in his mouth."

"How did you end up sending him here?" Dad nodded.

"As the rodeo officials were approaching, I told her I'd erase the video I was recording if she agreed to sell me the horse," I answered. "Once the officials got there, I talked them into letting us get the halter on the horse and as they waited, we went to her truck and she wrote out a bill of sale. Once I showed her that I deleted the video on my phone, she handed me the slip, I gave her a check; done deal."

"You rewarded her for that?" Dad huffed.

"I look at it as paying to get him away from her," I explained. "Then, when we got back out to the officials, they had just finished watching Craig's video of the confrontation."

"And?" He sighed.

"They kicked her off the property, banned her from ever riding there again, and have already sent the video to the WPRA for their review and actions," I answered.

"Good...good...no one should treat an animal like that and no one should stand for it. He's in Gaston's stall tonight, then I'll call and get the vet out here to check for ulcers and his dental work. When he clears, he can go out with the older horses so he can pretend he's retired for the next six months." He sighed then looked thoughtful. "So, you're in the truck headed to Sandpoint and no doubt those other five are wide awake in anticipation of this call."

I grinned and nodded.

"Awfully damn quiet in their defense of you," he continued with a raised brow.

Chuckles erupted in the truck.

"Well, you kids have a safe trip and text me when you get there," he sighed again.

"Good night, Dad," All six of us called out.

I caught a glimpse of his frown turning to a smile just before the screen went black.

Monday morning when I walked into the barn, Camille was leaning against Embers stall door staring at the horse. The rest of the family members were in the house so the barn was quiet.

"How was your ride?"

She turned slowly, "It was wonderful. I missed her so much and going riding by yourself like that is just so mind-clearing."

"It is," I agreed.

She stood away from the door and turned to me, "Mark and I haven't been together for a month."

"Yeah," I muttered in surprise.

"I've always been attracted to Craig but these last couple weeks it's just…"

"…has turned to more."

Her shoulders lowered in relief, "Yes, I know everyone knows but it still seems a bit new and we haven't even been together."

"Since you've spent most of those nights in a trailer with me, I can attest to that and I thank you," I smiled.

She chuckled, "When I was riding, he called and asked about this weekend in Omak…about an official date."

"And?"

Her cheeks reddened, "Lacie Jae and I are going to Redding on Wednesday to go through the storage unit where all our stuff from the house was taken. I don't know how long it will take. You and he will be in Hermiston on Wednesday, then he's helping a friend move to Middleton on Thursday while Logan and Brodie go to Hermiston…then we're all off to Omak on Friday. So, I suggested, since the rest of the week was so full, if he was interested, that maybe we would have a date tonight and just stay in town overnight."

I laughed, "I'm going to guess he took you up on the offer."

Her grin widened and eyes twinkled, "Yes, so he is picking me up in about an hour and we won't be back until tomorrow."

Happiness and excitement radiated from her.

An hour later, we sat on the steps of the porch watching Craig's truck turn from the main road down the driveway. Camille's overnight bag was set on the ground in front of us and her toes were tapping.

"You're not playing hard to get very well," I chuckled.

She laughed, "No games and this cowboy knows the truth."

Craig stopped in front of us with a wide grin appearing through the open window. As soon as Camille stood, he quickly opened the door and rushed to take the bag from her hands.

"A cowboy and a gentleman," She giggled as she leaned in to kiss his cheek. His grin widened.

"See you tomorrow," Camille waved over her should to me as he opened the truck door for her.

I didn't say anything, nor did I wave, because it really didn't matter. From the look on their faces as they looked at each other, they wouldn't have noticed or heard.

It wasn't until he slid back onto the driver's seat and turned to look at me through the open window that I spoke.

"Have fun."

His eyes sparkled, grin widened, and shoulders lowered, "Thanks, my big sister."

My heart nearly burst. With those few words, I knew, just how much Camille meant to him.

Tears welled in my eyes and all I could do was nod my happiness to him.

I watched them as the truck slowly made its way down the driveway.

I ran a hand down Madi's nose before releasing her into the pasture. She was coming along faster than I had predicted. With a nice turn and speed behind her she was shaping up to be a good backup for Gaston in barrels. I could just see, ten years down the line, my traveling with the pair of buckskin paints. They were such a cool looking pair.

As I dropped the halter and lead rope on the hook, the sound of an engine reached me. It was a very familiar one and I turned to see Dad's van making its way down the driveway. He turned toward me and the barn instead of stopping at the house.

"Evening, Daughter," He smiled that happy, relaxed smile as he opened his door.

"Evening, Father," I sighed.

"Seems like it's just you and me tonight."

"Where's Martin?"

"Meeting with clients then headed home for the night to work on a project tomorrow." He rolled out of the van and toward me. "Let's go for a ride."

"Oh, Dad, I would love that," I grinned. "It's been a long time since just the two of us rode."

"Go get Brutus and I'll get the tack."

We made our way into the barn.

I retrieved Gaston for the ride. It would be good for him to have a nice leisurely mountain walk. Then, I retrieved Ketchum instead of Brutus.

"You riding two?" Dad said with a raised brow.

"You know that without a rope around him, Ketchum is as gentle as Brutus."

"Brutus needs exercise just as much as Ketchum."

I smiled and took the saddle pad from him. He didn't put up a fight so I knew he was ready to step up. "Ketchum and Gaston both need a leisurely ride and that's what I need too."

"Yeah, it's been quite the year so far."

I saddled the horses while dad put the bridles on them. Both horses had been trained to lower their heads but they seemed to dip a bit farther down for him. A sense of ease spread through me.

Once mounted, we didn't talk for the first five minutes. We just enjoyed the rhythm of the horses and silence of the ranch. The air was still a bit warm for July, but the sun was hidden behind a large cloud making it bearable.

A hundred roping steers were in the pasture to our right. Some were tucked just into the trees where the fence line stopped them from wandering into the beef cows. We just rode along the edge and checked the fence.

"I'll come out tomorrow and tighten up that stretch," Dad pointed to the loosened barb wire.

"We'll be headed to Omak tomorrow," I reminded him.

"With Martin working, Craig in Middleton, Brodie and Logan in Hermiston..."

"...Camille and Lacie Jae in Redding..."

"It's too darn quiet." We said at the same time then chuckled softly.

"Why don't you come to Omak with us?" I asked, hopefully.

"I'll think about it."

The rest of the ride was peaceful as we just enjoyed each other's company and the horses, cows, and blue skies. When we finally entered into the house, we were greeted by silence.

Dad shook his head, "You three need to work on some grandkids to liven this place up." He grinned as he opened the door to the refrigerator.

"Well, Logan and Lacie Jae are your closest bet on that one," I retrieved two plates from the cupboard then took the bowl of spaghetti he handed me.

"Good thing Camille made this before they left," he gave me a teasing look.

"You're right," I nodded. "That's one way to ruin a perfectly good day of riding."

"By having to cook," he grinned.

He rolled to the kitchen table as I warmed the food in the microwave. He was staring at the coffee center when I set the plates on the table.

"Those two are such opposites...physically," He said. "But mentally, they just fit perfectly."

"They are what the other needed in life."

"Hmmm," Dad nodded and slid his fork into the noodles. "They are a lot like your mother and me."

I had noticed it, too. It was a calm aura about them when they were together. There was enjoyment and fun but that ease, also.

"You handling it alright?" He whispered.

I knew what he meant without him having to explain.

"I miss her every day," I sighed.

Dealing with my mother's loss was the hardest thing I battled.

Dad's phone ringing into the silence made us both jump.

"It's Brodie," Dad said as he lifted the phone to his ear.

"Logan must be up...and it's a video chat," I giggled.

Brodie's voice echoed into the room, "I would have bet a million dollars I was going to see your ear and not your face."

We all three laughed breaking the melancholy that had descended in the room.

Dad lowered the phone and I leaned in to grin at Brodie.

"I'll catch on someday," Dad huffed. "Until then, you can just continue with the ear exams."

I laughed and Brodie's face crinkled in disgust.

"Logan's up," Brodie turned the phone to the chutes.

"He was 3.9 on his first run," Dad said and we leaned over the phone to watch him run a 4.1.

"That's in third now," Brodie turned the phone back around. "I'll give the phone to Logan and he'll do your next ear examine when I'm up."

We laughed as the phone went dark.

"Wish we would have gone," Dad slid the phone back in his pocket.

"Then you're going to Omak with us this weekend," I carried both our plates into the kitchen then followed him to the sofas.

"Yeah, I am," he slowly stood from his chair and made himself comfortable on the sofa.

We had both relaxed to watch a movie when the phone rang again.

I was at his side when he held the phone as close to his eyeball as he could then answered the phone. We were both giggling when Logan appeared then his laughter boomed into the room.

"Ear and eye exam tonight," Logan grinned.

"Call when you're headed home and you can give me a tonsil exam," Dad huffed with a wide grin.

"Here's Brodie," Logan laughed and turned the phone.

"Damn, he missed a couple spur strokes," Dad said when Brodie slid from the pick-up man's horse.

"Scored an 82.5 for fourth," Logan nodded. "We'll be out of here in about twenty minutes."

"Full moon out there," Dad said. "Watch the animals moving around on the roads."

"Will do," Logan nodded. "The sisters are on their way back, too. LJ just texted a couple minutes ago."

"Good to know," Dad nodded then ended the call.

We settled back into the movie. What seemed like just minutes later, lights flashed across the room. I sat straight up and looked around. The movie was over, Dad was missing from the couch, and the clock said I had fallen asleep.

The room was still lit from the lights of the vehicle driving down the driveway. I slowly stood and walked to the back door to see if it was the sisters or the brothers that made it home first.

When I stepped out onto the porch, the lights momentarily blinded me but when the vehicle appeared, my heart dropped.

A county sheriff's car stopped in front of me.

CHAPTER THIRTY

My heart pounded as I walked down the steps. The door opened and an older sheriff gave me a look that I knew I would remember forever.

"Delaney?"

The voice was from inside the car so I leaned down and my breath stopped, "Martin?"

I looked to the sheriff then jogged around the car to open the passenger side door.

Even in the light from the car dash, I could see his face was ashen, eyes glassy, and chin quivering.

"What happened?" I leaned down.

"It's...Craig..."

"Is he alright?"

"He was in an accident...someone ran a red light and hit his car." There was an eerie hollow tone to his voice.

"Is he alright?" My breath stilled in anticipation.

"No...no...he's dead..."

My legs shook and knees began to give way...my body slowly melted against the seat. My hand reached out for his.

"I...I...my son, he's gone, Delaney."

My heart ached at the pure pain in his voice. My mind was ringing as it tried to stop his words from absorbing and making them a reality.

"What's going on?"

Dad's voice called out from the porch.

"Sir," the sheriff closed his door. "Mr. Houston asked me to bring him here. He shouldn't be alone right now."

"What the hell?" Dad growled and the whirl of the wheelchair motor made its way from the porch and around the back of the car.

Martin was staring out the front windshield then he slowly turned as Dad approached.

"Craig..." I whispered and the tears silently fell down my cheeks. Shock, sadness, disbelief crossed Dad's face as he looked at Martin.

"There was a car accident," the sheriff said.

"Where did it happen?" Dad asked.

"Just outside of Middleton on his way back," Martin exhaled. "I'd just talked to him...just an hour before the call."

I was stunned into silence as I held Martin's hand and cried.

Dad turned to the sheriff, "Where is he? What do we need to do?"

"In Middleton," The sheriff sighed. "I'll give you the number to contact them."

"I'm going in to get dressed," Dad said to me. "Stay here with him."

"Of course," I nodded and watched him roll away before turning back to Martin. "Let's go in Dad's van."

Martin nodded and slowly turned to slide out of the car. The sheriff and I had to physically lift him from the car and with shoulders slumped, he shuffled next to me as we slowly made our way to the van.

When he slid onto the seat, he automatically buckled his seatbelt, then stopped and looked down at it.

"They said he had his seatbelt on but the car hit the driver's side door and pushed him across the road into oncoming traffic...he was hit again."

My heart clenched and tears rose again as the vision played in my mind.

"He died on the scene," the sheriff added softly. "He didn't suffer."

Tears began to slide down Martin's face.

I leaned onto his shoulder and held him as tight as I could as Craig's grinning face appeared as if a vision. It was unthinkable to accept he would never tease me again...never laugh again...never ride again.

Oh, Lord in heaven! Brodie was going to be devastated. The last shreds of my heart ripped free as I sobbed into Martin's shoulder.

In the distance of my mind, I heard Dad's wheelchair return and the mumbling of his and the sheriff's voices.

The driver's door opened and I felt the weight of the chair and my father rock the van.

"Let me have your phone," Dad said to Martin and his hand seemed to float as he lifted it out of his pocket.

"Did you call anyone?" Dad asked.

"No…I didn't want…to…tell…Brodie…" His voice shook as his chin lowered to his chest. His whole body shook with the next wave of sobs.

I held him as tight as I could. Only the sound of his gasping and sobs filled the air…there were no words that could help him at that moment so we said nothing.

The light from the sheriff's car disappeared down the driveway.

"Hello? Who is this?" Dad asked and I glanced over to see him talking on the phone.

When Martin's tears stopped, I leaned back and shut the door, then quickly slid in the seat behind him.

I sat quietly in the dark as Dad spoke to the Middleton police department. Martin was silently staring out the window with eyes full of despair.

When he ended the call, he turned to Martin with a glance to me.

"They've told no one, they won't until we get there." He turned and looked at me. His expression was grim and uncertain. "Brodie and Logan will be here in 30 minutes but I don't want to wait."

"You want me to wait here for them?" I asked softly.

"I'm sorry, Delaney," Martin whispered.

"No…don't be. It's best he hear from me than on the phone," I said with desperate eyes to my father since Martin couldn't see me. "I love you, Martin. We'll help you through this."

Silence answered me as I stepped out of the van and watched them disappear down the road.

I stood in the middle of the driveway, in the dark with just the crickets interrupting the silence. I stared into the night, waiting for the lights of Logan's truck and trailer to turn down the drive.

When the lights appeared, my heart sighed in dread. The driveway was not the right place to tell him. Slowly, I walked into the house and stood in the living room staring at the entry from the hallway I knew they would walk through. I'd had my time to cry and let the unbelievable become believable. I needed to be strong for them. As horrific as it was going to be for Brodie, Craig had also been Logan's surrogate little brother, too.

I waited and prayed they came in together…my prayer was answered when Logan came through first with a very concerned look.

"Where is Dad?" He asked.

Brodie appeared with a worried frown.

I stared at both of them then took a deep breath. They stood staring at me with rising concern.

I looked into Logan's eyes then turned to Brodie.

"Craig was on his way home tonight…a car ran a red light and hit him," I spoke as calmly as possible.

"Where is he?" Brodie asked and turned back toward the hall.

"Is he alright?" Logan asked and took a step to follow.

"No, he's gone," I whispered.

Logan gasped and turned to Brodie who stopped and slowly looked back at me. He stared at me as if I was a vision.

"What?" He exhaled.

"The car hit him and shoved him into the opposite lane…another car hit him…he died there," I could feel the tears rising again as Brodie just stared at me. My chest hurt, skin began to itch, and mind still buzzing.

"No…no…no…" Each word shook as the realization made his eyes glisten.

Logan took his arm and pulled him back into the living room so we were within inches of each other.

"Where's Martin and Dad?" Logan asked with the pain reflecting in his eyes.

"On their way to Middleton," I answered and took Brodie's hand then Logan's. I squeezed tightly trying to use our combined strength to ease the pain. We had stood the same way when Dad told us Mom had passed away. We'd had a year to prepare for her death...this? There was no way to prepare for this.

Brodie just stared at me.

"How is Martin?" Logan asked.

I shook my head with the tears rising again.

Brodie's chin quivered. "I just talked to Craig," he whispered. "He is coming here to drive to Omak with us."

He pulled his phone out of his pocket and swiped it to unlock it. He called Craig.

There was silence as Logan and I waited for Brodie to understand that the phone wasn't going to be answered.

Brodie ended the call then dialed again. He hit the speaker button.

The phone rang and echoed into the silent house...goosebumps rose up my arm when the phone clicked and Craig's full of life voice filled the room:

"Hey, you've reached Craig...and I ain't answering...we're on the road because we believe!"

Brodie lowered the phone and looked at me with pure desperation in his eyes.

"I'm in a nightmare...this...isn't real," He whispered.

"It is a nightmare," Logan exhaled.

"And...it...is...real..." My words shook.

We stood silently for what felt like an eternity when lights flashed in the room.

Logan exhaled, "That is the sisters."

Brodie turned and walked down the hallway to our rooms.

"I'll go talk to them," Logan exhaled again.

"I have to stay with Brodie," I whispered and walked away.

Brodie was standing at Craig's bedroom door, staring at the closed door as I approached.

"It's unbelievable," Brodie whispered. "It's not right."

"No, it isn't right."

He turned and walked into his own room to slowly lower and sit on the bed. He stared at the pictures on the wall of him and Craig traveling together from the time they were small to just the week before.

I lowered next to him but remained silent.

In the distance, we could hear the door to the house open and close, then muffled sobs.

"I can't..." Brodie whispered.

A door opened then closed right across the hall then Logan appeared at the door. Without a word he sat on the other side of Brodie.

No words were spoken, we just stared at all the pictures of the happy rodeo partners traveling the country together.

The room began to lighten as dawn approached. The sound of Dad's wheelchair echoed in the silent hall. It stopped and a door was opened, mumbled words were followed by the door closing. The hum of the chair approached Brodie's door. When it stopped, I turned to see Dad. He looked tired as if he had aged ten years while he was gone. Brodie slowly lay back on the bed and stared at the ceiling, Logan did the same. Dad approached the bed and stopped just in front of us with his hand reaching out to lie on Brodie's knee.

"Where is Martin?" I whispered.

"At home...his sister is with him," Dad answered softly.

I leaned back and lay next to Brodie and stared at the ceiling as the sun rose and lightened the room. When I turned to him, his eyes were closed but the tears escaped down his temple and into his hair. I took his hand and squeezed.

"It's not right," Brodie whispered.

It was so wrong...the ache, the loss, the pain was overwhelming.

Within moments of the phones beginning to ring, Camille was at the door. Her eyes were red, cheeks streaked from tears but her eyes were focused on Brodie.

"Let me have your phone," she said to him. "I'll handle all the calls."

Without a word, he held out the ringing phone to her. Logan handed his to her also. Dad hesitated then held his to her, "If it's Martin or his sister..."

"I know..." she whispered and she turned to me. The tears welled again.

"I'll keep mine," I smiled my thanks.

She nodded then turned away.

I sat up and pulled out my phone to put it on vibrate. I had missed three calls from him.

Text from Huckleberry: Stunned, I'm coming to you

Text to Huckleberry: Give me a couple days

Text from Huckleberry: Delaney

Text to Huckleberry: I know, it's hard

Text from Huckleberry: My phone will not leave my hand, you call me when you can

Text to Huckleberry: I will

When I finally left the room, Camille was sitting at the kitchen table, a note pad in front of her with two of the phones next to it. The other was at her ear.

"Yes, I know," she was saying. "Thank you, Tyler...no, if you call his phone, I will answer, too...yes...I will tell the family."

She ended the call and wrote his name under a long list of names that were already on the notepad, then picked up the next phone as it vibrated.

"Hello? Yes, this is his number, no there will be no interviews for days, please understand and respect their grief...thank you."

She ended the call and picked up the next.

"Hello? Yes, this is his phone, I'll be handling the calls for now. Thank you, Johnny, yes, I'll let them know."

Lacie Jae walked in through the back hallway with a large dish in her hands. She set it down next to three others on the kitchen island.

She hesitated then looked up at me, tears glistened. "They don't know what else to do but to make sure you don't have to cook."

Her eyes moved behind me and I turned to see Logan. She ran to him. As they wrapped their arms around each other, he turned down the hallway and I could hear the office door close.

"Hello? Yes, this is his phone." Camille answered. "No, they are not accepting visitors right now and the funeral plans are not set yet."

A car turned down the driveway and the door to the office opened. Lacie Jae appeared and hurried past me to greet them.

Logan walked back to the bedrooms.

I glanced at Camille. All three phones were lying on the table and vibrating but her eyes were on me.

"I don't even know what to say," she whispered.

As I walked to her she jumped out of the chair and we came together for a strong, agony filled embrace. We held tightly until the phones were silent then began vibrating again.

"What can I do to help?" she whispered.

"Handling the phones," I leaned back to look into her concerned eyes. "When he shows up, don't let Martin be alone. I don't know how long his sister will be there but..."

"I'll take care of him," Camille nodded.

After a shared look, she reached for a phone and I turned to go back to Brodie's room.

It was dark when the phone call from Martin rang through on Dad's phone. After a brief muted conversation, Camille walked to Brodie's room.

"Martin is on his way here…his sister is driving him…he wants just Brodie to come out to the truck."

Brodie was standing on the back deck waiting when the truck arrived. Martin stepped out of the passenger side and, without hesitation, walked to the barn. Brodie followed.

I stood at the window and watched them disappear. My heart ached and tears fell unchecked.

The funeral was held graveside on top of the rise of the hill at the cemetery. The black coffin was covered in white roses with dozens of flower arrangements set around it. The image of Craig holding his Sisters rodeo buckle was on an easel near the front. To the right of it was an image of Craig as a boy standing between his parents. To the left was the photograph taken by the photographer at the Circuit Finals in January of the whole family.

I held Brodie's hand as we slowly walked up the hill to the waiting chairs. His black cowboy hat was low with black sunglasses covering his eyes. Logan, Lacie Jae, then Camille sat to the right of Brodie with Dad then Martin to my left.

As the minister stepped forward, a silence hovered in the air. He looked up with his gaze roaming the hundreds of people in attendance, then he stopped and took a step back. Martin's head turned. I followed his gaze and my heart shook.

CHAPTER THIRTY-ONE

Craig's mother slowly walked through the mass of people, her husband stood next to their car at the base of the hill. When Martin stood, his eyes met with his ex-wife as she walked right to him and without a word, their arms wrapped around each other. She buried her face into his chest.

The silence on the hill was laden with heavy hearts and tears.

When she leaned back, his hands cupped each side of her face as they stared into each other's eyes. He kissed her forehead as the tears slid down their faces.

My breath shook as I squeezed Dad and Brodie's hands tightly.

Craig's parents sat next to each other, held hands, but did not say a word through their son's funeral. When the final prayer was recited, they rose, the kiss to the forehead was repeated and Logan stepped forward to offer his arm to help her to her car. She hesitated in front of Brodie and his hand squeezed mine; his legs were visibly shaking. He slowly looked up with the tears escaping from under his sunglasses.

"Thank you," she whispered to him. "For giving Craig the life he loved. You are a special young man, Brodie. He loved you dearly."

Brodie's jaw tightened and more tears fell. He reached out a trembling hand and the two squeezed tightly before she turned and leaned against Logan as he walked her to her car.

When the mourner's line that walked by the casket and Martin began to thin, I stood and walked away to the edge of the cemetery.

Staring out at the open field and blue sky, a warm breeze caressed my hot skin and dried the tears before they fell.

My body hurt...I wrapped my arms around myself and squeezed hoping the ache would ease. It didn't...so I shoved my hands deep into the pockets of the dress and balled my hands into fists...deep breaths to calm my nerves.

Why did this happen? How were we supposed to understand when it made no sense and hurt so much? It just wasn't right.

I felt the tears rising again and closed my eyes to hold them in. I needed to hold on for just a while longer. Martin and Brodie would need our strength to get through the rest of the day.

I turned to look at the crowd gathered around Martin. He was standing with his hand resting on the back of Dad's chair...using Dad for support. Brodie and Logan were standing with Martin as if they were guarding him. Lacie Jae had a firm grip around Logan's arm; he was leaned into her slightly indicating he needed her there. Camille had already left to handle the crowd who were making their way from the cemetery to our ranch for the celebration of life.

I felt numb, lost, and on the edge of control. I needed an escape from reality.

My gaze swept the crowd that was slowly making their way back to their cars at the base of the hill. Everyone was sad...heartbroken...lost...holding onto the person they were with, but I needed someone...then, I saw him.

He was standing at the base of the hill looking up at me...watching me. When our eyes met, my whole body trembled and my eyes pleaded for him. Instantly, he began walking to me...comforting me with his eyes as he approached. He walked around dozens of people without a word to anyone as they turned and looked at him in curiosity and surprise.

My aching heart swelled as he approached and I could barely hold myself from sobbing as he grew nearer, arms lifting then pulling me to him. I buried my face into his chest as our arms wrapped around each other. We didn't speak...we just held each other as the ache in my heart became bearable.

His warmth calmed my trembling.

"You'll make it through this," he whispered in my ear.

I closed my eyes to hold in the strength of his arms and his words.

"Now that you're here, I feel I have a chance," I sighed. "But...everyone...will know..."

"YOU were more important than our clandestine meetings," he pulled me tighter to him.

"Thank you..."

"I will always be here for you, Delaney...always."

My arms wrapped around his neck and I held him closer...holding onto his strength and emotion. Once the trembling eased, I took a deep breath and leaned back just enough to look up into his eyes. They were comforting...warm...full of emotion.

My fingers caressed his chin, "You have no idea how much this means to me."

His answer was to lean down and kiss my forehead, then to each cheekbone, then ending with a soft kiss to my lips.

Our foreheads came together as my thumb played with the whiskers of his jaw.

"There is a celebration of life at your ranch now?" he whispered.

"Yes..."

"Can I drive you over?"

"Dad and my brother's will take care of Martin so yes...I so very much want you to stay with me."

His hand slid into mine and our fingers entwined tightly. I didn't look back. I didn't look at anyone, just to the ground as I watched my footing down the hill.

"I don't think we've walked out in public with each other since last summer in that little California town," I said.

He chuckled, "That was a fun couple of days of no one knowing us and we could do what we wanted."

"Well, I don't mind we can do this more often now."

"Me either," he opened the door of a blue truck.

He kissed me again before giving me a hand to brace me as I stepped into the truck.

The drive to our ranch was silent. I watched the line of cars ahead and turned back to see Logan's truck carrying all four men and Lacie Jae wasn't too far behind us.

"How long are you here?" I asked and pointed to a place to park by the barn. There were dozens of cars already parked in the field by the house and people sitting at the tables on the patio. Camille was just walking into the house.

"As long as you need me," he said and shut off the engine before turning to me. "Delaney...I'm here...as long as you need me."

Tears rose as my hand-stretched to his and our fingers interlocked.

"Let's go for a walk before we join everyone."

He nodded and our fingers slipped away for just a moment as we left the truck and met in front of it.

Without talking, but holding his hand and arm, we walked to the barn, through the aisle, and out the back. We walked across the pasture to the tree that nestled on the hill overlooking the main horse pasture. All the horse's heads rose to look at us then lowered to continue their grazing.

He leaned back against the tree and pulled me into his arms with my head resting on his shoulder and my arms comfortably around his waist. We stood silently, enjoying each other and watching the horses.

The phone in my pocket vibrated and with a sigh, I pulled it out.

Text from Logan: Come off the hill and face the inquisition

I chuckled and read it out loud.

Our finger came together again as we slowly walked down the hill.

"I'm glad I was wearing boots," I smiled.

"I would have happily carried you to the house," he chuckled with eyes dancing in humor.

That was what I needed...his strength and his sense of humor.

"You seriously think you could carry me?" I teased when we made it to the back of the barn.

He swooped me up into his arms with our laughter echoing in the barn.

"All the way to the house, My Lady?" he said in a terrible English accent.

"No, just here…for this…"

I wrapped my arms around his neck and pulled his lips to mine. For just a moment, we left the barn and disappeared into our own world. Memories of our clandestine rendezvous', stolen glances, and mid-night phone calls enveloped me. The pain in my heart eased.

He dropped my legs to the ground but our lips didn't part as we melted into each other.

When he leaned up away, his eyes were full of emotions and need but something else…an uncertainty.

"What?" I asked breathlessly.

"I know you know…but I've never said it to you," he whispered. "I want to, but I'm just not sure this is the right time…the right moment."

"Yes…I know," I smiled in our bliss. "And I've never said it to you but I know you know. You came to me when I needed you the most. You chose me over the gossip and drama that will happen as news of our relationship spreads."

"So many questions…" he teased.

"I know," I took his hand to walk through the barn. "This is our last few quiet moments for a while," I whispered, as we neared the doors of the barn and the noise of the crowd on the other side.

As we stepped into the light and to the view of dozens of heads that turned to us, he whispered;

"I will be here for you as long as you need me."

"I love you, Ryle."

"…and I love you, my Delaney."

337

CHAPTER THIRTY-TWO

Logan and Brodie met us at the edge of the yard. They didn't say anything...they just grinned at the two of us as they shook Ryle's hand. There were surprised raised brows and nods as we followed my brothers to our father and Martin. They were sitting at a patio table at the back of the house, surrounded by another dozen tables full of our guests.

Dad glanced between us then waved us to two chairs across from him.

Martin slowly shook his head, "Gotta say...you sure shocked the hell out of everyone."

I smiled at him and winked.

"This..." Dad waved his hand between Ryle and me. "How long?"

A guilty chuckle escaped me as I looked from him to Ryle, who was grinning, then back to Dad.

"Dad...Martin, this is Ryle Jaspers. Ryle? Well...you know everyone." I chuckled then turned back to Dad to answer him. "We met the night I won the Snake River Stampede."

Shocked and stunned gasped rang out.

"That was two years ago," Logan huffed.

"And you kept it hidden for that long?" Brodie asked.

"Why?" Martin added.

I turned and looked at Ryle who was watching me closely with humor twinkling in his eyes.

"At first, it was because of the gossipers and drama queens that we wanted to avoid," I answered honestly. "We didn't want any pressure...outside influences."

"And then?" Dad asked.

"Well..." I grinned at him. "Because it was fun."

Ryle and I chuckled.

"And today?" Dad turned and looked at Ryle.

"She needed me, sir," Ryle said and squeezed my hand.

"You gave up anonymity…the secret to come to her today?" Martin asked Ryle.

"Yes, sir, of course…like I said, I knew she needed me," Ryle nodded.

There was silence a moment until Martin stood enough to reach across the table and offer a hand to Ryle. Their hands met and shook firmly.

I felt the tears begin to rise again.

Dad broke the silence with a huff, "I'm kinda relieved."

"Relieved?" I asked in surprise. "Why?"

"Hell, girl," he drawled. "You haven't had more than 2 dates with a guy in the last couple years and I was beginning to think there was something wrong with you."

"Debate is still going on with that one," Logan laughed.

It brought a round of chuckles from everyone around us.

"Well…you must be Boots," Camille said as she walked down the steps of the porch.

Ryle grinned at her and stood. Much to my surprise, their arms wrapped around each other and they held each other tightly. I just watched with a dropped jaw until their grips loosened enough Ryle turned his head and whispered to her. Camille giggled.

"What?" I nearly yelled.

They both turned and smiled at me…their eyes were dancing in humor.

"What?" I repeated. "What did he say?"

Camille grinned, "He thanked me for taking you shopping for jeans."

The laughter erupted as a guilty grin spread across Ryle's handsome face.

"You knew about this?" Dad asked her.

Camille shook her head as she lowered onto the chair next to me, "Not really. I knew there was someone because Mark dropped me off early at the trailer one morning and I tripped on his boots at the door. So, I've just been calling him Boots."

I looked at her to gauge whether she was upset I hadn't told her who it was. She just smiled to reassure me.

"How did you meet?" Brodie asked.

Ryle laughed and I grinned sheepishly.

"Well," I started with a glance around the table. "After I won the Stampede, a bunch of racers and I went out to celebrate. We were at the bar when I felt a hand grip my butt."

Everyone looked at Ryle in a bit of disgust.

"It wasn't me!" he grinned and threw his hands up in the air. "I saw it happen, but by the time I got over to them, she had the guy laid out flat on the ground and was standing over him as he was gasping for breath. She told him she was raised with three brothers and bossed around 1400 pound animals. He should think twice before grabbing a cowgirl's butt again."

"That's my girl," Dad said proudly.

I smiled at him then turned to Ryle, "This cowboy walks up and looks at the guy on the ground then to me and says, 'Lady, is this guy bothering you? Because if he is, I'll be your huckleberry'," Another round of chuckles. "I thought it was hilarious and we partied together for the rest of the night and we've been in contact every day since."

"Every day?" Martin asked in surprise.

"Either by phone or text and, whenever we could, in person," Ryle nodded.

"Whether just a couple texts or all-night phone conversations," I added.

Dad turned to Ryle, "You're a team roper with Jess Corday…staying at Conner's 3.3 Ranch."

"Yes, Sir," Ryle answered.

"Call me, Evan," Dad ordered.

"Wait!" Lacie Jae sat up in her chair. She still had her arms firmly wrapped around Logan's arm. "You ride that pretty palomino?" She turned to me. "We saw them that first day in Vegas."

I chuckled, "Silas, yes. Then in Yakima at the Circuit Finals, but what you didn't see was me slide my room key into the edge of the sign on the fence."

"That I rode over and retrieved as soon as you two left." Ryle grinned.

"Seriously?" Camille laughed.

"Yeah," I laughed. "There were a couple of times we would leave keys for each other in potted plants in hotel lobbies."

"I had a key to her trailer so I would just leave gifts for her," Ryle added.

"The yellow M&M's in Vegas last year?" Logan asked and when Ryle and I nodded, he just shook his head. "I knew you didn't carry that dispenser all the way from that store."

"And," Ryle gave me a guilty grin. "If you ever want to kidnap her, just leave a trail of canned margaritas for her to follow."

"San Antonio?" Camille looked at me in surprise. "That's why all those cans were in the feed room?"

I laughed with a red flush of embarrassment, "Yes, but I also knew it was Ryle that left them there."

Dad was looking at me, thoughtfully. A tinge of worry crept up my spine until he turned to Ryle. "We've been thinking we should get a roping going instead of just sitting around." He said.

"Craig would rather us be riding and roping," Brodie nodded solemnly. "And I need something to do."

Ryle turned and smiled at me, "You going to ride in that dress?"

"I'll go change," I laughed and stood...with him standing with me.

"She can do it by herself," Logan growled.

My gaze shot to him and I could see the humor in his eyes.

I laughed with a sense of relief. I really didn't know how my family would take our hidden romance but I'm glad they were taking it well. The secret coming out would help everyone focus on something else besides why we were gathered together.

There was no doubt we were all going to use the new 'found' relationship and the roping to make it through the day.

341

The night Ryle left to join his team roping partner for the rodeo in Caldwell, I stood at the window in the living room looking out into the dark pastures. Camille had left with Martin so he wasn't home alone.

At one o'clock in the morning, I couldn't sleep nor stand to be alone in my room. The silence of the night was almost unbearable. A door opened and closed down the hall then two sets of footsteps walked down the hall.

I turned to see Logan and Lacie Jae appear.

"Just stay here," Logan whispered to her.

"But..." She pouted.

"No, I'll..." Logan started but stopped when he saw me.

"What's going on?" I asked.

"Northside bar called and said Brodie was there," Logan answered. "They said he's pretty wasted. They finally got him to eat something and have him quiet and calm."

"What?" I gasped. "I thought he was in his room. I'll go..."

"No," Logan said firmly. "I'll handle this."

He walked out of the room without another word.

Lacie Jae and I watched him walk away then turned to each other. Within moments, she was in my arms as we held each other.

"I hurt so much for him," she cried. "For all of you."

"For all of us," I whispered.

We stood at the window and stared into the night for an hour before the lights of Logan's truck turned down the driveway.

I was at the truck before it even stopped. Logan was tense, jaw clenched tight while Brodie was unconscious in the passenger seat.

With one fluid motion, Logan had Brodie over his shoulder and carried him toward the house. Lacie Jae and I scrambled up the stairs to get the doors open.

Dad was sitting in his wheelchair in the kitchen and didn't say anything as Logan carried Brodie to his room.

When Logan returned, the four of us just looked at each other then turned away. Our hearts were breaking but there was nothing we could do to help. Dad rolled back to his room as Lacie Jae and Logan went to his. I walked into Brodie's room and sat in the chair next to his bed. For hours I faded in and out of sleep until I heard a loud burp and a gasp. I jolted out of the chair and grabbed the laundry basket, barely getting it to the bedside before he rolled over and began vomiting.

When the last of the pungent alcohol filled the basket, Brodie looked at me with red depressed eyes, then turned and rolled over onto his stomach. Within seconds he was snoring.

"How long has he been sleeping?" I asked Camille over the phone as I leaned against Gaston.

"All day, what about Brodie? Has he recovered from the other night?"

"No, he's still sleeping, too. Basically for the last two days," I sighed. "Depression can take a toll on a body."

"I don't know what else to do besides be here for him," her voice was quivering from the tears.

"That is what he needs right now. Maybe try baking something so he gets an appetite and that will help with his energy."

"Bake what?"

"He likes pies so just make him what you can."

"OK, I can do that. Lacie Jae is here, I'll see if she will go to the store for me. Are you OK?"

I stepped out of the stall, "No, but Ryle is on his way here and can spend a few hours before they go to Moses Lake."

"Oh, good but please call me if you need to."

"I will."

I slid the phone back in my pocket and made my way down the aisle to check on each stall. Logan and I had both taken to cleaning stalls to keep busy; not one needed anything. Maybe riding Memphis would help. When my hand hit the door handle to the tack room, I could hear the sound of an engine so I walked out the end of the barn.

A white SUV had pulled alongside the house and a man was stepping out.

"Can I help you with something?" I asked and strode toward him.

His head turned and he smiled politely then leaned back into the vehicle and reappeared with a notebook and pen in his hand. A reporter, we had been dealing with phone calls for the last few days but this was the first to come to the house.

"I'm Paul Sampson, I was looking for Brodie Rawlins," he answered. "You're Delaney Rawlins."

"I know who I am and Brodie isn't available."

His head turned to the house then back to me, "I just have a few questions."

"He's not available," I repeated and stopped between him and the house.

"Well, since I came all the way out here," he said. "Can I talk to him for just a moment?"

"We didn't invite you out..."

"I tried calling..." he huffed.

"Alright," I sighed and his shoulders rose as if he was going to let him talk to Brodie. "Please, just get back in your car and leave."

He looked calm except his flaring nostrils, "I just need to..."

"Leave," I finished for him. "Or I can call the sheriff who is a great friend of ours."

"Delaney, don't overreact."

Fire coursed through me and from the look on his face he knew it was the wrong thing to say. "Can I make an appointment to talk with him?" He asked calmly.

"Give me your card and leave."

He looked at me thoughtfully but didn't move.

"That was the best I was going to offer you so, now, just leave," My jaw clenched and eyes narrowed.

His shoulders lowered and a deep sigh escaped. Without another word he turned back to his car and drove away. He turned onto the main road and passed Ryle and Jess as they turned down the driveway.

The anger that had taken over my aching stomach, melted away the closer their truck approached.

"Who was that?" Logan said from the door to the house.

I pulled my eyes from Ryle's smile to look at him, "Reporter."

Logan nodded and stepped back into the house.

Three hours later, Ryle and Jess drove away on their way to the rodeo in Moses Lake. Two steps to the house and I was stopped by Brodie stepping out the door.

His hair was limp against his head, showing just how long it had been since he had a shower. Thick whiskers covered his jaw. He was wearing a wrinkled blue shirt and dirty jeans that were gathered at the top of his boots. His bloodshot eyes glanced at me before he walked by me to the barn.

I wasn't really sure what to do so I just watched him until he disappeared into the barn. After a hesitation, I walked into the house and to the kitchen to pull a bottle of water from the refrigerator. Dad and Logan were watching a western on the large television but I couldn't sit still. I needed to do something so I walked back to the porch in time to see Brodie riding across the pasture on Bubba.

That's what I needed; to ride. Twenty minutes later, I was leading Memphis out of the barn and toward the arena. A slight breeze lifted the horse's mane and I heard a low thump by the trailers. The door to my living quarter's portion of my horse trailer blew open in the wind and hit the side again.

"Odd," I whispered and walked over to the trailer. After shutting the door, I stepped toward the arena then stopped. Ryle and I had slept there the nights he had stayed but there was no doubt I had shut the door when he left so why was it open?

I flipped the reins over the hitching post and stepped into the trailer. The air escaped and my whole body deflated when I saw the door to the alcohol cabinet open and two bottles missing.

"Son-of-a-bitch," I muttered and jogged back to Memphis.

We loped across the pasture in the direction Brodie had ridden. With thousands of acres in front of us, he could be just about anywhere.

CHAPTER THIRTY-THREE

We raced across the pasture and through the herd of cattle, making them scatter.

Where would I go? I had a few favorite places but I wasn't sure they were Brodie's. Running through the trees, I had to keep my eyes on the path and wasn't able to look in the distance but when we broke into the open I could see Bubba across the pasture. Relief washed through me. The horse was tied to a tree at the top of a hill that dropped into a deep ravine. Damn, it was a beautiful place to sit and look out at the mountains, but it was also a dangerous place to be when you were drinking.

After tying Memphis to the tree next to Bubba, I stepped over the edge of the hill and looked toward the ravine. Brodie was sitting halfway down with the bottle tipped to his lips. It was half gone already but the other bottle was on the ground next to him; it was still full.

I walked down the hill; his head turned to look at me with the bottle still in the air. After three large gulps, he finally lowered the bottle. There was no look of surprise, anger, or guilt.

I sighed, "This isn't the way to handle…"

"It doesn't hurt so fucking bad," he grumbled and lifted the bottle again.

My hand shot out to his forearm to lower the bottle but he yanked it away from me.

"Brodie, it's not…"

"TELL ME WHAT THE FUCK IS!"

My body jerked away from the sudden explosion.

"I don't know what is," I said honestly. "But, I do know that alcohol isn't the answer."

He stood but his body wobbled so I reached out to him to make sure he didn't tumble into the ravine. He twirled around with the anger, loss, and desperation radiating from his whole body. My breath caught and heart clenched. Tears instantly filled my eyes and fell.

"What the fuck am I supposed to do?" he exhaled in desperation. Tears filled his bloodshot eyes. "Tell me, Delaney! How do I handle this? How do I get over this anger? How do I fucking bring him back?"

"I don't know, Brodie," I cried. "I don't know how we get through this other than holding on to each other."

"I look at Martin…I don't know how he handles it, Delaney," Tears fell unchecked.

"Right now, he's leaning on Camille," My breath shook. "But, he's going to need you, a sober you."

He lifted his face to the sky and whispered, "I will never be me again."

My chin hit my chest; the tears continued as I realized just how right he was.

Arms held back, chest high, he let out a gut-wrenching anguished yell that echoed across the hills and into the ravine.

My whole body trembled at the loss, at the complete feeling of helplessness that washed over me. The tears were unending…I wrapped my arms around my body and sobbed.

After a moment, his arms encircled me and I tucked my face into his chest as his whole body sighed. We held each other tightly.

"I know I am not the only one hurting," He whispered. "But I don't know how to get past this and if I can't do that, I can't…"

We stood quietly a moment as the strength from his embrace and the love we shared helped ease the tears.

"Just this," I whispered. "Just this holding onto each other helps."

He sighed again.

I closed my eyes and thought of Dad and Logan and my body relaxed more. I thought of Gaston and the rest of my horses and my breathing returned to normal. I thought of

Craig, but this time with him on top of the chutes talking to Camille when she rode Popover. There was happiness and eagerness in his body. I thought of him like that and took a deep breath.

"Maybe," I whispered. "Instead of thinking of him as gone, think of him as if he was somewhere else."

"What does that mean?"

"Other than in the chute where you would be with him, think of his favorite place he would be if he weren't with you," I stepped back and looked up at him. "Think of him there, enjoying himself and laughing at whoever is with him."

He looked out over the ravine and took a deep breath.

"Maybe thinking of him being somewhere he loves, it will help us get through each day until it isn't so hard," I whispered.

After another deep breath, he closed his eyes and took another. Then, he nodded. "OK," he whispered. "OK...I'll try that."

He wobbled again, so I bent over and picked up the two bottles then grabbed his arm to steady him as we walked up the hill to the horses.

We rode in silence, but half-way to the house his eyes were closed, head down, and body loosely moving with the rhythm of the horse's stride. Then, he began to hum.

He walked into the house before me and didn't even look at Dad and Logan in the living room. I followed him as he walked straight to his room and fell onto his bed.

"I'm just going to sleep this off," he whispered and closed his eyes.

Dad and Logan were in the kitchen when I returned.

"He OK?" Logan whispered with brows drawn together in concern.

"I think he might be over the hump," I answered. "We'll see when he wakes up."

I spent hours in the arena working Madi and the two younger horses from Parkston's. I was tired, physically and mentally, but I needed the work to keep moving, to keep from dissolving into tears again.

When I was done training, I took a walk to the retired horses pasture to visit with the youngest of the crew; the horse from Tanya Morgan. Dad had renamed him after the team roper that delivered him to the property. So, I stood at the fence and looked at the sorrel with four white socks renamed Dillon.

The first five days he was released out on the 30 acres of pasture, Dillon did not come near the barn; even when the older horses came in for grain. On the sixth day he came in for grain then quickly went to the far side of the pasture. That had been his routine.

Today, he was grazing calmly in the middle of the pasture. Slowly, he was regaining trust.

I just stood and stared at him while the afternoon sun warmed my body. I wished I was in Moses Lake with Ryle. It would have been our first public appearance together but being here with Brodie was more important. I prayed that when he woke he could move forward.

Lacie Jae's SUV appeared and turned down the driveway with Martin in the passenger seat. My gut clenched in anticipation. This would be the first time since the night in the barn that Brodie and Martin had been together.

I walked through the gate as the vehicle came to a stop. Camille and Lacie Jae smiled as I neared but Martin was frowning.

"I need some help," Martin said and lifted a box out of the backseat.

To my surprise, the sisters giggled as they followed him into the house.

Logan and Dad met us in the kitchen.

"Where's Brodie?" Martin asked.

"I'll get him," I answered. My strides were wide and heart racing as I walked down the hallway.

He wasn't in his room, he was sitting on Dad's incline exercise bike; head tipped back, earbuds in and his eyes were closed. His legs pedaled slowly. I hesitated in disturbing him but the whole family was waiting.

When I tapped his shoulder, his eyes opened and he smiled. A real honest smile and it made my whole body tingle.

He pulled out the earbuds, "Where's Dad?"

"In the kitchen," I turned slightly down the hall. "DAD!"

"Shit, Delaney." Brodie cringed. "I have a bit of a headache."

"I bet you do," I chuckled to the sound of the wheelchair and multiple footsteps walking down the hall. Dad was first to appear but the rest were right behind him.

"What the hell are you doing on my bike, Son?" Dad huffed but couldn't stop the slight smile that appeared.

Brodie huffed, "I needed to move but figured I'd fall off the treadmill."

The relief was visible on all their faces.

"I was just sitting here listening to LJ's interview with Craig and me," Brodie explained.

Lacie Jae gasped.

"And?" Martin's jaw clenched.

Brodie's legs finally stopped pedaling and he set his feet on the ground but didn't rise.

"You were right, Dad. I need to do something for him, to honor him and in the interview, he said he wanted to win the Big Four saddle someday," Brodie explained and looked at Martin. "I want to win it for him."

My breath caught and I had to swallow hard to keep from crying.

"You're all entered in Kennewick next week," Dad said. "That's the first."

"Not just in saddle bronc," Brodie told him. "I want to ride in bareback for him and I'll do saddle bronc."

"Both, in all four rodeos?" Martin asked.

"Yes," Brodie answered and looked to Dad. "Is there time to get me entered in bareback in Kennewick?"

Dad nodded, "They announced a re-entry for tomorrow."

Martin huffed, "We'll get you in, but first, I need your help."

Brodie quickly stood, "Anything, what do you need?"

"These two sisters decided I needed something to eat and baked all damn day," Martin answered.

"Baked what?" Brodie's hand went over his stomach.

"Pies...a lot of them," Martin smiled at the two women. "Cherry, peach, strawberry-rhubarb, apple, banana and chocolate cream pie, even a damn pumpkin pie."

"We didn't know which one he liked so we just made a selection," Camille explained with a smile.

"I hope we have ice cream for over the apple," Brodie smiled.

Five minutes later, a dozen half-empty pie dishes were sitting across the kitchen island with everyone gathered around, eating a little of each one.

Logan and Lacie Jae were feeding each other pie and Camille was serving more to everyone with a quick reassuring smile to me. Dad, Martin and Brodie were talking about gathering horses for a week of bareback practice.

My mind eased...they had a mission...a goal to focus on. One thing I knew, it was going to be a long four weeks ahead of us.

I was sitting on the back porch looking out at the stars sparkling in the sky and listening to the horses wandering the pasture when he finally called.

"Hello, Sweetheart," I answered with a smile. "How was your run tonight?"

There was a pause before he answered, "Not too good," Ryle sighed. "Seems like every reporter came to town expecting to see the Rawlins family or at least you since I was on the day-sheet."

My heart sunk, "I'm so sorry."

"Nah, it ain't your fault," He sighed. "I could barely make a turn without someone asking me about Brodie. Some were just friends checking on him but others were just...well, pretty fucking rude when they found out you weren't going to be there."

"Damn, Darlin', I'm so sorry. We've dealt with phone calls but just one had the audacity to drive onto the property...a Paul something."

"Yeah, he was there; Paul Sampson, he was really pushy. I was going to try and talk you into coming to Caldwell Saturday for the finals there, but I'm not sure that's a good idea."

I sighed in relief then told him of Brodie's plan for a memorial for Craig.

"That's a lot of heart. With qualifiers, that is twelve rides altogether between the two," he whispered. "I have no doubt he can do it, but my advice is to get it out there in front of the media so you don't get hounded next week when you get to Kennewick."

"It was that bad?"

"Yeah, it was, and that was just being your new-found boyfriend. I can't imagine what it will be like for your family."

"Brodie is just barely hanging on but he needs this. I'm nervous that talking to reporters about his feelings and Craig's loss will just send him back...it will be too hard. And Martin...I just...he couldn't..." Pain shot through my stomach as nausea rose.

"I understand. That's why I called, to warn you."

"I'll talk to them. But, please, tell Jess I'm sorry."

"One more thing and I'm not saying you haven't been the best coach in the world for her, but Lauren is hosting a roping clinic at the 3.3 Ranch in between the Kennewick and Walla Walla rodeos. I think it would be good for Camille to go to it by herself, it would be a real confidence booster."

I exhaled the sudden wave of anxiety, "You're right. It's always best to have a couple of different coaches."

"I'll send you the flyer on it and you go talk to your family."

"I will," I sighed. "I love you."

He huffed and I could hear the humor in it, "I could shout it from the rooftops and see if you could hear it from here."

I giggled. The man-made me happy.

"I love you, My Delaney, and I'll talk to you tomorrow."

"Goodnight, Huckleberry," I whispered and ended the call.

A MESSAGE FROM THE HOUSTON AND RAWLINS FAMILIES

To honor Craig Houston, his childhood friend, traveling partner, and brother, Brodie Rawlins will ride in the bareback event for the Northwest Big Four Rodeos; Kennewick, Walla Walla, Lewiston, and Pendleton. This will be in addition to his riding in Saddle Bronc.

The families are still dealing with the sudden loss of this young soul, so we request the media to please be respectful of not only the focus it will take to complete this memorial but of the general overall feelings of the family and friends.

Within minutes of the release on our family's social media sites, Dad received a phone call from Sep Blackburn, an old steer wrestling buddy. He and his wife offered the use of their home and stables for the family to stay in Kennewick instead of staying at the rodeo grounds. We all immediately agreed.

"Bareback, breakaway, and steer wrestling on Thursday night then saddle bronc and barrels on Friday night," Dad told the group the next morning. "Saturday for the short-go."

Brodie turned to Logan with a smirk, "Sounds like you need to step it up a bit."

"Only one event per rodeo?" I added with a cocky raised brow.

Everyone at breakfast chuckled but Lacie Jae; she flat out laughed out loud.

The next morning, I walked out the backdoor of the house and stepped toward the barn. After more than twenty years of scanning the property as I walked, I automatically knew when something was out of place. I looked back to the arena, to the bucking chutes, something wasn't right.

CHAPTER THIRTY-FOUR

I turned to the arena and was halfway there when I saw Camille sitting on the platform behind the chutes. It was her legs dangling that I had seen. Her head turned to me as I walked through the gate. Tears slid down her red cheeks.

"You want me to leave?" I asked.

"No, it's OK," she took in a deep breath and began wiping away the tears

I leaned against the platform next to her and looked up at her glistening eyes. "Considering the circumstances right now, I know this is a stupid question, but are you alright?"

She huffed and wiped away another tear, "I feel close to Craig here."

"Great memories with Popover and your ride," I sighed.

"Yes," she smiled. "But...our first kiss was right here...followed by a few really great make-out sessions his last two weeks."

"Then I completely understand."

"Two weeks, Delaney," her voice faltered with shoulders lowering. "We only had two weeks."

I took her hand and squeezed tightly, "You had months of becoming friends, then you GOT to have two weeks with him before he left us."

She nodded with lips in a tight line and tears escaping again, "It was such a great two weeks, too. Between time on the road and time here? It was so wonderful and held so many promises for the future."

"Hold on to those memories."

She nodded with a shaking inhale, "We haven't spent much time together...since..."

"I know."

"How can I help?"

357

I shook my head with a sigh, "You've done nothing but help with the phones, taking care of the food, and staying with Martin. He shouldn't be alone."

"I…" She started, then stopped. After a big sigh she continued. "Craig knew that one of the issues between Mark and I was I didn't want to have kids yet. I was years away."

"Yeah, we all knew that."

She nodded, "Well, the night we were together in Bend?"

My stomach clenched, "Yeah?"

"We had made such an issue about birth control that we both used it…we were a bit overboard in protection because neither of us were ready."

"Yeah…" I exhaled.

"The last couple days…" She started and her eyes began glistening again. "I got to thinking…even praying that somehow…just somehow a miracle would happen…and I…" Her voice faltered and my stomach swirled. "I thought maybe I could give Martin a miracle…a child of Craig's…"

"Camille…are you…?"

"No," She bawled. "I started my cycle this morning. I screwed that up, too."

"Oh…"

"Ah, Hon," Martin's voice made us both jump.

I stepped back so he could wrap the crying woman in his arms.

"You didn't screw up anything," he whispered to her. "You made my boy over-the-top happy his last days and he was looking forward to a full future with you, too." Her cries shook. "I cannot express how much it means to me that you wanted that miracle. As wonderful as that would have been, you being in our lives is just as much a miracle." Her arms squeezed around his neck. "Sweet Camille, you have been by my side since the accident, making sure I was doing OK and watching over all of us. I know you didn't have the best draw in a father, but just so you know, I'll be looking out for you just as if you and Craig had completed your future and you were my daughter-in-law."

Tears streamed down my face as I turned away to give them this moment.

I walked to my bedroom to wash my face and try to pull myself together. These next few weeks were going to be hard on all of us so I couldn't let myself get out of control.

When I walked out of my room, Brodie was standing in front of Craig's bedroom door. He stared at the doorknob as his shaking hand reached for it. He stopped and his hand fell away.

"Brodie?" I whispered and walked to his side.

He didn't look at me but took a deep shaking breath, "Remember those chaps Mom had made for Craig just before she died but he didn't wear them?"

"Yeah, he didn't like the color but never told her…she never knew."

He nodded, "He liked the dark brown or black. Light blue or as he described them 'baby blue' with long white fringe was not a color he wanted to wear."

"He would have looked great in them, though."

"Yeah," he sighed. "He was going to wear them one day, in her memory."

"They are hanging in his room. He loved her that much to keep them."

"Yeah…and now," he took in a deep breath. "Now, I want to wear them when I'm riding for him…so I'm riding for both of them."

"Oh, Brodie," the words barely escaped and the tears fell again.

"I just can't get myself to open the door."

If I thought about it, I would never be able to do it. I reached for the doorknob and strode into the room as if it was just another day. Walking right to the chaps hanging on the wall I glanced at the bed. The covers were still thrown to the side and pillow indented as if Craig had just risen from the bed. A half-empty bottle of water and an opened bag of chips set on the bedside table.

I lifted the chaps from the hook and when I turned I expected Craig to be standing at the door, glaring at me for being in his room. It was Brodie standing as a statue, his skin pale and eyes filled with anguish. My heart began to hurt so I rushed to the door and shut it quickly behind me.

We stood quiet a moment as my heartbeat returned to normal before I handed him the chaps.

"Thanks…" He exhaled softly before turning away.

We both walked to our rooms to finish packing for the trip to Kennewick.

Our truck and horse trailer turned down the long entry drive of the Kennewick rodeo and fairgrounds. A small car was right behind it and the drivers of two other vehicles started their cars and turned to follow. I recognized Paul Sampson's car and had no doubt the others were reporters, too.

The truck drove past us and I lost them from view. I turned to Brodie who had his leg up on the bed stretching in preparation for his ride.

"Well, we fooled them," I sighed. "They are all following the truck back to the stables where Logan said he was going to take it."

Brodie didn't answer; he had his earbuds in and I could hear the music screaming in his ears.

We were in a small camp trailer that belonged to one of the rodeo committee members. He had loaned it to us for the weekend. Dad and Martin were staying at the Blackburn ranch to watch from the live-feeds. Ryle had ridden in slack and had qualified for the short-go on Saturday so he wasn't here either.

"I'm glad you thought of it," Camille nodded. She was lying on the top bed trying to make sure she stayed out of Brodie's way.

Brodie's eyes were closed as he twisted and turned. His right arm was already taped in preparation for the ride and chaps were around his waist but not buckled around the thighs yet. He just needed his hat and he would be ready to ride. I held it tightly in my hands. The longer we waited, the more sweat beaded on my forehead and slid down my back. The anxiety in my gut was beginning to eat the lining. I had no doubt I was at the first stages of an ulcer.

I leaned to the open window, "The announcer is introducing the directors and sponsors,"

"He's almost to the royalty," Camille added.

We glanced at each other and nodded. My stomach hurt as I reached over and touched Brodie's arm. His eyes darted to me as his hand pulled out the earplugs.

"Ready?" His voice was a growl; eyes narrowed in concentration as he took deep breaths and exhaled them quickly.

I glanced out the window and saw no one near.

"We're only four trailers over from the stands," I reminded him. "You concentrate and we have you covered."

"Then you go get on your horse and warm up," he grumbled and set his hat low on his head. The thick whiskers gave him a dark, rugged look.

Camille slid down from the bed. I nodded and opened the door.

When my foot hit the dirt, a man walked by on my right and I nearly jumped back in but he didn't even look at us. My nerves were ready to tingle out of my skin.

Brodie stepped out of the trailer and he took off with Camille and I having to jog to keep up with him. He walked around the first corner, which was right next to the horse pens and a brunette woman ran right into his chest.

"Get out of my way," the brunette said in a low voice.

"You're the one in the way," Brodie huffed and his hands came up to both of her upper arms and physically turned her to the side and out of the way as he continued his march to the chutes.

"Damn it!" The brunette yelled and took a step toward him.

Anger flared through me and I jumped in front of her with Camille at my side, "Back-off, bitch. Leave him alone."

"Are you kidding me?" She huffed and looked pissed. "LEAVE HIM ALONE? I didn't fucking manhandle him! Tell him to leave me alone."

My back stiffened and I started to take a step toward her when Camille took my arm and pulled me away, "Let's just go."

I instantly forgot about the brunette and jogged after Brodie.

"Seriously, Delaney," Camille whispered and I looked up at her. "You need to take a breather. Brodie ran into her, it wasn't her fault. I'd be pissed if a guy grabbed me like that."

"He didn't mean anything by it," I growled.

"We both know that but she doesn't and you looked like you were going to rip her head off."

We walked along the animal pens and to the back of the metal stairway where the cowboys entered the platform.

I blocked the entryway making sure no one could get to Brodie. He was standing in front of the chute where the dark bay horse he was going to ride was already loaded. The floor of the platform was even with the belly of the horse and Brodie's hands were resting on the top rail, his white vest and straw cowboy hat shown in the light. The long white fringe of his light blue chaps was still, which meant he wasn't moving...at all. He just stared out in the arena.

He looked so damn lost. I felt the tears rising and my body tremble. My gaze wandered to the other cowboys...Craig should be there. They should be pumping each other up for the ride like they had a thousand times before.

Camille's hand took mine and we squeezed tightly. I knew this first rodeo was going to be hard, but I didn't expect the physical pain in my heart.

"Delaney?"

I turned to a cowboy looking at me. It was Tate Owens, one of Brodie and Craig's saddle bronc friends.

"Hi, Tate," I whispered and wiped the moisture from my eyes.

"How are you holding up?" His voice was tender and soothing.

I just shrugged with a deep breath, "First time since..."

"I know," Tate sighed. "Can't even imagine what you're all going through, let alone Brodie." He took my elbow and smiled. "I'll take care of him on the platform during bareback and I'll talk to a couple bareback riders about taking care of him during saddle bronc."

Tears filled my eyes, these roughies had hearts.

"Are you riding tonight?" He asked.

"Breakaway tonight and barrels tomorrow night," I answered.

"It's up to you," Tate said. "But, we'll take care of him if you want to go warm-up."

"Go," Camille ordered and took my arm. "You go, I'll stay and between me, Tate, and all these cowboys back here, we got Brodie. No reporters will get to him."

My whole body trembled with the need to stay with him.

"Delaney," Camille turned me and glared. "Go get on Archer; he will make you feel better. He'll get you to relax." She nodded to Tate. "We got Brodie. Trust us."

"I do," I whispered and wiped away an escaped tear. "Ok, thank you," I said to Tate and with one glance out to Brodie standing like a statue over the horse, I turned away.

I jogged back to the warm-up arena where Logan was ponying Archer while he rode his horse, Fred. Three people I didn't recognize tried to talk to me but I just shook my head and kept going.

"How is he?" Logan asked as he handed me the reins.

"A statue over the chute," I answered and stepped up onto the saddle. "Camille and Tate are with him. Let's go watch from the entry gate."

We trotted the horses down to the arena and arrived as the second rider's chute gate was opened. Brodie was just stepping over the top of a tall bay horse.

"Delaney," Logan turned to me. "We have to concentrate or this isn't worth it."

I just nodded.

"It isn't going to do him any good if we can't get it together and he starts to worry about us, too." Logan continued.

"I'm trying," I whispered but it felt like my heart was beating right in my throat. "I just feel...honestly, a bit out of control." The tears started to rise again.

He gripped my forearm and squeezed, "You need to let it go and just concentrate on that one throw tonight."

"I know, I will."

"...Brodie Rawlins..."

We both looked back to the arena in time to see Brodie lean back on the horse, one hand in the air, chin tucked to his chest, then a nod.

"Ugh," I growled as my body rose as the horse bust out of the chute with two hard lunges. A high buck to the back followed by a fierce high back-humping jump with a dip to the right...a zag to the left then the horse straightened out to buck in a circle with strong high kicks all the way through the eight seconds. The pick-up men were quickly at his side.

I was gripping Logan's arm tightly as Brodie slid from the pick-up man's horse. Without hesitation, he walked across the arena and up and over the chutes.

My neck arched to see where he was going but he stopped in the back.

"I can't see him," I moaned.

"You take care of you," Logan grumbled then turned back to the arena. "What the hell was his score?"

"Yeah, see. It wasn't just me," I huffed.

"Brodie is riding bareback as a tribute to his late friend who passed away a few weeks ago," the announcer said solemnly.

"Damn, I don't want to hear that," I mumbled.

"And an 86 point ride takes him to the top of the leader board," the announcer continued.

His voice faded as Logan, and I turned away from the arena.

"That's a good start," Logan said then looked over his shoulder. "Take care of you and concentrate on that one throw."

"Back at ya, but throw yours to the ground," I smiled at our corny joke.

He huffed then trotted away to the opposite side of the arena.

I rode in circles as I listened to the announcer calling out the bareback rider's scores.

"And our last rider of the night is Trenten Montero," the announcer called out.

I stopped Archer to the side of the warmup arena and stared out across the mass of truck and horse trailers. My eyes closed as I listened to the crowd and the announcer. There was a gasp then a yell, then the announcer called out, "Nice ride, Trenten! The scores are coming in from the judges and...that's an 85 point ride! Which means Brodie Rawlins' first ride for his friend is the top ride of the night and we'll see him in the short-go on Saturday."

I wanted to be with him. He had to be happy to win the first night. Dad and Martin were watching the live feeds from Blackburn's ranch house, so I sent a quick text.

Text to Dad: Great start, Camille and cowboys are taking care of him behind the chute.

Text from Dad: You concentrate on you now.

Humph, if I didn't know any better, I'd think he and Logan had been talking.

I returned to the entry gate in time to watch Logan nod for his steer. The animal burst out of the chute with Logan sliding off his horse. In 4.1 seconds, he had a textbook turn and he and the steer were on their backs in the dirt.

"That was good," I whispered to myself then walked to the back by the timed-events chute to find a quiet spot, swing the rope, and concentrate.

As the team ropers finished their runs, I walked to the fence to watch the calves for the first of the breakaway ropers.

"They are quick tonight."

I didn't even turn to the voice, I just visualized a perfect run.

"Delaney Rawlins is our next roper..."

The announcer's voice faded away as I just concentrated on the men at the chute and the calf.

"Focus," I whispered to myself as I backed Archer back into the box. He stood quietly but his head always bounced from left to right as he anticipated the run.

I cleared everything from my mind but the horse, the rope, and the calf. The chute man was watching me; waiting for my nod.

One last breath and nod...

Archer lunged and three swings later I was pulling him to a halt and the rope flew from my saddle horn and bounced behind the calf trotting across the arena. Damn, that seemed too fast. I turned back to look for a broken barrier but there wasn't one. The reader board with our image trotting after the calf said it was a 2.5-second run. Not bad for this arena.

I retrieved the rope and was let out the gate and into an onslaught of questions.

"Where is Brodie? Can we talk to him?"

"How is Brodie feeling about the loss of Craig?"

"How did Brodie learn that his friend was dead?"

My whole body tensed, pain shot through my stomach, and I had to fight off the urge to hit them all with the lariat.

"How is the family holding up?"

"We'd like to update our readers..."

I nudged Archer into a trot down the road and away from all the questions.

Taking the long way around the parking lot and away from people, I made my way back to the stalls.

"Where the hell have you been?" Logan growled as I neared.

"Lots of questions at the gate," I answered and stepped down from the horse.

"I got them, too," He huffed.

"I took the long way around and away from people."

"Just tell them the family is dealing with the loss and Brodie is doing the best he can."

I pulled the saddle from Archer and glared at Logan; "I don't have to tell them anything. They should take in consideration what he is going through."

"They are only human, and most are just sympathetic and concerned."

"We're only human, too and trying to make it by one minute at a time."

"Delaney, they waited until after our runs, that was decent of them."

I just glared at him as I took care of Archer.

When I closed the horse's stall for the night, I looked around the trailers surrounding the long stable.

"Where's the truck?"

"Back toward the front," He turned without another word and started walking, thoroughly expecting me to follow.

So, I did.

He walked us right back to the little trailer we were using to hideaway before the rodeo.

"What are we doing here?"

He opened the door, turned, grabbed my arm, and nearly threw me up into the doorway.

"What the hell, Logan?" I gasped at the sudden movement and turned to glare at him.

He shut the door in my face with him outside and me barely a step inside.

"What the hell?" I gasped and reached for the door handle.

"Hello, Gorgeous."

Every nerve in my body that had been ready to attack Logan melted and I fell back against the wall. I turned to see Ryle standing with a hip comfortably resting against the counter and a roguish smile beaming from him.

I stared at him a moment before my mind settled from the shock of seeing him, "I thought you weren't coming until Saturday morning."

His grin widened, "That was the initial plan, but I got a call and was told to get my ass up here tonight."

"Why?"

"Because, Sweetheart, it seems as though you've been a bit on edge leading up to this rodeo and after I got here tonight, I heard you nearly decapitated a poor girl because Brodie ran into her."

My head fell back against the wall and I sighed, "Maybe I overreacted on that one."

We just stared at each other a moment.

"So you've been brought here to tame the savage beast?"

He laughed, "Never in a million years would I want you tame."

I smiled, "I'm still getting used to the fact they know about us."

"Me, too, and it came as quite the shock when your Dad called with a direct order."

"Can you imagine the call from him if he heard we got married in Vegas last year?"

CHAPTER THIRTY-FIVE

"I have a feeling it wouldn't have been a call, it would have been a face-to-face with a very disappointed father."

"Yeah…so it's probably a good thing you talked me out of it," I sighed with a wistful smile. "I still want to be your wife."

"And I want to be your husband," he nodded. "Just with our families with us."

"I agree, so how long do we have tonight?"

"It's about eight o'clock now, and we have this place for the next twelve hours without interruption…if you want."

"If I want?" I grinned and reached out to turn the lock on the door.

"Good decision," he grinned. "I stopped and bought you a few things. They are in the bathroom so you can take a hot shower to relax first, then I have something special planned."

"Oohhh, I love your something specials."

"Take a shower, no makeup, hair wet, and put on the items in the bag, then I'll tell you what it is."

My mind raced with the possibilities, "No makeup and wet hair?"

"Yes," he flipped a hand to the bathroom. "Go, so we can do this."

I giggled and hurried into the bathroom. The bag was on the counter, but I didn't look until after I had showered. Then I peered inside and started giggling in confusion.

"You want me to wear all of it?" I called out through the door.

"Yes."

I slid on a purple lace bra that didn't come close to covering my breasts, a matching demi-thong then, oddly enough, a pair of jeans. That was it. I tousled my damp hair to make it as sexy as I could then unzipped the jeans so just the top of the lace panties could be seen.

When I stepped out of the bathroom, the blackout curtains were drawn, lights turned off and the room was lit by a dozen small battery-operated candles. Their light flickered around the small trailer and danced off the man standing barefoot in just jeans. Our eyes met then his slowly lowered all the way to my toes and back up.

"Just as I imagined except the unzipped part; that is just fucking sexy," he whispered with a grin. "You...are more than any man could ever dream of."

With just a look, I told him how much I loved him.

"Well, I think the cowboy hat has to go back on." The flickering candles lit his flat abs as they twisted to grab the hat. He placed the hat back on low; just above his eyes. "How long have you imagined this?"

"I heard a song a couple of weeks ago and it instantly made me think of you. I've been imagining all different scenarios to listen to it with you and that outfit and a quiet dark room with just enough room to slow dance was exactly what I wanted."

"Intriguing...what is the song?"

He leaned over his phone that was sitting on the counter and hit the play button.

I recognized the first chords, "Chris LeDoux?"

"*Just look at you girl*," he whispered the lyrics with a warm smile as the song began to play. "*...standing here beside me, starlight on your hair, looking like a dream I dreamed somewhere...*"

My heart melted as he whispered the song and we slowly walked to each other as if in a dream. There may have been thousands of people outside the trailer at the rodeo and fair, but at that moment, no one else in the world existed besides the two of us. Our fingertips barely touched each other and caressed down arms, across necks, fluttered down a chest to the abs, then to trace across the back as we began to sway to the music. His lips kissed my temple and slowly moved down to my ear. He softly sang the words, "*You mean everything to me.*"

I leaned into him as our fingers continued the exploration of bare skin and lips barely touching. We swayed, kissed, touched and played out this fantasy he had dreamed for us. This man…how could it be that I loved him more this second than I did five minutes ago?

Gaston stepped up into the trailer as I threw the lead rope over his back, then followed him in to shut the divider.

When I closed the back gate, Brodie was walking out of the Blackburn's house. A slight smile escaped as he approached.

"You're sure about this?" The ache in my stomach increased.

"I need it to be normal," he nodded. "I need to get ready at the chutes, not hidden in a trailer."

"I understand," I wrapped my arms around him and squeezed tightly.

"Well," he chuckled and squeezed back. "I like this better than you growling at everyone. That Ryle guy must have some magic in him."

"To tame the wild beast?" I chuckled and stepped back.

"No one in this family wants a tame Delaney," he assured me with a smile. "Just a sane one."

"Ryle helps with that. He always has."

"It's been nice spending the day roping with him. That palomino of his is sure a quirky thing."

"Silas," I grinned. "And Dexter is the sorrel."

"Damn fine horses, and it was fun having our own mini-tournament."

"And who won?"

He laughed, and it made my heart relax just a bit.

"You, my sister, you won but then again, you have had more practice."

"True," I conceded with a smart-ass grin.

"You guys ready?" Logan approached with Lacie Jae, Camille, and Ryle right behind him.

It was still a bit bizarre to have Ryle in our group but I smiled at him and our hands instantly stretched to each other.

"What did Dad decide?" Brodie asked as we reached for the truck door handles.

"Since all three of us qualified for the short-go in our events last night, he is going to stay here with Martin tonight and then go to the arena tomorrow," Logan answered.

The closer we got to the arena, the quieter Brodie became and the more my stomach hurt. He was in the front seat with Lacie Jae sitting between the two men while I sat in the back between Camille and Ryle. Brodie began the low hum again as he stared out the side window; his body seemed to lower into the seat. My hand went over my stomach, causing a sideways glance to me from Camille.

"Nobody is going to approach him with Logan as his security guard tonight," she whispered.

Ryle squeezed my hand, "You want me to stay with you or Brodie?"

I wanted him with me but I also wanted him with Brodie. "Stay with Brodie."

"Lacie Jae and I will be with Delaney," Camille whispered.

"Anybody messes with her and we'll kick their ass," Lacie Jae huffed.

We all chuckled.

It was still early when we arrived. Very few cars were on the rodeo entrance side of the arena. I doubted after last night's covert arrival anyone would be expecting us to arrive so early or all together.

"I want an elephant ear," Lacie Jae declared rather loudly.

"Of course you do," Logan chuckled as he held her hand while she slid out of the truck.

"While you guys are getting ready, I'm going over to the fair and see if I can find one," she told him.

"It will help you focus better once you've had one," he grinned and they shared a quick kiss before she walked away.

An hour later, we were sitting in front of the borrowed camp trailer with Logan on the phone trying to find her.

"If she doesn't answer me back, we're sending out the search party," he growled.

CHAPTER THIRTY-SIX

Text to Lacie Jae: Logan is a bit frantic.

Within minutes she appeared around the end trailer by the stock pen full of bucking horses.

"What the hell, LJ?" Brodie grinned. "You trying to drive him insane?"

She didn't say anything, she just smiled as she wrapped her arms around Logan's waist and squeezed.

"Damn," Logan sighed while the rest of us chuckled.

There was something about her that seemed different than when she had left. The tired lines around her eyes were relaxed, shoulders lower, and there was a sense of ease about the way she was holding Logan. Since Craig's death, she had held him as if he was an anchor and she was afraid to let go. Now, she seemed calm.

When the rodeo began, I was riding Gaston in the warm-up arena behind the stables. The sun was just beginning to go down as we loped along the fence. Camille and Lacie Jae were standing at the gate encouraging the steer wrestlers as they left the arena and began their ride to the rodeo. When the team ropers began to depart, I was slowly walking in the circle. I didn't see the breakaway ropers leave. I was standing at the back corner of the arena, looking out in the distance and remembering the year before when we had ridden at this rodeo. Craig scored an 89 with his horse while Brodie had a 79. There had been teasing, laughter, shots of Pendleton whisky and both left the rodeo Saturday night with a new girl on their arms.

So much fun, so different than this year...it was so wrong...Craig should be here. A hollow ache in my heart caused my stomach to hurt again. Tears filled my eyes and slowly escaped. I wanted to curl into a ball in the bed and go to sleep until this overwhelming sadness went away.

Gaston began to walk and my whole body jerked to attention. Camille was leading him out of the arena.

"I got him," I whispered and lifted the reins with one hand and wiped the tears away with the other.

Her large glistening eyes looked up at me and our hearts ached in shared loss.

We were across the arena behind the roping chutes when the bronc riding began. Brodie was standing on the large platform behind his horse with hands on the rail and eyes staring into the arena. Behind him, standing in an arc, were five bareback riders that had already ridden. They were there for him as well as Ryle and Logan standing to the side.

"That's Johnny getting on now, isn't it?" Camille asked.

"Yeah," my breath shook as I exhaled the word.

She looked down at the day-sheet, "He's riding a horse called Fizzling Dud."

"Who in the world would call a horse Fizzling Dud?" Lacie Jae huffed. "Especially a bucking horse?"

Her question made me smile, "He'll probably be just the opposite."

When the gate swung open, the horse kicked high to the back, twisted in the air as he went down then kicked and twisted again. At the last second, he zig-zagged with his front hooves, and Johnny rode through it with fast spurring strokes.

"Oh, my gosh!" Lacie Jae gasped. "How did he hold on?"

"That was fun to watch," Camille applauded.

Johnny ran back to the chutes to be greeted with pats on the back and high-fives when his 88 point score was announced.

Brodie stood as a statue, not even flinching when the next rider burst out of the chute. Two bareback riders stepped up to him and his whole body startled from the intrusion. My heart clenched. It was all I could do to keep from bursting into tears.

We watched silently as the saddle was adjusted and tightened for the ride. Once Brodie rose above the horse, the judge and cameraman appeared at the chute. When he lowered, the horse rocked back and forth then stood still as Brodie lifted the buck rein, rolled his shoulders in, and tucked his chin to his chest. He nodded and the gate flew open.

Boom-boom-boom…my heart was pounding so hard I could barely hear the crowd yelling as the horse bucked in a large circle. Powerful kicks to the back and high into the air for the whole eight seconds. The pick-up-men helped him from the saddle and once his feet hit the ground, he marched to the bucking chutes without acknowledging anyone. He disappeared into the back when his 87 points was announced, which placed him second for the night, qualifying him for the short-go.

When the pounding in my ears eased, I could hear the announcer talking about Craig again so I quickly turned Gaston away from the fence and made my way to the opposite side of the arena. I didn't see Ryle, Logan, or Brodie.

The first barrel racer ran through the gate and into the arena. I leaned down to run a hand over Gaston's shoulder and took a deep breath. I tried hard to visualize the impending run but all I could see was the heartbreaking image of Brodie standing behind the chute. Another deep breath and I slowly released it. A hand appeared over the top of mine and I turned to look into Brodie's eyes.

The chaps were gone, he was back in his regular boots, and was wearing his grey Circuit Finals jacket. With the thick growth of whiskers and the low black cowboy hat, he looked rugged.

"Trust Gaston," he whispered.

I wanted to cry.

"You get in there and back out, then we'll go find somewhere and have a big banana split."

I chuckled and the rising anxiety began to subside, "We could just stop at the grocery store and get our own toppings."

"There you go," his lip twitched with the effort to smile. "Caramel, hot fudge…"

"Maraschino cherries on top."

He grimaced, "Those are nasty."

"Unless they are soaked in Fire Ball," I grinned.

"That would be true. We'll save those for tomorrow night." he smiled and my heart relaxed.

"Sounds like a plan," I nodded.

"Then go get this run done so we can get to the store," he patted Gaston on the shoulder then smiled one last time before walking away.

My body was relaxed as I rode up to the gate; my mind switched between ice cream toppings and visualizing the impending run as we waited our turn. When I rode out of the arena with a 17.27-second place run, my mind was focused on ice cream and Ryle.

We were at the grocery store, all six of us filling the cart with our favorite toppings when Brodie's phone alert rang out.

We stopped and waited as he read the message.

"I drew Yipee Kibitz for bareback and Blue Backsplash for saddle bronc," he announced.

"Seriously! Who the heck names those horses?" Lacie Jae huffed.

We all laughed and walked to the ice cream cooler.

Saturday morning, after Ryle had left to meet with his roping partner, I lowered myself onto the lawn chair on the back porch of the Blackburn's ranch house. It overlooked their personal arena where Camille was working the chute, Brodie was hazing, and Logan was on his tenth practice steer. Lacie Jae was sitting on top of the chute cheering him on.

I smiled at Dad who was beside me and had supervised the whole morning's arena activities.

"Memphis looked good," he said.

"He feels good, really getting the hang of it."

"Why didn't you ride Archer?"

"I rode him yesterday during our roping tournament," I smiled.

"That you won."

"That he helped me win. So, Memphis gets to practice today and Archer gets to work tonight."

"They are a good pair," he nodded thoughtfully. "You need a backup for Gaston."

"Well, Embers filled in alright."

"She won't for the long haul."

"I know…too bad I couldn't make up my mind about barrel racing before I sold Peppers."

"I give that an 8.3!" We turned to Lacie Jae's voice.

"An 8.3?" Logan called out to her with a grin as he walked back to the chute.

"Yeah, like in gymnastics. Your legs were wonky so you only get an 8.3," she explained with a teasing smile.

"Wonky?" Brodie laughed.

"Yeah, he didn't slide. He just hit the ground and tipped the steer over," Her arms and waist turned as if she was wrestling the steer.

"But, if I get it thrown in less time if I don't slide, it is better." Logan grinned.

"Maybe, but its funner to watch when you slide a long ways," She wrinkled her nose at him as he walked up next to her to wrap his arm around her and pull her in for a kiss.

"She is so good for him," I whispered.

"And your young man is for you."

"He is."

Martin walked out of the house and sat next to us. We quietly watched Logan and Brodie race down the arena with the steer between them.

"Brodie's doing better than I expected," I mused.

"We're keeping his mind busy…all of your minds busy. It will get harder for him with each rodeo," Martin nodded.

"I figured the first would be the hardest," I said.

Dad shook his head, "No…he's focused on this one. He'll start struggling the closer we get to Saturday at Pendleton."

"He really needs to place tomorrow to get the points to get that saddle," I sighed. "It'll be harder with each week."

They both looked at me with a solemn nod.

378

Logan and I resumed our positions at the arena gate entrance to watch Brodie stand on the platform behind the chute. His drawn horse, Yipee Kibitz, the big bay with a white blaze stood calmly watching the action in the arena.

Dad, Lacie Jae, and Camille were sitting in the lower reserved section next to the platform and close to the stock pens in the back. Just as Brodie lowered to tighten the cinch on the horse, Martin appeared to sit next to Dad. The announcer was standing in the arena right in front of them and turned to look at him with wide eyes, then cocked his head with a lift of a brow...silently asking him a question. Martin shook his head and the announcer turned away from him.

"He won't introduce him," Logan sighed. "He'll respect his wishes."

"Yeah," I swallowed hard and my gaze focused on Brodie.

Not once did he look in Martin's direction.

"What do you know on the horse?" I asked.

"Strong, good kick, can throw a few wicked jump turns in the middle...good points."

"Strong enough to help him get points?"

"Strong enough to get him the win."

The gate swung open and the horse burst out with Brodie's boots high up on his neck. Fierce, high bucks with Brodie matching each with a fast spur until the eight-second horn blared and I could breathe again. A gasp escaped when he tumbled off the back hip of the horse. It didn't seem to faze him as he rolled up to his feet and walked out of the arena with an 88.5 score.

Logan and I looked at each other then made our way to the other side of the arena where the roping chutes were. Ryle and Jess greeted us with welcoming grins as the last bareback rider walked out of the arena and Brodie was announced the average winner for bareback. With the win, he'd earned his first six points toward the saddle.

Minutes later, Brodie appeared and stood between Ryle's horse and Archer, well hidden from the crowd as we watched Logan chase the steer down the arena. He remained tucked between horses as the steer wrestling finished with Logan in second.

When Ryle rode into the arena, it was the first time I could openly cheer for him. Therefore, I let out a long, loud whistle and fist-pumped the air with a "woof woof woof"! Both Jess and Ryle grinned as they backed into the box.

"Go, Baby, Go!" I yelled and was rewarded with laughter from everyone around us.

I waited until they bust out of the box with ropes flying before I cheered again. When their 5.6 time was announced I cheered again with 'woof woof' and another loud whistle. As Ryle trotted across the arena to follow the steer, he turned back and looked over his shoulder…so I did it again. Then again, when they were announced the winners of the rodeo which was going to help them in the standings for the chance to go to Vegas and the NFR; Ryle was currently in 17th and Jess in 16th but needed to be 15th or better.

When Ryle returned to my side, he leaned in for a big 'public display of affection' kiss. We giggled and held hands until I entered in the arena for breakaway. I looked back at Logan and Ryle on horseback with Brodie standing between them. All three were grinning in encouragement. I would have given anything for a picture of that moment.

"Go, Baby, Go!" Ryle yelled and I grinned with the pressure in my stomach easing.

Archer's rump leaned back against the panel, his head bouncing left and right, my hand gripping the rope as I held it behind me. I tried to clear my mind of everything but the calf. Taking a deep breath, I timed my nod to Archer's bounce, and the lever was thrown and the calf bolted with Archer right behind him. In 2.2 seconds, we were skidding to a halt and the calf ran down the arena with my rope dangling behind him. I could hear the three men behind me cheering loudly and as I trotted down the arena, I could see Dad, Camille, Lacie Jae, and Martin cheering, too.

Family…they were my family and my heart filled with pride and love until the gate was opened and I rode out of the arena at the opposite end.

"Delaney, how is Brodie handling the death of Craig?"

"Where is Brodie now?"

"How did Brodie learn that his friend was dead?"

"Can I set up an interview with the family?"

They were all asked by one voice that I recognized but I didn't even acknowledge him. I just trotted down the road as my heart pounded in emotions. By the time I made it back to the stalls, Logan and Ryle were there unsaddling their horses and Camille was leading Gaston out of his stall.

I was greeted with congratulations for my second-place finish and Logan's questioning eyes.

"Same problem?" He asked.

"Yeah, just one reporter this time," I answered. "The guy that showed up at the ranch."

"You OK?" Ryle asked.

I just nodded as Camille took Archer's reins and I took the reins for Gaston.

Within minutes, I was riding Gaston out into the warm-up arena. Ryle appeared riding his sorrel horse bareback and smiling broadly.

"You have to warm-up, doesn't mean you have to do it alone," he grinned.

We rode quietly next to each other and listened to the announcer. When the saddle bronc was announced, we trotted over to the arena gate. Much to my surprise, Logan and three other steer wrestlers were there and made a space for the two of us.

"What…?" I started.

"Just making sure no reporters are around," Logan interrupted.

I looked around at the men and silently thanked each one.

The first chute was opened and a large bay horse made a spectacular leaping entrance into the arena. His first kick was nearly vertical, followed by high, powerful kicks with a twist in his back that had the rider tumbling before the 8 seconds were completed.

"Damn, that was something," Ryle muttered.

"Cowboy rides him to the horn and he'll walk away with a check," one of the steer wrestlers said.

Another four riders rode for the eight seconds before Brodie slid over the top of his horse; Blue Backsplash. He needed at least an 87 point score to win the average and the 6 points toward the saddle. Logan leaned against Gaston's shoulder just in front of my leg as we silently watched.

Brodie settled onto the horse, hand gripping the rope, he leaned back and nodded. The gate swung open with the horse taking two leaping strides then bucked high in the air. Brodie's body was elongated with feet deep in the stirrups at the horse's shoulder and free arm stretched high in the air behind him. It was a perfect position followed by boots and spurs curling back to the saddle and arm swinging down for balance. Fast spurring matched the horse's strong kicks in a tight circle. The horn blared and the free arm reached for the rein as the pick-up man rode in alongside of him.

My body relaxed and I caught the lowering of Logan's shoulders.

"Damn good ride," Logan began nodding as I began breathing again.

"He should place," I exhaled. "He should get points for that ride."

"Absolutely," Ryle added.

"Ladies and Gentlemen!" The announcer's voice called out. "That was an 87.5 ride for second place today but it gives Brodie a 174.5 average for the win. Remember, he also won the bareback average earlier. It was a great rodeo for Brodie and his commemorative rides for his late friend Craig Houston."

"Twelve points this rodeo," Logan turned to look up at me.

"Great start," I nodded with a smile but an ache in my heart.

"We'll take care of him; you and Gaston go kick some ass," Logan said with a nod to Ryle.

I backed away from the fence and trotted to the warm-up arena.

As I returned, I could see the reporter that had been to the house standing on the side of the road. When he saw me, he raised a camera toward me so I took a deep breath and rode past him as if he didn't exist.

At the entry gate, Logan, Ryle, and the other steer wrestlers were still there watching the tie-down roping. The other barrel racers, including Jess' girlfriend, Jamie Hamilton and I paced the horses just outside the entry gate. I was third in line so I stopped and watched the first ride on the distant video screen. Cheyenne Wimberley rode out with a 17.46, which was followed by Jamie's 17.85.

"Go get 'em, Sis," Logan called out as Gaston pranced into the arena then bolted to the first barrel. After the 17.51 seconds ride we trotted out to hear his, "Nice run."

When I pulled Gaston to a halt, Ryle and Logan were walking toward me then followed as we made our way back to the horses and trailer.

Camille joined us partway down the road, "Successful rodeo for the Rawlins family. Brodie got those saddle points on the board. He and Martin went back to the trailer. Evan and Lacie Jae stayed to watch the bull riding."

Once the horses were loaded into the back of the trailer, we joined Martin and Brodie in the living-quarters section. One of the four bottles of maraschino cherries soaked in Fireball was already devoured. The other three were gone before Lacie Jae and Dad arrived.

Sunday night, I carried the last load of laundry to my room. After arriving back from the Kennewick rodeo so late, the day had been quiet and lazy. Chores were completed, then movies and eating filled the day. I had finally managed to force myself to do the laundry.

Dad and Martin were leaned back in the recliners, both half asleep, while Logan and Lacie Jae were cuddled on the long sofa. Both were asleep. Brodie was sitting in the side chair, awake but staring out the window. He looked lost. I let him be. He was surrounded by family and if he needed anyone, they were right there.

I continued down the hall to my room. Camille's door was open and she had a suitcase open on her bed, but it was empty, and she was sitting in front of the laptop. Her roping clinic at the 3.3 Ranch began the next morning.

After putting the laundry basket in my room, I went back to talk to her, "I thought you would be packed by now."

She looked at me with a mean glare, "I'm not going."

CHAPTER THIRTY-SEVEN

I turned off the highway and followed the side road for a hundred feet then stopped. Just on the other side of the rise in the road was the 3.3 equestrian ranch. I could turn around now and never look back. But...I knew I couldn't. I had to face this...her...for him.

Slowly, the truck crept forward until I was at the base of the rise and I stopped again. The clock on the dash said the clinic started in 10 minutes. I should have been there at least a half-hour before to get signed in and have Memphis and Madi warmed up.

Moving forward again, my stomach ached as we approached the top of the hill. Once we crested the top, the truck would be visible from the estate and there would be no turning back. With a deep breath, I forced myself to hit the accelerator and continue.

A black wrought-iron fence spanned across the road and out into the field on each side, but the wide double gates were open as if inviting me in. There was no turning back now, so I passed through and stared at the property as I picked up speed to make it look like I was in a hurry.

The large house was next to the road leading into the driveway: a smaller building and large arena set between the house and the long horse stable. Metal panels created two additional arenas, as well as two round pens. Just on the other side of the large stable was the construction site of an indoor arena. The entire estate was surrounded by acres of pasture with horses grazing peacefully or standing along the fence watching us arrive.

It was beautiful...heavenly.

The pasture across from the house was covered with twenty horse trailer and truck outfits.

As I neared the house and slowed down to turn, a woman walked up to the road to greet me.

"Good morning," She said with a bright, welcoming grin. "You must be Camille."

My cowboy hat was low, hair captured in a braid down my back, and dark sunglasses covered my eyes. If anyone knew her, they would not guess I was Camille.

I just nodded…I didn't want to speak the lie out loud.

"They are getting ready to start so to make it quicker, why don't you park in the main driveway by the barn," She pointed to the opposite side of where everyone else was parked.

"Ok, thanks," I smiled and turned.

She walked alongside the truck. "I've got you checked in."

"I appreciate that."

"I'm Andrea, just let me know if you have any questions. Bathrooms are at the end of the barn, coolers of water behind the chutes. We'll break for an hour at noon for lunch."

I stopped the truck just where she pointed and with a deep breath, I stepped out of the truck.

She handed me a clipboard and a pen. "Just need your autograph on the release form."

I signed the paper with a scribble so it wasn't really legible, but she didn't even look at it when I handed it back to her.

Across from us was a small bleacher then the arena with horses and riders trotting in a wide circle to warm up.

I quickly had Madi unloaded and tied to the side of the horse trailer then Memphis made his appearance.

"Damn, those are nice horses…very beautiful and unique," Andrea said.

"Full brother and sister," I tied him to the trailer and opened the tack room.

"Do you rope with both?"

"Madi, the bald face mare, will be worked in roping and barrels, but Memphis here will be a breakaway horse." I swept the brush across his back.

386

"I'm going to go make sure they have what they need and will open the gate to the arena for you."

"Thanks," I whispered and quickly saddled the horse.

Madi whinnied softly and pranced as I stepped up onto the saddle and rode Memphis away from her.

My gaze went to the building that set between the house and the arena. It was called the bunkhouse, and Ryle had sent me numerous pictures of it because it was his home. My hands trembled slightly as I looked at the building. I knew he wasn't there, but it still made me a bit anxious to see his home for the first time.

When I walked through the gate to the arena, I smiled down at Andrea and nodded my thanks. I looked up to 21 riders on horseback, looking at me. Nineteen riders had stopped along a fence to face two riders standing in the arena; Jamie Hamilton and her mother and owner of the estate, Lauren Conners. I had managed to avoid Lauren since Cheyenne; she still made my gut hurt when I looked at her. This was going to be harder than I anticipated but I couldn't turn back now.

Lauren was watching me walk into the arena with her lips rolled into a thoughtful line and her eyes narrowed slightly. There was no doubt; she knew who I was. Jamie was watching me, too, with a curious look but no recognition.

Lauren nodded slightly, then turned her attention to the other riders. She made an introduction speech as I stopped at the end of the line.

There were barrels, poles, and cones spread through-out the arena and Jamie demonstrated a drill for everyone then each person took a turn going through the pattern. It was similar to the drill I had used at home so Memphis breezed through it effortlessly.

When he stopped at the end of the line again, I ran a hand down his neck and took a deep breath. My body had finally started to relax. Horses and riding did that to me.

Everyone went through the pattern a second time with Lauren critiquing as they went through.

I was the last one and she didn't say a word until halfway through the pattern.

"What's the horse's name?"

"Memphis," I answered.

After completing the pattern, we quietly trotted back down to the line. Jamie's eyes darted between her mother and me.

An anxious shiver tingled up my spine.

"Now that I've seen your riding level, I'm going to separate you into two groups so we can focus on what you need," Lauren said to the riders.

She slowly went down the line of riders and designated whether to remain on the pattern, or go to the adjoining arena and work in the box next to the chute.

When she came to me, she hesitated then asked, "Where would you like Memphis to go?"

All the riders looked at me curiously since she hadn't asked that question to anyone else.

I wanted to go to the opposite place she was going, but I had no idea where that was. "We'll go to the box," I answered.

Jamie remained in the arena as Lauren walked her large buckskin horse to the other arena and to the roping box. I sighed...there really wasn't any way of getting away from her. Wasn't the reason for coming here was to face my feelings for her?

The rest of the morning was spent 'learning' different drills and working with each horse and how she could help the riders get better. I was always the last to take a turn and completed what she had asked of the other riders without her saying a word to me. I was beginning to think she was irritated at me.

Just before noon, we gathered into the main arena with Jamie and Lauren facing us.

Lauren turned and looked up the road making everyone look.

I caught my breath when I saw the familiar truck and horse trailer making its way down the road and pull into the driveway behind my trailer and truck.

Lauren turned and looked at me.

"Does he know you're here?" She asked flatly.

Jamie's back straightened and she looked at me in surprise.

I shook my head then watched Ryle and his team roping partner, Jess, step out of their truck.

Ryle walked right to Madi and ran a hand down her back. She was very unique and easily recognized even if she was tied to my regular 4-horse trailer instead of the living-quarters trailer he knew so well. Then, of course, there was the truck but he would be expecting Camille to be here not me and she would not have brought Madi.

His head jerked toward the arena and he stared a moment, then he said something to Jess and with long strides started walking to the arena.

My heart was pounding, hands trembling, and I was trying very hard not to jump off the horse and run to meet him.

Instead of going to the gate, he didn't hesitate in climbing right over the fence, jumping to the ground and striding toward me. His eyes were on me and his grin widened as he approached.

I couldn't help but smile at the excitement that resonated from him.

"Damn, he's sexy," Someone from behind me said.

I giggled as he approached, and Memphis turned to watch him.

I stretched out a hand, and Ryle took it and pulled me from the horse and wrapped his arms around me.

"You have no idea how fucking excited I am to see you here," he grinned just before his lips were on mine for a short, fierce kiss.

Just being in his arms made the whole day better; facing Lauren easier.

He turned to Lauren, "I'm stealing her for a while."

I turned and looked up at her. There was no smile like there was on Jamie's face.

Lauren just nodded then turned back to the other riders. "We'll break for an hour. Andrea has lunch ready in the saloon at the barn."

"Come on," Ryle said and pulled me out of the arena with Memphis right behind us. "I thought Camille was coming here."

"She was..." We stopped at the trailer and I removed Memphis' bridle and replaced it with a halter so he could eat from the feeder.

"But?" Ryle loosened the cinch so the horse could relax during the hour.

"Last night she realized the connection between you and this place. She told me I needed to come and work out my issue."

"Did you tell her everything?"

I shook my head, "No...she has just seen how I react around Lauren, she doesn't know why."

"Well, I would like to know why," Lauren's voice was right behind us.

I jumped back and fell into Ryle's arms. Nausea of having to actually talk to her made my body tremble.

The initial surprise of her being there made me look right into her irritated eyes then I quickly looked away...out to the barn where I thought she had followed the riders.

His arms tightened around me and we stood in silence for a moment before he whispered, "Just say it."

I couldn't look at her and my gaze fell to the ground.

"What the hell did I ever do to you?" Lauren scoffed.

My body cringed and words stuck in my throat.

"It's not like that, Lauren," Ryle said. "Delaney, just tell her."

Still no words as I took a deep breath and tried to look at her but I looked to Memphis instead.

After another minute of silence, while I tried to talk, Ryle whispered again, "Tell Memphis what the issue is. Forget we are standing here."

I closed my eyes and fought off the tears. He knew me so well. I imagined I was standing in Memphis' stall at home, just him and me as I ran a brush across his back. My body relaxed and the words formed.

"She acts, encourages her daughter, and looks just like my mother," I whispered with my eyes closed but tears pushing to fall. "Mom died seven years ago...I miss her so much. Lauren rips out my heart every time I hear her or look at her."

The tears fell and my breath shook.

"Well..." Lauren whispered. "That is something I can understand."

My eyes opened and I looked up into hers. They had changed from irritated to a warmth that made the tears flow even more. I tried to wipe them away but I was embarrassed and a bit overwhelmed, they wouldn't stop.

"I'll be right back," Lauren walked toward the barn.

I turned into Ryle's arms and held him tightly. As much as I wanted to stay in his loving embrace, I also wanted to get away from Lauren. She knew what the issue was now so I could leave.

"I'm going to go home," I whispered to Ryle and his arms tightened but he didn't say anything.

When my body stopped trembling, I stepped back and looked up into his eyes.

"You OK?" His eyes were full of concern as he wiped away the trail of tears on my cheeks.

"Yeah...I think," I tried to smile. "I just need to go now."

"You're running away."

"Yes, I am. But I wanted to come here today to face this for you. I needed to get by this."

"You did this for me?"

I nodded anxiously, "I know she is such a big part of your life...what she has done for you by letting you live here so you could focus on your dreams. I just needed to get this initial face-to-face done but I need to leave now."

"You're stronger than this, Delaney," he whispered with love and understanding. "I can't say I know what you're going through but I know how hard this was for you to even drive here. So, you can be strong and finish the day."

"I don't think I can," I said honestly.

I heard footsteps and turned to see Lauren walking towards us. I didn't shrink away this time but my stomach quivered. She held a bottle of water out to me and with a trembling hand, I took it only to have my arm fall limply to my side.

Lauren smiled at Ryle then looked at me, "My uncle raised me from the time I was twelve until he died when I was twenty-six."

I nodded since Ryle had told me about her history. Her uncle had died in a terrible vehicle accident when someone tried to pass him while he was pulling a full horse trailer and they were hit by an oncoming truck.

"There is absolutely nothing I can say that will change how you are feeling right now," she smiled in understanding and my heart ached. "The only thing that will help is time and refocusing how you perceive me."

"What does that mean?" I whispered.

"Let me show you," she said and stepped back. "Will you walk with me a moment?"

I swallowed hard and leaned out of Ryle's comforting arms. For him, I would go with her to try and contain my feelings for her.

Instead of walking to the arena or to the barn, she walked toward the pasture gate. A dozen horses were grazing peacefully until we walked into the field. They all started walking toward us. I turned to look at Ryle but he was still standing at the horse trailer watching us walk away.

A warm, familiar sensation flowed through my body, causing tingles up my spine. I felt like I was walking with my mother as we made our way to the horses. It was unnerving and I had both the inclination to turn back and the need to stay with the lost memories.

"After I heard that it was you Ryle was seeing, I did research on you."

"Research?" I gasped.

"I love Ryle," Lauren smiled. "He's a special guy, and I wanted to make sure that the woman he was so enamored with was good for him."

I felt defensive now with a bit of the warm memories ebbing out of me.

"In that research, I read the story about Gaston being hurt in Salinas and you having sold your backup horse last January."

"At that time, I wasn't going to race full time," I explained. "But, Embers kept me in the running."

"Yes," Lauren nodded. "But as good as she is, Embers won't make you a full-time backup."

Irritation hit my gut, and again, I felt defensive but bit my lip instead of responding.

My hand went to the first horse we neared. She had scars across her shoulders and down her legs.

"That's Maggie," Lauren said. "She is the mother of all these horses."

"She was your uncle's last horse," I nodded. "The only survivor of the accident."

"Yes."

We quietly walked around the horses a few moments before she spoke again. Touching them made my nerves relax.

"I race a little still so I can ride with Jamie, but my main focus is roping," she said.

I just nodded and continued to give a young bay horse attention.

"Jamie has her two main barrel horses and has chosen two others that she is training."

I glanced at her, but she was looking over the horses.

"BlueDoc is my main barrel horse, but I have been riding a few others at races for training," She continued and pointed to a brown, a red bay, and a palomino. "Those three are five-year-olds and are ready to move on to the next level but I don't have time to take them there and Jamie's working herd is full."

I silently assessed all three horses and would easily love to take all three home.

"The brown with the wide blaze is a direct son of Dash Ta Fame, the palomino is a direct son of Frenchman's Guy," Lauren smiled. "And the bay is Corona Cartel."

I walked to all three and ran a hand down their necks, backs, and over the large quarter-horse rumps.

"Gaston is good with both the long and tighter patterns," Lauren said as she rest against the grazing Maggie. "These three are built just like him; the pali we call Andre, the brown is Maestro, the bay is just named Cartel."

I nodded thoughtfully then turned to look at her, "You're selling them?"

She nodded, "To the right person, and you need a horse ready to take to Vegas with you as Gaston's backup. These three will ride a bit different, but it shouldn't take too long for you to get in-sync. You've got a couple of months to get ready."

My breath caught, and I looked back at the three geldings. Andre, Maestro, and Cartel... I wanted all three. Dad was going to kill me for just bringing one home.

"You don't need the second half of the clinic," Lauren stated. "You can use the large round-pen this afternoon and ride all three to see if one will work for you."

I looked at her with wide eyes and tingles of excitement, "I would never turn down an offer like that."

We both chuckled and the anxiety I felt around her began to subside.

She pulled out her phone.

"I'll send a text to Ryle and ask him to bring halters and lead ropes out since I'm sure he is anxiously waiting for you."

I watched her as she typed on the phone and my heart trembled. She was so much like my mother in mannerisms, looks, everything but how she spoke to me. Lauren's was direct; my mother's was always with a hint of love in every word.

Maybe, the more I talked to her, the more I could actually handle talking to her. It sounded silly, but in my head, it seemed logical.

"Jamie wants to know if you're staying for dinner after everyone leaves," she looked up at me.

I needed to stay with Ryle. Everything in me wanted to be with him.

"Is it alright with you if I stay with Ryle tonight?"

"Of course, it is," she smiled. "So, you're OK now?"

I nodded slightly and saw Ryle walking across the pasture toward us. He always made me feel better...just looking at him smile at me made everything better. I turned back to Lauren.

"Honest...it may take a while," I whispered.

She nodded, "It's been 17 years since my uncle died and I still have problems seeing some of his old team roping partners."

"But, it does get easier?"

"It never goes away," she said softly. "But it will get easier."

"But it helps that you understand now."

"For both of us."

We nodded in understanding as Ryle arrived.

His eyes asked me if I was alright.

"Lauren is offering one of the three geldings as a team member with Gaston for Vegas," I informed him and he grinned broadly. "I'm going to spend the afternoon with them and I thought maybe I would spend the night with you instead of going home."

He laughed, "Did you seriously think I was going to let you leave?"

Lauren chuckled, "My fiancé, Kade, and his grandfather will be home tonight too, so I'll let Jamie know the seven of us can barbeque after everyone leaves."

We each haltered a horse then led them across the field. Ryle and I smiled at each other and our hands came together. Coming here today, as hard as it was, was the right thing to do.

The next morning, I drove down the driveway of the ranch in anticipation of Dad's reaction to the extra horse in the trailer. He was sitting on the porch with Camille and Lacie Jae as I pulled to a stop.

I stepped out of the truck and waved. Camille, of course, instantly stood and walked out to help unload the horses.

"How did it go?" She asked as we met at the back of the trailer.

"Very well," I smiled, and she sighed in relief. "It was a bit rough at first, but Ryle arrived, and we had a nice evening barbeque to help ease the emotions. How is it here? Where's Brodie?"

"He's with Logan and Martin pushing some of the cows somewhere."

"Well, that's some real technical ranch talk," I smirked and untied Memphis and backed him out of the trailer.

She took the lead rope with a laugh, and I turned to unload Madi. I tied her to the trailer and walked back in the trailer.

"What are you doing?" Dad called out.

My grin was filled with guilt when I stepped out of the trailer with the new gelding.

"Delaney! What the hell?" He shouted and instantly turned his wheelchair and drove to the ramp. Lacie Jae was right behind him with a bright grin.

The gelding whinnied loudly and was answered by a dozen new pasture mates.

"You hear that?" Dad yelled.

"Yes," I giggled.

"That's all the horses on the property wanting to know what the hell you're doing bringing *another* horse to eat their hay," he called out.

Camille and Lacie Jae joined in my laughter.

He stopped the wheelchair in front of the gelding, and the horse lowered his head and put his muzzle right in Dad's face and sniffed.

"What the hell?" Dad grumbled and gently pushed the horse's nose away.

"He likes you, Evan," Lacie Jae giggled.

"What's his name?" Camille asked as she slid a hand down the horse's neck and shoulder.

"Maestro," I answered.

"You have tons of M & M's now," Lacie Jae giggled. "Maestro, Memphis, and Madi!"

"You want to explain why you're 6 and 1 for the year?" Dad grumbled, but his hand was sliding gently down the horse's muzzle as it nibbled on the arm of the wheelchair.

"What does that mean?" Lacie Jae asked.

"It means one horse has left the ranch with six horses coming onto it," I answered with a grin.

"That's going to be a full ranch if you keep that up," Camille teased.

"My point exactly," Dad glared at me. "Want to explain?"

"Lauren Conners read about the incident in Salinas and knew I needed a backup horse for Gaston and offered me the choice of three geldings she had trained and ran herself. I rode all three but chose Maestro because we clicked from the first turn. On the final run going full throttle, we clocked a 17.13 standard pattern with a wide second."

"Damn, that's impressive," Dad nodded. "He's for Vegas. Alright, I'll give ya this one."

Camille, Lacie Jae, and I chuckled as the horse sniffed his face again.

The sisters walked the buckskin paints to the barn while I stood next to dad as he visited with the new horse.

"I have to say I was surprised when Camille told me you went to Lauren's place instead of hers."

I looked at him but didn't say anything.

"Daughter," he smiled in understanding. "I have eyes, too, and a woman that looks just like your mother isn't going to be unnoticed."

"She does," I nodded.

"She and her daughter remind me a lot of you and your mother."

"Very much so," I whispered.

"I also know that's why you go to some of the rodeos you go to, or I should say avoid, like Caldwell last year and the Stampede this year."

"She makes me physically ill," I conceded.

"And going to see her yesterday was because Ryle lives at her ranch."

"Yes, I just needed to try and face those demons…well, not demons, more like spirits, and get past it. He lives there, trains there, and his team roping partner is her daughter's boyfriend. It's not something I could just forget about; I needed to face it and try to work through it."

"You're OK with it now?"

I shrugged and let out a slow breath, "I think there is hope."

"Good," he smiled with love shining in his eyes. "I'm proud of you for making that effort, and it shows me just how much you care for that young man."

"A lot, Dad," I nodded. "More than I ever thought possible."

The day before the Walla Walla rodeo, the temperature lowered. The low-hanging dark clouds, slight bone-chilling breeze, and hint of rain in the air lowered everyone's mood. Martin had informed us he wasn't going to travel to Walla Walla. The whole family was quiet at breakfast with barely a word spoken.

Layering a hooded sweatshirt then denim jacket over my long-sleeve shirt, I slid on my gloves then a warm beanie as I walked to the barn. I had four more rodeos to run before the end of the season for breakaway roping and five more for barrels. I needed to focus on them so I was giving Ketchum the next month off.

Gaston, Archer, Memphis, and Maestro were walked to the arena and tied in preparation for training before the rain hit. Only a few sprinkles fell the whole morning. Occasionally, I would glance up at the house and Dad would be sitting in the window watching me ride. Camille and Lacie Jae did not leave the house while Brodie and Logan rode out into the fields.

The men arrived back at the house late in the afternoon so I could finally run fresh steers. With Brodie working the chutes, I hazed for Logan as he ran a dozen steers, then they both went in the house to work out on the fitness equipment.

I remained outside by myself, working drills, and patterns with Maestro. Pendleton was still going to be the last rodeo of the year but I wanted as much time with the new horse before the trip to Vegas, so I had added Othello the Friday night of the Pendleton week. I liked the horse on the ground. He had a curious personality and fondness for Dad's chair, which I thought was funny. He was even better to ride. Lauren had done a phenomenal job training him.

The first heavy raindrop fell just as I was walking the horses to the barn. By the time I had the tack put away and horses stabled and fed, the downpour began. I ran to my trailer and sat on the bench to watch the rain soak the arena I had just left.

Text to Ryle: Can you video chat?

It took ten minutes for a response.

Text from Ryle: Just started jackpot. In a couple of hours.

Text to Ryle: Good luck

I climbed up on the bed and stared at the ceiling. The rain hitting the roof was mesmerizing, but my gut began to ache.

The rain and dark skies did not help the depression in my heart. We needed sunshine and energy from the rodeo crowds, but if the rain continued and the Walla Walla arena was flooded, then the rodeo would be canceled. Brodie wouldn't be able to finish his rides for Craig.

CHAPTER THIRTY-EIGHT

"They aren't making the call until closer to rodeo time," Dad informed us as he rolled into the kitchen the next morning. "There's a good wind blowing, and they're hoping it dries out the arena."

"Well, let's just have a fucking positive attitude today," Logan huffed then grinned at Dad's glare.

"That's right, damn it," Brodie nearly shouted then returned Dad's glare with a bit of a smirk.

"You've raised 'potty mouths'," Lacie Jae quipped with a wide smile.

He looked expectantly at Camille and me.

"I'm your sweet loving angelic daughter," I smiled. "I would never swear."

Brodie choked just as he was taking a drink and squirted milk out of his nose.

"That's damn gross," I gagged.

"Yeah, way to make a liar out of yourself," Camille grinned at me.

Dad just shook his head in feigned exasperation and rolled right through the kitchen and out the back door.

Chuckling, we all followed him.

We were all traveling together in my truck for the five-hour drive to the rodeo. It was a three performance rodeo with no short-go round or average. All of our rides would be tonight, but wouldn't know the results for days.

Hopefully, with everyone trying to keep their sense of humor, Brodie would be relaxed since the absence of Martin was heavy on all our shoulders.

I turned into the dirt parking lot behind the Walla Walla Fairgrounds. Half the lot was already full of trucks, trailers, and horses. The carnival and fair were in full swing on the opposite side of the arena. A Facebook announcement had been sent during our trip stating the rodeo was to be held, but the arena would be muddy.

"Do we have time to go get carnival food?" Lacie Jae asked Logan.

"It's an hour or so before it starts," he nodded.

"Elephant ears again?" Brodie turned to her with a teasing smile.

He had been quiet the whole ride, just staring out the window and barely acknowledging when someone spoke to him. Once or twice, I heard him humming softly to himself.

"No rain in the forecast tonight," Dad stated. "You're all riding tonight with Delaney the last in the breakaway slack after the rodeo; then we'll decide if we want to stay the night here or just head to Ellensburg tonight."

We all just nodded, and the second the truck stopped, all four doors opened.

"Brodie Rawlins?"

We turned to a man walking toward us. His eyes were anxious and excited.

"Yeah," Brodie mumbled as he took a step back toward the trailer.

"I'd like to ask you a few questions..." The man started but was stopped when Logan stepped in front of him, blocking his path.

The man hesitated then silently watched as Brodie walked to the living quarters of the trailer and shut himself inside.

Lacie Jae stepped in front of Logan and glared at the man, "Leave him alone. Leave all of them alone. Give them time to heal. Just be a decent person and walk away."

"I...I...," The man stuttered and took a step back. "I'm sorry for your loss."

He turned and walked away.

No words were spoken as we unloaded the horses. The hollowness in my heart and pain in my stomach increased.

Camille, Logan, and I rode the horses to the warm-up arena while Dad and Lacie Jae disappeared into the trailer to be with Brodie.

When we returned, saddle bronc riders Tate and Johnny were standing at the trailer door.

"Is everything OK?" I asked anxiously.

"Yes, ma'am," Johnny nodded. "We just came to check on the family and wait on Brodie so we could walk together to the chutes."

"Thanks, Johnny," I smiled. "I really appreciate it, but stop calling me ma'am."

"Yes, ma'am," He grinned just as the door opened.

Brodie stepped out of the trailer with his saddle and bag. The pair escorted him toward the bucking chutes.

Three people tried to talk to Brodie but were very adamantly told not to approach by the cowboys. Without hesitation, Brodie walked through the door behind the chutes and disappeared. The rough stock riders that were present, gathered just outside the door to block the entrance.

The tension was making my back and head ache, so I stepped into the trailer to find ibuprofen.

"You relax; just take care of your business," Dad sighed. "He'll be taken care of by his friends."

I took a deep breath and closed my eyes to try and keep the tears at bay. "It's hard, Dad," I whispered.

"I know, Darlin'," he sighed. "It is for all of us, but we have to keep moving forward."

"I understand why Martin decided not to come, but I sure wish he was here."

"Delaney," He held out his phone to me.

There was an image on it; one of the Walla Walla rodeo grounds and it was taken from high on the bleachers across from us.

"Martin?" I whispered as my lungs ached and throat tightened. "Does Brodie know?"

"He does, I received it right before he left the trailer."

"Ok," I whispered and took a deep breath, "Ok…we can do this."

He slowly stood from the bench and opened his arms to me. I fell into them and absorbed as much strength as I could.

"I love you, Dad," I stepped back and looked up into his loving eyes.

He just kissed my forehead and sat down as I walked out of the trailer.

Gaston and I quietly watched the grand entry from the gate at the end of the arena next to the bleachers reserved for the competitors and family. Camille rode next to me on Archer and fellow breakaway ropers, Rylee Potter and Janey Reeves rode in behind me as we waited for Brodie to ride.

My gaze wandered to the bleachers as I tried to remember the angle of Martin's photograph.

"Who did he draw tonight?" Rylee asked.

"Smiling Bob for bareback and Flirtacious for saddle bronc," Camille answered.

Brodie's name was called, and we all turned to watch with my hand going over my stomach to cover the sharp ache. I held my breath from the moment the gate swung open. The horse had high kicks to the back as he turned out of the chute and bucked right past us. Brodie's spurring was fast and strong right up to the timer blaring out over the arena. It took him an additional dozen bucks before he was able to pull his hand from the riggin handle, then he lunged for the pick-up man. As the announcer waited for the score, he told the crowd of Craig's loss, and the memorial bareback rides for him.

I tried hard to keep my mind from thinking too hard, but my eyes were searching the stands where I knew Martin was sitting. My heart ached just a bit more when the 86 point score was announced. When the last bareback rider walked out of the arena, Brodie was in first place. He had a good chance after the rodeo Sunday to get a check and points for the saddle.

Logan passed right by us as he made his way into the arena and into the box. Lacie Jae appeared and stood in front of Gaston with her hands tightly gripping the metal panel.

A 4.5-second run put him in second place for the night.

"That looked good," Lacie Jae called out to him as he rode to the gate. He smiled down at her. "I'll give it an eight."

"Just an eight?" He asked with an eyebrow raised.

"From what I can tell from here, you didn't have your legs right again. You need to work on that." She teased.

His laugh was true and honest and made my heart sigh. She grinned mischievously at us then quickly made her way along the fence to follow him.

"They are such a cute couple," Rylee said.

"That they are," Camille smiled.

"Where's Ryle?" Janey asked.

"He's riding with the crew from the 3.3 Ranch," I answered. "So, he'll be riding here tomorrow night while we'll be in Ellensburg."

"We've ridden at the 3.3 a number of times," Rylee nodded with a smile. "I have to say; I was pretty darn surprised when I saw the picture of you and Ryle come through. I didn't have any clue."

"Neither did I," Janey added. "You two were pretty sneaky about it."

"We were having fun coming up with ways to keep the relationship hidden," I admitted with a chuckle, and the tension in my stomach eased.

We watched the team ropers, then Janey and Rylee roped in the breakaway. They ended the night in first and second place.

"I got my work cut out for me in slack," I grinned at the women.

The announcer's voice rang out, "You've already seen our first bronc rider when he rode in the bareback to an 86 second-place score. Brodie Rawlins is up against Flirtacious from the Brookman Rodeo. This gray mare…there's the nod!"

After a quick turn to the right, the horse had a perfect rocking high kick and Brodie's spurring matched buck to buck. The power and intensity between the two were strong throughout the whole ride.

"Wow…wow…wow…what a great ride!" The announcer called out. "Judge's scores are in and we have an 88.5 ride, which is currently second place."

Just to my left, I could see a man walk out between two trailers, stop, look right at me, then he turned and disappeared. I had no doubt it was the reporter that was at the ranch.

My stomach turned, and the pain made my hand rest on my abdomen. I looked for Brodie but he had disappeared behind the bucking chutes. The door that was blocked by the roughies was the only entry, so I knew the reporter couldn't get to him. Logan and Lacie Jae were standing in front of us watching the ride.

"That reporter is here," I told Logan.

"Which one?" He asked.

"The one that came to the ranch and kept approaching me at the gate in Kennewick," I answered.

He took a breath and sighed, "Maybe you should just…"

My whole body tensed, "Logan," I huffed. "His last question to me was, 'How did Brodie learn that his friend was dead?'. You really think I want to answer that? Why the hell would you even ask that two weeks after?" My voice cracked as my body shook

His shoulders lowered as he nodded, "We were just going over to sit with Dad in the VIP section, which is next to the chutes. I'll watch out for him." He walked to me and set his hand on my leg. "Take a breath, relax, and just go out and get the ride done. Get your job done."

I took a deep breath and nodded, "I just get so..."

"Trust me, I understand," he whispered. Pain reflected in his eyes. "Go get Gaston warmed-up and ready. We'll handle things here."

I turned away.

How did Brodie learn that his friend was dead? The words echoed in my mind. The image of Brodie's eyes when I told him Craig died haunted me. The realization, agony, and desperation.

Tears filled my eyes.

"Delaney?" Camille whispered.

"What?"

"Are you alright?"

"No."

I didn't even look at her. The tears blurred my vision, and Gaston came to a halt.

How did Brodie learn that his friend was dead?

It took a dozen blinks to clear my eyes as I wiped away the tears. Gaston had stopped behind the barrel racers waiting to enter the arena once the tie-down roping was complete.

"You're the second in?" Camille asked.

"Yes."

How did Brodie learn that his friend was dead? The agony in his voice...tears when the realization hit. My breaths began to shake, pain shot through my stomach, and the tears welled again.

How did Brodie learn that his friend was dead? The pain and loss standing on the hillside above the ravine...his yell to the sky...his pure devastation and my helplessness overwhelmed me.

"Delaney," Camille's hand rest on my arm.

My hand went to my stomach again as the gate in front of us opened, and Amberleigh Moore entered the arena. I desperately tried to wipe away the tears as her 17.02 seconds was announced and the gate opened.

The image of his smiling, happy face danced in my vision...that last time I saw him when he was picking up Camille. The first time he had called me his big sister. He had been so happy. My heart clenched.

Gaston pranced through the gate, and I held him back as I tried to stop the tears. The horse reared on his hind legs and the crowd cheered. After a deep breath, I gave up, and just let the horse run. The only thing I could do was rely on muscle memory as we approached the first barrel. It was wide, which caused the run to the second barrel to be off, and we ran in at a too tight angle. My leg scraped the barrel and pain jolted through it. At the last second, I was able to reach down and try to flip the barrel back. As we turned to the third, I had no idea if the barrel was up or down. The third turn was better, and thankfully, we were running for home. I felt numb and tired.

When I turned Gaston at the fence, I looked back to the second barrel. It was up but didn't really matter since the time was well out of placing. The horse instinctively pranced to the open gate while I leaned forward and patted his shoulder. Camille, still mounted on Archer, was waiting for me; her lip caught between her teeth and hand over her heart.

I trotted past her and down the warm-up area. When Gaston's breathing returned to normal, I walked him back to the trailer. Camille was at my side and we stepped off the horses at the same time. We didn't speak until the Gaston was taken care of, and Archer was tied to the trailer to wait for the ride in slack after the rodeo.

"You OK?" She whispered as we walked toward the arena.

"My leg hurts."

"Pretty cool grab, though," she smiled. "Will look good in the video."

"Worst run I've had in years, and it's going to be played over and over again on the internet."

"Well, they aren't streaming this for the Cowboy Network...so, there is that."

"I need a drink," my hand went over my aching stomach again. "...or maybe antacid."

In between the contestant's bleachers and the bucking chutes was the fenced VIP area filled with people sitting at round reception-style tables. It was on a rise, so the spectators were above the fence for easy viewing. Sitting at the table nearest the chutes was Dad, Logan, Lacie Jae, Sep Blackburn, and his wife. As we walked up the small hill to the gate into the area, Brodie walked out of the group of cowboys standing by the chutes.

I shook my head and rolled my eyes. Nothing was going to be worse than the teasing from my brothers, and the smirk on Brodie's face proved it. "Don't even..." I started.

"Brodie, can I ask you a few questions?"

All three of us turned to the voice. The reporter I had seen earlier was standing at the base of the rise. He looked up at us like he had won the lottery.

My lungs filled with air, a wringing began in my ears, and my body trembled. *How did Brodie learn that his friend was dead?* The anxiety from the last 20 minutes made the pain in my stomach surge.

"My name is Paul Sampson, I'd just like to ask you a few questions," The reporter continued.

"I..." My throat tightened, making my voice falter.

"What?" Brodie huffed. He was standing close enough behind me that I could feel his body tense.

"How are you holding up?" Paul asked.

"Just taking one day at a time," Brodie answered.

I could hear the announcer's voice talking about the bulls. "...Brady Portenier on the next bull..."

"You and your brother were at the Hermiston rodeo while Craig was in Meridian," Paul stated.

"Yeah..." Brodie exhaled.

The announcer's voice yelled, "Here we go! There's the nod!"

"Since he wasn't with you, do you consider it your fault that Craig died?"

The crowd behind us roared.

Other than fights with my brothers growing up, I had never hit a person.

CHAPTER THIRTY-NINE

I ran forward, arm pulling back, fingers curling into a fist. In the split second that Paul Sampson realized what was happening, he smirked, causing my shoulder to pull farther back. I was just above him enough that I could use my full body weight as I jumped from the rise and swung my fist to his face. The image of Brad Pitt's entrance into the movie Troy with the flying death jab to the giant warrior flashed in my mind.

Paul Sampson's mouth was open just enough that when my fist hit his jaw with all my flying weight behind it, I could feel the jaw adjust back and snap as the pain erupted in my wrist and up my arm.

The crowd roared at the bull ride as the reporter fell back onto the ground with me on top of him. I rolled off and jumped at him again with my arm pulled back, but I was suddenly rising above him. There was an arm around my waist lifting me up and I knew by its size that it was Logan.

The crowd roared, and the announcer's voice echoed, "Way to ride through that spin Brady!"

"What the fuck?" Paul Sampson bellowed with one hand going to his jaw and the other trying to push himself up from the ground.

Logan turned me away, and I could see the dozen cowboys that had been by the chutes running toward us.

"Get him out of here," Logan yelled at them. He was carrying me away from the commotion as if I was a rag doll tucked under his arm.

I was suddenly upright, and my arm grabbed and shoved into bitter cold.

"What the hell?" I gasped and looked down to my arm buried past my elbow in a large galvanized tub of ice and beer cans.

Logan was tossing the cans to the women behind the concession stand.

"Logan?" I growled.

"Hopefully, you didn't break your wrist," He said. "The ice will keep the swelling down."

"Delaney!" Dad's voice was right behind us.

"What?" I asked automatically and looked at him in surprise.

"That bitch!" Sampson's voice rang out.

We all turned back to him. The cowboys had formed a barrier between us and were forcing him away.

"I'm going to sue her," The reporter yelled.

"For what?" Tate yelled. "We didn't see a damn thing."

"We were all watching the bull ride," Johnny added just before the group disappeared around a trailer.

"You alright?" Dad asked.

My mind was still buzzing as if it was all just a dream, "My leg hurts."

"I'm sure it does," he huffed. "You hit that barrel pretty hard, but I think you hit that guy harder."

I looked down at my arm that was turning bright red, "I think I'm frozen."

"Hopefully, not broken," Brodie shook his head with a grin. "That was quite the sight to see...ya kind of shocked me."

"I sure hope someone got that on video," Lacie Jae quipped. "She looked like a superhero."

Logan chuckled and pulled my arm out of the tub, "Twist it, see if you're going to be able to handle the rope for breakaway."

After flipping my wrist a few times, I nodded, "It hurts from the ice...it's frozen."

"Keep it in there until slack starts," Dad ordered and turned to Camille. "Go get Archer."

She immediately turned and ran for the trailer.

We stood quietly and just looked at each other as if our life was on pause until Camille returned with the horse.

"There are still two bull rides," Logan said. "They'll start breakaway as soon as they are done."

"When are you up?" Dad asked me.

"Third," I answered as the dozen cowboys appeared from behind the trailer.

Most just looked at us with a smile then walked back to the chutes. Tate and Johnny approached.

"He's gone," Tate said.

"Headed to the hospital," Johnny smirked and looked at me. "I'm gonna guess his jaw is broken."

I gasped, "Really? I did feel a snap."

"Hopefully, it's broken for saying something like that to a pissed off barrel racer that just hit a barrel," Brodie huffed.

"She got it back up," Lacie Jae looked up at him. "Who was it, and what did he say?"

Brodie and I looked at each other then he turned to her, "A reporter that insinuated it is my fault that Craig is dead."

Everyone gasped.

"That son-of-a-bitch," Dad huffed with his eyes full of fury and body rising as if to jump up.

"I sure as hell hope you don't feel that way," Camille gasped.

"No, I don't," Brodie sighed. "But hearing someone else say they think it was...well..."

"No one thinks that," Tate growled. "NO ONE."

"I've never heard one person say that," Johnny shook his head.

Tears filled Lacie Jae's eyes as she looked up at him, "No one has said that or felt that."

Brodie just nodded and looked back at me.

"Damn," Logan growled. "Now, I wish I had hit him."

"If you had flown through the air like that," Dad muttered. "I don't think he would have ever gotten up again." He turned and looked at me. "I was going to lecture you on letting your emotions get the best of you for a tipped barrel, even if you did get it back up."

"And now?" Brodie asked.

"Now, I'm glad I taught you how to throw a punch properly," Dad answered.

"The bulls are done," Camille said and handed me the reins.

I took them with my left hand and pulled my arm out of the ice.

"I need some time for my arm to melt," I glanced at Logan. "You may have to help me up; I can't feel my fingers."

With a foot in the stirrup and my left hand on the saddle horn, Logan pushed me up into the saddle then I tucked my frozen hand under my thigh to help it thaw.

"I'll be back," Still in a numb haze, I turned toward the arena and entry gate.

The first roper was in the box ready to nod, so I trotted to get in line. The jolting of my body gave me the first inclination that the pain wasn't just in my wrist; my elbow and shoulder were throbbing. Well, this was going to be interesting.

When I came to a halt, I had to use my left hand to unhook my lariat from the saddle. I didn't even attempt to twirl the rope to warm up until I was backing into the box. Cold, trembling fingers gripped the rope as I focused on the calf in the chute.

Nodding, the chute was opened, the calf bolted, and Archer followed. I nearly screamed as I lifted the rope and twirled it once before throwing it at the calf. It didn't even come close.

I could just see the headlines:

NFR QUALIFIER DELANEY RAWLINS' WORST RODEO EVER

Maybe not exact, but it would be if I wrote it.

They were all waiting for me at the trailer but no one was smirking or even smiling.

I stopped Archer in front of them and looked at Dad.

"How do you feel?" He frowned.

"My leg hurts and wrist, elbow and shoulder..." I answered.

"Your stomach?" Camille whispered.

I looked at her then back to Dad, "I'm tired and don't want to be here anymore."

"Load up," Dad yelled. "We'll stop at the store on the way and get you something for your stomach."

I nodded then started to step down from Archer. Pain shot from my arm and Brodie stepped forward to help me down.

"...and we'll get something for your aches and pains," Dad finished.

An hour later, we were driving out of Walla Walla, and I was tucked between Camille and Brodie in the back seat. My head rest on his shoulder as my eyes closed.

"Thanks for being my superhero," he whispered.

I fell asleep to his humming.

Welcome to Coffee with Cowboys with me, Lacie Jae.

Greetings everyone! Lacie Jae with Coffee With Cowboys here. I'm a relocated city girl who will be adventuring into the ranching and rodeo world ... the cowboy way of life.

It's been a while since I posted, and to be honest, I wasn't sure I was ever going to do one again, but more on that later.

Today I woke up in Lewiston, Idaho. A town with rivers on two sides and farmer's fields surrounding the rest of it. They call it a valley because it's at the base of a mountain which, I'm told, the local people call a hill ... but it is a mountain.

Anyway, Logan and I came over from Ellensburg last night. Delaney made the championship round there, so everyone else stayed while we came here. If you saw or heard about her Walla Walla rodeo, you'll understand why she is trying so hard.

Logan said we came here early to get a prime spot in the back away from everyone and get his horses settled. He rides in slack on Tuesday morning. I think he wanted a day of peace and quiet. It's been such a hectic couple weeks and this place is quiet and peaceful. Just what we need right now.

The rodeo grounds set behind Lewiston with the farmer's fields around it so there's no hectic town life or traffic around us. It's early and quiet, but since we could hear people moving around Logan was OK with me walking by myself. It's not something I usually do but he said in this town it would be OK. He's protective and I love him for it.

Anyway, I wanted to see the whole rodeo grounds, so I'm standing at the top of the metal bleachers. The sky is pure blue, not a cloud in sight, a soft breeze blowing, just enough you feel like you should be in a chair on a quiet morning watching the horses graze, cows sleep, and dogs run. It's so peaceful.

I do have cows sleeping behind the bleachers, and I can look down over them wandering their pens. They are big, bad-ass bucking bulls sleeping after their morning breakfast.

There are a couple of bulls in one pen butting heads, another half asleep, and oddly one is licking the back of the bull next to him. A big black and white-speckled bull is standing next to the fence with his chin resting on the rail as if his head is too heavy in the morning sun.

I have horses in front of me, too. They have a huge pasture to roam in and there are bright red feed tubs spread out in the green grass where they had been fed their morning grain. I love watching horses eat, and now they are grazing across the green pasture with a few lying down sleeping in the sun.

The peace and quiet have been interrupted by the rodeo setup crew. The beeping of a tractor moving in reverse echoes across the arena. A large U-Haul sits in the middle as people unload the video equipment from inside. More people are calling out to each other as they place panels in the roping chutes, clean out the bucking chutes, and check the latches and hinges. There is a man placing garbage cans around the backside of the bleachers and another driving a large flatbed trailer to the field next to a large event tent.

In the open area behind the arena and stalls is our truck and trailer as well as another half-dozen competitors that arrived early. Some are already riding in a small arena toward the back. Off in the distance, slowly moving across a plowed field, is a farmer's tractor.

With all this activity around me, on one side as they prepare for the rodeo, and the stillness and peace on the other side with the horses grazing and bulls and steers sleeping, I feel numb, in a dream.

I want to enjoy this peace and relative calm before the rodeo storm, but I still feel a bit lost.

Brodie is halfway through his commemorative rides for Craig. He placed in Walla Walla, which was important, but he was bucked off in Ellensburg... which isn't in the Big Four rodeos, but this rodeo, in Lewiston, is and then we go to Pendleton to finish the Big Four. Delaney has decided to go to Othello to ride her new horse, Maestro. So, just a few more to go before we all have time off. I think we need that time to heal before we head to Vegas. Logan has already qualified for the NFR, as well as Delaney, and Brodie was sitting at fourteen last time I checked. If he finishes these commemorative rides as strong as he started, there would be no doubt he would qualify, too. When Craig died, he was sitting tenth, which had a lot to do with his spectacular second-place finish in San Antonio. That was so fun... what a great rodeo for him and Delaney.

(A pause...)

I don't know if you heard that round of laughter coming from the arena. There are a dozen people putting together the large screen that will show the rodeo to the crowd. The sound of them laughing and having fun makes me feel better. Watching all the preparations for the rodeo... there is an energy filling the grounds and my soul a little bit.

(Another pause...)

A few weeks back, in Kennewick, I had a chat with a fan of the podcast. She asked me why I hadn't been doing them. When I told her I didn't feel cheerful, she reminded me that I'm more…insightful sometimes rather than cheerful. She reminded me that life isn't always made of positive moments; there are those negative moments too. We need to remember the positive to help us get through the negative.

She had recently gone through a tough time in her life and was holding onto the good to help her get through.

I guess that's what we need to do with the loss of Craig. There truly isn't anything we can do to change what happened or bring him back; the only thing we can do is focus on the laughter he brought to our lives. Focus on the endearing love he had for his father and the Rawlins family. In the short time I had known him, he was always grinning with that internal light showing through. I will always remember how happy he was when he placed second in San Antonio. He didn't win, but he was still so damn happy with his performance and the pride that shone from his father.

I know in my heart and believe with everything in me that Craig will be there with Brodie in the chute while he is in Vegas, and he is here in Lewiston, too, as Brodie rides for him this week. Craig will forever be with Brodie; in his heart.

So, I will continue with the podcasts and share with you the good and the bad of this rodeo and ranching life. Before I sign off, I want to say one thing to the young woman; the fan that I talked to in Kennewick. You didn't understand why the negative incident happened to you…you were still searching for the answer.

But, think of this…if I hadn't seen the bruising, I wouldn't have stopped to talk to you and who knows if I would have continued with this podcast? I hope your life is filled with an overabundance of positive moments, and thank you for the chat.

With that, I am going to sign off and go have coffee with my cowboy. Have a great day, and a good cup of coffee.

"Well, you made up for Walla Walla," Logan handed me the cup of coffee then settled onto the chair next to me.

"Second in barrels and a shiny new buckle for breakaway," I yawned and looked around the Lewiston rodeo grounds. Our trailers were parked next to each other with the chairs and table hidden between them.

"Your wrist and shoulder must be better."

"They are. Other than rest, a lady had a Bemer so I did a couple sessions on it. Besides, the soreness made me concentrate a bit harder." I took a long swig of coffee then sighed. "Thanks for taking Camille last night so Ryle and I could have the night alone."

"You got here at two o'clock, and it's now seven, that's not much time," he huffed.

"For us, five hours together has always been a luxury," I grinned. "Besides, we have slack at 9:00 and we're both riding after you steer wrestlers."

"How long is he here?"

"He has to be in Puyallup on Thursday."

"So, you have all day tomorrow together with neither of you competing?"

"Yes, I run barrels in the perf Thursday night. So, after slack, we're going to a lakeside cabin and spending tonight and tomorrow there. I'll be back Thursday morning before Brodie and Dad get here."

"You need that mini-vacation."

"Well, I would have argued with you on that before Walla Walla," I glanced at him with a smirk. "I think I proved to everyone that I was beginning to lose it."

"Jackass was lucky it was you that hit him and not me."

I nodded then leaned back against the chair, "Martin said it was going to be hard on Brodie...this quest for the saddle. Each week would be harder but I didn't realize it was going to be that way for me, too."

"We're all adjusting...still trying to accept."

"Did you hear the podcast? Did you know she was going to quit?"

He took a drink of coffee then looked out into the distance, "Yeah, we had talked a couple of times. I didn't tell her either way, she needed to decide on her own. She's more emotional about Craig than she was about her father."

"Do you know the whole story?" I whispered with a glance at the trailer where the sisters were sleeping.

Logan nodded.

"He was a father, not a dad," My hand went over my stomach again. "Craig had a huge adventurous life ahead of him; their dad was living in a bottle and wasting his away."

Logan sighed, "Yeah..."

"Do you know who she talked to in Kennewick?"

He shook his head as he picked up his phone to look at the time.

"Team ropers and tie-down are between steer wrestling and breakaway," he stated.

"Yeah, so?"

His grin turned to me, "Bubba is here, why don't you come out and haze for me?"

The gloom that had begun to settle in me suddenly vanished as my heart jumped, "Yes! I love hazing."

We both chuckled, took one long last drink of coffee, then separated to our own trailers.

An hour later, we were sitting on the horses just outside the arena and were surrounded by all the other steer wrestlers and a few of the team ropers, including Ryle.

Camille and Lacie Jae were climbing the steps up the bleachers. Camille was carrying an umbrella and a cooler while Lacie Jae was carrying a large bag. We watched as they set up the large umbrella to block the morning sun, set the cooler between them at their feet, and spread out a blanket over the bleacher then placed stadium pillows over it. They sat down, pulled two 'Coffee With Cowboys' travel mugs and two breakfast burritos out of the cooler, then set their feet on the bleacher in front of them. Then, they turned and looked for us.

I looked at Logan, "I do believe they have adjusted to rodeo life."

Thursday morning, next to Jess' truck, I leaned away from Ryle and looked into his contented eyes.

"I'm going to miss you, Huckleberry," I whispered.

"We're taking more vacations together," he smiled.

"Oh, yes," I sighed and kissed him again.

"Alright, enough," Jess grumbled from the driver's seat. "We're going to be late for the rodeo."

One last kiss, then I leaned around Ryle to look at Jess, "Well, we can't have that now, can we?"

Jess and Jamie both grinned as Ryle sighed and stepped into the truck. As they drove away, I turned back to the trailer and Camille, who was sitting in the chair with a cup of coffee in one hand and phone in the other.

"You look so relaxed and happy," she smiled.

"It was a wonderful get-away," Sitting across from her, I relaxed back into the chair. "We arrived just before sunset on Tuesday and decided to take a walk around the lake and oh, what a sunset it was. Swirling, soft clouds in every hue of pink and blue and not just in the sky; it reflected on the water."

"Sounds spectacular."

"It was, then, we stayed in a Yurt by the lake and slept in yesterday until...well, I don't think we got out of bed until lunch, then we rented a canoe and played on the lake," I sighed at the memories. "Such a needed break before the next ten days."

My phone alert rang out.

I read the message with my hand going back over my stomach, the serenity that had come over me while Ryle and I were at the lake melted away.

CHAPTER FORTY

Text from Dad: We're on our way, should be there around 5:30. We're in Martin's truck so he is driving. Brodie is in the back seat staring out the window, and every once in a while, he starts that humming. Against my advice, they did phone interviews today since next week is Pendleton and the final rodeo for the Big 4. Lots of questions concerning emotions and memories. They had a good day yesterday moving herds and doctoring cows…being ranchers. Not good now.

I leaned my head back against the chair and closed my eyes to the whirl of emotions.

"What's wrong?" Camille whispered.

I handed her the phone without opening my eyes.

Her exhale was long and anguished, "How do we help?"

"We've been using food and activity to help," I reminded her. "He won't eat before the ride so we need something for after."

"We can run to the store, we have plenty of time."

I just nodded and rubbed my stomach over the pain. I heard her rise from the chair and enter the trailer then step out again.

"Here," she said.

I opened my eyes to the box of antacids.

"You need to go to the doctor," Her eyes were filled with worry.

"Lewiston tonight, then we go to Puyallup then Spokane, hopefully back to Puyallup, then down to Pendleton…I don't have time."

"You need to call today and make an appointment for when we get back," She sat back in the chair. "How are the points adding up for the saddle?"

"Tim Miller is team roping and tie-down, then there is Hanna Smith, who is barrels and breakaway. It will be one of the three that are placing in double events that will win it. I'm pretty sure Miller and Smith are doing all four rodeos…which is a requirement."

"Do they know?"

"No, we worded the announcement so he was just riding for Craig, not that he was after the saddle. Tim and Hanna rode slack here on Tuesday and are sitting 1st or 2nd in their events."

Camille sighed, "He really needs to keep up with them."

Text from Dad: Rodeo grounds in sight, where are you?

Text to Dad: Come in participant's entrance and drive straight forward until you can't go anymore then turn right. We are in the corner farthest away from arena.

We were standing in front of the trailer waiting when they arrived. My stomach was aching as I looked at the two men in the front, smiling at me. No one was in the back seat.

When the truck stopped, I walked to the back to retrieve his 4x4 wheelchair.

"Where is he?"

"Just relax, Daughter," his voice was soothing. "We passed by the roughies, and he saw Kirk and Trenten, so we let him out there. He needs their energy and that bit of normalcy."

"After last week, I don't think we have to worry about reporters approaching him," Martin grinned as he walked around the front of the truck with his arm over Camille's shoulders in a warm greeting.

"It's what the reporter said," I exhaled.

"I understand," Martin nodded with a sigh. "Honestly, we all would have hit him or wanted to; stupid question to ask.

Didn't have any of those this morning, but it was still pretty hard on him."

"And you," Camille added.

"Yes," he agreed. "But I sit in the bleachers and watch. After the interviews this morning, he realized the whole industry has their eyes on him."

"Yeah," Dad huffed with a bit of a glare to Martin. "I told you two…"

"Yeah, yeah…" Martin shook his head. "Always looking for the 'I told you so'."

"Especially when I'm right," Dad said as he wheeled toward the trailer.

We sat in the bleachers next to the roping chutes and watched the grand entry. Dad's wheelchair was tucked under the bleachers with a cover over it. It was family night at the rodeo with kids filling the stands. What seemed like a hundred riders were in the arena as they ran through carrying the rodeo sponsor flags.

Brodie was the last bareback rider out on a Sankey horse named Exotic Blonde. He was standing behind the chute, wrapping his wrist with white tape.

The anthem had been sung and the prayer recited, the pick-up men and judges were taking their places. The announcer boomed, "She's wild! Let's rodeo!"

The first chute gate was opened and a bay horse burst out with rider laid back low on the horse and his legs stretched out. His body flopped forward then back like a rag doll being tossed by the horse, his legs bounced over the neck with almost every buck. The horn blared and the cowboy rolled off the side and hit the ground right in front of the pick-up man. The horse jumped the cowboy then chased the bucking horse.

"Kinda ugly," I whispered and looked at the score on the screen. It was a 59 point ride.

"Had to be horse points," Dad muttered.

"What do you know about Exotic Blonde?" I asked.

"Wouldn't mind one myself," Dad chuckled with a smart ass grin.

Camille and Martin laughed while I gave him the ugly yuck face.

"Really depends on the rider," he answered. "She's about low forty average so he'll need to be pretty strong on her to get a higher score. Jamie Howlett got an 85 on her in Cheyenne last year."

"If he can stay focused," Martin added.

Kirk was the next rider, and Brodie was helping him get settled in the chute. When the gate opened, the horse lunged three long strides out of the chute before beginning a good strong buck with back legs bucking high and powerful all the way through. Kirk was able to stay with him through the buzzer. It was a decent 82 point ride.

Four riders later, Brodie was lowering himself onto the palomino horse. He bent over and adjusted his hand in the handle. The minutes ticked by as he continued to work his glove and give no nod.

"What the hell is he doing?" Martin's exhale shook in anticipation as Brodie finally leaned back. "He's going to get disqualified."

"Mindset," Dad grumbled. "He's having a..."

The gate finally swung open with Brodie leaned back, boots and spurs above the shoulders, and he spurred well for the first six seconds, then his legs quit moving. When the horn blared, he flew off the side of the horse to land stomach-first in the dirt.

I gasped and held my breath until he slowly rose. Normally, he would look to the giant video screen to watch the replay of the ride, but this time his shoulders were low and he strode out of the arena as if going to the principal's office. A 79 point score was announced.

"That's not going to help much," Dad sighed then looked to me. "Go get on your horse and get ready."

I stood without a word because I was so frustrated at not being able to help Brodie.

"Delaney?" Martin called out as I started to walk away.

Turning back, I saw understanding in his eyes, "You concentrate on you now. He'll be alright over there with his friends."

There was nothing to say, so I nodded and jogged out to the trailer. The exercise helped in getting my heart rate and energy back up.

Text from Dad: He placed fourth, still has a chance for points.

Gaston was prancing in excitement as we rode away from the trailer and to the arena. The steer wrestlers were gathered in the lane by the chutes, so I rode up into them and tried to relax by talking with the men I knew. Not one of them asked me about Brodie or Craig. It was evident how Brodie was dealing with the loss.

Logan was winning the steer wrestling at the end of slack on Tuesday and he kept his lead through the Thursday performance. As the steer wrestlers rode out, I inched closer to the gate so I could see across the arena to the bucking chutes.

Brodie was sitting alone on top of the chute divider with his feet resting on the gate. With arms crossed, he stared out into the arena. He looked lost. The tears rose again but I couldn't pull my eyes from him. Trenten suddenly rose up onto the chute to Brodie's left, then Kirk appeared to his right, then Johnny joined them. After a moment, Brodie's head turned to each man as a conversation began. Even from across the arena, I could see his shoulders rise as if waking.

I rode away to the warm-up arena until the bronc riders were announced then returned to the gate.

Brodie was the first rider and he was already sitting on the horse named Marquee with Tate Owens helping him with the cinch. Tate leaned down to look under the brim of Brodie's hat. He was talking to him, making Brodie nod. When Tate leaned back, Brodie's free arm rose and he nodded. The

424

brown horse burst out of the chute with Tate, Kirk, Johnny, and Trenton across the back, yelling at Brodie. Their energy resonated all the way across the arena to my heart.

The horse lunged out then started a leaping buck to the right. It was strong, rhythmic, and Brodie was in a perfect spurring motion with her. The mare had turned out of the chute and was bucking down the edge of the arena with the horn blaring when he was right in front of me. The pick-up men were at their side and Brodie leaned to them then slid from the horse and hit the ground on both feet. He stood motionless for a moment; then his whole body lowered as if in a large relieved sigh.

My heart was beating so hard, my hand rest over it. My neck was tight, causing it to ache down into my spine. Stomach pains were shooting through me.

"He did well this time," A voice beside me said, and I looked down at Martin. "I couldn't sit still." he explained.

"It was good," I whispered as the announcer called out the 84 point score. "That should hold for points, too."

"Go ride, Delaney," Martin patted Gaston's neck. "You concentrate on you now so he doesn't worry about a repeat of Walla Walla."

I smiled down at him, "I was hoping Ellensburg would wipe that out of everyone's memory."

Martin chuckled with a shake of the head, "I never want to forget that flying punch and I sure as hell wish someone had gotten it on video."

"I kind of wish that, too," I grinned. "Thanks, Martin."

"Go get him ready and kick some ass out there."

He walked away with a sigh.

As hard as it was for us, I couldn't imagine how hard this was for him. Thank the heavens we had each other to hold onto.

I returned to the gate when the tie-down ropers were done, and the royalty were in the back of the truck with the 3 barrels and driving into the arena. The crowd was clapping and yelling for the t-shirts the three women were throwing into the bleachers.

Martin had returned to the bleachers with Dad and Camille.

"Kick-ass, Sis."

I turned to Brodie standing next to me with his hand stroking Gaston's neck. I hadn't seen him in a few days; his whiskers were thicker, hair longer, and the wrinkles at the side of his eyes were deeper. It looked like he had at least tried to wash off the arena dirt.

"He likes these open arenas and all the energy of the kids," I said and tried to ignore the rugged, weary look.

"Well, he'll like this dirt," Brodie huffed. "I tested it for him."

My grin widened.

The first barrel racer trotted down the alley and into the arena.

He turned to watch, but we were on the flat behind the roping chutes, "Damn, you can't see anything from here."

"They are up there," I said and pointed to our family in the bleachers.

"Well, I'll go so I can watch Gaston win this thing for you." With that, he walked away.

I closed my eyes and listened to the next rider enter the arena, the yell of the announcer, the cheer of the crowd. Taking a deep breath, I opened my eyes and nudged Gaston into a walk down the road. Two riders later, I returned to make our way into the arena for 17.13 seconds.

"Delaney Rawlins just came from a 2nd place finish in Ellensburg to take over the lead in Lewiston! With two more nights of performances, there is a good chance that one will hold up!"

As my hand patted Gaston's rump, I looked up into the stands to my family as we trotted to the exit gate. The five of them were cheering me on and my heart sighed.

Welcome to Coffee with Cowboys with me, Lacie Jae.

Greetings everyone! Lacie Jae with Coffee With Cowboys here. I'm a relocated city girl who will be adventuring into the ranching and rodeo world ... the cowboy way of life.

What a whirlwind week this has been. Ellensburg, Lewiston, Puyallup, Spokane ... all in one week! In Lewiston, Delaney was first in barrels and fourth in breakaway while Logan won, too. Brodie was fourth and second. They placed in Puyallup and Spokane but didn't win.

We had two days at Blackburn's ranch to regroup, and now we're getting ready for the drive to Pendleton for their big roundup. It's the last of the Big Four rodeos that Brodie is riding in honor of his friend Craig and, except for a quick trip for Delaney to the Othello rodeo, it will be the last official rodeo for the Rawlins family for the year.

Logan drew a Tuesday slack and Friday afternoon performance, so he went to Pendleton with some fellow steer wrestlers, competed for his first round, then came back.

He and Delaney have qualified for the NFR and with his money earned so far in the Big 4 rodeos, we're pretty sure Brodie will jump in the standings and qualify, too. But we're following another odd twist. Delaney's boyfriend Ryle is a team roper with a cowboy named Jess. While Ryle was with Delaney after Craig's death, Jess won a rodeo with a friend and collected just over two thousand in earnings toward qualification. Jess is currently in 15th place for the heelers going to the NFR, but Ryle is in 16th place. If Ryle doesn't make it then Jess will have to choose one of the other headers whose partner didn't make it.

Honestly, I'm a bit heartbroken over this. I just can't imagine after working so hard to come in 16th and not get to go. Delaney reminded me that her first year trying she missed going by just $1639. That is awful, but when your roping partner, that you've traveled with all year, goes and you don't? Unimaginable!

Well, Pendleton is slack Monday and Tuesday, then performances Wednesday, Thursday, and Friday. They combine all those rides and the top twelve go to the championship round on Saturday.

Ryle and Jess roped in slack on Monday and Tuesday and are sitting in second place. So, fingers crossed and a lot of praying that they hold on and place Saturday to make sure Ryle gets to go with Jess. They are also going with Delaney on Friday night to Othello to try to add even more money to their year's total.

As for the Rawlins, tomorrow Brodie will compete in bareback and Delaney in barrels, then Friday is saddle bronc, steer wrestling, and breakaway. It's going to be busy!

It is Wednesday morning, and we're about to begin our drive to Pendleton. One of the trailers is already there so they had a good place to park. I guess it's pretty hard to find a spot at the last minute. If you remember, in the interview with Brodie and Craig last January, they both said Pendleton was their favorite. Logan and Delaney agree even though it's a bit tougher because their chute for the steers is different. I'm pretty interested in seeing what they mean.

They all love the history of the rodeo so I had to go online and research it. Wow, it goes all the way back to 1910! There is a Native Indian village, a theatrical performance about their history in the Happy Canyon arena, and parades! The bucking chutes are tall and wooden and painted bright colors. The arena is massive with a dirt race track around the grass arena. I can't wait to watch the horse races. They actually race bareback!

Needless to say, Camille and I are also excited for all the vendors and shopping, because, you know, we need more stuff! (giggles)

Looks like everyone is about ready to go so I'm going to make sure they have lots of caffeine for the trip. I'll do a follow-up once we get there and I get to see everything. I'm so excited but right now, I'm off to make Coffee for the Cowboys!

Logan brought his trailer days before to park so we had a good spot for the week, and we parked my trailer next to his. We were hidden behind a cement building. The area was for competitors, contractors, and specialty acts and away from the crowds. Our first half-hour was busy unloading horses and walking them to the barn, which held the stalls. Brodie, Martin, and Dad remained at the trailers to set up the living area between the two.

"What's on the agenda tonight?" Camille asked as we walked back to our campsite.

I sighed, "Brodie agreed to a couple more interviews."

"No," she exhaled in disbelief.

"Yeah, just the two, then he said no more so he can focus the next few days. I want to be there with him this time. Then we're going out for dinner to a friend's ranch out of town."

When we returned to the trailers, Brodie was gone.

"Where is he?" I asked Dad.

"He went for his Pendleton walk," He answered. "He's done it every year."

"But with Craig," I whispered and the heaviness in my heart increased.

"He'll need time to himself before the next three days," Dad argued. "He said he would be back before the interviews. They are still a couple hours away."

Text to Brodie: Interview is supposed to start in 5 minutes

Text to Brodie: Where are you? They are getting restless

Text from Brodie: Sorry, lost track of time, be there soon

Text to Brodie: What exactly do you consider 'soon'? It's been 30 minutes

Text to Brodie: Both interviewers are here. 1st one is determined to meet with you, I'm afraid they will stay until midnight if they have to.

Text to Brodie: OK, it's been an hour. In all honesty, do you just want me to tell them to come back tomorrow? I'm getting worried…well…have been for hours now.

He appeared at the end of the row of trailers, his head down looking at his phone. He was wearing a new cowboy hat and carried a number of bags in his hand. Much to my surprise he was smiling. But when his head rose, he saw the pair of reporters waiting to interview him and the smile disappeared. With shoulders lowering in resignation, he nodded to me.

"Which one first?" He sighed.

I slid the brush down Gaston's hip and glanced at Brodie who was keeping me company in the stall. His head was down, staring at his phone.

"Shouldn't you be headed to the chutes?"

"Just watching Sozo's ride from last year," He mumbled. "Good strong buck and goes to her right after the jump out of the chute."

"Rhythmic?"

"Yeah, rocking chair if I can get in sync with her."

"Dad and Martin said it was a good draw."

He stood and took a deep breath then walked to the stall door.

"Brodie?"

He turned and looked back at me.

I smiled slightly, "Toes out and don't bite the dirt this time."

"Thanks, Sis," he chuckled. "Same goes for you because that would just fucking hurt if you fell going that speed."

A half-hour later, the last of the grand entry was riding out of the enormous arena while Camille and I walked up the stairs behind the bucking chutes. The arena was the size of a football field with green grass growing in the middle and a dirt race track surrounding it. The large video screen was to my left and the timed event roping chutes to my right. Dad's wheelchair seat for the week was just above the first two sections behind the roping chutes. Martin sat in a chair at his side and Lacie Jae and Camille's empty seat were just in front of them.

The arena was large enough that just to the west of the bucking chutes, dozens of people were sitting in the grass waiting for the rodeo to start. Officials in black and white striped vests, photographers in tan vests, and the pick-up men on their horses were spread out across the arena.

We could see down into the chutes and Brodie was pacing the wide platform next to the brown horse, Sozo. His riggin was already on her back, but he was the seventh rider of the day. Johnny and Tate were standing to each side of him, but I didn't see anyone trying to approach him. Maybe my punching the reporter in Walla Walla discouraged anyone from trying but, more than likely, it was because he had already given interviews.

The first gate was swung open for the day and Brodie watched as the bay horse bucked, ducked, dived and finally threw the rider just before the horn blared.

"At least he isn't staring off into the arena like before," Camille whispered.

The next two riders busted out of the chute and made the eight-second rides. When Brodie stepped forward, Tate and the stock contractor moved in to help. A cameraman leaned over the chute.

Pain shot through my stomach again, but I stood as a statue. Both Tim and Hanna had ridden in slack, and Tim had already qualified for the finals in both of his events. Hanna had a second-place standing in breakaway and held second in barrels so she would qualify for Saturday also. Which meant Brodie had to have this ride and get to the finals to have any chance in earning the saddle for Craig. When he climbed up and over the chute to slide onto the horse, my hand covered my stomach.

"Please..." I exhaled softly with body tingling and back aching.

Both hands were in fists as Brodie nodded and the gate swung open. The horse launched and my body rose in anticipation. Her head dropped low to her hooves between each high buck to the back. Brodie spurred low and high with his chaps dramatically flying in the air and free arm jerking side to side, helping him balance. Horse and rider were in perfect unison as the horse had barely moved twenty feet from the chute before turning to the right. She bucked along the front of the chutes until the horn blared.

I exhaled the held breath, and my whole body relaxed with tension releasing. I felt like throwing up.

The men at the chutes were yelling at Brodie as the pick-up men rode in. The 87 point score was announced as Brodie walked out to sit in the grass with the crowd of cowboys.

Camille and I watched the remainder of the bareback riders with my heart pounding in relief as Brodie was announced in second place.

"That includes Wednesday's performance, too," I told Camille as we jogged down the stairs. "Even after tomorrow afternoon's perf, he should make it to Saturday."

"Now, you need to get Gaston there."

"I will," I said confidently.

When Gaston and I returned to the barn, the top three racers of the day were 28.77, 28.79, and 28.82, all three faster than Wednesday's performance, and I was more than thrilled to be in second. There was no doubt we would be going to Saturday's championship round.

I was the first person out of our trailers Friday morning. The air was just a touch crisp, but the sky was pure blue with not a cloud in the sky. It was going to be a beautiful day…perfect rodeo weather. I walked slowly down the road to the barn enjoying the sounds of the rodeo grounds waking up; generators started, horses calling out, the buzz of an ATV, a diesel engine roaring to life, and an occasional shout or laugh. It was peaceful, normal, and made me feel at home.

Gaston was in the first stall in our small section of the barn. He was lying on his side, legs tucked under him, and looking right at home. Memphis met me at his door and was looking for attention, which I happily gave him. Archer was next. He was in the back corner with head low and he didn't turn when I said his name. My gaze went to his feeder; the hay and grain I had given him the night before were untouched. There were no manure piles in the stall.

"Shit," he turned slightly to look at me when I opened the stall door. The pain in my stomach returned and this time my heart rate spiked. We always kept a halter safely hung on the fence in case of an emergency and I quickly reached for it.

"What's going on, Big Guy?" I whispered to him as I slid the halter on. Nausea swirled through me. "Looks like we need to take you for a walk."

"Good morning, Delaney."

I turned to Sammi Parkston, standing at the door. Peppers was behind her with his nose stretched out to his old traveling buddy, Gaston.

"Mornin'," I whispered as I ran a hand over Archer's stomach as if I could feel anything.

"Something wrong?"

"Looks like he's impacted," I led the horse out of the stall.

"Do you want me to get the vet?" She gasped.

433

I glanced at her then nodded, "Yes, please do, but send him to our trailer behind the building."

"I'll put Peppers away." She turned and jogged back to her stall.

I walked Archer out of the building and pulled out my phone.

Dad answered on the first ring.

"Archer is impacted," I huffed. "Sammi is on her way to call the vet, and I'm walking him to the trailers."

The whole family was waiting when we approached. The veterinarian drove in right behind us followed by Sammi. I felt numb...as if I was in a really bad but realistic nightmare. My hand covered my stomach again. We stood quietly as the veterinarian took the horse's temperature, pulse rate, and examined the gums.

"I'm not even going to bother to ask if you're OK," Camille whispered as the veterinarian began the rectal examination.

The horse was tubed and mineral oil pumped into his stomach.

Brodie slid an arm around me and I rest my head on his shoulder. I felt the overwhelming urge to just go to sleep until this weekend was past and my horse better.

"His temp and pulse are up and his circulation is good. There is also a bit of noise from his gut," the vet announced. "I gave him a bit of help for the pain and the mineral oil should clear out his bowels." He turned and looked at me in understanding. "He'll be ok, but I'll come back in an hour to see how things are."

"Thanks, Doctor," I whispered with a sigh.

"Was he competing today?" The doctor asked.

I noticed he said the word 'was'.

"Not anymore," I shook my head. "I have another horse I can use."

After giving Sammi a thankful hug, she and the veterinarian walked away.

I closed my eyes and tipped my head back. Memphis was used to the rodeo noise and commotion outside of an

434

arena. He was good inside an arena at a jackpot, but jackpots were quiet compared to crowds at a rodeo. I was going to ask him to rope in a massive outdoor arena, in front of one of the largest, loudest crowds in all of rodeo, AND, with a chute where the calf doesn't start standing next to us but instead is under the bleachers behind us where we couldn't see it. Plus, we had to run down a slight slope. This was going to be interesting.

"Just leave Archer here with us," Dad said and I turned and looked at him. "We'll watch over him this morning while you go lay down for a few minutes before the rodeo."

I didn't even argue, I just turned back into the trailer, crawled up on the bed and closed my eyes. With the knowledge Archer would be well cared for, I fell asleep with my stomach hurting and the depression beginning to settle over me, sapping me of any remaining strength or energy.

I felt the weight on the bed, and my mind began to wake. His arms wrapped around me and pulled me tight against him. I drifted off again as his kiss touched my forehead. His breath slid against my skin waking me just enough. I turned into his warmth.

"Feeling better?" Ryle whispered.

I wanted to complain that he was pulling me out of the peaceful slumber, but the reality was I needed to get up and check on my horse as well as get Memphis ready for his first big rodeo.

"How is he?" I whispered.

"Your dad is leaving the big pile of manure on the ground to let you see Archer is better."

"How sweet," I chuckled.

"I thought it was a special thing for a dad to do for his daughter," Ryle's chest shook as he laughed.

Leaning up on an elbow, I looked down into his humored eyes then back into the trailer to make sure we were alone. We were, so I turned back to him and kissed him to the point both our hearts were racing.

When we finally stepped out of the trailer, the whole family was there, but my gaze went to the blue roan horse standing behind them. His head was held high and eyes bright as he looked at me. And, as Ryle said, there was a big pile of manure waiting to greet me.

"Bit of bed-head, but you look better," Dad grinned.

"I feel better and thank you all for watching over Archer for me." I went to the pitchfork to remove the evidence.

Brodie was sitting at the end of the table looking at his phone. As I approached, he looked up with a grin while setting the phone down.

My gaze flickered to the phone in time to see a woman's picture on the background before the screen turned dark. I was shocked. Other than I didn't recognize the woman, the picture of him and Craig at the Sisters Rodeo had been on his screen since Craig's death.

"Who was that?" I huffed.

Brodie picked up the phone and slid it into his pocket, "Just the picture that accompanied the article I was reading."

It sounded plausible but he turned away too quickly.

Logan stood and took the pitchfork, "I'll clean that up while you go take a shower. We don't want you out there embarrassing the family with that bed-head going on."

Everyone chuckled as my hand went to my head, "Smartass." I grumbled at him before going back into the trailer.

I leaned down to pat Memphis' shoulder when we came to a halt under the bleachers. We were in the entry alley with the other ropers as we waited for the arena to be prepared for the roping events.

"You both look pretty calm," Dad said from the other side of the panels. Martin, Camille, and Lacie Jae were standing next to him.

I huffed and grinned at him, "Well, as we were warming up, I realized the run today couldn't be any worse than Walla Walla."

"Good to know you have your hopes up," Dad laughed.

The line of riders in front of me began to move.

"Best get to your seats so you can watch the spectacle happen in real life instead of on video," I shooed him away with my hand.

All four were giggling as they walked away.

Calf ropers, team ropers, and the other eight breakaway ropers walked through the tunnel that ran under the bleachers. I held Memphis' reins tight as we walked from the tunnel and out onto the wide-open arena. He began prancing as we made our way through the gate then to the other side of the long chute.

Memphis' head turned left and right as he looked at the large crowd in the stands and the riders around us. I walked him to the far corner and back then stopped along the fence just three horses away from the chute so he had time to get used to the commotion and noise. He was patient as we waited through the twelve tie-down ropers and seven of the breakaway ropers.

When we backed into the box, I had no doubt the horse was wondering what the hell we were doing.

The calf was behind us, hidden under the bleachers and when I nodded, a spotter nodded down the long chute to have the calf released. I still couldn't see the calf so the spotter called out when the calf was halfway down the long ally with a cowboy riding behind him to encourage the calf to run.

Memphis was still calm when I kicked him into action. He ran down the lane and when the calf appeared out the end, the horse focused right on it and charged after him. Luckily, he was a good draw, and the calf ran in a straight line as we raced after him. It was a quick throw and slide to a stop with the rope breaking off the saddle horn for a clean 4.3-second run.

"Good job!" I patted the horse with a wide grin and a silent cheer as we loped down the arena to follow the calf and retrieve my rope. I knew there were three riders faster than our time but I couldn't have been happier with the horse's performance. It had easily been his biggest challenge, and he couldn't have done better.

Ryle met me at the barn to take care of Memphis while I ran to the arena.

I stood at the top of the bleachers looking down at Brodie walking on the platform behind the chutes. His saddle was already cinched onto the Calgary stallion named Tiger Warrior. He was a big bay with a white blaze down his nose and long mane and tail that flew around him. I had seen him enough times I knew the horse could give Brodie the ride he needed to make the finals. Brodie just needed to stay focused.

The chute for Johnny and his horse, Calgary's Shoshoni Mountain, swung open, and Brodie watched the ride and cheered for him. That was a good sign.

One rider was between Johnny and Brodie and by the time Brodie was climbing over the chute, Johnny was hustling to the side to help. When Johnny stepped away and Brodie leaned back on Tiger Warrior my hands went over my stomach and breath caught in my lungs.

The nod and the green gate swung open. The horse lunged out and with the second stride dipped left, then ducked to the right with Brodie spurring through it, his seat solid in the middle of the horse's back and his eyes looking down at the horse's head. A high kick in the back and both horse and rider were stretched out in the perfect position. Brodie matched each buck with a strong spurring action with white chap fringe and black horse mane flying in the wind until the horn finally blared. Brodie grabbed the rein with both hands then turned to look for the pick-up man. When he slid from one horse to another then to the ground, he hit the ground with a hard drop that made me gasp.

Brodie stood and without a look to the horse, to the other riders, or even to the crowd, he walked to the out-gate and disappeared. A score of 87.5 was announced, making the crowd cheer. He won the day and made it to the short go on Saturday in second place.

Trick riders were next in the arena so I jogged down the stairs to find Brodie. He was below the stands with his chaps over his shoulder and a beer in his hand. He looked exhausted as he talked with Tate, Johnny and a half-dozen other men. He needed this normalcy so I walked away to meet Ryle behind Dad's chair when the steer wrestlers took over the arena.

"Jess and Jamie are going to load Maestro for you so Gaston doesn't realize you are leaving without him," Ryle slid his arm around my waist and pulled me in tight.

I chuckled, "Makes me feel a little less guilty."

Logan was the third rider with a successful run of 4.6, which easily put him in the finals for Saturday.

Twenty minutes later, I was in the back seat of Jess' truck cuddled next to Ryle on our way to the evening rodeo in Othello. It was odd...even if the four of us riding together was going to become a norm in the future...this first time, it was just odd.

Maestro was excited and ready to race...we took first place, Jamie was third, and Ryle and Jess took second.

The trip back to Pendleton was better than the trip to Othello...until my phone rang.

CHAPTER FORTY-ONE

"Dad?"

"Hey, Darlin'," he said in a hushed tone.

"What's wrong? Is Archer okay?" My hand went to my stomach again.

"He's fine; ate all his dinner and pooped it out. Now, put me on speaker so I can tell all of you and you won't have to repeat it." he ordered.

My hand shook as I lowered the phone and hit the speaker button.

"Alright, you're on speaker," I exhaled nervously. "What's wrong?"

"Brodie, Martin, and I left the roundup grounds and are staying at the Blackburn's' ranch for the night."

"What?" I gasped. "Why?"

"Brodie is fine, we're all fine," he said. "It's just an hour away so we'll have plenty of time tomorrow to get back."

"Dad, what the hell happened?" Pain shot through my stomach, strong enough I nearly doubled over.

"You alright?" Ryle whispered.

I nodded nervously.

"He went over to have dinner with some roughies and he returned back to the trailer just to be met by a reporter waiting for him," he answered.

"That jackass from Walla Walla?" I gasped.

"No, from what I heard, he went back to reporting on politics. This was a new one and the questions weren't too bad, but it still brings up the loss and the pressure of everyone watching him ride." He answered. "It was tough on both of them so I called Sep, and he said to come over."

I closed my eyes, "Are they alright?"

"They are just fine. Martin is in watching a movie with the Blackburn's, and Brodie is outside on the porch, getting some needed fresh air and alone time," he said. "They will both sleep better here at the ranch than on the trailer beds."

There was nothing I could do about it in the backseat of Jess's truck.

"Who did he draw for tomorrow?" I sighed.

"Both were at the NFR last year," Dad answered. "He has a good chance."

"Jess can drop me off..." I started.

"No, you go back to Pendleton, and we'll see you in the morning," Dad said.

"Dad..." I sighed.

"Darlin', it is quiet here right now. Peaceful and they have settled in so let's just let it be. Today has been a long day and tomorrow will be, too." His voice was firm and left no room for argument. "We'll see you in the morning for our final day of the year. You all drive safe and text me when you get to the trailers."

The call ended and I turned into Ryle's arms.

"Do you want coffee?" I whispered to Ryle as I cuddled into his side Saturday morning.

"Not yet," He whispered. "Damn, you are such an early riser."

I chuckled and kissed his jaw, "I'm going to go check on Archer."

"He will be fine, and it is going to be a good day," He whispered.

"And you are going to do your best today." I ran a finger over his bare shoulder and down his arm. It would be so nice just to lay there together and forget about the whole day.

"Don't focus on winning, focus on catching the steer and getting him turned for Jess," Ryle smiled.

I chuckled, "You've been talking to Dad. That's his main speech."

"Yeah, we had a talk yesterday and it really helped. I was focusing too much on placing and winning enough money to qualify instead of concentrating on just getting the job done."

"He is a wise ol' man," I leaned down and nuzzled into his neck.

"Say that to his face," Camille said from her bed.

I propped up on an elbow and looked down at her, "Oh, I have and was thinking about having a t-shirt made for him. Sorry if I woke you."

"You didn't," She smiled. "I've been awake for a while."

"I'm headed to the barn if you want to come with," I kissed Ryle on the cheek then slid off the bed.

After months of traveling together, we had a well-rehearsed routine of getting dressed, making the first two cups of coffee, and grabbing granola bars and bananas for breakfast.

With our 'Coffee with Cowboys' coffee cups placed in the cup holders, we drove away from the trailers in the ATV. We weren't even on the road yet when we stopped and talked to a couple of tie-down ropers. Just down the road from there, we ran into Trenten and his wife, Maria, then as we drove by the fenced-in area where the roughies camped and waved at the few men that were already awake and outside.

It took another ten minutes of stopping and talking to people then waving at people to get the short distance to the barn. When I stopped at the large door, I turned to see Camille with tears in her eyes.

"What's wrong?"

She sniffed with a shrug, "I was just thinking of that day last spring when I nearly begged you to let me go on the road with you. Evan said it was a long road through the summer and fall…to Saturday of the Pendleton Roundup."

"That seems so long ago, now," I sighed.

"Yes, but I can't believe it's already here," her gaze wandered over the trailers, tepees, bucking horses in their pens and people wandering down the roads.

"It has gone by fast," I smiled. "Was it as epic as you hoped?"

She grinned with a nod, "From the very first trip; the long drives, long nights, trailer parties, rodeos, jackpots, horses, horse injuries to triumphs and those damn hit barrels or missed throws. My first jackpot, to the work to get ready for traveling and practicing roping and then the shopping and shopping some more. I have a house full of stuff yet no house to put it in. The concerts! Toby Keith night, unbelievable and so many more artists. Making time to hit the beaches I love, our photoshoot, the laughter, seeing all those towns...the country I would have never seen in my old life. Then there is the heart of this world...the people." Her smile broadened. "Like all the ones we just passed...the people are so...tremendous. They absolutely love what they do and the way of life they live even when it's hard. It makes them all happy and fun to be around."

"So, the verdict is epic," I grinned.

"Very."

"Any regrets?"

She hesitated with a thoughtful look then shook her head, "No...no regrets of what I could control. The relationship with Mark...no regret, it was a solid relationship until I changed. I still care for him, always will and hope the best for him. I will never regret the time I got to have with Craig. We were friends first, and I truly believe we would have been together for a very long time if not forever. I knew what I wanted in life by then and so did he. No matter how my future turns out now, I will always wish he and I could have had our life together."

We shared a smile and sigh.

"Then, of course," she continued. "was spending all that time with my sister and you."

"As I said before," I grinned. "I like you even if you are beautiful."

She laughed.

We finally stepped off the ATV and walked into the barn.

After cleaning stalls and feeding, we slid back onto the machine and drove down the dirt road. We waved and talked to a dozen more people.

"I'm not ready for this adventure to be over," Camille sighed.

"Well, technically, it isn't. I have a few races planned next month to work with Maestro, then we still have ten long days in Vegas this December that will drag on but go so damn fast."

"Will I still be able to help you?"

"Yes, you and Martin will be needed for the half a dozen horses we'll have there. Gaston, Maestro, and Fred for competition then of course, our entry horses. Logan and I have both ridden Dad's horse in the grand entry, so this time, Brodie will ride him while I ride Mom's Embers, and Logan will take Bubba. At night, Dad can't walk me down the lane so you still get to do that."

"I am so excited."

I stopped the ATV next to the trailer and turned off the engine. "Besides, there is a best-dressed barrel racer competition every night and you happen to have great style."

Her eyes widened, "I get to dress you?"

I laughed at her eagerness, "Plus we have the back number night and the awards night we dress up for."

"And you're going to let me dress you? Pick out all your clothes?"

"I'll be your life-size Barbie doll so it's one less thing I have to think about."

"Well," She huffed. "I'll start planning tomorrow and make sure you stay in shape during your downtime, too. I already know the dress for one of the nights and you're going to need to be sleek and sexy."

We both giggled as we walked to the trailer as Logan and Lacie Jae stepped out.

"Horses fed?" Logan asked.

"Yes," I answered and plopped down into one of the lawn chairs.

"I need some exercise, so we're going to take Bubba for a walk," Logan slid onto the seat of the ATV.

Lacie Jae grinned, "Logan's walk is a run for me, so I'll be riding Bubba."

We all chuckled.

"I'll ride over and bring the ATV back," Camille said.

I watched them drive away, then jumped up and made my way to the man lying on my bed. He was on his stomach, arms curled around a pillow, and the sheet was barely covering his butt.

"I can't pass that up," I stepped up to crawl onto the bed and over his legs.

He chuckled.

After slowly running my hands up his sides then arms, I settled on his back and began a deep massage.

"I love you," he moaned.

"I know."

"I was lying here thinking you should come with us next week."

"To Texas?" I huffed.

"Yeah, Jamie's cousins are leasing us horses to ride the year's final rodeos down there. You can come to cheer us on."

"Hmm, well, I don't think I can stay the whole time."

"You need a vacation and I want you with me."

I stopped the massage and rolled down next to him.

"So, what I heard in all this was before I came in here, you were lying here thinking of me."

His eyes finally opened, and we shared a smile.

"I love you," I whispered.

"I know."

"Do you want me to go get Gaston?" Camille asked as she stepped out of the trailer. She wore the 343 t-shirt that Martin had given her and long dangling earrings that swayed as she walked. Her long dark hair flowed in bouncing curls down her back, and a blue flat-brimmed cowboy hat, blue denim jeans and ankle boots completed her casual yet very elegant look.

"No, but thanks. They award the prizes after each event and that takes some time so we have hours before we need to warm-up."

I brushed my hair back then settled the brown cowboy hat on my head to keep the hair held in place. Then, I tucked in my dark blue long sleeve western shirt covered in my sponsor's patches.

"Aren't you two just gorgeous?"

I turned in surprise at the voice. It was happy and full of life.

"Brodie?" Camille huffed.

Through the thick whiskers, his grin was wide, his eyes lit, and his whole aura was full of energy. He looked happy.

"I realized, I have ridden ten horses to get to today," he said proudly. "No matter what happens this afternoon, I'm happy, and I know Craig would be, too."

"Of course, he would," I gasped with heart pounding.

"Thank you, Sis, for everything," with sincerity ringing in his voice he stepped to me and pulled me into an embrace. "You are truly my superhero, and I couldn't be prouder than to call you my sister."

"Oh, Brodie," the tears rose.

"It's time to quit riding a memorial for Craig; it's time to rejoice in who he was and ride with that joy we always had." His smile was honest.

Tears of love and relief slid down my cheeks as we embraced.

"Now she's going to have to do her makeup again," Camille teased.

The sound of Dad's wheelchair made us all turn. The whole family was there between the two trailers, even Ryle who stepped in next to me and took my hand.

Brodie looked at Dad then Martin, "As LJ said on her podcast from Lewiston, Craig will always be with me when I ride."

"Yes, he will," Martin nodded. His jaw was clenched, lips rolled into a straight line, but his eyes were shining with pride as he looked at Brodie.

"He'll be with me in bareback today and probably in saddle bronc too but will be trying to push me off so I earn more in the rides for him than my own." Brodie grinned.

We all chuckled and nodded.

"I've also decided one more thing," Brodie looked to Martin. "I want to take the earnings for all the rides for Craig and start a roughstock riding scholarship program in his memory. Something to help beginners get to the clinics so they can learn like we did when we started."

Martin nodded, eyes glistening, "He'd really like that...talked about it."

Brodie took a breath and looked at the family around him, "It's been a hard month, and, I know, none of us could have done it alone. Thanks to all of you for helping me get through to this day. Now, we move forward and start living for him, and, as I said, we rejoice for who he was and what he brought to our lives."

My heart swelled and it took everything in me to keep from crying. Instead, I nodded, smiled, squeezed Ryle's hand tightly, and said, "Amen...let's rodeo."

Instead of standing in the bleachers behind him, hovering over him in the chutes below, I stood on the field with

Logan behind dozens of people sitting on the grass as Brodie lowered onto his bareback horse. There was an ease in my heart because I believed, with all my heart, that this last ride for Craig was going to be a good one. I believed.

"I believe," I whispered.

"We believe," Logan smiled.

As Brodie adjusted his hand in the riggin handle, the announcer spoke of Craig's accident and the memorial rides. This time, I did not hide away, flinch, or ignore the words; I rejoiced in pride and love.

There was no stomach pain when the blue gate swung open and the bay horse leapt out two strides then his fierce, high kick with nose touching the ground. The move was repeated in a large circle to the left until the last few seconds when he twist and turned to the right. They were beautiful high fierce kicks and Brodie's spurring and freehand kept up with him until the horn blared. The pick-up men were suddenly at his side and he was reaching for them. He slid to the ground and the second his boots hit the ground, he leapt in the air with both fists lifted to the sky.

"Yay! Yay! Yay!" He screamed over and over, then took his hat, pointed it to the end of the arena where Martin and Dad were standing in the bleachers and threw it.

The crowd was screaming, they were on their feet, giving him a standing ovation.

Brodie lifted his hands and eyes to the sky and yelled, "I BELIEVE!"

I was jumping up in down, hands gripping Logan's arm as we both screamed, "I BELIEVE!"

Everyone around us was standing and cheering for him. There were shouts of "I believe" ringing throughout the arena.

The 88 point score was announced and Brodie ran to Logan and I as the last three bareback riders took their turns.

When the last rider walked from the field, Brodie was first place for the day but third place in the average. He could not have been happier.

Text from Dad: Tim Miller missed his calf

I stared at the message, letting its meaning soak in. Even if Tim was successful with his team roping partner, Tim couldn't beat Hanna in points. If Brodie placed in Saddle Bronc, then he couldn't beat Brodie either. It would be between Brodie and Hanna and their final runs.

I ran the brush over Gaston again. It was a nervous habit. We were still an hour away from having to warm up, but I needed the horses to keep me relaxed.

Text from Dad: Awards are about over, SB starting soon, Brodie is last rider

When I began my walk over to the arena, Logan was riding Fred and ponying Bubba from the practice arena. The steer wrestlers were after the bronc riding so he needed the horses near.

He handed me the reins for Bubba, and I stepped up and rode next to him to the arena. Tyler was there and took the horse's reins so Logan could be on the field when Brodie rode. We walked under the bleachers by the roping chutes to make our way to the arena.

They were only on the second rider when we joined the crowd.

"I thought they would be farther along," I mused to Logan.

Kirk was there and turned with a grin, "They had a hard time catching the first horse."

The red gate swung open and Johnny rode out on a grey horse. The animal bucked high in the back with Johnny matching each buck with a strong fast spurring motion. The grey horse bucked right at the people sitting on the ground, making them rise and scatter. The announcer and crowd laughed while Logan grabbed my arm and pulled me out of the way and behind him.

When the horn blared, the pick-up men slid Johnny off and reached for the rope.

I looked up at Logan with a grin, "Well, aren't you my hero, willing to risk your body to protect me."

He didn't even look at me when he huffed, "Dad would have shot me if I let you get hurt."

I laughed, "Self-preservation then."

"Exactly," he nodded with a wide grin.

"Who did Brodie draw?" Kirk asked when we walked back to the crowd.

"Black Tie, Sankey's horse," I answered.

"NFR horse, he's a good one," Kirk nodded.

"Hopefully, he has a good day today," Logan exhaled.

When the tenth rider bust out of the chute, Brodie stretched out over the top of the dark bay horse and flipped his chaps back over his thighs. He was talking to the stock contractor who held the flank strap then to Tate and Johnny, who were behind the chute. All three men nodded.

The next rider was thrown from the horse's back with three seconds to the ahhs of the crowd.

Brodie lowered onto Black Tie's back, sliding his feet in the stirrup, adjusting his rein then shifting his body as he lowered back. With a tight grip on the rein, his free arm rose, chin tucked down and he gave the nod. Black Tie carried Brodie out into the arena and his powerful kicks brought cheers from the crowd and shouts from behind the chutes. Body quaking kicks, high fast spurring from Brodie, and the pair bucked their way to the middle of the arena as the buzzer went off.

I was bouncing again as the inhaled air I had held came out in a scream. Logan's hand was fist-pumping the air.

When Brodie slid from the pick-up man's horse, he jumped and yelled and fist-pumped in the air.

"He rode all twelve horses!" Logan hollered.

The announcer yelled the 90 point score and the crowd stood on their feet and cheered. Brodie was jumping and running with his hands in the air; Logan and I ran out to him. When he saw us, he jumped in the air and came down next to Logan who nearly tossed him in the air. Laughter rang out as Brodie's feet touched the ground and he reached for me in a strong, rib-breaking hug.

When he was announced the winner of the day and the winner of the average, he jumped and yelled again then pointed down to Dad and Martin.

He stopped, leaned back, and with his hands pointing to the sky, he yelled, "For you, Craig! I BELIEVE!"

Tears slid down my cheeks.

My heart was racing in excitement as he ran for the gate and mounted the horse to ride across the arena to receive the awards. When he burst from the gate, he was wearing his dark sunglasses under the black cowboy hat.

"Damn," Logan shook his head as we watched Brodie ride across the field where the people were setting up for the awards. "And I have to try to bulldog after this."

He looked down at me and I threw my arms around him for a strong hug.

"Dad and Martin…" I barely got the words out as we both turned to walk to the gate.

Then, something breathtaking and awe-inspiring happened. The cowboys behind the chutes began climbing down and onto the field while people walked out of the gates and onto the field to join them. They created a line where the dirt met the grass and took off their hats to cover their hearts.

"Logan," my breath shook as I reached out to grab his shirt to stop him.

He turned and lifted his eyes to the mass of people lining the field from one end to the other.

Whispered murmurs reached us, "For Craig…his procession."

I fell against Logan as we walked to the end of the line. I could not even imagine how Martin was feeling at that moment.

I turned to watch Brodie pose for pictures then step up into the saddle. When he turned the first corner, his hat was in

451

one hand, waving to the crowd. He waved at Martin, Dad, Lacie Jae, and Camille as he rode past them; they were standing and cheering. His head turned to the line of cowboys on the field and he slowed the horse to a trot. He moved his cowboy hat to cover his heart as he started in front of the long line of cowboys. His head turned to as if to look at each person, to recognize what they were doing for Craig.

The tears seemed unending as I leaned against Logan. I turned back to Dad but their seats were already empty.

When Brodie appeared at the far end of the arena, we walked to the gate. Within moments, Martin, Dad, and the sisters were there. We all impatiently waited for Brodie to appear through the gate. When he did, he jumped from the horse and ran to Martin and Dad.

"What do you think tomorrow is going to be like?" Logan asked as we sat on the horses and waited for the steer wrestling to start. The panels and chute were in place; the first rider backing into place.

"Exhausting, mentally and physically," I answered. "We'll get home late tonight then not want to do anything tomorrow."

"I want to just lie in bed and watch movies for a week," Logan nodded with a grin.

I chuckled, "You can't. Ryle asked me to go to Texas with him on Tuesday and I told him yes."

"Good, you need a vacation away. You taking your side-kick with you?"

"I'm not sure she would appreciate..."

"I call her that all the time, and she just laughs."

"Well, yes, I just haven't told her yet."

Logan chuckled as he walked forward to back Bubba into the box and haze for the first of two runs.

When he returned, he looked at me in concern, "It's done now, and no matter how good Brodie felt this morning, the reality is going to hit him whether it's here or at home."

I sighed, "I know. When life returns to normal, it's going to be a different normal that he'll have to adjust to. He's going to need a distraction and help to focus."

We switched horses just before he backed into the box. He looked down the chute, over to the spotter, then nodded. That few seconds it took for the steer to run down the chute seemed to take forever. He and the horse burst forward and when the steer burst from the chute, Fred and the hazing horse were right by its side. Logan leaned down, stretched out and slid from the horse with his arms wrapping the horns and his boots hitting the ground...they slid for a good fifteen feet before the steer slowed down enough that Logan could get his feet under him to turn the steer.

The 5.4 second time was not going to place him in first. He'd slid right out of that and into second place.

"Need some traction on them boots?" I teased with a grin when he approached.

"Won't win the rodeo, but I'm sure Lacie Jae is happy," he answered.

We both turned to see her standing with a grin on her face and both hands in the air with all fingers up.

"Ah, you finally got a ten," I laughed.

"The day we met her, I got my ten." Logan grinned at her with pure love and happiness.

"That you did, Brother, that you did."

I stood behind Dad as the team roping started. Ryle looked up at me from the arena and I smiled in encouragement. He nodded then turned away.

"Thanks for talking with him," I whispered to Dad.

"You're welcome. He's a good young man with a big future ahead of him."

"I agree."

"Where are they in the standings now?" Camille asked.

"They were 2nd after the slack but 4th now," I answered.

"For qualifying for the NFR?" Lacie Jae asked with a concerned frown.

"We won't really know how he stands until after the weekend is over," I answered and looked at Camille. "Which reminds me, we're headed for Texas on Tuesday."

"Really? Which horses?" She was excited and surprised.

"None, we're flying down for moral support," I answered and explained why.

"More adventure, I cannot wait," she grinned.

I rested my hands on Dad's shoulders as we watched the team ropers. His muscles began twitching.

"Dad?" I whispered.

"I'll be fine," he answered and adjusted himself in the chair.

"You have your muscle relaxers?" I asked.

"I do, but they make me tired so I'm not taking them until after we're done," he answered.

"You need to relax at the trailers for a while before you sit in the truck for hours," I said.

He just nodded and we were quiet until Ryle and Jess rode into the box.

I took a deep breath and stared hard.

Ryle swung his rope over his head a few times, then he took a deep breath and his shoulders lowered...he nodded.

Three times he turned to look down at the chute for the steer before he kicked his horse, Dexter, into action. He was going too fast and had to hold the horse back a stride so he didn't break the barrier. My heart jumped to my throat as he twirled the lariat once, twice, three times before letting the rope fly. It swirled around the horns and tightened as Ryle turned the calf for Jess, whose black horse had him in the perfect position. His rope flew and trapped the back hooves. Instantly, Dexter turned to face the black horse and the rope tightened with horns and both hooves trapped. Flag down, clock stopped at 5.7 seconds, no flag for a broken barrier.

"Yes!" I yelled. My heart was pounding in pride.

"Great run," Dad nodded.

"Mature decision to hold that horse back," Martin added.

Ryle loped down the arena to follow the steer. I was shaking in excitement for him.

"That puts Jaspers and Corday in third place with the leading team yet to go," the announcer reported.

Lacie Jae turned with wide eyes, "That's a good check, right?"

"Third or fourth will be," I smiled. "It should give him a solid chance."

She turned to watch the last team, "I'm still going to pray for him every day."

"Me, too," I whispered as the last team finished with a 9.5-second run leaving Ryle and Jess in third place.

As Gaston and I waited under the bleachers to go out onto the field, I began calculating the points for the saddle. Tim's no-time in calf roping took him out of the running. Hanna came into the day with a seven-point lead ahead of Brodie but with his first and third placing he earned ten points to take the lead by three points. Hanna was currently sitting in 3rd place in barrels. After today's race, if she averaged 3rd place she would earn 4 points and win. In 4th place, they would tie.

If they tied in points, the win would be based on the amount of money they had earned but I had no idea who had won more.

The gate was opened and we began our walk through the aisle and onto the field. Gaston walked calmly behind a couple of other racers, including Hanna with her long blonde hair bouncing as her black horse pranced. I have never ridden in a race to purposely beat another racer. I go in to win the whole thing…not just beat one person. We had ridden at a lot of races together and had even spent a few nights celebrating in bars. How was I supposed to look her in the face knowing I rode today only to beat her?

We had drawn for our racing positions, Hanna was second to go, I was eleventh.

When we walked out into the open, I was greeted by three very familiar faces sitting on the barrier from the track to the field. I walked the horse to Ryle, Brodie and Logan with the ache in my stomach rising.

"You've been calculating, haven't you?" Ryle sighed.

I glanced at him then to Brodie, "Yeah, couldn't stop myself." I hesitated and the ache in my stomach caused a grimace.

"Whatever happens, happens," Brodie said. "I'm satisfied and happy with what I've accomplished."

"And Craig would be, too," Logan added.

"Don't go in there racing against Hanna," Brodie said. "You go in and just race."

I looked out to the racers getting ready, "I need to warm him up."

We trotted away and had completed two large circles in the corner when the first racer was called. Maybe all the other racers would place better and I wouldn't have to worry about it. The first racer trotted down the line to the timer then broke into a run to the first barrel…which she knocked down. I sighed, that didn't help.

Maybe Hanna would knock one down…she didn't. Instead, she lowered her time by 2 one-hundredths of a second. That didn't help either.

"Delaney!"

I turned to Logan and walked over to him.

"What?" I huffed and watched the third racer run out onto the field.

"How old is Gaston?" He asked.

I turned and looked at him in surprise, "Thirteen."

"He is at the peak of his speed right now," Logan nodded. "Which means he'll start to slow down…"

"Logan, what the ever-living hell are you doing? Trying to psych me out?" I grumbled.

He huffed with a grin, "Just the opposite. You need to focus on winning this race for the right reason. You've ran this field a few times now and you haven't won it."

"Damn, Logan!" I gasped.

"Delaney," Logan shook his head. "I know you and Gaston can win this…we all believe you can but your head isn't thinking straight."

"Gaston has carried your butt around enough arenas and won, but you've never ridden him to a win on this field," Brodie added.

I stared at them both wide-eyed and a bit pissed. The fourth runner entered onto the field.

"He's got years ahead of him on the standard pattern," Ryle nodded. "But this one is different…you know that."

"You, too?" I glared at him.

"Delaney," Logan slapped his hand on my leg. "Look me in the eyes and tell me that next year Gaston is going to be faster and as healthy as he is right now."

I just glared but my mind started to focus on what they were saying.

"Right now, he is in the best shape of his life and he deserves to be on the books as a winner of this rodeo," Brodie added.

Ryle had stopped verbally agreeing with them but I could see it in his eyes.

I looked out across the field as the fifth runner charged for the first barrel.

"As much as I always hate to admit it," I huffed. "You're right."

I turned away from them and trotted to the edge of the field so I could concentrate.

I had watched the videos from runs at this field hundreds of times. I knew what I did wrong and at times when we just weren't fast enough but I knew, in my heart, we were fast enough this year. I believed it.

Closing my eyes, I ran through the last time we had ran in this arena. Over and over again, I mentally watched the run from my point of view and from the camera videoing me.

As the ninth rider rode into the field, I rode Gaston in a large circle. The crowd, the announcer, the people around us faded away as I concentrated on our movement. I glanced up as the tenth woman ran into the field.

I watched her make each turn but put Gaston and I in her place...she turned two strides too late for the first and overran it. I rode out far enough that I was at the edge of the crowd but out of her path when she ran to home. When she ran by, I trotted out to the spot I knew was the angle Gaston needed for the perfect turn at that first barrel.

"I believe, Gaston," I whispered when our name was announced. I inched toward the line. "I truly believe we can do this." His answer was to prance left then right.

The only short run in this pattern was the stretch from the timer to the first barrel. The angle for his turn was perfect; we couldn't have been any closer. There was no hesitation as he whipped around it and stretched out for the long run to the second. Having run this race before, he knew it was a distance to the second and didn't even attempt to turn before I cued him. It was another, couldn't have been tighter turn. There was barely a foot between my knee and the red and white barrel. My heart was racing, calves thumping on his sides to keep him moving as we raced to the last and third barrel. "We can do it...keep going." I huffed.

With one hand holding the rein high up on his neck and the other gripping the saddle horn tightly, we slid around the barrel with dirt flying behind us. As his body straightened for the final run, I leaned forward, hands high up his neck and did the one thing I had never done before. I gave him the John

Wayne 'hee yaw' yell, and he pinned his ears back with his body stretched out, digging deeper, and we flew across the green grass. I growled the 'hee yaw' twice more, giving him that extra verbal encouragement. We had never run faster than we did down the middle of that green field.

The closer we ran to the finish line, the clearer my thoughts became. Suddenly, the sound of the crowd cheering and the announcer yelling invaded my senses. I focused on Gaston's every stride so I could remember this moment.

In the distance, I could see Ryle and my brothers' arms in the air as they yelled and cheered us on. I'm not sure if it was the moisture in my eyes from the wind or the bouncing of the run but I could have sworn I saw four men standing where the three were supposed to be. We ran past them and turned. I could see Camille and Lacie Jae jumping and cheering in the stands with Dad on his feet with an arm in the air. The time of 27.15 was announced. I looked over my shoulder to see not only Ryle, Logan, and Brodie but Martin was there too. Tears welled as my heart raced. I trotted down to the corner of the track then back to cool down as the last racer ran into the field.

One more circle then Gaston and I trotted back to the four men and I jumped off the horse and into Martin's arms.

"You won," he yelled in my ear. "You won the whole damn thing." His arms squeezed tighter. "I am so damn proud of you...Craig is hollering and yelling in heaven."

"Delaney, come on," Ryle tugged at my shirt. "You need to get over there."

I looked at Martin as I was pulled away. "I love you."

"I know, Darlin'" He nodded with a wide grin.

I turned to Ryle and my brothers, "I want Gaston on the final lap. Can you switch the saddle while we're taking pictures?"

With the red roan trotting behind them, they ran to the side of the arena where the awards were to be given. I ran to the gate with the horse wearing the trophy saddle. My heart was racing and hands trembling, I could barely climb on the horse.

The whole awards presentation was a blur of excitement, smiles, and pictures.

The championship saddle was on Gaston when the last picture was taken. Logan nearly picked me up and threw me up into the saddle making everyone laugh.

As I started the victory lap, I searched for Dad in the stands and did a slow trot in front of him with a hand over my heart. Then Gaston was not to be denied his run as we loped away and around the arena.

On the last turn, I heard the announcer;

"The Big Four, Best in the Northwest points champion and winner of the saddle is Brodie Rawlins."

I screamed with a fist-pumping in the air. Concentrating so hard on winning the race for Gaston, I had forgotten to calculate each ride...which is what those three men had fully intended.

When I rode through the open gate, Martin and Brodie were in a strong embrace, with Logan grinning and pacing next to them. Ryle pulled me from the saddle, and I was barely able to hold Gaston's reins as we held each other.

"Delaney!"

I turned from Ryle and into Brodie's arms.

"Damn, girl, you did it," he squeezed hard.

"You did it," I whispered. "I'm so damn proud of you."

"I couldn't have done it without you," his body shook. "You were always there, pushing, helping, believing..."

I leaned back and looked up into his wide relieved eyes, "We all believed, and you did it."

"Where's Brodie?"

We both turned to Jess and Kirk under each of Dad's arms as they walked him through the arena gate. Trenten and Johnny were carrying the wheelchair.

"It's the fastest way to get him here," Jess explained with a grin.

Brodie ran to Dad as Camille and Lacie Jae ran to me. We shared a celebratory hug.

Dad's grin was electrifying, "Damn, Boy, you did it. I couldn't be prouder of you."

"We all did it," Brodie huffed and helped brace him as he lowered into the chair. "I couldn't have done it without all of your support and help."

"Excuse me."

We all turned to Lexi Maples, the media reporter for the rodeo.

"I hate to break up the celebration, but can I get a couple of interviews real quick?" She asked and looked at me. "You first then we'll talk about the Big Four win." She looked at Brodie with a broad smile.

A roar erupted from the crowd watching the wild cow milking in the arena.

"Let's step down here," Lexi said and waved an arm to just behind the bucking chutes.

"Let me have Gaston," Camille reached for the reins. "I'll get him to the trailer and bring the ATV over to collect all the prizes you and Brodie won today."

The next half-hour was another whirlwind of interviews and pictures. The last set taken, was of Brodie and I standing in the middle of the arena with the saddles and buckles. The very last shot was of Dad standing between us with Logan at my side and Martin at Brodie's.

I knew that shot was going to be enlarged and hung in the hallway at home.

When we finally walked out of the arena, Camille and Lacie Jae were standing at the ATV waiting for us. The area was nearly void of people.

"All the prizes are over at the trailer, including Ryle who is watching over it," Camille smiled as Logan placed the two saddles in the back of the ATV.

I looked back to Brodie who had stopped on the arena side of the open gate and was staring at the buckle in his trembling hands.

My breath caught...I knew the reality of the accomplishment was beginning to settle in him, but I didn't believe he realized the entirety of what he had done.

"You two sisters get in the back and hold the saddles down," Martin sighed. "I'll take you over and come back for the other four."

I shared a solemn glance with Martin then turned back to Brodie as the ATV drove away.

"Son?" Dad said softly.

After a long sigh, Brodie whispered as he continued to stare at the buckle, "It's kind of funny that all these weeks, I didn't once think of winning this rodeo. My whole focus was just trying to get each horse rode so I could get him that damn saddle." He shook his head. "Craig and I always wanted this one...dreamed of it...talked about it...and truly believed someday we would walk out of the arena carrying it."

His knuckles turned white as his grip tightened.

Tears slowly trickled down my cheeks, and it took all my will-power to keep from sobbing.

Dad turned his wheelchair and motioned for Logan and I to follow. We stopped at the stock pens and waited. It wasn't long before Brodie appeared and walked to us with his heels dragging the ground with every step. There was no swagger, no celebratory grin, and no sign that he had completed his memorial to his best friend.

He stopped and looked at the three of us.

"I want to go home," he sighed.

"I couldn't be prouder of you, Son," Dad said with a hand out to him. As their hands met in a firm grip, he continued. "You've accomplished something that no one in the family has done."

"You've all qualified," Brodie countered.

"Brodie," I smiled. I knew he had no idea...hadn't even considered it. "What you've won with the Big Four will put you a little over a hundred thousand for the year, which will place you about 7th or 8th for saddle bronc going into the Finals."

"I qualified, solidly, so I can take a week or two off now," he sighed.

"With the money you earned in bareback the last four weeks and the bit you won over the summer, you'll be around thirty-three thousand," Logan added.

"Son," Dad said with a humble voice. "You'll be sitting around 4th for the All-Around Cowboy going into the Finals."

Brodie's head lowered, "I didn't know..."

"You're the only rookie going into the finals. After the Big Four run, you earned the Saddle Bronc Rookie of the Year," I said proudly as the tears filled my eyes.

When his head rose, and he looked at us, I so desperately wanted to see pride, joy, happiness; anything besides the anguished weary eyes that looked back at us.

My body was shaking as I stepped up to wrap him in my arms with his head dipping enough into my neck that no one could see his tears fall. He was still holding Dad's handshake, and Logan's arm slid across his shoulders with the other hand gripping Dad's shoulder.

That was the image the photographer captured and was spread throughout the internet and was the cover of two magazines.

PART TWO

RIVER

(Three years before)

CHAPTER FORTY TWO

As I did with every trip out to the younger bucking horse herd, I searched for Destiny's Ignatius; my Iggy. He was two now and it would be another two or three years before he began his bucking career in the rodeos. One thing about raising bucking horses, there was no instant gratification. You had to wait YEARS and patience was NOT something I was known for.

Iggy was turning out to be a strong-willed, overly curious, and very smart young horse. With his strength and size, he was a full hand taller than the other horses born the same spring. I was hoping Dad would begin the horse's career at four-years-old instead of five.

At the moment, I was riding Iggy's mother, Destiny, who was pregnant with her third foal from our stallion, Chinook. The morning frost was already melting, but the chill in the air made my face red and tingle with the cold. If all predictions were correct, we were in for a long cold winter.

It was October, the weekend after our last rodeo of the season which meant I had more time to ride the hills and prairie with the horses. I would never get tired of that.

465

The herd of our younger male horses appeared in the bottom of the ravine. Two dozen colts, in all different colors, spread out over the land grazing on the last tufts of grass. Not all of them were gelded yet so the fillies and smaller young geldings were pastured separately.

Destiny's ears perked when she saw the herd and I didn't even have to tell her to go to them, she just turned and made her way down the slope. She was a good mother; nurturing even to those who weren't her foals.

As we approached, all their heads rose and looked at us curiously. A few trotted up the hill away from us while some eagerly trotted to us. I knew each horse by sire and dam. For most of them, Dad or I were the first humans they saw. While Mom worked as an operation's manager in a manufacturing plant, my twin brother, Caleb, was in his fifth year of veterinarian school at the Colorado State University in Fort Collins. He loved the school, classes, and learning. I could not stand being cooped up in the classrooms even if it concerned horses. I was where I wanted to be; outside with no walls confining me...and with horses.

Three of the young horses greeted us with nose to nose touches with Destiny and their little mouths opening and closing, letting the older horse know they were young and submissive to her. When Destiny greeted the horses with loving nudges, even more trotted to us.

I was in heaven with all these babes around me. I reached down and tried to touch a few. My fingers just touched a striking gold palomino's nose and he jumped back, shook his head, and nearly fell over himself getting away from me. He was a year younger than Iggy and Dad had named him Skitter since he hated to be touched.

"You're so silly, Skitter," I laughed. "You would think I was made of acid."

He took one more look at me and trotted away.

"Little brat," I called out to him with a laugh. His older sister, Betty, was in the filly herd and was the same way.

Only a few of the horses had names but all were branded for identification of their parentage.

Destiny and I wandered calmly through the little band with some following, others totally ignoring the fact we were there, and others trotting away with Skitter. I visually checked each horse to make sure they were alright. A few of them were scratched from their rough playing or from the brush but all were moving freely.

I looked through them all again, but didn't see Iggy. He was dominant of the group and usually would be the first to greet us. I had spent time with him when he was a foal at Destiny's side and he loved to have his back scratched. I'd yell his name and he would come running over for a scratch.

"Iggy!" I called out. Some of the horses startled away. "Iggy!"

I nudged Destiny into a circle around the herd but after completing the first loop, I did not see him.

My nerves tingled and my stomach ached.

"Iggy!" I yelled as loud as I could.

There was a movement in the distance to my right; he appeared over the rise. His strides were slow and there was no way he would be that far away from his buddies unless he was hurt.

"Son-of-a-bitch," I exhaled and pushed Destiny into a run to get to him.

As we neared, he stopped so I slowed her down to a walk and made a complete circle around him. There were a few scratches on his left side but nothing worse than I had seen before. His stride was normal so his legs were OK.

When I walked around his lowered head to his right side, my heart nearly stopped. I reached for my phone as I slid off Destiny's side.

He answered on the first ring like he always did when he knew I was riding by myself.

"Everything OK?"

"No, Dad. No, it is not."

"It's Iggy, his eye is swollen, matted, I can't even see the eyeball itself. There's blood on his face. It looks like there is something under his eyelid or it is torn. The whole side of his face is scratched."

"Where are you?"

"South of West Line pasture, Crocket Hill by the trees."

With nose nearly dragging the ground, Iggy slowly walked toward Destiny and me. His white blaze was dark from dried blood and dirt.

Normally, he was energetic and a bit too rambunctious for me to be on the ground with him but this time, as I was standing at Destiny's side, the colt slowly approached then tucked his head between us.

"Oh, Dad," The tears began to rise. "He's hurting something fierce."

"I'm on my way and will call the vet clinic. See if you can get a picture of it and send it to them so they know what they are dealing with."

The phone call ended and I leaned down to take pictures. The swollen mass of blood, mud, sticks, and skin just made my stomach sick. I sent the pictures then slid the phone in my pocket. The colt did not move, he just sighed as he leaned against his mother.

"Oh, sweetheart," I whispered and tentatively reached out to touch his shoulder.

He didn't move, so I stroked his neck and side and whispered softly to him until I saw Dad's truck on the horizon. He was pulling the four-horse trailer instead of the regular stock trailer.

The younger horses ran up and down the hill when they saw him. Destiny stood as a rock and watched him approach. Iggy didn't move.

Dad stopped just at the edge of the hillside about thirty yards away and closed the door as softly as he could. He lowered the ramp on the trailer then turned to us.

"He's going to have to be loaded and I figured it was easier for him to follow Destiny up a ramp rather than have him jump up."

I just nodded as he knelt next to us and looked at the eye.

"Damn," he grumbled and looked up at me with deep concern. "The clinic is sending Nellie out."

"She's a good vet," I whispered and continued to stroke Iggy's shoulder.

"Let's test it and see if he'll follow Destiny."

He walked to the mare's side and took the reins while turning her so her rump was next to the colt.

Four steps and the colt didn't move any more than leaning his head against me instead. My heart just ached for him.

"You walk, too," Dad whispered.

I turned and put my hand on the horse's shoulder near his uninjured eye and took a step toward Destiny. Iggy followed so we very slowly made our way to the trailer. As we walked, Dad stripped the saddle and blanket from the mare's back and dropped them on the ground.

Without hesitation, he led Destiny right up the ramp and into the trailer.

We looked at each other, both silently praying the colt would go into the confined quarters. He didn't waver; he just followed me up the ramp and tucked himself into Destiny's side.

I very slowly moved away from him and out of the trailer to quietly shut the doors then lift the ramp.

As I climbed up the side of the trailer to check on him, Dad ran back for the saddle and pad.

"I want to stay here and watch him," I said as he tossed the gear into the back of the truck.

He shook his head and my back straightened in determination.

"River, whatever happens, happens."

"Dad," I gasped.

"If he falls or lays down, then so be it, we'll still get him to the barn faster if you're in the truck and not hanging on to the side of the trailer."

Damn it! He was right, so I huffed in frustration and ran for the truck.

"Call the clinic and let them know we'll meet Nellie at the barn," he said.

I made the call then set the phone in my lap.

469

"It's bad, Dad," I whispered as the tears rose again. "It's bad."

"You just get yourself mentally prepared for the possibility that he'll be blind in that eye."

I didn't respond, I just stared out the windshield and willed the horse to remain standing quietly tucked into his mother.

Nellie was already in the barn with the canopy doors open on her work truck. A small table was setup next to it with bottles and other supplies resting on it. Dad backed up the trailer right next to her. She was in her forties with long dark hair worn in a braid but now covered by a thick beanie. She was also a marathon runner so she was very fit even though it was hard to tell with her baggy coveralls and puffy jacket.

The truck stopped and we burst out the doors and met the veterinarian at the back.

I climbed on the side and looked in.

"He's still just standing next to Destiny," I sighed in relief.

"Now, let's see if he will come out as easy as he went in," Dad lowered the ramp and we opened the doors.

Iggy's head turned slightly so Nellie could see his eye.

"He looks content where he is," Nellie said. "Let's see if he'll let me get a preliminary look while he's calm."

The second she stepped in the trailer, the colt reared back on his hind legs, banging his head on the roof. It was fast, shocking, and we all three gasped.

Nellie jumped out of the trailer and my first instinct was to step in. When Iggy's hooves hit the ground, I stepped cautiously in with Dad grabbing my arm to be able to yank me out if he reared again. He didn't, he just let me walk right up to him and lay a comforting hand on his shoulder.

After a few moments of smooth-talking and calming strokes, I took a step out and he followed me; one little step at a time. When we were clear of the ramp, Dad stepped in to get Destiny.

He walked the mare in front of us to guide Iggy into the barn. When we stopped, I stroked him and spoke to him until his head lowered as he relaxed. The second Nellie approached, he reared back up and Dad yanked me out of the way.

"Well!" Nellie cried out. "Little man is getting sedated."

Dad and I both nodded in agreement.

"River, leave the barn so he can't see you," Dad ordered.

"What?" I gasped.

"He obviously trusts you and we don't want that to be shaken when we give him the shot," Dad answered and pushed me toward the door.

I grumbled and stepped out.

There was a bang, a few swear words, then silence.

"Alright, come back in," Dad said.

Iggy's head slowly lowering to the ground, then his body melted with Dad and Nellie guiding him safely to the ground with his injured eye on top.

I sat next to him to calmly stroke his shoulder and neck as she examined the eye.

"Looks like the eyelid is torn," she mumbled. "But we should be able to stitch it back together."

"The eye?" Dad asked as he bent over and watched her.

"I've got it clean enough to get a stain in there to see where the problem is," she answered.

There was silence as she worked.

"Hmmm," she mumbled. "The cornea looks good...but there is a pinpoint puncture wound."

I took a deep breath and let it out slowly.

"He's a lucky little bucker," Nellie smiled and sat back on her heels to look at me. "The swelling makes it look worse than it is. He'll be alright, we just have to keep it clean and make sure an infection doesn't set in."

My shoulders lowered as a stress tear fell down my cheek. I wiped it away.

"Well, he's out now," Nellie glanced between us. "We can geld him now if you've changed your mind."

"We haven't."

Iggy spent two weeks in the corrals with me watching over him. I was the only one allowed to go near his eye with a medicinal eye drop. He still didn't like it, but he didn't rear back or fight me. He even allowed me to use a wet cloth to wipe down the muddy, bloody blaze down his nose.

When he was healed and ready to join his herd, we rode out to push them closer to the barn then opened the gate and he burst out of the corral with a high buck and a fart.

I took pictures of him running to rejoin his friends. They hung in my bedroom and a few in the living room of our house.

"River, what the hell are you doing?" Dad yelled.

"I've been waiting for this day for four years!" I pulled the video camera from the back seat of the truck. "You forgot to get the video camera."

"So we're tortured by having to watch it hundreds of times?" Caleb laughed.

I rolled my eyes at his teasing, "We record all of the first bust-outs every year so we can watch them hundreds of times."

Mom's eyes were filled with laughter as she took the camera from me.

"It's the most important thing I'm in charge of all year," She declared.

Dad shook his head, "I'd say that was keeping your day job so we can continue with this wild-ass dream we had a few years back."

"And it's providing medical insurance for us," I teased.

Caleb slid his arm across her shoulders and pulled her in for a kiss on the cheek, "The most important thing you're in charge of all year...is us and our dreams."

Dad and I nodded in agreement.

Mom placed the back of her hand against her forehead, "Oh, the pressure."

Dad laughed and looked over the full corrals. "Let's get these young horses through the chutes so you can feed us, too."

Mom grinned, "I made three fresh loaves of bread last night and we have steak stew and chili in crockpots ready for us."

"I love your fresh bread, Mom!" I said excitedly and stepped up into the saddle of the horse I was riding for the day.

We all turned to the corralled horses as Mom climbed over the fence and stood on the platform Dad had built for her. She prepared to video the first time our young herd of bucking horses were sent through the chutes.

Destiny's Ignatius, my Iggy, was standing in the corral waiting for his first 'performance'. He was three now, and from the moment Dad and I discussed breeding Destiny and Chinook while I was in the cold pond, we had anxiously waited for this moment. My heart was pounding in anticipation but I knew Dad was going to save him for last. I wanted him to be first but Dad just grinned and shook his head.

Six of Dad and Caleb's friends had come to ride the horses for the first time. It was our own private ranch rodeo. To show her support of her husband's dream, my mother had gifted him with two bucking chutes once the business license was purchased. They were installed in our home arena. Two more had been added from the profits of the first two years of horses, so we now had four chutes at the end of the arena. We only loaded two horses at a time for safety concerns since many of the horses would try to crawl out of the chutes.

Caleb was on the ground and responsible for opening the gate. He attached the rope to the handle of the first chute that held a three-year-old bay gelding. The horse's nose was inching over the top of the gate. A soft cotton rope was stretched over the top of the horse's neck to help hold it down so he didn't hurt himself.

Dad and our foreman, Nolan, were leaning down into the chute over the horse to attach the soft flank strap. Each of the young bronc riders had brought their own saddles and were standing impatiently waiting to ride.

Caleb was in the arena next to the chute and horse. He slid a wire hook under the horse's belly to push the strap and cinch through and carefully lift it to Dad and Nolan.

I trotted over next to Mom. When the horses were let free into the arena, they were unpredictable and I would use my horse to block Mom from the running horses. Since she was on a platform across the fence, it was highly unlikely she would be injured but it made Dad feel better to have the extra layer of security. He didn't say it, but I knew he also liked me out of the way of the initial bust out. Personally, I loved being with Mom so I didn't argue with him.

Nolan's two sons, both in their thirties and seasoned ranchers, were waiting on horses as the pick-up-men that would help the riders off the horses...if they hadn't already fallen off.

"Here we go!" Caleb yelled and lifted the rope attached to the gate to full tension. He waited for the young cowboy to nod then yanked the gate open.

The horse turned and jumped into the air landing on all four hooves then his back legs flew up in the air behind him...his head was nearly to the ground and as the back hooves hit the ground, the front rose high....he bucked and kicked straight ahead of him until Dad yelled, signaling the end of the 8-second ride. The cowboy jumped off with a fist-pumping in the air while the horse ran excitedly around the arena fence.

"Nice one!" Dad yelled.

The excitement of the horse's bucking intensity, resonated among all of us.

The horse ran past me but he was just curious as to what had just happened. None of our horses were dangerous to be around. They were all friendly when you stood next to them on the ground but some of them, like the palominos Skitter and Betty, did not like to be touched. Other than Iggy spending two weeks with me while he healed from his eye injury, we had not handled the horses. They had been allowed to run free in the pasture to grow strong enough for bucking.

I loped in front of the loose horse so he had a partner to follow and led him out the gate. The other two riders were right behind him to encourage his departure. As I turned around to go back to the arena, I looked over at the large dark bay gelding with the white blaze down his nose. He was standing in the corner of the pen watching me curiously. My stomach bubble in anticipation of his turn in the chute.

Dad, Nolan, and Caleb were already working on the next horse. It was Betty; the pretty palomino with a flaxen mane and tail who had a major abhorrence for being touched. We had high hopes for this little five-year-old, third-generation bucking horse filly.

She did not disappoint. A high buck with back legs flying behind her was followed by a leaping jump with all four legs in the air. Up and down she would kick out the back first then fly in the air again. It was rhythmic and looked pretty fierce.

I was entranced in watching her and my heart was pounding when the cowboy flew off her back before Dad yelled.

"Instead of just Betty, she needs to be Flying Betty!" Caleb yelled.

Dad laughed with a firm nod of the head as the filly ran around the arena with a high, proud prance. Her long white-blonde mane was flying dramatically behind her.

"Look at your father," Mom said from beside me.

He was standing on the platform behind the chutes and watching the filly run. The man resonated happiness. His grin, raised proud shoulders, laughter, and whole aura was happy.

"When you love someone and can help them reach that level in their dreams…what they want to do in life, it fills your heart and your soul," She whispered as we both watched him. "Although it helps I like my job, this is why I work, so he can fulfill that dream that burned in his gut."

I turned to Mom and saw the whole-hearted love she held for Dad beaming in her eyes as she looked at him. Slowly her eyes moved to me.

"Someday, I hope you know that love, that happiness, that total fire in your soul."

Tears welled, "I won't settle for anything less."

"Nor should you need to. Just remember that it isn't just about what YOU want in life, it's what you BOTH want. You are partners in life, not two people moving side by side through life together."

"I'll remember, Mom. I promise."

"Don't be in a hurry," She smiled.

I turned back to Dad in time to see him look across the arena…right at Mom. There was pride and love in his eyes too…pure happiness.

"Ready!" Caleb yelled and watched for the next cowboy's nod.

The next horse was released and hopped out of the chute. Then he hopped again…then again. There was no kick, no buck, and no intensity. The very disappointed cowboy slid off the horse's back with a shake of his head and flipped the flank strap lose before walking away.

The bay horse saw me on my horse along the fence and trotted over to us.

"Fizzling dud," Mom said softly.

With a smart ass grin to Dad, I trotted across the arena to lead the horse out to the corrals.

"Looks like Caleb's next saddle horse," Nolan called out and earned a few chuckles.

Dad looked at me as I rode back into the arena, "Let's hope your big boy beats that."

My heart nearly dropped and my stomach soured but I just smiled at him, "He will."

Caleb switched places with one of the cowboys and rode two of the younger buckers. Both horses were strong with rhythmic bucking and Caleb had no problem riding until Dad hollered. He had earned two trips to the National High School Finals for saddle bronc, placing second both years.

I had to wait through another dozen horses before Iggy was ushered through the lane and into the chute. When the gate was shut behind him, he rose on his hind legs and leaned out over the chute. My heart nearly stopped.

"Get the rope," Dad ordered.

I leaned over the saddle with my elbows on the horn. My whole body was tense and heart-pounding as I watched them calm the horse as he fought to get out again. Dad glanced up at me with raised brows then he focused on Iggy.

He patted the horse along the neck and spoke to him until Iggy stood quietly. The rider was behind the chute nervously shifting his weight from one foot to the other.

My lips rolled together as I stared hard.

Mom didn't speak.

We were all nervous. Destiny was such a sweet horse, a wonderful saddle horse to ride the ranch and push cows. Chinook was an outstanding bucking horse. He had helped many a cowboy win an event across the country and had been chosen to go to the National Finals Rodeo seven times. He was the reason we started the stock contracting business. We had liked Iggy so much that we rebred Destiny and Chinook every year. It was a gamble we hope paid off.

So, as Iggy stood quietly in the chute, I wondered if he would take after his mother or after his father.

CHAPTER FORTY THREE

"Ready..." Caleb said nervously instead of yelling like he had at all the others.

With one more glance up to me, Dad motioned for the cowboy to slide on the saddle. We all waited anxiously to see how the horse was going to take a rider on his back.

The rider leaned back in the saddle, one arm cocked up alongside of his head, and with a grimace on his face, he nodded. Caleb pulled open the gate and Iggy...did nothing. He stood calmly and looked out into the arena. My heart dropped again as I sat up straight.

"Shut it!" Dad yelled.

Caleb ran the gate forward and slammed it shut.

I moved my horse down the fence so I was straight across from Iggy, and he would be able to see me.

Dad nodded in agreement as Iggy's head rose over the gate, and it was clear to everyone when his ears perked up that he had seen me.

"Alright, let's do it again," Dad said to Caleb. Then looked at the rider, "You good?"

"Yes, sir! Let's do this!" He shouted and leaned back in preparation again.

Caleb pulled the gate rope tight, "Ready!" He yelled this time.

The rider nodded, and the gate swung open.

Iggy leaned back on his hindquarters and launched himself forward, exploding into the air with front legs twisted to the right. The rider flew from his back and landed with a thump on the ground.

Iggy landed on all fours, lowered and went straight up in the air, down again, and he went forward on his front legs braced in the dirt and his back legs kicking straight up in the air in a vertical line. Down again and he leaned back again on his haunches and flew up into the air with his front legs twisted to the left. Down again and the vertical lift of the back legs was repeated. When he hit the ground, he bucked and launched himself in the air twice more before the pick-up men rode in next to him to release the flank strap. Iggy took off at a run for a victory lap then came to a sudden halt. His sides were heaving from the sudden burst of energy and his head was high in the air, eyes looking at everyone until he saw me. As if on an afternoon trail ride, he trotted toward me.

Through the whole action, no one had said a word. Caleb had helped the cowboy from the ground and they were leaning against the gate watching the horse.

My mind was buzzing, skin tingling, heart pounding, but I simply smiled at Iggy and trotted in front of him across the arena and out into the corral. When I stopped, the horse was right next to me so I stretched out a trembling hand and stroked his neck until the energy in his body subsided and his breathing was back to normal. He walked away and lowered his head to a pile of hay on the ground.

I took in a slow breath to calm my nerves then turned my horse and somewhat calmly walked back to the arena. Everyone had gathered in front of the chutes with Mom walking across the dirt to join them.

I stepped out of the saddle and walked toward my smirking father. The excitement and joy racing through me began to boil as I approached until I finally couldn't hold back the scream of elation and my feet jumped in the air then stomped on the ground. Laughter erupted around me.

"He didn't even move twenty feet from the chutes!" Caleb hollered.

I jumped into Dad's arms and we held tightly.

"He's going to do it, Dad," I cried out. "I believe in him!"

"River, he just made believers in all of us," Mom announced.

"I'm not putting a high school kid or amateur on him," Dad squeezed. "He's headed directly to the pros."

The whole group couldn't move fast enough to put all the equipment away and release the new broncs out into their pasture. Some of the horses, as in the newly named Fizzling Dud, would remain for another year while others would go to work sooner.

We all quickly made our way into the kitchen, where Mom served the stew and chili with fresh homemade bread to the dozen chattering excited cowboys.

Caleb and I set up the computer and monitor at the end of the kitchen table so we could watch all the videos while we were eating.

We started with Iggy.

Dad looked down at the paper in his hand. It was his list of horses that would be used at the first spring rodeo we were contracted to work. His eyes rose and looked over the large corral that held over 40 bucking horses ready to make their spring debut. For some, this would be their second or third year of bucking. For others, like Iggy, this would be their first.

Dad turned to look at me, "Put Iggy upfront and shut the door."

I nodded with excitement coursing through me.

Iggy was a stallion and dominant in his manners to other horses so he would ride alone.

Once he was settled into the large hauler, I remounted and waited for the next instructions.

Dad started pointing and yelling orders;

"Henry the First, Flying Betty, Skitter..." He continued until 25 horses were loaded. It was a one day rodeo with eight cowboys entered in bareback and twelve in saddle bronc. Twenty horses were needed for the rodeo, with the rest available for re-rides. Fizzling Dud was on the re-ride list but was mainly brought along for the experience.

Two saddle horses were in with the calves and steers who were already loaded into the second truck that Nolan would be driving. We sub-contracted the bulls, and they would be delivered to the rodeo grounds after we arrived.

Three hours later, I was walking the pens of the rodeo grounds and looking for anything unsafe for the animals. I checked gates, bolts, and any wire I could see. The rodeo committee had done a great job in preparations for the horses.

"All good!" I yelled to Dad and climbed up the unloading chute to open the door of the large truck.

I waited for Dad to position himself along the alley between the pens to direct the horses to their designated home for the day.

"Let 'em go!" He yelled.

After pulling open the door, I jumped down to the ground to watch the horses make their way down the ramp. I loved to hear the hoofbeats in the trailer. Each horse would hesitate briefly at the top to look at their new surroundings, then they quickly make their way down the ramp and the aisle where Dad was waiting.

Nolan was inside the trailer, encouraging the horses to leave the trailer. "Clear, except for Iggy!" He yelled.

"I'll close the gate!" I yelled back and climbed over the fence to close the gate to the aisle until Dad was ready. I pulled it closed and chained it just in case then climbed back up and out of the way. "Let him go!"

There was a full minute pause before I heard Nolan; "Damn horse, just go!"

I didn't even hear Iggy's hoofbeats. What was he doing?

"He won't fucking get out of the pen!" Nolan yelled.

"Iggy!" I yelled with a grin. "Come out here."

Hoofbeats slowly made their way through the trailer until his nose peered out the door.

"Come on, Iggy," I chuckled.

He took another step forward enough so I could see his whole head. Slowly, it moved around as he looked out at the rodeo grounds.

"Come on," Nolan grumbled but the horse just stood and looked around.

"Iggy, you have to come out," I laughed.

He swung his head around until he saw me sitting on top of the fence, then he tentatively made his way down the ramp and next to me. A rumbling whinny escaped from him making the rest of the horses call out. His ears perked and nose inched over the gate toward his buddies.

"Let him through!" Dad yelled.

I slid off the fence in front of him and patted his shoulder as I opened the gate. He pranced through and down to the pen next to the other horses.

While Dad and Nolan switched haulers and began unloading the steers and calves, I scrubbed the water tanks then filled them.

Then the work began: bags of feed were dumped into feed tubs, bales of hay were thrown into each pen, meetings with rodeo committees, pick-up men, and rodeo secretaries. Then there was hauling the box pads to the roping chutes and stringing the barrier ropes.

With Dad and me in the saddle and Nolan on the ground, we ran the steers and calves through the arena twice so they would know where the exit gate was during the rodeo.

Then the bulls arrived. They were unloaded and separated into pens based on when they were performing. Just prior to the rodeo, the steers and calves were moved to the pens by the roping chutes and separated. As I strung the flank straps behind the chutes so they were ready to go, the cowboys began to arrive.

I was so busy prior to the rodeo start that I didn't have time to worry about Iggy. But, as the rodeo ceremonies began I helped Dad load the bareback horses into the chutes.

Flying Betty was going to be the first horse out in her rodeo debut. Due to her flying bucks, we had decided to by-pass the smaller rodeos and go straight to the professionals for her. The pretty palomino was watching the crowd around her as the riggin was placed on her back. She had become accustom to the equipment placed on her body, but she would stomp and toss her head, then lower it nearly to the ground if you dared to try and touch her above the shoulders. Once you were able to get a halter on her, she tolerated being led by another horse.

Dad and Nolan assisted the cowboys while I readied the camera and took pictures.

My heart was pounding in anticipation when the anthem was completed and the cowgirl running around the arena carrying a sponsor flag made her exit.

The cowboy was already on Flying Betty and he nodded. Two running jumps out into the arena and the palomino began her flying jumps then bucks. She put on a crowd-pleasing performance as they cheered for the rider. The horn blared followed by one pick-up man unhooking the flank strap while the other assisted the cowboy to the ground.

A score of 83 was announced for the ride with 39 given to the horse. I turned quickly to see Dad's expression. He was assisting the next rider but glanced up as Flying Betty was escorted out of the arena. He turned and looked right at me with a pleased grin. She did well for her first outing and would get stronger as she aged and gained experience. So a score of 39 was great for the first ride. I was proud of her.

Seven more bareback riders bucked out into the arena with all decent rides; most of the horses scored between 35 and 40.

I stuffed the camera into my pocket and made my way to help push the steers in the chutes for steer wrestling. I climbed up onto the rails above the alley. Each steer was numbered and in their own little pen and I double-checked each steer to the cowboy that had drawn him. Dad and a rodeo committee member worked the chute itself.

As the last of the larger steers made their rodeo appearances, the smaller team roping steers were loaded and the process continued. When the second to last of the team roper's steers was loaded into the chute, I quickly made my way to the bucking chutes. Nolan had the first two saddle bronc horses loaded; Legacy Baia Mare and Legacy Sibiu. They were the older experienced horses we had purchased when we started the business.

I helped load more as Dad made it back to load the last of the first group. There were eight chutes but twelve rides so we would have four more to load once the event started; Iggy was in that last group.

Henry the First was the first bronc out and he carried his rider to an 88 score; 44 for each. He was a horse we used for bronc riding and bareback and scored well in both.

Skitter was the next horse ready to go. It was his first time out, too, so I silently said a prayer for him. The gate opened and my prayer was not answered as he took two hops, stopped, then hopped again and stopped. When the horn blew, the cowboy slid off the side of the horse and turned to the judge who signaled for a re-ride.

Damn, I hated that and from the deep frown on Dad's face he was disappointed but we had learned a long time before that not all horses were going to give us 40 plus rides or even have good days.

The next two horses fared well, carrying the riders to 79's with each horse receiving a 19 score from both judges for a 38.

I jumped down from my perch to help Nolan load the last four horses.

"Who is the reride?" I asked him.

He smirked and shook his head, "Fizzling Dud."

"Oh, damn," I sighed. His first out in a chute had earned him his name. Two more times through the chutes in training and he had done a little better with each.

"We were pretty confident on the twelve drawn," Nolan shrugged. "I guess Skitter can have an off day, too."

Iggy walked excitedly into the chute and stood quietly, watching the action in the arena. I stood on the platform behind him and took videos and pictures of the rides leading up to his. Every minute or so the horse would try to push his nose through the panel to get to my leg. A couple of times he managed to reach my jeans with his lips and tug. I just looked down and giggled.

"Do not touch him," Dad said as he walked behind me.

I hated that rule. Do not touch or interact with the bucking horses on the day they ride. They need to keep their work mindset.

"I won't," I grumbled and moved so I could video Iggy's ride.

I stepped in between two cowboys who had already ridden and were looking at me like I was next on their lists.

"Not gonna happen," I smiled and leaned around them to be ready.

They chuckled and shrugged then watched as the chute was opened.

My heart leapt into my throat as Iggy exploded from the chute. It was a tremendous leap with his hips twisting to the side making the crowd roar. He was at the peak of his second buck when the rope sprung from the cowboy's hand and he flew off the horse's back.

Iggy took off at a run and did a full lap around the arena before the pick-up-men could catch him.

Dad and I shared a big grin with a nod to each other until we heard the scores. The first judge gave Iggy a 23 while the other was a 19.

"Nineteen!" I gasped. "What the fuckin' hell?"

"That should have been more," The cowboy to my right huffed.

I just opened my mouth to speak but my arm was grabbed and jerked.

Yanking my arm away, I turned with the swear words forming on my mouth but they stopped at Dad's glare.

"We've talked about this," he growled. "you do not over-react on scores."

"Dad," I whispered harshly. "That is just ridiculous."

"Don't say a word or you won't be back here next time," he let go of my arm and walked to the next chute.

The re-ride of Fizzling Dud was next.

I stood frozen in anger, my breaths escaping through gritted teeth.

"I agree with you," One of the cowboys looked at me. "And that ain't nothin' but the truth."

It was all I could do to raise the camera to catch the next ride.

Fizzling Dud was standing in the chute with his head too low. Dad and the rider were trying to get him to lift it. When he finally did, the cowboy quickly leaned back in the saddle, shoved his hat down harder, then lifted the rope with a death-grip.

Chin tucked to chest, he nodded and the gate swung open.

Fizzling Dud took two running jumps out of the chute then his back hooves flew back high in the air as stretched as far back as they could possibly go. He came down with a thud and with nose pushing the dirt of the arena he did it again three more times before he ducked left and did it again. Muscle shaking, spine-tingling, massive kicks to the back the whole 8 seconds and beyond.

When the horn blared, I was staring in utter shock at the horse.

"Damn, what a ride!" The cowboy to my right yelled.

I just nodded in stunned silence as the pick-up men chased the horse. I slowly turned to Dad whose eyebrows were high as he watched Fizzling Dud being led out of the arena.

He turned to me with a grin, "I hope you caught all that on video. Your mom will not believe us."

"I hope I did, too!" I laughed and turned off the video and scrambled to the ground to get to the timed-event chutes for the tie-down event.

While matching calf numbers to cowboys, my mind would go from angry to shock. I was anxious to watch both videos again but there was so much left to do.

When the last calf was waiting his turn in the chute, I ran to help Nolan with the bulls.

I jumped up on the platform behind the chutes and weaved between the bull riders that were getting ready for their turn or watching the barrel racers. Most had their pre-ride routines and I tried not to interfere.

Dad appeared to take my place and I went in the back to help with the gates and stripping chute.

The moment the rodeo ended, I was horseback, moving the steers and calves from the chute pens and back to the stock pens for loading.

While Dad was in a meeting with the rodeo secretaries, Nolan and I began to clean pens. Once enough contestant trucks and trailers were moved out of the way, Nolan backed up the first hauler and we started loading the steers.

Dad appeared with the box pads and stored them in the trailer then walked back with a smile.

"Well?" He asked.

I pushed the door closed and turned, "Well, what?"

"Iggy and Fizzling Dud are the talk of the committee," he grinned.

"Well, they should be," I stepped back from the truck so Nolan could switch trucks. "Nineteen damn points." I glared at him.

"Well, Darlin', most people agree with you but it is done, over, and we move on."

I took a deep breath and tried to exhale out the frustration, "And Fizzling Dud?"

He laughed, "We had them all fooled with the name of the horse."

"I can't guarantee the video, I was so stunned," I smiled and pulled out my phone.

We watched Iggy's video, which much to my surprise captured all of it, including the very blatant stunned, swear words at the end.

"That was the cowboys around me," my face flushed as I looked at him.

"They sure do have a feminine voice," he chuckled. "Get them sent to your mother."

I sent the pictures and videos then jogged down the aisle to get Iggy.

Halfway home I was fighting to stay awake.

"I'm so proud of the horses," I whispered as my eyes closed.

"Been a very long day," Dad said.

It was the first long day of the summer of my dreams; hauling the first of our home-grown horses along with the more experienced stock. Someday, down the line, all the horses in our trailer would be full of Destiny's offspring...all Westmoreland bred horses.

It all led to that one email we were waiting for the first of November. It came as we were dropping mineral tubs in the pasture for the livestock. It was only 29 degrees and there was five inches of snow on the ground. The wind whipped it around making it feel even colder.

"Here it is," Dad said as he scrolled through his phone. We were huddled in the truck on top of the mountain and with the heater blowing full blast.

I stared at him in anticipation, "Not Iggy?" I whispered.

"We didn't haul the younger ones much this year. He didn't get to the nine required outs. Not him but..."

"Who?" I asked anxiously.

"Four of our legacy and of our home-grown we have? ...none."

"What?" I gasped and the tears rose. "But..."

He turned and smiled, "Just kidding. He was named appropriately."

"Henry the First?" I cried out.

"Yeah, we now have our first home-grown NFR qualifier."

His eyes were full of pride and it was all I could do not to cry, "You call Mom and I'll call Caleb."

CHAPTER FORTY FOUR

"Where's Logan?"

The third time I heard the question, I turned to look to see who everyone was asking the question to.

There was a cowboy on a buckskin horse leaned down to talk to a very irritated man. The cowboy's back was to me so I couldn't see who it was but he said something to the man then shook his head and leaned back.

I was jostled to the side and the man next to me looked down.

"Sorry," he nodded his head to a man who had edged himself into the line of people watching the contestants prepare for the National Finals Rodeo grand entry.

I smiled in understanding.

"Where the hell is Logan?" The rude intruder yelled.

The cowboy turned to look at him and I had the first glimpse of apologetic brown eyes under the tip of his black cowboy hat that covered dark hair. He had a narrow, clean-shaven jaw, high cheekbones, and a perfect sympathetic smile. He was…all cowboy, which said something since he was surrounded by cowboys.

I could not pull my gaze away from him. After a moment, my vision blurred so I took the first breath since he had turned. My head cleared, but my body was frozen in place. I just stared with lips parted in a silent gasp.

"I called," The cowboy said and lifted a cell phone in the air. "They got stuck in an interview and will be here in minutes."

"He's got two minutes. If he's not here, you can just unsaddle the horse." The man turned away.

The cowboy took a deep breath and looked over his shoulder the other direction.

His whole body relaxed when a man and woman I recognized as Logan and Delaney Rawlins jogged up to him.

"Son-of-a-bitch!" He cried out to the pair. "What the hell took so long? I've had everyone and their families over here trying to find Logan."

I stood in a daze as I watched the three talk.

"Who is that?" I whispered to myself.

The man at my side answered with a chuckle, "Rawlins family; Logan, Delaney, and a very relieved Brodie."

Brodie…Brodie Rawlins…

I stared at the trio until Logan rode into the herd of horses and Delaney and Brodie disappeared into the crowd.

My gaze dropped to the ground as the vision of Brodie turning played in my mind…his eyes…that smile…I took a deep breath.

"Dammit, River," Dad's voice was next to me and I looked up at in surprise.

"What?"

"You going to stand back here all night?"

I shook my head and turned to make my way to my seat just a few rows above the announcer's platform as the mass of competitors were running out of the arena.

"What took you so long?" Mom huffed.

"Just excited and watching everyone behind the bleachers," I answered.

"Watching the cowboys," Caleb teased.

"Yes, because I don't see enough of those at home," I rolled my eyes.

Our attention turned to the bareback riders at the chutes. Henry the First was making his debut with Trenten Montero as his rider.

We silently watched the first three riders. In between each one, I looked around the arena for Brodie and his sister. I didn't see them anywhere, but then again, there were over 18,000 people in the arena; pretty much the same as looking for a needle in the haystack. I forced myself to forget about him and concentrate on the chutes.

"Your father is right where he is meant to be," Mom whispered.

He was standing on the platform behind the bucking chutes with Trenten as they waited for Henry's turn.

"He has been back there before," Caleb pointed out.

"Not with one of his own," I grinned.

"He'd never admit it, but he's a bit excitedly nervous," Mom smiled.

"I cannot wait for Iggy to be back there," I sighed.

"If he makes it," Caleb teased.

"You think he won't?" I asked in surprise.

"He's unridden after seven rides this year," Caleb grinned. "I'd be surprised if he isn't here next year."

"I agree," Mom nodded. "Knock on wood that he stays healthy."

"Oh, MOM," I groaned. "Don't jinx him. The eye puncture was bad enough."

They both chuckled as Dad and Trenten prepared the horse for the ride.

"Damn, I hope he scores well," Mom whispered.

"He's got a great rider for his first time out," I added.

"It's the top fifteen in the world…they are all great," Caleb chuckled. "We really can't get a bad draw here."

The gatemen and chute boss made their way to Henry's gate.

I took a deep breath in anticipation and leaned forward to rest my elbows on my knees. My hands came together under my chin and I prayed silently.

"Did you hear that?" Caleb asked.

"What?" Mom whispered.

"The announcer just said, 'Henry the First, born to and raised by the Westmoreland Rodeo Stock Contractors," Caleb answered.

"Dad's first," Goosebumps rose on my arm.

"Next year we'll have at least three more," Caleb added confidently. "There's a couple more that can do it, too."

"Iggy," I nodded.

"Flying Betty, Fizzling Dud, and Henry the First next year," Mom added.

"Depends on what he does right here," I said.

Trenten was just leaning back with hand wedged in the riggin, his arm high in the air, and chin tucked to his chest. He nodded and the gate swung open. As Henry bound out of the chute, Dad pulled the flank strap tight then stood as a statue as the horse's hind legs flew back in the air, stretching back as far as they could go. Trenten matched the horse spur for buck as Henry moved in a large circle in front of the chute. High powerful kicks from the horse and fast fluid spurring motion from the rider until the horn sounded and Trenten flew off the back of the horse and landed with both feet on the ground.

"Yes!" I screamed and looked over at Dad. He was standing proudly with a wide grin.

Mom, Caleb, and the cheering crowd grew louder when the second place 89 point score was announced; 44 for Henry!

We spent our days in Vegas hiking the trails around Hoover Dam and our evenings at the rodeos. The legacy horses kept all their riders in the money, while Henry took his second rider to another check. When we left Vegas, it was with full hearts and very high hopes for the next year.

After returning from the NFR, we spent a month recuperating, taking the horses to an annual Bares and Broncs competition in Cheyenne, and celebrating the holidays.

Our first rodeo was mid-January in Montana then for the next three months we were traveling to Denver, Houston, San Antonio, Arizona, Florida, and more. We received double the requests for sub-contracting out the horses then we had the year before.

"It's your decision, River," Dad leaned back in his office chair and looked between Mom and me. "We have to hire more people either way, so do you want to continue to be the boss with the foaling and breeding while I'm on the road or do you want to go on the road?"

I hated making decisions. It was much easier when I was a little kid and they just told me what to do. But, I wasn't a kid anymore and I wasn't just an employee but a partner of this business, so I needed to make the decision that was best for the company.

"It's more logical for me to be in charge of foaling and breeding while you're on the road," I said confidently.

They both nodded proudly.

"We'll get you out when we can...June, for sure, after the foaling is done and for the Christmas run through the end of the season."

"And live feeds from rodeos are getting more popular so you can watch the horses on those," Mom added.

"It's just for three months," I said with confidence.

It was still dark when I saddled my new buckskin gelding and began my morning ride to check on the horses. Nolan was in charge of the cattle and watched over that herd with his sons joining him when needed.

It was still early spring so the horses were pastured close enough I could ride to check on them instead of taking the truck. The gelding was a pleasure to ride and well-practiced at this pasture loop we made each morning. There were twenty-three broodmares to foal this spring with two already having given birth.

I rode over the rise of the wide ravine just as the sun made its appearance for the day. The blue sky was full of wispy white clouds touched with the rays from the pink sunrise. My winter beanie and scarf wrapped around my face helped guard my skin from the crispy morning breeze.

Stopping on the rise, I looked over the band of mares in front of me. Scanning each one, I found the two foals next to their mothers and another new foal on shaking legs as it nursed his mother.

"Baby buckers," I whispered with a wide smile. "I love them."

I continued scanning and found Destiny to my left halfway down the hill and lying flat on her side. Her body tightened with a contraction. Moving quickly, I stepped down from the gelding, tied him to the nearest tree, pulled my camera from the saddlebag, then stealthily made my way closer to the mare.

Lowering myself onto a rock, I silently watched the sunrise light the upcoming birth of Destiny's new foal. Pictures were taken of the three already born, then of the birth. After five minutes of silence, Henry the First's dam lowered to the ground. Her body was covered in sweat with sides clenching with each contraction.

Text to Dad: You somewhere I can video chat?

The video alert rang on my phone and I looked to the two mares in labor then answered. He was sipping a cup of coffee when I answered.

"What's up? Looks cold," he grinned.

"It is," I whispered. "Destiny and Brownie are in labor, hooves out on both. Want to watch Chinook's new offspring be born?"

"Stupid question, of course."

I chuckled and turned the phone so he could see Destiny then over to Brownie.

"We have another born overnight too," I whispered. "I haven't ridden over to check on him yet but he was nursing."

"Quit talking; you're ruining the moment," his voice whispered.

I had to bury my face in my gloved hand to keep from laughing out loud.

For a half-hour, we silently watched Destiny give birth to a black foal with white up both back legs. Brownie's foal, Henry the First's little brother, was dark brown with a crooked blaze down his nose.

The sound of hoof to rock made me turn to see the new foal and his mother walking toward the two mares. I turned the camera so Dad could see.

"Ah, 381 had hers," he whispered. "Big foal."

I moved the phone back to the two newborns that were trying to stand then set it on a rock, "Can you still see them?"

"Yeah."

I lifted the camera and documented our three newest additions to the Westmoreland Stock Contractors.

"Just a couple more days, Big Guy," I said to Chinook as I poured his grain and supplements into his feeder. "I personally hand-picked your harem this year; fifteen of the nicest ladies," I chuckled as the horse's large jaw worked its way through the feed. "Of course, your Queen Destiny is in the pasture waiting for you."

He was a big horse, 17 hands tall, with muscular arched neck highlighted with a thick wavy black mane that had flown dramatically around him when he would buck. The wide white blaze peeked its way through the black forelock that hung down his nose. His dark brown body was muscular and, to most people, very intimidating. But I knew he would never intentionally hurt someone, but you still had to respect his size and get the hell out of his way.

I leaned against the fence rail and watched Chinook eat. When the grain was done he lowered to the pile of hay. I reached out and pulled his forelock out of his eyes and created one thick strand down his nose. He was pretending to ignore me, but his big brown eyes occasionally flickered to me. After a few more bites of hay, he shook his head so the forelock spread across his eyes again.

I chuckled, "You don't like your hair done? Well, then…" I stood and turned dramatically. His head rose to look at me but his jaw continued to chew the hay. I flipped my hand in the air toward the large galvanized tank. "Your water is full, Your Highness, so you just continue to eat and build stamina for your months in the fields with your ladies." I giggled as his head bounced in the air as if he understood me then dipped back down for another bite.

My earliest memories were me pretending the horse was the queen's horse of my animal kingdom. I had always called him Your Highness because he was my imaginary magic steed. Many dark knights had fallen as I rode the fence next to the horse. He wandered the pasture peacefully but in my imagination, I was riding him to glory.

Chinook was born six months before me. Dad had worked for the Stiler Stock Company for 24 years; since he was twelve. He helped with every menial task the owner, Waylon, gave him until he was allowed to help with the bucking horses and bulls. Being the first one to touch Chinook, when the stock contracting company decided to close down eight years ago, Dad bought him with no real plans on what to do with him. He just couldn't bear the thought of the horse going to someone else.

I was only sixteen at the time, but I approached my parents with a plan. When my great-aunt had passed away, she left Caleb and me more than enough money to go to college. Since he was little, Caleb had assisted with any veterinarian that would let a kid help, so his future was set. I did not, in any way, want to go to college, so I offered my inheritance to my parents to start the Westmoreland Stock Contracting business. It took them three months to finally concede to my plan and they sold what they could and pooled all their savings together to match the amount of my inheritance. So, technically, I was half owner of the company. Of course, only my family knew that since I had made the decision to have Dad be the front of the business until my emotions were more...mature.

This big stout bay had begun this adventure for us, and his son, Iggy, would carry it on in the future. Our other stud, Windsor, wasn't as large as Chinook, but he had been a powerhouse in the rodeo. He was our first purchase after starting the business so we had a stallion to breed to Chinook's daughters. His black and white painted body and full-thick mane were reminiscent of his Night Jacket lineage. The sprinkling of color in our herd was mostly due to him.

As I walked out of the barn, I called over my shoulder, "I'm going to ride out and check on your harem to make sure they are ready for you."

We had the talk three more mornings before I finally backed the stock trailer to the gate.

Chinook knew what that meant and pranced excitedly around the perimeter of the corral. His mane flew in the air, tail flowing behind him as he pranced. This was one of those moments you respected the size and wish of the horse. I waited until he was on the opposite side of the corral and swung open the trailer door. The horse didn't hesitate running into the trailer. He was ready for his harem.

Nolan was assisting me for the day as the horses were moved from one pasture to another. Even though the man was old enough to be my father, I was his boss. Luckily, he respected the years that I had been around the business and breeding program, because it had been my whole life.

"I'd be running too if I knew a harem of women were waiting for me," Nolan chuckled and shut the door.

I laughed, "You couldn't handle fifteen women at the same time."

"Truer words have never been spoken," he grinned.

When we arrived at the pasture, fifteen mares lifted their heads to the arriving boyfriend. Thirteen foals were nervously skittering to their mothers.

I placed two video cameras along the route I guessed Chinook would take once released from the trailer. I also had a more expensive digital camera with a long lens I had purchased and positioned myself to capture his run. It was always so exciting and heart-pumping to watch the magnificent horse run.

"You ready?" Nolan asked as his hand rested on the trailer gate handle.

"Videos are running and camera is set," I nodded. "Release the beast!"

Nolan opened the door and stepped behind it so he wasn't in the way of the jump from the trailer.

Chinook pranced out twenty feet and let loose a neigh that vibrated over the rolling hills and down into the river canyon. His mares came running. In a scene for the movies, he reared back on his hind legs and shook his head with front hooves pawing in the air.

"Som' bitch!" Nolan called out. "I hope you got that."

I was too busy clicking the camera to respond. I just prayed it was all in focus.

With a high buck of the heels in the air, the horse took off at a run into the fields with his ladies trailing excitedly behind him. He ran, stopped, posed with head high and tail swishing then ran again. I kept taking pictures until he stopped and looked back at the mares. A few of them were letting him know they were ready to be bred. He got to work and I lowered the camera.

"No need for those pictures," I giggled to Nolan as I lowered the camera and looked back at the images of his magnificent entry into the field. "Perfect, Nolan!" I squealed excitedly and showed him the images.

"He is a beast."

"Let's not tell Dad about that rear-up," I said and retrieved the video cameras I had set up. "I'll send him pictures of him posing and bucking, but his birthday is coming up and I'll have a large print framed for him."

"Ah, he'd love that, River," Nolan agreed.

"You drive so I can look at the videos."

Two weeks later, and the day after his actual birthday, Dad arrived home to the new large portrait in his office. He was speechless and could do nothing more than hug both me and Mom then stare at it for days until he had to leave again.

While he was home, Iggy met his harem.

Text from Caleb: I know you don't listen to podcasts but check out Coffee with Cowboys, the girl is hilarious and refreshing

A week later, I was driving the truck on top of the hill, looking for the younger herd of horses. The rain was pelting the windshield causing the wipers to work overtime and the wind gust pushing hard enough on the truck I had a tight grip on the steering wheel.

I couldn't see a damn horse anywhere and it was pretty useless in the wind. If I were them, I'd be tucked into the trees by the river and shielded by the canyon wall.

After tiring of listening to the windshield wipers beat against the edge of the truck, I finally plugged in my phone and clicked on the link Caleb had sent me for the podcast.

Lacie Jae's voice was young, fresh, and joy-filled. She made me smile.

Welcome to Coffee with Cowboys with me, Lacie Jae.

Welcome to my first Podcast! I'm Lacie Jae, a relocated city girl who will be adventuring into the ranching and rodeo world … the cowboy way of life. Until a few weeks ago, I had never been around a horse or a cow, and now, that's changed.

I'll be sharing with you my adventures and discoveries as I travel with the Rawlins family. They are a three-generation rodeo and ranch family and also National Finals Rodeo qualifiers and champions. They have lived the cowboy way of life all their lives and are now generously letting me tag along and share their adventures.

To start, I want to explain the title of the podcast. I have been a coffee barista for the last five years and the last three as a manager over three coffee houses. So, obviously, I love coffee.

And so do cowboys!

The other morning, at the Rawlins Bar-R ranch, it was bright, beautiful blue skies and white frosted ground as they moved a small herd of cows into their corrals. I delivered coffee to them as they sat on their horses, stood in the dirt, or leaned against a gate. To clarify, when I talk about the Rawlins, it includes Craig, who is best friends and rodeo traveling partner to Brodie Rawlins and Craig's dad, Martin. They are family, too.

Brodie? The vision of him turning on his horse at the NFR played in my mind and my heart raced. His smile, eyes and laugh when he saw his family; I found myself leaning toward the phone as she spoke.

Even when the rain stopped and the pastures became quiet again, I sat in the truck at the rise of the hill and listened. Her fourth podcast was an actual interview with Brodie and his best friend, Craig. I listened to it three times before I forced myself to listen to the rest of them.

The younger herd appeared and I slowly made my way to the next pasture as I listened again to their night in the San Antonio bar. The third time I listened to it, I was looking out at a very drenched Chinook and his lovely band of mares and foals.

"We're headed west," was the first thing Dad said when he answered the video call.

I was standing in the barn with Destiny's newest foal. The six-week-old black filly was standing at my side with her nose inching toward the screen of the laptop.

"I see more of her nose than I do of you...I need to take a picture of that," Dad laughed and pulled out his phone. "You're taking Destiny back out to the pasture?"

"Yes, she was just in for a preg test and she's about four weeks."

"I'm sure they are all bred by now."

"How far west? Utah? Nevada?"

"Washington and Oregon, and maybe Idaho," he answered and took the picture. "Got a call for Henry, Iggy, Betty, and Fizzling Dud to go to Pendleton."

My heart warmed with pride, "Our Fearsome Foursome! That's awesome, Dad! We're going or are you sending Nolan?"

"We're going. You'll love Pendleton; it has that old history feel that you like in Cheyenne and Sheridan."

"I'm so proud of all four but Iggy still being unridden is unbelievable. As long as he doesn't get any more of those damn 19's then maybe he'll get to the NFR this year."

"You're getting ahead of yourself."

"I know," I huffed then laughed when the filly placed her nose on the screen.

Dad's laugh vibrated into the room, "You're making her too tame."

"Nothing different than I did with Iggy," I pushed her away.

"You have a name for her yet?"

"You know I do."

"Well...Destiny's what?"

"She's going to lure the cowboys to their doom," I giggled. "Destiny's Siren."

"I like that, maybe throw a wicked or enchanting in there."

"I like that. Perfect for His Highness' daughter, Destiny's Enchanted Siren," I grinned. "When do we head west?"

"Itchin' to get out?"

"I love all the babies but I'm ready for the road again."

"Well, that's not until mid-August to mid-September."

"We'll be there a whole month?"

"We're contracted at Kennewick and Pendleton and possibly Lewiston."

"Aren't they part of the Big Four?"

"I should have known you would know that."

I closed the laptop and gave little Enchanted Siren a scratch on the nose before saddling the buckskin gelding to ride the range. After loading him into a trailer, I waved goodbye to Mom as she left for her job. With a contented heart, I left the ranch behind.

"*All by myself, again,*" I sang with a smile. I needed to get a dog. Somehow, Dad had ended up with two loyal dogs that traveled with him all the time and I didn't have one.

I parked the truck at the crossroads of the four pastures which made it easy to go into all four to check the horses and fences in one ride.

It was a beautiful early May morning as I trotted across the green pasture. Blue skies, puffy white clouds, a slight breeze, and predicted temperatures of 70 degrees, just perfect for riding the range.

In the west pasture, I rode around the younger two and three-year-olds. They pranced, and whinnied, and curiously approached then would run away.

"Probably looking to see if I have grain for them," I said to the gelding. Hearing my own voice seemed out of place in the vast land.

I turned back and rode into the South pasture. The black and white, Windsor, was out with his band of twenty mares. They were all Chinook's daughters and they were all enjoying the spring day.

In the West pasture, Chinook and his harem were on the distant hill so I slow loped across to them. I truly was in heaven out riding the range under the sun and on a well-seasoned dependable horse. He was a pleasure to ride which made the whole morning that much more enjoyable.

The herd of horses was scattered across the green hillside. A few stood in the shadow of the trees that rest at the lowest point of the ravine. Three foals were chasing each other up and down the hill; such a peaceful scene.

I slowed the gelding to a trot as the horses became alert to our approach. A few ran back and forth then down to the trees and back up. The older mares just went back to grazing. Chinook was to the left of the herd, lying in the warm sun. His dark hide glistened.

I brought the gelding to a walk and slowly approached so I didn't startle him.

He was lying on his side with legs curled under him and his nose stretched out and resting on the ground. Twenty feet away, his head rose to look at me then dropped like a rock back to the ground and his legs uncurled and stretched out.

The air rushed out of me and I pulled my phone out of my pocket as I jumped down from the gelding.

CHAPTER FORTY FIVE

"River?"

"Nellie, Chinook is down."

"Bad?"

"I don't know."

"Where are you?"

"West pasture of the crossroads back at the ravine."

"It will take me thirty minutes to get there."

"Hurry," I gasped as my lungs filled with air. It was released in desperate shakes.

My feet stumbled over the rocks in my haste. I nearly fell twice before I was finally next to him.

There were no marks, scratches, bites, or any indication he had been kicked. There was no swelling in his legs or odd bend in a bone and there was no indication on the ground that he had been thrashing in pain.

His head lay flat against the ground, jaw slightly open with breaths fighting to get out. He took in a deep breath and it gushed out…seconds went by before he took another breath. His head rose again and turned to me only to have it drop again.

I knelt behind him, just at his neck so I could move the forelock out of his eyes. Life's hand was grasping my heart and squeezing. Every breath shook in desperation.

"Hold on," I whispered and ran a hand over his cheek. His eyes moved to me…there was no fear or anxiety reflected that I was so near to him and touching him. There was just a gentleness I had seen thousands of times. "She'll be here soon."

He lifted his head just inches then lowered it with a groan. I sat cross-legged behind his neck and slowly ran a soothing hand over his cheek, to his neck and down to his shoulder.

"You just stay down and calm, Your Highness," I whispered. "She's coming."

It was mentally frustrating that there wasn't a wound or injury visible where I could help him.

He took in a deep breath and it slowly released with a moan.

"Oh, Chinook, please hold on," I cried.

I swept his mane back and softly slid my hand down the warmth of his neck. Another breath was taken then slowly release. Memories of the horse from my childhood of watching him in the pastures or in the rodeo arena brought more tears as he took in another breath that was released with another moan. Hundreds of nights I had sat in the pasture watching him graze and nights of cheering for him at a rodeo.

Another intake of air…tears fell on him as his last breath was slowly released.

"No…" I cried into the silence of the morning. "No…don't go…please, Chinook, come back." With both hands, I gripped his mane as if to pull him back to life. With trembling chin to chest, the tears fell and the sobs racked my body.

Arms encircled me and pulled me in close. No words were spoken.

In the distance, I heard the ATV approaching. Then the quiet descended. I could hear gasps accompanied by sobs.

Mom's arms replaced Nellie's as I leaned into her. The tears had stopped, my body numb, and life's grip still held my heart tightly…it ached…it hurt.

It was two days before Dad and I could speak to each other. It wasn't really speaking, it was just looking at each other on the laptop video. Each time we'd open our mouths to speak, the words just wouldn't come out.

"We did as you wanted," Mom was sitting at my side with her arms wrapped around me. "He's buried on the rise just east of the house so the sun will rise over him. Have you thought of a headstone or marker?"

Dad shook his head with a deep breath.

"Well," Mom continued. "I thought we would take the image of him rearing that is in your office and have a wrought iron sculpture of him created and place that on the rise. It would be beautiful with the sunrise behind it."

His hand quickly rose to rub the crease of his brow. Mom and I both knew he was hiding the tears. Her arms tightened around me.

"We'll go with that, then," Mom whispered. "We'll see you in two days?"

He nodded without moving his hand.

"I love you, Adam," she whispered with a tight emotional break.

He nodded again with his hand reaching out to his laptop...the screen went black.

"So this is Kennewick," I looked out at the expanse of flat open space around the tall rodeo arena. There was a fair with carnival rides on the opposite side. "I like the walkway that surrounds the top."

"Nice view from up there," Dad nodded as we drove down the dirt road. "It's a nice arena, with a good staging area and platform behind the bucking chutes, too."

"I saw the circular turnstile for the horses on the internet."

"Unique."

"The pie shape pens are very unique. Iggy is going into one by himself...right?" I glanced at him as he turned the truck in preparation to backing to the stock pens gate.

"Yes, they confirmed it three times and our other three will be placed next to him on one side then the other will just be the aisle leading into the bucking chutes," he looked at me with determination. "I assured them you will only clean the pens and watch over our four horses…you won't interfere, at all, with anything else, including the performance."

"I know the drill," I smirked. "And I'll do my best not to make you a liar."

"There is no trying, River, you're just not going to interfere."

"No, I'm not," I huffed. "In fact, I'm going to sit here and let someone else help guide you back."

"No, attitude."

"What attitude?" I gasped in feigned shock. "I'm just not interfering."

He opened the door of the truck and stepped down while I leaned back and watched the people around the pens.

Kennewick was a four-day rodeo; the contestants were split between slack and three nights of rodeo performances with the top 10 overall moving to Saturday's short-go.

I pulled up the stock draw again on my phone and looked at the cowboys that our horses had drawn. Most of them were good riders that could really let the horses showcase their talent. I did like having Iggy unridden so far in his ten outings this year. The last two rodeos, the cowboys were off in the first three seconds which didn't really give the horse his time to shine. Although in those three seconds and those few that followed, he did look explosive and powerful and scored fairly well.

Dad slid into the truck and prepared to back up to the pens.

"You know anything about this Granger Miller that Iggy drew for Thursday night?" I asked him.

"Decent rider, just learning really," he answered.

I looked at Granger's riding stats on the rodeo website. He had only been pro for three months and had scored in the 70's on the ones he had made it to the 8 seconds. That didn't bode well for Iggy.

The truck engine was turned off and as Dad opened his door he glanced over his shoulder at me.

"This is me not interfering." I didn't even move.

"That is you having an attitude," he slid out of the truck and slammed the door.

I pulled the performance draw back up on the phone and looked at who was drawn on which night.

More specifically, I was looking at Brodie Rawlins. I knew Brodie was riding bareback on Thursday night, saddle bronc on Friday, then again Saturday if he qualified in either event. He didn't draw our horses, but he did have two really strong buckers for his first two rides. The championship round wouldn't be drawn until after the Friday night performance was completed.

Closing my eyes, I blocked out the world and thought of the moment I read about his best friend's death. I couldn't even imagine what that would be like. The closest friend I had was Caleb and the thought of him dying so suddenly, so unexpectedly, brought tears again. I cried every time I read about the accident and thought of what Brodie and his family were going through. I checked every day for a new podcast from *Coffee with Cowboys* but there wasn't even one. I had listened to the podcast with Brodie and Craig's interview at least a dozen more times.

There was an odd sense of fate when I heard that he was also going to be riding bareback in the Big Four rodeos as a tribute to Craig. Brodie didn't know me, probably didn't even know I existed, but it just felt right in my heart that I would be at three of the four rodeos to watch his memorial in person.

The wrought-iron sculpture of a rearing Chinook was placed on the eastern rise by the house. Mom was right; seeing the sunrise behind him in the mornings felt like we were giving him a tribute every day. I had gone from not wanting to look at it, to now wanting to put a bench under it so I could visit him and be near him. Mom said Dad wasn't ready for that yet, maybe someday. Dad and I still hadn't talked about Chinook's death other than him stating he was glad I was there the last moments of his life so that the majestic stallion didn't die on the hillside alone.

When the truck door opened, I squeezed my eyes closed real tight and took a deep breath to try and get control over my emotions. I had felt a bit out of control since Chinook's death; way too passionate about little things pertaining to the horses and ready to explode at any moment. Unfortunately, I had a few times.

"They kept asking where you were," Dad said as he slid back into the truck.

"Who?"

"The stock contractors and committee, they figured you would be there with the four horses."

"What did you tell them?"

"You were in the truck having an attitude and not interfering at all."

"You did not!" I huffed and sat straight up in the seat.

He chuckled, "Told them you were having a female moment."

"Dad!" I rolled my eyes.

He laughed as he pulled away from the pens. "I told them you were on the phone but you would be there to check on the horses as soon as you could."

"That just makes it sound like I don't trust them to look after the horses," I sighed.

"You can't have it both ways."

"So I take it they heard I yelled at the kid at the rodeo in Montana that let the water troughs go dry."

"Hon, it was on video and played on Facebook," he grinned.

"Well, I was right," I said petulantly.

"Yes, you were, and everyone that has horses would agree with you...just not with you calling him an ignorant jackass in front of dozens of people."

"And if they were honest, they would have called him worse in front of dozens of people."

He huffed and reached for the door handle but hesitated and looked back at me.

"You own this company as much as I do. Someday, it will be completely yours, which means you need to make sure you're the type of person people want to do business with. If not, there are a lot of stock contractors and they'll go

somewhere else." It was said in a matter-of-fact
tone...business...not family.

A mixture of emotions ran through me as he talked.

"I try to keep that in mind, Dad, honestly I do," I said.
"I just get so passionate about our horses and what is right and
wrong."

He smiled with a hint of pride shining in his eyes. "I just
keep reminding myself that even though I treat you as if you're
44, you are still 24."

I sighed in irritation, "Other people would have done
the same thing."

"I'm talking about everything, including you being one
of the faces...representatives of this company."

"What do you want me to do?" The frustration was
evident in my voice.

"Just think before you act."

"All I can say is, I'll do my best and if that doesn't work
out then I'll just go home and ride the open range where there
are no stupid people to irritate me."

He grinned and opened the truck door. "I love ya,
River."

Since the horses were taken care of, we setup our camp
for the next four days. The back of the trailer was an open
stock trailer with one section upfront so we could stall Iggy
away from the other horses. A short camper section protruded
to the front and over the back of the truck. Since the weather
promised blue sky and sunshine for the whole rodeo, we set out
coolers, chairs, and a camp table just outside the trailer door.

When we finally walked over to the horse pens, Henry
the First, Fizzling Dud, and Flying Betty were standing quietly
eating their hay. Iggy was pacing the pen. He liked pens he
could trot around but this pen wasn't big enough for that, so he
paced.

There were also three full water tanks in both pens.

I looked at the water for a moment then glanced around
for the people that were responsible for the over-the-top
arrangements. They were standing behind a truck watching
closely.

I glanced at Dad, "You know...I would have done the same damn thing."

We both grinned, and the men starting laughing, so we introduced ourselves to Wayne and Roy from the rodeo committee. We spent the evening barbecuing with them.

Our four horses were not drawn for Wednesday night so we stood on the top deck and watched the rodeo. There were small short-walled cubicle-like areas blocked off next to the arena for the different groups of spectators, and in the open area, multiple tables were scattered throughout. There were a few bars along the top walkway.

At moments, we walked to the back of the deck that overlooked the stock pens and watched the men move the horses and bulls in and out of the turn-style pens. It was fast, efficient, and the rodeo was entertaining and ran smoothly.

After cleaning the horse pens in the morning, we stayed in the trailer and watched movies until we were both bored. We went for a walk through the fair until it was time to get ready for the rodeo. I loved these days spending time with Dad.

Flying Betty, Henry the First, and Iggy were drawn for Thursday night. Zach Hibler and Mason Clements were riding Betty and Henry in the bareback section while Granger Miller had Iggy in saddle bronc. Fizzling Dud was drawn for Friday night.

It was 102 degrees outside when I stepped into my denim jeans, slid on my cowboy boots, and finally, our company long-sleeve western shirt. It was bright blue with our brand, WML, over the pocket and on the cuffs. Westmoreland was written down both arms. I swept my hair back and placed my cowboy hat on to keep it in place. The printed pass hanging from a lanyard was dangling from my neck and continually bounced against me so I tucked it into my shirt pocket until the rodeo started.

I had no idea where Dad had disappeared to but he would be helping with our horses in the chutes, so I knew I would run into him.

When I stepped out of the trailer, I felt the sweat instantly form against my skin. I couldn't wait for the sun to go down. Hundreds of truck and trailer outfits had pulled into the rodeo grounds in the last 24 hours and I knew one would be for the Rawlins family. I was a bit anxious to see Brodie in person again. We had been hundreds, if not a thousand-mile apart, but now we here...together. I walked a wide path through the new arrivals and very nonchalantly looked for him and his family.

I felt like a stalker, but I couldn't get myself to quit since the image of him turning on his horse and looking up toward me at the NFR kept playing in my mind. Maybe I wanted to confirm to myself that he was as handsome as I remembered. Or, perhaps, that he wasn't, so I could quit thinking of him.

In the distance, at least ten trailers away, I saw Logan Rawlins riding a bay horse and ponying a blue roan toward the warmup arena. I hesitated...should I follow him? No...they were there and we had three days for me to see Brodie. I'm not exactly sure what I was expecting but I was beginning to feel a bit obsessed. The anxiety started to increase as I walked away from the contestant's area and to our horses.

To the right of Iggy's pen was the path that led to the back of the bucking chutes and the rider's staging area. A wide metal stairway that led to the top deck split the path from the chutes and blocked the public from the riders.

The announcer was letting the crowd know the rodeo was starting within minutes so people filled the stairs as they made their way up to the second deck of the rodeo stands. Rodeo royalty were lined up between the arena gate and walkway in preparation for their runs.

Betty and Henry were already missing from their pens and Iggy was pacing in his until he saw me, then he approached the panel. With a sigh, I backed away.

"Go ahead and tell him hello," Dad walked up beside me.

"He bucks tonight," I grumbled.

"No, Granger turned out. He'll be at the end of the rerides."

I gasped in disappointment, "Are you kidding?"

"I wouldn't tell you to pet your horse if I was."

"Well, damn," I growled. "I guess if he's young and just learning it's best he doesn't get hurt on a horse like Iggy but it is so damn disappointing."

Dad nodded, "I'm going to help at the chutes."

Iggy's head was tilted to the side and stretched out as he stuck his nose through the panels to reach me.

I scratched the soft muzzle, "Damn frustrating to come all this way and you not get your turn for a ride." He pulled his nose back into the pen so I stretched my arm in to scratch his jaw. His head tilted into my hand. "Maybe Saturday…"

A hand gripped my forearm and yanked it out of the pen, making it bounce hard against the panels. Pain shot up my arm and made my fingers tingle.

CHAPTER FORTY SIX

"What the…?" Anger fired through me as I glanced over my shoulder and tried to pull my arm out of the grip. The fingers squeezed into the muscle and skin.

"That's a fucking stallion," A tall older man growled at me. He wore a red shirt that indicated he was part of the rodeo committee, but that fact did not stop my reaction.

As hard as I could, I stomped on the top of his foot with the heel of my boot, which made him cry out and step back…pulling me with him.

"You bitch," he howled.

"You bastard," I spat back. "Let go of me." I tried to yank my arm away from him, but he squeezed tight enough I could feel his fingernails dig in.

I raised my foot again, but he pushed against me and let go of my arm, so I bounced against the panels and began to stumble before I caught myself.

Fury was trembling out of me, "Who the fuck do you think you…?"

"Someone smart enough to know you don't reach into a stallion's pen to pet the pretty little pony," He fumed.

"But you're not fucking smart enough to know that I OWN that pretty little pony," My hands were on my hips and I was ready to battle.

"Whoa, whoa, whoa, whoa," Roy stepped between us and faced the man. "She's right; she owns the horse."

The older man's face contorted between anger and resignation, "We'll be putting up signs so no one can get to these panels."

"It won't stop me from petting MY pretty little pony," I growled petulantly.

"River, enough," Roy sighed. "It was just a misunderstanding."

The older man huffed and walked away.

I glared at him as I rubbed my sore arm, "You're telling me that, instead of to the man that tried to break my arm?"

He took a deep breath and looked at the older man's back, "Well, to be fair, his foot is going to be pretty sore when he takes off his boot."

I took a deep breath to cool down.

"You good now?"

I nodded to him and he smiled slightly and turned away.

I turned back to the pen and with both hands gripping the panel, I leaned against it and watched Iggy chew his hay. My heart was still pounding in anger.

I had enough time for five good deep breaths before a male voice spoke behind me.

"That's the stallion, Iggy," the man said.

"Yea, he's pretty awesome...heard Granger pulled out so he didn't have to ride him," A second man said.

Then a third male voice spoke, "Sad story about his sire."

My spine stiffened and lungs felt like they were going to burst.

The third voice continued, "He was fucking old, man. They shouldn't have had him out breeding in the first place."

A burst of white light flashed behind my eyes. The anger that had begun to diminish flared up like fire on the open range. I swirled around to the voice and with both fists hit him in the chest like a battering ram.

His eyes opened in shock as he stumbled back and nearly went to the ground with a hand to his chest.

"Oh, damn, River," the first cowboy gasped.

"What the fuck lady?" The second cowboy stepped between his friend and me.

"She owns Iggy," the first cowboy said and I turned to see Kirk St. Clair, a bareback rider.

My whole body was shaking in anger; my breaths felt like fire. My neck was so rigid that my spine was beginning to ache.

"It was a jackass thing to say," Kirk said in a soothing voice.

I had to get away before I attacked all three cowboys or ended up on video screaming at them.

Darting to my right, I sprinted between the stock contractor trailers and the horse's pens. I felt like my mind was losing control.

Just past the third trailer, I bumped into another cowboy.

"Get out of my way," My voice was low and coarse.

"You're the one in the way," The cowboy huffed and his hands came up to both my upper arms to physically turn me to the side and out of the way then strode away as if nothing happened.

"Damn it!" I growled at another person man-handling me.

I stepped forward to confront him but a blonde and brunette stepped between us.

"Back off, bitch," The blonde said. "Leave him alone."

"Are you kidding me?" I huffed and looked into fiery eyes. "LEAVE HIM ALONE? I didn't fucking man-handle him! Tell him to leave me alone." My body started shaking again.

The brunette stepped between us but spoke to the blonde who looked like she was ready to attack me, "Let's just go."

They both turned away without another word.

I stood as a statue as the anger and disbelief coursed through me. The two women followed the man toward the arena. When the blonde turned to the brunette, my heart sunk, breath escaped in a moan, and I wanted to scream at the top of my lungs. I recognized her...Delaney Rawlins, which meant the cowboy that I bumped into, was Brodie.

Son-of-a-bitch...why? I felt like I was a tornado and the only thing I wanted to do was pick up something and throw it.

516

Lawn chairs were sitting next to the trailer and I eyed them as potential targets.

More deep breaths…the announcer was introducing the royalty as they ran into the arena.

No matter what else was happening, I wanted to see Henry and Betty perform so in an anger haze I walked back toward the pens and right to the stairwell. Each step up was heavier than the last.

I caught a glimpse of Delaney on the backside of the stairs where the cowboys entered the staging platform. It looked like she was guarding it. I stopped a few steps up and looked to my right which had a perfect overview of the preparation area for the rough stock riders. I scanned each person until I saw Brodie standing on the raised platform just in front of a chute. The floor of the platform was even with the belly of the horse that was standing patiently in front of him.

Brodie's hands were resting on the top rail, his white vest and straw cowboy hat shown in the light. The long white fringe of his light blue chaps was motionless, which meant he wasn't moving…at all. He just stared out in the arena.

My heart sunk at the forlorn image; he looked so alone. I wanted to touch him.

"You're blocking the stairs," a woman said behind me so I slowly continued to the upper deck.

At the top, a man was sitting behind a large galvanized tub of ice and beer cans. The anger and now depression swirled in me so I pulled out a bill from my pocket and handed it to him, "I'll take however many this will buy."

I walked away with six tall silver beer cans wrapped in my arms, "Keep the change," I mumbled and kept walking along the deck until I stepped down to the next level to find a free table. They were all taken and all of the viewing cubicles were full except for one.

There was one woman sitting in the area that had six chairs and two taller cocktail tables. She glanced over her shoulder.

"You have anyone else with you?" she asked.

I slowly shook my head.

"My husband is busy and my kids couldn't make it tonight so have a seat," She waved a hand to the empty table.

Numbly, I just nodded and awkwardly set the six beer cans down. "Want one?"

She lifted a glass full of amber liquid in the air, "Already have another of these on the way, but thanks for the offer."

I pushed the table closer to the metal rail that created a barrier and kept people from falling directly into the arena. Perching on top of the tall chair and leaning against the railing, I opened a can. The first half, of the first can, was gone with the first tip.

I lowered it to see the woman raise an eyebrow to me.

"Bad night?" she asked.

I nodded and tipped the can a second time to finish off the whole thing.

Pushing that can away I opened the second as a very long, awful tasting, silent burp escaped. I could already feel the beer relax my muscles.

The anthem began and everyone rose. I stood next to the table to watch the rider carrying the red, white, and blue flag around the arena. I took a couple of long swigs after the rider stopped and before the prayer began.

Settling back in the chair with a numbness taking over my body, I looked for Flying Betty and Henry the First. My brain refused to let me remember in what order they rode.

The first rider was in the chute on horseback and ready. He had two men leaning over him to assist, plus a cameraman and a judge.

I was trying to decide if it was one of our horses when the gate flew open and a black horse appeared. Another swig of beer disappeared in the eight seconds the man rode the horse.

The second rider was announced as Kaycee Feild on Raggedy Ann.

Concentrating on the rest of the chutes, I leaned forward and squinted but I didn't see our horses. However, I did find my dad and two chutes down stood Brodie.

"No…" I whispered and leaned forward again. "Why did it have to be him?"

The third rider was announced as Brodie Rawlins.

"Oh, son-of-a-bitch," the breath exploded from me and my whole body melted into the chair.

This was his first ride in his memorial for his friend, Craig. Another long swig was taken as I tried desperately to keep from crying as the announcer told the story of the accident.

I closed my eyes and thought of Chinook...who was old...and shouldn't have been out... My eyes flew open and I looked around the crowd trying to find something to keep my mind busy.

The chute opened with Brodie riding a big tall bay horse. My breathing stopped as my body clenched until the horn blared and the crowd exploded in applause. When he slid from the pick-up man's horse, Brodie strode directly to the chutes without a glance at the crowd as his 86 point ride was announced.

I wasn't too far away from the chutes and could see him walking through the back of the platform and disappearing from view.

By concentrating so hard on Brodie, Flying Betty was in mid-flight before I noticed her. The cowboy hit the ground before the horn blared.

I flinched when my phone alert went off.

Text from Dad: She got a 41, where are you

I set the phone down and picked up a beer. The third one was gone when Henry was announced. My vision was fuzzy and I had to stare hard to see him run out into the arena and begin his powerful buck, kicks, and twists toward the end. The second the buzzer rang out, the rider flew over his shoulder.

"Here's to you, Henry," I lifted the can to him then took a long swig.

"You have a stock contractor shirt on," the woman said. "Is that your horse?"

"Henry and the pretty palomino that likes to fly...Flying Betty," My words were slow and a bit slurred.

The alert went off again and I tapped the front of the phone without picking it up.

Text from Dad: He got a 43, where are you

With a big sigh, I placed elbow on table, chin in hand, and melted against the table to watch the rest of the rodeo.

Brodie was announced as the winner of the night and the crowd cheered. I cried one tear, then wiped it away and forced myself to stop. My hand went from chin to forehead as I stared at the table. My first in-person encounter with Brodie and we were cursing at each other with him physically pushing me to the side.

"Son-of-a-bitch," I whispered.

"Hey, Maggie," a familiar male voice said as a chair scraped the ground and the table tipped slightly.

"Good rodeo, so far, great stock," The woman across from me said. "I really enjoyed last night."

"How are you enjoying it, River?" The man asked.

"Want a beer?" I raised my head and pushed one of the last beer cans toward him.

Wayne shook his head, "Still working, but maybe after we're done."

I nodded and leaned back in the chair to watch the steer wrestling.

"I heard about what happened earlier and want to apologize," he said.

A big sigh escaped as my eyes slowly rolled over to him, "For which one?"

His eyes narrowed as he hesitated before answering, "Your being asked to step away from Iggy."

"Asked..." I huffed.

"Well, it is unfortunate that it was physical and strong words said."

I huffed, took a deep breath, and looked toward the bucking chutes to see if Dad was there.

Wayne continued, "If you feel you need to go to the doctor..."

"What?" Maggie gasped and looked at me. "Are you alright?"

Without a word, I fumbled at the buttons at my cuff and slowly rolled the sleeve up to my elbow. Just below it, bruises were forming already and the skin was broken from the man's fingernails. The whole forearm was deep red.

I stretched it out on the table and twisted it for a complete inspection. It really looked like it should hurt but, presently, I couldn't feel a thing. I rolled the sleeve back down, fumbled at the buttons, then just gave up and reached for my beer.

Maggie leaned across the table and buttoned it for me. She turned and glared at Wayne before leaning back in her seat and finishing her drink in one tip of the glass.

My fourth empty beer was pushed to the side and I slowly leaned forward to grab the fifth can.

"You sure you need that?"

It was Dad, standing behind Wayne.

Emotions ran through my whole body, I felt nauseous and trembled. Tears rose as I looked at him and my lungs constricted to the point I could barely breathe, "He was too old to be in the pasture," The first of the tears fell. "I shouldn't have had him out there...it's my fault." My voice quivered as more tears slid down my cheeks.

"Why would you even think that?" Dad asked in clear surprise.

"That cowboy with Kirk said so. He said it was my fault," I could feel the tears falling, the snot beginning to run from my nose, and my voice sounded desperate and pathetic.

Maggie leaned over the table and handed me a napkin. Her eyes glistened.

"River," Dad's voice shook as he sat down between Wayne and me. "He was only 24, in excellent health. He was with his favorite harem...you not only picked the right number of mares for him but you chose his favorite mares."

My lips rolled together with chin shaking as my eyes begged for his forgiveness, "I loved Chinook...and so did you...I didn't do it on purpose."

He shook his head, "All the mares were bred; at least two to three weeks along when he died, which meant his last

521

two weeks he wasn't breeding. He was just hanging with his mares and offspring in his pasture in the sunshine. You didn't do anything wrong."

Tears formed in his eyes as he leaned forward and placed a hand on my arm…right over the bruises. I didn't feel it, but Wayne's hand went to Dad's to gently lift it.

"She has bruises from the first run-in at Iggy's pen," Wayne whispered.

"Damn it," Dad fell back in his seat and his hand went to his forehead.

"I wasn't interfering, Dad," I whispered. "I was just consoling Iggy…I was just so disappointed that cowboy backed out."

"None of this is your fault," Wayne said firmly.

"Chinook dying was not your fault either," Dad exhaled harshly. "I don't care what some stupid-ass cowboy, that doesn't know a fucking thing about horses has to say about it." He paused then glared at me. "The only reason you took what that jackass said to heart, was if you were already feeling guilty about it."

I nodded as I used my sleeve to wipe away the tears, then sniffed and wiped my nose.

Maggie was looking out in the arena with eyes still glistening. Dad had leaned back in his chair, his hands balled up in fists.

Wayne leaned against the table, and looked right in my eyes, "None of tonight's events were your fault. Twenty-four is not too old for a stallion that is in good health."

I nodded with a sigh, then leaned forward to that fifth beer and slid it across the table to stop in front of Dad.

"I'd be breaking windows and smashing chairs if I didn't have a few of these in me," I whispered, then reached for the last one and slowly twisted off the lid.

Dad huffed and reached for the beer.

The crowd roared and my mind finally took in the noise around us. The steer wrestling was done and the team roping had begun.

"I need to get back to work," Wayne stood and looked between the three of us.

"You don't worry about a thing," Maggie said. "I'll watch over them."

A few minutes later, two more beer cans arrived as well as four bottles of water and another amber-colored drink for Maggie.

The three of us quietly watched the rodeo until the horses for the bronc riders were ushered into the chutes. I sighed deeply, and the depression swirled in the beer haze.

I wanted Iggy out there. It was always exciting to anticipate his explosive departures and twisting bucks. I sighed again.

"Yep," Dad whispered then took another long swig of beer.

Neither Iggy nor Brodie were out there, but then again, the Brodie part didn't really have a bearing on my life...except for the fact I wanted to touch him.

I took a long swig of beer, then set the can aside and moved to the water.

When the last bull had bucked, and the announcer said the good-nights, we just leaned back and watched the people depart the stands.

I was on my second bottle of water and really needed to go to the restroom but wasn't sure if I was going to be able to stand, let alone walk.

The arena was nearly bare of people when Wayne arrived with a beer in hand and took a seat between Dad and Maggie.

She stretched across the table to place a hand over mine, "You need somewhere to hang out the next couple nights, you just come up here with me."

My smile was slow to appear through the haze but it was honest and sincere, "Thanks for tonight and I'll pro...lol..liby take you up on that."

The men rose as Maggie stood and said her farewells.

I placed my hands flat on the table and pushed myself up. I weaved a bit and both men reached for me.

"Let's get you to the trailer," Dad smirked. "Good thing it's a night rodeo, you'll have all day to sleep this off."

We walked slowly with me leaning into him while Wayne walked on the other side.

The stairs were descended very carefully. Halfway down, I turned and looked at the empty bucking platform and chutes. No horses, no cowboys…so sad. My mind flashed to Brodie standing next to the chute, looking so alone, "I want to touch him."

I didn't realize I had said the words out loud until both men turned to look at me.

"Touch who?" Dad asked.

My face warmed as I chuckled at my error, "I want to pet my pretty little pony."

Wayne grinned, "Yeah…we need…"

"That's what that old jackass called him," I interrupted and smiled between the pair. "Pretty little pony," I chirped. I felt my veins begin to wake as the blood started to boil again. "Handsome big-ass stud is what I should have said to the old fart," I growled.

"Let's get you to the trailer before you start throwing chairs," Dad grinned and wrapped an arm around my waist.

"I gotta pee, Dad," I chuckled.

"And I'm sure Wayne is real happy you told him that," Dad grinned and his arm grew tighter.

"Well, if he had five or six big beers and two or three waters, he'd have to pee, too." I slurred as my head swirled.

Wayne laughed and I grinned up at him. "You are correct there, young lady."

My head swung over so I could see Iggy in the shadows of his pen.

"Iggy's sad, too," I sighed.

"We all wanted to see him perform tonight," Wayne said.

"Can I say goodnight to him?" I asked.

"He's sleeping," Dad walked right past the pen.

Wayne left us at the trailer door, and as Dad shut it behind us, I stumbled toward the bathroom.

"So glad I don't have to pee in a por-lorta-polly," I slurred with a smile.

"Just make it into the bathroom and I'll be happy," He huffed.

I giggled and tossed my hat on the table then stepped into the small bathroom.

I settled onto the seat and my head fell against the wall. My body began to relax as the stream hit the water and kept going and going and going. I began to giggle.

"River, are you done yet?" Dad said through the door.

"River's peeing a river," I giggled again and my body began to melt against the wall.

When the stream stopped, the silence took over and I could feel my body begin to shut down.

"River! Are you awake?"

I tried to answer, but no words came out.

"Damn it, River," he huffed. "I'm not coming in after you, so if you don't wake up, you're sleeping in there tonight."

"Well, that would be uncom-forttata-able," I mumbled.

Forcing myself to lift my head away from the wall, I reached down to take off my boots but I couldn't do it with my jeans gathered at my ankles. I sat and stared at my jeans and boots as I wondered how I was going to get the jeans over the boots so I could take off the boots.

"River!" He pounded on the door.

My mind barely registered it but my body jumped. Using the wall and the sink cabinet as a brace, I slowly stood and leaned against the wall. I stared at my jeans and boots. Well, first things first, I pulled up my booty shorts. How did I usually get my jeans off with my boots on? Giggling, I realized I had to kick the boots off first. I bounced against the walls a dozen times before I finally had my legs free.

"What the hell are you doing?" Dad called out.

I opened the door and took a step but tripped over the pile of boots and jeans and nearly hit the ground. His arm came around my waist and he half carried and half drug me to the bed.

I didn't remember anything after that.

There was bacon, a cup of coffee, a bottle of water, three ibuprofen, and a note saying he was cleaning the pens.

He is the best dad, I smiled as I stood under the shower stream.

My head ached, wrists ached, and my forearm was killing me. There was a hand-width sized bruise that covered nearly the whole forearm and clear finger bruises around it. At the end of those it was easy to see the fingernail marks that had broken the skin. What the hell was the guy thinking to squeeze that damn hard?

After blow-drying my hair, I dressed in jeans and a dark blue t-shirt that had the WML brand across the front of it. Across the back shoulders, it said "Westmoreland Stock Contractors".

I took out the medicine kit and was dabbing antiseptic on the fingernail marks when Dad knocked then opened the door.

He was grinning when he looked up; then his gaze slid to my bruised arm. The grin changed to fury, and he turned to slam the door shut.

"Well, shit," I whispered and quickly slid into my tennis shoes to follow him.

CHAPTER FORTY SEVEN

I heard a shout but wasn't sure it was him but followed the direction anyway. Another shout and I darted between the trailers.

"Adam!" A man's voice called out.

I broke into a run as I entered the wide dirt opening between the entry gates and the animal pens.

The older man that grabbed me was standing next to the rodeo secretary's trailer. He was toe-to-toe, buckle-to-buckle, and nearly nose-to-nose with my father, who was talking so intensely, his face was red. His finger jabbed at but didn't quite touch the man's chest.

I couldn't hear what was being said; I could only hear the furious manner in which it was said. Three men were standing next to them; they were obviously trying to make sure the 'conversation' didn't get physical.

"...bruises already so fucking dark..." Dad was growling.

I placed my hand on his arm that was jabbing at the air.

His words stopped as he glared at the man then turned furious eyes to me. I'd seen that look before and it always made my stomach clench.

"Come on, Dad," I whispered and took a step back in hopes it would get him moving.

Instead, he reached out to my wrist and gently lifted my arm in the air.

The older man glanced at the bruising but didn't say a word. The three men standing next to us mumbled between each other.

"Come on, Dad," I repeated and pulled my arm back.

Without another word, he turned and we walked side-by-side to the trailer.

"Well, it's only 9:00 on a Friday morning and we have until late this afternoon to get ready for the rodeo," I said. "What would you like to do?"

"Well, I've read about some winery tours that offer taste testing," he grinned.

I laughed and shook my aching head.

We did go for a drive and stopped at a few wineries but I wasn't doing any taste testing. A half-dozen bottles were stored in the trailer as gifts for mom.

Being away from the rodeo grounds for hours helped release the tension I felt but walking into Iggy's pen just made my body sigh.

It was a couple of hours before the rodeo started so I was still in the T-shirt as I scraped the used bedding and horse manure into a pile.

It was Friday and he wasn't in the rodeo so I was allowed to play with him a bit. I'd scratch a shoulder or untangle a length of mane. He would nudge my hip with his nose, nibble at my jeans or tug at my shirt.

"So why do you go poop in your water bucket?" I asked him with a hand running down his blazed nose.

As I bent over to tip the water out of the bucket, there was a movement on the other side of the fence. I glanced up to see a pretty blonde looking at me.

"Excuse me," she said softly and glanced down at my bruised arm then back up. "Are you alright?"

I stood and took a deep breath. It was Lacie Jae Madison, the host of the Coffee With Cowboys podcast...about the Rawlins family...about Brodie.

My stomach swirled in anxiety but I smiled and nodded, "Yes, it was just an unfortunate incident."

She looked at me thoughtfully for a moment then stepped closer to the fence. There wasn't anyone else near us so no one could hear what she said.

"I was in a situation that caused bruising too," Her eyes were silently asking me if I needed help.

"Thank you for reaching out," I smiled in understanding. "But, this is just from a one-time overly aggressive stranger last night."

Her blue eyes widened, "Here at the rodeo grounds?"

I nodded, "It's been handled and once I'm done here I'll put on the long-sleeve shirt that covers it."

"I covered mine too," she whispered.

"No, I really am alright," I assured her. "I'm surprised you haven't already heard the story...there were a lot of people around."

"We're not staying here on the grounds," she shook her head. "They ride then we leave."

"Oh," No wonder I hadn't seen Brodie...except that once.

We stood quietly a moment, my holding the straw fork and her leaning against the panel and looking toward the bucking chutes.

"Can I ask you something?" I asked softly.

She looked back at me with her eyes looking a bit lost.

"Why haven't you done a podcast the last couple of weeks?"

Her eyes glistened, "I can't get myself to be cheery right now...since Craig died."

I nodded in understanding and my heart broke for the family just a bit more.

"But, you're not always cheery on them, sometimes you're more deep and spreading common sense that sometimes we forget."

She smiled, "I've never heard it like that."

"You talk about moments...like when you talked about that moment in Vegas when you met Logan...on the San Antonio one."

"Toby Keith night," she nodded and her eyes twinkled at the memory. "That was such a fun night."

"Yes, it was," I agreed. "But, you also talked about watching your sister riding a bucking horse and in that moment, you couldn't have been prouder."

She smiled a genuine smile that lit her eyes.

529

"And that's what I'm trying to say," I said earnestly. "You share moments…positive moments…but life isn't always that way. There are bad moments, like the jackass that grabbed my arm last night. I don't exactly know what that will mean in the future, but when we have those moments, we have to learn from them just as much as we learn from the positive."

"Yes…" she nodded thoughtfully.

"Life-altering moments, like what happened to Craig…well, we may never know why that had to happen but it did, and we still have to move on." I felt a little frustrated at not being able to put into words what I wanted to say without causing the tears that were filling her eyes. "We move on by remembering the positive moments…like you and Logan meeting in Vegas or when you said Craig helped your sister ride that bucking horse."

She took a deep breath and let it out slowly.

"By not sharing the bad moments on your podcast, you give the illusion that life is perfect when it's not." I lifted my arm and shrugged. "I had a horse die recently and it was the hardest thing I have ever gone through. He was six months older than me, so he was part of my whole life. We were basically raised together." Tears welled and my lungs ached. "I held onto feelings that maybe I should have let go at the time…but…"

I hesitated and looked down at the water in the trough.

"Using the positive moments of your life with him, will help you deal with his loss," She whispered.

I had to deal with the thought I had caused his death. I just looked at her and nodded. "He was majestic and I could just watch him for hours."

"Those are the good moments we need to hold onto when the bad ones get too hard."

"Yes," I whispered.

Iggy nudged my shoulder from behind and I turned to push his nose away with a laugh. "He was Iggy's sire," I said. "And moments of this brat trying to push me around make me smile…make me thank Chinook for giving me this obnoxious monster of a horse."

She chuckled when he took the back of my shirt between his lips and began pulling.

I reached for the hose and started filling the water trough and stepped aside so he could play in the stream of water. He bit at the water and pushed his nose into the end of the hose so the water sprayed out...that just caused him to bounce his head in the air as if he was laughing.

"He has quite the personality," Lacie Jae smiled.

I laughed, "Yeah, he does. Sweet on the ground, for me, but explosive in the arena."

"I look forward to watching your Iggy," She chuckled at his lipping the water again.

"Only if he is drawn tonight for tomorrow's short-go round," I shrugged. "Then Lewiston and Pendleton."

Her phone alert rang out and she read the message then looked at my arm then up to my eyes.

"We'll be in both places, too," She smiled. "I have to go, but thank you for the talk."

I just nodded as she turned away.

The bucket was full, so I leaned across the water to turn off the hose. I could feel Iggy nibbling at my jeans just above my boots but wasn't prepared for him to take them between his teeth and lift. My leg suddenly in the air tipped me off balance, and it was all I could do to keep from falling into the water trough.

I squealed and heard laughter behind me. After setting myself upright and turning to the horse, I looked at Wayne standing in one of the other pens. I waved with a giggle and finished cleaning the pen.

I watched Friday night's rodeo with Maggie in her viewing cubicle. She was the wife of one of the rodeo directors and after realizing who I was the night before, she had texted him to let my father know where I was.

"So, who do you have tonight in the performance?"

"Fizzling Dud; his name came from his first performance out the chute or I should say non-performance."

We talked horses the rest of the night until Fizzling Dud's gate was opened with Johnny Espeland along for the ride. The horse kicked high to the back, twisted in the air as he went down then kicked and twisted again. At the last second, he zig-zagged with his front hooves and his rider rode through it.

"Whoo-hoo!" Maggie applauded and turned to me with a grin. "Oh, he's fun to watch."

I laughed and applauded, "He's learning more each time. Not all outings have been the same."

Text from Dad: 44!

Both rider and horse had scored the same for an 88 in the round.

I continually searched the people behind the chutes for Brodie. I saw his brother, Logan, walk past the stairs with Brodie close behind. A few minutes later, I could see Brodie appear on the platform as he buckled on his light blue chaps. I wondered about the story behind the chaps; they seemed so unique. The pictures and videos of him riding at other rodeos, he rode in dark blue chaps with leather embellishments on the waistband and hips. So, why the light blue and white ones for this rodeo?

He slid his white vest on over white shirt then began stretching. I tried hard not to stare but when he stopped and stood behind the chute and looked out into the arena, my heart just ached. Everything in me wanted to lay a comforting hand on his shoulder or just wrap my arms around him and hold him tightly…let him know everything would be alright. I wanted to touch him.

This was saddle bronc riding but I recognized five bareback riders standing in an arc behind Brodie as if protecting him. Tears warmed my eyes at the solidarity these men had for each other.

Another rider bust out of the chute but Brodie's head didn't even turn to watch; he just stared straight ahead.

The horn blared, and two men stepped up behind Brodie. Even at this distance, I could see his body startle from the intrusion. Damn, it just squeezed my heart.

Brodie was the fifth rider out and leaned over to adjust his saddle and measure the length of the rein to the horse.

My mind was so focused on him that I didn't hear or see the riders before him bust from the chute.

Brodie was lowering down onto the saddle, with the flank man, judge and cameraman by his side. The brown horse rocked back and forth then stood still as Brodie lifted the rein up, rolled his shoulders in as his chin went to his chest. He nodded and the gate flew open.

My whole body clenched and rose as the horse bucked in a large circle, powerful kicks to the back and high into the air. For eight seconds, I held my breath until the horn blared. The crowd erupted in applause as the pick-up-men helped Brodie from the horse. Then, as he did the night before, he walked out of the arena and to the back of the platform without an acknowledgment to anyone.

The score of 87 left him short of the winning 88 Fizzling Dud had earned with his rider, Johnny. Brodie was second for the night, which meant he would be riding both bareback and saddle bronc on Saturday night.

"That boy is going to be tired, mentally and physically, by the time he is done," Maggie whispered and took a long swig from her drink.

After the rodeo, the draw for the championship round Saturday night was held. My stomach was in knots so I calmed myself by cleaning Iggy's pen again. He followed me around like a puppy...a really big puppy.

Just as I finished, Dad strolled up to the panel and rest his arms against it.

I stared at him until he smiled, "It's confirmed; Henry, Betty, and Iggy."

"Yes!" I huffed, then turned to Iggy and ran a hand down his neck. "You do your damnedest tomorrow...show them our Ignatius and I'll see you after the rodeo."

I made my way out of the pens and met Dad at the trailer.

"By the way," he said. "The volunteer that grabbed you last night was escorted off the property this morning."

I stepped into the trailer, "Who did the horses draw?"

I stood at the back of the upper deck which overlooked all of the animal pens. The horses and bulls were loaded into the pie-shaped pens as the stock contractor got ready for the rodeo. They were separated in order of performance so Henry and Betty were in a bareback pen with four other horses. Iggy was pacing back and forth in his pen. I had stayed completely away from him today. I wondered if he had gotten used to my attention the last few days and missed it today. Just a couple more hours and I would be able to talk to him again.

In the distance, by the horse stalls, I saw Delaney on a blue roan horse and Logan was next to her riding a big bay horse.

All three had made it into the short-go with Delaney in breakaway and barrels. I looked out to the expanse of trailers and trucks and wondered where Brodie was waiting.

Once bareback started, I leaned against the rail in Maggie's area while they bucked, then I ran to the back to watch the horses in the stripping chute…then back again. I'm not sure anyone would have found it as entertaining as I did.

Flying Betty was phenomenal for her rider and matched his 44 point score for an 88 point ride.

Henry the First's rider flew off at the 6.39-second mark but the horse scored 43.

Brodie was the last rider of the bareback section and I anxiously waited for any sight of him. He finally appeared when only three cowboys were left. He stood next to the chute but this time his head was down looking at the horse…or praying.

I clasped my hands under my chin for a silent prayer.

He carefully stepped over the rail to hover over the horse called Yipee Kibitz. I barely moved, barely breathed as I stared at horse and rider. The chute opened and I had to force myself not to jump in the air and yell.

Just as the horn blared, he tumbled off the back hip of the horse. The crowd gasped but he stood and walked out of the arena. He scored an 88.5. When the last chute for the bareback riders was empty, Brodie had won the night. His first ride for his friend was successful. He was nowhere to be seen but I so badly wanted to congratulate him. I wanted to touch him.

During the team roping, I was at the back of the deck overlooking the pens and watching them escort Iggy from his pen, through the center ring and down the lane to the chute. I ran back to the table to watch him load into the chute and Dad lean over to put the halter on him.

"It looks like your Iggy is the first out in saddle bronc," Maggie said.

As the cowboys stepped forward, I saw Brodie step up on the platform then to the chute right next to Iggy. He stretched his back and arms side to side then stood still again with hands-on rail and eyes down to the horse.

This time, his head turned and he looked right down at Iggy. That simple little move caused goosebumps up my arms.

"He's got a great rider tonight," Maggie mused.

"Yes, there is a part of me that wants him to remain unridden but another part that wants him to take a cowboy to the big check."

"He may be unridden, but the question is, is he rideable?"

"Well, you tell me after he's done here," I smiled at her as I took my camera out and prepared for the ride.

The rider stepped up over the rail and hovered over Iggy. The horse rocked forward in the chute then stood still.

"He's bored and wants to stretch his legs." I smiled.

The cameraman and judge took their places at the end of the chute with Dad holding the flank strap. The nod, the gate opening, and the horse was flying into the air...the crowd gasped and screamed in delight. He followed the dramatic bust-out with a nearly vertical buck with back hooves in the air, down on all four, and his back was hunched into an explosive lift with his back hooves to the right and the front hooves to the left. The second time, when he was completely air-born, the rider tipped to the side. When the horse's hooves hit the ground, the rider tumbled off just as the vertical buck was repeated.

"He made it to 6.8!" The announcer yelled.

"Holy hell, River!" Maggie gasped with wide eyes. "That was spectacular."

"Ridable?" I laughed.

"Absolutely, and when a cowboy can match him, they'll take home a check every time."

I proudly watched the pick-up men catch the rope that dangled from Iggy's halter. Dad turned and looked up at me with a wide grin. We gave each other a thumbs-up, then I ran to the back of the platform to look down into the stripping chute. Three men removed the halter and saddle before letting him jog down the lane and return to the turn style. When he was back in his pen, the horse began pacing.

I could see someone in a wheelchair sitting just outside his pen watching him. I jogged down the platform to the top of the stairs, which was right over Iggy's pen. Slowly, I leaned over to peer over the edge to see who the man was. My first thought was correct; it was Brodie's father. Lacie Jae was standing next to him.

The thought of walking down to talk to them flashed but was quickly denied. I walked back to join Maggie as we waited for Brodie's saddle bronc ride.

Three riders later, the gateman pulled the rope tight outside of Brodie's chute. I took a deep breath and my fingers interlaced under my chin. The gate swung open and I held my breath until the 8-second horn blared with horse bucking and cowboy spurring high to the saddle and low to the shoulders. It was a great ride that placed them second, which won him the average and the win for the rodeo.

His first rodeo of the Big Four was hugely successful.

CHAPTER FORTY EIGHT

I stood at the edge of the ocean, with the water caressing my bare feet and took a picture of the waves rolling in. Just to my right, my parents were walking hand-in-hand along the water. They looked entirely out of place but happy. I quickly took a picture then started a video. Caleb jogged up next to me to watch as I captured our parents in a quiet, relaxed moment. When they turned and saw the camera, I stopped the recording.

"Send me that," Caleb said then continued his jog down the beach.

"Are you enjoying the vacation?" Dad asked as they stopped in front of me.

"She would rather be in Walla Walla for the rodeo even if it is raining there," Mom chuckled.

I looked at Dad and smiled my agreement.

"I love that Mom and Caleb flew over to join us for Lewiston and Pendleton," I said honestly. "Even if Caleb is either jogging or has his head in his college books."

"And it was nice of Wayne to keep the horses until we head to Lewiston," Dad added.

"So," Mom smiled at me "What can we do so you enjoy this vacation?"

"I heard there were bumper cars in town."

"What is the Lewiston setup?" Caleb asked.

We were in the back seat of the truck as we pulled down the entrance of the rodeo grounds.

"They had slack Tuesday and bulls tonight then the rodeo Thursday, Friday, and Saturday. One performance, then the cowboys usually go to Puyallup and Spokane," I answered.

"Remember," Dad said as he carefully turned the truck and horse trailer behind a building full of stalls. "We're here as the sub-contractors which they usually don't do here. They had to split their horses between two rodeos and it was too costly to haul more over here. So ours are just fillers for here. The Sankey's take the lead."

There was silence in the truck until Caleb turned to look at me.

"You know, he was actually just talking to you," he grinned.

I rolled my eyes as my parents chuckled.

"Sometimes, I hate you, Caleb," I grumbled.

"You mean...times like now...when I just point out the truth," he chuckled.

"Yes," I glared at him and turned my attention back to the roundup grounds.

We were met by the stock contractors and after light-hearted banter, we unloaded the horses into their pens. Iggy, of course, had his own, which he pranced down the aisle to then thoroughly checked every neighbor around him.

When the horses were settled and the trailer parked by the pens and next to the pick-up men's trailer, I walked to the arena and up the empty bleachers to the top row and looked over the edge to the horses below. The pens and grass field were just how I imagined them...just as Lacie Jae and spoken in her podcast she had posted the day before. It was her first since Craig's death.

I put in the ear-buds and listened to the podcast again.

Welcome to Coffee with Cowboys with me, Lacie Jae.

Greetings everyone! Lacie Jae with Coffee With Cowboys here. I'm a relocated city girl who will be adventuring into the ranching and rodeo world ... the cowboy way of life.

It's been a while since I posted, and to be honest, I wasn't sure I was ever going to do one again, but more on that later.

Today I woke up in Lewiston, Idaho ...

... A few weeks back, in Kennewick, I had a chat with a fan of the podcast. She asked me why I hadn't been doing them. When I told her I didn't feel cheerful, she reminded me that I'm more ... insightful sometimes rather than cheerful. She reminded me that life isn't always made of positive moments; there are those negative moments too. We need to remember the positive to help us get through the negative.

She had recently gone through a tough time in her life and was holding onto the good to help her get through ... ...

...... Before I sign off, I want to say one thing to the young woman; the fan that I talked to in Kennewick. You didn't understand why the negative incident happened to you ... you were still searching for the answer.

But, think of this ... if I hadn't seen the bruising, I wouldn't have stopped to talk to you and who knows if I would have continued with this podcast? I hope your life is filled with an overabundance of positive moments and thank you for the chat.

With that, I am going to sign off and have coffee with my cowboy. Have a great day and a good cup of coffee.

I had to be standing close to where she had stood on the bleachers to be able to look down at the bulls, steers, and horses then out to the arena where the monitor she had spoken of was in place. In an odd way, I felt closer to her now, as if we were friends.

I knew Logan and Delaney had run in slack the day before. My eyes wandered out to the horse trailers in the dirt-covered parking lot. Were they still here? Delaney must be since she was still riding barrels on Thursday night. I had already checked the stock draw and knew Brodie was riding both bareback and saddle bronc that night. I wondered how he was handling the stress.

I listened to the podcast again. In the beginning, her voice was melancholy but by the end she seemed stronger and uplifted. The bruising on my arm had started to fade and as much as I wished the confrontation with the older volunteer hadn't happened, I'm glad it had helped her start the podcasts again. There were times her view on life and energy for the world she was discovering had helped me through a bad mood and made a day brighter. There was no doubt she was helping others, too.

We watched the bull riding event from the bleachers behind the bucking chutes. It was fun to cheer and tease the cowboys we knew. They met us for beer at our trailer for a fun relaxing evening…except for my constantly looking at everyone in my search to find a Rawlins.

Thursday night, I stood at the end of the bucking chutes with camera in hand. I was tucked into the far corner and out of everyone's way yet I had a good angle to get our horse's outings. All four bucked tonight.

My back straightened and I tried not to stare when Brodie appeared at the farthest bucking chute from me. He and the stock contractor were busy placing his riggin on the palomino horse called Exotic Blonde.

Fizzling Dud was the first horse out in bareback on two chutes from me. The gate opened and the horse lunged from the chute and began his powerful bucks. The cowboy was a ragdoll on top and flopped his legs on both sides of the horse's neck. It came with a 59 point score. The ride was ugly but the horse looked good as he garnered 40 of those points. I had no doubt that would not be a video we would be sharing, nor probably ever watch again.

Flying Betty was the third horse out and she was spectacular with an 88 point ride putting her rider in first place.

I watched Brodie as he moved two chutes closer to me and began helping Kirk St. Clair prepare for his ride. As hard as I tried, I couldn't stop watching Brodie. We were less than thirty feet apart. I had thought seeing him would end my obsession but when I saw him closer and realized he was as handsome as I first thought...well, I was wrong. Everything about him took my breath away.

I lifted the phone to take a picture of him then lowered it quickly. That would be crazy, wouldn't it? I began to lift it again but hesitated. No, I hadn't taken pictures of any of the other cowboys...it would be weird. I only had this one chance...I lifted the phone and took three pictures then lowered it quickly. My eyes searched for anyone that might have seen me. No, I was going nuts...I was becoming a stalker.

The chute opened with Kirk and the horse bursting into the arena but I couldn't pull my eyes away from Brodie. He was leaning on the back of the chute, yelling at Kirk. When the horn blared and the pick-up men swooped in, Brodie clapped his hands then turned away from me.

I stayed at the end of the chutes and just watched. He was already on the horse when his name was called; minutes went by before he finally nodded. My stomach trembled in anticipation when the gate was finally opened. He spurred most of the ride but his legs stopped moving toward the end.

"Damn..." I moaned then gasped when he flew off the palomino horse and landed flat on his stomach in the dirt.

He rose, then sauntered back to the chutes with shoulders low. A 79 point score was announced as he climbed up onto the chute and sat on the back panel. When the bareback was final, he was in 4th place.

"River!"

I turned to the stock contractor.

"Can you go help push the steers for the bulldogging and team roping? One of their volunteers hasn't arrived yet."

"Sure!" I jumped down into the arena and ran down the side to the roping chute. I was thankful for something to do to keep my mind busy.

When the last team of ropers burst from the box, I moved to the entry gate closest to the chutes for a good view of the bronc rides. Brodie was going to be the first out on the mare Marquee and Tate Owens was helping him prepare the horse for the ride.

The longer it took for him to prepare, the tighter my fingers gripped the rail. When the gate opened and the horse made her first lunge, my body rose with her. She bucked to the right then down the side of the arena toward me. When the horn blared, Brodie and Marquee were in a stretched out buck just ten feet in front of me. My heart was pounding, breath held, and the sound of horse and man grunting sent chills down my spine. Goosebumps covered my arms.

The pick-up men ran in to help Brodie from the horse; when he hit the ground, he stopped and took a deep breath. When he exhaled, his body lowered as if in relief, then he started the long walk across the arena. I watched him until he disappeared through the gate.

Iggy was going to be one of the last horses out so I jumped from the panel of the steer pen and made my way behind the bleachers to get back to the stock pens. I had been using my phone as a camera for the videos but, since I had time, I walked through the closed gates and into the pasture to retrieve my good camera from the truck to capture Iggy.

I could still hear the announcer so I could track who was riding.

"Ladies and gentleman, pay attention to this next cowboy, Chute 3, we have one of the top riders in the world, Brody Cress..."

I was halfway back to the mass of panels and pens holding the horses and bulls when I saw a movement to my right. The area was supposed to be void of people with a fence that blocked anyone from wandering into the horse pasture so I stopped and watched.

A man stumbled by a small building with the pick-up men's horse trailer parked next to it. Maybe he was drunk...his hand went to the front of the truck and he caught himself from falling. He leaned against the truck a moment before slowly walking down between the building and the trailer with a hand to the wall using it as a brace.

His light blue chaps had long white fringe that matched the white protective riding vest over a white shirt. It was a very unique look letting me know exactly who it was. My nerves tingled and heart began to race.

I looked back across the pens where I knew Iggy was standing in the chute. The flank man would be helping the rider, Tate Owens, prepare the saddle. Everything in me wanted to be there to watch the ride and cheer for my horse but my body turned to the direction Brodie had disappeared.

Hesitantly, I walked in front of the truck and peered around the side. There was a street light on the other side that cast an eerie light between the building and horse trailer. He was sitting on the ground, his back to the building, knees up, elbows resting on them and his head low. I couldn't see his face; the shadows and cowboy hat blocked the view. My heart constricted.

"Are you alright?" I called out softly.

There was silence.

"Are you alright?" I repeated a little louder.

"Yeah...fine..." he mumbled.

His voice was low but I could still hear the tremble.

"Can I help?"

"No...I'm fine..." he growled this time and there was a hint of desperation as if he was trying to hold back his emotions.

"OK," I walked around the truck and leaned against the door. I was still a good fifteen feet from him and he hadn't moved at all. "You be fine over there and I'll just be fine over here."

There was silence.

The announcer's voice boomed, "...that was a nice ride, Brody. We have a score of 85 points!"

Two more rides before Iggy's turn. I stared at the pens as if I could see through them and into the chute where I knew Iggy stood. I visualized Tate standing just over the chute, waiting his turn.

I glanced down to Brodie, sitting as a statue against the wall...I could hear shaking breaths escape him.

"Can I get someone for you?" I whispered just loud enough, I knew he could hear.

"Why do you think I came out here?"

"To be alone," my heart ached for him.

"So...go..."

I stood silently and listened to the announcer's voice, letting the crowd know that Jake Finlay on the horse called Big Bay would be next.

I should just go. Our first encounter had been disastrous, and this could even be worse. But, I couldn't get myself to move.

"I'll just stand guard for you," I whispered. "Make sure no one else bothers you."

I glanced down at him as his head lowered just a little more.

"There's no one out here...that's why I came here," It was said so low, I almost didn't hear him.

"But...I'm still going to just..."

"Why?" His head rose a few inches, but I could still just see the shadowy outline of him.

"I don't want you to be alone out here," I said truthfully.

"I can take care of myself."

"I know..."

"You know who I am?"

"Yes... Brodie Rawlins. I just watched you ride for your friend that died a couple of weeks ago and that has to be gut-wrenching...so I don't want to leave you alone."

He didn't answer, nor did he move. I heard another shaking breath that brought tears to my eyes. I couldn't imagine what he was going through and had no idea how to help him so

I just silently leaned against the truck and listened to the announcer.

"The judge's scores are coming in...and that's an 88 point ride for Jake! In chute 4, we have Allen Boore getting ready on the NFR horse Black Tie."

He was the last ride before Iggy so I still had time to get there.

I looked down at the camera in my hands...there would be all kinds of video and photos taken of the ride...I didn't need to be there. I glanced down at Brodie...his head bobbed slightly as more shaking breathes were released. No, I truly believed I needed to be here with him.

I jogged back to the truck and returned the camera to its case and pulled two bottles of water from the cooler.

When I returned, he hadn't moved but he was silent.

Slowly, I walked down into the shadows between us to set the water bottle next to him then walked back to lean against the door again. He didn't move.

The announcer's voice boomed again, "Tate Owens is our next rider on the young horse, Destiny's Ignatius ...commonly known as Iggy. This horse has really made a name for himself the last two years..."

I smiled proudly as I envisioned Tate sliding down onto the horse's broad back, his fingers wrapped tightly around the rope. Everyone knew Iggy didn't like standing in the chute once the rider was on his back so they would make it fast.

"Here we go...Tate gave the nod..."

The crowd roared.

"Wow! That was a spectacular bust out!" the announcer shouted. "Hold on! Hold on!"

My body ached to be there but my mind played out the horse's launch from the chute. Then he would turn whichever direction his ears had twitched...that's when most riders were thrown.

"Hold on! Watch out!" The announcer yelled as the horn blared.

A round of ahhhs vibrated from the stands and I knew Iggy had dislodged his rider.

"That horse has now been unridden in sixteen tries!" The announcer said. "Almost, Tate, but 7.3 just doesn't get you in the money. You can take pride in knowing that was the longest anyone has ridden Iggy."

My phone vibrated in my pocket.

Text from Dad: Where the hell are you?

Text to Dad: Helping a friend, sorry I missed it, I will watch video.

Text from Dad: Everything alright?

Text to Dad: Yes, I'll be there in a while.

I glanced over at Brodie. He still hadn't moved.

"You can go," he said as if he knew I had looked at him.

"No, I don't need to now."

"Now?"

"He's already ridden so I don't need to be anywhere."

"Boyfriend or husband going to be mad at you?"

"No…horse…that wouldn't know if I was there or not."

"A horse? Which one?"

"Iggy."

"Iggy is your horse? You're the stock contractor?"

"Sub-contractor here."

"River Westmoreland?"

"Yes…" I held back the gasp from the knowledge he knew who I was.

There was silence as he leaned back against the wall and his hand went to the bottle of water.

"I was told I was quite rude to you a couple of weeks ago."

"Well…it's understandable. I was having a terrible night…it was just bad timing." I hated that he knew it was me.

More silence as he drank from the bottle then set it down on the ground. His head leaned back against the wall.

"I just miss him so much," Brodie whispered with desperation hanging on every word.

"I imagine so."

546

"I was so focused at that rodeo…that first ride for him. I didn't really let it all sink-in until after the rodeo," he sighed. "Each week…it's getting harder to focus through the depression."

"You've made it three rodeos now. Only one left."

"Yeah…each one is harder."

"You rode Exotic Blonde in bareback. What was your score?" I asked even though I knew. I just wanted to keep him talking.

"79…."

"Fourth…your saddle bronc on Marquee was great and you're second there so far."

"Yeah…but every ride…it's just…getting so hard to battle the depression. I feel so…tired."

"Talking is the best thing to do."

"But my whole family is going through it."

"Which means they know how you feel and are probably the best shoulders to lean on right now, they need you, too. When you feel it coming on, go do something with one of them. Ride, play poker, work-out, just something physical so it helps pick your energy back up."

He didn't respond so we listened to the final two bronc riders.

He picked up the bottle and surprisingly poured it in his hand then splashed it onto his face.

"Good thing you're a man…you can do that…" I teased. "If it was me? I couldn't imagine how bad I would look."

He huffed with a big sigh, "I don't think there would be a problem…smudged makeup or not, you're a beautiful woman."

He'd said it as a statement…nothing more, but my jaw dropped in surprise, and my heart pounded.

"I guess I should say thank you," I managed to say.

He shrugged with another sigh, "Lots of women are beautiful…"

My heart dropped.

"...it's what's inside that matters," he continued. "And what you just did...staying here instead of going to watch your horse? Well...that's what matters...heart over beauty."

My heart fluttered again.

With a hand to the ground, he suddenly stood up.

I leaned away from the truck and looked up at him as he walked out of the shadows.

His black hat was low, barely showing his dark brown eyes. His long dark hair was pushed back and fell just past his collar. A thick layer of black whiskers covered his jaw and barely let the grim smile show through.

"Thank you, River," he said with a nod.

There was open honesty and emotion in his red-rimmed eyes.

I had no idea what to say, so I just nodded, stepped in front of the truck and out of his way. My whole body trembled in the need to touch him, so I shoved my hands into my pockets to keep from reaching out.

We both turned toward the bleachers and began walking side-by-side. At the pens he stopped and looked at me.

"I need to get over there...Delaney will be riding soon."

"Okay..."

With a tip of his hat to me, he turned and walked toward the back of the bleachers. I walked back to the pens under the bleachers with a few glances back toward him until he disappeared without a glance back to me.

I didn't see him again.

CHAPTER FORTY NINE

We were parked right by the pens filled with the bucking horses so I could see Iggy lying in the hot sun. Being a stallion, he was in his own pen, but in the next were his travel buddies Flying Betty, Fizzling Dud, and Henry the First. Just behind the horses were the tall bleachers of the Pendleton Roundup arena. Unlike most rodeos, the stock for this rodeo were personally selected from an array of stock contractors. This rodeo was one of the most historic rodeos in the country; it was an honor to have them here.

Our trailer was at the intersection where people would drive from the contestant's area to the front of the arena or to the back where the bucking chutes and announcers stand were. Just to the side of us were dozens of Indian tepees set up and displayed for people to walk through. Many of the occupants were in their official wardrobes. It was a busy place but I liked it because I could see our horses and I could people-watch.

Caleb was standing next to the trailer twirling a rope over his head then tossing it at a practice dummy. The rope swished around the horns then just as quickly swished off.

"Nice one," I teased as my gaze wandered to the arriving trailers. I had been watching for the Rawlins trailer all day and my breath caught when I finally saw them. There were two trucks but only one trailer that I recognized as Delaney's.

My heart raced in anticipation even though the vehicles turned and drove away from us then disappeared behind a concrete building. I wanted to run after them and talk to Brodie. We had talked in Lewiston, it wouldn't look that odd. Maybe talking to him wouldn't, but stalking him and running after him would, so I just turned my attention back to Caleb. We were here for days, I had to be patient.

"Where's mom and dad?" I asked.

"Meeting with all the other contractors," Caleb answered as he tossed the rope again, this time he pulled the slack of the rope and it tightened around the steer's horns.

"They need to get us involved in those," I sighed impatiently.

He shrugged as he coiled the rope and prepared for another throw.

"You should be involved right now. You're going to run the business someday. I'm too damn busy with finishing school and work."

"But you're going to be doing all my veterinarian work for free," I grinned.

"I think Nellie would miss the bucking horses," he smirked then glanced over his shoulder before making his throw. I followed his gaze to see the Rawlins family leading six horses toward the building to our right that was full of paneled stalls.

My heart pounded faster, eyes darting from one person to another, looking for Brodie. This was his last rodeo for the memorial for his friend, Craig. I hoped with all my might that he was able to ride his qualifying horse and make it to the short-go round on Saturday.

I had reviewed the stock draw for his round and was hoping he had drawn one of our horses. Not Iggy, because I wanted the horse to remain unridden, but the other three would give him a great chance of a high score. He had drawn a Sankey horse for bareback and a Calgary stallion for saddle bronc. They were good horses, NFR horses that were seasoned and champions. I truly believed he could get to the finals on both horses. That would be something.

"Who are you looking for?"

I turned with a jerk to Caleb, "No one, I was looking at their horses."

He turned to watch the Rawlins family as they made their way into the building.

"Why would they have six horses?" Caleb asked.

"It says in that podcast she does breakaway and barrels," I said innocently as if I hadn't listened to the podcasts dozens of times and stalked Brodie on the internet. "The big guy is Logan Rawlins, the world champion steer wrestler."

Caleb huffed, "I haven't been living under a rock, you know."

A chuckle escaped as I turned to him, "Just in a book."

"True," he sighed. "I should be in studying right now." With that, he tossed the rope over the dummy steer and walked into the trailer.

I sat and stared at the door of the barn waiting for the family to appear. I hadn't seen Brodie in the group so why was I watching for them? I needed to get a grip! A visit to the horses was in order. They didn't really need to be checked but what the hell else was I going to do?

Their water bucket was full and there was still hay on the ground. It was a warm 90-degree day and all four horses were laid out sleeping.

"Lazy horses," I whispered with a smile.

"Conserving energy to buck us off."

My heart nearly stopped, skinned tingled, and stomach a flutter; it was all I could do to keep from turning and jumping at him. That would have been a freakish thing to do.

So, I slowly turned and smiled at Brodie. His hair seemed longer, whiskers on his jaw thicker, but his eyes weren't at lost as they were in Lewiston.

"Not for you," I teased.

"You checked?" he asked in surprise.

Well, that was just damn embarrassing, but I just held the smile, "We always check to see who our horses drew for a rider."

He laughed and my heart nearly exploded at the sound.

"That's an interesting way of looking at it," He turned to the horses. "But I can see your point. Trying to get the horses a fair chance at a good ride so they can prove themselves."

I grinned, "Exactly."

"So, who has the pleasure of riding your unridden horse, Iggy?"

It made me swell with pride that Iggy was the horse he asked about.

"He is saddle bronc here and that would be Adler Spence."

"Huh," Brodie huffed then looked down at the sleeping horse. "Well, he's a…" He paused.

I chuckled, "Pretty much what Dad thought of him, too."

"At least in the first round, you have a chance with the unridden status remaining the same."

My grin widened, "Pretty much what I said to Dad."

We stood quietly for a moment watching the horses sleep. I was too tongue-tied and brain frazzled to think of anything to say.

"I was out for a walk after the ride and saw you standing here, so I thought I would come over and thank you again for talking with me last week."

I glanced up at him to see a warm smile.

"Anything or any time I can help, please let me know."

"Thank you," he nodded and looked toward the bleachers. "I love coming here. There is just something about this place that makes you feel like you've walked into history."

"This is my first time," I admitted. "The horses are starting to make names for themselves so we're getting invited to larger rodeos."

"These four have, for sure," he nodded and looked at the four sleeping horses. "How many do you have at home?"

"Right now, a hundred and eighty."

"Damn!" He huffed.

"Most are our homegrown horses, age 5 months to 6 years, and some older broodmares and bucking horses that we've purchased. We call them our legacy horses and name them after cities in Romania where Dad's family is from. We've also taken in a few retired older horses that just need pasture to wander in."

He looked around the area again. After a pause, he turned back to me, "You busy?"

My breath caught, and my stomach fluttered again, "Not really, I was just checking on the horses to give myself something to do."

552

"Want to go on a walk with me?"

I wanted to yell YES! But, I just smiled and nodded, "Sure, where to?"

"Today's rodeo is over and a lot of people have left already. I like to walk all the vendors before the weekend and mass of people arrive," he answered and turned away from the fence.

We walked toward the front of the arena.

"I've heard they have a lot."

"You haven't been yet?"

"No, just been hanging around the horses."

"Well, let me take you on a tour of the numerous ways to spend any extra money you might have in your pocket."

I laughed and followed him to the first group of vendors, where I bought a red and black wild rag scarf so I could remember the walk with him. Then there was a large over-the-shoulder bag covered in horses so I could carry all the treasures I found.

We walked, talked, and shopped for two hours. A dozen times I had to keep myself from reaching for his arm or hand or even just touching him.

Both of our phone alerts had beeped a dozen times but neither of us answered until we sat down on a bench with frozen lemonade drinks and hand-dipped corndogs.

Three texts from Dad: Where are you?

Text from Mom: River, if you don't answer your father, we are sending out the police.

Text from Caleb: Damn, Mom and Dad are starting to overreact so you better answer.

Text to all three: I am fine, just went shopping at all the vendors with a friend.

Text from Dad: Do NOT disappear like that again. What friend do you have in Pendleton?

Text from Mom: We were going to go together. Are you safe?

Text from Caleb: Now you've really done it. Dad's pissed and Mom's disappointed.

Text to all three: I am safe, I'm sorry but I was bored so I went shopping with a friend.

Text from Dad: Who?

Text from Mom: Who are you with?

Text from Caleb: Now you got them curious.

"Everything OK?" Brodie asked and slid his phone into his pocket.

"Yeah, I just disappeared on them and they were worried."

"Oh, sorry about that."

"Not your fault...sort of," I chuckled and when his eyes lit with a smile, my heart sighed and all I could do was grin at him.

"Well, let them know I will bring you back safe and sound."

"Just poorer," I giggled and sent the text as he chuckled.

Text to all three: I am with Brodie Rawlins, he will make sure I come back safe but broke.

Text from Dad: Good, he's respectable

I chuckled.

Text from Mom: I'll transfer $200 into your bank account. Have fun.

Text from Caleb: How the hell did you meet him? See if that tall brunette that was walking with the family this morning is single.

Text to Caleb: No, he's taken, we discussed that, his name is Logan and the little blonde is his girlfriend. ☺

Text from Caleb: Smartass

I laughed softly and looked up at Brodie.

"What?" he asked.

I shook my head, "Just a brother-sister joke."

He nodded with a grin and stood, "I have those with mine, too."

"We're twins so we have an overabundance of things to tease each other about. And, Mom is transferring more money into my bank account so we have more shopping to do." I grinned impishly.

"Good thing, because we're only halfway through them."

"Seriously?" I gasped.

We walked, talked, and shopped for another hour.

The best part of the day was at Hamley's western store in downtown Pendleton. Brodie decided he needed a new cowboy hat and I was able to stare at him to give my opinion. I liked the second one he tried on but still had him try another dozen.

"What about you?" he asked as we waited for a man to shape his new hat.

I stared at him a moment and thought, why not?

"I just have my riding ones at home and the one I brought for the rodeo was just the cleanest one I could find."

And so we spent another half hour on my hat. The fact that I could still stare at him while he was accessing my new hat was just a bonus I would never get tired of.

We walked out of the store wearing our new hats, walking just a bit taller, and with satisfied smiles. This truly was a day I wasn't going to forget.

"So, your family is here all week," Brodie stated when we stopped at the base of a giant statue of a man riding a bucking horse. It was right by the arena.

"Yeah, we pull out right after the final rodeo Saturday."

"Do you already have tickets?"

"Yeah, we're in the Z zone to the west of the bucking chutes. Up on top, it overlooks the horses but we're down just a couple rows up from the arena. I'll have a great view of Iggy dislodging Alder Spence."

We both chuckled then stood quietly next to the statue. I so desperately wanted to take a picture with him in front of it but was not going to ask.

"This is your first time here," he finally said. "You should have a picture in front of this famous Pendleton statue with the arena in the background." He set his bags down and pulled his phone from his pocket. "You go pose and I'll take it."

"Great idea," I dropped my bags and with hands-on hips posed with a wide grin.

He took my picture then started to walk to me when an older couple stopped him.

"Would you like us to take a picture of the two of you?" The man asked.

Yes! Yes! Yes! Yes! A thousand times yes!

"Thanks," Brodie handed them his phone and walked over to stand next to me.

We weren't touching, but we were next to each other and I was going to have this wonderful picture of our day together.

When he retrieved his camera and thanked the couple, he looked down at the image.

He lifted the phone closer then his fingers slid across the screen. He laughed.

"What?" I asked nervously, hoping I didn't have a weird look on my face. I would hate for him to have that.

The light of laughter was shining in his eyes when he looked up at me. With his black shirt and hat, long hair, and the thick dark whiskers around his grin he was old-western handsome and my body tingled. I so wanted a picture of that!

"Both our eyes are closed," he handed the phone to me.

"Well damn," I muttered and took a close look at the image. We looked happy, comfortable with each other, and asleep.

"Let's fix that," he took the phone back and lifted it in the air for a selfie.

We had to stand closer together with me leaned into him to get the shot and my whole body trembled in excitement as our bodies touched. It was not a surprise to see my wide grin and flushed face in the final image.

He handed me his phone, "Put your number in it and I'll send you the pictures."

"That better include the one with our eyes shut," I chuckled and typed my number into his phone.

"But of course," He laughed and started picking up our piles of bags.

My parents and brother were sitting in chairs in front of the trailer when we arrived. All three grinned when they saw us.

"Nice hat, Sis," Caleb nodded in appreciation.

"Hamley's?" Dad asked as they all stood.

"Yes," I set the bags down on the outdoor table and turned. "This is my shopping partner, Brodie Rawlins, and Brodie this is my brother Caleb and my parents Gloria and Adam Westmoreland."

Brodie's hand went to my mother first, "I'm going to assume you are Gloria."

We all chuckled and from the look on my mother's face as he shook her hand, he had instantly charmed her.

"An intelligent bronc rider does exist," Dad grinned as he shook Brodie's hand.

"Who knew?" Caleb added then shook the outstretched hand.

I blushed in a bit of mortification but Brodie just laughed.

"And how did you two meet?" Mom asked him.

Brodie looked at me with a raised brow then turned back, "She helped me out a bit last week in Lewiston so I came by this morning to thank her again."

"And we went for a walk to shop," I added and hoped they wouldn't ask about Lewiston. Of course, I had not told anyone about our encounter, not even Caleb.

"Do you have time for a beer?" Dad asked.

"Wish I could," Brodie answered. "But I'm a bit late for a couple of interviews I promised and my family is about ready to send out a search party."

"What?" I gasped. "I didn't mean to…"

"You didn't, River," he said smoothly. "I was enjoying our visit and didn't want to stop it for another damn interview, which will be nothing more than them asking me my feelings about Craig's loss."

"Oh," I whispered and flushed as the guilt washed over me. I had enjoyed our day so much that I had forgotten about Craig.

Brodie turned back to my family and nodded, "It was nice meeting you and hopefully sometime in the next day or so I can take you up on that beer."

"Anytime," All three of them answered.

Brodie turned back and looked down at me, "Thank you again, River."

I smiled, "Thank you for giving me something to do."

He chuckled then turned away.

I did not want him to leave. I wanted to help him. He was only twenty yards away when I jogged after him.

"Brodie?"

He stopped and turned. Before the smile appeared, I saw a glimpse of that loss in his eyes again. I nearly burst out in tears.

"Is something wrong?" he asked.

"Well, no," I said quickly. It hadn't been that far of a jog to catch up with him but I felt out of breath. "I just wanted to tell you, if you find you need someone to talk to, please call me. You have my number now."

His shoulders lowered and the smile softened, "I appreciate that."

"And," I smiled encouragingly. "I'll tell you the story about my name."

"Really?"

"Yes, it has quite the history."

"Alright, I may just have to call to hear the story."

"Anytime, anywhere, just call," I whispered. It took all the strength in me not to wrap my arms around him and just hold on. I hated the fact that the loss of Craig was so close to the emotional surface. "Good luck tomorrow…this whole week."

"Thanks," he sighed. "I look forward to talking with you again."

We both hesitantly turned away from each other. I wanted to stay with him; to hold him or just look at him. I wanted to touch him.

To hide my frustration of not being with him, as soon as I arrived back to the trailer, I went through each bag and showed my parents what I had purchased. Caleb had already returned to his studies.

Luckily, my bed in the trailer didn't face the road that led to Brodie or I would have been staring down it all night long.

In the morning, I had two messages from him. They were sent at 2:13 in the morning. He was going to be so tired.

One message simply said: Thank you for the walk. The second message contained three pictures; one by myself, the one with our eyes closed, and the wonderful selfie where we look so damned relaxed and happy. I wanted that moment back and must have stared at the picture for an hour before I finally rose to start the day.

As I walked to the horse pens containing our four horses, Iggy's head rose as he looked to me. He instantly started walking to the panel to greet me.

My hand rose to him but a hand on my wrist pushed it away.

"Don't touch him!"

CHAPTER FIFTY

I jumped back with the memory of the older man in Kennewick grabbing me. I turned ready for battle only to stop myself quickly.

"You know better than that," Dad grumbled and motioned me away from the horse.

"But…" I sighed.

I glanced over my shoulder at Iggy who was bouncing his head over the panel as if calling me back.

With a groan, I walked back to the trailer. I flopped down on the sofa and watched Mom clean the breakfast dishes and Caleb reading his veterinarian books.

"You two are boring," I whispered.

Caleb didn't say anything or even move.

Mom turned and looked at me with a raised brow, "You want to do the dishes the rest of the time we are here?"

I gave her a teasing smile and shook my head.

"Then we have a couple of hours before the rodeo starts so you can show me around all those vendors you shopped yesterday."

I sat straight up, "Can you transfer another $100 for me?"

She answered with a roll of the eyes.

After more shopping, with Caleb studying, we all three stood in the bleachers as the national anthem was sung and the horse and rider carrying the flag made their way around the enormous arena. I was stunned the first time I walked through the gates by how big it was. I had seen pictures and watched videos so I knew the field was grass surrounded by a dirt track. I just wasn't expecting the size.

One of the best parts was when an Indian in full regalia rode in riding a striking black and white paint horse whose name was Chinook. It made my heart ache for our big old stallion even if they didn't look anything alike.

The bareback event finally began and I anxiously watched each ride and for any glimpses of Brodie. He finally appeared behind the Sankey horse known as Sozo. Elbows on knees, hands clasped under my chin, I silently prayed as the chute was opened. It was a great ride; matching spur to buck.

"That looked good," Caleb clapped.

My heart was racing, fingers hurting from clenching so hard, and my whole body had tightened into a ball.

"Relax, River," Mom nudged me with an elbow.

I huffed and shook the tension out of my body.

"But his bareback rides are for Craig," I reminded her. "I just so badly wanted to see him ride and make it to the championship round."

A score of 87 was announced.

"That puts him in second place including the scores from yesterday's rodeo," Caleb said.

"I don't think they have the horse stock left for tomorrow that can get all the riders past an 87," Mom said.

"Unless there is a miracle," I whispered.

We watched quietly until the saddle bronc riders appeared on the back of the chutes.

"Should we bet on how fast Iggy tosses Alder Spence," Caleb asked as he read the day-sheet.

Mom and I just chuckled and watched Dad helping prepare the horse.

Ten minutes later, Iggy launched out of the chute and when his front hooves hit the dirt, Alder Spence was right next to them.

I sighed, "At least last week, Tate gave him almost a full ride so the judges could really score him."

"Seven rides last year and thirteen this year...all unridden," Caleb said. "And he had a horse score of 44 last week with Tate."

"But he's not going to have a chance to be chosen for the NFR at this rate," Mom added.

That just made my gut hurt.

"There is a chance he can still be drawn for the championship round on Saturday," I whispered.

We spent the evening at the Happy Canyon performance.

Friday, when Brodie appeared at the back of the chutes ready for his bronc ride, my heart was pounding in my chest.

"It would be pretty cool if he made it to finals for both events," Caleb muttered.

"Yeah," I sighed and watched Brodie's every move.

Fizzling Dud was first in the broncs and Dad was helping his rider, Cody DeMoss, prepare for the ride. The announcer was making fun of the horse's name and teasing Cody.

When Brodie walked past him, Dad looked up and they nodded to each other. It was a bit bizarre seeing them interacting.

"I can't imagine riding stock of this quality and having to do both events," Mom said. "That would be some major stress on the body."

"To go along with his mental stress by finishing his memorial for his friend," Caleb added.

My heart trembled at the thought of the amount of stress Brodie was going through. It was a good thing he had such a close family.

My eyes bounced from Brodie to Fizzling Dud then back until they finally opened the gate for Cody and the horse. The horse ran out his normal two strides then his back hooves flew in the air with the power in the kick stretching his legs far back into a straight line. Every third buck, the horse would almost turn 90 degrees to the left. It was repeated until the horn blared in the air.

I exhaled sharply.

"That's his best yet," Caleb said excitedly. "Those kicks are stronger."

"His power is growing," Mom nodded.

An 89 was announced and we all three cheered! Cody ran to the back of the chutes, he appeared on the podium and shook Dad's hand while both men grinned proudly.

"He's been consistent this year," Caleb nodded. "In the 40's with almost every ride."

"Maybe we'll be at the NFR with him too," I said and watched Brodie stepping over the chutes.

"Too?" Caleb chuckled.

"I'm not giving up on Iggy," I answered and stared at Brodie.

"It'll be interesting to see if Flying Betty can pull it off," Mom added.

"Who did Brodie draw today?" Caleb asked and lifted the day-sheet to read.

"Tiger Warrior from Calgary," I reminded him. "He's good...NFR good...big ducks and dives."

We grew quiet as the announcer made the same speech about Brodie's memorial for Craig we had heard in Kennewick, Lewiston, and the day before.

"How sad," a woman behind us said.

"Just tragic," another added.

"Do you think that affects him when he's in the chute?" Caleb asked.

I didn't answer. My mind went to Brodie sitting behind the building in Lewiston. My heart ached for him.

"No matter what happens," Mom sighed, "at least after tomorrow night, he'll have the rides off his shoulders and maybe he can move on."

"He's qualified for the NFR, though," Caleb reminded her.

"But that is different than this," She said.

In a way, I agreed with her, but I didn't think he would be able to move on until he rode his last bucking horse; whether this year or in ten years. Craig would always be there with him.

The chute opened and my whole body clenched as I prayed. This time, as Tiger Warrior bucked and Brodie spurred, my body lifted and fell with them.

The horn blared and Brodie's hand went to the rein. It was a wild race for the pick-up men to catch Tiger Warrior as he ran across the large field.

Finally, Brodie slid onto one of the pick-up men's horses but had a hard drop to the ground when he fell.

"Oh, damn," Mom whispered.

I stared and willed him to rise without being hurt. It probably didn't help, but Brodie wasn't limping when he walked to the large crowd of cowboys that were gathered in the arena.

An 86.5 was announced and we all gasped.

"That should have been more," Caleb huffed.

"You think he made it to the finals?" Mom asked.

"We'll see in three more rides," I sighed.

At the end of those rides, Brodie had qualified in both bareback and saddle bronc with his sister and brother qualifying in their events.

"That's going to be a big day for them tomorrow," Caleb said.

At the end of the rodeo, just before the wild cow milking event, Brodie was still in the arena with the large group of men. I had no doubt he was hiding away from anyone wanting to interview him. As the group of men walked toward the gate, I watched Brodie. A number of the other bronc riders had encircled him as they walked by. It made my heart warm that they were protecting him.

As they walked off the grass arena and into the dirt, Brodie's head turned toward us. His eyes were searching…until they met mine. We had just a moment to share a smile before he disappeared.

I didn't see him again, but at 10:40 when my parents were out with friends and Caleb was studying again, I received a text.

Text from Brodie: Is it too late for that story?

Text to Brodie: Of course not, give me two minutes then call.

"I'm going to check on the horses," I said to Caleb and stood quickly and slid on a hooded sweatshirt and my mud boots. Still in jeans, I was presentable as I stepped out of the trailer. It was dark out but many lights around the rodeo grounds lit the way to the horse pens. I could hear people laughing and an occasional whoop and holler as people celebrated the night.

I was halfway to the horses when my phone rang.

"Congratulations," I answered with a smile.

He chuckled, "Thanks."

"You OK?"

"Physically fine, mentally tired," he answered.

I was so glad he felt he could tell me the truth.

"Do you want to meet at the horses and talk in person?"

"Can't...I'm not there."

"Really?"

"Yeah," he sighed heavily. "Just a bit too much staying there...expecting Craig to be there. A reporter showed up wanting to talk about him again, so Dad, Martin, and I drove to a friend's place out of town. We won't be back until just before the rodeo."

"Well, that just sucks," I grumbled. "Don't they realize just how rude and inhuman that is?"

"I don't think they care. They just want to be the ones that tell the tragic tale."

"I'm sorry..." I leaned against the panels of the pen with Iggy slowly walking over to put his nose in my open hand. "So, that part is over and we don't have to talk about it anymore."

"Thanks."

"Well then, let me tell you the story about my name."

"I'm sitting here on the front porch of the house, looking out to a hundred head of Herefords in the moonlight, and waiting to be entertained."

I could visualize him with the smile on his face but the chair he was sitting in was on our family front porch at home instead.

"Well, my great-great-grandfather immigrated to the States from Romania. He didn't speak English, at all, so when he was on the boat coming over the ocean, he met a few men that tried to teach him. They kept telling him that he didn't want to stay on the coast they landed on, by New York, but he needed to go west past the Mississippi River where there was more land to buy. They had him repeat the sentence over and over again so when they landed, he could find help getting passage to keep going." I paused.

"I'm hanging on your every word," he chuckled.

I smiled and ran my hand down Iggy's nose, "When they arrived at the coast, they had to register, and the man behind the desk asked my great-great-grandfather his name. Of course, he had no idea what they were asking him so he just repeated the sentence the men on the boat taught him. But, he was flustered and didn't say it right. Instead, all he got out was river, west, more, land."

Brodie laughed, "So the guy wrote down River Westmoreland."

"Yes! My grandmother's name was River Westmoreland to carry on the story, and then mine or Caleb's grandchild will be named it, too."

"Every other generation," Brodie chuckled. "So, River Westmoreland, what was your great-great-grandfather's real name?"

"Raajyashree Iordanescu," I tried to say it with the given accent but I knew I messed it up every time.

Brodie laughed. A deep down from the gut laugh and my heart soared.

"I'm going to say you lucked out by the whole confusion," He finally said.

"When he finally found someone that spoke Romanian, they had a real good laugh about it and he decided to keep his new name for his new country."

"And where did he settle down?"

"He made it to California, to the coast, then turned back and settled in southern Arizona where it was warm all the time."

"What happened to him after that? What did he do for a living?"

We spoke for an hour as I distracted him from his reality with my great-great-grandfather's life. I tried to make it as entertaining of a story as I could to keep him laughing. I wished we were sitting on that front porch together.

When I heard him yawn, I looked at my phone. It was midnight.

"Ah, I heard that," I teased. "And you have a big day tomorrow so you need your beauty sleep."

He huffed, "I'm a bit scruffy to be considered a beauty."

"Someone once told me that real beauty comes from the inside, not what you look like."

"Damn, you got me on that one."

"Your dad teach you that?"

"Nah, Logan, my brother. He was a bit of a...well...a man-whore when it came to the women."

I chuckled and thought of his brother. With his height, looks, and aura of masculinity I could see that.

"He had women coming at him all the time and he wasn't one to turn them away until the last couple years. Three or four years ago, he found a girl that he liked and tried to settle down a bit but as beautiful as she was on the outside, she was a bitch on the inside."

"Is that what made him break it off?"

"No, she did," he huffed. "Logan was going to stick it out for some damn reason, but Anna couldn't take all the women throwing themselves at him...especially the ones that he'd already been with."

"That would take a strong person."

"Or one that really understands Logan, accepts his past, and will stand by his side like Lacie Jae does."

"She does the podcast," I nodded to the horses and thought of her approaching me in Kennewick. It took a strong person to reach out and try to help a stranger.

"Yeah, she's a bit fiery when it comes to Logan, and she's had to battle the same brain-dead, stupid women that just don't get the message that he's very taken now."

"But she's doing OK with it?"

"She had a couple of rough moments but we talked her way through it. Lacie Jae is cute as a bug on the outside and will be a great beauty as she gets older but her inside is where her beauty comes from. Logan saw it from the moment they met."

"And he told you, so you don't make the same mistake?"

Brodie chuckled, "I'm sure there were a number of the women he slept with that he would consider a mistake."

I laughed again and he yawned again.

"Alright, now you need to go to bed and rest up for tomorrow."

"Yeah…" he sighed. "I'm having that depression problem again…it's heavy. I just feel like if I don't get the horse rode tomorrow, then I will let everyone down."

"Oh, Brodie, that isn't it," I sighed and felt the tears well again. "It's not about you winning or even making it to the 8 seconds. It's about your love for Craig and your commitment to ride the Big Four for him. No one will care if you get bucked off or a low score. They care that you are riding for your friend."

There was silence.

"Brodie?" I whispered.

"You're right," he exhaled slowly.

"Quit thinking about everyone else and just get on the horse and ride. Enjoy it…have fun with the ride like you guys used to do."

"That is the part I've been missing the last couple weeks," he whispered. "I haven't enjoyed it. I've just ridden with the stress of it all weighing me down."

"Both rides tomorrow," I said earnestly. "Just enjoy them, let the fun memories take over and ride with those."

"Damn," he sighed. "Thanks, River…I really needed to hear that. I really needed to know that it was OK for me to enjoy it and not continue this…I guess funeral that I have dragged on."

"Who did you draw for tomorrow?"

He chuckled, "You didn't hear?"

"No, Caleb has had his head in his books. Dad and Mom were out to dinner…I haven't checked…who?" My heart caught at the thought of him riding Iggy.

"A Sankey horse again and a Westmoreland horse."

I could hear the smile in his voice.

"What ones?" I exhaled anxiously.

"Black Tie, who won a round here last year and Henry the First who, I hear, is NFR qualified last year…actually, both of them were."

I sighed in relief then instantly rejoiced, "Both horses are great and will give you a bit of a taste of what you're in for in Vegas in a couple of months."

He chuckled, "Yeah…I have my work cut out for me tomorrow."

"Well, I totally believe you can ride both."

There was silence.

"You believe and I believe and we'll end this call on that," he said in a very low voice. "I'll see you tomorrow after the rodeo."

"Good…"

The phone was already dead.

I was still rubbing on Iggy when the call ended. I hesitated in surprise that it ended so fast then texted Dad.

Text to Dad: Who did the horse's draw? Besides Henry who drew Brodie

Text from Dad: Flying Betty drew Orin Larsen, Iggy drew Mitch Pollock

Whoa…both great riders. Mitch would have a chance at giving Iggy a shot of showing off his buck.

I looked at all three horses standing quietly in their pens; Iggy, Betty, and Henry with Brodie, Orin, and Mitch. This was going to be a good rodeo.

CHAPTER FIFTY ONE

First thing in the morning, I printed off the day sheet and looked at the order of riders. Betty and Henry were bareback horses riding 3rd and 7th. Dad was going to be busy bouncing between the two. Iggy was saddle bronc and the first ride. Thank goodness! I wouldn't have to sweat through all the others waiting for him. Brodie and Black Tie were the last to ride.

I glanced outside for the weather; blue sky with just a few clouds but the temperature on my phone said it was only 55 degrees.

I dressed in a bright red shirt so Brodie could see me in the stands then slid on a dark blue vest for the morning. As I stepped out of the trailer, I slid a hand through my hair to push it to the back then placed the new black hat over the top to hold it in place.

I thought of Brodie and our trying on hats. I had to look at the pictures from the shopping trip again before I forced myself to stop and get to work.

Not once, did I even get a glimpse of any of the Rawlins family before Mom, Caleb, and I made our way up the bleachers.

As I stood for the National Anthem to play and the prayer to be recited, I searched the bucking chutes for Brodie. I saw just a flash of him just as he bent over, setting the riggin on the chute next to Henry the First. Dad was standing next to him when the first horse bust out of the chute. He was with Orin when the second horse and rider made their ride.

My heart raced, fingers twisted together, and feet tapped on the ground. Just as Orin Larsen rose above Flying Betty, my elbows hit my knees and fingers came together just under my chin for my silent prayer.

When the gate opened, Flying Betty lived up to her name by flying out of the chute then landing with a high kick to the back, then a buck with all four legs high in the air. They repeated the kick then the jump across the field with Orin matching her buck by spur stroke until the horn blew then he flew in the air with a thud of a landing.

I gasped right along with the crowd until he finally, slowly came to a stand with two men helping him.

Flying Betty received 45 points to match Orin's 44 for an 89 point ride.

"Yes!" I screamed and clapped for the pair.

"Damn, she flew!" Mom yelled and was looking at the platform behind the chutes.

Dad had already moved over to stand with Brodie behind Henry the First and they were both grinning broadly as they watched the blond horse fly around the arena. Even from a distance, I could see there was something different about Brodie today. He seemed more relaxed. I hoped telling him to have fun with the rides was the right thing to do.

As soon as the horse exited the arena, all focus went back to the next rider while Brodie and Dad prepared Henry for the ride.

Three more chutes were opened but no ride matched Orin's 89.

Then, too soon but not soon enough, it was time for Brodie's last ride for Craig. The announcer was telling the audience of the tragic loss and commemorative rides again so I just tuned him out and watched Dad and Brodie.

Brodie stepped over the chute to hover over the large horse then carefully slide down. My elbows to knees, fingers to chin position was being perfected at this rodeo. My body clenched as Brodie nodded and the gate was swung open.

Henry leapt out two strides then his fierce, high kick with nose touching the ground was repeated in a large circle to the left until the last few seconds when he surprised everyone with a twist and a turn to the right. They were beautiful high fierce kicks and Brodie's spurring and free hand kept up with him until the horn blared. The pick-up men were suddenly at his side and he was reaching for them. He slid to the ground and celebrated with both fists flying in the air, screaming 'yay, yay, yay' over and over until he pointed to the end of the arena. He took off his hat and threw it. Hands and eyes to the sky he screamed, "I BELIEVE".

My heart was racing, feet dancing, voice screaming, and hands beating together.

He had completed his memorial to Craig and I knew he could care less to what the points were but 88 points was announced over the cheering of the crowd giving him a standing ovation.

When the final ride of the bareback riding was completed, Orin won the title and the Westmoreland Stock Contractor's Henry the First won the bareback horse of the rodeo. The horse's chances of making it back to the National Finals Rodeo just increased and Mom, Caleb and I shouted and hollered!

"Got to have a good rider on them," Caleb said proudly.

"Now we hope Mitch can get Iggy showcased," Mom nodded with a glance to me.

I was still watching Brodie as he made his way out of the arena. At the last moment, he turned and looked right up at me. His hat had been replaced on his head, and he grinned as he tipped it to me.

There was that new light in his eyes as I happily grinned back.

"Iggy will be the first out," I finally said and turned back to the arena. Orin was still receiving the awards for winning the rodeo. "Just have to get past those damn timed events."

Mom and Caleb chuckled.

I wanted to watch Brodie's brother in steer wrestling so I remained in the seat while Mom and Caleb journeyed out into the mass of people to find us lunch.

His brother was second in the rodeo after the steer took him for a long drag in the grass.

The saddle bronc riders began appearing behind the bucking chutes. Brodie was one of the last to walk up behind his horse, Black Tie. Dad was already working with Mitch in preparing Iggy. They didn't do much because Iggy hated to be messed with in the chute.

Elbows on knees, chin in hands, praying silently, I waited. Even though the chute was tall and I could barely see some of the horses, Iggy was tall, and I could see him standing completely still as he looked through the slats of the gate and into the arena. I was becoming worried that he was going to repeat his refusal to come out of the chute.

"Please, please, please..." I whispered.

My breath caught when the gate swung open, and Iggy launched himself high up in the air and landed with a spine jolting thud and the crowd roaring in surprise. His front hooves went in the air then as he was going back down, his back hooves launched high and stretched back. At a point, he was completely flying in the air stretched out and four hooves off the ground. Another launch in the air and his shoulder rolled to the right and his hindquarters going left. Three more times he repeated the twisting buck. His front hooves hit the ground with his nose touching the dirt between them and his back hooves were high above his back. He was in a near vertical line when Mitch's hand loosened from the rein. When Iggy's front hooves hit the ground again, Mitch was tumbling off the side. The horn blared as his back hit the ground.

"Son-of-a-bitch!" Caleb screamed.

The crowd was erupting in applause as Mitch slowly stood.

My attention was on Iggy as he bucked across the field until one of the pick-up men was able to get close enough to release the flank strap safely. It was as if the man had waved the start your engine flag at Nascar. Iggy hit the dirt track that circled the arena and became a racehorse. He flew with hooves pounding on the ground, dirt flying and people scrambling to get out of his way. Long full strides and the horse outran the pick-up-men trying to catch him.

The rein dangling from the halter hit the ground then flew back into his legs. I squealed in fear and anticipation of his tripping and breaking a leg or neck. I jumped to my feet with my whole body ready to run out after him.

After a quarter-lap, the pick-up men stopped chasing him and rode to the middle of the arena and waited for the dark stallion to stop.

The rope hit the ground again, then bounced high enough to flip over his neck and safely away from his legs. My heart was racing nearly as fast as he was.

One lap around and the horse slowed to a prancing jog as if he was celebrating his derby win. His body was shiny with sweat and his mane and tail bounced and flew around him. The rope slid from his neck and dangled dangerously close to his legs. My fingers were at my temples in anticipation of covering my eyes if he went down.

The pick-up men began loping toward him as he made his way under the announcer's stand and in front of the bucking chutes. I quickly ran down the steps to the edge of the arena.

"Iggy!" I yelled but the crowd was cheering for the bucking racehorse.

"Iggy!" I yelled again, leaned over the rail, and waved my arms.

He turned his head and looked right at me. I would swear the horse danced and pranced across the dirt as if he was showing off with a 'did you see what I did, Mom?' attitude. The pick-up men were right behind him and as the horse approached me, they were able to grab the rein that was dangling from his halter.

"Damn horse," one of the men grumbled and ran the horse through the exit gate and disappeared.

I ran down the bleachers, down the steps, and back to the pens.

Iggy was still in the stripping chute as they released the saddle and halter from him before letting him trot to his pen. The other three horses were excitedly waiting for him and my heart was pounding as furiously as Iggy's sides were heaving.

As I grabbed the release to get in the pen, I could see Dad jogging toward us.

"Lady, get the hell out of there!" A man yelled.

I turned to him with a glare as I stepped into the pen. "He's my horse and I'll do what I want." I was so damned tired of men telling me to get away from my own horse.

I turned away and ignored him as Iggy jogged to my side. I began walking circles around the perimeter of the pen and the horse followed.

"Keep him moving until he cools off," Dad said as he leaned against the rail. "Then we'll check to see if he hurt himself."

I just nodded and nearly had to jog to keep in front of the puffing excited horse.

"Reminded me of your race across the field with Chinook running after Destiny," Dad called out.

I smiled and nodded but my whole body was tense; the anxiety was bubbling through me. It took five minutes of walking before the horse began to slow down and his breathing to return to normal. When he stopped on his own, I slowly walked to him and put a hand on his shoulder.

"He was walking normal, so...that's good," Dad said. I knew he was just as nervous as I was. "He'll be OK, but will be sore from the exertion in the morning."

"More from the racehorse run than the bucking," I nodded then startled as I looked at Dad. "That was a hell of an outing."

Dad nodded with wide eyes, "Yes, it was. Still undefeated, but Mitch came close and Iggy showed them what he's got."

"I can't wait to see the video! What was his score?" I asked as I left the horse's side and walked to the gate.

"River, I was scrambling just as fast as you were to get out here and make sure he was alright," He shook his head. "I know they announced it, but my brain was full of prayer the damn horse didn't trip on the rein."

"Mom and Caleb will know," I sent a text.

Dad was still watching Iggy with an occasional look back at the bucking chutes.

"I don't want to leave him either, but I want to watch Brodie," I bit my lip in concern.

"Here," he took off his pass and handed it to me. "I've been back there enough times I shouldn't have a problem. Stay here with Iggy and make sure he's alright. Call me if he lays down right away."

"But…"

"When it's Brodie's turn, come up the back way to the platform and stay on the opposite side of the chutes so he doesn't see you. You can come up and watch then come back here."

"Ok," I nodded anxiously as he walked away.

I watched the horses for three rides and the cheering from the crowd.

Text from Mom: He didn't make the 8

Text to Mom: Iggy's score mom, he'll still get scored whether it's a full 8 or not

Text from Mom: Yes, sorry, I knew that

Nothing… for three minutes, I listened to the crowd and stared at my phone.

"Our last rider of the day…" Boomed through the speakers.

I turned and ran for the back of the chutes. I made my way up and peeked around the corner to see where Brodie was then stepped up to hide behind one of the bareback riders, Trenten Montero.

My phone alert went off just as the chute was opened.

Black Tie, a big bay horse, carried Brodie out into the arena and his powerful kicks brought cheers from the crowd and shouts from behind the chutes. Body quaking kicks, high fast spurring from Brodie, and the pair bucked their way to the middle of the arena as the buzzer went off.

"He did it," someone down the chutes said. "Son-of-a-bitch, he placed in all 8 rides."

"Twelve if you count the qualifying rounds in Kennewick and here," Someone said.

"Man, that's some heart," Trenten huffed.

Tears rose as Brodie's arms flew over his head. Over and over, they flew in the air and the crowd grew louder. His brother was there, and nearly threw him in the air as a celebration, before Brody turned to his sister for an embrace. Then a fist pumped to the sky as the announcer called out the score: 90 points.

The crowd went wild as Brodie was announced the winner of the Saddle Bronc.

He ran for the gate where the horse that would carry the winner around for a victory lap was waiting. It already had Brodie's new prize saddle on its back.

"That kid has fucking heart," another man said.

"I'm impressed and proud," Trenten nodded.

Tears rose as I listened to the men talk about Brodie. I was so glad I was able to be on the chutes to hear their comments.

Brodie rode the horse across the grass-covered arena to the people waiting to give him the awards and take pictures.

"I didn't get to go to the funeral," a man on my right said.

"Me either," chorused from the men.

"He gave his friend one hell of a send-off," Trenten shook his head.

"Well, we should too," another man said. "Let Brodie know we understand what he went through and give Craig the send-off he should have gotten at the funeral."

"And how do we do that?" The man on my left asked.

"We'll give him the procession that he deserves...a salute to Craig and what Brodie did for him," Trenten declared. "Follow me."

All the men began to descend down the front of the chutes and out into the arena. I followed anxiously and looked for my dad. He was there, too. A line was formed where the dirt hit the grass and cowboy hats were lowered to their chests. I glanced down the line to see all the cowboys that had been sitting in the arena were also lining up with hats on chests. People were flowing out of the gates.

By the time Brodie started his victory lap, the whole length of the arena in front of the chutes was full of people with heads bowed and hats to chests.

As the announcer spoke of Craig's loss again, and Brodie came around the first corner, his horse slowed to a trot as he crossed in front of all the people saluting him and his friend. I was not the only person in line shedding tears.

Brodie wore dark sunglasses and his hair was flowing back in the wind as one hand held the reins and the other held his hat. He passed the procession at a trot with his head turned as if looking at each person as he rode by. I was wiping away tears as he neared. He smiled and nodded then rode by.

The crowd was cheering as he made the final turns, and everyone returned to their positions.

I jogged down to find Dad.

"Our job is done in the arena," he said and slid an arm around my shoulders. We walked to the exit gate together. "That, River, was one of the best moments I've seen in rodeo."

"Me, too," I whispered and watched as Brodie rode out of the arena and into the arms of his family. There were cameras everywhere.

Dad and I quietly walked past them and to Iggy. He was eating as if nothing had happened.

"Did you find out what he scored?" Dad asked.

"Oh! Mom texted," I pulled out my phone.

I stared at the number long enough, Dad leaned over my shoulder to look.

Neither of us spoke, we just turned as Iggy lowered to the ground and rolled onto his back for a good scratch.

"They have to choose him now," I whispered and gripped the phone tightly.

CHAPTER FIFTY TWO

As the rodeo continued, we finished cleaning the pens as best we could around the horses still waiting for their ride home. I watched Dad as I backed up the horse trailer to the horse's pen. He waved me to a halt and my gaze immediately wandered the grounds.

There were still people watching the departure process and others were waiting in line to get autographs from the cowboys and cowgirls that had ridden.

I hadn't seen Brodie since his win but I did hear over the speakers that his sister had won the barrel race.

Through the panels and across the pens, I could see a side-by-side ATV slowly making its way from the bleachers. I recognized Craig's dad driving while Lacie Jae and her sister were riding in the back, holding the two awarded saddles and trophies. All three of them looked unhappy.

My heart sunk; that couldn't be good for Brodie.

His father appeared in his wheelchair, then Logan and Delaney. They were slowly making their way toward the contestant's area. All three stopped and turned back to the bleachers where Brodie suddenly appeared. With head down, he was walking slowly, each step seeming to be weighted down. I recognized the box that held the prized trophy buckle in his hand. Halfway to his family, his head finally rose.

He stopped next to them, and his father's hand reached for his. After a moment, Delaney stepped forward and wrapped Brodie in her arms. Logan encircled them all in his arms.

The family stood together in a solemn embrace as the tears slowly slid down my cheeks.

"You going to get out and help?" Dad appeared at the window.

My gaze didn't leave the family. My chest ached for them.

"Damn," Dad whispered. "Maybe now they can move on."

"I have to say goodbye to him."

"I understand, River. Let's get the horses loaded and out of the other contractor's way then we'll go say our goodbyes."

He opened my door and it took all my strength to look away from the Rawlins family.

They were gone when we shut the gate to the horse trailer with the horses safely inside. With my parents up front and Caleb and I in the back seat, we moved slowly down the road and closer to where we knew the family was parked.

We stopped next to a net backdrop of a baseball field.

My phone alert rang out, and I quickly pulled it from my pocket. My heart was racing in anticipation.

Text from Brodie: Are you still here?

Text to Brodie: Yes, just stopped by the baseball field and were going to walk down to your trailer to say goodbye.

Text from Brodie: We're the only trailers left here, you can bring yours down. Plenty of room to turn around.

The Rawlins' trailers were backed up to the building but separated enough from each other that a dozen lawn chairs and a couple of tables were set up between them. Roping dummies set along the back. The horses were attached to the outside of the trailers and the family was sitting in the chairs. Except for Brodie; he was standing in front of the trailers watching us. My heart raced in anticipation.

Dad drove past their trailers to make a large loop and return to park right in front of them.

Our four horses whinnied, causing their six horses to call out.

As I stepped out of the truck, a loud bang echoed from our trailer. I turned back to Dad.

"It's Iggy; I'll calm him down."

I glanced over my shoulder to Brodie as I made my way back to the trailer and stepped up on the rail.

"Calm down," I told the horse. He turned his head, and I could see his whole body relax. "We're headed home, and you can run across your pastures again."

"Problems?" Brodie asked from behind me.

"No," I stepped down. "He is in a separated stall up front away from the others and he doesn't like being separated from Betty."

"He's a stallion, right?"

"Yes, and we don't want any Iggy-Betty babies yet," I smiled and faced him.

I looked right up into his warm brown eyes, and all I wanted to do was throw my arms around him and hold on. Instead, I shoved my hands into my vest pockets to keep from reaching out and touching him.

"Congratulations," I grinned at him.

"Thanks," he sighed. "I'm not sure which I'm happier about, winning or getting it over with."

Truthful, I liked that about him.

I stopped at a distance I knew the group at the trailer couldn't hear and turned to look up at him.

"Do you want my honest opinion?" I asked.

"Sure...of course," he answered with brows together in concern.

"Say that to me, but don't say it in front of anyone who will go to the media and repeat it," he smiled slightly so I continued. "Saying you're glad it's over puts a damper on the whole accomplishment, and that is what it is, Brodie. A huge accomplishment that everyone standing on that field with hats to chest understood and saluted you for."

He nodded with a sigh, "That's what Dad said too, and I understand. I truly appreciated and was overwhelmed at what they did. I could barely see enough to make it around the whole arena."

My hands balled into a fist in my pockets to keep from reaching out.

I smiled and glanced over at our families.

"Before we go over there," Brodie whispered. I looked up at him...he was so ruggedly handsome that I could just stare at him all day. I mentally shook myself so I could listen to what he was saying. "I can't thank you enough for talking with me last night."

"Anytime, Brodie," I said earnestly.

He shook his head, "Yeah, and I appreciate that, but last night after we left the rodeo, I couldn't shake the depression. It hit me so hard I didn't want to come back today…I had decided NOT to come back but hadn't told anyone yet. I couldn't show it to Martin. He's been having a hard enough time. Talking to you helped, more than you will ever know."

Tears tingled behind my eyes as I looked up at him.

"I am so glad that Raajyashree Iordanescu could help you through."

We both laughed as the tension dissolved and we walked back to the families.

"He alright?" Dad asked me.

"Yes, just wants back with Betty," I answered and glanced around the faces I hadn't met.

Brodie quickly introduced us to everyone. Logan and Lacie Jae were first, then her sister Camille was introduced, and my jaw clenched just looking at her and my stomach acid bubbled. I barely nodded to her then looked to Martin. Brodie's father, Evan smiled and nodded, but Delaney glared at me. She was holding the hand of a man introduced as her boyfriend, Ryle.

Behind the family was a long folding table. Displayed on the top were the two awarded saddles, buckles, saddle pads, coolers, boots, jackets, whiskey bottles, and other prizes. I imagined they were set up for pictures to be taken.

I looked at Delaney with a timid smile. Her nearly attacking me in Kennewick flashed in my mind. "Congratulations on your win."

"Thank you," She answered, but there was no warmth in her eyes.

"And to you," Brodie's dad nodded. "Damn fine set of horses you have there. That Iggy sure put on a show."

"Thanks," my parents, Caleb, and I said.

"How old is he?" Logan asked while looking at Dad.

"Five," I answered without hesitation. "He was big and smart enough; we gave him a half-year last year and he did well."

Dad chuckled and looked around the group and ended at Logan, "On paper, Iggy belongs to the business, but he actually belongs to River."

"Or I belong to him," I smiled.

"Since the day he was born," Mom added. "He hasn't had much of a chance to 'show his stuff,' but he did well in Lewiston, and today was just..." She hesitated while thinking of the word.

"Nearly perfect," Brodie nodded with an appreciative grin. "I'm not sure how many horses have scored a 48 at one of their first big rodeos."

I gushed with pride, "That score nearly rendered me speechless."

"Nearly," Dad teased then turned back to Brodie. "You and Henry the First had a pretty damn fine ride, too. Thanks for getting him Bareback Horse of the Rodeo."

"Good horses with good riders make for a damn good rodeo," Evan nodded.

Dad looked around the group who were relaxed back in their chairs, "Well, we don't want to interrupt your family time. We just wanted to come over and congratulate everyone and say goodbye to Brodie."

"We have plenty of chairs," Logan began to stand.

"Thanks for the invite," Dad said. "But we have a long road ahead of us."

Logan slowly leaned back down, and Lacie Jae wrapped her arm around his.

"And congratulations to all three of you for qualifying for Vegas," I added.

"We should see you and your horses there," Martin said.

"Hopefully," Mom whispered and looked at me.

"I'm not giving up on him, Mom," I whispered. "Iggy will be there...I believe he will be there."

"That's what you have to have," Martin nodded solemnly. "Belief...always believe."

There was silence…a very uncomfortable silence.

Dad turned to Brodie, "If you're over our way for another rodeo, stop by for that beer we discussed."

"Thank you, sir," Brodie nodded. "I'm not sure…I don't really know what…" his voice trailed off.

"You just need time to refocus," Delaney whispered to him. "You'll get there."

Brodie just nodded, and my heart dropped. I wanted so much to help him, but how could I from so damn far away? I did not want to be a thousand miles from him!

"Why don't you come work for us?" I blurted out.

Every single person there turned to me as if I was an alien. My face heated with an embarrassed blush.

"Where do you live?" Delaney finally asked.

"Cherry County, Nebraska," I answered hesitantly.

"Nebraska?" She whispered.

I frantically looked from Mom and Dad to Brodie, "Caleb is going back to school for his final exams, and Dad was going to hire someone to help the next month as we prepare for winter."

There was silence again but Brodie looked at my parents. Was he considering it? I silently and quickly prayed that he was.

Dad looked from me to Brodie, "If getting away for a while is what you need, then we'd be more than happy to have you at the ranch."

"Absolutely," Mom added. "I don't think we would need to check your references."

"Where is Cherry County?" Evan asked. He didn't have the look of disdain that Delaney had; his was more curious.

"Up at the northern border," Mom answered. "Pretty much in the middle and at the top."

"Basically, out in the middle of nowhere," Caleb smirked.

Dad turned to Brodie, "You are more than welcome. Between the horses and cattle, and with Caleb busy working on his finals, we have a lot of work to do the next month getting ready for winter."

Brodie smiled slightly then finally nodded. "Thanks for the offer. Let me think it over and I'll get back to you."

My heart pounded in excitement of just the possibility he would come to the ranch.

I glanced around the circle of people, and they all had different expressions; surprise, agreement, just a blank stare, concern, and then Delaney, who openly glared at me.

There was another loud bang from the horse trailer and I knew it was Iggy getting impatient so I turned back to Brodie then to his father. "It was nice meeting you, but he's already put himself under enough stress today so we should get going."

They all nodded and smiled in understanding, except Delaney. I felt a bit of irritation creep up my spine. What happened in Kennewick was in the past, she seriously needed to get over it.

Goodbyes were said and my parents and Caleb walked to the truck while I walked to the horse trailer. To my relief, Brodie followed me.

"You need to take him out and check him over?" Brodie asked.

"No, then we'd have a hard time getting him back in, let alone Betty, who hates to be touched," I answered.

"He'll be fine," Dad said and stretched a hand out to Brodie. "I know River said it first, but you are more than welcome to come to the ranch for a while if you need some time to get your head set before Vegas. We even have a few young horses you can practice on."

Brodie smiled and shook his hand, "Thank you, sir. Right now, I am leaning that way, but I want to talk to Dad and Martin first."

My heart jumped for joy and I shoved my hands further into my pockets to keep from reaching out to him.

Dad pulled a business card out of his wallet and handed it to him, "Call and we'll make arrangements."

"Thank you, again," Brodie nodded.

Dad glanced at me, then walked away.

Iggy kicked the side of the trailer again, and I nearly jumped a foot. Brodie and I chuckled as we walked to the truck door.

"Text or call anytime," I said softly and stared up at him. I wanted to remember everything about him.

"That goes both ways," he answered. His voice was low and earnest. "Thank you again, River."

There was nothing more to do except open the door and I just didn't want to! But, everyone was waiting, and I didn't want Iggy to kick again, so I opened the door and looked up at him one more time with my stomach swirling in anxiety, "Goodbye, Brodie."

He smiled warmly, "I'll talk to you later, River."

That was so much better than goodbye!

As we drove away, my heart ached that we were going to be so far away from each other. I glanced longingly at their trailers but only saw Delaney standing at the front of their truck, glaring at me. I just stared back.

CHAPTER FIFTY THREE

For the first time in five weeks, I crawled onto my own bed and under my soft bedspread. I curled into my pillows that I loved and closed my eyes to the comfort. I delighted in the familiarity to the point a slight sigh and smile escaped.

My mind began to drift off to the images of Iggy running out into his own pen. I could tell he was excited to be home, too. It was going to be an adjustment not to be with him every day. The other three horses were released out to hundreds of acres to rejoin the main herd. I drifted off to a solid, deep sleep.

Two weeks after returning home, as I did every morning when I woke, I reached for my phone to look for messages from Brodie. He had sent a few pictures of his family's ranch and a few of their steers and horses while he was out riding. There were pictures of him brushing a big sorrel horse he called Dillon, which had four white legs and a wide blaze. The horse had been through abuse with his old owner; Delaney and Craig had saved him. They were all pleased the horse had gained enough trust in people to approach them when they were out in the pastures. It was heart-warming that Brodie cared so much to share the horse with me.

Today's picture was of the ocean. His sister was riding in Red Bluff, California, and had won the open event and had qualified for The American Rodeo on her new horse, Maestro. Brodie had traveled with her and Camille to the race and spent their free time at the ocean.

The thought of him with Camille made me ache in jealousy, then remembering Delaney's glare made my mood sink even further. And I wasn't even out of bed yet!

My mind played scenarios of Brodie and Camille together until I finally growled into the quiet, dark room and rolled out of bed. It was only 5:30 and dark outside. I dressed quickly and shoved a beanie hat on my head without even brushing my hair and walked out of my room. It was quiet, so I left the house and marched out to the barn. There was a light dusting of snow on the ground with more bad weather predicted in the next couple of days.

Twenty minutes later, the sky was starting to lighten with a pink sunrise and I was trotting across the fields and out to the west pasture. These were the moments I treasured. This was the life I was meant for; riding with the sunrise on the open range.

The plan for the day was bringing in the older cows for pregnancy checks.

I rode across the pasture then down a ravine. I was just topping the west pasture hills when my phone alert went off.

Text from Mom: Where are you?

Text to Mom: Rise of the west pasture bringing in cows

Text from Mom: Well, you were up early

Text to Mom: I was awake and tired of lying in bed

Text from Mom: Will watch for you and open gates.

Text to Mom: Thanks, hot coffee would be good

Text from Mom: I'll have a big thermos ready for you

Text to Mom: Love ya

The older cows were well trained to this fall ride and flowed down the trail with barely a shout.

It took a half-hour pushing the herd to come within sight of the barns and corrals where I could see my parents waiting. Nolan was herding the cows through the gate.

The cows went into the corral without a straggler behind. They knew there would be grain in the troughs when they arrived. I rode through the gate with a warm, welcoming smile from both Mom and Dad.

"You're kind of handy to have around," Nolan smirked.

I chuckled and looked at my smiling mother, "Coffee?"

"Over on the branding table," she answered with a wave of her hand.

I rode to the side of the cows and stopped next to the table which was built into the corner of the corral. I stepped out of the saddle and tied the horse to the fence then turned. Two hands came up and grabbed my arms to stop me from colliding into him. I looked up into the brown smiling eyes of Brodie!

I gasped and nearly squealed, "You're here! I thought you were at the ocean."

"Yesterday I was," he grinned. "I flew in last night and Adam picked me up from the hotel a little while ago."

My heart was racing, a grin beginning to hurt my cheeks, and my hands fighting to reach out and touch him.

"I'm so glad you came to help," I finally managed to say.

He turned and looked at the cows that had filled the corral, "Looks like I got here just in time."

"Let's get to work!" Dad yelled.

I don't know that I had ever enjoyed a day working the cows as much as I did with Brodie. Once Nellie, our veterinarian, arrived, we spent nearly the whole day pushing the cows through the chute and letting them free again.

Only four cows weren't pregnant and they were kept in the corrals for the night to join the steers that would be sold to a rancher in Valentine in the morning.

The horses were turned out for the night and my parents went to the house as Brodie and I stood outside in the chilly night air.

"Thanks again for coming to help," I smiled at him.

"Thank you for inviting me even though it kind of shocked both our families."

"Yeah, it did," I didn't expand any more than that because I wanted to just handcuff us together so he could never get away again. But, I had to admit…that was a bit psychotic. "Mom made fresh bread last night." If I couldn't use handcuffs, then I'd hook him with homemade bread…it was more socially acceptable.

"I can always be lured by food," Brodie grinned.

My whole body trembled.

"I'll keep that in mind," I gave him a teasing grin, and he laughed.

Trembles…we had better get in the house before I fell apart.

With my hands shoved in my pockets, we slowly walked toward the house.

"The house isn't very big," I said quickly. "When we bought the place, there wasn't even a house on it, and we wanted to concentrate on the operation."

"Good business sense."

"Well, none of us like being inside anyway and we're on the road a lot so the middle of the house is a big open space with kitchen, sitting area by the fire, and the kitchen table. Mom and Dad's room plus a small office on one side and mine and Caleb's rooms are on the other. That's really about it."

"It sounds cozy," he smiled. "And I talked to Caleb; he said I could use his room."

"How long are you staying?" My gut clenched in anticipation.

He shrugged with a sigh and looked up into the sky, "At least two weeks. I'm entered in the memorial rodeo in Billings that weekend." He turned and looked down at me. "Then we'll see what happens."

I wasn't sure what to say, so I just smiled and nodded. I didn't want him to only be here for a few days but I was determined to spend every moment I could with him while he was here.

The evening was filled with ranching stories, laughter, and a lot of Mom's homemade bread.

I went to bed nearly giddy in excitement, yet anxious since Brodie was sleeping in Caleb's room right across the hall. It would take me ten steps to get to my door, six steps to go across the hall then another 10 to Caleb's bed where Brodie lay. Twenty-six steps and I would be with him…then what? Just stare at him sleeping?

I had once hidden in Caleb's closet to jump out and scare him. I was able to hide and watch him for 20 minutes while he was doing his homework. He had stood and lifted a glass of water to his lips when I jumped out. Water flew in the air as he fell back and tripped over his chair to hit the floor with a thud. I had absolutely scared the hell out of him and laughed for weeks. It took Caleb three months before he could laugh about it.

So…what the hell did that have to do with walking those 26 steps to stand at Brodie's side and stare at him while he slept? I closed my eyes, buried my face in the pillow, and laughed. First handcuffs and now this? I seriously needed to keep my crazy to myself.

The next day was filled with taking cows to the neighbors and setting up even more panel corrals around the property. At the end of the day, we went for a drive to check stock tanks that were close to the road.

It was just me, Dad, and Brodie in the truck as we drove toward the back hills. The conversation was full when we left the barn, but the longer we drove, the quieter it became. After a few miles, Brodie was staring out the side window, eyes distant, and his body beginning to sink back into the seat.

My heart ached for him, but I didn't know what to do. I looked to Dad for help.

"My old stallion Chinook loved these hills to stretch his legs," Dad said loudly.

"He was a handsome stallion," Brodie mumbled. "It's a beautiful sculpture you have of him."

"Every once in a while, I'd bring him out here so he could have a good stretch of the legs by himself and not be distracted by all the mares," Dad continued.

"Chinook loved dad," I added. "When they did that, the horse wouldn't run off or anything."

"Always stayed within eyesight," Dad nodded.

Brodie turned and looked out the windshield with his body sitting up straighter.

"A few years back," Dad continued. "I trailered him out here to check the stock tanks and let him have a good run. I slid off the halter to let him run free then walked around the trailer to shut the door. Much to my surprise, River was here with the new horse she had just purchased from the Billings Livestock Market."

I grinned, "I had no idea Dad was there and initially, I was pretty excited we were going to ride the riverbank together."

"Until the mare she was riding showed Chinook that she was ready for breeding," Dad said and Brodie turned to him. "Let's just say the stallion was ready to get to work."

We all three chuckled.

"Dad yelled and I took off at a run," I added. "The mare and I flew across the pasture with Chinook right behind us. Dad unhooked the horse trailer from the truck and raced down the road to catch up with us."

"I tell ya," Dad said and glanced at Brodie, who smiled in return. "That girl and that horse were flying...dead out run over the hills, across a creek, and turned toward a pond."

"Chinook hates water," I explained with a laugh. "Since the creek didn't stop him, and the river was too far, I thought the pond would be safe, so the mare and I splashed into the freezing cold water and were stuck there with Chinook dancing and screeching at the water's edge."

"It was early spring with a few drifts of snow still in the trees so it was snow-cold freezing," Dad laughed. "She was shivering with her feet out of the stirrups and tucked in under her."

Brodie chuckled and grinned at me. There it was...that light in his eyes.

"The mare was big, stout, and strong," Dad said. "She was able to stay ahead of the stallion even with a rider on her so the both of us decided we needed to just go ahead and breed them."

"After we got home and I changed into warm clothes," I chuckled.

"She asked for whiskey, but I gave her hot chocolate instead," Dad grinned. "...with a little whiskey in it."

Brodie laughed and my heart sighed.

"Since I just bought the mare, she didn't have a barn name yet," I said. "But that day she got it. I knew, in my heart,

that her offspring were going to be the future of our business,"
I turned and smiled at Brodie. "I named her, Destiny."

"Really?" He huffed. "As in Destiny's Ignatius?"

"Yes," I nodded. "Iggy was conceived that day."

"After he was born, we took the gamble and have bred
Destiny and Chinook each year," Dad added. "So, including
Iggy, who is five, we now have six direct Westmoreland bred
foals from Destiny, and she is in foal again."

"We researched Destiny's registry and found she'd
foaled three times before we bought her and all were mares. Of
course, we confirmed it through DNA then bought them two
years ago after Iggy turned out so dang big and bred them to
Chinook, too. There were no studs registered under her, which
was OK because we needed Chinook's dominating traits for the
bucking."

"In all, we have ten direct horses from Destiny right
now," Dad added. "We bred Iggy to the older legacy bucking
mares and the three Destiny mares we bought have been bred
both years we owned them to Chinook, so they have yearlings,
foals, and are in foal."

"Next year, we'll have twelve little Iggy's born," I
grinned. "I can't wait."

"The older retired bucking horses I've purchased the
last eight years we call the legacy herd," Dad said. "We also
have fifty working head now that we contract out. Good quality
geldings and mares. They'll help a good rider get in the
eighties."

As we told the story, Dad had changed his course and
driven toward the "Boys Pasture". As we topped the rise of the
hill, the gelding and mare herd came into view.

Brodie rose in his seat to look out to the herd.

"Chinook has Grated Coconut in his blood," I said.

"Many of our old bucking horse mares, that are retired
from performing and are now just broodmares, are from
Custer," Dad added. "He wasn't much of a bucker himself but
his offspring have been pretty dominant. Chinook and one of
the Custer mares produced Henry the First. Fizzling Dud is
from a different Custer mare."

"We've stayed pretty close to foundation bucking horses like Grated Coconut, Custer, and the paint stud, Night Jacket when we've purchased older broodmares, so we have a good proven foundation. Our third stud, Windsor, is Night Jacket lineage. He breeds Chinook's prodigy. Iggy's 4-year-old brother has half a dozen foals coming next spring, too." I added. "My dream is for Destiny to become the leading foundation mare for us with her offspring."

"Like Iggy," Brodie smiled.

"Yes," I nodded. "Next spring, if all foal, we'll have over 40 horses with Destiny as the foundation."

"That's a big gamble on one horse that isn't a bucking horse," Brodie shook his head.

"Very big," I agreed. "When I was freezing in that pond sitting on Destiny and watching Chinook try to stay out of the water, I just knew…something in my gut told me they were our future."

"Your destiny," Brodie nodded with a grin. "I don't think I've ever thought so much about the amount of work it takes to make a good string."

"Out of your own foundation," Dad added.

"And praying and loving on them every single day," I added. "Since we started the business, I have been in charge of the breeding program so I feel like they are my own kids."

"That's pretty impressive," Brodie grinned at me.

"She has been raised with bucking horses since she was born and used to sit with me and old Waylon when we would go through breeding plans and pedigree."

"How did Destiny's other foals turn out?" Brodie asked.

"Well, you can see for yourself," Dad said and turned the truck around.

"It's going to be dark soon, we only have time for one herd tonight," I said. "The closest are the yearlings and two-year-olds. We'll see the broodmares tomorrow; some still have foals at their sides."

"When do you wean?" Brodie asked.

"If they are working mares, then we breed for early foaling and wean at 3-4 months," Dad answered. "If they are part of the retired ladies band, then we wean the first of October."

"Which is on the list of things to do this week," I smiled. "So, you get to help with that, too."

"Love to and look forward to it," Brodie said. "We raise beef and roping steers but usually just buy our horses at a couple of years old, so I haven't been around many foals."

"We'll get you past that tomorrow," Dad smirked. "We have about twenty to separate and move the mares out to fall pasture down by the river." He turned the last corner for the herd of young horses to appear on the horizon. "Well doesn't that just figure; they are at the farthest point."

"We can come back tomorrow morning," I said.

"You two can ride out in the morning and check them," Dad said and turned the truck toward home. "Then ride over to the broodmares and we'll meet you there."

My heart swelled with anticipation of riding across my home, my piece of heaven with Brodie.

I glanced up at him and smiled. He looked pretty pleased with the idea, too.

"I have a question," Brodie said and looked over at us. "When you were on Destiney that first day and Chinook was let free...why didn't you just ride her into the horse trailer instead of out across the fields?"

"It happened so damn fast," I grinned.

"And you are not the first person to ask us," Dad laughed.

$$\text{WML}$$

"You get up this early all the time?" Brodie asked as he tightened the cinch on the bay horse.

I nodded, "Yes, I'd rather be riding the fields with the horses then just lying in bed."

"It's not even daylight yet," he stepped up into the saddle and rode through the gate.

I secured the latch then stepped up onto my buckskin gelding. "Sunrise is about twenty minutes out, I want to show you something before we go down to the horses."

Side-by-side, we rode the horses away from the barn and across the main pasture.

"Good thing there is a little moonlight left," Brodie chuckled.

"This gelding knows this ride by heart," I assured him.

I rode down a ravine then up a rocky bluff and stopped just at the edge of a cliff that dropped sixty feet down to the river's edge. The sun was just beginning to rise with a beautiful pink display against blue skies and puffy white clouds. The light shimmered on the water of the river below us giving it a pink silver morning hue. It curved through a timbered canyon with trees lining each side.

"This is Niobrara River," I said softly. "There are roughly two miles of it on our property."

Silently, we watched the sun lift in the sky and the light take over the dark canyons. Deer meandered along the river's edge, and wild turkeys could be heard as well as the distant cow mooing.

I could hear the distinctive sound of horses walking down a rocky path and pointed in the direction they would appear through the trees. It was the band of mares and foals. Just as they came into view, I retrieved my phone and took a picture and sent it to my parents. They loved these moments and Mom would share them on the business social media websites.

Brodie was taking pictures when I turned.

"It's beautiful up here," he whispered as he leaned on the saddle horn and looked out at the horses, river, wildlife, and, in the distance, rolling green hills.

"Dad calls this River's Point," I smiled.

"Little double entendre," Brodie grinned.

I nodded, "When we were looking at property for the business, we swore we would look at no less than five ranches before we chose. This was the third ranch, but when we came to this spot and looked out at the rolling hills, tree-covered ravines and canyon…the river itself with its beaches?" I turned and looked at him with a wide proud smile. "We knew…all four of us knew this would be home."

"It's absolutely peaceful and beautiful."

We rode down to the horses and stepped out of the saddle. My beautiful brown mare approached me.

"And this is Destiny," I ran my hand down the large mare's neck and turned to Brodie.

He was bending over, talking to one of the foals who were curious enough to come over and check us out.

"Hard to imagine this little guy is going to grow up to buck off cowboys," he chuckled.

My heart warmed as he walked around the mares and foals with his eyes wide and filled with peace. His whole body was relaxed as he stroked a neck or laughed as a foal would run away.

I took a picture of him then a quick video when he was surrounded by five foals and the vast expanse of flowing river behind him. There was no doubt I would watch that video a hundred times if not more.

"You'll have to send that to me so I can send to my family," Brodie grinned. "Let them know I'm still alive and doing well."

"You look like you are," The image of Delaney glaring at me flashed in my mind and I just shook it off as I slid the phone back in my pocket.

"How can you not when you're in such beautiful country and surrounded by baby horses?"

"That is how I feel with them, too."

Destiny's current foal nudged me in the back, but when I turned, she trotted away with a prance and a flick of the tail.

I chuckled, "Iggy's little sister. I named her Enchanted Siren."

"They are just tremendous babies," he turned to me. "Your family is raising some outstanding horses."

My heart swelled with pride, "I'll introduce you to the rest of his brothers and sisters in the other herds."

Dad's truck appeared on the horizon, which made me sigh. As much as I loved him, I just wanted more of Brodie all to myself.

We mounted the horses and made our way up the ravine path to the pastures.

"How does it work when your Dad said you owned Iggy?"

"All the horses belong to the company. But, because I bought Destiny with my own money, she is registered under my name and Iggy chose me for his human, so we just say he is."

Brodie nodded, "I could see the connection in Pendleton."

I thought of Brodie at the rodeo…the moments he would let the pain show. I hadn't seen that but once in the truck since he arrived.

"I wasn't surprised she brought you here," Dad grinned as we arrived at the truck. "Early enough to watch the sunrise, I bet."

"We'll have to do that again tomorrow." Brodie sighed. "How many acres do you have here?"

"1600 hundred in the company name and another 1200 leased," Dad answered and his eyes moved back down to the river. "Looks like the mares are headed back up here." He dropped the tailgate of the truck to reveal two bales of fresh green hay and three bags of grain. "Once they see these, they should just follow me back to the house, but you two stay behind just in case and shut gates as we go."

I turned to Brodie with a wide grin, "You ever push a hundred bucking horses across a range before?"

"No," he looked between the two of us. "You're doing that today?"

"The three of us are," Dad nodded. "We'll get this group into the west-line pasture then ride out to push the main herd into the east-line pasture. It's easier to feed them there rather than down by the river where they are now."

"Let's get going then," Brodie grinned.

Dad drove the truck away from us with the mares and foals following him.

I turned to Brodie as we trotted behind. "It can get a bit tricky on the big push when the horse you're riding decides he wants to run free, too," I warned him.

CHAPTER FIFTY FOUR

"I'll ride up front and lead the way," Dad told Brodie. "You and River will follow on each side to encourage them forward. When they get moving, if they follow the older horses, they should move in a good flow. If a horse is lagging behind, stay with them and we'll come back."

"Try to watch for any that have a limp or any injuries," I added.

Dad stayed along the trail as Brodie and I rode side-by-side at a distance from the main herd to get to the back of them. Most had their heads high watching us. A few older horses began to walk down the road toward Dad. They had an instinct that told them it was time to move to winter pasture, where they would be fed daily.

Brodie was sitting high in the saddle and a smile graced his handsome face. It made my heart beat a bit faster. I couldn't wait for him to experience the ride.

We dropped down into a ravine and when we rode back to the top we were right behind the herd. The horses in the back trotted forward away from us and stopped to watch us approach.

"Hee-ya!" I yelled.

The horses in the back trotted away from us and into the herd which caused the whole group to move toward Dad. He turned his horse and started trotting toward the gate. I rode off to the right while Brodie moved left of the herd.

Within minutes we were loping along beside them. I kept glancing at Brodie as we rode. He was such a natural horseman and so damn good looking he could easily have been in the movies; up on the big screen. More than once, I wished I had a camera to capture him and the horses running across the pasture.

It was exhilarating to watch the bucking horse's legs stretching, manes bouncing, and tails trailing behind. The pounding of their hooves to the hard ground was another heartbeat for me. It was racing just as fast as they were, and my buckskin had no problem keeping up with them.

I glanced at Brodie and saw a wide elated grin.

Dad led them down a dirt road and right through the gate that led them to the winter pasture. The grass was a little longer in the field, and when we didn't ride into the field, the horses spread-out then stopped; heads instantly went down to graze.

"Ride through," Dad waved to us, and we walked the horses into the pasture as he closed the gate.

I turned to Brodie. His eyes were lit with adventure, face a bit flushed, and his whole body was taller in the saddle.

"What did you think?" I grinned.

"An experience I'll never forget," Brodie laughed. "Just wish I had a Go-Pro or camera I could have filmed it."

"I think it would be awesome to attach one on the head of one of the horses as they run in the herd," I agreed.

Dad stepped up into the saddle and we slowly started walking around the grazing herd. The horses were relaxed but still watched us for any indication they were supposed to run somewhere.

"That black horse to the right with the one white hoof and the mass of mane and forelock," I pointed for Brodie. "That is Iggy's four-year-old-brother, Destiny's Inferno."

"Damn, he's as huge as his big brother," Brodie huffed.

"He went to a handful of rodeos this year," Dad said and we continued to walk around the herd. "He doesn't have the explosive bust-out as Iggy does, but he has the power behind each buck and so far just does a big circle as he kicks."

"This big bay mare with the wide blaze is the three-year-old I called Destiny's Spirit," I pointed then turned to look at Brodie. "The yearling and two-year-old are in the younger horse herd. They are Destiny's Mayhem, a gelding and Destiny's Black Shadow, not a speck of white on her."

"Do you name all of them?" Brodie asked.

"Just Destiny's direct offspring when they are born," Dad answered. "The rest earn their names as they go like Fizzling Dud and Flying Betty." He pointed to both horses. "When we purchased the Legacy horses, if they didn't have a name, they were named after cities in Romania where my father's family originated."

"Henry the First was the first foal born after Dad purchased Chinook." I walked the buckskin to the horse and he just stood calmly as if he knew we were talking about him.

"In two weeks, we'll pull thirty from this herd for a Bares and Broncs competition down in Cheyenne," Dad said.

We spent another half hour talking about the herd before riding to the house.

Mom was standing at the computer with a wide grin. She was blocking the monitor until we were standing next to her, then she stepped aside to reveal a large image of the horses running along the trail with Dad in the lead and Brodie and I alongside.

"Damn," Brodie gasped in surprise as he leaned in. "I didn't even see you out there."

She smiled, "I was hiding behind a large rock so the horses didn't see me."

My heart was full as she began scrolling through the images. Brodie looked like a whole different person than the man I met at the rodeo in Lewiston.

For the next week, we moved cows and horses, built more pens, and added roofs over them. We even framed in a large coat-room out the backdoor of the house with wide steps down to the ground. Brodie was handy to have around, and I couldn't believe how fast the days were going by. I hated it...but loved every second of it.

With a day of light rain outside, we built stalls inside the barn. Brodie was kept busy all week and not once did I see that lost look in his eyes.

It may have been a spur of the moment, desperate request for him to come work for us, but it had been the right thing for him. The weekend of his departure to Billings was

only days away. It nearly killed me thinking of him being gone
and never coming back.

Handcuffs…no, still too unacceptable.

With no thick socks helping to tighten my knee-high
mud boots, my feet slid with each step. The bib overalls were
also too large without the extra layer of clothes on underneath,
but the air was comfortable with just the overalls and hooded
sweatshirt underneath. Most importantly, they were waterproof
and would be needed when the large rain clouds arrived.

I adjusted the wide suspender straps over my shoulders
then pulled my hair out from being trapped under the
sweatshirt. I liked leaving it down when it was chilly to help
keep me warm. I shoved my dark brown oil-skin cowboy hat
over the messy hair.

The house was quiet when I stepped out of my room.
Caleb's door was slightly open, which meant Brodie was already
up and outside. I had to force myself not to peek in the door
and look at the bed. I rolled my eyes at myself and turned into
the kitchen.

When I stepped out of the house, I slid my thin leather
gloves on while standing on the front steps. The wind had just
a hint of crispness to it, so I took a deep breath to fill my lungs
with the fresh air. I could see the mist as I exhaled.

My eyes wandered across the yard, wide driveway, and
to the corrals. I saw no animals at the barn, which was odd so I
headed there.

Our older retired horses had access to the back of the
barn and a ten-acre pasture. Three of them were standing at the
back of the barn, tucked inside out of the wind. I could see
another dozen grazing in the lower part of the pasture that was
hidden from the house.

To the left, a single cow and her calf were lying in the middle of the field, while the rest of the herd were scattered throughout the trees.

"Hmmm," I watched them for a moment then decided it was best to check.

I glanced around the barn again and saw no one. Dad's truck was gone, which meant he and Brodie had probably gone to town.

A disappointed sigh escaped me. I really loved seeing Brodie first thing in the morning. We were days away from him leaving, and he still had made no overt hint if he liked me…as in really liked me anywhere near how I liked him.

"Just let it the hell go, River. He has a lot to mentally get over," I mumbled to myself and slid onto the seat of the 4-wheel ATV just as the first raindrops began to fall.

No matter, it would be a quick trip out to check the pair, then I'd get back in and find something to do in the barn to keep my mind busy.

The engine roared to life and I made my way through two gates and out into the field. By the time I was halfway to the pair, my clothes were speckled with raindrops, which were getting bigger and falling thicker. I tipped my head down so the wide brim of the hat would protect my face.

As I approached the pair, the cow stood and revealed the good-sized black calf curled on the ground next to her. The cow turned to look at me with big curious eyes. She was tag number 32, an older, gentle cow that had been in our herd for at least ten years. Being well seasoned, she knew exactly what to do when she saw the 4-wheeler; she started walking toward the barn. However, her calf, who I guessed would weigh 300 pounds, just watched her walk away.

I stopped the ATV ten feet from the calf and he watched me with rising alarm but he didn't stand. Between me approaching him and his mother walking away, the calf should be bounding toward her. I slid off the machine and walked around the calf with his eyes watching me closely. He didn't make a move to stand and I couldn't see anything wrong with him.

I looked back at his mother, but she was continuing her walk to the barn.

"Alright, Big Guy," I said to him. "You have to get up on your own or I get the rope and the ATV pulls you up."

Hands-on hips, I stared him down, but he didn't flinch so I walked within a foot of him. He finally rocked forward to stand so I took a couple of steps back to give him room. After a full minute of rocking back and forth, he finally managed to stand. I carefully walked around him and grimaced when I saw the back leg he had been laying on. It was three times its normal size with an apparent open wound on the side that was matted with mud and dried blood but no oozing pus.

"Looks ugly, Big Guy," I said and walked toward him to encourage him to move so I could assess the damage.

He took a few tentative limping steps to follow his mother then paused to look back at me.

"You get to the barn and we'll get that cleaned up so you don't hurt anymore," I promised him.

He turned and slowly limped his way toward the corrals, barn, and his mother.

I slid back on the ATV and started it. The engine roar caused the calf to double his speed.

I felt sorry for him and was already deciding what I was going to need to get the injury cleaned and pain-free.

With his mother walking through the corral gate, the calf was moving at a good pace to follow her, so I just enjoyed the moment. The scent of the rain, the sound of it hitting my hat, and the peaceful scene of horses and cows grazing reminded me of why I loved my life.

Brodie lived in Oregon with his family and I lived in Nebraska with my family. Neither of us would be inclined to move so why was I dreaming of him every night? Why did I want to spend every moment with him...or at least just stare at him? He made my heart flutter and my whole body warm.

The calf scampered to the right and away from his mother so I turned the 4-wheeler to cut him off. He turned quickly and headed the other direction but ran right past the open gate.

"Your mother is right there!" I yelled at the calf and roared past him to turn him again.

Three times…back and forth.

"You stupid cow!" I yelled.

I stopped the ATV and parked it next to the gate to block him from running past it again.

When I slid off the machine, I instantly slipped in the mud but kept myself from falling.

"Stupid cow!" I yelled at him again then ran ahead to turn him back.

He turned and I jogged alongside him to keep him next to the fence. Hopefully, he would turn at the 4-wheeler. He didn't, instead he tried to run around it but I ran ahead of him to stop him. My tripping and falling onto my hands and knees in the mud managed to get him stopped.

He just stood and stared at me as I glared at him while standing back up. I wiped my hands down the front of my wet overalls.

"Turn the hell around and go in the corral with your mother!" I yelled at him.

He trotted back down the fence.

"Damn you!" I screamed and ran back down the fence to cut him off. We repeated the action one more time.

When he neared the gate, I took off my hat and started waving it in the air, screaming at him and running toward him. He stared again until I was just feet from him, then he turned into the corral and trotted toward his mother. I ran to shut the gate behind him.

I placed my wet hat on my wet hair and glared at the cow again as I opened the next gate that led into the corral next to the barn.

The rain was now near a downpour, causing puddles to form with the mud and manure.

Momma cow trotted right through. She knew she would be fed at the barn. Her calf did not and again refused to go through the gate.

I ran back and forth, waving my arms, and swearing at him. He just trotted back and forth in front of the opening.

"You would think with the hurt leg you wouldn't run so damn much, Stupid Cow!" I yelled again.

He stopped and turned to look at me so I charged at him…he, in turn, charged at me. I barely managed to avoid getting a calf head in the stomach. Instead, I spun around and fell back to land on my ass in the mud, which in the corrals was also a mixture of manure. Grabbing a handful of mud and manure mixture and throwing it at him was just an immediate reaction which he didn't really worry too much about it. He just limped himself to the other side of the corral and watched me.

I stood up with wet legs, hands, and my ass covered in mud and took deep breaths to calm myself. It was useless to get angry at a cow because they just didn't care.

Slowly, I walked behind him and calmly motioned my hands to make him move. He did…slowly…one little limp at a time until he walked through the opening toward his mother. I ran for the gate to get it closed, but he twirled around and shot back into the corral.

"Fucking cow!" I screamed and swung the gate back open with as much force as I could muster.

More deep breaths, I calmly walked behind him again, and he slowly limped through the opening to his waiting mother.

I ran for the gate. Two steps forward and my foot was sucked down into the mud…the fourth step pulled my socked foot out of the boot and it squished in the mud…the sixth step and I fell forward into the puddles. I landed on my knees and stuck my hands out to keep from falling entirely, but they just slid out from under me. As my stomach and chest hit the ground, I bent my head back to keep my face from smashing into it too. The mud and manure mixture splashed up my neck and over my cheeks. I closed my eyes to keep it from going into them.

As soon as my sliding fall stopped, I glanced up at the calf…he was headed for the opening again, so I stumbled up to my feet, and with one boot on and one off, I charged at him again. He slid to a stop and slowly limped back to his mother as I gripped the gate and flung it closed.

"You stupid son-of-a-bitch!" I yelled at him and chained the gate closed.

I stood soaking wet, covered in mud and manure, and swore at the damn calf again.

With deep breaths, I lifted my face to the rain hoping it would help wash off the dirt and manure. I could feel it moisten the skin and I raised a muddy hand to wipe it away the best I could.

"Here, let me help."

I nearly jumped a foot as I twirled around to see Brodie walking through the gate next to the abandoned 4-wheeler. He had a wide grin with laughter dancing in his eyes.

Oh, damn it! I couldn't have looked worse!

He stopped close enough I had to bend my head back to look up into his eyes.

"How much did you see?" I asked in exasperation.

"About the time you charged each other, and you landed on your...ass," he chuckled.

"Ah...I must look like a freaking mess."

"Whether you wear makeup, mud, or...manure, you are a beautiful woman," he chuckled again and with a tender touch, wiped said manure off my cheek.

He made my heart tremble.

His hand rose, and I thought he was going to wipe away more mud, but he took off my hat, and with one arm behind my shoulders and the other around my waist, he pulled me to him.

"Do you mind if I kiss you?" He whispered when our lips were just inches apart.

"Do you mind if I kiss you back?" I sighed as our lips met.

My body warmed to the point I melted against him. I was finally allowed to touch him so I swung my arms around his shoulders and gripped his coat tightly. Standing on tip-toes, I pulled him tighter to me as he lowered more. My stomach swirled, mind in a heavenly haze, and heart beating wildly.

I held on until Brodie slowly raised just enough our eyes connected and we were both protected from the rain by his wide-brim hat.

We grinned at each other.

"Well, that was a bit…gritty," he chuckled.

The light and laughter in his eyes made my heart sigh.

"That makes it memorable," I sighed.

"Yeah," he grinned. "I'll be remembering that one…and this one."

We came together for another soft, lingering kiss with the rain creating a shield around us as the world disappeared.

With a sigh, he rose just inches above me.

"I could stand here and kiss you all day," he whispered.

I lowered down and looked up into his eyes, "Me too…but I have a stubborn calf to doctor."

He leaned back and replaced my hat on my head, "Let's take care of him and find somewhere dry so I can kiss you again."

"I'm good with that plan, but I seem to be missing a boot."

A wave of pure romance rushed through me when he swooped me up into his arms and carried me to the 4-wheeler with the rain showering us. I wrapped my arms around his neck and let the moment absorb into my heart. I was going to remember this moment forever.

He lowered me onto the ATV then leaned in for another kiss before rising just high enough to smile at me.

"I'll go grab your boot and get the gates for you."

"Watch that little calf! Don't let him out."

The sound of his laugh as he turned and walked away filled my heart.

"Without being able to get him in a chute, I think it is safest to sedate him," I said as I knelt down next to the calf's swollen leg. "We've been meaning to get a chute setup in the

barn for rainy days but there has just been so much more to do
we haven't gotten to it yet."

The calf was tucked into a stall inside the barn with the
floor covered in straw. His mother calmly stood in the stall
next to him and watched us while chewing her hay. She seemed
content out of the rain and let us take care of her calf.

I walked into the tack room where we kept a small
locked cabinet with the medicine. Brodie followed me into the
room and filled a bucket with warm water and soap. When our
eyes met, I smiled happily then glanced in the mirror behind
him. My eyes widened in horror.

"Oh, hell!" I gasped at my image. The raindrops had
created streaks down my cheek so I looked like a damn zebra.
My hair was tangled and drying in a mixture of mud and
manure. The creases at the edge of my nose were black with
mud as well as the crease in my eye lids. My chin and neck were
splattered with the black mud.

Brodie grinned with a devilish chuckle.

I looked at him with wide astonished eyes, "You kissed
THAT?" I reached for the towel on the counter.

"No, I kissed you...which is more than just your looks,"
he pulled me into his arms and away from the sink and towel.
"And I want to keep kissing you so go give him the shot so we
can get on with more kissin'."

"Let me just wash..."

"No."

He turned me and shoved me out the door.

"Brodie!" I grumbled with a laugh.

The calf was sleeping soundly as I scrubbed the wound
the best I could.

"It doesn't look infected," I said as I used a razor to
clean away the loose skin, mud and dried blood.

"He charged you pretty strong so it doesn't look
broken," Brodie grinned.

"Ha ha..." I teasingly rolled my eyes.

"I'll give him antibiotics and keep him inside for a while
to keep him from moving," I stood to clean the mess.

"What are you guys doing in here?"

I turned to my parents looking into the stall. Their eyes were on the calf but when I turned, they looked at me. Mom gasped and Dad laughed.

"What the hell happened to you?" Dad asked.

"And why didn't you wash up?" Mom asked with eyes darting to Brodie then me.

"I found the calf injured and had a few muddy mishaps getting him to the barn," I said to Dad then turned to my grinning mother. "Because Brodie wouldn't let me."

Brodie chuckled, "She looks fine. I've heard mud facials are good for you."

We all four laughed.

"We're going into town to meet the Baxter's for bowling, dinner, then the movie," Mom said. "Would you like to join us?"

"No," I said, probably too quickly.

Their eyes danced in knowing smiles as they looked at Brodie.

"I thank you for the offer," He smiled. "But I'd like to spend some time with River before I have to leave."

My body tingled in excitement as my mind sighed at the thought of him leaving.

Dad turned and looked at me with a smile, "You two have fun, but River?"

"Yes, Dad?" I giggled.

"You're starting to stink," he grinned.

"Dad!" I gasped with cheeks warming.

My parents laughed then turned to walk out of the barn. I quickly gave the calf the antibiotic.

"He's fine for now. I'm going in to shower and change," I said.

"What would you like to do for the day?" He asked as we walked down the aisle of the barn.

His hand slowly moved over to take mine. My whole arm tingled as our fingers interlaced.

"Kiss you," I said honestly with a quick glance at him.

611

"I like that plan, but nourishment may be advantageous. You know how to use your mother's bread machine?"

"Yes," I said in surprise.

"So in between the kisses, what if we made spaghetti and bread?"

"I love to cook and make fresh bread," I grinned.

"And I love to eat."

After my shower, I happily spun around my room in a simple blue knit sweater that flowed comfortably to just above my knees and over black leggings. My hair was still damp as it brushed against my shoulders and since we weren't going to go anywhere, I was barefoot.

When I walked into the kitchen, Brodie had the bread maker on the counter and all the ingredients set out next to it. He was wearing a black t-shirt that already had a smear of flour across the stomach. But best of all, he was barefoot too.

After a long lingering kiss to start the afternoon, we made bread, cookies, a cake, and the spaghetti. It was a wonderful rainy afternoon in which I couldn't keep my hands from reaching out to touch him.

When my parents arrived back at the house, the oven was off, counters full of food, and we were cuddling on the couch watching John Wayne in *Big Jake* and enjoying cookies and milk.

The next morning, we rode out to River's Point to watch the sunrise. This time, instead of watching from horseback, we stood in front of the horses with our arms wrapped around each other.

I was in absolute heaven as we silently watched the sunrise. The sky was bright blue and as the sun lit the horizon, a white mist hovered over the river and ravines.

"Beautiful," Brodie whispered as he took a picture of the river then a selfie of the two of us together. "River?"

"Yes?" I cuddled into his shoulder with his arms tightly around me.

"I have to leave tomorrow night."

"I prefer not to think of that."

"Well, I was wondering...because I don't want to leave, but I really need to ride this weekend...but I don't...would you consider...if we got two rooms...would you consider going with me?"

YES! I wanted to scream, jump, and do a happy dance but I hid my crazy and just smiled sweetly, "I would love to go but I don't see any reason to waste that second room."

He paused, "You sure?"

"Yes..."

He looked out at the river then up to the sky, "I don't know what's going to happen in the future. I can't guarantee after Vegas..."

"It's OK, Brodie," I whispered. "There are no guarantees in life. I know what I want now...and that is you. After? Well...we'll just take one day at a time and see where it leads us."

He turned me in his arms so we could look into each other's eyes. After a moment of silent searching for an answer, he smiled and nodded.

WML

"You're sure about this?" Mom stood at my bedroom door and watched me pack my overnight bag.

"Yes," I answered firmly. "I knew you and Dad would be worried, but it is what I want."

"Since we met Brodie in Pendleton, we knew you liked him. It's as if you're at ease and at peace when he is around."

I laughed, "Oh, Mom. I'm really not. I'm just working really hard at hiding my crazy, so I don't scare him off."

Her body relaxed as a grin spread across her beautiful face, "That was what I was worried about. Not that you didn't like him, but that you were so calm. Now I know better. I felt the same way about your father."

I laughed, "Half the time I have to keep myself from doing a weird happy dance or tackling him when I see him."

"Then you truly like him," she sighed.

"Since the moment I saw him, I've been a bit obsessed with him...as in stalking him on the internet."

She laughed and sat on the edge of the bed.

"The first time I talked to him in Lewiston, I was so overwhelmed with emotions and shock that I could barely speak. Then, in Pendleton, when he showed up at the horse pens, I had to shove my hands in my pockets just to keep from touching him or, I should say, grabbing him."

"And when you invited him here?"

I sat on the bed next to her and our hands came together, "I honestly couldn't bear the thought of him being so far away and I wouldn't be able to help him." Her eyes were understanding and the worry had eased. "I knew if he was here, riding with the herd or watching the sunrise at River's Point that it would help him...ease his soul in some way."

Her arm slid around me to pull me into an embrace, "I love your heart, young lady."

An hour later, Brodie held open the passenger-side door of my own truck for me to slide in. I chuckled, "You can drive there. I'm driving us home."

"It's a deal," he chuckled and shut the door.

I rolled down the window so I could turn to Mom as she walked to the truck. Dad was on the other side talking to Brodie. Quickly, I crossed my eyes, twisted my lips out to the side to make a face, and stuck my tongue out. She was the only one to see it and drew glances of confusion when she started

"GPS says we have eight and a half hours to our destination," Brodie said as we drove down the long driveway.

"You think we can hold a conversation that long?" I teased with a grin.

For the first four hours it was non-stop talking about horses, rodeo, childhoods, and I told him of my fairytale dreams of riding Chinook in my enchanted kingdom. Then I told him of the first spring we had released the stallion into the lush pastures of our new ranch and how exciting it was. We all knew it was his forever home.

"And it is," Brodie nodded.

"Yes," I sighed and released the last remnants of guilt and remorse on how the stallion had died. I would always have the memories and he would always be with us.

His phone chimed instead of its normal alert.

"Lacie Jae posted a podcast," Brodie explained and plugged his phone into the speaker of the truck.

Welcome to Coffee with Cowboys with me, Lacie Jae.

Greetings everyone! Lacie Jae with Coffee With Cowboys here. I'm a relocated city girl who will be adventuring into the ranching and rodeo world... the cowboy way of life.

Have you ever seen a horse throw a fit? Well, I did and wouldn't have believed it if I didn't see it with my own eyes.

Evan, Logan, and I were enjoying our coffee yesterday when Delaney and Camille loaded the horse trailer and took off for the next barrel race.

As you know, Delaney qualified for the NFR this coming December and she decided to give her main horse, Gaston, a month off from competition. They are just riding the hills here at the ranch to keep him in shape.

She has been taking her new horse, Maestro, around to different rodeos and races to get in-sync with him ... as she put it.

So this morning, all her horses are in the front pasture that runs along the driveway. Besides Maestro and Gaston, she also has Ketchum, Memphis, Madi, and Archer. All were peacefully grazing and wandering the pasture this morning when Delaney walked out and haltered Maestro. Gaston's head rose, and he watched them walk away but didn't seem too concerned. I'm sure he was used to them practicing here at the ranch.

So, it was normal ... peaceful ... we sipped our coffee and watched over the herd as Delaney loaded the big black horse into the horse trailer. Still no problem ... quiet and relaxing ... until she started the truck.

Gaston's head jerked up and looked over at the truck and trailer. I've witnessed it before, this horse knows the sound of Delaney's truck and he trotted a few steps toward the fence but hesitated because the truck didn't move.

But when it did, the horse ran to the fence, whinnied as loud as he could, and then pranced back and forth. The truck started down the driveway and Gaston threw his fit! Bucking, snorting, farting, kicking in the air, running in circles, bucking more, tossing his head ... he ran down the length of the fence next to the driveway as if he wanted to run in front of it to stop it.

Back and forth he ran and bucked while Delaney slowly moved down the driveway.

Gaston became a racehorse up and down the fence, head tossing, kicking out ... throwing a tantrum.

Well, Logan and Evan guessed right. As we were chuckling at the spectacle, Delaney stops the truck just past the gate that is three-quarters of the way down the long driveway. Gaston begins pacing back in forth in front of it; whinnying at her the whole time.

She gets out of the truck, opens the back of the horse trailer. Maestro is behind a panel in the middle of the trailer so the door is wide open when Delaney walks to the gate. Gaston bucks and kicks as she opens the gate and ... well ... he could have run down to the road or back here to the ranch but he didn't. That dang horse, without a halter or rope on him, runs right into the back of the trailer and turns to look at her as if "What was she thinking leaving him behind!"

We can see the big grin on Delaney's face as she closes the trailer door then turns to look back at the ranch house.

We laughed and waved at each other before she got in the truck and drove away.

I talked to her last night and she said she didn't run him in the race itself but she did ride him in the time-only's. Which, if you didn't know, is when they run a practice pattern and are timed on it. After he ran the barrels twice, she put him in a stall and he was happy and satisfied, then she got to work with Maestro ... and they won the race.

The moral of this little story is that Gaston LOVES his job. He loves traveling, he loves her, and he loves competition.

For those people that crazily think that humans are forcing the horses to do what they want them to do, remember this story. And, also the fact that Gaston is 1300 pounds ... Delaney might be 125. If he didn't want to run the race or even move, she couldn't physically make him do it.

Bucking bulls are 2000 pounds. If they didn't want to buck, they just wouldn't. Bucking horses love to buck. I've witnessed that with Popover, the bucking horse here that Camille rode last spring. He loved doing it and trotted into the chute when they opened the gate. He looked ten years younger when they finished the ride. Popover loves to buck; he loves his job!

Evan says it's more about making sure you have the right horse and discipline matched together. Gaston is phenomenal as a barrel horse, but Evan says he hates being around ropes and would never make a breakaway or team roping horse.

So, Gaston's tantrum was a first for me, and what I love the most is that Delaney loved him enough to stop and take him with her.

I hope you enjoyed this podcast, I'm off to have coffee with cowboys.

Have a good day and a great cup of coffee!

We were quiet a moment before Brodie finally glanced at me. "Can I ask you something?"

"Anything."

"Were you the one that LJ talked to in Kennewick?"

"Yes, how did you know?"

"She mentioned in the Lewiston podcast that 'if it weren't for the bruises' she wouldn't have stopped to talk to you." He paused. "One of the directors told me it was you that the guy nearly yanked your arm off by the stock pens right before we ran into each other."

"Yeah, hurt for weeks."

"Until I heard that podcast I didn't realize how hard LJ was taking Craig's loss…that she had considered stopping."

He was deep in thought so I remained quiet and waited for him to speak.

"Her father died right before she came to live with us at Christmas last year."

"I didn't know that."

He nodded thoughtfully, "She has never mentioned it on her podcast and doesn't talk about it at home. She wasn't close to him…neither was Camille, I really don't know why but I do know that they took Craig's loss harder than their father's."

"Well, obviously, they either have the same mother or father because they can't possibly be full sisters."

"You've met LJ but how do you know Camille?"

My bottom lip was quickly caught between my teeth and my eyes narrowed thoughtfully.

Was this really the right time to tell him?

618

CHAPTER FIFTY FIVE

"Well," I hesitated in answering.

"Oh...you did meet her in Pendleton."

"Yeah...that's where," I said as nonchalantly as possible.

"Who did you draw?" I asked to change the subject.

"Bob Cat."

"He's good..." for the rest of the drive, we talked bucking horses.

I was in heaven.

"It's four o'clock now," Brodie said as we drove into Billings. "The rodeo starts at seven so do you want to drop off the bags at the hotel and get checked in then go to the arena?"

My stomach swirled, heart pounded, and toes curled in my boots to keep myself from screeching. I kept my voice calm, "Sounds like a plan."

I stood in the lobby of the hotel and stared at the pictures on the wall as Brodie checked into the hotel. With a pounding heart and trembling hands, I forced myself not to look at him until he approached with key in hand. My overnight bag was on the floor at my feet, and my hands were firmly shoved into my vest pockets.

My face was flushed as I turned to him. His smile was sweet and eyes questioning.

"I was just thinking," I whispered. "Maybe I should wait down here while you take the bags to the room." The last thing I wanted was to attack him once we got to the room and miss the rodeo.

He chuckled and I could have sworn his cheeks turned red before he turned away, "Probably a good idea."

When we arrived at the arena, I was barely a foot away from the truck when I heard my name called. I turned to see a grinning face.

"River," Trenten Montero smiled. "I didn't know you were providing stock for here. You bring that pretty palomino with you?"

I grinned and shook my head, "No, Betty is home being a ranch pet and I'm just here as co-pilot."

Brodie walked next to me and gently placed his hand on the small of my back. I nearly melted and all words failed me as the two men shook hands.

"Good to see you here," Trenten told Brodie. "You riding bares and bronc this time?"

"Just saddle bronc," Brodie answered.

With his bronc saddle comfortably resting over his shoulder and rodeo bag in his free hand, they talked as we made our way to the contestant's entrance.

When we were alone, Brodie turned to me with a pleased smile.

"You need your game-face on," I huffed. "I'm going to take my first ever companion-pass and go sit in the bleachers. I can already see half-a-dozen people I know."

He chuckled, "Probably a good idea."

We both started to turn away, then I turned back.

"Brodie?" I said just loud enough only he could hear me.

He stopped and looked over his shoulder at me. With the whiskers, sweet smile, and dark brown eyes under his black cowboy hat, he made my heart flutter.

"Yes, River?" He said in a long-drawn-out drawl.

"When you get on that horse, you stay on that horse past the eight seconds, then wait for the pick-up man to help you off where he can very carefully place you on the ground," I smiled. "Do NOT get hurt."

His grin widened and eyes danced with laughter, "There is no way that will happen. I have plans for tonight."

I gave him a wicked grin, "So do I, Cowboy."

I sat in the bleachers with Trenten's wife, Maria, and more people I knew and barely had a moment's peace before the rodeo began and the first bareback rider bust from the chute. Trenten was second to ride and ultimately finished in third to win a check.

Text from Brodie: I have been asked if we would like to join everyone for dinner and a beer after. What do you think?

My first thought was hell no! Then it was…that's too much crazy…keep your composure.

Text to Brodie: Nourishment would probably be advantageous.

I turned to the chutes to see if he was within sight when he read the message. I could just barely see him as he looked at his phone and a wide grin spread across his face.

Text from Brodie: I was going to turn them down, but you do have a point.

Well, damn! I chuckled to myself.

"Are you leaving after the saddle bronc?" I asked innocently.

Maria confirmed they were, and I felt a little better.

Brodie appeared over the back of the chutes with a few cowboys at his side to help him out. I knew they were there for mental support because Craig should have been here, too. Craig should be there; my throat constricted, so I pushed the thought to the back of my mind. What help would I be to Brodie if I was too emotional?

When he stepped over the panels and over the horse, my elbows went to my knees, hands clasped just under my chin and I silently whispered a prayer.

The gate opened and the horse lunged out two strides before beginning his bucking. Brodie was leaned back, eyes between the horse's ears, seat centered, rein gripped tightly and lifted up and down as the horse bucked. When the horn blared, Brodie looked for the pick-up man and easily slid from horse to horse then to the ground. As he walked out of the arena, a bit of a smirk appeared even though the given score placed him second for the night.

Just in front of our seats, he turned and looked up at me with a swaggering grin. I laughed.

We were one of the last to arrive at the restaurant and Brodie held the door open for me.

"I had planned on stopping for something to eat on the way to the hotel," he whispered.

"Me, too," I chuckled.

"Then how in the hell did we end up here with this crew?"

"Because I just HAD to hide the crazy," I said flippantly before realizing what I was saying.

"Your what?"

"Nothing..." I muttered as we approached the table.

"There she is," Brody Cress grinned at me. "What's your stock contractor's opinion on difficult horses in the chute?"

"Don't draw them," I teased with a smart-ass grin.

The dozen roughies, spouses and girlfriends laughed as we slid onto our chairs.

"No, seriously," Trenten huffed.

"Well, we don't have many fighters, biters, or layer-downers, but we do have Betty who will put her head down and not raise it if she thinks you're going to touch her head," I answered. "We just suggest, after she is in the chute, not to let anyone near her head from the riggin forward."

"She's just bareback?" Trenten asked.

"For that reason," I nodded. "Some horses you can work around it, some are worth the battle, but there are those that won't get you a score high enough to make it worth it. With Betty, she scored better with her head up as she exits but still gets a good score when her head is down, so she's worth it."

The next hour was filled with beer, laughter, jokes, teasing, food, and best of all, bucking horse talk.

"Isn't a brodie when you spin circles in your car?" Maria asked with a grin to the two men.

"Isn't that called doughnuts or cookies?" I laughed.

"It's both," Trenten answered.

"So, you two are just like doughnut and cookie spinners," I teased.

"Dessert spinners," Maria giggled.

"Damn, cookies and doughnuts sounds really good right now," Brodie's head tipped toward the kitchen.

"Cookies, spinnin', then flying into my mouth," Brody nodded.

"Doughnuts, they got to have some back there," Brodie stood.

"I got your back," Brody grinned and followed.

A round of laughter erupted from the table.

"That was so much fun," I sighed as we finally walked down the hallway to our hotel room door.

"I agree. They are a great group of people."

The beer had managed to calm my anxiety, but when he slid the plastic key into the door lock, the calm jolted out of me.

"Do you mind if I take a shower and get the arena dirt off me?" He asked as we walked through the door.

"No, go ahead."

He picked up his bag and disappeared into the bathroom, leaving me standing alone. There was nothing special about the room; it looked like a hundred other rooms I had been in. Which, usually the first thing I did was get rid of the ugly bed cover, so that is what I did.

The shower water turned on and my head jerked to the door. My face warmed as I imagined him on the other side.

"Oh, stop that, River!" I grumbled to myself.

I concentrated on taking off my boots and jacket then getting my bag ready for my turn in the shower. The room was quiet. I could turn on the television but didn't really want that to be on when he joined me. Music...I pulled out my phone and looked through the different playlists...what would be a good song to begin the evening? There was "Ain't Your Mother's Broken Heart" about hiding your 'crazy'. I chuckled and scrolled past that one.

The water turned off, and my head went to the door again. That was fast. My mind started to wander to the other side of the door again, so I pulled it back to the playlist.

I was still scrolling when the door opened. My eyes flew to him, then slowly down him as my skin began to heat. Black boxer briefs were the only thing he wore and his hair was still wet...the hair on his chest. I forced myself to take a breath as my eyes went down his flat abdomen to his long muscular legs. It was all I could do to keep from jumping at him.

"Damn, Brodie," I blurted then instantly flushed when he grinned.

"Was I supposed to get fully dressed?" He chuckled.

"I...no...I...I..." I could not get another word out, so I grabbed my bag and walked into the bathroom with the reddest face I had ever felt.

Closing the door behind me, my hands trembled as I undressed.

When I turned off the shower, I could hear music playing in the room.

At the bottom of my bag, I had carefully placed a blue nightie. It had thin straps, lace that hugged my breasts then fell loosely across my stomach then down to mid-thigh. It also had a tiny matching thong. I had no doubt he would like it.

Anxiety flowed through my veins. My hands trembled as I opened the door.

The room was darker with only the side lamp on but I could see him clearly standing in front of the dresser with his back to me.

His bare back was muscular with two small bruises, long legs with a few scars, and under the black material, a very firm round butt.

My face heated again with the desire to just run at him but, instead, I slowly closed the bathroom door behind me.

He glanced over his shoulder and looked into my eyes then slowly lowered to the nightie and my bare legs. A loud long exhale escaped him as his eyes rose again. Then, he turned away.

That was unexpected...now what was I supposed to do?

"I heard this song a couple of weeks ago, and it made me think of you."

"Really?" I huffed. "Please don't tell me it's *Crazy Women*."

He chuckled and looked over his shoulder again, "You're not crazy."

"Oh, good," I rolled my eyes. "I've hidden it well."

He chuckled and turned away, "No, it's Chris Stapleton's *Tennessee Whiskey*."

"I would think *Whiskey River*."

He shook his head and the song began to play, "Listen to the first verse."

I used to spend my nights out in a barroom
Liquor was the only love I've known,
but you rescued me from reachin' for the bottom
and brought me back from being too far gone.

My breath caught as he turned. The look in his eyes was thankful, warm, and held a twinkle from his smile.

"Friday night, in Pendleton, you rescued me from the bottom...from giving it all up and being too far gone," he whispered and took a step to me.

I was surprised when my legs were able to take a few steps without falling.

"You are just like Tennessee whiskey; strong when you fight for your family and horses," he continued as I stepped to him.

625

My fingers slid slowly over his bare arms and up to his broad shoulders.

"Then, those moments when you're not charging a calf but doctoring it instead, you're just as sweet as Strawberry wine."

One of his hands slid to the small of my back, while the other gently cupped my jaw. We slowly came together as we chuckled.

"And now, you're as warm as a glass of brandy."

I leaned into his warmth.

To the rhythm of the music, we began dancing across the floor.

"I can drink this in all night long." He whispered into my ear.

Leaning against his shoulder and wrapping my arms around his neck, I closed my eyes to this perfect moment.

When the song faded away, I lifted my lips to his. The song began again as we swayed to the music with a kiss that lasted the whole song. When it faded away the second time, he lowered and lifted me into his arms. My body melted into him. The song began again as he gently lowered me onto the bed.

Somewhere in the distance of the peaceful sleep, I heard humming and turned to it... into Brodie's warmth. It ran the whole length of my body as he turned into me with his arm curling over my shoulders. My arm slid across his flat stomach as I turned my face into his warm shoulder.

The humming continued.

"I've heard that before," I whispered behind closed eyes.

"*Seven Spanish Angels...*"

"Oh…yeah…" I sighed. "And where did that come from?"

"It was Craig's favorite go-to song for karaoke or middle of the night drives. We must have sang that song thousands of times. "

His voice was soft…wistful…full of memories. My eyes slowly opened to the dark room.

"Have you ever watched *The Man from Snowy River*?"

"Of course, and that song was not in it," I whispered.

"The scene where they are all waiting for the great horseman Clancy…and you see him on his horse trotting across the prairie, sun on him, and looking like he doesn't have a care in the world as he hums his song."

"Yes, I love that."

"After Craig died, Delaney told me to imagine him in his heaven…the place he loved more than anything…besides in a chute. Craig's aunt lives in Hamilton, Montana, and he loved to ride the mountains there. All-day he would ride with no real destination; he'd just trot across the mountains like Clancy did…with a smile of pure contentment with life. It is his heaven. When I begin to fall…when I think of him…I think of him there, trotting across the mountains with the sun on his face, that contented smile…humming *Seven Spanish Angels* and enjoying his heaven."

A tear slowly slid from my eye, "That's so beautiful," I whispered.

"I don't know why he died…I just don't understand…but if he can't be here with us then he needs to be in his heaven. The pain isn't so bad knowing he's there."

Another tear fell as he kissed my forehead.

"Is there anything I can do to help?" I whispered.

"You have…are…did by inviting me to your place to get away. Why did you?"

"I was so shocked to hear of his death and I followed the news coverage…then when we talked in Lewiston, you just tore at my heart. We had just lost Chinook, so I knew the weight of a heavy heart at such a sudden loss. He was six months older than me so he was part of my whole life."

Another tear fell but he didn't say anything. "I know that isn't totally the same, but if I'd lost Caleb that way? I just don't know what I would do and...well, I didn't know how I could help when we were a thousand miles apart."

He was silent, so I turned onto my stomach with hands crossed on his chest and chin resting on them. His glistening eyes were looking through the dark toward the ceiling.

"Why did you accept the offer?"

"I tried the getting drunk and fighting in a bar...Logan saved me from that. Then I did the riding off alone in the mountains and getting totally wasted...Delaney saved me from that. Dad told me to find something to honor Craig and not destroy my life."

"The Big Four rides?"

"Yeah...then when I went home, it was so...I kept expecting him to call or drive down the driveway. Then I saw the picture of my family consoling me after Pendleton ended."

"We were loading the horses and I saw you...it just broke my heart."

"I've only seen the picture once...I don't want to see it again."

"I have a picture like that," I whispered with eyes scrunched tightly together.

"You do?"

"Yes, you met Nellie, our veterinarian. She took a picture when she arrived after Chinook died."

"Of what?"

"Of me, sitting next to him on the hillside...leaning over him and holding his mane in both fists as if I could bring him back."

"Damn..."

"Mom sent it to me...I've only looked at it once."

"You've seen mine, so let me see yours," he whispered.

My phone was in my bag, so I slid on the nightie and walked to retrieve it. I sat cross-legged on the bed as I found the image. Without looking at it, I handed him the phone.

He stared at the image and after a moment, his eyes began to glisten and my heart ached at the memory.

"That's just sad," his words trembled. "You look so tiny next to him."

"He was as big as Iggy."

He handed me the phone and leaned back on the bed to stare at the ceiling again.

The energy in the room had drained and I hated it.

"I do like the first picture of us," I smiled, hoping it would help bring him back to 'the now' instead of with Craig.

"Lewiston?"

"No," I frowned. "We didn't take a picture together in Lewiston it was Pendleton next to the statue."

He turned slightly to smile at me, "You don't know about the Lewiston picture?"

"Which picture?"

"When I rode Marquee."

"No…"

I leaned against his shoulder as he swiped through pictures on his phone then stopped.

The mare was in mid-buck; front legs curled back to her belly, head tucked between them, causing her neck to arch high. Leaned back on her back hooves, preparing for the next launch into a high kick, the muscles in her hips and legs were taut from the tension. On her back, with hand gripping the rein, free-arm high in front of him for balance, was Brodie. The spurring motion had his boots all the way to the back of the saddle, butt a foot from the leather, and head tucked to his chest looking down her arched neck. Arena dirt scattering from the back hooves, mane and tail of the horse and the long white fringe of his chaps flying made you feel the action and power of the ride.

Just in front of him at the exit gate was Delaney watching from her horse. Just behind him and perched on the panel by the entry gate, was me.

"Well, I'll be damned," I muttered.

"When I first looked, I just saw Delaney then wondered who that cute chick was that was watching, too."

"Cute chick?" I chuckled.

"After we spent the day together in Pendleton, I went back and looked at it and realized it was you."

"Huh, I've been in the background of pictures so many times because I'd be on the chute or helping push steers, I just don't think of the photographer being there anymore."

"Yeah, but they sure capture some great memories. The long hallway at home is covered with pictures of us. We even have one of the first time Craig and I met."

His voice trailed off and the heaviness of lost memories began to hurt my heart.

This was not what I wanted, I needed to do something.

I looked at him then gently ran my hands up his chest, neck, then cupped his jaw with both hands. Slowly, my fingers curled to tug into his beard. He smiled as he looked at me.

"How do we get out of this funk and move on?" I whispered and playfully wiggled his beard enough I knew it wouldn't hurt him.

His eyes narrowed then widened, "Well, let's take care of that first."

"What?" I rubbed his beard to smooth the whiskers I had ruffled then set back in time for him to sit up and wrap an arm around my waist.

As he swung himself out of the bed, he pulled me up into his arms.

"Now what?" I giggled.

He was bare butt naked as he walked across the hotel room floor to set me onto the bathroom counter next to the sink. Then he turned and walked out.

"Brodie?" I asked a bit nervously and leaned to peek out the door. He pulled on his boxer shorts then leaned down into his bag. "What are you doing?"

"Moving on," he mumbled and returned with a black bag in his hand. "Hold this."

I took the bag and anxiously waited to see what was inside...it was a razor, a trimmer, and a pair of scissors.

"You're going to shave?" I gasped.

"Yeah, I haven't for a couple of months now...it is past time to do it." He took the scissors and cut the long whiskers along his cheek line.

"Are you going to leave stubble or a mustache?"

He smiled and glanced at me, "We're at a point now I can try anything. What would you like to see?"

"Mustache and goatee," I giggled and leaned back against the mirror and crossed my legs.

As he cut away the length, I watched him. His long hair was swept back away from his face, thick eyelashes framed brown eyes, and almost invisible freckles touched each cheekbone. A few wrinkles crinkled from his eyes as his gaze flickered to me, but he didn't say anything. He started the trimmer and slid it across his cheeks to reveal the skin that had not been seen since Craig died.

"You have to stop that," he whispered and spread shaving cream across his jawline and cheeks.

"I'm just watching."

"No, you're looking at me, not watching me."

"That bothers you?"

"With that look, yes...I'm very bothered ... but I need to focus."

My face warmed again when I realized what he meant.

"What would you like me to do?"

He grinned as the razor began its way through the white cream, "Tell me why you keep calling yourself crazy."

I laughed, blushed, and shook my head.

He stopped and looked at me, "Why not?"

"I hide my crazy to keep from scaring you away," I said with a guilty giggle.

He laughed and resumed shaving, "I can't imagine that. Tell me..."

"I don't know...it might take some hard thinking to come up with something that isn't too overboard for you."

"Tell me one thing," He finished revealing the left cheek and started on the right.

"Alright," I teased. "I keep my hands in my pockets to keep from touching you."

He cocked his head to me with a frown, "I wondered why you always had your hands in your vest." A devilish grin appeared. "You can touch me anytime and anywhere you want."

We both chuckled as my face turned red again.

631

He finished the right cheek and washed away the shaving cream from his face. Then, he started trimming around the goatee and taming the mustache. I couldn't pull my gaze from him as he seemed to reveal a different man in front of me. From the softening of his eyes, I could tell he saw it, too.

"How does it look?" he asked.

"Roguish, masculine, and just damn sexy," I exhaled.

"So, stop shaving?" he grinned.

My whole body sighed at the image. "Yes, stop."

"Whatever you would like, my lady," He chuckled. "So, while I clean up this mess, tell me another crazy thing."

I laughed, and even to me, it sounded a bit evil...crazy.

He stopped wiping the counter and looked at me, "What just went through your mind?"

"My first thought when I saw you in the corral at the ranch...your first day."

"And that was...?"

I bit my bottom lip as I tried to decide whether I should say it out loud.

When he finished cleaning, he placed a hand on the counter to each side of me and leaned within inches of our lips touching.

"And that was...?" he repeated.

Oh, what the hell!

"That I needed a set of handcuffs to keep you from leaving," My face flushed again as I grinned.

His head tilted back as he laughed. It was a deep from the soul laugh that I hadn't heard for a while.

"Well," He turned to the room and lowered down into his bag.

"Don't tell me you have handcuffs!" I gasped.

He laughed again and returned with a roll of white tape he used when he rode.

"Let's experiment," He chuckled and pulled off a long strip of the tape and twisted the middle. Then he took my arm and wrapped one end around my wrist and the other around his own.

We both laughed as we held up our 'handcuffs'.

"You came up with that pretty darn fast," I chuckled. "So, you got some crazy in you, too."

His devilish grin went perfectly with the new mustache and goatee…and with that look, I made him put his hat back on.

CHAPTER FIFTY SIX

"It's good to see he shaved," Mom mused as she looked out the kitchen window at Brodie.

He and Dad were carrying a metal panel across the driveway to begin to extend Iggy's turn-out. The horse was prancing in circles then leaning over the fence inspecting their work.

"A big step," I agreed as I leaned into her and watched the men.

"Have a good time?"

"The best," I sighed.

"I'm not too sure your father is going to let the two of you sleep together in your room."

"We talked about it and Brodie wants to respect my parent's house," I smiled. "So, tonight he will be in Caleb's bed and I in mine then tomorrow night, after we run the horses through the chutes, I'm going to take him down for a night at the river."

"River! It's going to be freezing out there."

I laughed, "Mom, this is me. Have you seen my winter fires by the river?"

"Twenty-footers," she chuckled. "You can stand twenty-feet from it and still sweat."

Monday morning, Brodie and I rode behind the herd of two and three-year-old buckers as they galloped down the road and into the corrals. His smile was wide, and body relaxed as he rode my buckskin gelding. With the new mustache and goatee, he looked a bit outlaw in his dark ranch coat and black hat. I had already taken pictures of him as we prepared for the ride.

When we stopped, I slid off Destiny and greeted him between the horses so we were hidden away from Dad and shared a quick kiss.

The air was chilly and our breath misty as we began separating the horses and running them through the chutes. Manes and tails were tugged and brushed so they could get used to handling and halters were slid on and off. Shots were given and health assessments documented. Then they sat in the bucking chutes for a while before we released them into the arena. It was busy, arduous work that I loved. Doing it with Dad and Brodie was wonderful. The only thing that would make it better was if Caleb was there, too.

I drove the side-by-side ATV down the rocky path to the river using only the headlights and the bright shine of the full moon.

"Good thing you know where you're going," Brodie chuckled.

"Making you nervous?" I teased with a laugh.

"I'm pretty confident you've done this before."

"Caleb and I basically lived here in the summers. We floated the river on rafts and would throw marshmallows in the water to use as target practice with our 22's. We fished and camped out nearly every night. Mom and Dad came along a few times, too. This river has been our playground for the last seven years."

A half-hour later, the fire lit the sky and reflected on the water's glassy surface. Thick saddle pads were laid against a fallen log for comfort as we snuggled against them. A thick bedroll lay under us and a winter sleeping bag lay over us. I nestled into his arms and we silently watched the river flow in the moonlight and the embers from the fire drift into the breeze.

"I'm jealous of your summer nights here," Brodie whispered.

"Heaven…this place has been heaven to us."

"Tell me something about your life before this place."

"Pick an age."

"Eight."

"Oh, that is an easy one," I smiled. "Dad was still working for Waylon who adored Caleb and I, and treated us like we were his grandkids. When we traveled to rodeos or other places with the horses, while Dad worked, our sanctuary was on top of the horse trailer, so we were safely tucked away from drunken man or wild bucking beast. We had the best seats at the arena." I chuckled. "That started when we were five. Everything was great until we got a little…let's say mischievous and we were racing up and down the trailer ladder and I slipped and fell; broke my damn leg."

"Ouch."

"Yeah, I was so upset because they put me in this huge cast and I couldn't go to the rodeos with Dad for a couple months. Worst months of my life which got worse because Waylon stopped us traveling with Dad altogether."

"Well, that sucks."

"It did…but only when Waylon traveled with us," I giggled. "If he wasn't there, then we were stowed away so we could go. There was one time when we were nine, Waylon showed up unexpectedly. Caleb was hidden behind the chutes, but I was standing on top. Nearly everyone behind the chutes knew we weren't supposed to be there, so the world champion bronc rider stands in front of me to block me from Waylon, who walked up to talk to him." I laughed at the memory. "I'm huddled behind the cowboy trying to be as small as possible until Dad distracted Waylon so I could be quickly lowered to the ground. One of the other cowboys took my hand and hustled Caleb and me over to sit with his family in the bleachers."

"Sounds like your dad was a bit devious."

"He knew Waylon was over-reacting and would relax a bit, but he never did. We weren't allowed back on the trailers, but were allowed to travel when we were around ten and could help."

"You and Caleb are pretty close."

"It's a twin thing and we didn't have many other friends outside of school since we traveled most of the summer."

"Our friends were mostly members of the rodeo associations and each other. Logan played football so he had those friends but Craig, Delaney, and I stuck with horses and the ranch."

"After we moved here, it was just basically the four of us and all the friends on the road."

"I don't know if there is a day I regret being on the road with my grandfather, Dad, and Logan bulldogging and a bit of team roping...no rough stock at the big rodeos."

"Same here, but all rough stock. Funny isn't it? That we both spent our youth traveling for rodeos, just on the opposite side of the arena."

"Could be we were at some of the arenas at the same time."

"You're right." I smiled at the image of us as children playing around a rodeo together. "When we got older and started the business, we stayed mostly on the East side of the states until this year when we went west."

"And when we got older, we concentrated on club and high school and stayed West of the states." He squeezed me in tighter to his side.

The night was filled with the sound of the river flowing and the fire crackling. The cold air on our faces was refreshing compared to the warmth of lying next to each other under the sleeping bag and heat from the fire. I took a deep breath and closed my eyes to take a moment to appreciate Brodie and the night.

When my eyes opened, the fire was low, the sky beginning to lighten, and Brodie was missing from my side.

Damn! I had fallen asleep!

A movement behind the fire pit drew my attention. Brodie was walking along the water's edge. He stopped when the moon's glow shone on four deer appearing from the trees and walking to the river. I lay quietly watching Brodie watch the deer drink from the small inlet then gracefully make their way up-river. When the deer disappeared, Brodie continued his walk.

The air was cold, but under the sleeping bag I was warm. My hand slid to the spot Brodie had vacated. It too was cold. He had been up for a while. Hopefully, not upset that I fell asleep.

He disappeared and it was a good twenty minutes before he reappeared walking toward me. There was no hurry in his stride, hands deep in his jacket pockets, and head turned to watch the light sparkle from the water's surface. When he neared, he turned to me, and our eyes met. We shared a soft smile, but there seemed to be something different in his eyes.

"Good morning," he whispered and lowered to one knee at my side. A finger gently moved my hair away from my eyes and tucked it behind my ear.

"I'm sorry I fell asleep," I whispered.

He shook his head, "No need to be sorry, we both did. It was a long day of work and between the fire, river, and holding you...it was just too damn peaceful."

"You've been up for a while."

He nodded with his gaze going out to the river, but he didn't say anything.

My hand slid into his and squeezed, "Are you alright?"

His eyes returned to mine, and he sighed, "A couple of friends are driving by here tomorrow, headed back to Oregon."

My heart dropped, "You're leaving with them?"

"It just makes sense. I'll meet them in Chadron early in the morning."

He rose and walked to the back of the ATV to retrieve a bucket. Scooping water from the river, he poured it over the fire.

No cuddling by the fire? No taking advantage of our last moments alone together? An ominous ache grew in my stomach.

Afraid disappointment would hang on my words, I remained silent as I stood and began to roll-up the sleeping bag. When the last camping item was stowed in the ATV, I stood at the river's edge and let the sound of the water soothe my heart.

His arms encircled my waist as he stepped in behind me. I leaned back and closed my eyes as I willed away the tears that rose.

"I'll see if Nolan or Adam will take me to Chadron in the morning."

Couldn't he say something about us? Why was it about his leaving?

"I can..."

"I want to remember you here at your ranch, not at a gas station being harassed by cowboys."

"But..." the tears finally escaped.

"It's only for a few weeks," he kissed my temple. "Then we'll be together for two weeks in Vegas and we can make plans for after."

"Yeah..."

"Until then, I plan on annoying you a couple of times a day with phone calls and video chats."

I turned into his arms and buried my face into his jacket.

"Let's just forget I'm leaving in the morning and have a good day today," he whispered. "What's on the agenda?"

I leaned back and brushed away the tears but I couldn't get myself to look at him, "Moving the Corrientes herd to the North Line pasture."

"Let's head back before Nolan and Adam start without us." He tried to make it light-hearted but it fell a bit flat.

Once we crested the hill coming out of the river canyon, a chilly breeze stung at our skin.

"Going to be a cold ride this morning," I muttered.

From the look on my parent's faces, they were just as surprised as I was at us arriving back to the house so early.

When I walked out of my room after taking a shower, Brodie was nowhere to be seen.

"Where is he?" I asked Mom as she handed me a cup of coffee.

"He asked to borrow the office for a while," She looked confused. "Why are you home so early? It looks like you're still getting along."

I shook my head with an exasperated exhale, "I have no idea."

The door to the office was closed and since it didn't have a window, I couldn't see him.

"Well, I'm not just going to wait around. I'm going to work," I huffed and walked to the door.

As I slid on my coat, thick beanie hat, warm boots, scarf, and gloves, his voice filtered through the door but it was nothing more than a mumble.

Mom and I looked at each other with a shrug and I stepped out into the freezing morning.

Every five minutes I looked at the house without a sign of Brodie. My heart began to ache and stomach acid began to bubble in anger the longer he was in the house.

After dropping off a large bale of hay in the horse's feeder, I drove the tractor back through the fence Dad was holding open for me. We had not mentioned Brodie, but he did give me an inquisitive look. I just shrugged.

Brodie appeared from the back of the house as I parked the tractor in the shed. I didn't make a move that I had seen him as I stepped down from the machine and walked in the feed room for a bag of feed for the cows. With the bag over my shoulder, I walked out to the ATV and dropped it in the back. I went in for another bag. The anger-adrenaline had two more bags hefted and strode out to the ATV before Brodie approached.

He stepped in the feed room behind me and before I could lift the next bag he was wrapping his arms around my waist and jerking me back to him. I tried to turn but he squeezed tighter.

"Brodie..."

"Shhhh..." He whispered in my ear as he turned me toward the door and lifted my feet off the floor.

All my anger at him began to dissolve, "What are you doing?" I giggled.

"Apologizing for how long the phone call took and making sure you're not mad at me." He walked us out to my truck.

Without letting me go, he opened the door and leaned inside.

"There," he chuckled and relaxed so I could turn in his arms.

"There, what?"

He had slid on sunglasses so I couldn't see his eyes.

"What the...?"

He leaned back in the truck and retrieved mine from the dash then, with a grin, slid them on my face.

"The sun isn't very bright today," I chuckled.

"No, I wanted to tell you about the phone call but I didn't want to see your eyes...or you see mine."

"Why?" I asked with a bit of anxiety creeping in my stomach.

He smiled and looked at me...I think, because I couldn't see his eyes.

"The phone call I received wasn't just about going back to Oregon."

I sighed at the thought of him leaving in just hours.

"Then what?"

He was forcing his lips into a fine line instead of grinning, "I was meeting with all the saddle bronc qualifiers and choosing the horses for the NFR."

I inhaled in surprise and was so frustrated, but glad I couldn't see his eyes and try to read them. We stared at each other a full minute before I talked myself into not commenting. It wasn't fair to him if I quizzed him about my horses.

I turned away and walked back into the feed room. Brodie was right behind me as we both picked up a feed bag and walked it to the ATV.

When Mom and Dad found out why, they put their sunglasses on, too. We spent the whole day wearing the dark glasses, even inside.

Well, after my parents disappeared into their bedroom after dinner, Brodie and I were stretched out in each other's arms on the couch, supposedly watching *Wyatt Earp*. When my phone alert dinged, we were in a full-fledged deep passionate kiss with my arms wrapped around his neck and both legs wrapped around one of his. Brodie rose just enough to whisper against my lips.

"You need to check that?"

With a groan, I grabbed my phone and had to lift the sunglasses enough to read the message.

Text from Mom: Is it safe to come out?

I giggled.

Text to Mom: Just canoodling…we'll take a break.

I giggled again and pushed my hands against Brodie's chest to sit up.

"Mom needs to come out and was checking to see if it was safe."

He leaned back with a laugh.

"I told her we were just canoodling and would take a break."

"What the hell is canoodling?" Brodie chuckled.

"What we were just doing," I grinned.

The bedroom door opened, and Mom slowly stuck her head around the corner, then giggled and walked to the kitchen.

"So, in Nebraska, making-out is called canoodling?" Brodie looked between Mom and me.

Mom chuckled, "When the kids started traveling with Adam, he would have a Weird Word Wednesday, and they would spend the week finding odd words to use all day on Wednesday."

"It was Dad's way of making us read and keep learning through the summer," I said and sat back down next to him. "Bamboozled was one of my favorites. I said it all the time when I was little."

"*That horse just bamboozled that cowboy!*" Mom said in a rodeo announcer's voice. "We heard that a thousand times when she was eight."

"Then there was the summer Caleb got hooked on skedaddle," I laughed. "We skedaddled everywhere we went for years."

"He still says it," Mom nodded.

"The only one we just can't get right is tenterhooks," I huffed. "It's an old fashioned saying but it just doesn't make sense."

"What is a tenterhook?" Brodie asked.

"It literally means a hook used to fasten cloth on a drying frame or tenter," Mom answered.

"But the phrase is used like…being nervous about what is going to happen," I finished.

"So," Brodie shifted his sunglasses. "You're on tenterhooks on whether your horses are chosen for the NFR."

"Brodie!" I gasped and hit him with a sofa pillow. "You're not supposed to mention that."

"That is exactly how it would be used," Mom laughed and disappeared into her room.

Brodie chuckled and jumped at me, smashing me back on the cushions with his lips firmly pressed against mine so I couldn't ask any questions.

"I may have to upgrade my cell phone so I can video chat with you," I nuzzled into his ear.

"I'll be on the big computer screen for the late-night sexy stuff," he bit my ear lobe.

"I don't think I can get myself to do that," I giggled.

He leaned up just enough so we could see each other through the dark sunglasses, "Well, we can practice every night until we get it perfect."

We both laughed.

"Sexting?" He lifted a brow.

"I'll have to find some weird words to throw your way."

"Just searching for weird sex words could be interesting," His chuckle was deep and roguish.

I laughed and wrapped my fingers in his long hair to lower his lips back to mine.

It was nearly midnight when we separated into our bedrooms. I lay on the bed, staring at the ceiling…26 steps and I could be by his side. I fell asleep imagining I had taken those 26 steps.

WML

I heard the faint thump of Caleb's bedroom door closing, and my eyes opened into the dark room. The clock on the bedside table said it was only 5:21. Dad was taking Brodie to Chadron to meet with the cowboys by 7:00. I sat up and listened. There was a faint murmur in the kitchen, so I quickly slid from bed and dressed.

Nolan was pouring a cup of coffee when I stepped out of my room.

"Mornin'," he said and leaned against the counter.

"Have they left?"

"Your dad just walked out the door," he answered. "Had to go over to Valentine to help the Baxter's round-up their runaway cows again."

"I can take…"

"I'll be taking Brodie to Chadron," he smirked. "He took his bags to my truck, then went out to the barn."

"Oh, I'll go out there." I stepped forward, but Nolan held up a hand.

"River, just stay here," he sighed with a look of concern. "I get the feeling he just needs a few moments to himself."

"Why?" I gasped.

Mom stepped out of her room, fully dressed for the day.

I glanced at her then back to the foreman, "Why?"

He shook his head and turned to pull two coffee cups from the cupboard and fill them for us. "That's why he went out there."

"Let's get breakfast going so you can eat before you leave," Mom said.

My stomach churned in worry. I helped her make bacon and egg omelets while constantly glancing out the window to the barn. The sun was just beginning to rise in the distance, but the bright outdoor lights were illuminating the driveway and revealed Nolan's truck sitting half-way between the house and the barn.

Text to Brodie: Breakfast is ready

I stood at the window and waited for him to appear.

Text from Brodie: Didn't think Gloria would be up this early so I just had a protein bar. Thank your Mom for me.

The worry bubbled.

"He won't be in," I sighed and slid Brodie's omelet onto my plate then set them in the refrigerator.

Nolan walked out the door.

Picking up my winter boots, I sat at the table.

"He's had a good time here," Mom sighed and set the last plate into the dishwasher and closed the door.

"Yes, lots of good memories and time to relax."

"Now what?" She whispered and folded the dishtowel, then set it on the counter. Her fingers played with the edges as her lip caught between her teeth.

"Now what, what?"

"Where do you two go from here?"

"We talked about Vegas," I could feel a blush and didn't look at her. "Caleb will be in a room alone this year,"

"And then?"

"We haven't really mentioned what happens after."

"Are you going to Oregon?"

"I suppose...maybe...yeah..."

Her eyes were narrowed, brows together in concern, "River, what happens when he heals?"

"What are you talking about?" I glanced at her as my foot slid into the boot.

"You take on projects...animals. Since you were a child, you'd adopt anything that was wounded and take care of it then just get tired of it. Horses, calves, cats, squirrels..."

"Seriously, Mom?" I slid the other boot on with a shake of the head. "I didn't get tired of them, they healed and moved on."

"That's my point," She huffed. "What happens when Brodie heals enough to move on? You just let him go, too? You..."

The back door slammed loud enough I jumped and turned. Through the window, I could just see the back of Brodie's head…he was walking away.

"Son-of-bitch…" I gasped and strode to the door and yanked it open. He was almost to the truck with Nolan already behind the wheel. The foreman looked confused but the engine roared to life.

"Brodie!" I yelled.

He whirled around, his eyes were an angry glare, "I'm not a fucking project."

"I never said you were," I took the first step down. "That was Mom, not me that…"

"Evidently, that's who you are," He growled, his eyes were narrowed and held that hurt lost-look that had been absent the last few weeks. "You can't use me, River."

"Brodie," I stepped down in disbelief. "That's not…"

"If that's all you've wanted…just to heal me…then you're wasting your time. I don't know if I will ever heal." He opened the truck door and slid inside.

My heart leapt to my throat. Was he just going to leave and not finish the conversation? The door slammed, and my whole body flinched.

I needed to stop him and explain, but two steps down my left boot hit the dirt and froze. The truck moved forward and our eyes locked with no emotion from either of us.

It was as if a sliding glass door closed in front of me. I could see him, but the sound faded away.

I knew I wasn't using him. The moment I first saw Brodie, he wasn't wounded…Craig was still alive yet I was entranced by him…obsessed with him. So, if he wasn't willing to talk…if he was just going to drive away because of a comment Mom said…did that mean he had just been using me? He was just using me to distract himself from Craig's death. The realization hit like a kick to my chest. If he could walk away so easily, then he didn't feel the same way about me as I felt about him.

As the truck neared, I took a deep breath, and the anxiety I had held in my heart for him this past year exhaled out.

A calm penetrated my thoughts and veins. With one final, slow blink, I pulled my gaze from his and turned away. As the sound of the engine passed, the door of the house closed behind me.

For two weeks, I rode the hills, checked on horses, and repaired fence.

I was walking the buckskin through the herd of pregnant mares, when Destiny appeared at my side. She looked at me like she was expecting something so I stopped and dismounted.

My hand slowly ran under her mane and through her thick winter hair.

"You are so beautiful," I whispered to her. "Why am I not riding you right now?"

There really wasn't an answer, so I switched the saddle and bridle from one horse to another.

"You are rather round," I chuckled at Destiny as I lengthened the cinch so I could tighten it. "Not sure why you wanted to go riding with me, but this may be the last time until weaning next year."

When I stepped to her side, her nose came back to me. She didn't usually do that and a bit of alarm touched my heart.

I hesitated a moment and ran a hand down her nose, "You're obviously still in foal, so what are you trying to tell me, Destiny?"

With a bit of a nervous stomach, I looked around at all the mares. The headcount was right so I anxiously stepped up into the saddle and waited for her reaction. Her body rose in anticipation of the ride, just like it had a hundred times before.

From the higher vantage point, I looked out at the other mares. All were in-foal and large. Nothing seemed different so I just took a deep breath and nudged Destiny forward.

Instead of going straight ahead, she turned sharply to the right and started walking.

The anxiety rose again as I looked ahead of us to see if a horse was in need, or if something was out in the pasture. I was a bit surprised to see she turned toward the barn.

"Well, I didn't intend to go there," I whispered to her. "But, let's see what you're doing."

I relaxed back in the saddle and took a deep breath. My gaze wandered over the rolling hills and ravines that led down to the river. There was no snow yet but it was predicted in the next two days so the pastures were tan dormant grass and dirt roads. Not the most pleasing to the eye but I still loved it.

Destiny stopped at the gate and I quickly had us through and remounted again. As soon as I was in the saddle, she began trotting toward the barn. The anxiety in my stomach rose again.

CHAPTER FIFTY SEVEN

Dad was standing in the driveway near Chinook's sculpture, Mom was standing on the new porch by the back steps, and Caleb's truck was just turning down the driveway. I sighed, everyone was alright so what was Destiny up to?

When we approached, Dad turned to me with wide eyes, "Why are you on her? I thought you were on the buckskin."

I smiled, "I was checking the herd and she came up to me like she wanted to ride so I switched."

"She did?" Mom walked to Dad.

"Yeah, why?" I asked in concern but turned to watch Caleb step out of his truck.

Caleb waved but turned toward the house.

"Come out here a moment," Dad called out to him.

I could see the impatient lowering of my brother's shoulders before he dutifully turned to join us. Not wanting to hover over all of them, I stepped down from the saddle.

"I'm a bit tired from the drive," Caleb sighed as he stopped next to me.

It had been six weeks since he had been home, so we gave each other a 'just give the parents what they want' look.

Dad held out his phone to me, "Here, read that."

"What is it?" I asked and took the phone.

The headline of the document on the phone read, "Official List of NFR Stock"

My hands began to tremble. The list of animals was in order of the rodeo event so I scrolled through to the bareback horses.

"Three legacy horses; Baia Mare, Arad, and Sibiu," I gasped with an excited glance to my family. My heart was racing as I continued to read. "Henry made it again and...oh!" I started bouncing in excitement. "Flying Betty is now an official bareback NFR horse!" I screamed.

"And the saddle bronc?" Caleb inhaled in anticipation.

I scrolled up through the list...my heart was pounding...Dad wouldn't tell me to keep looking if Iggy wasn't there, he wouldn't have had me read it if...

"Iggy!" Tears rose as I looked up to the very excited, joy-filled eyes of my family. "He is an NFR horse!" My whole body trembled, the tears fell, and my legs weakened to the point I leaned against Destiny for support.

"Destiny!" I cried and turned to her to wrap my arms around her neck. "Your little boy is National Finals Rodeo bound!"

"He will just be her first offspring to go to Vegas," Caleb chuckled with a hand running down her nose.

"And to think, she wanted to be here when you heard the news," Mom whispered.

We all four laughed as I wiped the tears from my eyes.

"And next to Chinook, too," Dad whispered and his lips rolled into a thin line with eyes beginning to glisten.

"You knew it, River," Mom said proudly. "We all believed and now it's happened."

"How many horses in all?" Caleb took the phone from me. "Oh, hell! Fizzling Dud made it too! Legacy Craiova, in the saddle bronc with Iggy and Fizzling Dud, so that's three and five total in the bareback...eight horses this year."

"Half of them Westmoreland bred and raised," I grinned.

"We have at least ten more bucking like they could go next year," Dad nodded and looked up at Chinook's sculpture. "Home-grown and all the old man's prodigy."

Mom threw herself into Dad's arms and held him tight as Caleb and I wrapped both of them into a big, corny, heart-warming, memorable family embrace.

All of our phones started chiming with alerts for the congratulatory messages that poured in.

I sat on Caleb's bed and fell back to look up at the ceiling. My fingers were interlaced across my stomach and my bare feet kicked up in the air. He sat on the opposite side and fell back so we were shoulder-to-shoulder, just like we had done thousands of times growing up.

"You want to talk about it?" he asked.

"My mind is all kinds of discombobulated! I am bursting with energy and pride."

"Not what I'm talking about," he chuckled.

A twinge hit my heart but I shook it away, "Unless it has to do with the horses, NFR, and anything else that makes me happy, then no, I don't want to talk about it."

He exhaled, "Well, I was asked to come home this weekend to talk to you."

"And it's great timing, so we were all together when we learned who was going to the NFR."

"River…"

"Caleb…"

"They are concerned."

"I don't know why. I've been working just like normal."

"Not like normal, that's the problem."

"What does that mean?"

"Dad said at the Bares and Broncs event last weekend, you worked without an…"

"…emotional breakdown?" I sighed. "I didn't yell at anyone or get upset at a score? I just worked and got the job done."

"Yeah."

I leaned up on my elbows and looked down at him, "Why is that bad? Isn't that what they've wanted all these years; for me to get over my immature outbursts and just work?"

He leaned up on his elbows so we could see eye-to-eye. There was concern in his and it just made my stomach hurt.

"Mom said it was like a switch went off in you when Brodie left."

My lips twisted to the side and I sighed, "Honestly, Caleb, it was more of a door closing."

"No future there?"

"I don't believe there ever was one," I fell back and looked up at the ceiling.

He did the same with a heavy sigh.

"With three of our horses in saddle bronc, there is a pretty big chance Brodie will draw one of them."

"Dad is behind the chutes, not me," I whispered. "It doesn't make any difference to me…it doesn't matter."

I truly wished I believed that.

Dad and I rode over the crest of the hill and looked down at the river's edge. It was a chilly 40-degree day with no wind but plenty of blue sky and sunshine.

The main horse herd was there drinking, lying on the sand in the morning sun, or grazing on the last remnants of the summer grass.

"They look awfully peaceful down there," Dad grinned.

"Well, those seven we're after will look awfully peaceful in Vegas, too."

Dad laughed, "There is nothing peaceful about Vegas. They have airplanes flying overhead all day and night. Then there's all the people and traffic."

"Maybe I should take a picture of them on their river beaches and hang it in their pens so they can remember what they will be going home to."

We grinned at each other.

Henry the First was stretched out as he lay in the sun, Flying Betty was pawing at the water, and Fizzling Dud was standing next to one of the legacy horses as they groomed each other.

"Well, let's go interrupt their day." Dad nudged his horse forward.

The horses heard us as we rode down the trail to the beach and trotted toward the second trail that led them to the pastures above. Henry the First rolled up onto his side and waited until we were nearly on top of him before he stood, stretched out his body then slowly followed the rest of the herd.

"Well, he's in no hurry for Vegas," I chuckled.

We followed Henry up the trail and when we reached the pastures above, Nolan and his sons had the main herd trotting toward the barn and corrals.

When Henry took off in a run to follow, Dad and I did the same. I would forever cherish these moments riding next to my father behind a herd of bucking horses.

An hour later, the seven horses going to Vegas were in the corrals watching the herd running back to the pastures.

The eighth, Iggy, was in the chute as we brushed his mane and tail in preparation for his first trip to the National Finals Rodeo.

Once they were all groomed, they were loaded into the long 5th wheel stock trailer.

"River, how many pictures of those do you have to take?" Dad laughed.

"I want to make sure I get the right angle," I positioned the camera again to make sure the sun's light reflected on Destiny's Ignatius' very first NFR sticker that was stuck to his large rump. He had one on each side, and I already had at least a dozen pictures, but one more couldn't hurt…I took five. His

NFR number was 188…I think I had that many pictures taken of the stickers for the eight horses we had in the pens.

"You have plenty of the other horses already, too," Mom chuckled and tugged at my shirt. "Let's get going."

"But…" I whined loudly.

"No, buts!" They both called out.

I chuckled and climbed down from the fence panel. Iggy's head turned away from the pile of hay he was devouring to look at me…briefly, as he turned to grab another mouthful.

"Pretty much just morning visits," Russ, the security guard, smiled at me. "I promise we'll take care of them."

"I know," I said with a sigh. "You guys always do."

A low flying jet airliner flew right over us and had all of us looking up at it.

"They'll get used to that, too," Russ nodded.

"Thanks," I smiled and gave in to leaving since my parents were walking out of the stock pen grounds and to our truck.

On the tailgate of the truck sat a brown cardboard box. The box was taped shut and there was no shipping label but my name was written across the top.

It wasn't there when we left so I turned and looked at my parents, "Where did that come from?"

They both shook their heads as Dad pulled his knife out of his pocket and began to slide the blade through the tape.

I huffed and pulled the box away from him, "It has my name on it."

He glared at me but I just took the knife out of his hand with a smile.

"She is right," Mom chuckled but didn't leave my side.

With a smirk, I finished opening the package. Slowly, I opened the top flaps of the box and looked in…both my parents leaned forward to peer inside.

All I could see was the Styrofoam shipping peanuts so I took out a few handfuls before my hand hit something hard. It was a glass bottle…my fingers slid around the long neck and lifted. A black and white label greeted me and a knot formed in my stomach.

"Whiskey?" Dad gasped.

"Someone sent you whiskey?" Mom huffed.

"Tennessee whiskey," I whispered.

The nerves tingled down my spine as my hand went back in and pulled out the bottle of strawberry wine.

"Wine? What the hell?" Dad stood taller as if ready to battle someone.

Another dip into the box and I pulled out a glass with just a short stem.

I took a deep breath and slowly released it. One last time into the box and I pulled out the brandy bottle.

"What the hell?" Dad grumbled.

"River?" Mom gasped. "You know what this is? Who sent it?"

"Yes, Brodie…" I whispered as his vision played in my mind. His smile surrounded by whiskers, dark eyes twinkling in mischief, and his body against me…holding me…slow dancing throughout the hotel room. "It's from a Chris Stapleton song we danced to."

"Well," Mom said softly. "So, he's reaching out…he must forgive what I said." She looked at me hopefully.

"I can't imagine why he would leave it here if he didn't," I exhaled with my spine straightening.

Dad frowned thoughtfully, "But, do you forgive him?"

Although we had not discussed Brodie since he left the ranch, it did not surprise me that Dad knew why I was upset.

Without answering, I placed the bottles and glass back in the box and carried it into the trailer. My phone began ringing but I didn't recognize the number so I just stared at it.

"You going to answer that?" Dad asked.

"I don't know who it is," I sat down on the sofa and pushed the button. "Hello?"

"River, this is Delaney Rawlins."

I lowered the phone and ended the call.

"Who was it?" Mom asked.

I just shrugged and walked out of the trailer. Every fiber in me wanted to go see Iggy, but I couldn't. I wanted to talk to Caleb, but he was still on the plane flying to Vegas, so I couldn't do that either. I just walked to the truck. "I want to be early for the meeting to make sure I can get a small stock contractor vest," I called over my shoulder. "You can have the coat."

As I stepped into the truck for the drive to the SouthPoint Hotel & Casino where we were staying for the next twelve days and where the stock contractor's meeting was held, my phone alert went off again.

It was from Delaney but this time it was a text message…an image…the picture of Brodie and I standing in front of the Pendleton Roundup statue with our eyes closed. I just stared at it. Out of all the pictures we had taken, that one was my favorite.

I put the phone on silent.

A half-hour into the meeting, I glanced at the phone to see I had missed another call from Delaney but there was no message left. Another picture was sent but I didn't open it. Caleb had also sent a message.

Text from Caleb: Just arrived, where are you?

Text to Caleb: Stock Contractor meeting at SouthPoint

Text from Caleb: OMW, I had no formal clothes at college so we have to go buy some for the ceremony party tonight

Text to Caleb: Yes! Something to do!

Text from Caleb: You can't find anything to do in Las Vegas? Sad, sister, just sad

I started giggling then quickly looked around me. No one was looking; they were listening to the speaker. The harder I tried to listen, the more my curiosity rose on what picture Delaney had sent. I finally sighed and pushed the button to reveal the image of Brodie and I at the river's edge as the sun rose. We looked so happy. I slid the phone in my pocket.

"What are you wearing?" Caleb asked as he set the new Wranglers, black dress shirt and dark grey suit jacket on the cashier's counter.

"Blue jeans and a WML t-shirt," I grinned.

"If you could get away with it," he chuckled.

"I brought my black lacy, high-neck tank dress with a little jacket and the Victorian black lace ankle boots."

"That sounds hideous," he said as he handed cash to the cashier.

She looked at him with wide eyes then looked at me, "I don't think anything would look hideous on her."

We both laughed.

"Twin brother, inside joke," I chuckled. "He would never be caught complimenting me so everything is just hideous."

"Oh," she handed him his change. "Hair up or down?"

"I was thinking I'd keep the back down but lift the sides," I said seriously. "The little jacket is silver so I brought my grandmother's sterling silver barrettes."

"Oh, pretty, add a little height on the top," she nodded then looked at Caleb. "With you in these and her in the black lacy number, you'll both look perfectly hideous."

We all laughed.

The alert on my phone to notify me of a new Coffee With Cowboys podcast beeped when Caleb started the truck. I plugged my phone into the truck speaker system and started it.

CHAPTER FIFTY EIGHT

Welcome to Coffee with Cowboys with me, Lacie Jae.

Greetings everyone! Lacie Jae with Coffee With Cowboys here. I'm a relocated city girl who will be adventuring into the ranching and rodeo world ... the cowboy way of life.

We are finally in Las Vegas! It has been quite the week getting to the point we were all here. Logan spent the last two weeks with a big group of steer wrestlers on one of their ranches practicing for the finals. Brodie was off training with some of his friends, too. Delaney prepared at home and helped the rest of the family to come here.

I haven't been back in Las Vegas since last year when I met Logan and Delaney while I was lost trying to get to the Thomas and Mack Center for the rodeo. I had the privilege of spending two days with them before going home.

Delaney had a meeting at the MGM so I asked if I could go with her. I wanted to go back to the casino, to the very spot I was standing when Logan asked me if I was lost. Boy, he just didn't know how much!

As we're walking into the hotel, my heart was beating so fast. Not because of the memory of being lost, but because of how much my life had changed since that moment. So many memories: the Rawlins and Houston's, the rodeos, animals, travel, all the new friends I've met, and becoming true friends with my sister, Camille. It truly was a joy-filled walk as we made our way down the hallway.

When we got to the spot, I recognized it immediately and just hugged Delaney so hard because that was how I felt last year when I first met her. We talked about that night while we stood there and she pointed to the path I was supposed to walk down. I turned and looked at the path ... the one, that if I had known where it led, I would not have met them and my life would be so different.

When I turned back around, Delaney was gone; nowhere to be seen. My heart ... well ... instead of Delaney, Logan was there ... on bended knee and a ring box held out to me. There was so much love and happiness in his eyes as he looked up at me. I cannot put into words how I felt at that moment; flushed, trembling, light-headed, and oh so deliriously happy. I don't think I have to tell you my answer. Even before I looked at the ring, I stepped forward and placed a hand on each side of his handsome face and told him how happy and in love with him I was. Then, right there, in front of all those people watching, I kissed him with every fiber of my love. Nothing could make me happier than becoming Mrs. Lacie Jae Rawlins.

I was pleasantly surprised to see the whole family amongst the crowd watching.

While wrapped in my new fiancés' arms, I took a picture of the path I didn't take last year just to remind myself of how that one crossing-point in my life, had affected me so much. I will let go of the 'what ifs' of what would have happened if I had kept up with the group I was with instead of standing in one place until help arrived. Sometimes, moving isn't the answer. Sometimes, we have to wait for life to catch us before we can move forward.

Needless to say, it was a wonderful family night of celebration before the long days ahead of us and no matter what happens with our family competitors, I am going home as a winner ... as the future Mrs. Rawlins.

But for now, we have a big twelve days in front of us. They have practice and autograph sessions each day and tonight is the big welcome reception and back-number presentation. Lots of meetings going on too, but the big one is tomorrow before the awards banquet. You'll remember that Brodie rode the Big Four rodeos last fall as a memorial for his best friend Craig. Tomorrow is the presentation where Brodie will receive the trophy saddle.

In last year's podcast, when I interviewed Brodie and Craig, Craig had stated he would like to win the Big Four saddle someday. Therefore, Brodie's goal last fall wasn't just to ride the bareback for the 4 rodeos, but it was to win that saddle for Craig to give to his dad, Martin. He did, by one point.

Brodie and the committee have asked the saddle bronc and bareback riders that helped him throughout the four rodeos to join in the celebration. He has also asked the stock contractors of the horses he rode to be at the meeting. He could not have done it without such outstanding horses.

I'll try to touch base a couple of times this week but for now, Camille is waiting for me so we can get everything ready for tonight's big party. She is Delaney's personal stylist this week, and I can't wait for all of you to see the outfits she has designed.

Well, I'm off to have coffee with just one cowgirl this morning.

Have a great day and a good cup of coffee.

I turned off the podcast and looked at Caleb as he drove the truck back into the parking lot of the hotel, "Did you know that?"

"That Brodie was after the saddle?"

I glared at him, "He rode Henry the First, which means our company would have been invited to the ceremony tomorrow."

"No, I didn't, but I haven't seen Mom and Dad since I arrived, so they haven't had a chance to say anything yet."

"You haven't heard of texting?"

Caleb parked the truck and turned to look at me, "I have not heard about it, but what are you going to do?"

"Flibbertigibbet," I huffed.

He chuckled at our code swear word we used when we were in school.

"Just because you go, doesn't mean you have to talk to him."

"I know."

"I'll be there with you, then we'll go party at the awards banquet."

I reached for the door handle, "It will just be for a few minutes. I can survive that."

Caleb and I shared a hotel room just down the hall from our parents; where we were currently waiting for Mom to finish getting ready. I tapped the toes of the Victorian boots to the rhythm of the song playing on the television. The dress stopped at mid-thigh and was figure-hugging, but the silver lace jacket was loose with a small pocket strategically placed so I could slide my phone and tiny wallet into it. It meant I didn't have to carry anything and the thought made me shimmy across the room to the song.

"Someone is ready to party," Dad chuckled.

He was dressed the same as Caleb but wore a white shirt and his black cowboy hat.

"You are absolutely debonair," I told him with a proud smile. "Too bad your son looks like roadkill."

"But my daughter and wife make up for it," Dad winked with a grin to Caleb.

"Hey, now," Caleb huffed as he placed his dark grey cowboy hat on is head. "You're going to make me self-conscious."

"All those girls out there tonight will cure that," Mom giggled as she walked out of the bathroom. She wore a knee-length white lace dress, with a long black lace vest over the top. Her dark brown hair was curled to perfection and her eyes shown of love as she looked at us.

"Stunning, Mom," I gasped.

"Absolutely," Caleb nodded. "But it sure doesn't look like we're very colorful in our white, blacks, and greys."

"Your personality will make up for it," Dad teased and slid an arm around Mom's waist to pull her in for a back-bending kiss.

"Ewwww!" Caleb and I called out.

As we made our way down the wide hallway, Caleb looked over at me. "You know you'll run into them."

"May tonight, but will tomorrow," I reminded him. "We just go with the flow."

As we rode down the escalator, he turned again, "Tonight's the welcome ceremony and back number presentation, but tomorrow is the award ceremony."

"Yeah," I nodded.

"I should have at least bought another shirt today for it. What are you wearing tomorrow?"

I smiled, "Why don't we just save some money and just switch outfits?"

He grinned, "Me? In that dress? Now, that would really look hideous."

I giggled as we arrived at the main floor of the hotel and turned to follow our parents to the wide hallway that led to the ceremony.

"I want our picture together at the backdrop," Mom said over her shoulder.

"But Caleb is hideous tonight," I whined with a teasing elbow poke to his ribs.

"We'll put him on the end so we can cut him out later," Dad laughed.

"Yeah, I love my family," Caleb chuckled.

At the entry of the hallway leading to the ceremony, stood a life-size bronze statue of Benny Binion on a horse. On the wall to the left was a backdrop for the official golden-carpet portraits for the attendees. Currently standing on the carpet with his family was bareback rider, Kaycee Feild. They were smiling for the long row of photographers taking their pictures.

The next family waiting in line was the Rawlins.

"Well," Caleb sighed. "That didn't take long."

"River?" Mom glanced over her shoulder to me.

"It's no big deal. We'll be seeing them tomorrow at the Big Four saddle presentation you forgot to mention we were invited to." My stomach swirled at the sight of Brodie in the black hat that we had purchased together in Pendleton. It went well with his black jacket. He still had the mustache and goatee, his hair fell to the collar of his white shirt, and his wide smile brought back the memory of the first time I had seen him horseback the year before. He looked so much older.

"You're going?" Dad turned to look at me.

"Am I not part owner of this company?" I tried to sound mature. "It is only right that the whole company accepts the invitation to celebrate such a large accomplishment."

He smiled proudly as Caleb took my arm and tucked it under his elbow then squeezed tightly.

As the Feild family walked off the carpet, the Rawlins took their place. Brodie and Logan assisted their father as he stood in the middle of the group. Martin pushed the wheelchair to the side. The men looked handsome and happy in their suit jackets, dress cowboy hats, and jeans. Camille walked to the end to stand next to Martin and his arm wrapped protectively around her waist. She wore a simple black dress and heels with her long dark hair curled to perfection and flowing down her back. She was stunning and my stomach clenched in dislike.

Lacie Jae stepped in between her sister and Logan, wearing a silky pale pink dress that flowed to her ankles and pink shoes. As tiny as she was and with her short white-blond hair, she looked like she should have fairy wings protruding from her back. Her laughter floated in the air as her hand went up to show the photographers her engagement ring.

Delaney came into view as she stepped in next to Brodie. Her dark blond hair was down her back and lay over a spectacular form-fitting dress of silver-metallic with a soft purple Aztec pattern. Her smile was dazzling as she turned and held a hand out to her boyfriend, Ryle.

The family grinned at the row of photographers and the lights flashed. My eyes went back to Brodie. He looked happy, truly happy. I took a deep breath and slowly let it out as Caleb tightened his arm around mine. The last moment I was with

Brodie replayed in my mind making my back straighten and eyes move away from him to look at the families just in front of us.

The Rawlins made their way off the carpet, all but Ryle and Delaney. They stayed and posed with Ryle's team roping partner, Jess and his girlfriend and their family. My gaze moved past them and down the hallway to see Brodie standing next to his father and looking right at me. He smiled and my stomach clenched. I turned away to look at Caleb.

"Gobbledygook," I whispered.

He lifted a brow to me with a concerned expression, "Cattywampus?"

"Persnickety."

"Doohickey."

"Just a bunch of damn malarkey."

"That bad?"

"Just bamboozled," I nodded.

Dad turned and looked at us, "What the hell is the brouhaha back there?"

Caleb and I giggled.

"Just their twin gibberish," Mom sighed. "Up to their usual shenanigans."

"I'm just flummoxed," Dad shook his head.

All four of us started laughing. I could always depend on my family.

When I turned back, the Rawlins family was walking away from us and down to the banquet.

All four of us handed one of the volunteers our phones to take our pictures. Once the pictures were taken, I retrieved my phone then turned to see Caleb walking down the hallway to the main doors.

"What's he doing?" I asked Dad as we followed.

"Finding us the right table," He answered.

I loved my brother.

He found a table at the back of the room with another stock contracting company. There was a sea of cowboy hats between us and the stage. I couldn't help but smile and be happy for Brodie when he was introduced and walked on stage. He held up the back number then flipped it around to show

Craig's name written on the back. My heart swelled with emotion, then I quickly downed the rest of the Pendleton to try and drown the tears.

Logan, Delaney, and Ryle also flipped their numbers around to show Craig's name written on the back.

"What a family," Mom whispered.

When the last contestant left the stage and the announcer said his goodnights, the murmur in the room increased and the drinks began to flow. Caleb's head turned quickly. I followed his gaze to see Camille walking from the corner bar with a drink in each hand. I watched him, watch her all the way across the room. Irritation tickled down my spine, but I didn't say anything.

I turned my chair so I couldn't see the Rawlins family and relaxed. We laughed, teased, joked, and had a fun-filled night talking about bucking horses and their accomplishments of throwing cowboys into the air.

"We're going to the room," Mom finally sighed.

I looked at Caleb, "I'm not ready."

He shook his head, "No, I'm hungry. Let's go down to the Steak n' Shake."

I jumped up, "Chocolate covered strawberry milkshake, yes!"

The restaurant was packed when we arrived with a waiting line twenty feet out of the door.

Sitting at a table just inside the door was Lacie Jae and Logan. I started to turn away when Lacie Jae's eyes lit up in surprise, and she waved. I did like her, so there was no reason to be rude so I waved back.

Then, she waved for us to join them.

"There's no way out of it without looking like jackasses," Caleb whispered.

I sighed, "Yep."

CHAPTER FIFTY NINE

"You look so beautiful!" Lacie Jae grinned. "I love those boots."

"Vintage Victorian from my mother last Christmas," I sat in the chair next to her with a smile and nod to Logan. A glance at their table showed they were at the end of their meal. "You look like you need a set of fairy wings."

She giggled, "That's what Logan said, too."

"Congratulations on the engagement," Caleb nodded.

I held out my hand in expectation, "It was very romantic."

She giggled again and slid her hand in mine. There were three perfect diamonds in a row.

"Isn't it beautiful?" Lacie Jae smiled at me then turned to her grinning fiancé.

"Yes, it is," I sighed. Could these two be any more perfect for each other?

"We haven't seen each other for two whole weeks," Lacie Jae said. "And once the rodeo starts, we'll just have our evenings together until after it's over."

"Gives her plenty of time to start planning the wedding," Logan grinned.

"Not much to plan," She laughed. "We'll get married in the backyard of the ranch and have a barbeque catered for dinner while you have a wedding team roping jackpot."

Logan glanced between me and Caleb, "And now you know why I asked her to marry me."

We all chuckled as the waitress stopped by to take our order.

"So, how long have you two been here?" Logan asked.

"My parents and I brought the horses down over the weekend," I answered.

"I was at college and flew in this morning," Caleb added.

"What's your major?" Logan asked.

"Veterinary Medicine," Caleb answered.

"He has his Bachelor's Degree in Animal and Veterinary Science with a Pre-Vet emphasis; at the top of his class," I added proudly. "And is in his first year of Vet school."

"Very impressive," Lacie Jae smiled.

"What are your plans after you graduate?" Logan asked.

"I'll work with our ranch vet clinic and the owner, Nellie, has offered me a full-time job with her," Caleb answered. "She said she would work with my long-term goal."

"Which is?" Logan asked.

"PRCA on-call veterinarian," Caleb answered.

"That would be an adventure," Logan nodded.

"Growing up, we traveled to a lot of rodeos with Dad, and Caleb always helped the veterinarians when they let him," I added proudly. "He rode broncs through high school."

"Are you in college rodeo?" Lacie Jae asked.

"No, I wanted to focus on school," Caleb answered. "I can get my fix on riding anytime I go home."

"He went to High School National Finals twice," I said proudly. "Came in second both times."

"Sounds like you have a good goal and a strong background to carry you through," Logan nodded.

"I just have to get through this next week," Caleb huffed. "I'll be studying this weekend during the day, rodeo at night, then fly out Sunday night. Exams Monday through Friday mornings then I'll fly back Friday afternoon and be celebrating all next weekend."

"Wow," Lacie Jae gasped.

Two men stopped by the table to talk to Logan, when they left, he turned to us with a smile. "That's our cue to head-out."

"We stay much longer and we'll run into even more people and be here all night," Lacie Jae stood. "He needs his beast-sleep."

I chuckled, "Beast-sleep?"

She grinned up to him then to me, "He needs to go into beast-mode to throw those steer."

Logan stretched out a hand to Caleb, "Good luck on your exams. Look me up when you get back, and I'll buy you a line of shots."

Caleb laughed as he shook his hand, "I'll be ready for them by Friday. Good luck this week."

They walked away as the waitress brought my milkshake and Caleb's huge steak burger.

"How many meetings did you have?" Caleb asked as he buttoned the white WML dress shirt.

"Quite a few, but it was fun meeting everyone and listening to all the business talk."

"Did you join in?"

"When it came to the breeding program. Dad took the lead deciding where the horses went and which rodeos we contracted."

Deciding for a more fun and formal look for the night, I was in the matching white stock contractor shirt that Caleb had on but I wore black western gaucho pants and black boots. Both the pants and boots had matching blue stitching. The black cowboy hat had a dark, wide leather hatband with the WML brand and running horses tooled onto it. My belt matched the hatband, and my dark hair was straightened then pushed back behind my ears, allowing the black and blue feather earrings to show.

Caleb glanced at me, "And I didn't think you could look any more hideous than you did last night."

I chuckled and handed him his black hat, "You look like twice ran-over roadkill."

There was a light tap on the door and he opened it to find our parents.

"Let's go, we're going to be late," Dad ordered.

"It's like a five-minute walk," Caleb huffed.

As we walked down the hallway, I continually tucked and re-tucked my shirt then added adjusting my hat.

"Stop fidgeting," Caleb whispered. "It's just a few minutes then we'll escape to the awards banquet."

After lying in bed all night, knowing that I would be facing the whole damn Rawlins family at the presentation my heart was rather calm. Refusing to let myself dwell on the weeks on the ranch with Brodie, I focused on his last words instead. They allowed the calm, cold reserve to ease my nerves...or so I thought.

I don't think it even took the whole five minutes to get to the room filled with people. Just before entering, I took a deep calming breath and let it out slowly.

"I'm very proud of you," Mom whispered as we lowered on the chairs in the back of the room.

"It is business," I focused on keeping my heart calm but my stomach still swirled as I looked across the smiling faces in the room.

Brodie and his family were toward the front by the podium greeting everyone and mingling with all the Big Four rodeo committees. Camille rose from a chair and wrapped her arm protectively around Martin's arm. Her dark hair was in a braid down her front shoulder and over a caramel-colored suede dress that flowed to mid-calf. Intricate leather ankle boots that matched her low-slung belt perfected her style.

I glanced at Caleb, whose eyes kept flickering from the prize saddle to Camille. He was having a very hard time keeping his eyes off her. I honestly wished she was ugly...or even a blonde since he had never dated a blonde.

"Please take your seats so we can get started," A voice echoed through the speaker system in the room.

The room grew quiet as everyone sat except four men who stood behind the podium. The saddle was on a stand to the left and next to it a jacket hung from the back of a chair.

The logos of all four rodeos and the words "Big Four" were embroidered onto the back of the jacket.

"Good evening, everyone," The speaker began. "I've known this year's winner of the Big Four Best of the Northwest challenge since he was six-years-old and traveling with his father, grandfather, and big brother. I don't think there was a doubt, in anyone's minds, that this young man would succeed in the rodeo world. Even before he began competing in junior high and high school rodeo and the different associations, he already had thousands of miles clocked on the rodeo road, been to just about every rodeo arena across the country, and practiced his spurring on every fence, cooler, or old bucking horse he could find.

This year, he competed in all four rodeos in bareback and in saddle bronc. He rode all twelve horses that were put in the chute in front of him placing with each ride while winning bareback and saddle bronc in Kennewick and then saddle bronc in Pendleton. That, in itself, was a tremendous feat. Myself, alongside the rest of the committee members, rodeo volunteers, competitors and the fans in the stands or over the internet, were blessed to witness such an amazing journey this young man took to honor his friend."

The room erupted in applause.

The announcer continued; "He joins the prestigious list of former winners such as Tuf Cooper, Trevor Brazile, Austin Foss, Stevi Hillman and many many more. Please help me welcome your Big Four Best of the Northwest winner from Bend, Oregon, Brodie Rawlins."

As Brodie rose and made his way to the front of the room, he received a standing ovation. Placing a piece of paper on the podium, Brodie looked at the crowd and nodded his appreciation.

When the room grew quiet, Brodie took a deep breath.

"First, and foremost, I would like to thank everyone involved in the Big Four rodeos. I will wear the jacket with pride and display the beautiful saddle with honor."

The room erupted in applause again.

Brodie nodded and took another deep breath, "It goes without saying that this would not have happened without my family. Dad, Martin, Logan, and Delaney have been my foundation forever. This year, we were fortunate to add a couple of sisters with Lacie Jae and Camille. These six people, from the moment I said I wanted to win this saddle, believed in me. They have helped me, battled with me, and prayed with me when times were tough. I'd also like to thank Delaney's barrel horse, Gaston, who won the Pendleton rodeo for her and solidified the one-point lead I needed to win." Delaney's laugh could be heard over all the chuckles. Brodie smiled at her then continued, "To my bucking horse brotherhood, bareback and saddle bronc, I could not have done this without you helping me with every ride. There is a special bond between roughies and it didn't shine any better than in those twelve rides. You were all there for me. Thanks to Kirk, Tate, Johnny, Brody, Trenten, and every one of you that pulled a riggin' or saddle, said an encouraging word, or even a few cuss words when I had a hard time nodding for the gate.

"Of course, it doesn't matter if that gate opens if you don't have the quality of horse to match you in points to win. The stock contractors supplied high quality, point gettin' horses that made it possible. I have already purchased a picture from all twelve rides and they are on the table along the back. I would ask that each contractor sign the photograph for me. They will be framed and hung on the wall at home just above the spot waiting for this saddle. Just under those pictures will be a carved wooden sigh that simply says 'believe'." He took another deep breath as he paused.

"My Pops says you have to believe...you just got to believe you can do it before you can do it." He paused again then wiped tears from his eyes. "Those were some of the first words Craig said to me when we were five-years-old." The silence in the room was heavy. "His last words were, '*I'll see you tomorrow; then we'll go buck some broncs and kick-ass in Omak because we are on the road to believing'.*

Believing is the foundation of our lives. 'Jesus said to her; I am the resurrection and the life. Whoever believes in me, though he die, yet shall he live'.

When he paused, the room was filled with 'amen'.

"Martin told me that he believes that when your soul leaves this earth, it is not the end of your life. Your life will continue with those who it has touched. Craig lives through us." He took another deep breath and looked around the room. "I have decided to create a roughstock scholarship program in Craig's name using the winnings from the bareback rides at the Big 4 rodeos and the bonus money. Martin has committed to matching that amount as well as our family ranch. Craig's life will continue in the hearts, minds, and beliefs of roughies."

The room erupted in applause as he received a standing ovation. I wiped away my tears.

When seats were taken and the room grew quiet he turned and looked at the four men standing behind him who represented the Big 4 rodeo committees. "I'd like to thank all of you again. I appreciate everything your committees have done to put on the rodeos." He turned back to the room and looked around the crowd. "I have one more thank you to add." He picked up the piece of paper and put it in his pocket. Another deep breath before he continued, "Friday night of the Pendleton Roundup, Dad, Martin, and I had left to spend the night at a friend's house. Only one person in this room knows that I did not intend to return to the rodeo on Saturday."

Surprised gasps echoed in the room. My breath caught and fingers curled in fists.

"What?" Delaney huffed.

He looked at her then across the room as if looking for me, "I was tired, beaten up, every muscle ached, and so damned depressed I could barely put one foot in front of the other. I had met her briefly in Lewiston then we were able to spend more time together in Pendleton. That Friday night we shared a phone call that literally changed my life. I stopped the weeks' long funeral I was leading for Craig and began celebrating his life instead. I began enjoying riding again instead of seeing it as a burden."

Mom's hand from the left and Caleb's from the right slowly moved to grip my hands. My heart was pounding and my stomach was a knot.

Brodie continued, "She didn't have to step forward and help me, but she did. Her family didn't have to help me, but they did. They took me in for a couple of weeks on their ranch and let me work, play with their younger horses, and take time to heal before getting ready for this next week. Adam, Gloria, Caleb, and River Westmoreland, thank you for being a true example of the heart of this industry."

Brodie took another deep breath and smiled at the room. "Thank you to everyone who came here today to celebrate this award. There is an open bar and hors d'oeuvres to start the night before we go to the awards banquet."

He took a step back and I took a deep breath.

"Well, that was nice of him," Mom whispered.

I looked at her and thought of Brodie's last words to me at the ranch.

Pictures were being taken of Brodie behind the saddle. Martin joined him then the entire family. The crowd stood and began to mingle.

Dad signed the picture of Brodie and Henry the First that caught them in full stretch. I couldn't help myself and looked for the picture of his ride with Sankey's Marquee in Lewiston. It was the one he had shown me on the bed in Billings with Delaney behind the gate and me on the fence panel. The vein in my temple began to throb.

"I forgot my wallet," Caleb said as we stepped out of the room. "Stay here, I'll be right back."

I was watching him walk away when I heard her behind me.

"River?"

I slowly turned and looked at Delaney.

Her eyes flickered between me and my parents.

"Thank you, to all of you, for letting Brodie rest at your ranch," Delaney said.

"He didn't rest much," Dad smirked. "He worked and earned his keep."

"That is Brodie," Delaney smiled at him then turned to me. "Can I talk to you for a moment?"

I didn't even have to think about it, "I'm going to help my brother." I walked away from her to follow the path Caleb had taken. I waited for him at the escalator while watching for any of the Rawlins to appear. After ten minutes, I pulled out my phone.

Text from Mom: That was rude. He did not need help getting his wallet from the room.

I didn't answer her back.

Text to Caleb: Where are you?

Text from Caleb: Standing outside the meeting room looking for you. Parents went searching for you.

Text to Caleb: I'll be right there.

When I walked down the hallway toward Caleb, he turned and walked into the room that had held the Big 4 meeting.

"Geez, Caleb," I huffed. "Why...?"

My words and feet stopped when I walked into the room.

The room was empty except for Camille who was sitting on a table that had been pushed up against a wall. Her feet were resting in a chair in front of her and a book rest on her knees. Delaney and Lacie Jae were huddled in next to her as they laughed at something in the book.

"Delaney," Camille chuckled. "I can't believe you did this...all these pictures."

"They are just wonderful," Lacie Jae giggled. "Look at that one, you're on Popover, and that one, you're in bikinis at the ocean, then the photo shoot, and the muddy rodeo. Oh, that one with your birthday filly, Piper. She is so little there."

I took two steps backwards as Caleb walked toward them. All three looked up with laughter shining in their eyes; then surprise.

Delaney looked from Caleb to me. I took another step backwards, and started to make a hasty retreat.

"Wait," Delaney huffed. "Please, I just want to..."

I hesitated, "Considering the last time we talked, there is no…"

"We talked?" She asked in surprise.

I huffed impatiently, "In Kennewick…"

"We talked in Kennewick?" Her voice rose in confusion.

"Yes, and you were ready to rip my head off, so why…?" I huffed.

"Wait," Camille slid off the table.

My spine tightened as Caleb's head quickly turned to her.

"I don't…" Delaney started.

"You were the woman Brodie ran into?" Camille asked.

"Just before the rodeo?" Delaney gasped. When I nodded she shook her head. "I'm sorry, but I didn't know that was you. I was so focused on Brodie, I had no idea who it was."

"Really?" I shook my head. "Then why in the hell did you continue to glare at me in Pendleton?"

"I glared?" Delaney shook her head. "I didn't…I just look like that when I'm concentrating."

"She really does," Lacie Jae added softly.

I rolled my eyes in disbelief.

"The first time I remember seeing you, was Friday of Pendleton when I saw your picture as the backdrop of Brodie's phone," Delaney explained.

He had me on his phone the day after we took the picture? I was shocked.

"When I saw you after the rodeo at our trailers, I was trying to figure out why you would be on his phone and why would you replace the picture of him and Craig at Sisters Rodeo."

I was stunned and just stared at her.

"Then you suggested he go with you and your family to Nebraska," Delaney shook her head. "I couldn't even…"

"She is very protective of Brodie," Camille added.

"You surprised all of us," Lacie Jae nodded with a smile.

Delaney shook her head; "The first time you see him and you're…"

I sighed in a bit of a haze, "It wasn't the first time…"

"Well, he said you met in Lewiston," Lacie Jae nodded.

I just shook my head at her, "No…San Antonio…and…"

Lacie Jae's eyes narrowed in thought, "When WE talked in Kennewick, you said San Antonio was fun…you were there? Toby Keith night?"

"Yes," I shook my mind out of the haze. "This doesn't matter…"

"What color shirt did you wear?" Camille asked.

"What the hell difference does that make?" I growled.

My phone alert beeped and I turned away from her to look at the message then to Caleb, "Let's go."

"You were in the pink shirt," Delaney gasped. "You left with Craig that night."

"You slept with Craig?"

I jumped to the sound of Brodie's voice. He had walked in the door behind us.

"You slept with Craig?" He asked again with eyes wide in disbelief.

CHAPTER SIXTY

"What difference would it make if I did?" I huffed with face heated in anger. I turned to Caleb, "Let's go."

He turned and to my dismay, he shut the door, "I remember that night and you weren't in pink. You and I both wore red so we could find each other in a crowd."

"In red?" Camille huffed.

I turned to glare at her.

"Oh, I recognize the look now," She chuckled and my stomach clenched in anger.

"Let's go," I grabbed Caleb's arm instead of the chair. I so wanted to grab that damn chair and throw it at Camille.

She turned to Delaney, "You remember the girl in the red shirt in San Antonio?"

Tingles of irritation trickled up my spine and my hand went from Caleb's arm to the nearest chair. My fingers curled tightly around the top.

"Yes," Delaney nodded and looked at Brodie. "She didn't sleep with Craig. She only danced with him."

I lifted the chair up then slammed it down hard on the ground. All three women jumped but Brodie and Caleb just looked at me in surprise.

"This has nothing to do with anything," I growled. "It makes no damn difference in our lives. It does not matter!" I turned to Caleb again. "Let's go."

"River?" Brodie's voice was soft and soothing.

Instead of popping the chair again, the irritation, and anxiety made me kick it down the aisle instead.

I twirled at Brodie, "None of this matters, leave me the hell alone."

"Why are you so angry?" Delaney gasped.

"River," Brodie took a step to me. "I just want to…"

"What you have to say, makes no damn difference to me," I began trembling as the anger I had been holding tight inside my heart began to take over.

"River, let's go," Caleb knew I was at the brink of losing control.

"I'm sorry for leaving so abruptly," Brodie said quickly.

It was a slap to my senses, "That's it?" I nearly screamed.

"Calm down," Camille flinched.

I shot her a glare that was filled with so much anger she took a step back.

Caleb grabbed my arm but I shook it away from him.

I turned to Delaney, "You want to know why I'm so damned angry?"

With wide eyes, she nodded, "Yes."

Fire coursed through me when I turned back to Brodie, "What did you say to me when you left?"

He hesitated, "I didn't know if I would ever heal but…"

"Before that," I growled.

"You couldn't use me as a project…you couldn't use me…" He shook his head "But I realized…"

"Where did you hear those words?" My hand gripped the next chair and Caleb's hand went over the top of mine to keep me from throwing it.

Brodie's gaze flickered to the chair then back to me. His eyes narrowed in concentration then widened.

"How the hell do you think that went over?" I snarled.

"Where did you hear it?" Delaney stepped to her brother.

Brodie closed his eyes and exhaled. When they opened, they were full of dread.

"Where?" Delaney asked again.

"Where is she?" Brodie asked.

"Who?" Camille asked.

"Mom?" Caleb huffed.

"Where is she?" Brodie repeated.

"Her mother?" Delaney gasped and took a step away from him.

"You used her mother's words to break up with her?" Lacie Jae whispered with wide eyes.

"And she knows?" Camille murmured.

"Where IS she?" Brodie stepped forward.

I turned away from him and walked to the door.

"River, where the hell is she?" Brodie pushed the chairs to the side as he strode toward me.

Glaring over my shoulder at him, I reached for the door handle.

"RIVER...!" He bellowed.

I opened the door and looked out. "Mom?" My parents turned to me as Brodie stopped.

"We've been searching for you two. Are you ready to go to the banquet or not?" Mom huffed.

"Brodie wants to talk to you," I stepped back.

Her brows rose in surprise as she and Dad walked into the room.

I walked out and down the hall.

By the time I hit the top of the escalator, Caleb was at my side.

Normally, I would go to the horses for a distraction but that wasn't an option so I walked through the main casino and out the front doors. Caleb followed me down the side of the casino until we reached the wide stairway that led to the side doors.

"Why didn't you talk to me?" He asked in frustration and pulled me to the steps.

We sat to the side and out of the way then I looked up into the sky and took a deep breath before answering.

"I walked in the house and she was already in tears. She kept saying, over and over, how sorry she was and offered to call him."

"It makes my gut hurt."

"It killed me, Caleb. For days I would catch her wiping away tears."

"Why didn't you say anything to me?"

"I was so angry, I was beyond throwing anything," I sighed. "Other than that, I was hurt and shattered that he didn't really feel about me how I felt for him. It just burned in me that he could leave so easy. That was hard." I leaned my head on his shoulder and we sat quietly watching people hurry in and out of the hotel.

Caleb's phone alert rang out.

"They want us to meet them at the stock-draw post by the front door," Caleb said.

They both looked concerned as we walked through the front doors.

"We'll say this once then move on," Mom said. "He was very thorough and honest in his apology. I accepted it because I knew he truly meant it...he was quite upset."

My stomach swirled, "And we move on."

Dad nodded, "We have three horses in the rodeo tomorrow night; Flying Betty and Baia Mare ride with Craiova as a re-ride. Friday night is Henry the First and Arad."

"Henry made the eliminator pen this year? Awesome," Caleb added. "We have the Binion sale tomorrow, then the rodeo."

"And Futurity Bronc sale on Friday followed by the rodeo," I added.

"Then we shop on Saturday," Mom grinned at me.

"Three days of money out the window," Dad sighed in feigned exasperation as we walked to the banquet.

I stared at the ceiling long after Caleb had turned off the television and lights. A light snore echoed in the room, and I glanced over to his bed and sighed. I was jealous of his sleeping.

Turning back to the ceiling, I thought of the confrontation in the meeting room. I still didn't like Camille, really liked Lacie Jae, and came to realize that I had misjudged

Delaney. Kennewick was a non-issue because she didn't even know it was me. Her glaring at me in Pendleton was just because she loved and protected her brother. I could understand that. I couldn't count how many times I had protected Caleb from buckle bunnies and just terrible women.

Then there was Brodie. His apologizing to Mom was a relief off my shoulders but it did not change the fact that I had cared more for him than he did for me. He left too damn easy.

I rolled over and curled around the pillow and heard a soft ding. Caleb's snoring stopped and a light flickered. He instantly sat up.

"Really, Caleb?"

His whole body jerked as his head twisted to me. The light from his phone highlighted his face enough I could see genuine shock. It made me giggle.

"Why aren't you sleeping?" He huffed.

"Why aren't you? Ten seconds ago you were snoring."

He looked at his phone, "I was waiting for a question to be answered."

"Was it?"

Seconds past without an answer; he just stared at the phone.

"Well?" I asked.

The light on the phone went dark, "Yeah."

After setting the phone on the side table, he lay back down with his back to me.

"Well, goodnight again to you, too," I smiled.

"Yeah, night," he whispered.

What the hell was that about?

"That was a good price."

Dad and I were settled into the seats at the indoor-arena at the SouthPoint Hotel. The bucking horse sale was nearing a close with Mom and Caleb disappearing to the Steak and Shake to get us a table for lunch.

"She was a decent bucker but stopped about the six-second mark," Dad nodded.

"How many left to go?" I asked.

"Ten, but we can go," He stood. "That's two today which gives us the option to buy more tomorrow. Nolan made arrangements for a total of five to be shipped up to him."

"We still need to consider another stallion," I sighed. The thought of replacing Chinook in the pasture still made our hearts hurt.

I followed him up the stairs of the bleachers only to have him stopped twice to talk before we even reached the top.

"I'll just meet you at the cafe," I whispered and shimmied past him.

At the end of the walkway that led to the vendor booths, stood Lacie Jae. Her smile was wide as she waved at me.

"Well, you're a surprise," I grinned.

"I thought I might see you when I saw a bucking horse sale was in progress," She giggled. "Logan is signing autographs in the other room so I just went for a walk to buy more stuff I don't need. He's had steer wrestling practice, grand entry practice, interviews, and autograph signings like crazy the last three days."

"Well, you were right the other day. You'll only have him to yourself after the rodeo each night."

"We're taking Wednesday off from everything during the day and just going to go for a drive," She chuckled. "I'm already looking forward to it."

"Hoover Dam isn't too far. We go there every year during the day to hike and get out of the city."

I looked down as the last bid was called for the horse in the arena. When I turned back, her relaxed expression had become pensive.

"What?"

"Well, I really like you and I consider us friends," she sighed. "But, I just want to say this once, then we don't need to talk about it again."

"Alright…"

"Delaney and Brodie just want to talk with you…"

"Why?"

"I'm guessing for closure," she said softly.

"Isn't that what happened yesterday?"

She shook her head, "No, that was everything just thrown against the wall…now it needs to be cleaned up and put away."

"He apologized to my mother and she has accepted. I've had my closure."

"I adore you for how much love and hurt you had for your mother," Lacie Jae smiled. "I can't imagine how upset I would be if someone had done that to my mom." She hesitated then continued. "Just think about it before closing the door. Make sure you truly got the closure you need."

"Alright," I said to end the conversation.

From the look on her face, she knew it, too.

Her phone alert chimed.

"That's Logan," Lacie Jae smiled. "He's ready to go. Another signing tomorrow, then he has two on Saturday at the convention center."

"At Cowboy Christmas?"

"Both of them, I didn't get much of a chance to shop there last year, so I'll be able to shop while he is busy."

"With your sister," I tried to keep myself from snarling the word.

"No, she's with the horses and Delaney all day to help her. I stay with Logan to help him and Martin and Evan stay with Brodie to help him."

I hesitated but I did like her and she was a joy to be around, "My mother and I are going there Saturday morning to shop. Would you like to go with us?"

Her eyes widened in surprise, "I'd love to."

"We both need to go now. I can text you the details."

"Here's my phone. Type your number in it for me."

When she turned to leave, I walked back to the arena to look for Dad. He was in a large group of people and looked to be in an intense conversation.

Text to Mom: You at café?

Text from Mom: All by myself, I've ordered for everyone

Text to Mom: I'm on my way

Where the hell was Caleb? He was supposed to be with her. I had my answer when I walked past the restaurant at the end of the hallway. He was sitting toward the back at a table with a woman...a brunette.

I stopped in disbelief and just stared at Camille. They were both leaning over the table toward each other so there were only inches between them as they talked.

"What the hell, Caleb?" My hands curled into fists to keep myself from yelling at him. He knew how I felt about her.

They fell back in their seats with Caleb shaking his head and Camille shrugging with her eyebrows together in clear confusion.

I had no idea what to do. If I confronted the pair it would cause one heck of a scene. So, I'd wait until after lunch with our parents...if he showed up.

Turning away, the irritation ran through me, and I stomped to the café where Mom was waiting.

Her smile was bright and happy when she saw me. The irritation eased. I did not want to ruin her day. Dad appeared within minutes and Caleb joined us as the meals were delivered to the table.

"And where have you been?" Mom greeted him with a teasing smile.

I glared in anticipation.

"I ran into a couple of buddies from college and lost track of time," he answered.

What? He lied? My back straightened in irritation. It just proved he knew how I felt about Camille.

"Night number one!" Mom grinned as we settled onto our usual seats at the Thomas and Mack Center. We were just a few rows behind the announcer's platform. "Always so exciting."

"Until day six or seven," Caleb chuckled.

"Well, hopefully, they have a Westmoreland horse drawn every night so we have something to look forward to," Mom smiled then turned to me. "You've been quiet all afternoon. Are you feeling well?"

"Yes, I'm fine," I thumbed through the souvenir program until I came to the page showing the bareback for the night. Flying Betty and our Legacy Baia Mare were listed as the fourth and ninth rides.

I took a picture of the page, circled the two horses and posted it to the company social media sites with a note that Henry would be Friday night. I turned to zoom in to get a picture of Dad standing on the platform then posted that. It was just busy work to keep from having to talk.

The opening festivities started with a light show and the traditional heart-pumping loud 'Viva Las Vegas' song with Elvis Presley. We stood as the anthem was sung then sat as a large square podium was lowered to the arena floor from the rafters and the band took the stage for an upbeat country song that was accompanied by another light show.

"I wonder how Betty is handling all this noise and lights?" Mom mused. The horse was just behind the stage.

"Probably wishing she was back on the open range," Caleb answered.

"Once she realizes she gets to buck after all this noise, she'll love it," I huffed.

There was too much attitude in my comment to him and they both turned to look at me. I did not look back. Instead, I looked for Dad behind the chutes.

The parade of contestants began their run into the arena. I tried not to anticipate the run of the Rawlins siblings, but I couldn't help but smile when Delaney's boyfriend rode in with the broadest smile. When the Rawlins rode into the arena, Logan led the way with Delaney following and Brodie right behind her.

To my surprise, they rode into position in the large U-shape, and stopped right in front of us. All three were grinning at each other then, their eyes rose above me, to the suites along the top of the bleachers. They waved and I had no doubt it was to their father. I couldn't imagine the pride he held for seeing his three kids together.

As the entry continued, I watched the siblings. Logan and Delaney looked elated. Brodie was smiling but his shoulders began to lower and his head dipped a few times enough I couldn't see his face.

Craig should be on the horse next to him and I knew that was what Brodie was thinking.

When all the contestants lifted their hats and tipped them to the crowd, the Rawlins trio held them out and pointed toward their father. Brodie was forcing a smile.

I bit my lip to try and stop the tears as they began to rise. I took in a deep breath and released it. By the time the contestants started their run out, Brodie's smile was gone.

I turned back to the bucking chutes and saw Dad standing with Trenten Montero behind Flying Betty. They were both standing toward her rump. Anytime anyone walked close to her head Trenten would block them.

"I'll be damned," I chuckled.

"What?" Both Mom and Caleb asked.

"When Brodie and I went to the Nile Rodeo, we had dinner with a crowd of cowboys including Trenten and his wife," I answered. "We were talking about horses in the chutes and I told them Betty hated having her head touched so, if I were the rider, when she was loaded into the chute, I'd make sure no one got near her so she didn't lower it to the ground. She would buck better if her head was up."

"That's why Trenten is keeping people away?" Mom asked.

"Yeah, I said from the riggin forward." I nodded.

When the third rider bust out of his chute, Trenten rose above Betty with a wave to everyone to stay back. Dad nodded in agreement to the men as he positioned the flank strap to her back. Betty's head was up and she was looking out into the arena.

"Damn, I hope she bucks," Mom gripped my hand.

"You are the worst at trying to jinx our horses," I groaned.

CHAPTER SIXTY ONE

Trenten slowly lowered onto the horse while watching her head. By the time the arena was clear and they had the rope on Betty's gate, Trenten had his glove wedged into the riggin. With his free hand, he kept motioning for people to stay away from the horse. He leaned back, tucked his chin to his chest, and with one last wiggle on her back, he nodded.

I stopped breathing when Betty lunged out of the chute. Her first buck was high in the back with the follow-up buck being high in the air with all four hooves. With every jump and buck I was rising and lowering with her. My eyes were so focused on her, I didn't pay any attention to Trenten.

Betty's hooves were at least four feet off the ground when the eight-second horn blared. The announcer was yelling, the crowd applauding, and I was screaming.

"Beautiful for her first outing," Mom shook Caleb and my hands up in the air.

"I hope they got that last jump," Caleb laughed. "She lived up to her name on that flight!"

The beautiful blonde horse with flowing mane and tail pranced out of the arena as the score of 87 was announced. Both judges scored her at 22 points.

"That's just outstanding," Mom grinned.

I pulled out my phone.

Text to Dad: I LOVE THAT BLONDE

Text from Dad: I do too

I looked behind the chutes and caught him looking at us. I stood and gave him a big thumbs-up.

The Flying Betty giddiness remained until Legacy Baia Mare bust out of the chute and completed a good strong buck straight down the arena. Her rider was a first-time qualifier and was more than happy when he rode past the eight-second horn and received an 81.

"She is just a solid mare," Caleb sighed with a grin. "Now, we can sit back and relax."

Logan hazed for three men before he finally rode into the box. There was no way a woman like Lacie Jae could be so in love unless the man had a kind heart and soul. After our talk in the restaurant where he put so much focus on Caleb and his dreams, I liked him and silently prayed for him.

The leading time was 3.9 until Logan charged out of the box and he threw his steer in 3.6 seconds. The last rider came in and beat him with a 3.5 second run with Logan greeting him behind the chute with a low five and a wide grin.

When the team roping started, I looked back down to the bucking chutes. Brodie was leaned over his horse adjusting his saddle. He was the third rider on a horse named Spotted Blues. I turned back to the team roping and watched Delaney's boyfriend and partner back into the box. Ryle was on a flashy palomino horse and Jess on a black. Both horses were completely still as they waited. With the nod, the steer was released and ran straight ahead. The horns were captured and the steer turned with the heels trapped in the rope. The palomino completed a turn that whipped around to face the heeler and saved them time on their run of 5.8 seconds.

"Wow, that horse is impressive," Caleb said.

I nodded and watched the grinning pair ride out of the arena through the gate between the bucking chutes. Brodie was standing just to the left behind his horse, hands tucked into vest, and staring blankly into the arena. It reminded me of his first rides for Craig in Kennewick.

I sighed; it was obvious he was so lost he didn't see Ryle and Jess's run. After watching him stare blankly through two more runs, I pulled out my phone.

Text to Dad: Go talk to Brodie

I glanced behind the chutes where Dad was standing along the back wall. He pulled out his phone and read the message. His head lifted and looked at Brodie then to me.

Text from Dad: I'm not bothering him before his ride.

Text to Dad: Stand behind him and listen then. Is he humming?

He read the message then shrugged at me.

Text to Dad: If he is humming, he is not here. He is in the mountains riding with Craig.

Dad's shoulders lowered and he looked back at Brodie. After a hesitation, he walked in behind him, waited until the announcer was quiet a moment, then stepped forward. Another hesitation, then he reached out to Brodie's elbow making his body jolt. My heart ached for him.

I turned back and watched the team roping until the final run was made with Ryle and Jess placing fourth.

Our focus turned back to the bucking chutes where Brody Cress was on the horse known as, Smoke Rings. The gate opened and horse lunged three big leaps then began a solid rocking motion in a large circle with high kicks and head low to the ground with each buck. The horn blared and the pick-up men swooped in.

"Good horse for the first night," Caleb mused as Brody ran through the gate as his 86 point scored was announced.

The next horse burst from the chute but my focus was on Brodie as he lowered onto the blue roan, Spotted Blues from the Flying 5 and Big Bend stock contractors. Cress had rushed up to help the stock contractor, Chad Hutsell, ready the horse.

The crowd roared as the horn blared. The rider in the arena jumped from the horse and landed on his feet with ease.

"That has got to be hard on their knees," Mom huffed.

The gatemen had already wrapped the rope on the gate outside of Brodie's chute. My heart began to pound and stomach tremble but I remained still.

The nod, the gate flying open, and the horse leapt out into the arena…my body tensed and fingers curled into a fist.

After the first jump from the chute, the roan kicked high and fast with Brodie's legs spurring to match the pace. With each strong buck, the horse stretched out but Brodie's feet were deep in the stirrups and arm high in the air for balance. Twenty feet out, the horse turned to the right as the horn blared and the pick-up men rode in.

I took my first breath since the gate opened and starting clapping to relax the tension. A score of 86 was announced.

"That was great," Mom turned to me with wide eyes. "His first ride at the NFR and it was just beautiful."

"Brodie tied Brody," Caleb chuckled.

I nodded with a smile as my phone alert rang out.

Text from Dad: You made that happen

Text to Dad: Let's keep that opinion between the two of us

A vendor walked by and I bought three tall silver Coors Light cans from him.

Text to Dad: Look at me

Mom, Caleb, and I were holding up our beers to him when he looked across the arena to us. His grin was wide as he laughed.

Text from Dad: You are the worst family I could have

We giggled and took a big swig of the beer while he watched.

The saddle bronc came to a close with 86 landing the two riders in third place in the standings.

As the tie-down roping began, the bucking platform cleared with just a few people standing toward the back. When the roping completed and the truck carrying the barrels for the barrel race made its way into the arena, Ryle, Logan, and Brodie were standing on the platform behind the bucking chutes.

The first racer ran into the arena. I glanced at the day sheet to see Delaney was fourth to run.

"Why won't you talk to her?" Mom asked.

She was sitting between Caleb and me so I turned and looked at her with a quick glance to Caleb. Mom was watching the second racer turn the first barrel, and Caleb was staring down the tunnel where the racers entered. No doubt, he was thinking of Camille who would be down there with Delaney. The irritation ran down my back.

My attention went back to Mom, "Because there is absolutely no reason to. Lacie Jae said they want closure and I don't really care what they want. He apologized to you, and that ends it."

691

Her lips pursed and eyes narrowed.

We watched the third rider race into the arena.

I relaxed back in my seat with hands tucked deep into the vest pockets. They curled into fists as Caleb continued to stare down the tunnel with a blank expression.

Delaney and her red roan horse sped into the arena. She wore a black hat with leather tooled hat band that matched her belt and the cuffs that ran from her wrist to just below her elbows. Matching tooled leather ran across the front shoulders of her black shirt. Her dark blonde hair was flying behind her.

Damn, she looked fantastic but more importantly, she was soaring and my heart was pounding almost as hard as the horse's hooves.

Two barrels turned and they aimed for the third. The turn was so close the whole arena gasped then started yelling. As they ran out of the arena, the crowd erupted at her 13.65 run. She was in first place.

"Wow," Mom gasped. "That was great and didn't she look beautiful?"

"Probably win the best-dressed contest the racers have," Caleb nodded.

And Lacie Jae said Camille was styling Delaney for the week, which made me glare at him again. Why were he and Camille in the restaurant together? And why did he lie about it?

The race came to an end with Delaney placing second.

"Are you going to the buckle ceremony at SouthPoint?" Mom asked.

I looked at Caleb but he didn't answer; his focus was on that damn tunnel.

"The futurity sale is in the morning," I answered. "I don't want to stay out too late. Maybe tomorrow night."

"I need to study," Caleb mumbled and turned to watch the first bull rider bust from the chute.

Friday morning, I slid my vest over a white shirt with our WML brand on the cuff of each sleeve and on the left pocket. It was subtle but there. The black hat I had purchased in Pendleton was the last touch before walking to the door to meet with Dad. I looked over my shoulder to Caleb, who was already leaned over a book with the laptop open next to him. A pencil moved across a white notebook. To anyone else, he looked deeply focused, but I knew better. When he focused, his eyes would narrow as he concentrated, but now his eyes were relaxed and shifting from book to computer to paper as he wrote.

"See ya," I mumbled and stepped out the door.

"Have fun."

I pulled the door closed but stopped just before the latch hooked. I waited until I could hear muffled talking then pushed the door open. He was leaned back in the chair, phone to ear, and looking up at the ceiling.

"Any luck?" He paused then exhaled. "Tonight or tomorrow? I leave on Sunday."

His head slowly turned to look at me with eyebrows rising in surprise.

"Yeah, I understand," he said. "I'll just wait and hear from you. I have to go…yeah."

He lowered the phone and ended the call.

"What?" He sniped.

"You know how I feel about her," I huffed. "Why would you…?"

"Who?"

"I saw you with Camille yesterday," I glared. "Knowing how I feel…"

He shook his head and rolled his eyes, "It has nothing to do with you. Just go to the sale."

"Caleb…" I fumed.

"I know how you feel and don't worry about it." He turned back to the books and picked up the pen to dismiss me.

With a final glare, I turned away.

Dad was already waiting for me at the top of the escalator.

693

"Just you and me today," he grinned.

"Well then, we better spend all our money today on horses before I go shopping with Mom tomorrow."

He laughed and I relaxed.

We sat a short distance from the crowd in the bleachers of the equestrian arena in the SouthPoint hotel. Both of us holding a catalog and making notes as the horses were bucked out of the chutes. For the next few hours, I forgot about Brodie, Caleb, Camille and everyone else and just got lost in talking and buying bucking horses with Dad. I loved it.

"I like that pick-up man's horse, too," I pointed at the dark bay horse. "I could use another riding horse to give the buckskin gelding a rest."

"You ever going to name him?"

"Who?"

"The buckskin gelding."

"That is his name."

"Seriously, River?"

"Yeah, and I can buy that one and call him the bay gelding."

We grinned at each other and by the end of the day, we were loading the bay gelding and four bucking horse mares into the back of the transport truck.

As the large truck drove away headed to Nolan in Nebraska, I turned to Dad.

"We bought mares…not a stud or even a potential stud."

"No," he sighed. "You've been on me about picking from our own herd, so I'll relent. Let's go have lunch and talk over what homegrown boys we should consider instead."

"Food and horses; doesn't get much better."

Caleb was still hovering over his laptop when I arrived back at the room.

"Still?" I fell onto the bed.

"Hmmm," He nodded. "Give me five minutes."

I leaned back on the bed with my arms flayed to the side and stared at the ceiling while thinking of the bucking horses we had purchased. Minutes passed by and my eyes began to close...my mind went to Brodie standing behind the chutes. It always went to Brodie when I had nothing to do to keep it busy.

"After studying all morning, I called the teacher and asked if I could do the test today instead of next Friday," Caleb sighed. "That way I can come back Thursday afternoon."

"You finished it?" I asked behind closed eyes.

"Crushed it."

"Shall we go out and celebrate after Henry bucks tonight?"

"A friend offered me a pair of Bill Engvall tickets."

My eyes flew open and I twisted to him, "Did you take them?"

"Absolutely."

I didn't arrive at my seat until the first horse bucked out of the chute. It was Trenten on Sankey's Prairie Rose, and boy did that horse buck, duck, and dive with Trenten doing a spectacular job of riding the beast. They rode along the wall right under us.

If it wasn't for the beer and the three containers of French fries I was holding, I would have been applauding right along with the rest of the fans.

"Damn, good," Caleb yelled.

"You have enough fries?" Mom chuckled.

"Never in this place," I popped the first one in my mouth and held them out to share. Caleb took the first container from the pile. "See, never enough with Caleb around."

She took the second container with a smirk, "Just trying to help out your figure."

"By destroying yours?" I grinned.

"I can use a couple pounds," She smiled sweetly.

"And I can't?" I gasped with a giggle.

"I would never say that...out loud," she said and Caleb laughed.

The announcer's voice interrupted her teasing when Henry the First's name was called.

Our attention went back to the chutes as the big bay was released. The horse and rider scored an 89 for a second-place finish. Henry's third go-around at the two NFR's and he had placed second in all three.

"He's going to get that damn go-round buckle one of these days," I muttered.

"Well, do you want to stay for the rest of the rodeo or go ahead and go to dinner?" Caleb asked.

Logan Rawlins walked his horse into the arena and backed into the hazing box.

"I'm fine either way," I answered.

"I'm going to be honest," Mom sighed. "I really want to see how she is dressed tonight."

I knew she meant Delaney so I pulled out my phone and found the image that had been posted on the network's Facebook page of Delaney getting ready for the rodeo.

"Here," I muttered and handed Mom the phone.

Delaney's pants, body-hugging vest, and hat were made of dark, distressed oil-skin leather, which were complemented with a black shirt, hatband, belt, and boots. Her sponsor's patches were visible down her arms, and their family brand was over her left chest of the vest. A dark red wild rag was wrapped perfectly around her neck, and her long, dark blonde hair was in a thick braid down her back.

"Wow," Mom whispered.

"Damn," Caleb huffed. "Very western but also elegant."

It was an excellent way to describe it.

"*All she needs is a pair of six-shooters strapped around her hips,*" Mom chuckled. "That's what the quote under the picture says."

I watched Logan back into the box and prepare for his run. He was wearing a black shirt and hat...very standard for him. My mind instantly wandered to Brodie and what he would be wearing. Oddly enough, I could not remember what chaps he had worn the night before, the bright blue chaps he had worn during the Big Four rodeos or the navy blue chaps he had always worn before Craig died.

Logan placed second with a 4.1-second run. Delaney's boyfriend and his partner caught both ends for a 5.2, and it was irritating the hell out of me that I was anticipating all their family rides. By the time Brodie was standing behind the chute, I had slumped down into the chair with fists shoved deep in the vest pockets. As hard as I tried, I couldn't help but watch the big monitor hanging from the ceiling to see the man close-up as he measured the length of rein for the ride.

He wasn't wearing the light or dark blue chaps. Black chaps with golden leather-tooled trim hugged his hips. With the close up it was easy to see the family brand on one thigh of the chaps and the word 'believe' on the other. To one side of the buckles at his waist was the replica of the NFR back-number with his 88 in red ink and the other side was the initials CH. Long black and dark blue fringe swayed as he stepped over the panel and the horse. His black vest covered a white shirt, and the black hat and whiskers gave him a rugged outlaw image. My fists curled in my pockets.

"Next we have Brodie Rawlins, the saddle bronc rookie of the year on Nutrena's Hammer Stone, who is a force to be reckoned with," the announcer said.

The gate swung open and after two long strides, the horse started a strong powerful, rhythmic buck in a large circle. Brodie matched him stride for stride. The 84.5 point ride landed him in fourth place for the night.

I tried not to care.

Delaney and her roan horse flew into the arena, and 13.85 seconds later they stopped the clock when they ran out. It placed her third.

Again, I tried not to care.

CHAPTER SIXTY TWO

Saturday morning, Mom and I met Lacie Jae at the front entrance of the convention center. Her wide grin and happy light in her eyes helped boost my energy. She was a joy to be around.

Two hours of shopping, there was not one word spoken of the Rawlins family beside Logan. Lacie Jae stopped in front of a vendor with beautiful rugs for sale and ended that reprieve.

"Delaney said their ranch house is a showroom for the vendors here," she giggled. "Now that I see a lot of the merchandise, I have to agree."

"Sounds beautiful," Mom smiled.

"It is," Lacie Jae answered. "Ever since Evan qualified for the NFR, they have purchased one or two pieces each year to add to the look. I informed him, just because Logan and I were getting married did not mean I was moving out. So he said I get to choose this year."

She and Mom laughed, my stomach ached, but I managed to smile.

The rug she was standing in front of looked like a large piece of tooled leather. The black and gold swirled pattern circled a long-horned steer head. "This rug in front of the fireplace would really add to the room," Lacie Jae said and waved at the vendor.

As she purchased the rug and made arrangements for it to be shipped, I held her bags and Mom bought two lamps from the vendor next door. Lacie Jae loved them and bought two, also.

"Since we're parked in front, I'm going to take the lamps to the truck so we don't have to carry them," Mom said and turned to Lacie Jae. "Would you like me store yours there?"

"Yes, but I'll help carry them out," Lacie Jae answered.

"I'm going down to the Rock & Roll Denim booth," I smiled. "Have a nice walk."

They both chuckled and walked away.

I stopped at the NFR booth and bought a few items then turned down the aisle only to be met by Delaney and Camille. Not them in person, but a 60 foot long, 20-foot high picture of them standing in front of a horse trailer parked by an old abandoned gas station. The sun was rising behind them and the women looked strong in their wide-stance poses and fierce eyes boring into the camera. They both looked like they were staring right at me. A dozen people were standing next to the long wall, just looking at the picture. Whether I liked them or not, it was a stunning image.

The shorter wall on the side had additional images of them in different positions. Not one image was a sexy 'come hither' look, they were all strong, confident women's expressions. There were also a few of the two women laughing and looking like they were having a fun time.

A lone woman was standing at the sidewall staring at the images. She had long black hair to her waist, pretty blue eyes, and the deepest, darkest red lipstick I had ever seen. There was something about the way she was sneering at the two women that made me watch her for a moment. She reached in her purse and pulled out a pen.

"Nice pictures," I stepped up next to her.

She startled, then caught herself and gave me a broad smile and dropped the pen back in her purse.

"Yes…they are," she drawled. Her sneer returned as she looked at an image of Delaney standing in the back of the horse trailer with hands-on hips, feet apart, and chin tipped up in a proud, defiant look. Camille was holding the back gate open and looking over her shoulder at the camera as if she were pissed they were interrupted. It was stunning.

"You know them?"

She huffed with a slight shrug, "I know *of* the blonde, but I know the brunette. She was here with me last year."

"Oh, so she's a friend of yours?" I asked in surprise.

"Was…" Her gaze never left the image. "You know them?"

I shook my head, "Know *of* them."

She huffed again, "She was a good friend or so I thought. I even helped her find a job after her father died and we shared an apartment with a friend."

"What do you mean 'or so I thought'?" My stomach clenched in anticipation.

After a heavy sigh, her head turned to look at another image, "She was jealous of me. Ever since we met she wanted what I had so she seduced my boyfriend so I would break up with him."

I gasped in shock. It confirmed that I had to keep Caleb away from Camille. "Did you?"

"Of course, I did," She rolled her eyes and shook her head as if I were crazy for even asking. "Then I kicked her out of the house we shared."

The pen was in her hand again and she pulled off the cap. When she leaned toward the picture, I grabbed her arm.

"What are you doing?"

An older couple walking down the aisle toward us stopped and watched as I lowered the woman's arm.

She grinned and pulled her arm away, "I think Camille would look great with a pig nose, deviled horns, and maybe a mustache."

She leaned in again with pen-raised. The couple watching started waving at someone as I stepped in between the wall and the pen.

The woman glared at me, "What the hell difference does it make to you?"

"For me? Not a damn thing," I smiled coldly. "But for the people that paid for the images and this vendor display it means a lot of hard work and money."

A man walked to the older couple and they pointed at the woman and me.

"Can I help you?" The man asked us.

The woman looked at him, then turned and walked away. She disappeared into the mass of people.

He turned and growled at me, "The couple said you were drawing on the pictures?"

"Not her, the other woman," The older man said. "This woman stopped her."

He looked at me then down to my vest, "You're a stock contractor here?"

"Yes," I nodded.

He turned back to the older couple, "Thank you for stepping in."

They both nodded and made their way down the aisle.

He turned back to me with an outstretched hand, "I'm Terry Halsted."

"River Westmoreland," I smiled.

"I appreciate your stepping in. It would have been a shame to have the image destroyed and have to cover it up for the week. We were all pleased at how well they turned out. They are costly, too."

"I imagine so."

"Tell you what," he smiled and took a step back. "If you're looking for a new trailer for your company, I'll make you one hell of a deal."

What better way to spend the money the horses had earned for coming to the NFR then to buy them a new transport? I had no doubt Dad would agree.

We were standing in his booth looking through the catalog when Mom and Lacie Jae found me.

"Terry?" Lacie Jae laughed. "So good to see you."

He gave her a quick hug, then looked at me. "I didn't realize you knew Camille and Delaney."

"I know Lacie Jae," I corrected with a smile and tucked the catalogs in my bag.

"River just kept a woman from writing on the image of Camille and Delaney," Terry told them. "So, I'm working on a great deal for her on a trailer."

"Adam will like that," Mom smiled. When talking business, she always called Dad and I by our names so no one would look down to me as just the 'owner's daughter'.

I exchanged cards with Terry and we started shopping again.

A half-hour later, as all three of us were trying on boots, Lacie Jae turned to me with a frown, "Who in the heck would want to draw on that wall?"

I shoved my foot into the boot, "She said she was here with Camille last year."

"WHAT!" Lacie Jae gasped. "Eve or Kendra?"

"I have no idea," I shrugged.

"Short hair or long?" She asked.

"Down to her waist," I stood and shuffled my feet for the feel of the boot.

"Kendra...ooh, I don't like her," Lacie Jae growled.

"Well, I love these boots," I said to distract her. "What do you think of yours?"

She stomped the boots on the ground. No doubt, she was smashing Kendra under them.

"I like them," She finally mumbled.

"What do you think of these?" Mom asked and showed us her pair.

"Yes," Lacie Jae and I said at the same time.

We grinned at each other and bought all three.

Nothing more was said about Kendra or the incident, and we managed to cover the whole convention center before we had to leave to get ready for the rodeo.

"So, since he is in a wheelchair, is Evan allowed to help with the contestants?" Mom asked Lacie Jae.

She shrugged, "I don't know; he likes to watch from a suite with some of his old riding buddies."

"Then, if everyone else is taking care of one of the contestants, who do you sit with during the rodeo?" Mom asked Lacie Jae as we left the building.

"I just sit down by the roping chute," Lacie Jae shrugged.

"By yourself?" I asked.

She nodded, "Yeah, I still enjoy it because it happens so fast, and I've gotten to know a lot of the riders."

Mom and I glanced at each other and smiled.

"We have four tickets and only use three because Adam is behind the chutes," Mom said. "Would you like to sit with us?"

Lacie Jae's eyes opened wide in excitement, "I would love to. Today was so fun."

Mom gave her one of the tickets, and she was in her seat before we arrived. She was wearing her new black boots and a cute black dress with a turquoise and silver belt around her tiny waist. Caleb, Mom, and I were in our black cowboy hats and white WML shirts. I wore my vest over mine.

She sat on the edge of her seat through the opening and when the three Rawlins siblings stopped in front of us and looked up at their father, she stood and waved at them.

I grinned at her exuberance when Logan spotted her and pointed her out to Brodie and Delaney. All three waved. Brodie smiled at me and my stomach swirled again as I nodded in return then turned away to look for Dad behind the chutes.

As the riders streamed out of the arena, Lacie Jae turned to us, "Do you have any horses in the performance tonight?"

"No, we have three more horses that haven't been drawn yet so hopefully this is our only free night," I answered.

"Last year, I didn't know anyone here besides my sister and her two friends but I enjoyed it anyway. It's so much more exciting when you know the competitors," She said and pulled out her phone. "I hope you guys don't mind, but I like to video all three of them...and Ryle, so that is four."

"Why would we mind?" Caleb asked. "We'll just make sure not to swear while you're videoing."

"It would be River that would swear," Mom quipped.

I just shrugged because she was right.

Logan was the first of her targets. She lifted the phone, "OK, starting in 1, 2, 3 now..."

Logan backed into the box as I relaxed back in my seat.

His reins were tight as he held back the big bay horse. With a nod, the steer bust from the chute with the horse and a leaning Logan right behind him. Stretching out, Logan slid from the horse with arm around the right horn and hand gripping the left. The official's flag fell, stopping the clock at 4.1 seconds when six legs were in the air as the steer rolled over and nearly on top of Logan. The steer jumped to his feet and right over the top of him with a hoof caught in Logan's shirt. As the steer ran off, the material tore from shoulder to waist. When Logan stood, the front of the shirt fell to his knees, exposing a hairy chest and abs with the crowd and announcer cheering.

Lacie Jae started giggling. She stopped the video then pointed it to the large screen over the top of the arena as they replayed the run and Logan standing. The crowd cheered again and she took the picture just as the shirt fell and Logan looked down.

With a mischievous laugh, she waved at him as he looked up at her. He shook his head but didn't even lift the material to cover himself as he walked out of the arena.

"I'll have to show him that picture when he decides to eat something fattening or not exercise," She giggled with a wide grin to us. "You just never know when you're going to expose your tummy to 18,000 people."

Mom, Caleb, and I laughed. She truly was one of a kind.

"And the millions of people watching online or on TV," I added.

Her laugh was a bit devilish as she typed on the phone. Moments later, she was giggling again, "I sent it to Evan and he said he is going to have it enlarged and put it in front of the treadmills at home."

When the attention shifted to the bucking chutes, Brodie was leaning over the horse and adjusting his saddle.

"It was really nice of Adam to talk with Brodie Thursday night before the ride," Lacie Jae said without looking at us. "I could see he was struggling to focus but there wasn't anything I could do about it."

"He didn't want him to get hurt," Mom sighed.

As much as I didn't want to talk about Camille around Caleb, I wanted the conversation away from Dad and Brodie. "You said on your podcast that your sister was Delaney's stylist for the week. I really liked the leather cuffs the first night."

"And last night's," Mom added.

Lacie Jae's face lit with excitement, "I can't wait for you to see tonight's outfit. Do you know who Annie Oakley is?"

"Of course," All three of us nodded.

"There is a famous picture of her posing with her rifle. She is wearing this embroidered skirt with flowers down her hip and thigh and fringe at the bottom. Camille had the whole outfit designed from that portrait except she had the skirt and leggings made into denim jeans instead." Her grin was wide. "Wait until you see it!"

"She's going to have to do a whole photoshoot just for the clothes," Mom smiled.

"They are next Thursday," Lacie nodded. "Camille designed a shirt to honor Lillian Rawlins, their mother. She died of heart disease so the shirts and pants are black with red ribbons embroidered on them." Her hand covered her heart. "It was so special when she showed the design to everyone for just Delaney, then Logan and Brodie wanted matching shirts. They'll wear them the last night."

"Damn," Caleb muttered.

"Yes," Lacie Jae nodded.

She chatted about the different designs until the team ropers entered, and she prepared to get another video.

For the third night in a row, Ryle and Jess managed a perfect run but in 5.3 seconds, which placed them fourth.

The action turned to the saddle bronc, and I resumed the position of hands deep in vest pockets and body slumped in the chair.

"Do you go to the buckle ceremony?" Caleb asked Lacie Jae.

My stomach burned. I knew he was just asking if Camille was going to be there.

"Just Logan last night as a friend to Tyler who won," Lacie Jae answered. "They are all such a wonderful group of men that really support each other. If no one wins tonight, Camille wants to take Martin out on the town. He's having a hard time so she wants to get him active instead of laying around the hotel until he can get himself to sleep."

"Huh," Caleb hummed. "What do you have planned?"

My stomach ached.

"She's been so busy with the horses, styling Delaney, and helping with autograph signing, I'm not sure she has planned anything yet," Lacie Jae answered.

"If you don't want to go too far, bowling at SouthPoint is a lot of fun," Mom said. "They have a great bar, too."

"I'll text Camille right now," Lacie Jae giggled.

Five bronc rides later, Lacie Jae's phone beeped.

"Bowling it is," Lacie Jae smiled, then lifted her phone as Brodie lowered himself over the horse Ricky Bobby.

The gate opened and three jumps in Brodie was toppling forward in the saddle. Lacie Jae gasped and my breath caught as he righted himself back up and finished the 78 point ride.

"Well, he got a score," Caleb huffed.

Brody Cress was next with an 84 point ride. At the end of the saddle bronc section, the announcer informed us that nine of the fifteen riders had ridden all three horses and all were still in contention to win the average, which could lead to the World Championship.

"That's going to be a hell of a contest," Lacie Jae said.

My feet began to tap on the floor impatiently. I was ready to go but knew we were going to stay to finish the rodeo with Lacie Jae. It would be pretty rude to leave her.

When Delaney raced into the arena, I watched the big monitor to see her outfit, but the 13.62 seconds didn't leave much time to see it.

"I should take pictures to show you before I get here," Lacie Jae giggled. "If you don't mind, since we are going out tonight, I'm going back to find Logan."

"No problem," Mom smiled.

We sat through half of the bull riders then walked up to the aisle to watch the remaining on the monitors. Dad appeared at the glass doors and we escaped before the mass of people.

"Now what?" Mom asked.

I thoroughly expected Caleb to suggest bowling.

"Dinner?" Dad asked.

"Yes," Caleb and I answered.

I was a bit stunned when Caleb turned to me, "Movie after to let the old folks go back to their room?"

"Yes," I giggled at Mom's glare.

Half-way through the movie, I received a text.

Text from Dad: Mason Clements vs. Legacy Sibiu, Zeke Thurston vs. Destiney's Ignatius

Caleb and I looked at each other with wide eyes.

"Damn glad I'll be here for that," he whispered.

CHAPTER SIXTY THREE

Text from Dad: You're eating already? The grand entry just started

Text to Dad: Of course, you hiked our butts off this morning

Text from Dad: It was good for you after days in this town just sitting around.

Text to Dad: Yes…I think you told us that about at the three-hour mark and then the four

Text from Dad: I promised you a big dinner after Iggy bucks and before Caleb flies out

Text to Dad: We only bought beer and French fries, so we still expect the big dinner

Text from Dad: How many orders of fries?

Text to Dad: Just 6

I turned and looked at him on the back of the platform as the contestant grand entry parade began to run out of the arena. He was standing next to Mason Clements, who Legacy Sibiu had drawn for the ride. They were the last of the bareback to buck so the horse was still in the tunnel.

Text to Dad: What's all the kerfuffle about? It is an easy four hours before dinner and three of us are eating the six orders…I think this is where I should have paid attention to algebra…but I didn't…so college boy did the calculating. It's a half an order per thirty minutes. That's not bad. ☺

Text from Dad: But the question is, how many have you already eaten?

Text to Dad: 15 minutes = 4 orders gone ☺

Text from Dad: So much for algebra

Text to Dad: I think college boy forgot the hunger-factor in his equation

I glanced over to see Mason looking over Dad's shoulder reading the text. I started to giggle when they both grinned.

"How did the bowling go last night?" Caleb asked Lacie Jae.

"Not as long as I expected," she chuckled. "I think we got home around 12:30 with a very drunk Martin. He and Camille got into a drinking and bowling competition and she won and he...well, let's say he just got out of bed around three."

"Oh, damn," Caleb cringed. "Hangover?"

"Merciless one," She nodded with a smirk. "He cussed her out all day whether she was around or not."

They giggled and I wondered why Camille would do something like that to someone she cared about.

The first bareback rider burst out of the chute and was on the ground in 3.4 seconds.

"That's not a good start on the night," I muttered and my hands curled into fists and were shoved deep in my pockets.

When the black and white, Legacy Sibiu was finally ushered into one of the arena chutes, I leaned forward, elbows on knees, and hands clasped under my chin. "Come on girl...you got this." I whispered to the mare.

When the gate opened, she juked right then left with the Mason flying to the side then sitting square on her back as she finished the eight seconds with strong bucks that barely moved her twenty feet into the arena.

"Yes!" I yelled and applauded the horse with a fist pump toward Dad.

He grinned proudly as the 86 point score was announced; 43 points for the cowboy and 43 for the horse.

"Now to get past these damned timed events so we can get to Destiny's Ignatius," I grumbled then sneaked a peek at a giggling Lacie Jae.

"What's the fastest Logan has turned one here?" Caleb asked.

"I think it was 3.6," Lacie Jae answered. "I saw him do a 3.8 here last year, my first night with Delaney. That was pretty exciting."

Logan was the last rider into the box. He needed a run faster the 3.9 to win and faster than 4.2 to even get a check for the round.

"This has been a smokin' night," Caleb huffed. "Everyone has just killed it."

Logan nodded and seemed to slide from the horse before I could blink. Quick stop, fast turn, and the steer turned with four legs in the air. Logan was rolling up and looking at the clean barrier before we could even take a breath and Lacie Jae could squeal.

"That, ladies and gentlemen," the announcer yelled. "Is why he is a 2 time world champion! On one of the toughest nights I've seen at the NFR, he takes the round with a 3.8 second run. Did you see that horse work for him?"

Lacie Jae was bouncing in her seat. When he turned to look at her, she blew him a two-handed kiss and his grin widened. He blew one back then, tipped his hat to his father behind us.

"We're going to the buckle ceremony!" She stomped her feet. "I hope one of the other three make it, too."

Ryle and Jess' run was good but only one back hoof was caught for a 5 second penalty and out of contention for a check.

When the saddle bronc started, my boots started bouncing on the ground and fingers curled into the side of my jeans to hold the material tightly. A deep breath and then another. The four of us remained quiet as the first four riders burst into the arena. Two rode for a score, two did not.

Brodie lowered onto his horse, Kesler's Artificial Colors. The gate flew open and 9 seconds later Brodie was in the dirt.

"Well, it wasn't the best ride he's ever made," Lacie Jae sighed after turning off the video. "But at least he'll still get a score."

The 81.5 points were two short of Brody Cress's ride on Flying 5 Rodeo's, Blue Feather.

"So Cress just went up 4 points over Brodie in the average race," Caleb said.

"They both rode," Lacie Jae nodded.

Dad and Zeke were standing on the podium behind Iggy. They were the last ride of the night.

"I'm getting sick to my stomach in anticipation," Mom whispered.

"Let me have your phone," Lacie Jae said. "I'll record it for you."

I didn't even look at her when I dropped it in her hands.

"That horse fills the whole chute," the announcer pointed out. "This should be a good one...world champion Zeke Thurston against the unridden horse, Destiny's Ignatius."

Elbows on knees, fingers clasped together under my chin, and prayers whispered.

Zeke rose above the chute and lowered onto the dark bay that stood quiet and still.

Boots deep in the stirrup, rein tight in his hand, Zeke leaned back, braced, then nodded.

The gate swung open and Iggy launched into the air. Three powerful, twisting bucks, followed by a high-kick buck and an unexpected shake of his large head and the rein pulled from Zeke's hand. The next high-kick with the back hooves had the cowboy launching out of the saddle.

"Tremendous bucking from that horse!" The announcer yelled over the screaming crowd. "With the clock stopping at 6.9 seconds, Destiny's Ignatius remains unridden."

I jumped up and cheered as the pick-up man approached Iggy. They were barely able to get the flank strap off before the horse took off for his victory lap.

"Go Iggy!" I shouted and stomped my boots.

"Damn, I'm glad I was here for that," Caleb huffed and my heart pounded.

Text from Dad: 47!!!

"YEAH!!!!" I stomped my boots even harder and gave Dad a grin and a double thumbs-up.

For the rest of the night, my legs shook, feet tapped the ground and fists bounced on my thighs.

"You need a drink," Caleb grinned just as the first barrel racer ran into the arena.

"A couple of them at dinner before we take you to the airport, then I'm going back to the room to re-watch the rodeo and listen to what they said about Iggy on the network telecast."

All three of them laughed at me, but I didn't care.

"So what can you tell us about Delaney's outfit tonight?" Mom asked Lacie Jae.

"Pure white, head to toe, and Gaston has white everything, too. Saddle pad, head-stall, boots, everything but her saddle," She answered. "Looks really cool next to his red roan hair."

"And the significance?" Caleb asked.

"Look at her back when she comes out," She grinned.

When Delaney entered the arena, the announcer and the crowd cheered their encouragement and appreciation of the all-white outfit and the silver angel wings stitched onto the back of the shirt. The extra energy in the room had them racing out with a 13.64 second-place finish.

"We have to go so we can get Caleb to the airport," Mom told Lacie Jae.

"I'm going to find my buckle winner," She laughed and stood with us.

It was late by the time I crawled onto my bed and turned the laptop on. I looked over at Caleb's empty bed and sighed. I missed him already.

Text from Dad: Fizzling Dud vs. Brody Cress tomorrow night

Text to Dad: That will be a good one!

I watched Iggy's performance a dozen times before finally falling asleep.

After our morning trip to see the horses, we hiked for hours at the dam. On the way back to Las Vegas, we listened to Lacie Jae's new podcast.

Welcome to Coffee with Cowboys with me, Lacie Jae.

Greetings everyone! Lacie Jae with Coffee With Cowboys here. I'm a relocated city girl who will be adventuring into the ranching and rodeo world ... the cowboy way of life.

My fiancé ... let me say that again a little louder ... my fiancé won the go-round last night so we were up late at the buckle ceremony. It is so exciting to walk onto stage and see the crowd having fun. I got to show off my ring last night and the announcers were so nice to congratulate us and get the crowd to cheer. So ... much ... fun!

Today is day 5 of the rodeo so we are almost halfway there. The highlights ... well, Logan is sitting well in the standings but having to get into beast-mode to retain the championship. Brodie is still in the hunt for the average title. Eight cowboys have ridden all the horses so far with Brodie and his good friend Brody Cress in the mix. Each ride is added to their total. The rider with the most points on all ten rides, wins the average. It's REALLY important they ride all ten.

And then there is Delaney. She is just having fun. She and Camille started the year just wanting to have an epic year, and that is what they are doing. Delaney is having fun with Gaston and Camille is having fun dressing Delaney.

Tonight is Tough Enough to Wear Pink night and Camille outdid herself on this one ... well she has on all of them. Did you see Saturday night's Annie Oakley outfit? I LOVED it! And next Saturday night will be in honor of her mother and both Brodie and Logan will be wearing the same shirt. So darn touching.

Anyway, tonight Delaney will be an ombre of pink starting with really dark pink at her boots and jean's bottom and fading to white until halfway up her shirt then it goes back to the ombre pink to match the bottom. Hat is pink as well as a pink VERY sparkly belt and earrings. Seriously, folks, watch tonight to see.

I have had the pleasure of sitting at the rodeo with one of the stock contracting families, the Westmoreland's. They have eight horses here this year, and it has been so much fun seeing the rodeo from their point of view, as in the horse's performance and not just the cowboy. They love their horses so much and really want them to perform well and get good scores for the cowboys.

River is one of the owners and is the daughter in the family. She lowers into this little ball, with her elbows on her knees and says a little prayer before each of the horses perform. Then, she shouts and yells, and, last night for her beloved Iggy, she was stomping her boots and cheering when he performed so well he got a 47 out of 50 score. That's impressive and she was so happy. The whole family was.

And a funny thing, Brodie reminded me that in Kennewick last fall I was wondering who in the world would name their bucking horse Fizzling Dud. Well, it was the Westmoreland's and the horse performs tonight. I can't wait to talk to them about it and find out where they got that name because he's here at the NFR, so he's not a fizzling dud.

We have been so busy since we arrived last week with meetings, parties, practices, autograph signings, shopping, and the rodeo that I have barely been able to stop. We have one event today then Logan and I are taking the afternoon off and just going to relax.

Everyone is getting ready for the Exceptional Rodeo at the convention center which the NFR contestants help special needs kids with different rodeo events in the arena. We've been part of these a few times this past year and it is always so heartwarming to see the smiles on the kid's faces.

I have been looking forward to this morning all week, and for tomorrow when Brodie will be recognized as the rookie of the year for the saddle bronc. They have a brunch set to award all the prizes including a saddle. That will be two saddles Brodie is taking home as awards.

I better get the coffee going and get myself ready. I'll post again this week as we lead up to the championship night on Saturday.

For now, I have a bunch of cowboys drinking their coffee without me!

You all have a wonderful day and a great cup of coffee!

Text from Dad: I have had three people ask me how Fizzling Dud got his name.

Text to Dad: Her podcast is pretty popular in this crowd.

Mom and I made our way down to our seats and were met by the announcer. He wanted to know how Fizzling Dud got his name. I laughed and blamed it all on Mom.

Lacie Jae appeared in the middle of the explanation.

"I've been told a dozen times, my next podcast better have Fizzling Dud's story," She giggled.

"Did you have a good day?" Mom asked as we settled into our seats.

"Wonderful morning at the kid's rodeo then we went out to the team roping and sat quietly watching all the ropers. It was relaxing and fun," Lacie Jae answered. "I did miss Delaney not roping out there this year."

As they chatted about the day, I leaned back in my seat, hands in vest pockets, and sighed. I missed Caleb.

Text to Caleb: You watching rodeo?
The contestants made the entrance into the arena.
Text from Caleb: Not yet, had to run an errand. On my way back to apartment.
Text to Caleb: You're going to be here for Thursday night?
I glanced up in time to see the Rawlins siblings waving at their dad and Lacie Jae. Brodie smiled at me and I looked at my phone.

Text from Caleb: Not sure, maybe Friday morning
Text to Caleb: Why?
Text from Caleb: Friend needs help and may drive down overnight instead.
Text to Caleb: Why?
Text from Caleb: Watch the rodeo and stop the inquisition.

I slid my phone in my pocket with an irritated huff.

Lacie Jae's phone rose to capture Logan's 5.1 second run to place him fifth, and Ryle's roping of 5.3, which brought them a third-place check.

Brodie was the second rider in saddle bronc on a rematch with Black Tie who had helped him win the Pendleton Roundup. I was watching the chute behind him with Brody Cress adjusting the rein on Fizzling Dud while Dad positioned the flank strap.

The gate swung open for Brodie and Black Tie. The horse began rhythmic high-kicks down the arena. Brodie matched him spur for buck and they looked phenomenal together. When the horn blared, they were on full out stretch in a vertical line. It was a perfect picture.

The pick-up men swooped in and helped him from the horse and Brodie raised both fists up to the sky in a celebratory salute. He did it again when the 89 point score was announced.

"Good job, Brodie!" Lacie Jae called out before ending the recording.

I hated the fact that my heart was racing from the ride.

I turned back to the chute and the gatemen were already prepared to open Fizzling Dud's gate.

Elbows on knees, hands clasped together under my chin, and a prayer whispered.

The gate opened and Fizzling Dud did not move. Didn't even turn his head and ignored the people trying to wave him out.

CHAPTER SIXTY FOUR

"Fuck," I whispered as the gate swung closed.

"River?" Mom said softly.

"What?"

"It's pretty easy to lip-read that word."

"What's that got to do with anything?" I stared at the chute as they prepared to open it again.

"The camera was on you."

My face instantly warmed, and my jaw clenched, but I remained focused on the chutes.

"Well, imagine I just said it again a dozen times," I whispered.

She and Lacie Jae giggled.

The gate swung open again and the horse lunged out and hit his rump on the gate making it fly back and knock over two of the gatemen.

My whole body rose with Fizzling Dud as he launched his body in the air then kicked high to the back, twisted in the air as he went down then kicked and twisted again. At the last second, he zig-zagged with his front hooves. Brody spurred him through every kick and zig-zag.

My heart was pounding, and fists in front of me as if I was holding the reins when the horn blared. Brody gripped the rein with both hands and looked for the pick-up men. Fizzling Dud zig-zagged again, causing Brody to lean to the side just as the pick-up man rode alongside him. It was too late, and Brody tumbled down between the horses with the pick-up man's horse nearly kicking him in the head.

I was standing, fist frozen in the air, and a look of worry on my face. I knew that, because my image flashed on the large screen hanging from the ceiling. When Brody stood, I turned to the horse and cheered for him as his rein was captured, and he was led out of the arena.

"Yes!" I clapped frantically for the horse and looked to Dad.

We grinned at each other.

"You look pretty good on that big screen," Lacie Jae chuckled.

My eyes went to the screen just as the score of 89 was announced. Brodie and Brody had tied again.

"Yes!" I hollered and plopped back down in my seat just to stomp my boots on the ground while clapping.

When my mind cleared, I could hear the announcer saying he had talked to the owners of the horse and repeated how the horse earned his name.

"He almost did it again," Mom chuckled.

"He loves the roar of the crowd when he gets to bucking," I grinned. "You don't buck, you don't get a roar."

The slow motion replay of the ride showed the two men that were knocked down by the gate slowly rise and look to each other with a grin and for one, a wipe of blood off his brow. They were OK and so was Brody and the horse. I sighed in relief.

Zeke Thurston had an 89.5 point ride on the sorrel horse, Major Huckleberry, which took away Fizzling Dud's win. It was a bit depressing. I really wanted the horse to win his first buckle. But, my horse-high remained into the barrel race.

Delaney's white and pink outfit received a loud reaction from the crowd which fueled the energy in her and the horse. They ended the night with a 13.45 second run and in first-place.

"Back to the buckle ceremony!" Lacie Jae cheered.

Half-way through the bull riding, we walked up the stairs and out into the wide aisle, both Brodie Rawlins and Brody Cress were in a group of men talking and laughing. I looked at Cress and we both grinned.

"Are you OK, Cookie?" I asked and gently slid my arm around his waist as his went over my shoulders. "You didn't crumble, did you?"

"Just the usual bumps and bruises, nothing crumbled," he laughed.

"We could all see how worried you were over him," Brodie drawled.

I ignored his comment and didn't move my gaze from Brody Cress. I tightened my arm around him, "For as much as what was going on in the arena between you, Fizzling Dud, the pick-up men, and the gatemen, it was pretty odd to have the camera on me."

"If it weren't for the fact I was riding the most talked about horse of the day, they probably wouldn't have," Brody grinned.

We all looked at the Cheshire-cat grin on Lacie Jae as a guilty giggle rumbled out of her.

"Thank you for show-casing him so well," Mom added with a polite smile to both men.

"We're going to take off before the crowd starts leaving, but you go get yourself down to the Sport's Medicine room and let them take care of you," I squeezed Brody again and smiled at the group of men…except for Brodie.

"We are headed there now," He said with a quick hug to me and glance to Brodie.

"Take care, Cookie, and good luck the rest of the week," I chuckled at him just before we walked away.

"I understand why you didn't acknowledge Brodie, but why did you call the other one Cookie?" Mom asked.

The answer made my heart hurt.

I lay in bed watching the rodeo on my laptop. Caleb's empty bed just depressed me. I was going to be glad when he was done with college.

Text to Caleb: Did you get to watch rodeo?

Text from Caleb: The camera loves you...although, you probably shouldn't swear anymore.

I forwarded the recording of the rodeo to the saddle bronc and pushed play.

When Brodie and Black Tie burst from the chute, I pushed pause in the middle of the first stretching kick to the back. Both horse and rider were elongated out...the standard saddle bronc photograph. I stared at Brodie. How could he walk away so easily? We could have had a wonderful life together. My heart ached and the tears began to rise again so I forwarded the video past his ride until the first shot of me appeared.

The camera focused on me in my curled praying position and staring hard at the bucking chute. The swear word was quite evident. Although I'm sure Dad would think I should be embarrassed, I thought it was quite funny.

The camera caught me jumping into a standing position and yelling at the horse, then again the shot of my reaction when Brody fell between the horses.

"We could all see how worried you were over him." He was the one that walked away, he didn't have a right to be jealous.

I watched Fizzling Dud's ride three times before signing onto the app that played the buckle ceremony. I was four floors up in the hotel from where the ceremony was in full swing. Delaney and the entire Rawlins family were on stage laughing with the announcers, Flint and Randy. Camille was grinning with her arms looped through Martin's and Brodie's and talking about having fun designing Delaney's outfits. My stomach soured and I turned off the laptop.

Thundering hooves against the dirt road, flying manes and tails as they ran, my heart calm, at ease, at home behind the herd. Pounding echoed and the herd dissolved; my eyes open.

My phone rang, and the pounding continued.

Mom was calling and I could hear Dad yelling my name through the door. It was 8:01, we were supposed to meet at 7:30 to go hiking.

"I was asleep," I answered the phone and crawled out of bed.

"Who do you have riding tonight?" Lacie Jae asked as we settled into the seats.

"Flying Betty and Legacy Baia Mare with Craiova third in the re-ride pen," I answered.

"Oh, fun," She chuckled. "They have two rides to watch you tonight."

I laughed, "Anyone watching Betty knows how she got her name."

And the horse flew. A strong kick to the back followed by leaping, four hooves in the air jumps. It was rhythmic and beautiful. She helped her rider take home a check for third place. Legacy Baia Mare was one spot out of the money.

"Logan says the steers tonight are really big and strong," Lacie Jae said five minutes before Logan's drawn steer drug him six feet down the arena before he could turn the nose. The clock stopped at 6.3, well out of the money.

"I was reading this morning that all three still have a chance at the title," Mom said.

"Statistically, yes," Lacie Jae nodded. "In reality, it is all in the luck of the draw. The animal for Brodie and Logan or placing in the night run for Delaney; whether she is running in deep dirt or not. After Gaston winning last night on the top of the ground, she made the tough decision to let him rest for a night and let Maestro run in the deep dirt tonight."

I shoved my hands in my vest and watched the stagecoach drive into the arena carrying the delegation celebrating the Rookie of the Year recipients. Brodie walked out from behind the chutes and stood with the other winners while holding his new buckle. He looked up at his dad and waved, then without looking at us, he walked away. I guess my ignoring him the night before pissed him off. I internally shrugged.

The saddle bronc began with Brodie falling two more points behind Brody Cress in the running. Three riders landed in the dirt before the buzzer leaving just five cowboys riding all their horses for the week.

We were ten barrel racers in before Mom finally asked Lacie Jae what Delaney was wearing.

"Maestro is a dark brown, so she is dressed completely in black except a long-coat that flows down to mid-thigh. It looks like one of those civil war coats with all the brassy buttons and the high-collar. It is in dark suede that nearly matches the horse perfectly," Lacie Jae answered and lifted her phone.

It was odd seeing Delaney on a horse that wasn't a red roan, but the coat? I wanted one.

"They look great," I muttered before realizing I had admitted it out loud so it would be on the recording.

The announcer's voice rang out, "Look at that horse turn those barrels. He is the fourteenth out, which means deep dirt and they are going to be in the top…if not…yes, folks, there it is! Delaney Rawlins' backup horse just took her to the lead with only one rider left to go."

Lacie Jae was nearly screaming as she cheered and before turning off the phone. That was going to be a hard one to listen to, I thought with a snicker.

The last rider was a full second slower than Maestro and Lacie Jae was squealing.

"Back to the buckle ceremony!" she laughed. "I can't believe it! Three nights in a row!"

She was gone before the first bull rider bust out of the gate. Mom and I sat quietly and watched. Dad appeared and took a seat next to her. Their hands came together as they smiled at each other.

Text to Caleb: They are doing it again.

Text from Caleb: Canoodling parents?

Text to Caleb: Would be if we weren't still sitting at the arena watching the bulls. You here tomorrow night?

Text from Caleb: Not sure until morning

Irritation bubbled through me.

Text to Caleb: Isn't that why you took your Friday exam last Friday?

Text from Caleb: Shit happens, depends on if I am flying tomorrow afternoon or driving down with a friend tomorrow night.

Well, at least he wasn't here with Camille.

Thursday afternoon, when we arrived back to the hotel after checking the horses and hiking, I received the text I was expecting and sighed.

Text from Caleb: Driving overnight from Denver. Won't be there until tomorrow, late morning.

I walked down to my parent's room with feet dragging the floor. It was more fun getting ready with Caleb there so we could tease each other than the silence I was walking away from.

Mom opened the door with a smile, "Your father has already left, so it's just you and me tonight."

"Great," I gave her a half-hearted smile. "He took the truck, so we're shuttling."

She grinned, "Henry and Arad buck tonight. Remember that and it will make you feel better."

I nodded as we walked out of the hotel and to the shuttle bus.

"So we can leave after the bareback is done?" I asked.

Mom looked at me with wide, annoyed eyes, "I enjoy watching the rodeo with Lacie Jae and you...so, I'm not leaving."

The shuttle ride was very quiet.

"I'm going to get fries," I huffed as she walked down the stairs to the seats and a waiting Lacie Jae.

Watching the monitors to follow along with the opening of the rodeo, I wandered along the concourse and purchased popcorn to take to the seats and a new NFR t-shirt to wear the next day. I plopped down into my seat just as the first bareback chute opened.

Henry the First was the third horse to buck with Trenten Montero on his back. Elbows on knees, fingers clasped under my chin, I said the silent prayer.

"Don't swear," Mom whispered.

My jaw gritted together, but I couldn't help my body rise when Henry's gate opened, and the horse launched out. Powerful kicks to the back and nose tucked to the ground as he prepared the next buck had my heart racing.

"Go, Henry!" I yelled as the horn blared.

My arms went into the air as a holler escaped and I looked over at Dad as the 88 point score was announced. Dad and I grinned at each other.

When the bareback was complete for the night, Henry the First was second again.

"Four for four placing second," I grumbled with a smirk.

"He'll have his day and no cowboy would turn him away if they knew they were getting a check," Mom said.

Arad was the last to buck and there was barely a chance to cheer when the cowboy lost his grip and flew over the horse's shoulder.

I sighed, shoved my fists in the vest pockets, and leaned back to silently watch the rodeo as Mom and Lacie Jae chatted like long lost friends. Even that irritated me.

With a 4.9 second turn, Logan was fourth for the night. He still grinned at his dad and at Lacie Jae. He was a very handsome man and very nice. *I bet he couldn't leave Lacie Jae as easy as his brother left me.*

I gritted my teeth at allowing myself even to think that thought but when Brodie appeared on the platform, all I could do was glare at him. Every movement was watched and mentally cursed. By the end of the saddle bronc section, two other cowboys were out of the race for the average. Brodie's 84 point ride left him farther away when Brody Cress who had earned an 86.

Delaney rode out on her brown horse, Maestro, wearing an outfit that looked like it was from the 1950's. They were .04 seconds out of the lead and ultimately placed fourth for the night.

"Are you alright, River?" Lacie Jae asked.

"Yes, just tired," I lied. What was I supposed to say to her? That I was mad at Dad for taking the truck, Caleb for not being there and mad at Brodie for…everything?

Halfway through the bulls, Lacie Jae had left for the night and Dad appeared with three beers and 3 orders of fries.

When the last fry was eaten, I turned to my parents, "Where's dinner tonight?"

They both chuckled.

"I want ice cream," Mom said and rose from the red seat.

"I'm OK with an ice cream dinner," I grinned at Dad.

"Well, if that's what my favorite women want, then let's go have ice cream."

We were still sitting in the little café by the front entrance of SouthPoint when the stock draw was posted. I watched the man take down the old draw and put up the new. Iggy would be in the pen for Friday night. It would be a huge disappointment if he didn't get drawn or ended up in the re-ride pool.

With ice cream cup in hand and spoon in mouth, I walked to the post and read down the list of names and stopped at the saddle bronc.

"Flib…ber…ti…gib…bet."

CHAPTER SIXTY FIVE

"Why aren't you going with us?" Mom asked as she stepped up into the truck. "You love hiking there."

"I'm going to hang with Caleb since I can't go see Iggy this morning," I smirked at Dad who had already told me three times not to go see the horse.

"It's only 45 minutes to Hoover Dam," Mom continued. "You'll have plenty of time…"

"Mom, I've gone all week with you," I shook my head with a smile. "You two go on a date-for-the-day by yourselves and enjoy. You have all day with no worrying about us because we'll be together. I have to keep my mind off of tonight, so I'm going to talk Caleb into going to Freemont Street and zip-line over the crowd."

"You two be careful and check-in when he gets here," Dad ordered.

The door was finally closed and I turned to walk back to the front of the hotel. Walking to the draw post again, I reread the names. It did not miraculously change overnight: Brodie Rawlins vs 188 Destiny's Ignatius was still on the list.

Flibbertigibbet was repeated and my body sighed. I had barely slept through the night. When I dreamt, I was running behind the herd of bucking horses. I woke up exhausted.

Maybe buying myself something would ease my nerves so I walked to the small gift shop just inside the doors to look at their earrings. I set two pair on the glass countertop and pulled my wallet from my vest pocket. While I waited my turn, I watched the people that seemed blended into the numerous slot machines. The tables with different card games were also full of people. It was only 8:00 in the morning; had they been there all night?

I saw a flash of Camille walking behind the first table and disappearing into the mass of slot machines. Right behind her, was Caleb.

What the hell?

I was stunned and it took a moment to shake myself out of the shock and walk away from the counter leaving the earrings behind. My eyes were darting from each person trying to find where the pair had disappeared; maybe the café where I had first seen them together. I hurried and barely caught a glimpse of them just past the café and turning up the escalator to the next level.

My body shook in anger at him. Had he really arrived the night before and spent it with her?

They were at the top of the escalator when I saw them next so I had to sprint up the stairway. At the top, my heart was racing in anger and exertion. Camille disappeared into a room to the right.

"Caleb!" I yelled.

His head jerked over his shoulder and eyes widened in surprise. In a flash, the expression turned to pure irritation, which made my eyes narrow in a fierce glare.

"What the hell?" I growled. "Did you just lie to all of us?"

He looked into the room then back to me, "River, this has nothing to do with you."

"You lied to us."

"No, I didn't," he huffed. "We drove all night and got here twenty minutes ago. Why aren't you with Mom and Dad?"

"Because I wanted to hang-out with my lying brother," I fumed.

"I don't have time for this," he huffed. "If you want to know, come with me but keep your mouth closed. This isn't about us."

"What isn't?"

"Trust me," he turned. "Just be quiet."

With body at full tension and ready to go to battle, I walked into the room behind him.

My stomach swirled as he closed the door behind us.

There were dozens of chairs spread out in the room and a few tables set along the side. But, it wasn't just Camille in the small conference room. It was the whole damn family that turned and looked at us in surprise. Lacie Jae and Logan were sitting with her arms wrapped around one of his. His long legs were stretched comfortably out in front of him. Martin was sitting next to them and it looked like we had interrupted their conversation. Delaney and Ryle stood behind her father, who was sitting in his wheelchair. Camille stared at me as if I was an illusion while Brodie stood next to her and glared at me.

"What is this?" Brodie huffed as he looked from me to Camille. My jaw clenched to hold back the words.

Camille turned away from me and looked at him, "We needed to talk to everyone…"

"Who?" Brodie glared. "What the hell does River and Caleb have to do with anything?"

"Brodie," Camille sighed. "Please, just give me a few minutes to explain."

He glowered at her but remained silent. The sneer he directed at me left it clear he didn't want me there, which was OK because I didn't want to be there either. I just couldn't figure out how to leave without him thinking I was doing it because of him.

Camille looked around the small group. "I'm going to ask that you all sit down before I explain."

"Alright," Delaney whispered with a curious glance to me as she took a seat next to her father. Ryle was right next to her.

Brodie hesitated with another glare then finally sat next to Martin.

Camille looked at Caleb who nodded to her. She took a deep breath that made her whole body lower when she released it. She pulled a chair in front of the group to face them then slowly lowered to sit on the edge.

She tipped her head down to look at the floor and another deep breath was taken. When her head rose she was wiping away tears.

"Camille?" Martin whispered in concern.

Lacie Jae sat up in her chair, "You OK? Is something wrong?"

Camille shook her head then turned to look at Caleb. Her dark brown eyes were pleading with him, "I can't say the words."

"It's OK," he whispered and walked to stand behind her.

I stood frozen in confusion.

"What the hell is going on?" Evan growled.

"I'll explain," Caleb said calmly. "I have to go back to last week so you understand." He glanced back to me then to the family. "Last week, after the Big Four saddle presentation, I witnessed a confrontation between River and some of you."

I stared at him in surprise as the heat slowly moved from my neck and up to my face. My stomach ached.

"It wasn't meant…" Delaney started.

She stopped when he nodded and lifted a hand.

"I know, but during the…conversation, there was a question of whether River was wearing a red shirt or a pink shirt at the bar the night Toby Keith sang," Caleb continued.

"What does that have to do with anything?" Brodie grumbled.

"Let him explain," Camille whispered.

Caleb began again, "I knew River was in red and that she had only danced with Craig."

Martin and Evan both looked at me in surprise. I didn't move, but my face was warm and flush.

"River and I went to the bar that night with Eric, one of my college classmates, and his sister, Gail," Caleb continued. "When Craig walked River back to the table, Gail took his arm and pulled him out onto the dance floor. They danced together on and off all night."

"She was the one wearing the pink shirt," Camille explained.

"…and left with Craig." Brodie huffed.

"Yes," Caleb answered. "Last week, after the conversation, I was lying in bed thinking about that night and I remembered something I had seen on Facebook from Eric. I sent him a few texts and when he answered back, I contacted Camille the next day to help me."

"Help you with what?" Logan asked.

Camille took a breath, "Remember Saturday night?" She looked at Martin.

"Barely," he huffed. "I can't remember the last time I drank so much and passed out."

The family chuckled into the tense atmosphere.

"That was by design," Camille smiled. "I needed to get something without you knowing."

Martin's eyes narrowed. "What?"

Another deep breath from Camille before she answered, "A DNA sample."

Gasps rang out with Martin's body sitting up straighter.

"Are you telling me…?" he whispered with eyes wide. "You wouldn't tell me if…" His eyes darted from Camille to Caleb.

I slowly melted onto the closest chair with my heart racing in anticipation.

"I remembered that Gail was pregnant," Caleb explained. "I flew back to Fort Collins for the college exams Sunday night then met with them."

The room was hushed.

Caleb continued, "Gail gave birth last week, and I was able to get a DNA sample and sent it in on Monday to compare to the sample Camille got from you. I received the results yesterday."

Martin's body slowly leaned back in the chair, his eyes wide in anguish and wonder, "You're telling me, that my son…"

"It was a positive match," Camille whispered and rose just enough she could kneel in front of him and take his hand. "You are a grandfather."

"Oh, my God," Delaney whispered through tears.

Lacie Jae wrapped her arms around Logan and buried her face into his chest.

Evan placed a trembling hand on Martin's shoulder while Brodie fell back in his chair.

"Where?" Martin finally huffed. "I want…"

"First," Caleb interrupted. "I need to finish."

"They will not keep me away from my son's child," Martin growled.

"She isn't," Camille's voice was smooth and calming.

"When I talked to Gail," Caleb said. "She was going through a very rough time. It's just the two of them and they were struggling. She was quite relieved when I told her about you and the Rawlins family because...she was about to call an adoption agency."

"What?" Evan roared.

Martin's jaw dropped, his body started to rise, but Camille gently pushed him back down.

Caleb continued, "I contacted an attorney and had the paperwork completed because if the DNA test came back as a match, Gail said she would relinquish her rights to you for you to adopt..."

"Where do I sign?" Martin huffed.

"I'll get the paperwork," Caleb nodded and walked to the door. When it opened, a woman entered with a file folder in her hand.

"Caleb explained everything to you?" the woman asked.

"Where do I sign?" Martin nodded.

"I am a notary and will sign the papers for you if you will show me your identification," she said.

With a trembling hand, Martin pulled his wallet from the pocket inside his jacket and handed her his driver's license. Camille moved the chair she had been sitting in so it could be used to sign the papers.

Except for a sniffle or gasp of disbelief, the room was quiet as Martin signed the papers. The woman pulled a long metal bar out of her bag and scanned it over each page.

"Your contact information is in the paperwork so I will send you the official file by email," the woman said.

"When does he get custody?" Evan asked. "We can fly..."

"No," Camille whispered with a smile. "Last night, after the rodeo, I flew to Denver to meet Caleb and drive back with him."

"The baby is here?" Lacie Jae whispered and wiped away tears.

Martin stared at Camille in disbelief, "You have seen him...her? Did she have a boy or girl?"

Camille smiled warmly at him as tears slowly slid down her cheeks, "Both."

"What?" Everyone gasped.

"She gave birth to twins," Caleb smiled. "Craig has a daughter and a son."

Martin's body shook and the whole family moved to him as the tears began to fall.

"Take a few minutes," Caleb whispered then turned to look at me as if he just remembered I was there. Tears fell unchecked down my cheeks as my body tingled in disbelief.

"Where are they?" Logan exhaled.

Caleb looked from him to the questioning eyes of the new grandfather.

"Just outside that door," Caleb whispered.

"I can't believe this," Martin's head fell back as the tears fell again, his whole body shook. "I want my son so bad my heart and body ache with the need to see him." Pure anguish radiated from him and tears slid down every cheek in the room.

After a moment, Martin looked to Camille who was still kneeling in front of him. With a gentle hand he cupped her jaw and smiled, "And you were so upset you couldn't provide me with a grandchild...something of Craig...and now you have brought me two."

She chuckled through the tears and wrapped her arms around him for a strong, rib breaking embrace.

"And I now forgive you for that hellacious hangover last Sunday," he whispered.

When she leaned back, and Martin looked around the family, it felt like the whole room sighed in realization. Caleb felt it too and as he walked to the door he looked at the stunned family, "Stay seated, it's a bit overwhelming when you first meet them."

"Them..." Brodie exhaled in disbelief.

After looking at each person in the room, as if trying to prepare them, Caleb opened the door and stepped out. I caught a glance of the woman that had brought the papers and another woman standing with her that had a hand on a wide stroller with two car seats attached. A blanket covered the top of each.

Caleb nodded to them, then pushed the stroller to the door. I stood to open the door wider for him. Our eyes met and he smiled.

"You are my hero," I whispered then shut the door behind him.

"I think I'm going to explode," Delaney's voice shook as she stared at the car seats.

Caleb pushed the stroller next to Camille and with a trembling hand, she removed the blankets and positioned the chairs so the babies could be seen.

The whole family moved in to hover over them.

"They are so tiny," Ryle whispered.

Brodie looked to Caleb, "Are they healthy?"

"Very healthy; Gail is a tiny person," Caleb answered. "At birth, the boy weighed in at 4 pounds, 3 ounces and the girl at 4 pounds, 1 ounce."

"They are so small they could fit in Logan's palm," Lacie Jae gasped.

"What are their names?" Brodie asked as he stared at the twins.

"Paperwork is in the file for Martin to rename them," Camille answered. "I spoke with the mother on the phone and she knew you would want to change them and didn't have a problem with it."

"There is one more thing," Caleb said and all their eyes moved to him. "She knows who you are and can follow the twin's progress on your social media websites, but she wanted to know, when the time was right, if she could come visit."

"Of course," Martin nodded, but his eyes moved back to the babies. "You let her know I will buy her a plane ticket once we get them settled in at the ranch."

"Are you ready to hold one?" Camille whispered to him.

With a deep breath, Martin nodded and leaned back in his chair in emotional preparation.

Camille slowly lifted the little boy out of his chair and carefully nestled him in the crook of Martin's arm. The baby could barely be seen.

"So tiny…" I whispered to myself.

The girl was lifted from the carrier and Camille smiled at Martin.

"I'm terrified of just holding one right now," Martin huffed with wide eyes.

"Give her to me," Evan ordered with outstretched arms.

I sat in the back of the room and watched as each family member met the two newborns; the children of their lost son and brother. Life began for them again. I could see it in all their faces. It had been less than thirty minutes since they had known of the babies and yet all their lives had changed and I knew it was because of my brother. My heart swelled in love and pride for him as he smiled and spoke with the family.

Having barely met Craig, the whole situation was a bit shocking and overwhelming for me. I couldn't imagine how it was going to be for this family, especially when, in just a couple hours, they were going to have to focus back on the rodeo and not on the two little miracles that were already so loved.

Caleb sat down next to me and we watched the family.

"Forgive me?" he whispered.

"Of course," I answered without hesitation.

Moments passed until Logan finally stood to walk over to Caleb. We both stood and Logan wrapped Caleb in a strong embrace.

"Thank you," Logan whispered.

"Caleb!" Martin's voice rang out. Everyone looked at him. His eyes were wide with wonder. "When I get my legs back and I don't have a GRANDCHILD in my arms…" He hesitated with a deep breath before continuing. "I thank you for bringing them to me. There are no words."

"But there will be a line of shots on the bar tonight," Logan grinned. "I did promise to take you out after your week of exams."

"How did you manage this and all your finals?" Evan asked.

"Compartmentalizing," Caleb answered. "It was the only way I could focus to take an exam in the morning then studying all afternoon for the next morning."

"And watching our horses in the rodeo at night," I added with pride.

Brodie stood, his eyes still dazed from the events.

When our eyes met, I just turned away as if he was a stranger on the street.

"Did you see the draw for the night?" he huffed with a smirk.

"Of course, I did," I sighed as if it was a stupid question.

"He's got his work cut out for him tonight with your Iggy," Evan grinned.

"Cress has Brodie by 5 points," Logan added. "He has to ride the unridden horse to keep in the race for the average."

"I'm glad I made it back for it," Caleb added.

I remained quiet.

"Nothing to say?" Brodie huffed at me.

"Iggy will do all the talking," I said boldly.

"You don't believe I can ride him?" Brodie sneered.

I turned to look at the babies cradled in Evan and Martin's arms then turned to Brodie, "Well, if nothing else today, we did learn that miracles do happen." I huffed with a dismissing glance at him and started to turn away. His eyes narrowed, nostrils flared, lips in a fine line, and a low growl escaped. Plain and simple, I had managed to piss him off, royally.

I strode out of the room without a look or word to anyone. My heart and head were in a deep emotional storm.

I was only fifteen feet down the corridor when I heard my name called.

"River!"

CHAPTER SIXTY SIX

It was not who I was expecting but I stopped and turned to face him. He was pissed, too.

"What the hell has gotten into you? You are never that rude."

I saw her step out of the room and glance both ways. When she took a step toward us I turned to Caleb knowing full-well that he had no idea she was behind him.

"You know how I feel about Camille and yet here we are."

Camille stopped, took a step forward then stopped again. She started to turn away, looked right at me with brows high, then stopped again.

"And we both know why and that is something you have to deal with yourself."

"So, you just dismiss my feelings because she's beautiful?"

Camille turned and looked at the back of his head; her eyes wide in anticipation of his answer.

"You know it doesn't have a damn thing to do with how she looks," Caleb growled. "You know I'm not that immature or insecure to be attracted to someone just because of their looks."

"Then what is it?" I huffed with cheeks warming. I had no doubt my face was flushed a deep pink.

"Damn, River, it sounds weird and it...damn it...it's...," He exhaled heavily. "It's because she reminds me a lot of you."

I scoffed, "We don't look a damn thing alike."

He glared, "It's not the looks, River. It's everything I have learned about her from listening to those damn podcasts, to the pictures on their Facebook, and stories I've heard...and damn it. She wants adventure and has fun doing it, but she also isn't afraid to get her hands dirty with work. You may have a couple of dozen rides over her but she rode a damn bucking horse and loved it. She has grit, just like you."

Even without looking directly at her, I could see Camille's shoulders relax and a smile appear.

I rolled my eyes at him causing his glare to return, "You and I both know you can't believe everything that is written about people, and pictures can be manipulated to look one way and not another."

"Damn, River." He growled. "Even if I fell for her in pictures and stories, working with her this last week, behind everyone's back...the integrity she had, the deep concern she had for the mother, yet knowing how life-changing this was for Martin and the Rawlins...she was a rock and handled everything with grace and love. That is normally you."

"Yeah, I got no grace here," I scoffed. "So, are you saying all this just to piss me off or are you actually going to tell her?"

"How in the hell am I supposed to approach her when I know how upset you would be?"

"Well, I love you, Caleb," I huffed.

"Yeah, that doesn't really help much though does it?" He hissed with a glare.

"Turn around," I growled.

Confusion flashed in his eyes before he slowly turned. When their eyes connected, I turned and walked away. My phone rang four times and the message alert vibrated ten times before I slid into the back of the taxi. On the way to the Thomas and Mack Center, I turned off my phone.

I needed to just disappear. What I really needed was to be on the buckskin gelding at River's Point watching the sunrise over the top of a hundred bucking horses and winding river. Closing my eyes, I imagined myself there enjoying the tranquility. I could almost hear the wild turkeys gobbling, the cows mooing, and the click of horse hooves hitting rock as they walked down the trail to the river.

Within just hours of Iggy's second out at the NFR, I wanted nothing more than to be home.

Russ was talking with a group of people when I arrived. He smiled and waved me through.

Iggy was standing at the opposite side of the pen with his eyes closed and head low. I leaned against the paneled fence and watched him as the morning's surprising revelation played in my mind. As shocked as I was, I couldn't imagine what Martin and the Rawlins were going through. They were going to have a hard time concentrating on the rodeo tonight. Except, maybe, Brodie since he was now pissed and I knew he would be focused on proving me wrong when it came to riding the horse in front of me.

"Was glad to see him on the draw tonight," Russ stepped in next to me.

"Yep," I smiled politely. "He gets another chance to shine."

"Pretty spectacular on Sunday," He nodded and we stood quietly and watched the sleeping horse. He finally turned to look at me. "I have a message for you."

"Really?" I huffed in surprise.

"From your dad," he grinned.

I rolled my eyes with a sigh, "He told you to tell me that Iggy is working tonight so don't touch him."

The guard chuckled again, "That and to turn your damn phone on."

"Oh," I blushed and reached for the phone. "Thank you."

He walked away to the tune of the message alerts ringing. Iggy's head turned to the sound, then rose when he saw me. He slowly walked across the pen.

I glanced at the guard who had his back to me. With a guilty grin, I reached out to Iggy's nose.

"Don't tell anyone and you damn well better perform tonight," I grinned at the horse. "You do spectacular tonight and make an impression so we can get you back here under all these flying planes next year."

He followed me along the fence as I walked down to the pen that held the rest of our horses. They were eating their morning hay or snoozing in the sun. I turned back and Iggy followed me back down the fence again until we came to the corner. I stopped and looked over to him…into his big brown eye that was watching me. My heart grew calm and warm just looking into the golden brown depth. I never felt confused around him.

"I know you don't understand," I whispered. "But you are my dream and fill my heart with so much pride and love," I gently caressed his soft muzzle and took a deep breath as my stomach tingled at the memory of his first performance and in anticipation of his next ride. "I wish I could spend the day here and just tell you all day how special you are to me and get you pumped up for tonight."

I chuckled softly; there was that crazy coming out again. It had been a while since I felt that bit of anxiety simmering in me.

I glanced to the security guard who was facing me but talking with two barrel racers. Smiling, I reached out and ran my hand down Iggy's nose.

Stepping back I took in his massive presence; height, dark brown muscular body, thick mane, and arched neck. Even as calm as he stood watching me, power radiated from him. "Destiny's Ignatius, you go out and light a fire under his ass and make him earn every damn point and I'll be back in the morning with a pocket full of treats."

With a wicked grin and a lifted heart, I walked away from the horse.

On the ride back to the hotel, I read the messages. Four from Mom and five from Dad stated basically the same thing; do not turn off your phone in this damn town and call immediately.

Text to Mom and Dad: I am fine, Iggy needed a pep talk, on my way back to the hotel.

Text from Caleb: What the hell? What is going on with you? Keep your phone on

Text from Caleb: I called parents and told them about babies

Text from Caleb: I'm not sure if I should thank you or kick your ass

Text from Caleb: WTF River!

Text from Unknown Number: This is Camille, I know you refuse to talk to any of us about Brodie, but will you please meet with me about Caleb? I am so confused.

"Well, so am I," I whispered to myself.

Text from Mom: Ice Cream, meet me at the little café by the front entrance.

Caleb and Dad were sitting at the table with her when I walked through the doors. The energy I had gained with Iggy began to drain. I slid on the seat in front of a large bowl of chocolate ice cream and brownie chunks and braced myself for the inquisition.

"So how did the talk go with Iggy?" Dad asked.

I smirked, "You remember the day he was born and the reason I named him Ignatius?"

All three nodded.

"Well, I told him to light his ass on fire and make sure he earns every point he gets."

All three chuckled, and we finished the ice cream without a word of Brodie, Camille, or anyone outside the family and horses.

"So," Mom leaned back and looked straight at me. My stomach clenched in anticipation. "There are a few hours before we have to go to the arena and I thought we should go upstairs and see if there is a bowling lane free."

"Yes!" I stood as the relief washed through me.

Lacie Jae was already at the seats when we arrived. She was standing and began an excited bounce when she saw us. Her arms wrapped around Caleb with a strong embrace as she grinned with a few tears escaping.

"You are such a savior," she whispered to him.

He blushed as he grinned at her, "How are they?"

Tears escaped big blue eyes as her hands went to her chest. "I am so in love. It was so hard to leave, Martin couldn't so he is at the hotel with them and the nurse who will stay with us until we leave Sunday."

"They need a nurse?" Mom gasped. "Are they alright?"

"Oh, yes," Lacie Jae nodded. "She is the daughter of one of Evan's friends and they wanted to be very careful with them…they are so tiny and it's been a long time since any of us have been around a baby."

"Any names yet?" Caleb asked as we took our seats with Lacie Jae sitting between Caleb and me.

"Oh, no," Lacie Jae giggled. "They are going to wait on changing them."

"What were…or are their names?" Mom asked.

"Cindy and Oscar," Lacie Jae grimaced. "Right for some people, but not for Craig's babies. They also decided to change Craig's room into the nursery. Delaney is the only person that has been in there when she got the light blue chaps for Brodie. There is a lady they trust that is going over to their ranch tomorrow to remove the furniture and clothes but leave everything on the walls. They want the twins to be surrounded by their father as they grow."

Tears rose and fell; I had to look away.

"I've been doing that all day," Lacie Jae whispered and took my hand. "We all have. It's just so overwhelming at moments and it will take a while to come to grips with it."

"Yes," I sighed. My head and heart ached.

The Viva Las Vegas light show started in the arena and the blaring of the song stopped all conversation. As the flag riders raced around the arena on the stunning black horses, I turned to look for Dad. He wasn't on the platform.

Text to Dad: Where are you? Having a beer in the back?

Text from Dad: Not yet. What the hell did you say to Brodie? He's on a terror back here.

Text to Dad: I'm innocent

I giggled to myself.

Text from Dad: Poppycock! You haven't been innocent since you started crawling

I laughed.

Text to Dad: I am gobsmacked you would even think that of me. ☺

Text from Dad: You are a dingleberry

Text to Dad: Now you're down to name-calling, you old whippersnapper.

I glanced up as the parade of contestants ran into the arena.

Text to Dad: I'm flabbergasted you would just be lollygagging in the back and not out front enjoying the hullabaloo.

Text from Dad: I had to get the whatsit thingamajig, and then the whatchamacallit and whatnot

I turned to see him appear at the back of the chutes and sliding on his NFR jacket. He glanced over at me and I could just make out his grin as someone stepped between us and started talking to him.

Text to Dad: Thanks Dad, I've been a bit coddiwomple today

I slid my hands into the vest pockets, slumped back in the seat, and relaxed as if I didn't have a care in the world.

Lacie Jae was waving at the Rawlins siblings that were stopped in front of us.

Logan and Delaney were waving at her while Brodie was glaring at me. A scowl was nearly hidden behind his whiskers. I just looked back as if I was bored. It disguised the aching stomach that was making me nauseous but I wasn't going to let him know that he affected me in any way.

We stared at each other until the ride out of the arena started and he had to turn away.

My phone vibrated an alert.

Text from Dad: That was a new one. I had to look it up. Chin up, my little Nincompoop. It will be a grand night.

My stomach settled as I glanced at him. His hand was over his heart and even from a distance I could feel the love and comfort he was sending me. Tears rose and I just nodded and slid the phone back in my pocket.

Confusion, frustration, and, at moments, the waves of just not caring and giving up swarmed through me as the rodeo began. I turned down the offers of a beer. It wouldn't help if I let down my defenses or even let them ease and became too emotional. I just needed to make it through another 36 hours and we could go home and ride across our open range.

"Do you have any horses in bareback?" Lacie Jae asked.

"Legacy Sibiu is first on the re-ride list," Caleb answered.

She giggled, "Is that another Romanian city?"

"Any name starting with Legacy are named after the cities," He answered.

The bareback riding started and I silently judged each horse to practice to see if I matched the judges and it kept my mind busy. The last rider bust from the chute and the horse ran down the arena with barely a buck.

"Reride," Caleb and I said at the same time.

"Sibiu gets to buck tonight," Mom chirped.

"But next, bulldogging," Lacie Jae grinned.

Logan hazed three times before backing in the box himself as the last steer wrestler of the night. Lacie Jae lifted her phone and captured the bust from the chute with Logan sliding from his horse, arm stretched over the steer's back then the steer stopped with Logan falling to the ground in front of him. A hand had managed to grip one horn and he struggled to pull the steer back to him. Scrambling to his feet, precious seconds ticked off the timer as he maneuvered himself behind the steer to reposition for the turn.

When the clock stopped at 14.4 seconds the crowd sighed in disappointment as he stood. Then they cheered when he nodded with a grin up at his dad then turned to Lacie Jae and blew her a kiss.

Lacie Jae stopped the video and lowered the phone. "He probably just lost the championship but look at that grin," she whispered. "That's why I love him."

"That's the way rodeo goes," Caleb stated. "Not everyone can win."

Lacie Jae had the phone ready to video Ryle and Jess when they entered the arena.

"I love how that palomino faces," Mom said.

"That's Silas, he loves this arena," Lacie Jae nodded. "They've caught them all so far this week."

Caleb huffed, "Saying things like that, before it's all over, jinxes them."

"Oh, my gosh!" Lacie Jae cried.

"I do it all the time," Mom chuckled with a glance to me.

Ryle nodded, and 5.9 seconds later, Lacie Jae was sighing in relief as the official's flag dropped. Her hand slapped Caleb's leg. "Don't do that!"

"Well, there is tomorrow night," Caleb chuckled.

Even their teasing couldn't get my stomach to settle. Iggy was the last horse of the night, so I stood while forcing myself not to look at the bucking chutes. "I'll be right back."

"Before saddle bronc," Mom ordered.

I nodded and made my way up the stairs and down the hall. Stopping in front of the monitors I watched the rest of the team roping with hand over my stomach and shifting from foot to foot.

When the flag rider rode into the arena to announce the saddle bronc, I exhaled a deep breath and slowly walked down the stairs to my seat. I had barely sat down when the chute opened and Legacy Sibiu launched into the arena on the bareback re-ride. The black and white mare kicked high in the back then launched into a long leap then repeated until the horn blared. They were barely 20 feet from the chutes when the rider toppled off the horse's side. The 85 point score gave the pair a third-place finish for the night.

I whistled and yelled for the horse as she trotted out the exit gate. My stomach swirling eased and the excitement of seeing Iggy perform started to build. Leaning forward with elbows on knees, I waited.

Brody Cress completed his ride with 82 points. He was pulling ahead of Brodie for the average win.

After the fifth rider bust into the arena, Iggy walked through the chutes with Dad and Brodie approaching him from the platform. The knot in my stomach returned, but it was nerves and excitement.

"Iggy fills the whole damn chute," Caleb murmured.

Dad and Brodie situated the flank strap and saddle on the stallion's back. I focused on what I could see of Iggy's head and glanced at the large monitor for the close-ups.

Brodie rose above the panel and over the chute. My elbows hit my knees, hands clasped together and a prayer said as my pulse raced.

"Come on, Iggy," Caleb whispered.

"River, don't swear, you're on camera again," Mom exhaled and my jaw clenched together.

Lacie Jae had the phone up to video the ride. The announcer was telling the crowd that Destiny's Ignatius from the Westmoreland Stock Contracting company had never been ridden the full eight seconds. The energy in the arena increased.

With rein gripped in his hand, Brodie leaned back, wiggled down into the saddle, took a deep breath and nodded.

The gate swung open and my heart leapt to my throat.

CHAPTER SIXTY SEVEN

Iggy launched high and powerful to make a grand entry into the arena. Brodie held his spurs high on the horse's neck until the front hooves finally hit the ground. The horse kicked back so high he was nearly vertical in the air with Brodie leaned back as far as he could go. The back hooves were barely on the ground when the horse launched into the air with such power I gasped. Another high kick in the back with the horse's hips twisted to the left, another buck and he twisted to the right, then he launched himself in the air with all four hooves in the air and Brodie deep in the saddle. At the peak of the next buck with back hooves high in the air, the horn blared. When the hooves hit the ground, Brodie was flying over the horse's shoulder.

I found myself screaming along with the rest of the crowd. My boots were pounding against the ground before I even realized I was standing.

Brodie stood just as the pick-up man released the flank strap from the horse and Iggy took off in a race around the arena. When the large proud stallion, with mane and tail flying, finally slowed down to prance another lap, horse and cowboy watched each other. With hat in hand, Brodie tipped it to the horse as he neared.

The crowd erupted in another cheer as the announcer's voice echoed into the building letting them know they had just watched a record-tying ride in the Thomas and Mack Center.

"93 points!" I yelled with both fists in the air and my eyes flying to Dad whose own arm was fist pumping in the air.

Brodie was walking through the arena, fingers to the sky and yelling; "That's for you, Craig!"

As if deciding he had made his mark on the night, Iggy pranced out through the gate. Every fiber in my body wanted to follow him out into the corrals and throw my arms around his huge sweaty neck. I laughed at the thought and looked back at Dad. Our eyes met and we just grinned and nodded to each other.

Brodie's arms rose to pump up the crowd again then he turned and threw his hat in the air as his eyes rose above us and he pointed to his father. I turned into my mother's arms then over to Caleb's as Lacie Jae giggled between us.

With hand over heart, I finally fell back into my seat with another whoop and holler escaping. There was no doubt, Brodie and Iggy had won the night.

When Brodie took his victory lap around the arena on a large black horse, he took his hat off and waved to the crowd. My heart was pounding at the sight of his grin. I turned away to look at Dad behind the chutes but he was nowhere to be seen.

As Brodie rode out of the arena, I trotted up the stairs and into the aisle.

Pacing circles in front of the monitors, I watched the tie-down roping until my heart rate returned to normal. Just as I turned to go back to the seats, Dad walked through the large glass doors. His grin was wide when he saw me.

"I believed in him!" I yelled and ran to jump into his arms.

"A dream come true," Dad laughed.

A crowd of friends joined us to congratulate us on the ride. I caught glimpses of the barrel race on the monitor. The final placings were on the screen showing Delaney Rawlins in second place for the night with a 13.64 second ride.

Within minutes of the final racer exiting the arena, Mom and Caleb appeared.

"Lacie Jae went to meet up with Evan," Caleb said.

"And we have a trip to the buckle ceremony to get ready for," Mom wrapped her arms around me.

The thought of sharing the stage with Brodie and his whole family put a damper on the night but I was determined that no matter what Brodie said or did, it would not ruin the first go-round buckle ceremony for one of Destiny and Chinook's prodigy.

It was a long, loud, non-stop talking trip from the rodeo to the SouthPoint hotel where the buckle presentation was held. My hands were shaking as I replayed the video of the ride that had already been posted on the social media websites.

"Play it again," Caleb laughed as he leaned over my shoulder.

I didn't hesitate in hitting the play button at least three more times.

"My Lord, what a beautiful ride," Mom had tears in her eyes.

"I want to go hug that damn horse," I laughed. "First thing in the morning."

"Call Nolan," Dad ordered with a grin.

We talked to the elated foreman until we parked at the hotel.

After the rodeo completed, the hallway behind the stage of the bar where the ceremony was held, filled with contestants, families, and media. The excitement rang in the air.

Just in front of us, stood Lisa Lockhart and her family as they waited their turn on stage. In front of them, were the Rawlins family and Martin.

We could hear the crowd in the bar laughing at something the announcers, Flint and Randy, said. It just filled my soul with even more excitement.

"I want a picture of the four of us back here," Mom declared.

We positioned ourselves so the entry onto the stage was visible behind us then I took the picture. Roscoe Jarboe had won bull riding and offered to use my phone and took another photo of us.

I hugged him a thanks then immediately posted the two
pictures to our company website:

Post: The son of our beloved Destiny and the late NFR
spectacular stallion, Chinook, has his first go-round
buckle ceremony tonight after a record-tying ride of
93. Destiny's Ignatius! This will be the first in many
more to come in the future.

My heart raced when I looked up to see Brodie and the
rest of the family walk onto the stage.

"We'll need the Westmoreland's next," a man waved at
us. It just made my heart beat even faster.

Brodie began his family introductions. The crowd
cheered when he introduced Delaney and Logan.

"You want to talk or do you want me to?" Dad
whispered.

"He's my horse, remember?" I grinned. "I'll take the
buckle too, but you can have the bottle of Pendleton."

He chuckled, "You'll steal that later."

"Probably," Caleb nodded.

"I'll also try to keep from swearing," I teased.

My mind was racing with what I was supposed to say. I
hated being in the spot-light, riding alone on the vast rangeland
was more my style.

"Brodie and Brody are good friends," Randy, the
announcer was saying. "They are the only two left that have
ridden every horse and tonight's ride pulls you three points
ahead of Cress."

"Yes, sir," Brodie answered.

"With a good ride tomorrow night, you'll walk out with
the average payoff and be in the running for the world," Randy
continued.

"I'll just be riding a bucking horse tomorrow and the
rest will play out whatever way it plays out," Brodie nodded.
"It's the same way I walked into tonight knowing I had one of
the top horses in the pen. I didn't worry about yesterday,
tomorrow, money, or awards. When you draw an unridden
horse, you focus on him."

"Speaking of the horse, let's bring the stock contractors out here," the announcer said.

I led the walk onto the stage with my stomach quivering in nerves. My whole focus was on the two announcers as they handed me a microphone. I had never held one before and my hands trembled. The crowd in front of me cheered as I stopped next to Brodie. I didn't look at him or his family. I needed my mind clear.

"This is River Westmoreland of the Westmoreland Stock Contracting Company," Flint said to the crowd then turned to me. "Let's talk about that horse,"

"I can talk about him all day," I laughed and my nerves eased. "He's big, spectacular, sweet, fierce, and everything we dreamed he would be."

"He is out of a past NFR horse named Chinook," Flint nodded.

"Yes," I answered. "We lost him last spring and Ignatius is stepping into the big horse shoes and really is living up to our belief in him."

Flint turned to the crowd, "It takes years of being patient, hoping, and dreaming before you find out if that horse is going to buck."

He looked right at me as if waiting for an answer.

"Whether it is the day a bucking horse is born, or the day a cowboy sits on an animal the first time waiting for him to buck, it is a very long process of growing, time in the chutes for experience, hours on the road, many rodeos, and lots of prayers. You live off of the belief that someday you can make it to those infamous yellow chutes."

"Amen, to that," Brodie said from beside me.

Flint grinned as if he liked my answer, "And one that will have a record ride."

"It takes both the cowboy and the horse to come together to make that happen," I nodded.

"I also understand that you're in charge of the breeding operations at your company," Randy said.

"Yes, sir," I nodded. "I was born to a stock contracting dad and used to sit on his knee as they discussed breeding programs. Then, when we started our own company, we worked on it together."

"She basically took over the year before Destiny's Ignatius was born," Dad added. "So he is all hers…just ask him."

Chuckles and giggles erupted from the stage.

"Introduce your family and we'll watch the ride," Flint said.

I turned to my parents and saw the proudest filled eyes I had ever seen, and my voice faltered, "Well…first is my business partner who happens to be my dad, Adam Westmoreland. Then the woman that holds us all together, my mother, Gloria. And the guy on the end is my future veterinarian, who happens to be my twin brother, Caleb. I'd also like to give a shout-out to our foreman who stayed home, Nolan Stokes. We couldn't do this without him."

"Nice," Flint grinned at me. "Now for the ride, Brodie talk us through it."

We turned to watch the video screen. One hand gripped the microphone and the other fell over my heart as Iggy bust out of the chute and Brodie talked of the ride.

Tears filled my eyes as Dad leaned in to whisper in my ear, "I love you, Darlin'. So proud…"

"Just a fantastic ride," Flint said.

Brodie nodded, "I had the pleasure of spending a few weeks with the Westmoreland's at their ranch in October and I have to say they have another dozen horses that will be honored on this stage in the future. They have a tremendous herd. Ignatius' little brother, Inferno, is just as big and strong and it wouldn't surprise me if both horses made it to this stage next year and I hope I am here next to them."

The crowd applauded and I heard words of agreement from his family.

"Brodie, this is your first time here and I'm sure your brother and sister have given you instructions on what to say since both have been here numerous times, but this is your moment to say whatever you want and thank whoever you want," Randy said and waved his arm to 'give' Brodie the stage.

752

Brodie chuckled with a smile at his family then lifted the microphone, "My thanks to God for giving me the ability and talent, my sponsors to helping me get down the road, and to my family for giving me the example of how to get here. My biggest thank you is to Martin who took his son to a rodeo one day and let him get on a sheep for the first time, which got him hooked. And, to my best friend, Craig Houston, who left this earth way too damn soon." The crowd erupted in applause. "Craig pushed me every day to be better. He gave me the encouragement I needed when things got tough, and he just made the whole learning and growing experience, and the traveling so much damn fun. He was the absolute best friend any man could ask for."

He lowered the microphone and stepped back as the crowd applauded again.

My jaw clenched to try to stop the flood of tears.

"Well said, young man," Randy nodded. "Let's get that first go-round buckle in your hands."

I was handed the bottle of whiskey which I quickly handed to Dad, then a check which I handed to Mom, but the buckle, encased in a windowed box, was gripped tightly in my hands. Without looking at him, I stepped next to Brodie as we posed for the pictures then held back as he and his family began to exit the stage. We slowly walked behind them.

"Good job," Randy said to me with a smile.

"Thanks," My nerves began to relax.

Just off stage, Caleb, Mom and Dad walked to Camille. I was standing next to Martin and Evan with the rest of their family having walked away to talk with friends. In his chair, Evan was just a bit lower than me and our eyes met.

"First time talking on stage?" he asked and I nodded with a relieved grin. "Couldn't tell; you were confident and had a good story."

"Thanks," I whispered. "I'd rather be facing a bitchy bucking mare with a new foal than stand in front of people."

He chuckled, "Except for this stage."

"Yes," I laughed. "This is the exception."

753

"Brodie shared the pictures of your place and the herd of horses," he said. "Very beautiful and impressive."

I nodded proudly, "I've thought of you a few times this week and how proud you must be to have all three of your children on the arena floor waving at you each night."

He sighed with eyes glowing of love, "No doubt their mother was smiling from heaven."

"And Craig was next to her cheering them on," Martin added.

I looked up at him with a twinge in my heart, "I am so very, overly happy for you to be united with his children."

"Damn miracle," he whispered and with glistening eyes looked at Caleb to Camille then to me. "My name is Charles, but I go by my middle name, which makes my initials CMH. Craig's middle name was Martin so he had the same initials." He took a deep breath. "To continue that and to honor the man who brought them to us, my grandson's name is Caleb Martin Houston."

"Oh!" My tears instantly rose. "He will be so astonished."

"My granddaughter...I called Craig's mother to let her know of the twins and we both agreed on a name," Martin continued. "She will be named after Craig's mother, Eloise, and the Rawlins mother, who he adored and considered a second mom. So, my granddaughter's name is Lillian Eloise Houston."

My heart nearly burst with pride and love.

"So beautiful," I whispered.

"Just you and Evan know tonight," Martin nodded with a firmer voice. "I'll tell everyone else in the morning."

"I never knew wearing a red shirt would become the beginning of a miracle," I smiled.

They both chuckled.

"I was surprised to hear you met Craig," Evan said.

"He was a gentleman, funny, and one heck of a dancer," I said truthfully.

"I didn't realize you and Caleb were twins," Martin said. "Since I'll be raising a set of boy-girl twins now, you have any advice?"

I laughed, "It was fun because we went through the same stages together like favorite cartoons and same classes at school. It was also a challenge because we were going through the same stages together and fought over everything."

Both men laughed. They were comfortable to talk to...I liked them.

When we stepped out of the hotel and into the cool air, I said goodnight to the two men and turned to follow my family. Brodie blocked my path with a sneer.

"And you didn't think I could win," he huffed.

"It depends on who is looking at it," I said and walked around him.

"What the hell does that mean?" Brodie growled.

His entire family stood behind him while mine stood next to me.

"You went the eight seconds and won the buckle," I shrugged. "Iggy doesn't worry about the 8 seconds, he just works to get the cowboy off his back...and he got you off his back at eight and a half seconds and so in his mind, he won."

Brodie glared so I just shrugged with a smirk and turned to walk away. We were barely 30 feet away when I heard him yell.

"Damn it!"

I turned to see Brodie striding toward us with a determined gleam in his narrowed eyes that were focused on me. His whole family was quickly following behind him; none of them looked happy.

CHAPTER SIXTY EIGHT

"Brodie, get your ass back here," Evan growled.

I took a breath and turned to face him with the buckle gripped tightly in front of me as if it was a shield.

My parents and Caleb stopped to look back, too.

Ten feet away, Brodie's eyes were twinkling in 'I told you so'.

The moment he began to speak he stopped in surprise.

Dad had stepped between us, his stance braced for battle and face tinted red.

"Before you say a word, you jackass," Dad growled. "Remember that YOU are the one that hurt my daughter and my wife."

The family stopped behind him with Delaney gripping Brodie's arm and trying to pull him back.

"I apologized to Gloria and to you," Brodie huffed. "River wouldn't even talk to me until this morning and that was just to throw a 'miracle' remark at me about Iggy."

"It amazes me how empty-headed and immature you twenty-somethings are at times," Dad growled. Brodie's eyes narrowed and lips rolled into a straight line. "You know why I talked to you opening night?"

"Dad!" I huffed and tugged at his shirt-sleeve but he just yanked it out of my fingers.

He continued as if I hadn't spoken, "I'm standing there wanting to do nothing more than kick your fucking ass for hurting my family. I wanted to knock you into that bucking chute and let that horse trample you."

Gasps rang out...including mine. Brodie's eyes widened and jaw dropped.

"But I get this damn text from my daughter, who you broke her heart, and she tells me to go up and see if you're fucking humming," Dad huffed.

"What?" Delaney whispered.

Dad continued, "She tells me if you're humming, you're not in the arena, you're in the mountains in Montana riding with Craig."

"Oh..." Delaney gasped.

"Knowing what my daughter wants and wanting to make her happy," Dad continued. "I didn't kick your ass into the chute. I walked up and talked to you like it was just another damn rodeo."

I glanced around the startled faces of his family. No doubt, Mom and Caleb's were too.

"Dad," I whispered and pulled on his arm again. "This doesn't matter."

Brodie glanced at me, "Why doesn't it matter?"

"Because it does not affect us anymore," I said. "Congratulations on riding Iggy and good luck tomorrow, but stop this."

In the silence, I heard the announcer from the NFR yelling into the night, "...on the unridden horse Destiny's Ignatius..."

Lacie Jae had her phone up, speaker on, and was playing the video from the ride.

The announcer continued with the crowd cheering in the background, "There's the nod and here we go!"

"Hold on," My voice echoed from the phone.

"Wow, what a bust out!" The announcer yelled.

As the ride continued, my voice whispered from the phone, "Get 'em...toes out...you got it...spur...hold on...hold on...you got it...damn...you can ride him...just seconds...you can...ahhh...yes..." Then I was screaming in elation.

The video ended and silence hung in the air.

I was shocked because I had no idea I had said anything.

"When she made the miracle remark this morning," Evan said. "You had just met Craig's babies and everyone was overcome in emotion; definitely not focused on rodeo."

"Would you have been as driven to ride Iggy if she hadn't said it?" Caleb asked.

Brodie looked at him with shoulders lowering and he shook his head.

"Both times," Mom said. "River knew what you needed and reached out to help you, even after what you did to her."

"And if it wasn't for me losing my temper," Dad huffed. "You would have never known."

I pulled on Dad's shirt again, this time he turned and looked at me.

"This is over now, it doesn't matter," I whispered. "Let's just get something to eat and celebrate Iggy's win."

Without a glance to anyone, I turned and walked away with my family right behind me.

When we finally made it to our room at 2:00 in the morning, Caleb and I both fell onto the beds fully dressed. My mind was so exhausted.

"What a damn day," Caleb muttered.

"Why can't life be easy?" I sighed.

"For being the most drama-free person I've ever known as we grew up, you sure have made up for it this week."

At 8:00 the next morning, I was stepping out of the bathroom showered and dressed for the day. I glanced at Caleb, expecting him to be sleeping, but he was texting on his phone.

"I was going to go with you this morning," he grumbled.

I picked up the boxed trophy buckle, "You can still come over."

"Hmmm…would you mind if…"

"If Camille came, too?" I glanced at him as I walked to the door.

He nodded with pure hope in his eyes, "I'd like to spend more time with her before we leave tomorrow."

"No, I don't mind."

"I'm a bit confused on this whole thing with Camille...why you did what you did."

I opened the door and walked out with a shout over my shoulder, "Me, too."

When I slid onto the back seat of the Uber car, I wrapped my arms around the buckle box and held it close to my chest. Then, I asked myself the one question I had been avoiding since we arrived. If anything Brodie or is family had to say to me didn't really matter, then why did I have such an issue with Camille?

The first time I had seen her was in San Antonio the night Toby Keith had surprised everyone at the bar. Craig had surprised me by asking me to dance and he was nice, funny, but not Brodie who had danced with Camille all night. Jealousy... plain and simple. I was disappointed, but he lived in Oregon and I lived in Nebraska so I let it go. But, later on Lacie Jae's podcast she said Camille had a boyfriend named Mark. In my mind, she was cheating on Mark with Brodie and there, combined with the jealousy, began the first embers of dislike.

The Uber stopped and I slid out of the car and walked toward the gate with the security guard greeting me with a wide grin.

"What took you so long?" Russ smirked.

I smiled, "I wasn't sure if you would let me in."

"He earned himself an early visit from his favorite human," He walked along the side of me as we made our way to the pens. "I've watched that ride a couple of times already this morning."

"I bet I got you beat on that," I grinned.

"I'm sure you do."

"Have they been in the exercise pen yet?"

"They have a few herds ahead of them."

Iggy was at the back of the pen inching his nose over the panel of the fence trying to pester the horse next to him.

"He's in a mood," I chuckled.

The horse didn't see me as I walked along the fence to the gate, but he did hear the chain rattle against the panels. His head turned, lifted, and he trotted to me.

My heart just sighed as I looked at him. So much love and pride.

I held the box out to him and his nose pushed against the glass. "Truly wished you understood how significant this was."

"Let me have your phone and I'll get a picture of the two of you with the buckle," the guard said.

Iggy stood still for the pictures but he didn't pose. Instead, he pushed my hat, my hip, sniffed my boots then up to my knees then started on my hands as if looking for a treat. His last move was to put his muzzle to my ear. I giggled the whole time.

The guard returned my phone and disappeared with a wave.

I posted three images on the company website and was leaning against the fence panel reviewing the rest of the pictures while Iggy nibbled at my pant leg.

"I thought I'd find you here."

Confusion swirled through me again as I leaned around Iggy to see Brodie standing at the gate. He was wearing his go-round buckle he had won the night before, his NFR coat and the black hat we had purchased in Pendleton. With a black shirt and dark goatee and mustache, he looked very rugged and handsome. Damn, that man. Why was he pushing so damn hard?

The chain rattled when he opened the gate, making Iggy turn to look.

"OK if I come in?"

I hesitated, then sighed. Maybe it was finally time, with just the two of us, to talk so he would walk away.

"He's not too fond of people besides Dad and me," I finally said. "Just stay by the fence until he decides you're OK."

"And I'll know that when?" He asked hesitantly.

"He'll approach you. If his ears go back, then I'd suggest you move out quickly," I smirked.

Brodie hesitated and looked at me then the horse.

"He's never hurt anyone...never charged anyone..." I assured him. "Just don't approach me until he says you're OK."

He closed the gate, then slowly walked up the fence so he was across the corral from me with the horse in between.

"Why are you here?" I asked.

"Because my two fathers informed me I was a bigger jackass than your father said I was," he smiled. "They were impressed with you on stage last night, and evidently, you had a conversation with them after."

"We did not discuss you," I grumbled.

"I don't doubt that," he smirked. "Logan likes you too, and he 'suggested' that I find out why talking to me doesn't matter to you."

"Why should it matter to me?"

Iggy took a step toward him with his head low, but ears pointed toward him in curiosity.

Brodie spoke to me but kept his eyes on the horse, "I've been trying to apologize and..."

He stopped when Iggy's head lowered to the ground and approached his boots. The horse began his sniffing until he got to Brodie's chest then turned back to me as if to ask a question.

"It's OK, boy," I whispered with a reassuring smile.

Iggy took a step forward to block our view of each other but looked from Brodie then back to me as if he wasn't quite sure if he should be OK with the man in the corral.

"Excuse me!"

All three of us looked over at a woman standing by the gate.

"Yes?" I asked.

"I'm looking for the Westmoreland stock contractor," The woman smiled as her eyes moved between Brodie's belt buckle and the trophy box in my hand. "I heard he was back here."

"SHE is the contractor, River Westmoreland, and is the owner of the horse," Brodie stated firmly and my stomach clenched at the pride in his voice.

The woman's eyes widened, "Oh, good, both of you are here with the horse. I'm with the network, and I'd love to get a picture of the record-tying bronc rider, horse, and stock contractor since you're all here," She lifted a camera. "Would that be OK?"

I sighed but smiled brightly since at the moment I wasn't the woman Brodie jilted, I was the 'face' of our company. Lifting the buckle to display it in front of me, I put one hand on Iggy's shoulder. His neck arched and head rose to make him look huge next to me. Brodie stood away from the fence so his buckle was on display also. Iggy's head swung to him then back to me.

"So, are ya'll comparing notes from last night?" The woman asked as she took the pictures.

I grinned a bit wider, "Why yes, that is exactly what we're doing."

Brodie chuckled.

"Just a quick question for a caption," She said. "What do you think is the biggest factor in a record ride?"

"Experience, and the belief that you can do it," Brodie answered.

"Belief, faith, and a damn good mare and stallion," I added.

"Thank you!" She waved and walked away.

"Can I buy his acceptance with food?" Brodie asked and pulled a cube from his pocket.

"You carry horse cubes?"

"For Cinco, Dad's old bulldogging horse that I ride in the grand entry."

Iggy's head turned and took the cube from his hand.

"Evidently, you can," I sighed.

"Tennessee Whiskey," Brodie said softly. "I hoped to break the ice with a little alcohol and a perfect memory."

My heart ached as the vision of our dance played in my mind. It was a perfect memory.

"When you didn't respond, I asked Delaney to send the sunrise picture. I didn't think you would open it if I sent it."

"Why do you keep pushing?"

"Because of the next picture...the first one of us together."

"With our eyes closed...as in the way we walked into the relationship."

"Blind but hopeful," His eyes were searching mine for the answer.

"There were no promises...on either side."

Iggy took a step forward and blocked our view of each other again.

"Getting between us again," Brodie mumbled. There was a long pause as we stood on each side of the horse. "That's it, isn't it?" he finally whispered.

I leaned back and watched a plane fly over us. "What?"

"That's why it doesn't matter...because..."

"YOU are the one that left."

"By the time we got to the end of the driveway, I knew I had made the biggest mistake of my life. I knew you wouldn't..."

"And yet you didn't stop or call."

"No...that was because of the look in your eyes when we left; like you were just letting go."

"You left without talking," I whispered and lowered my gaze to the ground. "It was quite clear you didn't care for me as much as I cared for you and that hurt."

"That's not true..."

"You were using me to fill the void Craig left." My heart ached and I wanted to cry but clenched my jaw to keep the tears from falling. Thankfully, Iggy still blocked us from one another so he couldn't see me struggling.

"Maybe in Pendleton after I thanked you. Craig and I usually went for a vendor walk before we settled in but I wasn't going to go at all until I realized, after I thanked you, that I wanted to spend more time with you. So, maybe then I did, but definitely not after. It was you I was calling on the phone because I wanted to talk to YOU. Accepting your offer to go to your ranch wasn't about him either. I wanted to be with you."

"Brodie," I forced my voice to remain calm. "There is no reason to rehash all the emotions or reasons or excuses or whatever…"

"Because it doesn't matter, because the horses are between us. You'll choose them…"

Iggy walked away from us and our eyes connected. There was hurt in his.

"No," I whispered. "I chose you."

His eyes narrowed.

"I was enamored with you since the first time I saw you behind that building." I nodded to the arena.

"You saw me there?" He asked in surprise.

"Last year, you were sitting on a horse with people asking you where Logan was."

"Really?"

"Then I saw you in San Antonio at the bar."

"Why didn't you ever tell me you danced with Craig?"

I shrugged, "There never seemed to be a right time."

"Then I literally ran into you in Kennewick and you ran into me in Lewiston," He smiled softly. "Then Pendleton…when I couldn't wait to find you."

"…and I was searching for you." I relented. "But the moment I offered for you to come to the ranch was the moment I chose you over my own world."

"How?"

"In Lewiston and Kennewick, to that last moment in Pendleton, we were just a person from Oregon and one from Nebraska. From the moment I asked you to come into my world was the moment I chose you over it."

Our gaze held for a few moments, then he shook his head, "I didn't realize that."

"When you walked away without even talking to me, so quickly, I realized you didn't care for me enough to stay and talk. You were just using me to keep from thinking of Craig."

"No…not at your ranch."

"The ranch I was willing to walk away from for you. Everything I had dreamed of, my business, my family, I was willing to leave to walk at your side where ever you went."

"I would not have asked or expected that of you." He took a step to me and Iggy's head turned to him so he stopped.

"It doesn't matter now," I whispered. "Iggy, Destiny, Siren, Inferno, Henry, Skitter, Betty, Fizzling Dud, Spirit, Windsor...I won't leave them. I won't leave my life for someone who would walk away from me so easily."

His shoulders lowered as he nodded, "Alright, I understand that now."

I took a step toward Iggy.

"But River?"

Hesitantly, I stopped.

"At no point did I ever think of you in Oregon and away from your ranch."

"It doesn't..."

"Yes, it does matter," he interrupted and walked toward me.

Iggy's head turned to watch him so he stopped and took a step back.

"It matters," Brodie pleaded. "The night on the river...I just..." His voice faltered. "After working the younger horses all day then going to the river for a camp-over in 30-degree weather? What woman would want to do that?"

"Me..." I started.

"Exactly," His hand flew toward me making Iggy's head swing around and watch him. "We laid there listening to the river and watching the fire while you told me stories of growing up at the arena...your dad stowing you away and hiding you from the boss. Damn, River...you fell asleep in my arms and you were so damn beautiful and perfect," He stepped back and exhaled gruffly. "It was fucking perfect and scared the hell out of me."

"It was perfect," I nodded and the tears began to well. "So why in the hell did you throw it away...run away...? Did you...?" I gasped with pains of betrayal piercing my heart. "Did you call the cowboys to come pick you up that morning?"

CHAPTER SIXTY NINE

He shook his head, "No…of course not."

"It was awfully convenient…" My voice lowered in accusation.

"I did NOT call them," he growled. "We had talked in Billings about the group conference call about the NFR horses. They knew I was with you so they called about the ride home." His eyes bored into mine. "That is the truth…absolute truth."

I took a shaking breath and nodded I believed him.

"I want you to understand," His voice was low and pleading. "Why I left…you did nothing wrong. I just want you to know what I should have told you that morning instead of getting mad and leaving."

I inhaled a shaking breath to ease the tension in my lungs and heart.

"The night before I left, we were talking about the weeks leading up to Vegas and how we could communicate."

"Yes…"

"I went to bed that night thinking of the night before at the river and wanting you with me every second of every day. You made my life bearable, tolerable, and…honestly…worth living," His eyes began to glisten and voice softened. "I went to bed wishing that I could introduce you to Craig. He would have loved you, which is evident since out of all the women in the bar that night, he asked you to dance. After pushing away the disappointment at the loss of that chance and knowing that it wouldn't happen, I finally managed to fall asleep only to wake in the middle of the night." His eyes moved to the horizon. "Craig kept appearing in my dreams…so fucking vivid I thought I could reach out and touch him. It all stemmed from that one thought of introducing you two and I got mad." He looked at me with anger, hurt, and agony. "All the weeks since he was killed, I was mad at the world, mad at the people that ran the stop sign, and, more than anything, I was mad at God for taking him away. Those feelings I dealt with, but that morning, for the first time, I was mad at Craig. So mad I was shaking." Tears slowly slid from his eyes. "I miss my best friend so fucking much my chest hurts, physically hurts, each morning when I wake up and remember he's gone. It's all I can do some mornings to even get out of bed and face life without him there." He took a deep shaking breath. "You, River, gave me every reason to get out of bed. You, River, made me mad at Craig so I got mad at you because my feelings for you made me mad at him. It was a vicious circle that I fought for an hour before I threw my bags in Nolan's truck and went to say goodbye to you."

"And Mom's words of my just using you as a project just fueled the fire." My hands trembled as I wiped the tears from my cheeks.

"Yes, and I just lost my head long enough to yell at you and lose you," he groaned. "Like I said, by the time we were at the end of the drive…the look on your face when you turned away…I knew I had lost you." He shook his head. "The first couple of weeks I was furious at myself and just focused on working out, working cows, and working hard not to think about you." With a heavy exhale he looked at Iggy then back to me. "It had only been just over two months since Craig died, and I just…"

Iggy turned to walk toward us and Brodie took a step away from me. The horse stopped next to him and nudged his elbow.

"You better have another cube in there," I took a deep breath.

A cube appeared from his pocket and quickly disappeared between the horse's lips. As if he forgot the horse was a petulant stallion and not a saddle horse, Brodie ran a hand down his neck. The horse did for him, what he does for me…it calmed his heart and the tears ceased. He wiped away the remnants from his cheeks.

"I could not imagine you away from him and the other horses," His eyes were soft in understanding. "They are a part of who you are."

"And your family, Martin, and now Craig's children are part of who you are."

"But I'll see them at rodeos and I can call, visit, or video chat with them," He smiled. "You can't exactly do that with the horses."

"And Craig's babies?"

"Caleb and Lillian," he smiled warmly. "They are going to be raised with the most doting grandfather and loved by all their aunts and uncles. I will be there for them whenever they need me. I will provide if Martin can't and I will cherish every second I have with them."

The gate chain rattling had all three of us turning. Caleb was walking through the gate with Camille standing just to the outside looking at me pensively.

"River," Brodie whispered as his hand went in his jacket and came out with a white box the size of his palm. "Take this…when you have a moment and if you'll give me the chance…"

I took the box and slid it into my pocket as he turned to greet Caleb.

"Good morning," Caleb grinned and shook Brodie's hand. "I have to say this is a surprise."

I nodded and looked back at Camille, "Would you two give me and Camille a few moments please?"

"Only if you promise not to push her under the horse and make him trample her," Caleb snickered.

I chuckled, "Wasn't that a shocking revelation?"

"It sure came as a surprise to me," Brodie huffed. "Damn glad he said it though."

"I promise I won't let Iggy attack," I smiled and patted the horse on the shoulder.

Brodie pulled out one last horse cube to feed to Iggy before the three of us met Camille at the gate.

"Looks like he thinks Brodie is acceptable," Caleb teased.

"Well, it took a few range cubes to make it happen," Brodie nodded then turned to me. "I have an autograph signing I have to get to but can we talk later?"

I stared at him a moment then finally nodded. His smile widened as he nodded at Camille. When the men walked away, Camille turned to me as if bracing for an attack.

"Who is Mark?"

"What?" She said in surprise.

"Who is Mark?"

"I met him last January through Delaney and we dated until July."

"So, when you were with Brodie in San Antonio you were cheating on Mark?"

Her shoulders relaxed as she shook her head, "Mark couldn't go with us so Brodie promised him that he would look after me while we were in Texas."

"So, Mark and Brodie knew each other?"

"Mark takes care of their ranch when they are traveling, Delaney ropes with him, and he went to high school with Logan."

I stared at her a moment trying to decide if I trusted her answer.

She smiled in understanding, "Mark and I separated after it became clear that he wanted me to stay home and have kids, but I wanted to stay on the road with Delaney and live for the adventure. I didn't have any growing up." She hesitated then continued, "Craig and I were together."

"What?" I gasped.

"Craig and I were friends, of course, but we grew into more after Mark and I separated. We were together for two weeks before the car accident."

If she was with Craig, then there was no way she would have been with Brodie. They were friends then lovers, then he was gone.

"Well, that just sucks," I grumbled.

"Yes, it did."

"Lacie Jae said the lady writing on the display walls at the convention center was Kendra."

"Horrible person," Camille grimaced. "We met in college and after my father passed she helped me get a job near her so we could share an apartment with a friend. I started dating a guy and after a few weeks, she informed me that they were sleeping together behind my back, so I broke it off and went looking for Lacie Jae but ended up meeting Delaney and Mark instead."

"She said you were jealous of her and seduced her boyfriend."

Camille rolled her eyes, "Of course, she did. As I said, she is a horrible woman; a person that would spitefully ruin a vendor's display and childishly draw stupid things on a person's image. I talked to my ex-boyfriend, that she said she slept with, and he said they didn't and he wouldn't because he thought she was a bitch."

I glanced down the road to see Caleb walking toward us.

"I'm not sure exactly why I did what I did yesterday," I said. "Maybe I wanted to hear the truth about you while he was angry. That seems to be the best way to get my family to talk."

Camille smiled, "Well, I was a bit shocked, then very pleased. I like your brother...very much."

I turned and looked at her, "I am extremely protective of my family."

"As I am of Lacie Jae and now the Rawlins and Martin."

"Don't sway him from the path he has mapped for himself."

"Absolutely not," she smiled. "We had a long talk about his plans when we were driving from Denver the other night. I'm excited for him and will encourage him in every step." She hesitated with a frown. "But, there is one thing you should know."

"What?" I exhaled.

"I very much like your brother for his looks," She grinned with a soft giggle.

I chuckled, maybe she wasn't so bad after all.

Caleb stopped in front of us with a grin.

"No horse trampling yet," I assured him. "But I do want to say, since you're both here, what a remarkable thing you two did in finding and bringing those babies to Martin."

They smiled and I could see a sparkle of light in their eyes as they looked at each other. There was already a special bond between the two of them.

"You two have fun today," I turned away. "I'm going to go take a nap."

My body moved to the rhythm of Destiny's stride as we galloped behind the herd of a bucking horses racing down the road of the open range. My heart soared from the freedom as my lungs took in the crispness of the air. I turned to my left to see Brodie on the buckskin gelding running behind the excited and nervous horses. He was grinning as he watched the horses run.

A ding rang out and I looked to the horses to see what was wrong. Another bell chimed and Brodie had disappeared. A ringing sound pierced the air and the horses began to dissolve.

Another bell and my mind cleared enough to know that I had once again been dreaming of us riding with the horses. The phone's ring began again.

My eyes were still closed when I answered it.

"What?"

"Nice," Brodie's voice chuckled.

My heart clenched.

"Sorry," I whispered and sat up on the bed. "Trying to catch up on my sleep from last night."

"Well…I'd say I was sorry to wake you but, I'm really not," He chuckled and I had to smile at his honesty. "You said we could talk later."

"Yeah," I sighed.

"Are you here at SouthPoint?"

"No, I'm at our trailer."

"Oh…well, damn."

"It won't take long to get back to the hotel."

"Can you meet me at the Bellagio instead?" His words were full of hope.

I slid from the bed to clear my groggy mind, "Yeah, I guess. What time?"

"We have to be there at 1:00."

"It's 12:15," I moaned.

"Please?"

"Alright, but I won't have time to change."

"You don't need to, you're beautiful just the way you are."

His words made my stomach flutter, but the reflection in the mirror in front of me did not reinforce those words.

"I'll get there," I finally whispered.

"I'll meet you at the main front doors."

I ended the call and hurried to try to freshen what makeup was left and brush my matted hair. Luckily, the cowboy hat would hide most of the nap's damage.

It was 12:59 when I walked through the doors. My heart was racing from the last jog to the doors and the anticipation of another talk with Brodie.

His grin was wide and eyes bright when he saw me. A hand reached out to grab mine but quickly waved to the side instead. "This way."

His long strides had me nearly jogging to keep up.

"This is a bit rushed and weird," I finally huffed as we walked down a corridor toward two large doors. "There are no restaurants down here."

"We can eat after."

"After what?"

He didn't answer as he opened one of the doors and we walked into a large room then walked to another set of doors.

"Why are we here?" I gasped.

Again, no answer as he opened the next set of doors that revealed pews filled with people running down each side of a small chapel and a wide aisle in front of us that led to a man standing with a bible in hand. A bride in a sleek white satin dress faced a grinning groom wearing a grey cowboy hat and a wide, happy grin. To the left of the bride, was a woman my age and to the right of the groom, was an older man.

Brodie slid onto one of the pews in the back and took my arm to pull me down next to him.

I looked at him in disbelief and whispered, "Who is that and why did you bring me to a wedding?"

He looked at me and smiled, "The bride is Lauren Conners; she owns the estate where Ryle lives. Groom is Kade Weston."

"You rushed me to your sister's boyfriend's landlady's wedding?"

He chuckled and shook his head, "She also sold Maestro to Delaney...the horse that won the buckle the other night."

Still in a bit of shock, I glanced around the room. I didn't know anyone there except Martin, Logan, and Lacie Jae. They were sitting on the far side of the room.

Laughter and clapping erupted as the bride and groom shared their first marital kiss.

The bride turned to hug the younger woman.

"That's her daughter, Jamie," Brodie whispered.

The groom turned to hug the older man.

"That is his grandfather, Pete."

I turned and shook my head, "Why did you bring me here?"

CHAPTER SEVENTY

The bridal party turned to walk down the aisle and sit four rows back from the front. Lacie Jae, Logan, and Martin stood and moved to the front.

"For this," Brodie whispered, stood and motioned for me to move into the aisle. I numbly complied then was shocked when he took my hand and walked me toward the alter, then onto the seats in the front row.

"Hi, River," Lacie Jae greeted me with an excited grin.

"Hi…" My voice faltered.

Ryle walked down the aisle in denim jeans, white shirt, and black cowboy hat. His roping partner, Jess, was right behind him. They stood at the front of the room.

"Brodie?" I whispered with wide eyes.

He turned to me and grinned, "They nearly got married here last year but Ryle talked her out of it because he knew she would want her family here."

"Delaney and Ryle are getting married right now?" I exhaled softy. "On the tenth day of the National Finals Rodeo where they are both competing?"

"Yes, they figured they would be too tired tomorrow and we have that interview setup with the whole family. This morning, when Lauren announced their wedding, Ryle and Delaney decided to get it done right after. It will be quick but official."

"You didn't know about this when we were at Iggy's pen?"

"No, they told me after the signing."

"She doesn't want to get married at the ranch?"

"No," he whispered. "Not without Mom."

My heart ached. I couldn't imagine a big wedding without my mother at my side.

"But," he continued. "Dad wasn't going to miss out on his father and daughter dance."

Everyone in the room turned to look at the door. To my surprise, Caleb was sitting on the pew Brodie and I had just left.

Camille appeared at the door in a simple, figure-hugging dress the same brown color as her flowing, curled hair. A turquoise necklace matched the belt around her tiny waist. She wore brown and turquoise cowboy boots. Her smile was wide as she walked down the aisle carrying a small picnic basket with a red and white checkered napkin covering the top. She stopped across from Ryle and the two grinned at each other.

Evan appeared at the door in his wheelchair but he stopped and slowly rose from the chair. Someone on the outside of the room moved the chair out of the way. He turned and held out a hand and Delaney appeared and slid her hand in his. She was wearing the complete Annie Oakley outfit she had ridden in the Saturday before. The father and daughter grinned at each other then she stepped into his open arms.

Music echoed into the room and the pair slowly danced down the aisle together with their eyes barely moving from each other. Both had tears glistening and wide smiles as they reached the front of the aisle. A strong embrace with Delaney's eyes closing in love and happiness was completed before Evan held his daughter's hand out to a very emotional groom. Ryle wiped away tears with chin quivering as he nodded at something Evan whispered to him.

Evan sat on the pew next to Martin as the bride and groom grinned at each other. Pure love radiated from them as my heart warmed.

"We are gathered here today," the minister said. "To marry Delaney and her huckleberry in wedded bliss."

Half the people in the room chuckled, the other half were like me...a bit confused.

The minister continued until another song began to play.

"I recognize that voice," I whispered and turned to Brodie.

"Kind of fitting, isn't it?" He chuckled. "We thought it was fate that the only song we could find about being someone's huckleberry was sung by Toby Keith. AND, it is about getting married."

Baby I'll be your Huckleberry, you don't have to double dare me...

"I'll tell you the meaning after the wedding," Brodie whispered with a broad smile as he watched his sister take the small picnic basket from Camille.

I'm gonna be your Huckleberry...

As the song continued, Delaney took a small bottle out of the basket and handed it to Ryle.

He laughed and held the bottle up for the crowd to see, "Huckleberry syrup."

Everyone chuckled as the syrup was followed by; Huckleberry taffy, jelly, candy sticks, pancake batter, and finally a dozen huckleberry bon-bons.

You're so extra ordinary sweet like maraschino cherry...

When the basket was empty, Ryle handed all the items to Jess then reached into his pocket and pulled out four over-sized chocolate and huckleberry candy bars.

"Yes!" Delaney laughed and yanked them out of his hands.

I'm gonna be your Huckleberry...

"The rings?" The minister chuckled.

The rings were exchanged as the song finished. *We grew up and we got married...*

"Perfect song!" Lacie Jae giggled.

"...I pronounce you husband and wife." The minister finished.

The room cheered as the wedded couple shared another kiss.

I stood down the hall from the two wedding parties and waited for Brodie. Loud chatter and laughter was endless. Lacie Jae appeared and excitedly approached.

"A five-minute wedding," she giggled. "Wasn't that fun?"

"Yes," I answered. "Quite the surprise."

"I saw the picture on Facebook earlier of the two of you with Iggy and you looked happy. So, you being here with Brodie...does that mean you two are...?" she hesitated.

"We just talked this morning," I nodded. "Then he asked if we could talk this afternoon and I relented...without knowing it was a wedding. I'm not sure how much time we're going to have to talk before he has to go to the arena."

"Sometimes," Lacie Jae smiled. "Just being together and not talking is better than actually saying words. You feel them instead."

I groaned, "I've had enough feelings for the last twelve days. I'm ready to go home and ride the nice quiet open range."

"I understand that," she huffed. "I can't wait to go home and just sit on the porch with Logan and a cup of coffee and watch the horses and cattle graze."

"This time of year, you might want to add a crackling fire to that," Brodie said from behind me.

"Forty-eight hours," Lacie Jae chuckled and looked at me, "I'll see you tonight at the arena." She walked away with a slight wave.

"Any more weddings you need to drag me to?" I asked with a smirk.

He looked at me to gauge my reaction then shook his head, "No, I just wanted to spend some time with you and didn't think you would go if I said what we were doing first."

"Well, you're probably right. So, what else did you want to do?"

"Are you hungry?"

"Starving."

We were quiet as we walked through the lavishly holiday-decorated atrium to the elegant Sadelle's cafe. My stomach ached with anticipation as we took our seats.

"Tell me about the huckleberry wedding," I smiled.

He laughed and told me the story of how Ryle and Delaney met. Knocking a guy on his back for grabbing her ass? Well, I liked her even more.

When our food arrived, we both started as if we hadn't eaten in days. After my first initial devouring of the food, I hesitated long enough to talk.

"So, the huckleberry theme for the day continues since you have Flying 5's Major Huckleberry tonight and Cress has Black Tie, the horse you placed with on Monday night."

"And I won the Pendleton Roundup on," He nodded. "Zeke won the round with Major Huckleberry Monday night and tonight has Rodeo Houston's Womanizer who Brody won the 10th round on here last year and won the average. But, unless both Brody and I get bucked off, Iggy bucking Zeke off last Sunday night ruined his chance at the average this year."

"That's a hell of a pen tonight," I grinned.

"I saw Fizzling Dud is in the pen tonight."

"He has a rematch with Cody DeMoss. They had an 89 in Pendleton."

"I'm three points ahead of Brody right now for the average...thanks to Iggy," He grinned. "Up until Wednesday it was all just numbers and what-if's, now it is starting to get a bit...real. Grandfather won it, then dad the year after Mom died, Logan his first attempt, and Delaney her second. It's my turn and I'm starting to feel the jitters."

He had always been open and honest with me from the moment we met in Lewiston and I was a bit happy he continued.

"You can only do, what you can do, then let the chips fall as they may," I quoted my father.

We talked of horses and riders until our meal was finished and his phone beeped.

A heavy sigh escaped as he picked up his phone.

"My ride is outside waiting for me," he said as he lifted his wallet out of his jacket and placed cash on the table. "I'm sorry I have to rush off, but I don't want to keep them waiting."

"That's fine, I understand."

He stood and looked down to me as if looking for an answer, "I've enjoyed this...just the two of us."

Tingles shivered down my spine, "So have I."

With a smile, he turned, hesitated, then turned back.

"Do you still have it?" His voice was low as if afraid I would say no.

I reached in my vest pocket and pulled out the box he had handed me in Iggy's corral. The gold ribbon tied around it to hold the lid closed clearly indicated I had not opened it. I set the box on the table.

He looked at the box then up to my eyes, "I want more of this. I know the mistake I made and how much it hurt you. It will never happen again. It seems, almost every night, I dream of riding with you behind your herd of horses and want nothing more than to kiss you in the pouring rain as the world just disappears. I hope you will find it in your heart to forgive me for leaving and give me another chance...I will never hurt you again."

Anxiety raced through my veins and into my stomach; no words formed so I just nodded. With a final sigh and a hopeful smile, he walked away. I watched him through the café and into the atrium. When he disappeared from sight my eyes lingered on the last moment. My body was flushed, heart pounding, but anxiety lay over me not letting me focus.

Laughter from the table next to me brought me out of the haze. To distract myself, I slid my phone out of my pocket to check for messages.

Text from Caleb: Good to see you at the wedding. You two together again?

Text to Caleb: No, just lunch at café by atrium, he just left.

Text from Mom: LOVE the pictures of you showing Iggy his buckle. And the one with Brodie. You were both smiling so was that a work smile or a personal smile?

Text to Mom: Work

Text from Dad: Great professional shot of you and Brodie with Iggy. Good representation, proud of you.

Funny, how he didn't ask if it meant Brodie and I were back together.

Text to Dad: Very proud of you, Dad.

Text from Nolan: You best give me a call.

I hit his speed dial button.

"Hey," He answered.

"What's up?"

"Well, we have a problem."

"Ok…"

"The horses you and Adam bought arrived here the other day."

"Something wrong with them?" My stomach sunk.

"Nah, the bucking horses are fine. Spent some time in the corral then I let them out with the smaller herd. I checked on them this morning and they've blended in well."

"So, what's the problem?"

"That would be with that bay gelding Adam said was yours."

"The saddle horse, yeah."

"Well…"

"Is he OK?"

"I walked by him the other day and he called out to me so I just went ahead and threw a saddle on him."

"You rode my horse before I did?" I chuckled.

"He needed a good stretch of the legs so we checked on the cattle in the back pasture."

"So what is the problem? Did he do alright?"

"Well, that is the problem," He sighed. "By the time we got back, the damn horse had a name."

"Ah hell, Nolan, you just stole my horse. Didn't you?" I grinned.

He chuckled, "Well, you know I ain't one to be a horse thief."

I loved this man; he was a true heart of gold.

"So, if the Westmoreland Stock Contracting business were to give you the horse as your bonus for the year, it wouldn't be stealing."

He laughed, which made me grin.

"I was leaning toward buying him from you...that would be bit of an extravagant bonus," He chuckled.

"Well, you are a bit of an extravagant foreman and you've more than earned him. So, what name did you give him?"

"Xavier."

I laughed again, "Seriously?"

"If you can come up with Ignatius, I can come up with Xavier."

"How did you come up with that?"

"He has an X brand on his back hip so it just seemed fitting."

I nodded in agreement, "Yeah, it does."

A body sliding into the seat Brodie had left made my body visibly startle.

"That's the greeting your mother gets?" She grinned at me.

"Nolan, that money-bags lady just landed in the chair next to me. I have to go so I can be nice to her because I have to buy myself another saddle horse." I sighed dramatically.

They both laughed.

"I thought you just bought a new saddle horse," Mom said as I slid the phone into my pocket.

"I just gave him to Nolan as a bonus."

As I told her about the phone call, my finger traced the top of the small white box.

"How did you get here so fast?" I asked.

"Your father and I were picking up Caleb and Camille to take back to the hotel. He told me where you were so I came to see if you needed to talk. I do like that young woman. Beautiful but down to earth and she has those eyes for your brother."

"Yes, she isn't what I expected."

She pointed to the box. "And what is that?"

"A 'please give me another chance' gift from Brodie," I answered honestly.

"What's in it?"

"I don't know. I can't get myself to open it.

781

The waiter stopped to pick up the plates from the table.

"What did you have?" Mom asked.

"Eggs benedict."

She huffed, "Well, I know that isn't enough to satisfy your appetite." She turned to the waiter. "Do you have chocolate éclairs or frosted brownies, or…anything chocolate?"

I loved my mom. She always knew what I needed.

"We have pudding, Babka A la Mode, ice cream, chocolate pumpernickel…"

"Pumpernickel?" Mom gasped. "I haven't heard of that in ages."

"What's pumpernickel?" I asked.

"It's a very dense, sweet rye bread," the waiter explained. "With a chocolate coating."

"Well, let's give it a try and a Babka A la Mode to share," Mom said.

"And hot chocolate," I added.

When the waiter walked away, she pointed at the box again.

"What is the holdup in opening it?"

I hesitated in answering.

CHAPTER SEVENTY ONE

"What we talk about, stays with us," she said firmly.

"Because we don't want anyone trampled?"

She laughed with an exaggerated roll of the eyes, "I knew he was angry, but that one surprised the hell out of me." She leaned forward. "But, he doesn't regret finally saying it and getting those emotions out in the open."

"Brodie was glad he said it."

She leaned back, "What else did he say?"

I told her everything.

"So, what is keeping you from forgiving him?" she frowned.

I closed my eyes and took a deep breath to control my emotions. When they opened, I looked into her loving, concerned eyes, "Fear...he left so damn fast, and yet I was willing to give up everything to be with him. Fear...I hurt so bad I could barely breathe. When I started focusing on the anger I had for him because he hurt you, I could handle it. But, when I saw the look on his face when he realized what he did, it's just...every time it gets harder to stay angry."

"Then why not just let it go?"

"What he did...changed me," My voice trembled but I felt a sense of relief that I said it out loud. My lungs constricted with anxiety and the emotional upheaval swirled through me, bringing tears to my eyes. "You all saw it and I felt it. I'm not the same because of him and that scares me. He left so fast and easy the first time, what if I said yes and he did it again? I couldn't take that, Mom." I wiped away the tears. "I am afraid it would destroy me."

The waiter arrived and placed the desserts on the table. Neither of us picked up a spoon or fork.

"He was two months out of losing his best friend," She said. "It takes a long time to heal and move on from emotions like that. He realized what he did and why...he told you that."

"Yes," My finger started pushing the little box in circles.

"You understand why, so take off the ribbon to make that one step forward."

I hesitated, and then pulled the gold ribbon until it fell away. My finger pushed the box in circles again.

"You cannot go through life being afraid. Your father and I were afraid to take your offer to use your inheritance to start a business. What if we failed and YOU lost your future?"

"But we..."

"We realized that the fear keeping us from accepting your offer, could be keeping you from the future you were meant to have. Our fear nearly cost us not only your future, but it could have cost..." She stopped and her eyes narrowed. "Finish that sentence."

I gasped, "How am I supposed to know?"

"Exactly, River," She smiled. "No one knows what the future holds. If you decide to hold onto the fear and let the chance of happiness with Brodie go, what else are you letting go? What future are you seeing? Can you be as happy with someone else as you were with Brodie in just those few weeks you had together? Do you truly believe that those feelings you have for him are just going to go away?"

"So, you're saying I should just forgive him and let it go? Just like that?"

She leaned back in the chair and nodded, "He knows what he did, emotions over Craig's loss will ease with time and it was more than enough for me to forgive him."

"Just let it go?" I swept my hand over the little box.

"You have been supportive of him since before you knew him. What is the difference from supporting and helping him through the tough times in Lewiston and Pendleton, than understanding why he left and forgiving him and supporting him now?" She stopped and our eyes met for a moment and my heart began to ache again. "What do YOU want? Is it Brodie or not?"

"When he appeared this morning, I was irritated but not mad because he came alone to talk to me. When he told me about the dream of Craig and me, it broke my heart. When he asked to meet this afternoon, I could have easily said no, and yet I took this box without hesitation."

"That should tell you something. Open the box and see what he is offering as a bridge to get to the other side."

With the tip of my finger I flipped the top of the box off only to reveal a square of thick cotton.

"Must be fragile," Mom whispered as she leaned forward.

I pinched the cotton and tossed it to the side. I gasped, reached for the lid of the box, slammed it down over the top and shoved the box back into my pocket.

My face flamed red as our wide, startled eyes looked at each other. Then, we started giggling, which soon turned to subdued laughter.

"You will never tell your father about this," she demanded when the laughter trailed away.

"Never," I gasped and the embarrassment flushed through me again. "But I do think I should explain."

"I don't think I want to know why he gave you that for a forgiveness gift," She shook her head.

I giggled again, "The first day, when he came to the ranch and I saw him in the corral, my first thought was to handcuff him to me so he couldn't leave. I told him that when we went to Billings."

"So he bought you handcuffs," Mom grinned and picked up her fork. "That is very...oddly...romantic."

Within minutes, the Pumpernickel bread and Babka A la Mode were gone.

"River, come with me," Dad ordered as we walked away from the truck.

"OK," I looked at Mom and Caleb in surprise.

Mom smiled, "We'll see you inside."

With hands shoved in my NFR vest pockets, we made our way to the back of the Thomas and Mack center. Horses and cowboys were everywhere.

"Probably don't have time to go see the horses," I mused.

"We don't really need to, they are fine and you would just stare at each other with nothing to do."

I chuckled and silently agreed.

We walked along the side of the group of competitors waiting for the grand entry and stopped just before the tunnel. It was the same spot where I had seen Brodie for the first time the year before. I looked for him; he was on the same buckskin gelding but talking with his brother and sister instead of searching for them.

The siblings were wearing the matching shirts Lacie Jae had told us Camille designed to honor their mother. They were black with the sponsor's logos on the front. The front and back shoulders were covered in small embroidered red ribbons that symbolized the National Heart Association. The red ribbons covered from the black cuff on the wrist to the elbows. Each of their black cowboy hats had a red ribbon pin attached to the side. The shirts were beautiful.

Brodie looked so different from that wide-eyed cowboy I had seen the year before, but I still couldn't get myself to stop staring.

"Dad, do you remember last year when we were here, just like now, and you asked me if I was going to stand back here all night?"

He looked down at me, his eyes narrowed, "Vaguely."

"I had just seen a cowboy on top of a buckskin horse and he made my whole world stop." I whispered.

"The same cowboy, on the same buckskin horse that you were just staring at?"

"Yes."

"When you and Brodie walked up to us after your shopping in Pendleton, I knew you liked him. You seemed to glow and your eyes were bright."

I turned to look up at him but he was looking at Brodie.

"I liked him, too," His voice was low enough that no one else could hear him but me. "I've known of the Rawlins family for twenty years. Respected the grandfather and father...watched Logan grow into a world champion and Delaney become a hell of a roper and racer. But, from afar, as I had never met them. When I met Brodie, I had no doubt he would be a true cowboy, living up to his family name. Although I was surprised when you suggested he come to the ranch, I knew you wouldn't unless you really cared so I agreed." He turned and looked at me with thoughtful eyes. "Every day that passed when he was there, I could see you two growing closer and just seeing you two work together...well, I just couldn't believe the luck." He paused with a long exhale. "If I could create the perfect man for my daughter, who I cherish more than life, it would be Brodie Rawlins."

Tears filled my eyes.

With a smile, he continued, "Your lives growing up emulated each other and even if you weren't in the same atmosphere, you were in the same world with the same friends and beliefs, and the same love of horses and rodeo. You both are the hardest working people I know and respect your way of life. Your dreams entwine."

"Dad..." I whispered and wiped away a tear.

"I cannot tell you how upset I was when Nolan called and told me what happened. I wasn't even mad at Brodie at the time, I was mad at the fact that it happened when I wasn't there." He turned to me. "I would not have driven Brodie away from you until you talked. I was so pissed at Nolan for doing that but he didn't have any idea...he just thought he was doing the right thing."

"I know..."

He shook his head, "I didn't get mad at Brodie until I got home and your mother told me what happened...while she

787

was crying uncontrollably because she thought she had ruined your life."

More tears fell as I remember the moments I had consoled her.

"That, just fucking pissed me off," He growled then turned back to look at Brodie. "I figured when we got here, and you two were in the same place that maybe you'd have the chance to talk so I kept my mouth shut and feelings to myself."

"Until the whole trampling thing," I whispered.

He huffed, "After watching you fighting so hard not to care and him fighting so hard to get you to talk, I just figured I'd get it out there and stop him from saying something stupid and drive that wedge between you two."

I slid my arm through his and squeezed.

"From the pictures this morning of the two of you in Iggy's pen...did you get a chance to talk? Just the two of you?"

"Yes."

"And you've made up your mind?"

"I think so...yes..."

"So, you finally realized how much you love him?"

I gasped and my eyes shot to his, "No one has said that word."

He looked at me with eyes twinkling in humor, "Then maybe that's the problem. You don't have the emotions you two have had for each other when you just 'like' each other. It takes a whole lot of deep-in-the-heart love for you both to hurt so much or fight so hard."

I sighed, "You don't think he was just using me to fill the void that Craig left?"

He shrugged, "In some ways, he was because if Craig were still here, would we be having this conversation?"

I looked at him in surprise.

"It's not a bad thing, River. It is how life works. A person is taken away and something has to step in to fill a void, whether it's a friend, work, or a relationship. Do I think he would have found anyone to fill that void like you have? No. It might have taken years, but that doesn't mean he doesn't love you for who you are or want to spend time with you for who you are."

"But," I whispered and the anxiety touched my heart again. "He...when he left...he changed me."

"That is how love works, Hun," he sighed. "When you fall in love with someone like I did with your mother, it will change who you are...hopefully for the better. Before he left, you had a wide-eyed attraction with him. After he left, you were...more mature because you had to deal with all those feelings he left behind and caused. That will always change a wide-eyed attraction to a more realistic one. If your feelings survive that, then it's real emotion."

"Which, I guess, isn't all that bad...sort of."

"When I met your mother, my life was bulls, horses, and work. After Gloria came into my life, that all changed. I wanted to be with her all the time and not work. I wanted a life with her, a family with her and I changed my outlook, who I was at the time, so I could make sure I had her the rest of my life."

I nodded with a sigh, "I see your point and I'm really glad you changed who you were then."

"And if you stop for a moment and look at who you were when he arrived at the ranch and who you are right now...did he change you for the worse?"

We both looked out as the herd of contestants began their ride through the tunnel and into the arena. As Brodie rode by he looked behind him then to the side then forward then his head jerked to the side again and he looked right at us. We barely had a chance to see the smile on his face before they disappeared.

When the area was clear with the last runner going in, Dad started walking.

"Come on."

He took off down the tunnel and I was not going to refuse. I had been in the arena before but never during the rodeo with the platform full of bareback riders and stock contractors. Some of the horses were still in the chutes in the tunnel making my heart race with anticipation.

"What if someone asks who I am?" My voice shook in excitement.

"You're the Westmoreland Stock Contractor."

"That has been you. What are they going to say to you?"

"If they ask?" He turned and grinned. "I'm going to tell them I'm the stock contractor, River Westmoreland's, dad."

My heart nearly burst.

As we approached the stairs to the platform, the tunnel grew brighter and louder. The announcer was still yelling out contestant names and states when I took the first step up to the platform and my pulse was pumping. I could barely breathe as I took that last step to the top with the full arena opening before me. The red seats were full, the lights bright, horses and riders celebrating their last night of the rodeo. I stood motionless and took it all in.

Dad's hand grabbed my arm and pulled me half-way down the platform and behind the horse-filled chutes and bareback riders getting ready.

"About time you're back here."

"Hey, River. Exciting night."

"Good to see you, River."

"Can't wait to see your Fizzling Dud of a horse perform tonight."

…more greetings than I could wrap my head around as I just grinned at each and nodded.

The contestants began their ride out of the arena and I took a step back against the wall as stock contractors and riders prepared for the beginning of the rodeo.

Dad was standing right next to me as we searched the seats for our family.

My hands trembled as I pulled out my phone.

Text to Mom: Look at Dad

I watched her read her phone then look over. Her head turned left and right then locked onto us. She stood with arms waving in the air.

Dad turned and looked at me with a grin, "Some people, River, are worth changing for. Every accomplishment in my life would mean nothing, if she wasn't there with me."

"Ah, Dad," I grinned. "That's so romantic."

"What's even better, is that I make sure she knows it."

I leaned into him, "I love you both so much."

"Well, enough mush stuff, let's rodeo. You want to pull Fizzling Dud's flank strap?"

My heart dropped at the thought.

"No," I chuckled nervously. "You get it done here then we'll work on that for next year."

He grinned proudly, "It's a deal partner."

We stood next to each other through the round of bareback riders.

Dad stepped away from the wall and within seconds, the spot filled. I knew who it was without looking at him.

"So, you here all night?" Brodie whispered.

I watched the first steer wrestler back into the box.

"Will it bother you if I am?"

"I am bothered every time I am near you."

I bit my lip to keep from grinning.

"Seriously, do you need me to leave?" I asked in concern.

"No, I can ride whether you are back here or in the seats watching."

The second steer wrestler rode into the box.

"We have a family interview tomorrow," he whispered. "Are you leaving first thing in the morning? I'd like to talk to you again when we're done."

"We have an assigned time slot to pick up the horses. I'm not sure when it is but if we miss it, we have to wait to the end of the day."

"You're OK with talking more?"

I stared out into the arena as the third steer wrestler rode into the box. I wasn't sure what to do or how my answer would affect his ride.

"So...no?" He sighed.

I had no doubt that a 'no' answer would negatively affect his ride.

CHAPTER SEVENTY TWO

My hands moved behind me then I took his hand that was closest to me and placed it behind me. His fingers squeezed mine and I heard a long breath escape.

When his fingers relaxed, I slid them up my arm, under the sleeve cuff I had just undone, and up until they stopped against the metal. He turned and looked down at me, but I just turned away and looked into the audience. His fingers slid over and around the handcuffs fastened to my left wrist.

As the steer wrestlers made their runs, we stood quietly with him playing with the handcuffs.

"River?" He whispered when only two steer wrestlers remained.

Hesitantly, I turned and looked up at him.

His smile made my heart tighten.

"Would you mind if I kissed you?" He whispered.

I gasped, hit him in the chest with my free hand, and growled, "You even try it, and I'll throw you under one of those horses and let it trample you."

He laughed, but I was serious!

"Do you know how many cameras are back here?" I huffed.

His grin was wide, "Not quite up to that kind of attention?"

"NO!" I turned and pulled my hand away to button the cuff again and hide the handcuffs.

As the reigning world champion, Logan was the last steer wrestler to ride. Throwing the steer in 4.1 seconds placed him third for the night and the average, which left him short of his third world championship. When he walked out of the arena with a proud wave to his dad and a kiss blown to Lacie Jae, the crowd roared.

"Your brother is a class act," I sighed.

"He is," Brodie nodded.

The saddle bronc horses were being moved into the chutes as the team roping began. Since Brodie was one of the last to ride, his horse wouldn't be brought from the tunnels yet.

"River? I need to tell you something."

"What?"

"When you were fighting that calf in the pasture before I kissed you the first time?"

"Yeah?"

"No matter how much mud and manure was on you, you were the most beautiful woman I had ever seen."

I chuckled.

"Last week," he continued in a low voice. "The first time I saw you was before the back-number celebration...on the media carpet."

"Yeah?"

"When I saw you, in that little black dress, little silver shoulder jacket, your hair just perfect, and those cool boots...well, I could barely get my eyes off you."

The anxiety bubbled through me. My face flushed and hands trembled at the need to reach out and grab him so I shoved my hands deep in my vest pockets.

I couldn't give in so I turned and looked up at him, "You need to go get your game face on. Major Huckleberry isn't an easy ride."

Brodie grinned, "No, he's pretty powerful." He took a step away.

"Brodie?"

He turned and looked back at me with a smile.

"When you get on that horse, you stay on that horse past the eight seconds, then wait for the pick-up man to help you off where he can very carefully place you on the ground," I smiled. "Do NOT get hurt."

His grin widened and eyes danced with laughter, "There is no way that will happen. I have plans for tonight."

I gave him a wicked grin, "So do I, Cowboy."

"Just so you know," He lowered to whisper in my ear. "While we're in this building, I'll keep my distance, but once we leave? Well, consider yourself warned."

My face flushed as I chuckled.

He walked away without a glance back and disappeared.

Within a minute, Dad walked back on the platform and stood by my side.

"Everything back the way it should be?" he asked without looking at me.

"Yes."

"Good, back to work then," he nodded. "When DeMoss gets on Fizzling Dud, I want you at the horse's head. I don't want a repeat of Monday night. When the gate opens, push his head to remind him that he's supposed to go to work."

My heart raced.

The moment the cowboy rose above the panel, I knelt at the horse's head.

"You remember," I whispered to Fizzling Dud. "You only get the roar of the crowd if you go out there and buck."

As I knelt with my hand on the horse's neck, watching Dad adjust the flank strap and Cody adjust the rein, I realized that this was what my 16-year-old self, had dreamt about. I had practiced my speech to my parents for a week before going to them to offer my inheritance to start the stock contracting business.

This moment in time with my father, my partner, behind the chutes and beside me at the National Finals Rodeo was my dream coming true. His Highness Chinooks' offspring was at my fingertips getting ready to shine in front of the crowd of 18,000 people and millions on television and the internet. A homegrown horse, that my father and I had watched be born, was now preparing to bust out at the ultimate stage for a bucking horse with both of us at his side.

The gate swung open and I pushed the horse out onto that stage. The crowd roared, Mom and Caleb cheered from the stands, and I rose to stand next to my business partner...my dad. In the eight seconds, my eyes took in the crowd, the lights, the large monitor hanging from the ceiling showing a close-up of the horse and rider, and my mother and brother cheering them on from the red seats.

My heart calmed; happier at that moment then I had ever been in my life. This dream came true.

The 90 points Fizzling Dud and Cody earned to put them in first place was just icing on the cake.

Brodie was next then Brody Cress riding last.

Dad and I stepped back to the wall to watch the battle for the average and possibly the championship.

The horses, Major Huckleberry and Black Tie walked into the chutes and both men stepped forward. The stock contractors, Chad Hutsell and Wade Sankey, were at their sides.

The eleventh horse and rider bust from the gate and my eyes flickered between the ride and the men preparing the horses for the next ride. An 86 point score was announced.

When the twelfth horse broke from the chute, Brodie was tightening the cinch around Major Huckleberry. An 84 point score was announced.

The thirteenth horse had Brodie crawling over the chute and Brody tightening the cinch around Black Tie. An 83.5 point score was announced.

"How many separate them?" Dad whispered.

"Brodie is…Rawlins is ahead by 3 points."

Brodie lowered onto Major Huckleberry, reached down to adjust the stirrups, then flipped his black chaps out of the way.

Brody rose above the chutes and Black Tie.

Shoving his hat down tighter, Brodie leaned back, lifted the rein, took a breath, grimaced, then nodded.

The gate swung open and the red horse leapt out two strides before beginning the high kicks to the back, head tucked low then thrust up to start the next buck. Each kick had his back legs high in the air and muscles rippling with the force of the landing of the front hooves. Brodie's spurring was smooth and fast, matching the horse in perfect unison. Toes out, arm lifting the rein with each buck, free arm moving high and low, chin tucked, and eyes focused down the horse's neck. The fierceness of the kicks did not ease even when the horn blared into the arena.

Both my hands were in fists at my side, my body swaying with the movement of the horse. When the horn blared, I turned and grabbed Dad's arm in a powerful grip.

"He did it, Dad," I squealed.

"Yes, and it looked damn good."

Brodie slid from Major Huckleberry to the pick-up man's horse then dropped to the ground. One arm rose to remove his hat and hold it to his chest, as the other arm pumped in the air. His grin was wide and relieved when the 85 point ride was announced.

"He did what he could do," Dad sighed.

I didn't have to do the math in my head, the announcer did it for me.

"Rodeo fans, that means Brody Cress has to make a 90.25 ride on Black Tie to win. Last year during the 5TH round, the pair rode to an 88 point ride. Brodie Rawlins rode Black Tie for a 90 on Monday night and an 89 in Pendleton so it is more than doable. If they tie in the accumulated points then the total money won throughout the Finals decides the winner. That would be Cress. These two men are friends and they'll wish the best to each other, but they dang sure want to take the average title for themselves."

Brody was already sitting on Black Tie. The bay horse with mass of black mane was looking out into the arena as if plotting his course. Shoving his hat on his head tighter, Brody looked up at the stock contractor and said something. He lifted the rein high and tight then lowered it again and adjusted the rein in his hand. He leaned back, lifted the rein, focused on the horse's head, and nodded.

I caught my breath as man and horse burst from the chute and began a high-kick, leaping-buck down the arena. The spurring was perfect, the kicks fierce, and the crowd loud. When the horn blared my hands tightened around Dad's arm again.

"It was perfect," I whispered and watched the pick-up men retrieve Brody.

"Just as good, if not better than Rawlins," Dad nodded.

Everyone around us began throwing out numbers and guesses on which cowboy won.

Breathes were held and eyes stared at the reader board.

"Ladies and gentleman, the judge's scores, are in and that was an 87.5 point ride. Which means Rawlins wins the average and Cress comes in second for the night, the average, and second in the world standings."

"HE DID IT! I squealed and threw my arms around Dad and squeezed.

"You best go back and find him," Dad chuckled. "I'm going to go sit and watch the rest of the rodeo and the awards presentations with your mother."

"I love you, Dad."

We walked down the steps together, and just as I was ready to turn into the media room where the interviews would be underway, I gasped.

"DAD!"

His head jerked to me with brows together in concern. "What?"

"They were 87.5 and 85!"

"Yeah?"

My fingers curled into fists, and feet starting bouncing, "Fizzling Dud was 90! HE won the night and his first buckle!"

I ran back into his arms.

"Thank you, Dad," I whispered and squeezed a little harder. "Thank you for believing in the 16-year-old that had a dream."

"Your drive, your passion, and your love made it easy to believe."

Brodie was finishing his first interview when I stepped into the room. We grinned at each other but he was pulled away to the next interview. I looked up at the monitors to see the first barrel racer run into the arena.

"When does Delaney run?" I interrupted.

"Second..." he stepped away from the interviewer and to the monitor.

"This should be good then," I smiled. "She'll still have the energy of your win in her."

"And Gaston feeds on it."

The video showed Delaney and the horse slowly walk down the long tunnel toward the arena. She ran a soothing hand down the horse's neck and her lips were moving as she spoke to him. Within feet of the opening, they burst into a run. The turn on the first barrel couldn't be tighter.

"Come on, Sis," Brodie whispered.

The second turned and they raced to the third. As they lunged away from the third barrel, Delaney's boot hit the barrel. We all gasped but the barrel fell back into place as horse and rider flew out of the arena with long strides. The camera angle changed to the end of the tunnel as Delaney approached the exit gate. Her time of 13.25 was announced, and her hand swept down Gaston's neck.

"Her fastest time of the week," Brodie grinned and turned back to the interview. "Second on the ground will get that."

I watched seven more riders run with an occasional glance to Brodie as he moved from one interviewer to the other.

"Congrats, River!" Someone in the room hollered.

I turned to look, and half the people in the room were looking at me.

"For what?" I asked in surprise.

"He got second..." Dad said from behind me. "...reserve saddle bronc horse of the Finals Rodeo,"

My breath caught as I turned to him and my feet started bouncing in anticipation, "Fizzling Dud..."

Dad's grinned widened, "Destiny's Ignatius."

My scream of elation echoed in the room as I jumped into Dad's arms then turned to Brodie.

When my heart beat returned to normal, Delaney was standing at the door of the interview room. Her eyes were searching until they saw Brodie. A grin spread across her face as she watched him talking to a reporter. Her gaze continued around the room until she stopped at me.

Her smile faded, eyes became questioning.

I did not need her to thank me for helping Brodie, but I knew she needed to so I walked to her with a welcoming smile. Tears glistened in hers and we wrapped each other into a strong embrace. No words were spoken aloud. There was a new sense of ease between us when I stepped back.

My eyes went behind her when Camille appeared. Delaney's eyes went behind me to her brother.

"That was fast," I said to Camille since I knew she took care of Gaston after the ride.

"Had a volunteer take him so I could come in with Delaney," Camille explained with a grin.

We turned to the monitor as the last barrel racer sped into the arena. When she ran out of the arena the room grew quiet.

"Delaney!" The reporter at the door yelled. "Rawlins!"

Delaney turned away from Brodie, "What?"

"I need an interview!" The woman waved her over.

"It held up? We won the round?" Delaney grinned.

"Delaney," The woman huffed. "You won the round, the average, and by $472 you just won the world championship."

"I DID NOT!" Delaney gasped with hands covering her chest. The room erupted in shouts and applause.

"YYYEEESSS!" Camille screamed with hands going in the air and boots running in place.

The two women ran to each other and hopped in a celebratory circle.

"Delaney!" The reporter laughed. "We have to get this done before the bull riders finish."

She turned to Brodie and hugged him, then to me for another hug, then to Camille. She even hugged my dad.

"Delaney!" The reporter shouted again.

She stepped up to the reporter, then back again as her hand went to her chest and eyes to the ground.

"Give me a second," Delaney whispered and took a dozen deep breaths.

The microphone was instantly in front of her when she stepped forward and the cameras began rolling.

"Delaney, you just learned you won the day, average, and world championship. How do you feel?"

"Overwhelmed," Delaney gasped and wiped away tears. "I want to see my dad and my husband and..."

"Your husband?" The reporter huffed. "You're married?"

"Yes," Delaney laughed. "Ryle Jaspers and I were married this morning, so there is going to be one hell of a party tonight."

BLAZING TRAILS PODCAST TRANSCRIPT

Introduction- Sponsor Announcements

Devan: Hello everyone, this is Devan Reilly your host of the Blazing Trails podcast. Today will be a little different. Normally, I'm just with one or two people, but today I'm with ten people sitting around a big round table in a conference room at the SouthPoint Casino and Hotel. I'll start by going around the room and introducing you to everyone that is here. First though, after two weeks of seeing everyone in western dress; you all look like you're part of a summer league baseball team. For the listeners, they are all wearing a black t-shirt with different saying on the front in white.

Lacie Jae: We found a T-shirt shop and had a little fun.

Evan: In the middle of the night, after a few hours of celebrating.

(Everyone chuckles)

Devan (laughing):   I'll introduce each of you and tell the listeners what your shirts say since it's different for each person. To my left is the patriarch of the family, Evan Rawlins, a 2-time NFR qualifier in steer wrestling and father of Logan, Delaney, and Brodie. Evan's shirt says, 'Wise Ol' Man'.

Laughter

Evan: They've been threatening to get me this shirt for a couple of years now.

Martin: He finally got wise enough to earn it.

Laughter

Logan: Or drunk enough to let us make it.

Devan: You're not that old.

Brodie: Oldest in the family.

Chuckles

Devan: Next to Evan, is his oldest son, Logan, and his shirt says, 'Future Mr. Lacie Jae Rawlins', which leads us to his fiancé Lacie Jae next to him and her shirt, fittingly, says 'Future Mrs. Logan Rawlins'. Congratulations to both of you on the engagement.

Lacie Jae: Thank you.

Devan: Lacie Jae is the host of the podcast 'Coffee With Cowboys' and myself and all your other fans listened to your podcast last week telling about the proposal.

Lacie Jae: Devan helped me get started with the podcast. I couldn't have done it without him. He gave me lots of advice and taught me the equipment I needed. He is also very fun to be around.

Devan: Thank you, Lacie Jae. Next to Lacie Jae is her sister, Camille, and her shirt says 'Just here to pick up roadkill', which leads to Caleb Westmoreland, whose shirt says 'Roadkill'. That's awesome. For our listeners, Caleb is part of the Westmoreland Stock Contractors and is going to school to be a veterinarian.

Caleb: My dad and sister are the stock contractors. Mom and I just get the privilege of riding along with them.

Devan: Which leads to his sister, River, and Brodie Rawlins. Her shirt says "Bucker's Life- I raise 'em'." and his shirt says "Bucker's life- I ride 'em'". Two of River's horses won a go-round at the National Finals Rodeo and one of those, Destiny's Ignatius, was ridden by Brodie who is the Average Champion this year with a final 4th place for Saddle Bronc and 8th place in All-Around Championship.

Applause from everyone

Devan: Well deserved. Also, River's horse Ignatius was reserve saddle bronc of the rodeo.

Applause

Devan: Next to Brodie is Martin Houston, who is part of the Rawlins family. His shirt says 'Ask me about my Grandchildren'. We'll get to that later in the broadcast. Delaney is next, and her shirt says, in large, all-capital letters, 'FEED ME' and goes along well with the large tray of food that was placed in front of her when we entered.

Laughter

Evan: We kept it soft food, so she doesn't crunch into the microphone.

Laughter

Devan: Next to Delaney is her new husband Ryle Jaspers, NFR team-roper, who placed 6th as a header this year. His shirt says 'My WIFE is the World Champion Barrel Racer' That is two life-changing events that happened in one day.

Ryle: Best damn day of my life.

Devan: So those are the people we have in the room. I usually do a five random question section to start the program but since we have ten of you, I wrote 12 questions and threw them in a hat so you can each draw your own random question. We'll just go around the table, starting with Evan.

Evan: Alright, I'll pull the first one.

Devan: Read it out loud, then give it your best answer.

Evan: What is your favorite holiday? Easy, Christmas with the kids and any straggler cowboy or cowgirl that needs a place to celebrate.

Logan: Favorite exercise. Rowing machine. I can do it sitting down and it works the whole body.

Camille: And if you and the steer keep doing a strip routine in the middle of the NFR arena, you best keep using it.

Laughter

Lacie Jae: Favorite dessert.

Everyone: Elephant Ears.

Lacie Jae giggling: That's no fair.

Devan: I have a couple of extra questions in there, pull another.

Lacie Jae: What is my favorite movie? Well, if you asked me a year ago, it would have been 'Sleepless in Seattle'', but now, I would have to say 'Blazing Saddles'. I would never have understood the humor in it until this last year living with all these cowboys and horses.

Chuckles

Camille: My turn and the question is, what was your biggest challenge this last year? Keeping nachos out of Delaney's mouth the last couple months.

Laughter

Delaney laughing: That is probably true.

Devan: Which goes along with your FEED ME shirt.

Delaney: Exactly.

Devan: OK, Caleb, you're next.

Caleb: What is your favorite moment from this last year? Well, I'll have to go with, when Mom, Dad, River, and I were together to read that Flying Betty, Iggy, and Fizzling Dud became NFR horses.

Devan: That's a great family moment. River?

River: What is your favorite television show? Oh, well, I don't watch television much. I'm always outside.

Devan: On a cold stormy day and you're stuck inside, what do you watch?

River: Usually old movies like Big Jake, Silverado, Rio Bravo, Sons of Katie Elder.

Evan: Excellent choice in movies.

Devan: I agree. Brodie your turn.

Brodie: What is your go-to food when traveling? Beef jerky.

Martin: What is your go-to alcoholic beverage? I'm gonna go with a beer on a hot day and a Pendleton straight the rest of the time.

Delaney: If you were going to do another professional sport, what would it be? Olympic biathlon, which is cross-country skiing with rifle shooting.

Devan: I did not expect that.

Delaney: I would add skiing behind a horse if that was an official sport.

River: Skijoring, that is fun. We do it at home.

Brodie: So do we.

Devan: And Ryle has the last of our quick questions.

Ryle: What western movie would you have liked to be in? Wow…just one?

Devan: You can do two or three.

Ryle: Butch Cassidy and the Sundance Kid, Tombstone, and any movie with John Wayne.

Devan: Good choices, I'd have to add Jeremiah Johnson. Everyone's answers were excellent.

Evan: What's the last question in there?

Devan: This last year, what was your favorite rodeo?

Evan: We can all answer that. Mine would be Joseph, Oregon. That was the first time all four of the kids were in the top 15 of the standings.

Camille: …and then there was the celebration at the bar after.

Laughter

Logan: Denver…it was the first big one that Lacie Jae went to and it was a massive amount of fun watching her take it all in. She is always saying how much her life has changed since coming into our family. But, she has also changed mine by bringing her joy and wide-eyed appreciation to what we do.

Brodie: We've been around the arenas and rodeos all our lives and seeing her experience all of them has made us appreciate it even more.

Devan: Every rodeo is different in its own way from small-town arenas to the large ones like Denver or AT&T stadium. Lacie Jae, you're next. What was your favorite rodeo?

Lacie Jae: San Antonio, watching everyone cheer for Craig then Delaney

Camille: Salinas…it was a damn roller coaster and pretty much represented the whole year.

Caleb: Pendleton. I loved the history and, even though it was a bit stressful at the moment, I loved watching Iggy do the whole victory lap. He's a bit independent-minded. Then Henry the First won bareback horse of the rodeo.

River: Night 9 of the NFR with Iggy taking the cowboy to the bank.

Laughter

Brodie: The cowboy? I was going to say Lewiston where I first talked to that stock contractor lady, but I'll say Sheridan. That was a big goal I accomplished.

Martin: San Antonio

Delaney: Houston

Logan: You knocked a damn barrel down your first run.

Delaney: Yeah, but it was the first one Camille and Lacie Jae were both with us and by knocking it down, I was more focused for San Antonio...and we know how that turned out.

Laughter

Ryle: Kennewick, it was an emotionally stressful rodeo, but it was the first one I could openly yell and cheer for my future wife.

Devan: Great answers and a good way to start the conversations. We've all heard the phrase 'the elephant in the room'; well, there are a lot of elephants in this room.

Camille: I hope you're not talking about our weight.

Laughter

Devan (laughing): Oh, hell no. Just that there are a lot of big stories in the room and it's hard to decide where to start. But, I think we will start with you, Camille.

Camille: Why me?

Devan: Martin, the Rawlins and Westmoreland's have lived the trail for many years. This was your first year around animals and traveling the rodeo trail. This was your and Lacie Jae's year of blazing a new trail for yourself. What was your impression?

Camille: It is hard and I love it. I can say that when someone makes it to the NFR, they have EARNED it. It wasn't given to them. They worked hard, nearly every day.

Evan: There is no down time in rodeo.

Devan: That's for sure.

Camille: Before we went on the road, I would have absolutely dreaded a three-hour drive anywhere. Now, it's just a blink or 'piece of cake'. Thousands and thousands of miles were driven. There was a stretch that we took turns behind the wheel and were driving for four days straight with just enough time to stop for Delaney to make a run in barrels or breakaway, then off we went again.

Brodie: While taking care of the animals so they can make it through that grueling schedule.

Camille: Exactly. Then there are those moments you decide to get fuel in the next town and end up praying on fumes as you finally roll into one. That was a mistake we won't do again. We fixed flat tires, broken windshield wipers, changed oil, did our laundry in some questionable truck-stops, dealt with mean people and wonderful people. Got tired of each other...

Delaney: Amen to that.

All chuckle

Camille: I think the most important thing I would say is, you can't go on the rodeo trail thinking everything is going to be picture perfect. We had a section in Wyoming that was a lot of fun, traveling worked out, we got some sleep, and Delaney did well. Then we went to Salina's and Gaston was hurt. You are up one day and down the next. You win one day, and the next day you walk away feeling like you might as well quit and go home. This whole journey was an adventure. That is how you should take it. Enjoy it as that adventure. Not everyone gets to do it.

Lacie Jae: One thing you have to learn in all those miles on the road, is having to realize there will be moments that are out of your control and you just have to sit and wait or move on.

Logan: Only stress over what you can control.

Lacie Jae: Before I met the Rawlins, my life was pretty much even...kind of boring. Now, I love the people and life so much that I get too passionate about different

807

things. Logan and Evan have been trying to contain my exuberance.

Evan: Never contain, just focus.

Devan: It's good to have passion about your life. That's the way you want to live your life.

Camille: Delaney gave me a book last week that has pictures from January when we met to last month. Every challenge I took on, road trip we ventured on, and a lot of the people that we met. It was truly amazing to see the trail I blazed this last year and how much it changed me. I love it and can't wait to keep going. You have to have passion for this rodeo life. If not, you're just going to hate it and you'll make everyone and yourself miserable.

Lacie Jae: I love the rodeo life, whether traveling with just Logan and me or with a bunch of other steer wrestlers, then we fly sometimes, and then you get to go home and it just makes home that much better.

Delaney: Then there is listening to Lacie Jae's take on the world in her podcasts.

Lacie Jae: I have really had to step out of my comfort zone. There is just so much to this rodeo and ranching world that it gets overwhelming at times. I researched some of the rodeos I went to, like Pendleton, and the history itself is so, full...rich...truly overwhelming.

Camille: Intimidating.

Devan: What do you mean?

Camille: It's...well, even though I'm just Delaney's sidekick...

Chuckles

Camille: ...I have met people that have blazed the trail of this industry. Talking to them, I'm like, who am I to be a part of this? Part of this group of people? True legends and sometimes I feel like I can't live up to what they have laid before us.

Lacie Jae: It isn't just one person or two, it's the whole industry...the rodeo world celebrates, holds onto, and cherishes their past.

Evan: My father was alongside those legends. I was with a good portion of them, and my boys were raised traveling with the greatest rodeo cowboys to walk the earth. As someone new, trying to step into that world, it takes grit, belief you can do it, but most importantly, perseverance to continue. Do that, and in ten years, people stepping into the world will be intimidated by you, too.

Logan: Each generation of rodeo cowboys is more than willing and eager to help the new generation. Clinics, amateur rodeos, or just finding a mentor will help build that confidence to know you can be that intimidating legend someday.

Chuckles and nods of agreement

Devan: Let's go back to that 'just Delaney's sidekick'. I've seen the videos of you jumping in the alley as she runs in and out. I've seen the video of Delaney's reaction when you caught your first calf in competition. We've all seen the sponsor pictures with the horse trailer, and you handle her social media. And let's not forget you dressed her for the NFR, which won the best-dressed category by a long shot. I'm not much of a judge of women's fashion, but they were truly amazing and I couldn't choose a favorite, but the gunslinger one stands out. You also took care of all their horses while they were busy. That's not just a sidekick.

Logan: I started calling her that and will forever because she's about to become my sister-in-law, and it's funny. But in all the years I've traveled and rodeod, I've never seen anyone support another person like she did Delaney this year.

Evan: She is the reason Delaney got back on the rodeo road this year instead of just roping.

Camille: That was the win in San Antonio.

Brodie: That was you in the lane with her, cheering her on, and bringing back the excitement of racing that was lost when Mom passed away.

Martin: It's not just the competitor; it's the people around you that get you to a championship.

Logan: You may be the sidekick, but never JUST a sidekick.

Camille: Now, you all made me cry.

Lacie Jae: We need to get you another t-shirt; Not JUST Delaney's Sidekick.

Chuckles

Devan: So we've covered the blazing trails…let's tell some tales. Who has a good story to share with our listeners?

River: Well, that's not good.

Laughter

Devan: For the listeners, River is between her brother and boyfriend and I barely had the question out of my mouth when both their hands went up.

Chuckles

Brodie: Mine isn't about you.

Caleb: Mine is

Devan: Well, let's start with yours Caleb

River: Be careful, twin brother, because I got just as many stories about you.

Laughter

Caleb: River and I started traveling with Dad when we were really young. Our perch was on top of the horse trailers where we were safely out of the way. River had a special attachment to our late bucking horse, Chinook. She always oversaw when he was loaded into a trailer and always wanted to be close at a rodeo when he went through the chutes. We were at this rodeo when we were seven…

River laughs

Caleb: …and Chinook was seven, beginning of his illustrious career, and this judge gives him a horse score of eighteen.

Brodie: That couldn't have gone well.

Caleb chuckling: River is a bit passionate and protective of our horses and she didn't agree with the judge and neither did the crowd that was booing the low score.

She also has a tendency to throw things when she's mad. She's standing between the arena fence and one of the stock pens and very stealthily reaches down to the pile of horse manure, picks one up, and launches it at the judge.

Laughter

Caleb: The damn thing hits him in the forehead.

River: As the arena camera was on him so it was seen by everyone watching the screen.

Caleb: The judge gasps, stands away from the fence he was leaning on while waiting for the next ride and the whole crowd erupts in applause and laughter.

River: I was not on camera when I threw it, so they didn't know it was me.

Caleb: She threw three more that hit him, then turned, ran to the trailer, and crawled up on top. No one ever knew it was her, and until this day and Dad hears this podcast, he had no clue why she wouldn't come down until the horses were loaded and we were on our way home.

River: I love my horses...don't piss me off.

Laughter

Devan: Brodie? Your story?

Brodie: Camille mentioned a little while ago about the flat tire they had...I believe it was in Reno.

Camille: Yeah

Brodie: When we all woke up, Delaney saw the flat tire and thought since we were safely at a rodeo grounds and were waiting for the rodeo later in the day, that it would be good for Camille to change the tire and learn how to do it.

Camille: It was and I got it changed.

Brodie: Yeah, you did and by the time you were done, we had a couple of dozen people watching and bringing food over for a large potluck breakfast.

Delaney: Most fun we've ever had changing a damn tire.

Camille: So...what's your point?

Evan, Logan, Martin, Brodie laugh

Delaney: You did not!

Camille: Did what?

Lacie Jae giggling: Who flattened the tire to start with?

Brodie laughing: It was Craig's idea, but he was too lazy to get
                 up and actually do it. So...

Camille: YOU flattened that tire on purpose?

Laughter

Delaney laughing: Well, it was a lot of fun.

Camille: Did you know?

Delaney: Not until just now.

Brodie: You did a good job of changing the tire and
             entertaining a bunch of road-weary rodeo family.

Camille: It was fun...but I will have my revenge.

Devan: Anymore tales?

Logan: Granddad's shortcut.

Evan chuckles: Keep in mind this is well before cell phones
                and GPSs. You used a Rand McNally journal. We
                were leaving a rodeo, headed to the next one, when
                Dad decides to take a short cut. I make an excuse
                and tell him the boys and I are going to ride with a
                friend that isn't feeling well and he and a couple of
                fellow doggers take off down the road on their
                shortcut. We get to the rodeo and there is no sign of
                them. Rodeo starts, I win, Dad hasn't arrived so we
                drive down the shortcut in the opposite direction.
                Still, no Dad, so we call the rodeo secretary to see if
                he ever made it. He didn't, so we called the police in
                the area. Well, they had already received a call from
                Dad stating when I called, just to tell me he would
                meet me at the next rodeo. He was alright; they had
                just convinced themselves they were supposed to go
                to Springfield, Missouri, and not Springfield, Illinois.

Devan: They went to the wrong city?

Evan: Yeah, they are only about four hours apart. I knew
             they were going to the wrong one, but my dad was a
             bit of a stubborn man and I couldn't convince him
             otherwise, so I went and won the rodeo without him
             and three other bull doggers.

Chuckles

Devan: That's classic. Other than GPS and cell phones, what's the most significant change you have seen since you started?

Evan: Signing up for rodeos. Instead of standing in line at a phone booth, we can enter online now. There were times a dozen of us would stand at the phone booth and just pass the phone to the next cowboy to enter without having to hang up and pray you got through again.

Delaney: Our success is because of Dad. He knows the industry inside and out, which rodeos to go to which to bypass, how to arrange your schedules to make the most out of possible payouts.

Logan: He learned the hard way. We have GPS, mapping programs, and cell phones.

Brodie: With the new technology, we get our draws days before, so we can see if the horse we drew is worth the money to go to the rodeo.

River: We don't get that option. We just have to deal with the cowboys that draw-out on a horse that may just be learning. Their chance to buck in front of a crowd is taken away. It is, however, our goal to raise bucking horses that every cowboy would have confidence they could pull a check. We had a little gelding that barely got out of the chute on his first try. The second was a little better. He had chances to prove himself and buck in front of a crowd and loved it enough he won his first NFR go-round buckle last night.

Evan: Both sides, we all want a great performance and points on the board.

Caleb: Very true, I was on both sides by raising bucking horses and riding them in high school and amateur rodeos.

Devan: You ever want to go pro?

Caleb: No, my goal and focus has and will be veterinarian school and taking care of the animals.

Devan: You have a clear goal. How about the rest of you?
            Where do you go from here? What's next year look
            like?

Delaney: I want back on that podium. No other feeling like it.
            Last night…winning is always a dream, but it was
            more than I could imagine, standing there with all the
            world champions, crowd cheering, and seeing my
            family so proud.

Logan: I agree with her. But, last night, somewhere in the
            celebration, Brodie and I talked about our sister
            walking away with so many damn all-around saddles
            this last year.

Brodie: Kind of pissed us off and made us proud at the same
            time.

Chuckles

Logan: So, as well as both our main events, Brodie and I will
            be team roping.

Devan: PRCA?

Brodie: Yes, we've roped together since we were kids. We
            rope in jackpots and series together so it's time to
            take it on the professional road, too.

Logan: It's a competition between the two of us.

Brodie: We'll only rope with each other so our team roping
            money will be even, so it will be bull dogging or
            saddle bronc that will make the difference in our
            standing.

Logan: We both want to win the All-Around championship
            here next year.

Brodie: But, there is a side competition between the two of
            us on who is at a higher placing.

Lacie Jae: What do you win?

Evan: Besides bragging rights.

Logan and Brodie laugh

Logan: It ranged from a bottle of Pendleton to a new truck.

Brodie: We decided to settle on the prize before we get to
            Houston.

Devan: River? What does the next year look like for you?

River: We're working on a new stallion that has to step into Chinook's breeding program. We have a number we're considering, including Henry the First's little brother, but I'll be working on a breeding program to make sure we have the horses no cowboy will want to pull-out from.

Chuckles from Brodie

Devan: Lacie Jae and Camille?

Camille: I'm the side-kick keeping nachos away from Delaney and getting her back on that podium. And, picking up some roadkill along the way.

Laughter

Camille: Delaney and Evan have convinced me to branch out to other equine disciplines besides roping. So, I will be going to different clinics for reining, cutting, western pleasure, and I added polo because it sounds adventurous.

Devan: That will make you a well-rounded horsewoman.

Camille: There's another crack on my weight.

Laughter

Devan chuckling: Figuratively...the more you know overall, the better you can be in just one discipline.

Lacie Jae: I want to continue to learn and explore this industry and, hopefully, entertain and educate people along the way with the podcast. And, get married.

Logan chuckling: Put that on my list, too.

Devan: Martin? Evan?

Evan: I'll be focused on the ranch, the wedding, and getting these kids on the road to fulfill their dreams.

Martin: Brodie and I will be working on developing the scholarship and clinic program in honor of Craig. As much as I love all the people in this room, my focus this year will be on Craig's twins; Lilly and Caleb. I will continue with my regular job, and go to a rodeo when they are close, but I will be with my grandchildren.

Devan: The story of those two babies is truly a miracle. We talked about it before the show, and you'll be sharing

	that in your own time and not here. We'll move to the three competitors. Your first year here all together. What moment, as a family stands out to you?
Brodie:	That grand entry ride the first night. I'd seen Dad, Logan, and Delaney ride in it. It had been a dream I believed would happen, but it was supposed to be with Craig at my side. I'm not going to lie, it was hard not having him there, very hard, but Logan and Delaney did what they could to help me through it.
Logan:	Last night when the three of us walked into the suite wearing the shirts dedicated to our mother. Those pictures we took with just the family will be on our wall at home and treasured.
Delaney:	I agree with that…but I would also say the night we all had our back numbers and posed for pictures. That was the first night that made it a reality that we had all made it together.
Devan:	With the full year's success comes money in the bank. First thing you're spending your money on?
Logan:	A wedding and honeymoon.
Chuckles	
Delaney:	My horses won it for me, so I've already ordered a new trailer for them with top of the line safety and comfort.
Brodie:	I haven't really thought about it. A new truck with camper to get around better makes sense.
Devan:	One last question you can all answer, and we'll go around the table like we did before. Where will you be Tuesday morning?
Evan:	Drinking coffee on horseback at the ranch while riding through the herd of cattle on a very quiet mountain.
Logan:	Drinking coffee alongside Dad.
Lacie Jae:	Drinking coffee at the kitchen table while going through Brides magazines and looking for a wedding dress.

Camille:	Drinking coffee alongside Lacie Jae making sure I approve of the Maid of Honor dress she chooses.
Caleb:	Home in Nebraska helping Mom and Dad…and drinking coffee.
Chuckles	
River:	Drinking coffee in Oregon while loading a rescued horse named Dillon, to take home, and become my new saddle horse. He'll spend the rest of his days riding the quiet sunset mornings across beautiful pastures.
Brodie:	Drinking coffee, watching River load the horse, and preparing for our drive to Nebraska
Martin:	Drinking coffee while taking turns holding my grandchildren and shopping for baby stuff on the internet.
Chuckles	
Delaney:	Drinking coffee at an undisclosed honeymoon location.
Ryle:	Drinking coffee alongside my World Champion Barrel Racer wife on our honeymoon
Chuckles	
Devan:	I always end the show with words of advice to the listener. This time I put all your names in a hat and I'll draw five random people to answer the question; what is your advice to everyone listening? So the five are; River, Martin, Logan, Ryle, Delaney
River:	Believe in your dreams, fight for them. If it's something you believe with all your heart you can do, then keep fighting for it. Not just in rodeo but everything in your life; find a way to make it happen.
Logan:	Don't give up. There will be times you just want to throw in the towel and walk away after a bad day. Don't. Just don't. Vikings Hall of Fame Quarterback Fran Tarkenton once said, "It's perfectly okay to want to quit – as long as you don't."
Ryle:	Make sure you are with the people that are there to support your dreams, those that truly believe in you. My parents have been supporting me since I picked

up a rope. I have a team at home; Marty, Kade, and Pete that push me to my dream, are our practice partners, and they quite often travel with us. My roping partner Jess…well, if I didn't believe he was the best person to get us here then I would have found another partner and vice-versa. After our first few months roping together, we knew we meshed well, understood each other, worked well together and shared the same dream. Then there is Lauren Conners. She believed in us enough to open up her home, which is a team roper's dream estate. She helped take the financial burden off our shoulders so we could concentrate on getting the roping done. She is one hell of a roper herself and has roped with the best. Knowing she believed in us, just helped grow our confidence. So, my advice is to surround yourself with the right people.

Evan: My advice is not to leave out your wife.

Devan: That was a pretty mean glare.

LAUGHTER

Ryle laughing: I was just teasing. No matter what else was happening in my world, the ups and downs, successes and failures, this woman, my wife, was there since we met. Every day we talked about dreams and beliefs and staying focused. She has a tremendous mentor in her father that showed her not only how to believe in herself, but also to encourage those people around her. He also showed her how to put a rude guy flat on his back which is why we met. So, thank you, Evan.

Chuckles

Lacie Jae: She also throws a mean superhero punch so you all best watch out.

Laughter

Delaney: My advice…if you are truly fighting to get into that top 15 and make it to Vegas, remember that every dollar counts. Don't slack off thinking you can just take a weekend off. My first attempt I was $1639 short and found myself in 16th place...in the crying hole. Trust me, it lives up to its name. This is your job, you work on it every day. If you're not competing, then you should be practicing. I won this year by $472. There are a dozen 'ifs' in there. In Salinas, after Gaston was hurt, I had to use my late mother's horse to try to get to the short-go. She just happened to be with me because Camille rides her and had her in phenomenal shape. I was lucky she still remembered how to run the pattern. She didn't win money but gave Gaston the time to heal and run in the short-go. Then there is Pendleton when my brothers and husband guilted me into trying so damn hard to win for Gaston. My going to the 3.3 Ranch and meeting Lauren Conners? If I didn't go and end up buying Maestro, I wouldn't have gone to the Othello rodeo and won $865 to add to the standings. So many things added up for me this year, but because I kept fighting, it worked out. Like Logan said, don't give up.

Devan: All excellent advice. The last one is Martin. You've had a very long year with the success of your son at the beginning of the year, then to his death and the miraculous discovery of his twin children. How do you move forward? What advice do you have to keep someone going when you're thrown such momentous life-altering turns?

Long silent pause

Martin: My advice is the same advice I told my son when he wanted to start riding sheep or mutton bustin'. It's the advice he gave to Brodie the moment they met at the chutes at five-years-old.

Brodie, Logan, Delanie: "My Pops says you have to believe...you just got to believe you can do it, before you can do it.'

Martin: Take one day at a time. Hold onto those people that you love that will be there when you need them most, and be there for them when they need you.

You never know what the future holds for you. Find something to focus on whether it is a personal goal or something to help others. Find what is important to you and make it happen. Believe in yourself, believe in your dreams, and believe you can make a difference.

Devan: No better way to end this podcast, so thanks to all of you for being on the show. For everyone listening, keep blazing trails and telling tales and I'll see you down the road.

COMMERCIALS AND CLOSE

ACKNOWLEDGEMENTS

Tracy Hammond
Crystal Longfellow
Devan Reilly
Kirk & Katie St. Clair
Brody Cress
Ike Sankey
Cody Yates
Lewiston Roundup Association
Trenten & Maria Montero
Martee Pruitt
Dillon Holyfield

Lindsey and Chad Hutsell
Brady Portenier
Tate Owens
Johnny Espeland
Lori Smith
Darryl Kirby
Rylee Potter Hansen
Kim Grubb
Jessica Gates
Amberleigh Moore

ABOUT THE AUTHOR

I was raised with Shetlands and ponies and have loved horses since I watched a Shetland colt born when I was four.

Growing up, the TV show Bonanza was my favorite. I loved that western life and wanted to be Little Joe and Hoss' little sister. I wanted to live at the Ponderosa. Watching rodeos on television and attending when I could, was the closest I could get to the cowboy way of life.

That changed when I purchased my first 'big horse' when I was twenty-one. I now have the granddaughter and great-granddaughter of that horse in my pasture.

I am also a photographer specializing in the equine industry; shows, races, jackpots, and rodeos. With my photography, I create my own covers.

The Tagger Herd Series was my first venture into fictional writing and I love the family and horses in the series.

My first 'stand-alone' novel was Hoofbeats in the Wind which ventured into rodeo.

Coffee With Cowboys delves deeper into the rodeo world and researching for the book has been an adventure. I have met wonderful people from fans, stock contractors, and competitors. I thank every one of them that have helped make this book a possibility.